The House on the
Borderland
and Other
Mysterious
Places

The House on the Borderland and Other Mysterious Places

Being The Second Volume of
The Collected Fiction of William Hope Hodgson

Edited by Jeremy Lassen

Night Shade Books · New York · 2018

This series is dedicated to the readers, editors, publishers and scholars who have worked tirelessly since William Hope Hodgson's death to ensure that his work would not be lost or forgotten. Without their efforts, these volumes would not be possible.

In particular, the editor would like to thank S. T. Joshi, Mike Ashley, Jack Adrian and George Locke for their generous support.

Contents

Contents

The Cosmic Circle of Wonder and Imagination

...if you have so much as a splinter of wonder in you, you read Hodgson, and you know without question he is a master. – China Miéville

This outstanding ability of Hodgson, to plunge into a dream world and stay there for a book-length sojourn, fits with his seriousness and lends to his tale a straightforward, desperate convincingness. – Fritz Leiber

THIS, THE SECOND VOLUME of The Collected Fiction of William Hope Hodgson, brings together two of his most enduring and influential creations—*The House on the Borderland*, and the supernatural detective Carnacki. This book is also a detailed exploration of the duality (only hinted at in the first volume of this series) that suffuses his fiction—the "wonder" and "dream world(s)" of his prose versus its "straightforward, desperate convincingness." To put it more simply: the Cosmic versus the Mundane.

The House on the Borderland was Hodgson's second published novel, and is the penultimate example of his narrative duality. Half the book is devoted to the cosmic exploration of the nature of reality, while the other half of the book is a tightly paced, suspenseful siege narrative. Critics have cited this duality as a reason for its effectiveness; or conversely, the reason for its failure. In either case, *The House on the Borderland* remains a stunningly memorable achievement. Like a vast, burning star at the center of the universe of fantastic literature, the influence of this novel has been felt continuously since its publication.

Chapman & Hall (who a year earlier had published *The Boats of the "Glen Carrig"*) published *The House on the Borderland* in 1908, and like *Glen Carrig*, *Borderland* was greeted with nearly unanimous critical praise. Despite this it apparently did not sell well, and would be the last Hodgson title published by Chapman & Hall. It seems that Hodgson's contemporary readers were not as accepting of his cosmic extravagance as were the critics and later readers such as H. P. Lovecraft, who deemed it "The greatest of all of Mr. Hodgson's works."

Carnacki, the Ghost-Finder arose out of Hodgson's desire to build a reliable market for his short fiction. A popular series character all but guaranteed regular sales to the magazine markets. Carnacki is at once an example of his pursuit of commercial markets, and at the same time, and an indication of his fascination with the fantastic. This fusion of popular formula and personal fixation resulted in one of the most enduring figures of the ghost breaker/psychic detective genre. It is also another great example of the duality that inhabits his work—a *detective*... of the *supernatural*.

"The Gateway Monster," "The House Among the Laurels," "The Whistling Room," "The Horse of the Invisible," and "The Searcher of the End House" were published in *The Idler* in 1910, from January through May. "The Thing Invisible" had been scheduled to appear in the June issue, but was not published until January 1912, in *The New Magazine*. It would be the last Carnacki story to see publication during Hodgson's lifetime.

Several of these stories were slightly re-written for their 1913 republication in the Eveleigh Nash book entitled *Carnacki The Ghost-Finder*. In addition to rewriting them, Hodgson also reworked the order in which they were presented. In 1910, for copyright reasons, an abridged edition was published in the US. This edition was titled *Carnacki, The Ghost Finder, and a Poem*. It featured events of the Carnacki stories as part of a single narrative. It is an interesting and effective enough variant that it will be reprinted in the fifth volume of this series.

The final three Carnacki stories were not published until after Hodgson's death. "The Haunted *Jarvee*" was revised by Hodgson's wife at the request of the editor of *The Premier Magazine* in 1919, and it eventually saw publication ten years later in the March 1929 issue. It was further (but only slightly) revised by August Derleth for its publication in the 1947 Mycroft & Moran edition of *Carnacki the Ghost-Finder*. "The Hog" was published for the first time (via Derleth's efforts) in the January 1947 issue of *Weird Tales*, and was subsequently reprinted in the Mycroft & Moran edition, which also featured the previously unpublished story "The Find."

It has been suggested that these last two stories might have been fabricated by Mycroft & Moran/Arkham House publisher August Derleth. However, noted Hodgson scholar Sam Moskowitz confirmed the existence of the manuscript for "The Find" and has noted that Derleth changed "virtually nothing." Moskowitz also found several notes from Hodgson's letters that refer to the submission of a story called "The Hog." Without a doubt, these two stories were revised and edited by Derleth, but at their core, they are Hodgson's work. The editorial changes make them stand out from the earlier Carnacki stories, but they are an artifact of their time—edited and published posthumously due to Hodgson's inability to find a venue for their publication during his lifetime.

The last section of this volume captures another facet of the duality of Hodgson's writing—the seemingly supernatural story with a natural explanation. Hodgson could lead his readers to the brink of the fantastic and then, teasingly, frustratingly, reel them back down to earth. This formula found its way into a Carnacki story, and also reappeared in several of his mystery and adventure pieces. Whether straight mystery, adventure, or the formula described above, the stories in the final section of this book are a revealing strata that spans his career... from his first published story, "The Goddess Death," to several that did not see publication until more then sixty years after his death.

Whether on land, at sea, or in the places beyond and between, Hodgson kept one foot firmly planted in the real world and one foot in the ether. From popular mystery fiction to ghost breakers to cosmic visions, Hodgson knew how to give the reader glimpses into the unseen vistas of the universe. These flights of cosmic fantasy... these explorations that begin *here* and go *elsewhere*, have been inspiring readers and writers for generations. From H.P. Lovecraft and Clark Ashton Smith, to Fritz Leiber and China Miéville, with hundreds of others in between—the cosmic circle of fantastic fiction that began with William Hope Hodgson remains unbroken.

Jeremy Lassen
San Francisco,
November, 2003

The House on the Borderland

From the Manuscript, discovered in 1877 by
Messrs. Tonnison and Berreggnog, in the
Ruins that lie to the South of the
Village of Kraighten, in the West
of Ireland. Set out here,
with Notes

by William Hope Hodgson

To My Father
(Whose Feet Tread The Lost Aeons)

"Open the door,
  And listen!
Only the wind's muffled roar,
  And the glisten
Of tears round the moon.
  And, in fancy, the tread
Of vanishing shoon—
  Out in the night with the Dead.

"Hush! and hark
  To the sorrowful cry
Of the wind in the dark.
  Hush and hark, without murmur or sigh,
    To shoon that tread the lost aeons:
  To the sound that bids you to die.
Hush and hark! Hush and Hark!"

Shoon of the Dead

Introduction to the Manuscript

ANY ARE THE HOURS in which I have pondered upon the story that is set forth in the following pages. I trust that my instincts are not awry when they prompt me to leave the account, in simplicity, as it was handed to me.

And the MS. itself——You must picture me, when first it was given into my care, turning it over, curiously, and making a swift, jerky examination. A small book it is; but thick, and all, save the last few pages, filled with a quaint but legible hand-writing, and writ very close. I have the queer, faint, pit-water smell of it in my nostrils now as I write, and my fingers have subconscious memories of the soft, "cloggy" feel of the long-damp pages.

I recall, with just a slight effort, my first impression of the worded contents of the book—an impression of the fantastic, gathered from casual glances, and an unconcentrated attention.

Then, conceive of me comfortably a-seat for the evening, and the little, squat book and I, companions for some close, solitary hours. And the change that came upon my judgements! The emergence of a half-belief. From a *seeming* "fantasia" there grew, to reward my unbiassed concentration, a cogent, coherent scheme of ideas that gripped my interest more securely than the mere bones of the *account* or *story*, whichever it be, and I confess to an inclination to use the first term. I found a greater story within the lesser—and the paradox is no paradox.

I read, and, in reading, lifted the Curtains of the Impossible, that blind the mind, and looked out into the unknown. Amid stiff, abrupt sentences I wandered; and, presently, I had no fault to charge against their abrupt tellings; for, better far than my own ambitious phrasing, is this mutilated story capable of bringing home all that the old Recluse, of the vanished house, had striven to tell.

Of the simple, stiffly given account of weird and extraordinary matters, I will say little. It lies before you. The inner story must be uncovered, personally, by each reader, according to ability and desire. And even should any fail to see, as now I see, the shadowed picture and conception of that, to which one may well give the accepted titles of Heaven and Hell; yet can I promise certain thrills, merely taking the story as a story.

On final impression, and I will cease from troubling. I cannot but look upon the account of the Celestial Globes as a striking illustration (how nearly had I said "proof"!) of the actuality of our thoughts and emotions among the Realities. For, without seeming to suggest the annihilation of the lasting reality of Matter, as the hub and framework of the Machine of Eternity, it enlightens one with conceptions of the existence of worlds of thought and emotion, working in conjunction with, and duly subject to, the scheme of material creation.

— William Hope Hodgson
"Glaneifoin," Borth, Cardiganshire,
December 17, 1907

Table of Contents

Grief[1]

"Fierce hunger reigns within my breast,
   I had not dreamt that this whole world,
      Crushed in the hand of God, could yield
Such bitter essence of unrest,
      Such pain as Sorrow now hath hurled
      Out of its dreadful heart, unsealed!

"Each sobbing breath is but a cry,
   My heart-strokes knells of agony,
      And my whole brain has but one thought
That nevermore through life shall I
      (Save in the ache of memory)
      Touch hands with thee, who now art naught!

"Through the whole void of night I search,
   So dumbly crying out to thee;
      But thou are *not*; and night's vast throne
Becomes an all stupendous church
      With star-bells knelling unto me
      Who in all space am most alone!

"An hungered, to the shore I creep,
   Perchance some comfort waits on me
      From the old Sea's eternal heart;
But lo! from all the solemn deep,
      Far voices out of mystery
      Seem questioning why we are apart!

"Where'er I go I am alone
   Who once, through thee, had all the world.
      My breast is one whole raging pain
For that which *was*, and now is flown
      Into the Blank where life is hurled
      Where all is not, nor is again!"

---

[1] These stanzas I found, in pencil, upon a piece of foolscap gummed in behind the fly-leaf of the MS. They have all the appearance of having been written at an earlier date than the Manuscript.—Ed.

I
The Finding of the Manuscript

RIGHT AWAY IN THE WEST of Ireland lies a tiny hamlet called Kraighten. It is situated, alone, at the base of a low hill. Far around there spreads a waste of bleak and totally inhospitable country; where, here and there at great intervals, one may come upon the ruins of some long desolate cottage—unthatched and stark. The whole land is bare and unpeopled, the very earth scarcely covering the rock that lies beneath it, and with which the country abounds, in places rising out of the soil in wave-shaped ridges.

Yet, in spite of its desolation, my friend Tonnison and I had elected to spend our vacation there. He had stumbled on the place, by mere chance, the year previously, during the course of a long walking tour, and discovered the possibilities for the angler, in a small and unnamed river that runs past the outskirts of the little village.

I have said that the river is without name; I may add that no map that I have hitherto consulted has shown either village or stream. They seem to have entirely escaped observation: indeed, they might never exist for all that the average guide tells one. Possibly, this can be partly accounted for by the fact that the nearest railway-station (Ardrahan) is some forty miles distant.

It was early one warm evening when my friend and I arrived in Kraighten. We had reached Ardrahan the previous night, sleeping there in rooms hired at the village post-office, and leaving in good time on the following morning, clinging insecurely to one of the typical jaunting cars.

It had taken us all day to accomplish our journey over some of the roughest tracks imaginable, with the result that we were thoroughly tired and somewhat bad tempered. However, the tent had to be erected, and our goods stowed away, before we could think of food or rest. And so we set to work, with the aid of our driver, and soon had the tent up, upon a small patch of ground just outside the little village, and quite near to the river.

Then, having stored all our belongings, we dismissed the driver, as he had to make his way back as speedily as possible, and told him to come across to us at the end of a fortnight. We had brought sufficient provisions to last us for that space of time, and water we could get from the stream. Fuel we did not need, as we had included a small oil-stove among our outfit, and the weather was fine and warm.

It was Tonnison's idea to camp out instead of getting lodgings in one of the cottages. As he put it, there was no joke in sleeping in a room with a numerous family of healthy Irish in one corner, and the pig-sty in the other, while over-head a ragged colony of roosting fowls distributed their blessings impartially, and the whole place so full of peat smoke that it made a fellow sneeze his head off just to put it inside the doorway.

Tonnison had got the stove lit now, and was busy cutting slices of bacon into the frying-pan; so I took the kettle and walked down to the river for water. On the way, I had to pass close to a little group of the village people, who eyed me curiously, but not in any unfriendly manner, though none of them ventured a word.

As I returned with my kettle filled, I went up to them and, after a friendly nod, to which they replied in like manner, I asked them casually about the fishing; but, instead of answering, they just shook their heads silently, and stared at me. I repeated the question, addressing more particularly a great, gaunt fellow at my elbow; yet again I received no answer. Then the man turned to a comrade and said something rapidly in a language that I did not understand; and, at once, the whole crowd of them fell to jabbering in what, after a few moments, I guessed to be pure Irish. At the same time they cast many glances in my direction. For a minute, perhaps, they spoke among themselves thus; then the man I had addressed, faced round at me, and said something. By the expression of his face I guessed that he, in turn, was questioning me; but now I had to shake my head, and indicate that I did not comprehend what it was they wanted to know; and so we stood looking at one another, until I heard Tonnison calling to me to hurry up with the kettle. Then, with a smile and a nod, I left them, and all in the little crowd smiled and nodded in return, though their faces still betrayed their puzzlement.

It was evident, I reflected as I went towards the tent, that the inhabitants of these few huts in the wilderness did not know a word of English; and when I told Tonnison, he remarked that he was aware of the fact, and, more, that it was not at all uncommon in that part of the country, where the people often lived and died in their isolated hamlets without ever coming in contact with the outside world.

"I wish we had got the driver to interpret for us before he left," I remarked, as we sat down to our meal. "It seems so strange for the people of this place not even to know what we've come for."

Tonnison grunted an assent, and thereafter was silent for awhile.

Later, having satisfied our appetites somewhat, we began to talk, laying our plans for the morrow; then, after a smoke, we closed the flap of the tent, and prepared to turn in.

"I suppose there's no chance of those fellows outside taking anything?" I asked, as we rolled ourselves in our blankets.

Tonnison said that he did not think so, at least while we were about; and, as he went on to explain, we could lock up everything, except the tent, in the big chest that we had brought to hold our provisions. I agreed to this, and soon we were both asleep.

Next morning, early, we rose and went for a swim in the river; after which we dressed, and had breakfast. Then we roused out our fishing tackle, and overhauled it, by which time, our breakfasts having settled somewhat, we made all secure within the tent, and strode off in the direction my friend had explored on his previous visit.

During the day we fished happily, working steadily up-stream, and by evening we had one of the prettiest creels of fish that I had seen for a long while. Returning to the village, we made a good feed off our day's spoil, after which, having selected a few of the finer fish for our breakfast, we presented the remainder to the group of villagers who had assembled at a respectful distance to watch our doings. They seemed wonderfully grateful, and heaped mountains of, what I presumed to be, Irish blessings upon our heads.

Thus we spent several days, having splendid sport, and first-rate appetites to do justice upon our prey. We were pleased to find how friendly the villagers were inclined to be, and that there was no evidence of their having ventured to meddle with our belongings during our absences.

It was on a Tuesday that we arrived in Kraighten, and it would be on the Sunday following that we made a great discovery. Hitherto we had always gone up-stream; on that day, however, we laid aside our rods, and, taking some provisions, set off for a long ramble in the opposite direction. The day was warm, and we trudged along leisurely enough, stopping about midday to eat our lunch upon a great flat rock near the river bank. Afterwards, we sat and smoked awhile, resuming our walk only when we were tired of inaction.

For, perhaps, another hour we wandered onwards, chatting quietly and comfortably on this and that matter, and on several occasions stopping while my companion—who is something of an artist—made rough sketches of striking bits of the wild scenery.

And then, without any warning whatsoever, the river we had followed so confidently, came to an abrupt end—vanishing into the earth.

"Good Lord!" I said, "who ever would have thought of this?"

And I stared in amazement; then I turned to Tonnison. He was looking, with a blank expression upon his face, at the place where the river disappeared.

In a moment he spoke.

"Let us go on a bit; it may reappear again—anyhow, it is worth investigating."

I agreed, and we went forward once more, though rather aimlessly; for we were not at all certain in which direction to prosecute our search. For perhaps a mile we moved onwards; then Tonnison, who had been gazing about curiously, stopped and shaded his eyes.

"See!" he said, after a moment, "isn't that mist or something, over there to the right—away in a line with that great piece of rock?" And he indicated with his hand.

I stared, and, after a minute, seemed to see something, but could not be certain, and said so.

"Anyway," my friend replied, "we'll just go across and have a glance." And he started off in the direction he had suggested, I following. Presently, we came among bushes, and, after a time, out upon the top of a high, boulder-strewn bank, from which we looked down into a wilderness of bushes and trees.

"Seems as though we had come upon an oasis in this desert of stone," muttered Tonnison, as he gazed interestedly. Then he was silent, his eyes fixed; and I looked also; for up from somewhere about the centre of the wooded lowland there rose high into the quiet air a great column of haze-like spray, upon which the sun shone, causing innumerable rainbows.

"How beautiful!" I exclaimed.

"Yes," answered Tonnison, thoughtfully. "There must be a waterfall, or something, over there. Perhaps it's our river come to light again. Let's go and see."

Down the sloping bank we made our way, and entered among the trees and shrubberies. The bushes were matted, and the trees overhung us, so that the place was disagreeably gloomy; though not dark enough to hide from me the fact that many of the trees were fruit-trees, and that, here and there, one could trace indistinctly, signs of a long departed cultivation. Thus it came to me, that we were making our way through the riot of a great and ancient garden. I said as much to Tonnison, and he agreed that there certainly seemed reasonable grounds for my belief.

What a wild place it was, so dismal and sombre! Somehow, as we went forward, a sense of the silent loneliness and desertion of the old garden grew upon me, and I felt shivery. One could imagine things lurking among the tangled bushes; while, in the very air of the place, there seemed something uncanny. I think Tonnison was conscious of this also, though he said nothing.

Suddenly, we came to a halt. Through the trees there had grown upon our ears a distant sound. Tonnison bent forward, listening. I could hear it more plainly now; it was continuous and harsh—a sort of droning roar, seeming to come from far away. I experienced a queer, indescribable, little feeling of nervousness. What sort of place was it into which we had got? I looked at my companion, to see what he thought of the matter; and noted that there was only puzzlement in his face; and then, as I watched his features, an expression of comprehension crept over them, and he nodded his head.

"'That's a waterfall," he exclaimed, with conviction. "I know the sound now." And he began to push vigorously through the bushes, in the direction of the noise.

As we went forward, the sound became plainer continually, showing that we were heading straight towards it. Steadily, the roaring grew louder and nearer, until it appeared, as I remarked to Tonnison, almost to come from under our feet—and still we were surrounded by the trees and shrubs.

"Take care!" Tonnison called to me. "Look where you're going." And then, suddenly, we came out from among the trees, on to a great open space, where, not six paces in front of us, yawned the mouth of a tremendous chasm, from the depths of which, the noise appeared to rise, along with the continuous, mist-like spray that we had witnessed from the top of the distant bank.

For quite a minute we stood in silence, staring in bewilderment at the sight; then my friend went forward cautiously to the edge of the abyss. I followed, and, together, we looked down through a boil of spray at a monster cataract of frothing water that burst, spouting, from the side of the chasm, nearly a hundred feet below.

"Good Lord!" said Tonnison.

I was silent, and rather awed. The sight was so unexpectedly grand and eerie; though this latter quality came more upon me later.

Presently, I looked up and across to the further side of the chasm. There, I saw something towering up among the spray: it looked like a fragment of a great ruin, and I touched Tonnison on the shoulder. He glanced round, with a start, and I pointed towards the thing. His gaze followed my finger, and his eyes lighted up with a sudden flash of excitement, as the object came within his field of view.

"Come along," he shouted above the uproar. "We'll have a look at it. There's something queer about this place; I feel it in my bones." And he started off, round the edge of the crater-like abyss. As we neared this new thing, I saw that I had not been mistaken in my first impression. It was undoubtedly a portion of some ruined building; yet now I made out that it was not built upon the edge of the chasm itself, as I had at first supposed; but perched almost at the extreme end of a huge spur of rock that jutted out some fifty or sixty feet over the abyss. In fact, the jagged mass of ruin was literally suspended in mid-air.

Arriving opposite it, we walked out on to the projecting arm of rock, and I must confess to having felt an intolerable sense of terror, as I looked down from that dizzy perch into the unknown depths below us—into the deeps from which there rose ever the thunder of the falling water, and the shroud of rising spray.

Reaching the ruin, we clambered round it cautiously, and, on the further side, came upon a mass of fallen stones and rubble. The ruin itself seemed to me, as I proceeded now to examine it minutely, to be a portion of the outer wall of some prodigious structure, it was so thick and substantially built; yet what it was doing in such a position, I could by no means conjecture. Where was the rest of the house, or castle, or whatever there had been?

I went back to the outer side of the wall, and thence to the edge of the chasm, leaving Tonnison rooting systematically among the heap of stones and rubbish on the outer side. Then I commenced to examine the surface of the ground, near the edge of the abyss, to see whether there were not left other remnants of the building to which the fragment of ruin evidently belonged. But, though I scrutinised the earth with the greatest care, I could see no signs of anything to show that there had ever been a building erected on the spot, and I grew more puzzled than ever.

Then, I heard a cry from Tonnison; he was shouting my name, excitedly, and, without delay, I hurried along the rocky promontory to the ruin. I wondered whether he had hurt himself, and then the thought came, that perhaps he had found something.

I reached the crumbled wall, and climbed round. There, I found

Tonnison standing within a small excavation that he had made among the *débris*: he was brushing the dirt from something that looked like a book, much crumpled and dilapidated; and opening his mouth, every second or two, to bellow my name. As soon as he saw that I had come, he handed his prize to me, telling me to put it into my satchel so as to protect it from the damp, while he continued his explorations. This I did, first, however, running the pages through my fingers, and noting that they were closely filled with neat, old-fashioned writing which was quite legible, save in one portion, where many of the pages were almost destroyed, being muddied and crumpled, as though the book had been doubled back at that part. This, I found out from Tonnison, was actually as he had discovered it, and the damage was due, probably, to the fall of masonry upon the opened part. Curiously enough, the book was fairly dry, which I attributed to its having been so securely buried among the ruins.

Having put the volume away safely, I turned-to and gave Tonnison a hand with his self-imposed task of excavating; yet, though we put in over an hour's hard work, turning over the whole of the upheaped stones and rubbish, we came upon nothing more than some fragments of broken wood, that might have been parts of a desk or table; and so we gave up searching, and went back along the rock, once more to the safety of the land.

The next thing we did was to make a complete tour of the tremendous chasm, which we were able to observe was in the form of an almost perfect circle, save for where the ruin-crowned spur of rock jutted out, spoiling its symmetry.

The abyss was, as Tonnison put it, like nothing so much as a gigantic well or pit going sheer down into the bowels of the earth.

For some time longer, we continued to stare about us, and then, noticing that there was a clear space away to the north of the chasm, we bent our steps in that direction.

Here, distant from the mouth of the mighty pit by some hundreds of yards, we came upon a great lake of silent water—silent, that is, save in one place where there was a continuous bubbling and gurgling.

Now, being away from the noise of the spouting cataract, we were able to hear one another speak, without having to shout at the tops of our voices, and I asked Tonnison what he thought of the place—I told him that I didn't like it, and that the sooner we were out of it the better I should be pleased.

He nodded in reply, and glanced at the woods behind, furtively. I asked him if he had seen or heard anything. He made no answer; but stood silent, as though listening, and I kept quiet also.

Suddenly, he spoke.

"Hark!" he said, sharply. I looked at him, and then away among the trees and bushes, holding my breath involuntarily. A minute came and went in strained silence; yet I could hear nothing, and I turned to Tonnison to say as much; and then, even as I opened my lips to speak, there came a strange wailing noise out of the wood on our left. . . . It appeared to float through the trees, and there was a rustle of stirring leaves, and then silence.

All at once, Tonnison spoke, and put his hand on my shoulder. "Let us get out of here," he said, and began to move slowly towards where the surrounding trees and bushes seemed thinnest. As I followed him, it came to me suddenly that the sun was low, and that there was a raw sense of chilliness in the air.

Tonnison said nothing further, but kept on steadily. We were among the trees now, and I glanced around, nervously; but saw nothing, save the quiet branches and trunks and the tangled bushes. Onwards we went, and no sound broke the silence, except the occasional snapping of a twig under our feet, as we moved forward. Yet, in spite of the quietness, I had a horrible feeling that we were not alone; and I kept so close to Tonnison that twice I kicked his heels clumsily, though he said nothing. A minute, and then another, and we reached the confines of the wood coming out at last upon the bare rockiness of the countryside. Only then was I able to shake off the haunting dread that had followed me among the trees.

Once, as we moved away, there seemed to come again a distant sound of wailing, and I said to myself that it was the wind—yet the evening was breathless.

Presently, Tonnison began to talk.

"Look you," he said with decision, "I would not spend the night in *that* place for all the wealth that the world holds. There is something unholy—diabolical about it. It came to me all in a moment, just after you spoke. It seemed to me that the woods were full of vile things— you know!"

"Yes," I answered, and looked back towards the place; but it was hidden from us by a rise in the ground.

"There's the book," I said, and I put my hand into the satchel.

"You've got it safely?" he questioned, with a sudden access of anxiety.

"Yes," I replied.

"Perhaps," he continued, "we shall learn something from it when we get back to the tent. We had better hurry, too; we're a long way off still, and I don't fancy, now, being caught out here in the dark."

It was two hours later when we reached the tent; and, without delay, we set to work to prepare a meal; for we had eaten nothing since our lunch at midday.

Supper over, we cleared the things out of the way, and lit our pipes. Then Tonnison asked me to get the manuscript out of my satchel. This I did, and then, as we could not both read from it at the same time, he suggested that I should read the thing out loud. "And mind," he cautioned, knowing my propensities, "don't go skipping half the book."

Yet, had he but known what it contained, he would have realised how needless such advice was, for once, at least. And there, seated in the opening of our little tent, I began the strange tale of "The House on the Borderland" (for such was the title of the MS.) ; that is told in the following pages.

II

The Plain of Silence

"I AM AN OLD man. I live here in this ancient house, surrounded by huge, unkempt gardens.

"The peasantry, who inhabit the wilderness beyond, say that I am mad. That is because I will have nothing to do with them. I live here alone with my old sister, who is also my housekeeper. We keep no servants—I hate them. I have one friend, a dog; yes, I would sooner have old Pepper than the rest of Creation together. He, at least, understands me—and has sense enough to leave me alone when I am in my dark moods.

"I have decided to start a kind of diary; it may enable me to record some of the thoughts and feelings that I cannot express to any one; but, beyond this, I am anxious to make some record of the strange things that I have heard and seen, during many years of loneliness, in this weird old building.

"For a couple of centuries, this house has had a reputation, a bad one, and, until I bought it, for more than eighty years no one had lived here; consequently, I got the old place at a ridiculously low figure.

"I am not superstitious; but I have ceased to deny that things happen in this old house—things that I cannot explain; and, therefore, I must needs ease my mind, by writing down an account of them, to the best of my ability; though, should this, my diary, ever be read when I am gone, the readers will but shake their heads, and be the more convinced that I was mad.

"This house, how ancient it is! though its age strikes one less, perhaps, than the quaintness of its structure, which is curious and fantastic to the last degree. Little curved towers and pinnacles, with outlines suggestive of leaping flames, predominate; while the body of the building is in the form of a circle.

"I have heard that there is an old story, told amongst the country people, to the effect that the devil built the place. However, that is as may be. True or not, I neither know nor care, save as it may have helped to cheapen it, ere I came.

"I must have been here some ten years, before I saw sufficient to warrant any belief in the stories, current in the neighbourhood, about this house. It is true that I had, on at least a dozen occasions, seen, vaguely, things that puzzled me, and, perhaps, had felt more than I had seen. Then, as the years passed, bringing age upon me, I became often aware of something unseen, yet unmistakably present, in the empty rooms and corridors. Still, it was, as I have said, many years before I saw any real manifestations of the, so called, supernatural.

"It was not Hallowe'en. If I were telling a story for amusement's sake, I should probably place it on that night of nights; but this is a true record of my own experiences, and I would not put pen to paper to amuse any one. No. It was after midnight on the morning of the twenty-first day of January. I was sitting reading, as is often my custom, in my study. Pepper lay, sleeping, near my chair.

"Without warning, the flames of the two candles went low, and then shone with a ghastly, green effulgence. I looked up, quickly, and, as I did so, I saw the lights sink into a dull, ruddy tint; so that the room glowed with a strange, heavy, crimson twilight that gave the shadows, behind the chairs and tables, a double depth of blackness; and wherever the light struck, it was as though luminous blood had been splashed over the room.

"Down on the floor, I heard a faint, frightened whimper, and something pressed itself in between my two feet. It was Pepper, cowering under my dressing-gown. Pepper, usually as brave as a lion!

"It was this movement of the dog's, I think, that gave me the first twinge of *real* fear. I had been considerably startled when the lights burnt first green and then red; but had been momentarily under the impression that the change was due to some influx of noxious gas into the room. Now, however, I saw that it was not so; for the candles burned with a steady flame, and showed no signs of going out, as would have been the case had the change been due to fumes in the atmosphere.

"I did not move. I felt distinctly frightened; but could think of nothing better to do than wait. For perhaps a minute, I kept my glance about the room, nervously. Then, I noticed that the lights had commenced to sink, very slowly; until, presently, they showed minute specks of red fire, like the gleamings of rubies, in the darkness. Still,

I sat watching; while a sort of dreamy indifference seemed to steal over me; banishing, altogether, the fear that had begun to grip me.

"Away in the far end of the huge, old-fashioned room, I became conscious of a faint glow. Steadily it grew, filling the room with gleams of quivering green light; then they sank quickly, and changed—even as the candle-flames had done—into a deep, sombre crimson, that strengthened, and lit up the room with a flood of awful glory.

"The light came from the end wall, and grew ever brighter, until its intolerable glare caused my eyes acute pain, and, involuntarily, I closed them. It may have been a few seconds before I was able to open them. The first thing I noticed, was that the light had decreased, greatly; so that it no longer tried my eyes. Then, as it grew still duller, I was aware, all at once, that, instead of looking at the redness, I was staring through it, and through the wall beyond.

"Gradually, as I became more accustomed to the idea, I realised that I was looking out on to a vast plain, lit with the same gloomy twilight that pervaded the room. The immensity of this plain scarcely can be conceived. In no part could I perceive its confines. It seemed to broaden and spread out, so that the eye failed to perceive any limitations. Slowly, the details of the nearer portions began to grow clear; then, in a moment almost, the light died away, and the vision—if vision it were—faded and was gone.

"Suddenly, I became conscious that I was no longer in the chair. Instead, I seemed to be hovering above it, and looking down at a dim something, huddled and silent. In a little while, a cold blast struck me, and I was outside in the night, floating, like a bubble, up through the darkness. As I moved, an icy coldness seemed to enfold me, so that I shivered.

"After a time, I looked to right and left, and saw the intolerable blackness of the night, pierced by remote gleams of fire. Onwards, outwards, I drove. Once, I glanced behind, and saw the earth, a small crescent of blue light, receding away to my left. Further off, the sun, a splash of white flame, burned vividly against the dark.

"An indefinite period passed. Then, for the last time, I saw the earth—an enduring globule of radiant blue, swimming in an eternity of ether. And there I, a fragile flake of soul-dust, flickered silently across the void, from the distant blue, into the expanse of the unknown.

"A great while seemed to pass over me, and now I could nowhere see anything. I had passed beyond the fixed stars, and plunged into the huge blackness that waits beyond. All this time, I had experienced little, save a sense of lightness and cold discomfort. Now, however, the atrocious darkness seemed to creep into my soul, and I became filled with fear and despair. What was going to become of me? Where was I going? Even as the thoughts were formed, there grew, against the impalpable blackness that wrapped me, a faint tinge of blood. It seemed extraordinarily remote, and mist-like; yet, at once, the feeling of oppression was lightened, and I no longer despaired.

"Slowly, the distant redness became plainer and larger; until, as I drew nearer, it spread out into a great, sombre glare—dull and tremendous. Still, I fled onward, and, presently, I had come so close, that it seemed to stretch beneath me, like a great ocean of sombre red. I could see little, save that it appeared to spread out interminably in all directions.

"In a further space, I found that I was descending upon it; and, soon, I sank into a great sea of sullen, red-hued clouds. Slowly, I emerged from these, and there, below me, I saw the stupendous plain, that I had seen from my room in this house that stands upon the borders of the Silences.

"Presently, I landed, and stood, surrounded by a great waste of loneliness. The place was lit with a gloomy twilight that gave an impression of indescribable desolation.

"Afar to my right, within the sky, there burnt a gigantic ring of dull-red fire, from the outer edge of which were projected huge, writhing flames, darted and jagged. The interior of this ring was black, black as the gloom of the outer night. I comprehended, at once, that it was from this extraordinary sun that the place derived its doleful light.

"From that strange source of light, I glanced down again to my surroundings. Everywhere I looked, I saw nothing but the same flat weariness of interminable plain. Nowhere could I descry any signs of life; not even the ruins of some ancient habitation.

"Gradually, I found that I was being borne forward, floating across the flat waste. For what seemed an eternity, I moved onwards. I was unaware of any great sense of impatience; though some curiosity and a vast wonder were with me continually. Always, I saw around me the breadth of that enormous plain; and, always, I searched for some new thing to break its monotony; but there was no change—only loneliness, silence and desert.

"Presently, in a half-conscious manner, I noticed that there was a faint mistiness, ruddy in hue, lying over its surface. Still, when I looked more intently, I was unable to say that it was really mist; for it appeared to blend with the plain, giving it a peculiar unrealness, and conveying to the senses the idea of unsubstantiality.

"Gradually, I began to weary with the sameness of the thing. Yet, it was a great time before I perceived any signs of the place, towards which I was being conveyed.

"At first, I saw it, far ahead, like a long hillock on the surface of the Plain. Then, as I drew nearer, I perceived that I had been mistaken; for, instead of a low hill, I made out, now, a chain of great mountains, whose distant peaks towered up into the red gloom, until they were almost lost to sight.

III

The House in the Arena

"AND SO, AFTER A time, I came to the mountains. Then, the course of my journey was altered, and I began to move along their bases, until, all at once, I saw that I had come opposite to a vast rift, opening into the mountains. Through this, I was borne, moving at no great speed. On either side of me, huge, scarped walls of rock-like substance rose sheer. Far overhead, I discerned a thin ribbon of red, where the mouth of the chasm opened, among inaccessible peaks. Within, was gloom, deep and sombre, and chilly silence. For awhile, I went onward steadily, and then, at last, I saw, ahead, a deep, red glow, that told me I was near upon the further opening of the gorge.

"A minute came and went, and I was at the exit of the chasm, staring out upon an enormous amphitheatre of mountains. Yet, of the mountains, and the terrible grandeur of the place, I recked nothing; for I was confounded with amazement, to behold, at a distance of several miles, and occupying the centre of the arena, a stupendous structure, built apparently of green jade. Yet, in itself, it was not the discovery of the building that had so astonished me; but the fact, which became every moment more apparent, that in no particular, save in colour and its enormous size, did the lonely structure vary from this house in which I live.

"For awhile, I continued to stare, fixedly. Even then, I could scarcely believe that I saw aright. In my mind, a question formed, reiterating incessantly: 'What does it mean?' 'What does it mean?' and I was unable to make answer, even out of the depths of my imagination. I seemed capable only of wonder and fear. For a time longer, I gazed, noting, continually, some fresh point of resemblance that attracted me. At last, wearied and sorely puzzled, I turned from it, to view the rest of the strange place on to which I had intruded.

"Hitherto, I had been so engrossed in my scrutiny of the House, that I had given only a cursory glance round. Now, as I looked, I began to realise upon what sort of a place I had come. The arena, for so I have termed it, appeared a perfect circle of about ten to twelve miles in diameter, the House, as I have mentioned before, standing in the centre. The surface of the place, like to that of the Plain, had a peculiar, misty appearance, that was yet not mist.

"From a rapid survey, my glance passed quickly upwards, along the slopes of the circling mountains. How silent they were. I think that this same abominable stillness was more trying to me, than anything that I had, so far, seen or imagined. I was looking up, now, at the great crags, towering so loftily. Up there, the impalpable redness gave a blurred appearance to everything.

"And then, as I peered, curiously, a new terror came to me; for, away up among the dim peaks to my right, I had descried a vast shape of blackness, giant-like. It grew upon my sight. It had an enormous equine head, with gigantic ears, and seemed to peer steadfastly down into the arena. There was that about the pose, that gave me the impression of an eternal watchfulness—of having warded that dismal place, through unknown eternities. Slowly, the monster became plainer to me; and then, suddenly, my gaze sprang from it to something further off and higher among the crags. For a long minute, I gazed, fearfully. I was strangely conscious of something not altogether unfamiliar—as though something stirred in the back of my mind. The thing was black, and had four grotesque arms. The features showed, indistinctly. Round the neck, I made out several light-coloured objects. Slowly, the details came to me, and I realised, coldly, that they were skulls. Further down the body was another circling belt, showing less dark against the black trunk. Then, even as I puzzled to know what the thing was, a memory slid into my mind, and straightway, I knew that I was looking at a monstrous representation of Kali, the Hindu goddess of death.

"Other remembrances of my old student days drifted into my thoughts. My glance fell back upon the huge beast-headed Thing. Simultaneously, I recognised it for the ancient Egyptian god Set, or Seth, the Destroyer of Souls. With the knowledge, there came a great sweep of questioning—'Two of the—!' I stopped, and endeavoured to think. Things beyond my imagination, peered into my frightened mind. I saw, obscurely. 'The old gods of mythology!' I tried to comprehend to what it was all pointing. My gaze dwelt, flickeringly, between the two. 'If—'

"An idea came swiftly, and I turned, and glanced rapidly upwards, searching the gloomy crags, away to my left. Something loomed out under a great peak, a shape of greyness. I wondered I had not seen it earlier, and then remembered I had not yet viewed that portion. I saw it more plainly now. It was, as I have said, grey. It had a tremendous head; but no eyes. That part of its face was blank.

"Now, I saw that there were other things up among the mountains. Further off, reclining on a lofty ledge, I made out a livid mass, irregular and ghoulish. It seemed without form, save for an unclean, half-animal face, that looked out, vilely, from somewhere about its middle. And then, I saw others—there were hundreds of them. They seemed to grow out of the shadows. Several, I recognised, almost immediately, as mythological deities; others were strange to me, utterly strange, beyond the power of a human mind to conceive.

On each side, I looked, and saw more, continually. The mountains were full of strange things—Beast-gods, and Horrors, so atrocious and bestial that possibility and decency deny any further attempt to describe them. And I—I was filled with a terrible sense of overwhelming horror and fear and repugnance; yet, spite of these, I wondered exceedingly. Was there then, after all, something in the old heathen worship, something more than the mere deifying of men, animals and elements? The thought gripped me—was there?

"Later, a question repeated itself. What were they, those Beast-gods, and the others? At first, they had appeared to me, just sculptured Monsters, placed indiscriminately among the inaccessible peaks and precipices of the surrounding mountains. Now, as I scrutinised them with greater intentness, my mind began to reach out to fresh conclusions. There was something about them, an indescribable sort of silent vitality, that suggested, to my broadening consciousness, a state of life-in-death—a something that was by no means life, as we understand it; but rather an inhuman form of existence, that well might be likened to a deathless trance—a condition in which it was possible to imagine their continuing, eternally. 'Immortal!' the word rose in my thoughts unbidden; and, straightway, I grew to wondering whether this might be the immortality of the gods.

"And then, in the midst of my wondering and musing, something happened. Until then, I had been staying, just within the shadow of the exit of the great rift. Now, without volition on my part, I drifted out of the semi-darkness, and began to move slowly across the arena—towards the House. At this, I gave up all thoughts of those prodigious Shapes above me—and could only stare, frightenedly, at the tremendous structure, towards which I was being conveyed so remorselessly. Yet, though I searched earnestly, I could discover nothing that I had not already seen, and so became gradually calmer.

"Presently, I had reached a point more than half-way between the

House and the gorge. All around, was spread the stark loneliness of the place, and the unbroken silence. Steadily, I neared the great building. Then, all at once, something caught my vision, something that came round one of the huge buttresses of the House, and so into full view. It was a gigantic thing, and moved with a curious lope, going almost upright, after the manner of a man. It was quite unclothed, and had a remarkable luminous appearance. Yet it was the face that attracted and frightened me the most. It was the face of a swine.

"Silently, intently, I watched this horrible creature, and forgot my fear, momentarily, in my interest in its movements. It was making its way, cumbrously, round the building, stopping, as it came to each window, to peer in, and shake at the bars, with which—as in this house—they were protected; and whenever it came to a door, it would push at it, fingering the fastening stealthily. Evidently, it was searching for an ingress into the House.

"I had come now to within less than a quarter of a mile of the great structure, and still I was compelled forward. Abruptly, the Thing turned, and gazed, hideously, in my direction. It opened its mouth, and, for the first time, the stillness of that abominable place was broken, by a deep, booming note, that sent an added thrill of apprehension through me. Then, immediately, I became aware that it was coming towards me, swiftly and silently. In an instant, it had covered half the distance that lay between. And still, I was borne helplessly to meet it. Only a hundred yards, and the brutish ferocity of the giant face numbed me with a feeling of unmitigated horror. I could have screamed, in the supremeness of my fear; and then, in the very moment of my extremity and despair, I became conscious that I was looking down upon the arena, from a rapidly-increasing height. I was rising, rising. In an inconceivably short while, I had reached an altitude of many hundred feet. Beneath me, the spot that I had just left, was occupied by the foul Swine-creature. It had gone down on all fours, and was snuffing and rooting, like a veritable hog, at the surface of the arena. A moment, and it rose to its feet, clutching upwards, with an expression of desire upon its face, such as I have never seen in this world.

"Continually, I mounted higher. A few minutes, it seemed, and I had risen above the great mountains—floating, alone, afar in the redness. At a tremendous distance below, the arena showed, dimly; with the mighty House looking no larger than a tiny spot of green. The Swine-thing was no longer visible.

"Presently, I passed over the mountains, out above the huge breadth of the plain. Far away, on its surface, in the direction of the ring-shaped sun, there showed a confused blur. I looked towards it, indifferently. It reminded me, somewhat, of the first glimpse I had caught of the mountain-amphitheatre.

"With a sense of weariness, I glanced upwards at the immense ring of fire. What a strange thing it was! Then, as I stared, out from the dark centre, there spurted a sudden flare of extraordinary vivid fire. Compared with the size of the black centre, it was as naught; yet, in itself, stupendous. With awakened interest, I watched it carefully, noting its strange boiling and glowing. Then, in a moment, the whole thing grew dim and unreal, and so passed out of sight. Much amazed, I glanced down to the Plain from which I was still rising. Thus, I received a fresh surprise. The Plain—everything, had vanished, and only a sea of red mist was spread, far below me. Gradually, as I stared, this grew remote, and died away into a dim, far mystery of red, against an unfathomable night. Awhile, and even this had gone, and I was wrapped in an impalpable, lightless gloom.

IV
The Earth

"THUS I WAS, AND only the memory that I had lived through the dark, once before, served to sustain my thoughts. A great time passed—ages. And then a single star broke its way through the darkness. It was the first of one of the outlying clusters of this universe. Presently, it was far behind, and all about me shone the splendour of the countless stars. Later, years it seemed, I saw the sun, a clot of flame. Around it, I made out, presently, several remote specks of light—the planets of the Solar system. And so I saw the earth again, blue and unbelievably minute. It grew larger, and became defined.

"A long space of time came and went, and then, at last, I entered into the shadow of the world—plunging headlong into the dim and holy earth-night. Overhead, were the old constellations, and there was a crescent moon. Then, as I neared the earth's surface, a dimness swept over me, and I appeared to sink into a black mist.

"For awhile, I knew nothing. I was unconscious. Gradually, I became aware of a faint, distant whining. It became plainer. A desperate feeling of agony possessed me. I struggled madly for breath, and tried to shout. A moment, and I got my breath more easily. I was conscious that something was licking my hand. Something damp, swept across my face. I heard a panting, and then again the whining. It seemed to come to my ears, now, with a sense of familiarity, and I opened my eyes. All was dark; but the feeling of oppression had left me. I was seated, and something was whining piteously, and licking me. I felt strangely confused, and, instinctively, tried to ward off the thing that licked. My head was curiously vacant, and, for the moment, I seemed incapable of action or thought. Then, things came back to me, and I called 'Pepper,' faintly. I was answered by a joyful bark, and renewed and frantic caresses.

"In a little while, I felt stronger, and put out my hand for the matches. I groped about, for a few moments, blindly; then my hands lit upon them, and I struck a light, and looked confusedly around. All about me, I saw the old, familiar things. And there I sat, full of dazed wonders, until the flame of the match burnt my finger, and I dropped it; while a hasty expression of pain and anger, escaped my lips, surprising me with the sound of my own voice.

"After a moment, I struck another match, and, stumbling across the room, lit the candles. As I did so, I observed that they had not burned away, but had been put out.

"As the flames shot up, I turned, and stared about the study; yet there was nothing unusual to see; and, suddenly, a gust of irritation took me. What had happened? I held my head, with both hands, and tried to remember. Ah! the great, silent Plain, and the ring-shaped sun of red fire. Where were they? Where had I seen them? How long ago? I felt dazed and muddled. Once or twice, I walked up and down the room, unsteadily. My memory seemed dulled, and, already, the thing I had witnessed, came back to me with an effort.

"I have a remembrance of cursing, peevishly, in my bewilderment. Suddenly, I turned faint and giddy, and had to grasp at the table for support. During a few moments, I held on, weakly; and then managed to totter sideways into a chair. After a little time, I felt somewhat better, and succeeded in reaching the cupboard where, usually, I keep brandy and biscuits. I poured myself out a little of the stimulant, and drank it off. Then, taking a handful of biscuits, I returned to my chair, and began to devour them, ravenously. I was vaguely surprised at my hunger. I felt as though I had eaten nothing for an uncountably long while.

"As I ate, my glance roved about the room, taking in its various details, and still searching, though almost unconsciously, for something tangible upon which to take hold, among the invisible mysteries that encompassed me. 'Surely,' I thought, 'there must be something—' And, in the same instant, my gaze dwelt upon the face of the clock in the opposite corner. Therewith, I stopped eating, and just stared. For, though its ticking indicated, most certainly, that it was still going, the hands were pointing to a little *before* the hour of midnight; whereas it was, as well I knew, considerably *after* that time when I had witnessed the first of the strange happenings I have just described.

"For, perhaps a moment, I was astounded and puzzled. Had the hour been the same, as when I had last seen the clock, I should have concluded that the hands had stuck in one place, while the internal mechanism went on as usual; but that would, in no way, account for the hands having travelled backwards. Then, even as I turned the matter over in my wearied brain, the thought flashed upon me, that it was now close upon the morning of the twenty-second, and that I had been unconscious to the visible world through the greater portion of the last twenty-four hours. The thought occupied my attention for a full minute; then I commenced to eat, again. I was still very hungry.

"During breakfast, next morning, I inquired, casually of my sister, regarding the date, and found my surmise correct. I had, indeed, been absent—at least in spirit—for nearly a day and a night.

"My sister asked me no questions; for it is not, by any means, the first time that I have kept to my study for a whole day, and sometimes a couple of days, at a time, when I have been particularly engrossed in my books or work.

"And so the days pass on, and I am still filled with a wonder, to know the meaning of all that I saw on that memorable night. Yet, well I know that my curiosity is little likely to be satisfied."

V

The Thing in the Pit

"THIS HOUSE IS, AS I have said before, surrounded by a huge estate, and wild and uncultivated gardens.

"Away at the back, distant some three hundred yards, is a dark, deep ravine—spoken of as the 'Pit', by the peasantry. At the bottom, runs a sluggish stream, so overhung by trees, as scarcely to be seen from above.

"In passing, I must explain that this river has a subterranean origin, emerging, suddenly, at the East end of the ravine, and disappearing, as abruptly, beneath the cliffs that form its Western extremity.

"It was some months after my vision (if vision it were) of the great Plain, that my attention was particularly attracted to the Pit.

"I happened, one day, to be walking along its Southern edge, when, suddenly, several pieces of rock and shale were dislodged from the face of the cliff, immediately beneath me, and fell, with a sullen crash, through the trees. I heard them splash in the river, at the bottom; and then silence. I should not have given this incident more than a passing thought, had not Pepper, at once, begun to bark, savagely; nor would he be silent when I bade him, which is most unusual behaviour on his part.

"Feeling that there must be some one or something in the Pit, I went back to the house, quickly, for a stick. When I returned, Pepper had ceased his barks, and was growling and smelling, uneasily, along the top.

"Whistling to him, to follow me, I started to descend, cautiously. The depth, to the bottom of the Pit, must be about a hundred and fifty feet, and some time, as well as considerable care, was expended before we reached the bottom in safety.

"Once down, Pepper and I started to explore along the banks of

29

the river. It was very dark there, due to the overhanging trees, and I moved warily, keeping my glance about me, and my stick ready.

"Pepper was quiet now, and kept close to me all the time. Thus, we searched right up one side of the river, without hearing or seeing anything. Then, we crossed over—by the simple method of jumping—and commenced to beat our way back through the under-brush.

"We had accomplished, perhaps, half the distance, when I heard, again, the sound of falling stones on the other side—the side from which we had just come. One large rock came thundering down through the tree-tops, struck the opposite bank, and bounded into the river, driving a great jet of water right over us. At this, Pepper gave out a deep growl; then stopped, and pricked up his ears. I listened, also.

"A second later, a loud, half-human, half-pig-like squeal sounded from among the trees, apparently about half-way up the South cliff. It was answered by a similar note from the bottom of the Pit. At this, Pepper gave a short, sharp bark, and, springing across the little river, disappeared into the bushes.

"Immediately afterwards, I heard his barks increase in depth and number, and, in between, there sounded a noise of confused jabbering. This ceased, and, in the succeeding silence, there rose a semi-human yell of agony. Almost immediately, Pepper gave a long-drawn howl of pain, and then the shrubs were violently agitated, and he came running out, with his tail down, and glancing, as he ran, over his shoulder. As he reached me, I saw that he was bleeding from what appeared to be a great claw wound in the side, that had almost laid bare his ribs.

"Seeing Pepper thus mutilated, a furious feeling of anger seized me, and, whirling my staff, I sprang across, and into the bushes from which Pepper had emerged. As I forced my way through, I thought I heard a sound of breathing. Next instant, I had burst into a little clear space, just in time to see something, livid white in colour, disappear among the bushes on the opposite side. With a shout, I ran towards it; but, though I struck and probed among the bushes with my stick, I neither saw nor heard anything further; and so returned to Pepper. There, after bathing his wound in the river, I bound my wetted handkerchief round his body; having done which, we retreated up the ravine and into the daylight again.

"On reaching the house, my sister inquired what had happened to Pepper, and I told her he had been fighting with a wild cat, of which I had heard there were several about.

"I felt it would be better not to tell her how it had really happened; though, to be sure, I scarcely knew, myself; but this I did know, that the thing I had seen run into the bushes, was no wild cat. It was much too big, and had, so far as I had observed, a skin like a hog's, only of a dead, unhealthy white colour. And then—it had run upright, or nearly so, upon its hind feet, with a motion somewhat resembling that of a human being. This much, I had noticed in my brief glimpse, and, truth to tell, I felt a good deal of uneasiness, besides curiosity as I turned the matter over in my mind.

"It was in the morning that the above incident had occurred.

"Then, it would be after dinner, as I sat reading, that, happening to look up suddenly, I saw something peering in over the window-ledge the eyes and ears alone showing.

" 'A pig, by Jove!' I said, and rose to my feet. Thus, I saw the thing more completely; but it was no pig—God alone knows what it was. It reminded me, vaguely, of the hideous Thing that had haunted the great arena. It had a grotesquely human mouth and jaw; but with no chin of which to speak. The nose was prolonged into a snout; this it was, that, with the little eyes and queer ears, gave it such an extraordinarily swine-like appearance. Of forehead there was little, and the whole face was of an unwholesome white colour.

"For, perhaps a minute, I stood looking at the thing, with an ever growing feeling of disgust, and some fear. The mouth kept jabbering, inanely, and once emitted a half-swinish grunt. I think it was the eyes that attracted me the most; they seemed to glow, at times, with a horribly human intelligence, and kept flickering away from my face, over the details of the room, as though my stare disturbed it.

"It appeared to be supporting itself, by two claw-like hands upon the window-sill. These claws, unlike the face, were of a clayey brown hue, and bore an indistinct resemblance to human hands, in that they had four fingers and a thumb; though these were webbed up to the first joint, much as are a duck's. Nails it had also, but so long and powerful that they were more like the talons of an eagle than aught else.

"As I have said, before, I felt some fear; though almost of an impersonal kind. I may explain my feeling better by saying that it was more a sensation of abhorrence; such as one might expect to feel, if brought in contact with something superhumanly foul; something unholy—belonging to some hitherto undreamt of state of existence.

"I cannot say that I grasped these various details of the brute, at the time. I think they seemed to come back to me, afterwards, as though imprinted upon my brain. I imagined more than I saw, as I looked at the thing, and the material details grew upon me later.

"For, perhaps a minute, I stared at the creature; then, as my nerves steadied a little, I shook off the vague alarm that held me, and took a step towards the window. Even as I did so, the thing ducked and vanished. I rushed to the door, and looked round, hurriedly; but only the tangled bushes and shrubs met my gaze.

"I ran back into the house, and, getting my gun, sallied out to search through the gardens. As I went, I asked myself whether the thing I had just seen, was likely to be the same of which I had caught a glimpse in the morning. I inclined to think it was.

"I would have taken Pepper with me; but judged it better to give his wound a chance to heal. Besides, if the creature I had just seen, was, as I imagined, his antagonist of the morning, it was not likely that he would be of much use.

"I began my search, systematically. I was determined, if it were possible, to find and put an end to that swine-thing. This was, at least, a material Horror!

"At first, I searched, cautiously; with the thought of Pepper's wound in my mind; but, as the hours passed, and not a sign of anything living, showed in the great, lonely gardens, I became less apprehensive. I felt almost as though I would welcome the sight of it. Anything seemed better than this silence, with the ever present feeling, that the creature might be lurking in every bush I passed. Later, I grew careless of danger, to the extent of plunging right through the bushes, probing with my gun-barrel as I went.

"At times, I shouted; but only the echoes answered back. I thought thus, perhaps to frighten or stir the creature to showing itself; but only succeeded in bringing my sister Mary out, to know what was the matter. I told her, that I had seen the wild cat that had wounded Pepper, and that I was trying to hunt it out of the bushes. She seemed only half satisfied, and went back into the house, with an expression of doubt upon her face. I wondered whether she had seen or guessed anything. For the rest of the afternoon, I prosecuted the search, anxiously. I felt that I should be unable to sleep, with that bestial thing haunting the shrubberies, and yet, when evening fell, I had seen nothing. Then, as I turned homewards, I heard a short, unintelligible noise, among the bushes to my right. Instantly, I turned, and, aiming quickly, fired in the direction of the sound. Immediately afterwards, I heard something scuttling away among the bushes. It moved rapidly, and, in a minute, had gone out of hearing. After a few steps, I ceased my pursuit, realising how futile it must be, in the fast gathering gloom; and so, with a curious feeling of depression, I entered the house.

"That night, after my sister had gone to bed, I went round to all the windows and doors on the ground floor; and saw to it, that they were securely fastened. This precaution was scarcely necessary as regards the windows, as all of those on the lower storey are strongly barred; but with the doors—of which there are five—it was wisely thought, as not one was locked.

"Having secured these, I went to my study; yet, somehow, for once, the place jarred upon me; it seemed so huge and echoey. For some time, I tried to read; but, at last, finding it impossible, I carried my book down to the kitchen, where a large fire was burning, and sat there.

"I dare say, I had read for a couple of hours, when, suddenly, I heard a sound that made me lower my book, and listen, intently. It was a noise of something rubbing and fumbling against the back door. Once the door creaked, loudly; as though force were being applied to it. During those few, short moments, I experienced an indescribable feeling of terror, such as I should have believed impossible. My hands shook; a cold sweat broke out on me, and I shivered, violently.

"Gradually, I calmed. The stealthy movements outside, had ceased.

"Then, for an hour, I sat, silent, and watchful. All at once, the feeling of fear took me again. I felt as I imagine an animal must, under the eye of a snake. Yet, now, I could hear nothing. Still, there was no doubting that some unexplained influence was at work.

"Gradually, imperceptibly almost, something stole on my ear—a sound, that resolved itself into a faint murmur. Quickly, it developed, and grew into a muffled, but hideous, chorus of bestial shrieks. It appeared to rise from the bowels of the earth.

"I heard a thud, and realised, in a dull, half comprehending way, that I had dropped my book. After that, I just sat; and thus the daylight found me, when it crept wanly in through the barred, high windows of the great kitchen.

"With the dawning light, the feeling of stupor and fear left me; and I came more into possession of my senses.

"Thereupon, I picked up my book, and crept to the door, to listen. Not a sound broke the chilly silence. For some minutes, I stood there; then, very gradually and cautiously, I drew back the bolt, and, opening the door, peeped out.

"My caution was unneeded. Nothing was to be seen, save the

grey vista of dreary, tangled bushes and trees, extending to the distant plantation.

"With a shiver, I closed the door, and made my way, quietly, up to bed.

VI

The Swine-Things

"IT WAS EVENING, A week later. My sister sat in the garden, knitting. I was walking up and down, reading. My gun leant up against the wall of the house; for, since the advent of that strange thing in the gardens, I had deemed it wise to take precautions. Yet, through the whole week, there had been nothing to alarm me, either by sight or sound; so that I was able to look back, calmly, to the incident; though still with a sense of unmitigated wonder and curiosity.

"I was, as I have just said, walking up and down, and somewhat engrossed in my book. Suddenly, I heard a crash, away in the direction of the Pit. With a quick movement, I turned and saw a tremendous column of dust rising high into the evening air.

"My sister had risen to her feet, with a sharp exclamation of surprise and fright.

"Telling her to stay where she was, I snatched up my gun, and ran towards the Pit. As I neared it, I heard a dull, rumbling sound, that grew quickly into a roar, split with deeper crashes, and up from the Pit drove a fresh volume of dust.

"The noise ceased, though the dust still rose, tumultuously.

"I reached the edge, and looked down; but could see nothing, save a boil of dust clouds swirling hither and thither. The air was so full of the small particles, that they blinded and choked me; and, finally, I had to run out from the smother, to breathe.

"Gradually, the suspended matter sank, and hung in a panoply over the mouth of the Pit.

"I could only guess at what had happened.

"That there had been a land-slip of some kind, I had little doubt; but the cause was beyond my knowledge; and yet, even then, I had half imaginings; for, already, the thought had come to me, of those falling rocks, and that Thing in the bottom of the Pit; but, in the first

35

minutes of confusion, I failed to reach the natural conclusion, to which the catastrophe pointed.

"Slowly, the dust subsided, until, presently, I was able to approach the edge, and look down.

"For a while, I peered impotently, trying to see through the reek. At first, it was impossible to make out anything. Then, as I stared, I saw something below, to my left, that moved. I looked intently towards it, and, presently, made out another, and then another—three dim shapes that appeared to be climbing up the side of the Pit. I could see them only indistinctly. Even as I stared and wondered, I heard a rattle of stones, somewhere to my right. I glanced across; but could see nothing. I leant forward, and peered over, and down into the Pit, just beneath where I stood; and saw no further than a hideous, white swine-face, that had risen to within a couple of yards of my feet. Below it, I could make out several others. As the Thing saw me, it gave a sudden, un-couth squeal, which was answered from all parts of the Pit. At that, a gust of horror and fear took me, and, bending down, I discharged my gun right into its face. Straightway, the creature disappeared, with a clatter of loose earth and stones.

"There was a momentary silence, to which, probably, I owe my life; for, during it, I heard a quick patter of many feet, and, turning sharply, saw a troop of the creatures coming towards me, at a run. Instantly, I raised my gun and fired at the foremost, who plunged headlong, with a hideous howling. Then, I turned to run. More than half-way from the house to the Pit, I saw my sister—she was coming towards me. I could not see her face, distinctly, as the dusk had fallen; but there was fear in her voice as she called to know why I was shooting.

" 'Run!' I shouted in reply. 'Run, for your life!'

"Without more ado, she turned and fled—picking up her skirts with both hands. As I followed, I gave a glance behind. The brutes were running on their hind legs—at times dropping on all fours.

"I think it must have been the terror in my voice, that spurred Mary to run so; for I feel convinced that she had not, as yet, seen those hell creatures that pursued.

"On we went, my sister leading.

"Each moment, the nearing sounds of the footsteps, told me that the brutes were gaining on us, rapidly. Fortunately, I am accustomed to live, in some ways, an active life. As it was, the strain of the race was beginning to tell severely upon me.

"Ahead, I could see the back door—luckily it was open. I was some half-dozen yards behind Mary, now, and my breath was sobbing in my throat. Then, something touched my shoulder. I wrenched my head round, quickly, and saw one of those monstrous, pallid faces close to mine. One of the creatures, having outrun its companions, had almost overtaken me. Even as I turned, it made a fresh grab. With a sudden effort, I sprang to one side, and, swinging my gun by the barrel, brought it crashing down upon the foul creature's head. The Thing dropped, with an almost human groan.

"Even this short delay had been nearly sufficient to bring the rest of the brutes down upon me; so that, without an instant's waste of time, I turned and ran for the door.

"Reaching it, I burst into the passage; then, turning quickly, slammed and bolted the door, just as the first of the creatures rushed against it, with a sudden shock.

"My sister, sat, gasping, in a chair. She seemed in a fainting condition; but I had no time then to spend on her. I had to make sure that all the doors were fastened. Fortunately, they were. The one leading from my study into the gardens, was the last to which I went. I had just had time to note that it was secured, when I thought I heard a noise outside. I stood perfectly silent, and listened. Yes! Now I could distinctly hear a sound of whispering, and something slithered over the panels, with a rasping, scratchy noise. Evidently, some of the brutes were feeling with their claw-hands, about the door, to discover whether there were any means of ingress.

"That the creatures should, so soon, have found the door, was— to me—a proof of their reasoning capabilities. It assured me that they must not be regarded, by any means, as mere animals. I had felt something of this before, when that first Thing peered in through my window. Then, I had applied the term superhuman to it, with an almost instinctive knowledge that the creature was something different from the brute-beast. Something beyond human; yet in no good sense; but rather, as something foul and hostile to the *great* and *good* in humanity. In a word, as something intelligent, and yet inhuman. The very thought of the creatures filled me with revulsion.

"Now, I bethought me of my sister, and, going to the cupboard, I got out a flask of brandy, and a wineglass. Taking these, I went down to the kitchen, carrying a lighted candle with me. She was not sitting in the chair, but had fallen out, and was lying upon the floor, face downwards.

"Very gently, I turned her over, and raised her head, somewhat.

Then, I poured a little of the brandy between her lips. After a while, she shivered slightly. A little later, she gave several gasps, and opened her eyes. In a dreamy, unrealising way, she looked at me. Then her eyes closed, slowly, and I gave her a little more of the brandy. For, perhaps a minute longer, she lay silent, breathing quickly. All at once, her eyes opened again, and it seemed to me, as I looked, that the pupils were dilated, as though fear had come with returning consciousness. Then, with a movement so unexpected that I started backwards, she sat up. Noticing that she seemed giddy, I put out my hand to steady her. At that, she gave a loud scream, and, scrambling to her feet, ran from the room.

"For a moment, I stayed there—kneeling and holding the brandy flask. I was utterly puzzled and astonished.

"Could she be afraid of me? But no! Why should she? I could only conclude that her nerves were badly shaken, and that she was temporarily unhinged. Upstairs, I heard a door bang, loudly, and I knew that she had taken refuge in her room. I put the flask down on the table. My attention was distracted by a noise in the direction of the back door. I went towards it, and listened. It appeared to be shaken, as though some of the creatures struggled with it, silently; but it was far too strongly constructed and hung to be easily moved.

"Out in the gardens, rose a continuous sound. It might have been mistaken, by a casual listener, for the grunting and squealing of a herd of pigs. But, as I stood there, it came to me that there was sense and meaning to all those swinish noises. Gradually, I seemed able to trace a semblance in it to human speech—glutinous and sticky, as though each articulation were made with difficulty: yet, nevertheless, I was becoming convinced that it was no mere medley of sounds; but a rapid interchange of ideas.

"By this time, it had grown quite dark in the passages, and from these came all the varied cries and groans of which an old house is so full after nightfall. It is, no doubt, because things are then quieter, and one has more leisure to hear. Also, there may be something in the theory that the sudden change of temperature, at sundown, affects the structure of the house, somewhat—causing it to contract and settle, as it were, for the night. However, this is as may be; but, on that night in particular, I would gladly have been quit of so many eerie noises. It seemed to me, that each crack and creak was the coming of one of those Things along the dark corridors; though I knew in my heart that this could not be, for I had seen, myself, that all the doors were secure.

"Gradually, however, these sounds grew on my nerves to such an extent that, were it only to punish my cowardice, I felt I must make the round of the basement again, and, if anything were there, face it. And then, I would go up to my study; for I knew sleep was out of the question, with the house surrounded by creatures, half beasts, half something else, and entirely unholy.

"Taking the kitchen lamp down from its hook, I made my way from cellar to cellar, and room to room; through pantry and coalhole—along passages, and into the hundred-and-one little blind alleys and hidden nooks that form the basement of the old house. Then, when I knew I had been in every corner and cranny large enough to conceal aught of any size, I made my way to the stairs.

"With my foot on the first step, I paused. It seemed to me, I heard a movement, apparently from the buttery, which is to the left of the staircase. It had been one of the first places I searched, and yet, I felt certain my ears had not deceived me. My nerves were strung now, and, with hardly any hesitation, I stepped up to the door, holding the lamp above my head. In a glance, I saw that the place was empty, save for the heavy, stone slabs, supported by brick pillars; and I was about to leave it, convinced that I had been mistaken; when, in turning, my light was flashed back from two bright spots outside the window, and high up. For a few moments, I stood there, staring. Then they moved—revolving slowly, and throwing out alternate scintillations of green and red; at least, so it appeared to me. I knew then that they were eyes.

"Slowly, I traced the shadowy outline of one of the Things. It appeared to be holding on to the bars of the window, and its attitude suggested climbing. I went nearer to the window, and held the light higher. There was no need to be afraid of the creature; the bars were strong, and there was little danger of its being able to move them. And then, suddenly, in spite of the knowledge that the brute could not reach to harm me, I had a return of the horrible sensation of fear, that had assailed me on that night, a week previously. It was the same feeling of helpless, shuddering fright. I realised, dimly, that the creature's eyes were looking into mine with a steady, compelling stare. I tried to turn away; but could not. I seemed, now, to see the window through a mist. Then, I thought other eyes came and peered, and yet others; until a whole galaxy of malignant, staring orbs seemed to hold me in thrall.

"My head began to swim, and throb violently. Then, I was aware of a feeling of acute physical pain in my left hand. It grew more severe, and forced, literally forced, my attention. With a tremendous effort, I glanced down; and, with that, the spell that had held me was broken. I realised, then, that I had, in my agitation, unconsciously caught hold of the hot lamp-glass, and burnt my hand, badly. I looked up to the window, again. The misty appearance had gone, and, now, I saw that it was crowded with dozens of bestial faces. With a sudden access of rage, I raised the lamp, and hurled it, full at the window. It struck the glass (smashing a pane), and passed between two of the bars, out into the garden, scattering burning oil as it went. I heard several loud cries of pain, and, as my sight became accustomed to the dark, I discovered that the creatures had left the window.

"Pulling myself together, I groped for the door, and, having found it, made my way upstairs, stumbling at each step. I felt dazed, as though I had received a blow on the head. At the same time, my hand smarted badly, and I was full of a nervous, dull rage against those Things.

"Reaching my study, I lit the candles. As they burnt up, their rays were reflected from the rack of firearms on the side wall. At the sight, I remembered that I had there a power, which, as I had proved earlier, seemed as fatal to those monsters as to more ordinary animals; and I determined I would take the offensive.

"First of all, I bound up my hand; for the pain was fast becoming intolerable. After that, it seemed easier, and I crossed the room, to the rifle stand. There, I selected a heavy rifle—an old and tried weapon; and, having procured ammunition, I made my way up into one of the small towers, with which the house is crowned.

"From there, I found that I could see nothing. The gardens presented a dim blur of shadows—a little blacker, perhaps, where the trees stood. That was all, and I knew that it was useless to shoot down into all that darkness. The only thing to be done, was to wait for the moon to rise; then, I might be able to do a little execution.

"In the meantime, I sat still, and kept my ears open. The gardens were comparatively quiet now, and only an occasional grunt or squeal came up to me. I did not like this silence; it made me wonder on what devilry the creatures were bent. Twice, I left the tower, and took a walk through the house; but everything was silent.

"Once, I heard a noise, from the direction of the Pit, as though more earth had fallen. Following this, and lasting for some fifteen minutes, there was a commotion among the denizens of the gardens. This died away, and, after that all was again quiet.

"About an hour later, the moon's light showed above the distant horizon. From where I sat, I could see it over the trees; but it was not until it rose clear of them, that I could make out any of the details in the gardens below. Even then, I could see none of the brutes; until, happening to crane forward, I saw several of them lying prone, up against the wall of the house. What they were doing, I could not make out. It was, however, a chance too good to be ignored; and, taking aim, I fired at the one directly beneath. There was a shrill scream, and, as the smoke cleared away, I saw that it had turned on its back, and was writhing, feebly. Then, it was quiet. The others had disappeared.

"Immediately after this, I heard a loud squeal, in the direction of the Pit. It was answered, a hundred times, from every part of the garden. This gave me some notion of the number of the creatures, and I began to feel that the whole affair was becoming even more serious than I had imagined.

"As I sat there, silent and watchful, the thought came to me— Why was all this? What were these Things? What did it mean? Then my thoughts flew back to that vision (though, even now, I doubt whether it was a vision) of the Plain of Silence. What did that mean? I wondered—And that Thing in the arena? Ugh! Lastly, I thought of the house I had seen in that far-away place. That house, so like this in every detail of external structure, that it might have been modelled from it; or this from that. I had never thought of that—

"At this moment, there came another long squeal, from the Pit, followed, a second later, by a couple of shorter ones. At once, the garden was filled with answering cries. I stood up, quickly, and looked over the parapet. In the moonlight, it seemed as though the shrubberies were alive. They tossed hither and thither, as though shaken by a strong, irregular wind; while a continuous rustling, and a noise of scampering feet, rose up to me. Several times, I saw the moonlight gleam on running, white figures among the bushes, and, twice, I fired. The second time, my shot was answered by a short squeal of pain.

"A minute later, the gardens lay silent. From the Pit, came a deep, hoarse Babel of swine-talk. At times, angry cries smote the air, and they would be answered by multitudinous gruntings. It occurred to me, that they were holding some kind of a council, perhaps to discuss the problem of entering the house. Also, I thought that they seemed much enraged, probably by my successful shots.

"It occurred to me, that now would be a good time to make a final survey of our defences. This, I proceeded to do at once; visiting the whole of the basement again, and examining each of the doors. Luckily, they are all, like the back one, built of solid, iron-studded oak. Then, I went upstairs to the study. I was more anxious about this door. It is, palpably, of a more modern make than the others, and, though a stout piece of work, it has little of their ponderous strength.

"I must explain here, that there is a small, raised lawn on this side of the house, upon which this door opens—the windows of the study being barred on this account. All the other entrances—excepting the great gate-way which is never opened—are in the lower storey.

VII
The Attack

"I SPENT SOME TIME, puzzling how to strengthen the study door. Finally, I went down to the kitchen, and with some trouble, brought up several heavy pieces of timber. These, I wedged up, slantwise, against it, from the floor, nailing them top and bottom. For half-an-hour, I worked hard, and, at last, got it shored to my mind.

"Then, feeling easier, I resumed my coat, which I had laid aside, and proceeded to attend to one or two matters before returning to the tower. It was whilst thus employed, that I heard a fumbling at the door, and the latch was tried. Keeping silence, I waited. Soon, I heard several of the creatures outside. They were grunting to one another, softly. Then, for a minute, there was quietness. Suddenly, there sounded a quick, low grunt, and the door creaked under a tremendous pressure. It would have burst inwards; but for the supports I had placed. The strain ceased, as quickly as it had begun, and there was more talk.

"Presently, one of the Things squealed, softly, and I heard the sound of others approaching. There was a short confabulation; then again, silence; and I realised that they had called several more to assist. Feeling that now was the supreme moment, I stood ready, with my rifle presented. If the door gave, I would, at least, slay as many as possible.

"Again came the low signal; and, once more, the door cracked, under a huge force. For, a minute perhaps, the pressure was kept up; and I waited, nervously; expecting each moment to see the door come down with a crash. But no; the struts held, and the attempt proved abortive. Then followed more of their horrible, grunting talk, and, whilst it lasted, I thought I distinguished the noise of fresh arrivals.

"After a long discussion, during which the door was several times shaken, they became quiet once more, and I knew that they were going to make a third attempt to break it down. I was almost in despair. The props had been severely tried in the two previous attacks, and I was sorely afraid that this would prove too much for them.

"At that moment, like an inspiration, a thought flashed into my troubled brain. Instantly, for it was no time to hesitate, I ran from the room, and up stair after stair. This time, it was not to one of the towers, that I went; but out on to the flat, leaded roof itself. Once there, I raced across to the parapet, that walls it round, and looked down. As I did so, I heard the short, grunted signal, and, even up there, caught the crying of the door under the assault.

"There was not a moment to lose, and, leaning over, I aimed, quickly, and fired. The report rang sharply, and, almost blending with it, came the loud splud of the bullet striking its mark. From below, rose a shrill wail; and the door ceased its groaning. Then, as I took my weight from off the parapet, a huge piece of the stone coping slid from under me, and fell with a crash among the disorganised throng beneath. Several horrible shrieks quavered through the night air, and then I heard a sound of scampering feet. Cautiously, I looked over. In the moonlight, I could see the great coping stone, lying right across the threshold of the door. I thought I saw something under it—several things, white; but I could not be sure.

"And so a few minutes passed.

"As I stared, I saw something come round, out of the shadow of the house. It was one of the Things. It went up to the stone, silently, and bent down. I was unable to see what it did. In a minute it stood up. It had something in its talons, which it put to its mouth and tore at. . . .

"For the moment, I did not realise. Then, slowly, I comprehended. The Thing was stooping again. It was horrible. I started to load my rifle. When I looked again, the monster was tugging at the stone—moving it to one side. I leant the rifle on the coping, and pulled the trigger. The brute collapsed, on its face, and kicked, slightly.

"Simultaneously, almost, with the report, I heard another sound—that of breaking glass. Waiting, only to recharge my weapon, I ran from the roof, and down the first two flights of stairs.

"Here, I paused to listen. As I did so, there came another tinkle of falling glass. It appeared to come from the floor below. Excitedly, I sprang down the steps, and, guided by the rattle of the window-sash, reached the door of one of the empty bedrooms, at the back of the house. I thrust it open. The room was but dimly illuminated by the moonlight; most of the light being blotted out by moving figures at the window. Even as I stood, one crawled through, into the room. Levelling my weapon, I fired point-blank at it—filling the room with a deafening bang. When the smoke cleared, I saw that the room was empty, and the window free. The room was much lighter. The night air blew in, coldly, through the shattered panes. Down below, in the night, I could hear a soft moaning, and a confused murmur of swine-voices.

"Stepping to one side of the window, I reloaded, and then stood there, waiting. Presently, I heard a scuffling noise. From where I stood in the shadow, I could see, without being seen.

"Nearer came the sounds, and then I saw something come up above the sill, and clutch at the broken window-frame. It caught a piece of the woodwork; and, now, I could make out that it was a hand and arm. A moment later, the face of one of the Swine-creatures rose into view. Then, before I could use my rifle, or do anything, there came a sharp crack—cr-ac-k; and the window-frame gave way under the weight of the Thing. Next instant, a squashing thud, and a loud outcry, told me that it had fallen to the ground. With a savage hope that it had been killed, I went to the window. The moon had gone behind a cloud, so that I could see nothing; though a steady hum of jabbering, just beneath where I stood, indicated that there were several more of the brutes close at hand.

"As I stood there, looking down, I marvelled how it had been possible for the creatures to climb so far; for the wall is comparatively smooth, while the distance to the ground must be, at least, eighty feet.

"All at once, as I bent, peering, I saw something, indistinctly, that cut the grey shadow of the house-side, with a black line. It passed the window, to the left, at a distance of about two feet. Then, I remembered that it was a gutter-pipe, that had been put there some years ago, to carry off the rain water. I had forgotten about it. I could see, now, how the creatures had managed to reach the window. Even as the solution came to me, I heard a faint slithering, scratching noise, and knew that another of the brutes was coming. I waited some odd moments; then leant out of the window and felt the pipe. To my delight, I found that it was quite loose, and I managed, using the rifle-barrel as a crowbar, to lever it out from the wall. I worked quickly. Then, taking hold with both hands, I wrenched the whole concern away, and hurled it down—with the Thing still clinging to it—into the garden.

"For a few minutes longer, I waited there, listening; but, after the first general outcry, I heard nothing. I knew, now, that there was no more reason to fear an attack from this quarter. I had removed the only means of reaching the window, and, as none of the other windows had any adjacent water-pipes, to tempt the climbing powers of the monsters, I began to feel more confident of escaping their clutches.

"Leaving the room, I made my way down to the study. I was anxious to see how the door had withstood the test of that last assault. Entering, I lit two of the candles, and then turned to the door. One of the large props had been displaced, and, on that side, the door had been forced inward some six inches.

"It was Providential that I had managed to drive the brutes away just when I did! And that coping-stone! I wondered, vaguely, how I had managed to dislodge it. I had not noticed it loose, as I took my shot; and then, as I stood up, it had slipped away from beneath me.... I felt that I owed the dismissal of the attacking force, more to its timely fall than to my rifle. Then the thought came, that I had better seize this chance to shore up the door, again. It was evident that the creatures had not returned since the fall of the coping-stone; but who was to say how long they would keep away?

"There and then, I set-to, at repairing the door—working hard and anxiously. First, I went down to the basement, and, rummaging round, found several pieces of heavy oak planking. With these, I returned to the study, and, having removed the props, placed the planks up against the door. Then, I nailed the heads of the struts to these, and, driving them well home at the bottoms, nailed them again there.

"Thus, I made the door stronger than ever; for now it was solid with the backing of boards, and would, I felt convinced, stand a heavier pressure than hitherto, without giving way.

"After that, I lit the lamp which I had brought from the kitchen, and went down to have a look at the lower windows.

"Now that I had seen an instance of the strength the creatures possessed, I felt considerable anxiety about the windows on the ground floor—in spite of the fact that they were so strongly barred.

"I went first to the buttery, having a vivid remembrance of my late adventure there. The place was chilly, and the wind, soughing in through the broken glass, produced an eerie note. Apart from the general air of dismalness, the place was as I had left it the night before. Going up to the window, I examined the bars, closely; noting, as I did so, their comfortable thickness. Still, as I looked more intently, it seemed to me, that the middle bar was bent slightly from the straight; yet it was but trifling, and it might have been so for years. I had never, before, noticed them particularly.

"I put my hand through the broken window, and shook the bar. It was as firm as a rock. Perhaps the creatures had tried to 'start' it, and, finding it beyond their power, ceased from the effort. After that,

I went round to each of the windows, in turn; examining them with careful attention; but nowhere else could I trace anything to show that there had been any tampering. Having finished my survey, I went back to the study, and poured myself out a little brandy. Then to the tower to watch.

VIII
After the Attack

"IT WAS NOW ABOUT three a.m., and, presently, the Eastern sky began to pale with the coming of dawn. Gradually, the day came, and, by its light, I scanned the gardens, earnestly; but nowhere could I see any signs of the brutes. I leant over, and glanced down to the foot of the wall, to see whether the body of the Thing I had shot the night before was still there. It was gone. I supposed that others of the monsters had removed it during the night.

"Then, I went down on to the roof, and crossed over to the gap from which the coping stone had fallen. Reaching it, I looked over. Yes, there was the stone, as I had seen it last; but there was no appearance of anything beneath it; nor could I see the creatures I had killed, after its fall. Evidently, they also had been taken away. I turned, and went down to my study. There, I sat down, wearily. I was thoroughly tired. It was quite light now; though the sun's rays were not, as yet, perceptibly hot. A clock chimed the hour of four....

"I awoke, with a start, and looked round, hurriedly. The clock in the corner, indicated that it was three o'clock. It was already afternoon. I must have slept for nearly eleven hours.

"With a jerky movement, I sat forward in the chair, and listened. The house was perfectly silent. Slowly, I stood up, and yawned. I felt desperately tired, still, and sat down again; wondering what it was that had waked me.

"It must have been the clock striking, I concluded, presently; and was commencing to doze off, when a sudden noise brought me back, once more, to life. It was the sound of a step, as of a person moving cautiously down the corridor, towards my study. In an instant, I was on my feet, and grasping my rifle. Noiselessly, I waited. Had the creatures broken in, whilst I slept? Even as I questioned, the steps reached my door, halted momentarily, and then continued down the passage. Silently, I tiptoed to the doorway, and peeped out. Then, I experienced such a feeling of relief, as must a reprieved criminal—it was my sister. She was going towards the stairs.

"I stepped into the hall, and was about to call to her, when it occurred to me, that it was very queer she should have crept past my door, in that stealthy manner. I was puzzled, and, for one brief moment, the thought occupied my mind, that it was not she, but some fresh mystery of the house. Then, as I caught a glimpse of her old petticoat, the thought passed as quickly as it had come, and I half laughed. There could be no mistaking that ancient garment. Yet, I wondered what she was doing; and, remembering her condition of mind, on the previous day, I felt that it might be best to follow, quietly—taking care not to alarm her—and see what she was going to do. If she behaved rationally, well and good; if not, I should have to take steps to restrain her. I could run no unnecessary risks, under the danger that threatened us.

"Quickly, I reached the head of the stairs, and paused a moment. Then, I heard a sound that sent me leaping down, at a mad rate—it was the rattle of bolts being unshot. That foolish sister of mine was actually unbarring the back door.

"Just as her hand was on the last bolt, I reached her. She had not seen me, and, the first thing she knew, I had hold of her arm. She glanced up quickly, like a frightened animal, and screamed aloud.

" 'Come, Mary!' I said, sternly, 'what's the meaning of this nonsense? Do you mean to tell me you don't understand the danger, that you try to throw our two lives away in this fashion!'

"To this, she replied nothing; only trembled, violently, gasping and sobbing, as though in the last extremity of fear.

"Through some minutes, I reasoned with her; pointing out the need for caution, and asking her to be brave. There was little to be afraid of now, I explained—and, I tried to believe that I spoke the truth—but she must be sensible, and not attempt to leave the house for a few days.

"At last, I ceased, in despair. It was no use talking to her; she was, obviously, not quite herself for the time being. Finally, I told her she had better go to her room, if she could not behave rationally.

"Still, she took not any notice. So, without more ado, I picked her up in my arms, and carried her there. At first, she screamed, wildly; but had relapsed into silent trembling, by the time I reached the stairs.

"Arriving at her room, I laid her upon the bed. She lay there quietly enough, neither speaking nor sobbing—just shaking in a very ague of fear. I took a rug from a chair near by, and spread it over her. I could do nothing more for her, and so, crossed to where Pepper lay in a big basket. My sister had taken charge of him since his wound, to nurse him, for it had proved more severe than I had thought, and I was pleased to note that, in spite of her state of mind, she had looked after the old dog, carefully. Stooping, I spoke to him, and, in reply, he licked my hand, feebly. He was too ill to do more.

"Then, going to the bed, I bent over my sister, and asked her how she felt; but she only shook the more, and, much as it pained me, I had to admit that my presence seemed to make her worse.

"And so, I left her—locking the door, and pocketing the key. It seemed to be the only course to take.

"The rest of the day, I spent between the tower and my study. For food, I brought up a loaf from the pantry, and on this, and some claret, I lived for that day.

"What a long, weary day it was. If only I could have gone out into the gardens, as is my wont, I should have been content enough; but to be cooped in this silent house, with no companion, save a mad woman and a sick dog, was enough to prey upon the nerves of the hardiest. And out in the tangled shrubberies that surrounded the house, lurked—for all I could tell—those infernal Swine-creatures waiting their chance. Was ever a man in such straits?

"Once, in the afternoon, and again, later, I went to visit my sister. The second time, I found her tending Pepper; but, at my approach, she slid over, unobtrusively, to the far corner, with a gesture that saddened me beyond belief. Poor girl! her fear cut me intolerably, and I would not intrude on her, unnecessarily. She would be better, I trusted, in a few days; meanwhile, I could do nothing; and I judged it still needful—hard as it seemed—to keep her confined to her room. One thing there was that I took for encouragement: she had eaten some of the food I had taken to her, on my first visit.

"And so the day passed.

"As the evening drew on, the air grew chilly, and I began to make preparations for passing a second night in the tower—taking up two additional rifles, and a heavy ulster. The rifles I loaded, and laid alongside my other; as I intended to make things warm for any of the creatures who might show, during the night. I had plenty of ammunition, and I thought to give the brutes such a lesson, as should show them the uselessness of attempting to force an entrance.

"After that, I made the round of the house again; paying particular attention to the props that supported the study door. Then, feeling that I had done all that lay in my power to insure our safety, I returned to the tower; calling in on my sister and Pepper, for a final visit, on the way. Pepper was asleep; but woke, as I entered, and wagged his tail, in recognition. I thought he seemed slightly better. My sister was lying on the bed; though whether asleep or not, I was unable to tell; and thus I left them.

"Reaching the tower, I made myself as comfortable as circumstances would permit, and settled down to watch through the night. Gradually, darkness fell, and soon the details of the gardens were merged into shadows. During the first few hours, I sat, alert, listening for any sound that might help to tell me if anything were stirring down below. It was far too dark for my eyes to be of much use.

"Slowly, the hours passed; without anything unusual happening. And the moon rose, showing the gardens, apparently empty, and silent. And so, through the night, without disturbance or sound.

"Towards morning, I began to grow stiff and cold, with my long vigil; also, I was getting very uneasy, concerning the continued quietness on the part of the creatures. I mistrusted it, and would sooner, far, have had them attack the house, openly. Then, at least, I should have known my danger, and been able to meet it; but to wait like this, through a whole night, picturing all kinds of unknown devilment, was to jeopardise one's sanity. Once or twice, the thought came to me, that, perhaps, they had gone; but, in my heart, I found it impossible to believe that it was so.

IX

In the Cellars

"AT LAST, WHAT WITH being tired and cold, and the un-easiness that possessed me, I resolved to take a walk through the house; first calling in at the study, for a glass of brandy to warm me. This, I did, and, while there, I examined the door, carefully; but found all as I had left it the night before.

"The day was just breaking, as I left the tower; though it was still too dark in the house to be able to see without a light, and I took one of the study candles with me on my round. By the time I had finished the ground floor, the daylight was creeping in, wanly, through the barred windows. My search had shown me nothing fresh. Everything appeared to be in order, and I was on the point of extinguishing my candle, when the thought suggested itself to me to have another glance round the cellars. I had not, if I remember rightly, been into them since my hasty search on the evening of the attack.

"For, perhaps, the half of a minute, I hesitated. I would have been very willing to forego the task—as, indeed, I am inclined to think any man well might—for of all the great, awe-inspiring rooms in this house, the cellars are the hugest and weirdest. Great, gloomy caverns of places, unlit by any ray of daylight. Yet, I would not shirk the work. I felt that to do so would smack of sheer cowardice. Besides, as I reassured myself, the cellars were really the most unlikely places in which to come across anything dangerous; considering that they can be entered, only through a heavy oaken door, the key of which, I carry always on my person.

"It is in the smallest of these places that I keep my wine; a gloomy hole close to the foot of the cellar stairs; and beyond which, I have seldom proceeded. Indeed, save for the rummage round, already mentioned, I doubt whether I had ever, before, been right through the cellars.

"As I unlocked the great door, at the top of the steps, I paused, nervously, a moment, at the strange, desolate smell that assailed my nostrils. Then, throwing the barrel of my weapon forward, I descended, slowly, into the darkness of the underground regions.

"Reaching the bottom of the stairs, I stood for a minute, and listened. All was silent, save for a faint drip, drip of water, falling, drop by drop, somewhere to my left. As I stood, I noticed how quietly the candle burnt; never a flicker nor flare, so utterly windless was the place.

"Quietly, I moved from cellar to cellar. I had but a very dim memory of their arrangement. The impressions left by my first search were blurred. I had recollections of a succession of great cellars, and of one, greater than the rest, the roof of which was upheld by pillars; beyond that my mind was hazy, and predominated by a sense of cold and darkness and shadows. Now, however, it was different; for, although nervous, I was sufficiently collected to be able to look about me, and note the structure and size of the different vaults I entered.

"Of course, with the amount of light given by my candle, it was not possible to examine each place, minutely; but I was enabled to notice, as I went along, that the walls appeared to be built with wonderful precision and finish; while here and there, an occasional, massive pillar shot up to support the vaulted roof.

"Thus, I came, at last, to the great cellar that I remembered. It is reached, through a huge, arched entrance, on which I observed strange, fantastic carvings, which threw queer shadows under the light of my candle. As I stood, and examined these, thoughtfully, it occurred to me how strange it was, that I should be so little acquainted with my own house. Yet, this may be easily understood, when one realises the size of this ancient pile, and the fact that only my old sister and I live in it, occupying a few of the rooms, such as our wants decide.

"Holding the light high, I passed on into the cellar, and, keeping to the right, paced slowly up, until I reached the further end. I walked quietly, and looked cautiously about, as I went. But, so far as the light showed, I saw nothing unusual.

"At the top, I turned to the left, still keeping to the wall, and so continued, until I had traversed the whole of the vast chamber. As I moved along, I noticed that the floor was composed of solid rock, in places covered with a damp mould, in others bare, or almost so, save for a thin coating of light-grey dust.

"I had halted at the doorway. Now, however, I turned, and made my way up the centre of the place; passing among the pillars, and glancing to right and left, as I moved. About half way up the cellar, I stubbed my foot against something that gave out a metallic sound. Stooping quickly, I held the candle, and saw that the object I had kicked, was a large, metal ring. Bending lower, I cleared the dust from around it, and, presently, discovered that it was attached to a ponderous trapdoor, black with age.

"Feeling excited, and wondering to where it could lead, I laid my gun on the floor, and, sticking the candle in the trigger guard, took the ring in both hands, and pulled. The trap creaked loudly—the sound echoing, vaguely, through the huge place—and opened, heavily.

"Propping the edge on my knee, I reached for the candle, and held it in the opening, moving it to right and left; but could see nothing. I was puzzled and surprised. There were no signs of steps, nor even the appearance of there ever having been any. Nothing; save an empty blackness. I might have been looking down into a bottomless, sideless well. Then, even as I stared, full of perplexity, I seemed to hear, far down, as though from untold depths, a faint whisper of sound. I bent my head, quickly, more into the opening, and listened, intently. It may have been fancy; but I could have sworn to hearing a soft titter, that grew into a hideous, chuckling, faint and distant. Startled, I leapt backwards, letting the trap fall, with a hollow clang, that filled the place with echoes. Even then, I seemed to hear that mocking, suggestive laughter; but this, I knew, must be my imagination. The sound, I had heard, was far too slight to penetrate through the cumbrous trap.

"For a full minute, I stood there, quivering—glancing, nervously, behind and before; but the great cellar was silent as a grave, and, gradually, I shook off the frightened sensation. With a calmer mind, I became again curious to know into what that trap opened; but could not, then, summon sufficient courage, to make a further investigation. One thing I felt, however, was that the trap ought to be secured. This, I accomplished by placing upon it several large pieces of 'dressed' stone, which I had noticed in my tour along the East wall.

"Then, after a final scrutiny of the rest of the place, I retraced my way through the cellars, to the stairs, and so reached the daylight, with an infinite feeling of relief, that the uncomfortable task was accomplished.

X

The Time of Waiting

"**T**HE SUN WAS NOW warm, and shining brightly, forming a won-drous contrast to the dark and dismal cellars; and it was with comparatively light feelings, that I made my way up to the tower, to survey the gardens. There, I found everything quiet, and, after a few minutes, went down to Mary's room.

"Here, having knocked, and received a reply, I unlocked the door. My sister was sitting, quietly, on the bed; as though waiting. She seemed quite herself again, and made no attempt to move away, as I approached; yet, I observed that she scanned my face, anxiously, as though in doubt, and but half assured in her mind that there was nothing to fear from me.

"To my questions, as to how she felt, she replied, sanely enough, that she was hungry, and would like to go down to prepare breakfast, if I did not mind. For a minute, I meditated whether it would be safe to let her out. Finally, I told her she might go, on condition that she promised not to attempt to leave the house, or meddle with any of the outer doors. At my mention of the doors, a sudden look of fright crossed her face; but she said nothing, save to give the required promise, and then left the room, silently.

"Crossing the floor, I approached Pepper. He had waked as I entered; but, beyond a slight yelp of pleasure, and a soft rapping with his tail, had kept quiet. Now, as I patted him, he made an attempt to stand up, and succeeded, only to fall back on his side, with a little yowl of pain.

"I spoke to him, and bade him lie still. I was greatly delighted with his improvement, and also with the natural kindness of my sister's heart, in taking such good care of him, in spite of her condition of mind. After a while, I left him, and went downstairs, to my study.

"In a little time, Mary appeared, carrying a tray on which smoked a hot breakfast. As she entered the room, I saw her gaze fasten on the props that supported the study door; her lips tightened, and I thought she paled, slightly; but that was all. Putting the tray down at my elbow, she was leaving the room, quietly, when I called her back. She came, it seemed, a little timidly, as though startled; and I noted that her hand clutched at her apron, nervously.

" 'Come, Mary,' I said. 'Cheer up! Things look brighter. I've seen none of the creatures since yesterday morning, early.'

"She looked at me, in a curiously puzzled manner; as though not comprehending. Then, intelligence swept into her eyes, and fear; but she said nothing, beyond an unintelligible murmur of acquiescence. After that, I kept silence; it was evident that any reference to the Swine-things, was more than her shaken nerves could bear.

"Breakfast over, I went up to the tower. Here, during the greater part of the day, I maintained a strict watch over the gardens. Once or twice, I went down to the basement, to see how my sister was getting along. Each time, I found her quiet, and curiously submissive. Indeed, on the last occasion, she even ventured to address me, on her own account, with regard to some household matter that needed attention. Though this was done with an almost extraordinary timidity, I hailed it with happiness, as being the first word, voluntarily spoken, since the critical moment, when I had caught her unbarring the back door, to go out among those waiting brutes. I wondered whether she was aware of her attempt, and how near a thing it had been; but refrained from questioning her, thinking it best to let well alone.

"That night, I slept in a bed; the first time for two nights. In the morning, I rose early, and took a walk through the house. All was as it should be, and I went up to the tower, to have a look at the gardens. Here, again, I found perfect quietness.

"At breakfast, when I met Mary, I was greatly pleased to see that she had sufficiently regained command over herself, to be able to greet me in a perfectly natural manner. She talked sensibly and quietly; only keeping carefully from any mention of the past couple of days. In this, I humoured her, to the extent of not attempting to lead the conversation in that direction.

"Earlier in the morning, I had been to see Pepper. He was mending, rapidly; and bade fair to be on his legs, in earnest, in another day or two. Before leaving the breakfast table, I made some reference to his improvement. In the short discussion that followed, I was surprised to gather, from my sister's remarks, that she was still under the impression that his wound had been given by the wild cat, of my invention. It made me feel almost ashamed of myself for deceiving her. Yet, the lie had been told to prevent her from being frightened. And then, I had been sure that she must have known the truth, later, when those brutes had attacked the house.

"During the day, I kept on the alert; spending much of my time, as on the previous day, in the tower; but not a sign could I see of the Swine-creatures, nor hear any sound. Several times, the thought had come to me, that the Things had, at last, left us; but, up to this time, I had refused to entertain the idea, seriously; now, however, I began to feel that there was reason for hope. It would soon be three days since I had seen any of the Things; but still, I intended to use the utmost caution. For all that I could tell, this protracted silence might be a ruse to tempt me from the house—perhaps right into their arms. The thought of such a contingency, was, alone, sufficient to make me circumspect.

"So it was, that the fourth, fifth and sixth days went by, quietly; without my making any attempt to leave the house.

"On the sixth day, I had the pleasure of seeing Pepper, once more, upon his feet; and, though still very weak, he managed to keep me company during the whole of that day.

XI

The Searching of the Gardens

"NOW SLOWLY THE TIME went; and never a thing to indicate that any of the brutes still infested the gardens.

"It was on the ninth day that, finally, I decided to run the risk, if any there were, and sally out. With this purpose in view, I loaded one of the shot-guns, carefully—choosing it, as being more deadly than a rifle, at close quarters; and then, after a final scrutiny of the grounds, from the tower, I called Pepper to follow me, and made my way down to the basement.

"At the door, I must confess to hesitating a moment. The thought of what might be awaiting me among the dark shrubberies, was by no means calculated to encourage my resolution. It was but a second, though, and then I had drawn the bolts, and was standing on the path outside the door.

"Pepper followed, stopping at the doorstep to sniff, suspiciously; and carrying his nose up and down the jambs, as though following a scent. Then, suddenly, he turned, sharply, and started to run here and there, in semicircles and circles, all around the door; finally returning to the threshold. Here, he began again to nose about.

"Hitherto, I had stood, watching the dog; yet, all the time, with half my gaze on the wild tangle of gardens, stretching round me. Now, I went towards him, and, bending down, examined the surface of the door, where he was smelling. I found that the wood was covered with a network of scratches, crossing and recrossing one another, in inextricable confusion. In addition to this, I noticed that the door-posts, themselves, were gnawed in places. Beyond these, I could find nothing; and so, standing up, I began to make the tour of the house wall.

"Pepper, as soon as I walked away, left the door, and ran ahead, still nosing and sniffing as he went along. At times, he stopped to investigate. Here, it would be a bullet-hole in the pathway, or, perhaps, a powder-stained wad. Anon, it might be a piece of torn sod, or a disturbed patch of weedy path; but, save for such trifles, he found nothing. I observed him, critically, as he went along, and could discover nothing of uneasiness, in his demeanour, to indicate that he felt the nearness of any of the creatures. By this, I was assured that the gardens were empty, at least for the present, of those hateful Things. Pepper could not be easily deceived, and it was a relief to feel that he would know, and give me timely warning, if there were any danger.

"Reaching the place where I had shot that first creature, I stopped, and made a careful scrutiny; but could see nothing. From there, I went on to where the great coping-stone had fallen. It lay on its side, apparently just as it had been left when I shot the brute that was moving it. A couple of feet to the right of the nearer end, was a great dent in the ground; showing where it had struck. The other end was still within the indentation—half in, and half out. Going nearer, I looked at the stone, more closely. What a huge piece of masonry it was! And that creature had moved it, single-handed, in its attempt to reach what lay below.

"I went round to the further end of the stone. Here, I found that it was possible to see under it, for a distance of nearly a couple of feet. Still, I could see nothing of the stricken creatures, and I felt much surprised. I had, as I have before said, guessed that the remains had been removed; yet, I could not conceive that it had been done so thoroughly as not to leave some certain sign, beneath the stone, indicative of their fate. I had seen several of the brutes struck down beneath it, with such force that they must have been literally driven into the earth; and now, not a vestige of them was to be seen—not even a bloodstain.

"I felt more puzzled, than ever, as I turned the matter over in my mind; but could think of no plausible explanation; and so, finally, gave it up, as one of the many things that were unexplainable.

"From there, I transferred my attention to the study door. I could see, now, even more plainly, the effects of the tremendous strain, to which it had been subjected; and I marvelled how, even with the support afforded by the props, it had withstood the attacks, so well. There were no marks of blows—indeed, none had been given—but the door had been literally riven from its hinges, by the application of enormous, silent force. One thing that I observed affected me profoundly—the head of one of the props had been driven right through a panel. This was, of itself, sufficient to show how huge an effort the creatures had made to break down the door, and how nearly they had succeeded.

"Leaving, I continued my tour round the house, finding little else of interest; save at the back, where I came across the piece of piping I had torn from the wall, lying among the long grass underneath the broken window.

"Then, I returned to the house, and, having re-bolted the back door, went up to the tower. Here, I spent the afternoon, reading, and occasionally glancing down into the gardens. I had determined, if the night passed quietly, to go as far as the Pit, on the morrow. Perhaps, I should be able to learn, then, something of what had happened. The day slipped away, and the night came, and went much as the last few nights had gone.

"When I rose the morning had broken, fine and clear; and I determined to put my project into action. During breakfast, I considered the matter, carefully; after which, I went to the study for my shotgun. In addition, I loaded, and slipped into my pocket, a small, but heavy, pistol. I quite understood that, if there were any danger, it lay in the direction of the Pit and I intended to be prepared.

"Leaving the study, I went down to the back door, followed by Pepper. Once outside, I took a quick survey of the surrounding gardens, and then set off towards the Pit. On the way, I kept a sharp outlook, holding my gun, handily. Pepper was running ahead, I noticed, without any apparent hesitation. From this, I augured that there was no imminent danger to be apprehended, and I stepped out more quickly in his wake. He had reached the top of the Pit, now, and was nosing his way along the edge.

"A minute later, I was beside him, looking down into the Pit. For a moment, I could scarcely believe that it was the same place, so greatly was it changed. The dark, wooded ravine of a fortnight ago, with a foliage-hidden stream, running sluggishly, at the bottom, existed no longer. Instead, my eyes showed me a ragged chasm, partly filled with a gloomy lake of turbid water. All one side of the ravine was stripped of underwood, showing the bare rock.

"A little to my left, the side of the Pit appeared to have collapsed altogether, forming a deep V-shaped cleft in the face of the rocky cliff. This rift ran, from the upper edge of the ravine, nearly down to the water, and penetrated into the Pit side, to a distance of some forty feet. Its opening was, at least, six yards across; and, from this, it seemed to taper into about two. But, what attracted my attention, more than even the stupendous split itself, was a great hole, some distance down the cleft, and right in the angle of the V. It was clearly defined, and not unlike an arched doorway in shape; though, lying as it did in the shadow, I could not see it very distinctly.

"The opposite side of the Pit, still retained its verdure; but so torn in places, and everywhere covered with dust and rubbish, that it was hardly distinguishable as such.

"My first impression, that there had been a land slip, was, I began to see, not sufficient, of itself, to account for all the changes I witnessed. And the water—? I turned, suddenly; for I had become aware that, somewhere to my right, there was a noise of running water. I could see nothing; but, now that my attention had been caught, I distinguished, easily, that it came from somewhere at the East end of the Pit.

"Slowly, I made my way in that direction; the sound growing plainer as I advanced, until in a little, I stood right above it. Even then, I could not perceive the cause, until I knelt down, and thrust my head over the cliff. Here, the noise came up to me, plainly; and I saw, below me, a torrent of clear water, issuing from a small fissure in the Pit side, and rushing down the rocks, into the lake beneath. A little further along the cliff, I saw another, and, beyond that again, two smaller ones. These, then, would help to account for the quantity of water in the Pit; and, if the fall of rock and earth had blocked the outlet of the stream at the bottom, there was little doubt but that it was contributing a very large share.

"Yet, I puzzled my head to account for the generally *shaken* appearance of the place—these streamlets, and that huge cleft, further up the ravine! It seemed to me, that more than the land-slip was necessary to account for these. I could imagine an earthquake, or a great *explosion*, creating some such condition of affairs as existed; but, of these, there had been neither. Then, I stood up, quickly, remembering that crash, and the cloud of dust that had followed, directly, rushing high into the air. But I shook my head, unbelievingly. No! It must have been the noise of the falling rocks and earth, I had heard; of course, the dust would fly, naturally. Still, in spite of my reasoning, I had an uneasy feeling, that this theory did not satisfy my sense of the probable; and yet, was any other, that I could suggest, likely to be half so plausible? Pepper had been sitting on the grass, while I conducted my examination. Now, as I turned up the North side of the ravine, he rose and followed.

"Slowly, and keeping a careful watch in all directions, I made the circuit of the Pit; but found little else, that I had not already seen. From the West end, I could see the four waterfalls, uninterruptedly. They were some considerable distance up from the surface of the lake—about fifty feet, I calculated.

"For a little while longer, I loitered about; keeping my eyes and ears open, but still, without seeing or hearing anything suspicious. The whole place was wonderfully quiet; indeed, save for the continuous murmur of the water, at the top end, no sound, of any description, broke the silence.

"All this while, Pepper had shown no signs of uneasiness. This seemed, to me, to indicate that, for the time being, at least, there was none of the Swine-creatures in the vicinity. So far as I could see, his attention appeared to have been taken, chiefly, with scratching and sniffing among the grass at the edge of the Pit. At times, he would leave the edge, and run along towards the house, as though following invisible tracks; but, in all cases, returning after a few minutes. I had little doubt but that he was really tracing out the footsteps of the Swine-things; and the very fact that each one seemed to lead him back to the Pit, appeared to me, a proof that the brutes had all returned whence they came.

"At noon, I went home, for dinner. During the afternoon, I made a partial search of the gardens, accompanied by Pepper; but, without coming upon anything to indicate the presence of the creatures.

"Once, as we made our way through the shrubberies, Pepper rushed in among some bushes, with a fierce yelp. At that, I jumped back, in sudden fright, and threw my gun forward, in readiness; only to laugh, nervously, as Pepper reappeared, chasing an unfortunate cat. Towards evening, I gave up the search, and returned to the house. All at once, as we were passing a great clump of bushes, on our right, Pepper disappeared, and I could hear him sniffing and growling among them, in a suspicious manner. With my gun-barrel, I parted the intervening shrubbery, and looked inside. There was nothing to be seen, save that many of the branches were bent down, and broken; as though some animal had made a lair there, at no very previous date. It was probably, I thought, one of the places occupied by some of the Swine-creatures, on the night of the attack.

"Next day, I resumed my search through the gardens; but without result. By evening, I had been right through them, and now, I knew, beyond the possibility of doubt, that there were no longer any of the Things concealed about the place. Indeed, I have often thought since, that I was correct in my earlier surmise, that they had left soon after the attack.

XII

The Subterranean Pit

"ANOTHER WEEK CAME AND went, during which I spent a great deal of my time about the Pit mouth. I had come to the conclusion, a few days earlier, that the arched hole, in the angle of the great rift, was the place through which the Swine-things had made their exit, from some unholy place in the bowels of the world. How near the probable truth this went, I was to learn later.

"It may be easily understood, that I was tremendously curious, though in a frightened way, to know to what infernal place that hole led; though, so far, the idea had not struck me, seriously, of making an investigation. I was far too much imbued with a sense of horror of the Swine-creatures, to think of venturing, willingly, where there was any chance of coming into contact with them.

"Gradually, however, as time passed, this feeling grew insensibly less; so that when, a few days later, the thought occurred to me that it might be possible to clamber down and have a look into the hole, I was not so exceedingly averse to it, as might have been imagined. Still, I do not think, even then, that I really intended to try any such fool-hardy adventure. For all that I could tell, it might be certain death, to enter that doleful looking opening. And yet, such is the pertinacity of human curiosity, that, at last, my chief desire was but to discover what lay beyond that gloomy entrance.

"Slowly, as the days slid by, my fear of the Swine-things became an emotion of the past—more an unpleasant, incredible memory, than aught else.

"Thus, a day came, when, throwing thoughts and fancies adrift, I procured a rope from the house, and, having made it fast to a stout tree, at the top of the rift, and some little distance back from the Pit edge, let the other end down into the cleft, until it dangled right across the mouth of the dark hole.

"Then, cautiously, and with many misgivings as to whether it was not a mad act that I was attempting, I climbed slowly down, using the rope as a support, until I reached the hole. Here, still holding on to the rope, I stood, and peered in. All was perfectly dark, and not a sound came to me. Yet, a moment later, it seemed that I could hear something. I held my breath, and listened; but all was silent as the grave, and I breathed freely once more. At the same instant, I heard the sound again. It was like a noise of laboured breathing—deep and sharp-drawn. For a short second, I stood, petrified; not able to move. But now the sounds had ceased again, and I could hear nothing.

"As I stood there, anxiously, my foot dislodged a pebble, which fell inward, into the dark, with a hollow chink. At once, the noise was taken up and repeated a score of times; each succeeding echo being fainter, and seeming to travel away from me, as though into remote distance. Then, as the silence fell again, I heard that stealthy breathing. For each respiration I made, I could hear an answering breath. The sounds appeared to be coming nearer; and then, I heard several others; but fainter and more distant. Why I did not grip the rope, and spring up out of danger, I cannot say. It was as though I had been paralysed. I broke out into a profuse sweat, and tried to moisten my lips with my tongue. My throat had gone suddenly dry, and I coughed, huskily. It came back to me, in a dozen, horrible, throaty tones, mockingly. I peered, helplessly, into the gloom; but still nothing showed. I had a strange, choky sensation, and again I coughed, dryly. Again the echo took it up, rising and falling, grotesquely, and dying slowly into a muffled silence.

"Then, suddenly, a thought came to me, and I held my breath. The other breathing stopped. I breathed again, and, once more, it re-commenced. But now, I no longer feared. I knew that the strange sounds were not made by any lurking Swine-creature; but were simply the echo of my own respirations.

"Yet, I had received such a fright, that I was glad to scramble up the rift, and haul up the rope. I was far too shaken and nervous to think of entering that dark hole then, and so returned to the house. I felt more myself next morning; but even then, I could not summon up sufficient courage to explore the place.

"All this time, the water in the Pit had been creeping slowly up, and now stood but a little below the opening. At the rate at which it was rising, it would be level with the floor in less than another week; and I realised that, unless I carried out my investigations soon, I should probably never do so at all; as the water would rise and rise, until the opening, itself, was submerged.

"It may have been that this thought stirred me to act; but, whatever it was, a couple of days later, saw me standing at the top of the cleft, fully equipped for the task.

"This time, I was resolved to conquer my shirking, and go right through with the matter. With this intention, I had brought, in addition to the rope, a bundle of candles, meaning to use them as a torch; also my double-barrelled shotgun. In my belt, I had a heavy horse-pistol, loaded with buck-shot.

"As before, I fastened the rope to the tree. Then, having tied my gun across my shoulders, with a piece of stout cord, I lowered myself over the edge of the Pit. At this movement, Pepper, who had been eyeing my actions, watchfully, rose to his feet, and ran to me, with a half bark, half wail, it seemed to me, of warning. But I was resolved on my enterprise, and bade him lie down. I would much have liked to take him with me; but this was next to impossible, in the existing circumstances. As my face dropped level with the Pit edge, he licked me, right across the mouth; and then, seizing my sleeve between his teeth, began to pull back, strongly. It was very evident that he did not want me to go. Yet, having made up my mind, I had no intention of giving up the attempt; and, with a sharp word to Pepper, to release me, I continued my descent, leaving the poor old fellow at the top, barking and crying like a forsaken pup.

"Carefully, I lowered myself from projection to projection. I knew that a slip might mean a wetting.

"Reaching the entrance, I let go the rope, and untied the gun from my shoulders. Then, with a last look at the sky—which I noticed was clouding over, rapidly—I went forward a couple of paces, so as to be shielded from the wind, and lit one of the candles. Holding it above my head, and grasping my gun, firmly, I began to move on, slowly, throwing my glances in all directions.

"For the first minute, I could hear the melancholy sound of Pepper's howling, coming down to me. Gradually, as I penetrated further into the darkness, it grew fainter; until, in a little while, I could hear nothing. The path tended downward somewhat, and to the left. Thence it kept on, still running to the left, until I found that it was leading me right in the direction of the house.

"Very cautiously, I moved onward, stopping, every few steps, to listen. I had gone, perhaps, a hundred yards, when, suddenly, it seemed to me that I caught a faint sound, somewhere along the passage behind. With my heart thudding heavily, I listened. The noise grew plainer, and appeared to be approaching, rapidly. I could hear it distinctly, now. It was the soft padding of running feet. In the first moments of fright, I stood, irresolute; not knowing whether to go forward or backward. Then, with a sudden realisation of the best thing to do, I backed up to the rocky wall on my right, and, holding the candle above my head, waited—gun in hand—cursing my foolhardy curiosity, for bringing me into such a strait.

"I had not long to wait, but a few seconds, before two eyes reflected back from the gloom, the rays of my candle. I raised my gun, using my right hand only, and aimed quickly. Even as I did so, something leapt out of the darkness, with a blustering bark of joy that woke the echoes, like thunder. It was Pepper. How he had contrived to scramble down the cleft, I could not conceive. As I brushed my hand, nervously, over his coat, I noticed that he was dripping; and concluded that he must have tried to follow me, and fallen into the water; from which he would not find it very difficult to climb.

"Having waited a minute, or so, to steady myself, I proceeded along the way, Pepper following, quietly. I was curiously glad to have the old fellow with me. He was company, and, somehow, with him at my heels, I was less afraid. Also, I knew how quickly his keen ears would detect the presence of any unwelcome creature, should there be such, amid the darkness that wrapped us.

"For some minutes we went slowly along; the path still leading straight towards the house. Soon, I concluded, we should be standing right beneath it, did the path but carry far enough. I led the way, cautiously, for another fifty yards, or so. Then, I stopped, and held the light high; and reason enough I had to be thankful that I did so; for there, not three paces forward, the path vanished, and, in place, showed a hollow blackness, that sent sudden fear through me.

"Very cautiously, I crept forward, and peered down; but could see nothing. Then, I crossed to the left of the passage, to see whether there might be any continuation of the path. Here, right against the wall, I found that a narrow track, some three feet wide, led onward. Carefully, I stepped on to it; but had not gone far, before I regretted venturing thereon. For, after a few paces, the already narrow way, resolved itself into a mere ledge, with, on the one side the solid, unyielding rock, towering up, in a great wall, to the unseen roof, and, on the other, that yawning chasm. I could not help reflecting how helpless I was, should I be attacked there, with no room to turn, and where even the recoil of my weapon might be sufficient to drive me headlong into the depths below.

"To my great relief, a little further on, the track suddenly broadened out again to its original breadth. Gradually, as I went onward, I noticed that the path trended steadily to the right, and so, after some minutes, I discovered that I was not going forward; but simply circling the huge abyss. I had, evidently, come to the end of the great passage.

"Five minutes later, I stood on the spot from which I had started; having been completely round, what I guessed now to be a vast pit, the mouth of which must be at least a hundred yards across.

"For some little time, I stood there, lost in perplexing thought. 'What does it all mean?' was the cry that had begun to reiterate through my brain.

"A sudden idea struck me, and I searched round for a piece of stone. Presently, I found a bit of rock, about the size of a small loaf. Sticking the candle upright in a crevice of the floor, I went back from the edge, somewhat, and, taking a short run, launched the stone forward into the chasm—my idea being to throw it far enough to keep it clear of the sides. Then, I stooped forward, and listened; but, though I kept perfectly quiet, for at least a full minute, no sound came back to me from out of the dark.

"I knew, then, that the depth of the hole must be immense; for the stone, had it struck anything, was large enough to have set the echoes of that weird place, whispering for an indefinite period. Even as it was, the cavern had given back the sounds of my foot-falls, multitudinously. The place was awesome, and I would willingly have retraced my steps, and left the mysteries of its solitudes unsolved; only, to do so, meant admitting defeat.

"Then, a thought came, to try to get a view of the abyss. It occurred to me that, if I placed my candles round the edge of the hole, I should be able to get, at least, some dim sight of the place.

"I found, on counting, that I had brought fifteen candles, in the bundle—my first intention having been, as I have already said, to make a torch of the lot. These, I proceeded to place round the Pit mouth, with an interval of about twenty yards between each.

"Having completed the circle, I stood in the passage, and endeavoured to get an idea of how the place looked. But I discovered, immediately, that they were totally insufficient for my purpose. They did little more than make the gloom visible. One thing they did, however, and that was, they confirmed my opinion of the size of the opening; and, although they showed me nothing that I wanted to see; yet the contrast they afforded to the heavy darkness, pleased me, curiously. It was as though fifteen tiny stars shone through the subterranean night.

"Then, even as I stood, Pepper gave a sudden howl, that was taken up by the echoes, and repeated with ghastly variations, dying away, slowly. With a quick movement, I held aloft the one candle that I had kept, and glanced down at the dog; at the same moment, I seemed to hear a noise, like a diabolical chuckle, rise up from the hitherto, silent depths of the Pit. I started; then, I recollected that it was, probably, the echo of Pepper's howl.

"Pepper had moved away from me, up the passage, a few steps; he was nosing along the rocky floor; and I thought I heard him lapping. I went towards him, holding the candle low. As I moved, I heard my boot go sop, sop; and the light was reflected from something that glistened, and crept past my feet, swiftly towards the Pit. I bent lower, and looked; then gave vent to an expression of surprise. From some-where, higher up the path, a stream of water was running quickly in the direction of the great opening, and growing in size every second.

"Again, Pepper gave vent to that deep-drawn howl, and, running at me, seized my coat, and attempted to drag me up the path towards the entrance. With a nervous gesture, I shook him off, and crossed quickly over to the left-hand wall. If anything were coming, I was going to have the wall at my back.

"Then, as I stared anxiously up the pathway, my candle caught a gleam, far up the passage. At the same moment, I became conscious of a murmurous roar, that grew louder, and filled the whole cavern with deafening sound. From the Pit, came a deep, hollow echo, like the sob of a giant. Then, I had sprung to one side, on to the narrow ledge that ran round the abyss, and, turning, saw a great wall of foam sweep past me, and leap tumultuously into the waiting chasm. A cloud of spray burst over me, extinguishing my candle, and wetting me to the skin. I still held my gun. The three nearest candles went out; but the further ones gave only a short flicker. After the first rush, the flow of water eased down to a steady stream, maybe a foot in depth; though I could not see this, until I had procured one of the lighted candles, and, with it, started to reconnoitre. Pepper had, fortunately, followed me as I leapt for the ledge, and now, very much subdued, kept close behind.

"A short examination showed me that the water reached right across the passage, and was running at a tremendous rate. Already, even as I stood there, it had deepened. I could make only a guess at what had happened. Evidently, the water in the ravine had broken into the passage, by some means. If that were the case, it would go on increasing in volume, until I should find it impossible to leave the place. The thought was frightening. It was evident that I must make my exit as hurriedly as possible.

"Taking my gun by the stock, I sounded the water. It was a little under knee-deep. The noise it made, plunging down into the Pit, was deafening. Then, with a call to Pepper, I stepped out into the flood, using the gun as a staff. Instantly, the water boiled up over my knees, and nearly to the tops of my thighs, with the speed at which it was racing. For one short moment, I nearly lost my footing; but the thought of what lay behind, stimulated me to a fierce endeavour, and, step by step, I made headway.

"Of Pepper, I knew nothing at first. I had all I could do to keep on my legs; and was overjoyed, when he appeared beside me. He was wading manfully along. He is a big dog, with longish thin legs, and I suppose the water had less grasp on them, than upon mine. Anyway, he managed a great deal better than I did; going ahead of me, like a guide, and wittingly—or otherwise—helping, somewhat, to break the force of the water. On we went, step by step, struggling and gasping, until somewhere about a hundred yards had been safely traversed. Then, whether it was because I was taking less care, or that there was a slippery place on the rocky floor, I cannot say; but, suddenly, I slipped, and fell on my face. Instantly, the water leapt over me in a cataract, hurling me down, towards that bottomless hole, at a frightful speed. Frantically I struggled; but it was impossible to get a footing. I was helpless, gasping and drowning. All at once, something gripped my coat, and brought me to a standstill. It was Pepper. Missing me, he must have raced back, through the dark turmoil, to find me, and then caught, and held me, until I was able to get to my feet.

"I have a dim recollection of having seen, momentarily, the gleams of several lights; but, of this, I have never been quite sure. If my impressions are correct, I must have been washed down to the very brink of that awful chasm, before Pepper managed to bring me to a standstill. And the lights, of course, could only have been the distant flames of the candles, I had left burning. But, as I have said, I am not by any means sure. My eyes were full of water, and I had been badly shaken.

"And there was I, without my helpful gun, without light, and sadly confused, with the water deepening; depending solely upon my old friend Pepper, to help me out of that hellish place.

"I was facing the torrent. Naturally, it was the only way in which I could have sustained my position a moment; for even old Pepper could not have held me long against that terrific strain, without assistance, however blind, from me.

"Perhaps a minute passed, during which it was touch and go with me; then, gradually I re-commenced my tortuous way up the passage. And so began the grimmest fight with death, from which ever I hope to emerge victorious. Slowly, furiously, almost hopelessly, I strove; and that faithful Pepper led me, dragged me, upward and onward, until, at last, ahead I saw a gleam of blessed light. It was the entrance. Only a few yards further, and I reached the opening, with the water surging and boiling hungrily around my loins.

"And now I understood the cause of the catastrophe. It was raining heavily, literally in torrents. The surface of the lake was level with the bottom of the opening—nay! more than level, it was above it. Evidently, the rain had swollen the lake, and caused this premature rise; for, at the rate the ravine had been filling, it would not have reached the entrance for a couple more days.

"Luckily, the rope by which I had descended, was streaming into the opening, upon the inrushing waters. Seizing the end, I knotted it securely round Pepper's body; then, summoning up the last remnant of my strength, I commenced to swarm up the side of the cliff. I reached the Pit edge, in the last stage of exhaustion. Yet, I had to make one more effort, and haul Pepper into safety.

"Slowly and wearily, I hauled on the rope. Once or twice, it seemed that I should have to give up; for Pepper is a weighty dog, and I was utterly done. Yet, to let go, would have meant certain death to the old fellow, and the thought spurred me to greater exertions. I have but a very hazy remembrance of the end. I recall pulling, through moments that lagged strangely. I have also some recollection of seeing Pepper's muzzle, appearing over the Pit edge, after what seemed an indefinite period of time. Then, all grew suddenly dark.

XIII
The Trap in the Great Cellar

"I SUPPOSE I MUST have swooned; for, the next thing I remember, I opened my eyes, and all was dusk. I was lying on my back, with one leg doubled under the other, and Pepper was licking my ears. I felt horribly stiff, and my leg was numb, from the knee, downwards. For a few minutes, I lay thus, in a dazed condition; then, slowly, I struggled to a sitting position, and looked about me.

"It had stopped raining, but the trees still dripped, dismally. From the Pit, came a continuous murmur of running water. I felt cold and shivery. My clothes were sodden, and I ached all over. Very slowly, the life came back into my numbed leg, and, after a little, I essayed to stand up. This, I managed, at the second attempt; but I was very tottery, and peculiarly weak. It seemed to me, that I was going to be ill, and I made shift to stumble my way towards the house. My steps were erratic, and my head confused. At each step that I took, sharp pains shot through my limbs.

"I had gone, perhaps, some thirty paces, when a cry from Pepper, drew my attention, and I turned, stiffly, towards him. The old dog was trying to follow me; but could come no further, owing to the rope, with which I had hauled him up, being still tied round his body, the other end not having been unfastened from the tree. For a moment, I fumbled with the knots, weakly; but they were wet and hard, and I could do nothing. Then, I remembered my knife, and, in a minute, the rope was cut.

"How I reached the house, I scarcely know, and, of the days that followed, I remember still less. Of one thing, I am certain; that, had it not been for my sister's untiring love and nursing, I had not been writing at this moment.

"When I recovered my senses, it was to find that I had been in bed for nearly two weeks. Yet another week passed, before I was strong

71

enough to totter out into the gardens. Even then, I was not able to walk so far as the Pit. I would have liked to ask my sister, how high the water had risen; but felt it was wiser not to mention the subject to her. Indeed, since then, I have made a rule never to speak to her about the strange things that happen in this great, old house.

"It was not until a couple of days later, that I managed to get across to the Pit. There, I found that, in my few weeks' absence, there had been wrought a wondrous change. Instead of the three-parts filled ravine, I looked out upon a great lake, whose placid surface reflected the light, coldly. The water had risen to within half a dozen feet of the Pit edge. Only in one part was the lake disturbed, and that was above the place where, far down under the silent waters, yawned the entrance to the vast, underground Pit. Here, there was a continuous bubbling; and, occasionally, a curious sort of sobbing gurgle would find its way up from the depth. Beyond these, there was nothing to tell of the things that were hidden beneath. As I stood there, it came to me how wonderfully things had worked out. The entrance to the place whence the Swine-creatures had come, was sealed up, by a power that made me feel there was nothing more to fear from them. And yet, with the feeling, there was a sensation that, now, I should never learn anything further, of the place from which those dreadful Things had come. It was completely shut off and concealed from human curiosity for ever.

"Strange—in the knowledge of that underground hell-hole—how apposite has been the naming of the Pit. One wonders how it origi-nated, and when. Naturally, one concludes that the shape and depth of the ravine would suggest the name 'Pit'. Yet, is it not possible that it has, all along, held a deeper significance, a hint—could one but have guessed—of the greater, more stupendous Pit that lies far down in the earth, beneath this old house? Under this house! Even now, the idea is strange and terrible to me. For I have proved, beyond doubt, that the Pit yawns right below the house, which is evidently supported, somewhere above the centre of it, upon a tremendous, arched roof, of solid rock.

"It happened in this wise, that, having occasion to go down to the cellars, the thought occurred to me to pay a visit to the great vault, where the trap is situated; and see whether everything was as I had left it.

"Reaching the place, I walked slowly up the centre, until I came to the trap. There it was, with the stones piled upon it, just as I had seen it last. I had a lantern with me, and the idea came to me, that now would be a good time to investigate whatever lay under the great, oak slab. Placing the lantern on the floor, I tumbled the stones off the trap, and, grasping the ring, pulled the door open. As I did so, the cellar became filled with the sound of a murmurous thunder, that rose from far below. At the same time, a damp wind blew up into my face, bringing with it a load of fine spray. Therewith, I dropped the trap, hurriedly, with a half-frightened feeling of wonder.

"For a moment, I stood puzzled. I was not particularly afraid. The haunting fear of the Swine-things had left me, long ago; but I was certainly nervous and astonished. Then, a sudden thought possessed me, and I raised the ponderous door, with a feeling of excitement. Leaving it standing upon its end, I seized the lantern, and, kneeling down, thrust it into the opening. As I did so, the moist wind and spray drove in my eyes, making me unable to see, for a few moments. Even when my eyes were clear, I could distinguish nothing below me, save darkness, and whirling spray.

"Seeing that it was useless to expect to make out anything, with the light so high, I felt in my pockets for a piece of twine, with which to lower it further into the opening. Even as I fumbled, the lantern slipped from my fingers, and hurtled down into the darkness. For a brief instant, I watched its fall, and saw the light shine on a tumult of white foam, some eighty or a hundred feet below me. Then it was gone. My sudden surmise was correct, and now, I knew the cause of the wet and noise. The great cellar was connected with the Pit, by means of the trap, which opened right above it; and the moisture was the spray, rising from the water, falling into the depths.

"In an instant, I had an explanation of certain things, that had hitherto puzzled me. Now, I could understand why the noises—on the first night of the invasion—had seemed to rise directly from under my feet. And the chuckle that had sounded when first I opened the trap! Evidently, some of the Swine-things must have been right beneath me.

"Another thought struck me. Were the creatures all drowned? Would they drown? I remembered how unable I had been to find any traces to show that my shooting had been really fatal. Had they life, as we understand life, or were they ghouls? These thoughts flashed through my brain, as I stood in the dark, searching my pockets for matches. I had the box in my hand now, and, striking a light, I stepped to the trap-door, and closed it. Then, I piled the stones back upon it; after which, I made my way out from the cellars.

"And so, I suppose the water goes on, thundering down into that bottomless hell-pit. Sometimes, I have an inexplicable desire to go down to the great cellar, open the trap, and gaze into the impenetrable, spray-damp darkness. At times, the desire becomes almost overpowering, in its intensity. It is not mere curiosity, that prompts me; but more as though some unexplained influence were at work. Still, I never go; and intend to fight down the strange longing, and crush it; even as I would the unholy thought of self-destruction.

"This idea of some intangible force being exerted, may seem reasonless. Yet, my instinct warns me, that it is not so. In these things, reason seems to me less to be trusted than instinct.

"One thought there is, in closing, that impresses itself upon me, with ever growing insistence. It is, that I live in a very strange house; a very awful house. And I have begun to wonder whether I am doing wisely in staying here. Yet, if I left, where could I go, and still obtain the solitude, and the sense of her presence[1], that alone make my old life bearable?

---

[1] An apparently unmeaning interpolation. I can find no previous reference in the MS. to this matter. It becomes clearer, however, in the light of succeeding incidents.—Ed.

XIV
The Sea of Sleep

"FOR A CONSIDERABLE PERIOD after the last incident which I have narrated in my diary, I had serious thoughts of leaving this house, and might have done so; but for the great and wonderful thing, of which I am about to write.

"How well I was advised, in my heart, when I stayed on here—spite of those visions and sights of unknown and unexplainable things; for, had I not stayed, then I had not seen again the face of her I loved. Yes, though few know it, none now save my sister Mary, I have loved and, ah! me—lost.

"I would write down the story of those sweet, old days; but it would be like the tearing of old wounds; yet, after that which has happened, what need have I to care? For she has come to me out of the unknown. Strangely, she warned me; warned me passionately against this house; begged me to leave it; but admitted, when I questioned her, that she could not have come to me, had I been elsewhere. Yet, in spite of this, still she warned me, earnestly; telling me that it was a place, long ago given over to evil, and under the power of grim laws, of which none here have knowledge. And I—I just asked her, again, whether she would come to me elsewhere, and she could only stand, silent.

"It was thus, that I came to the place of the Sea of Sleep—so she termed it, in her dear speech with me. I had stayed up, in my study, reading; and must have dozed over the book. Suddenly, I awoke and sat upright, with a start. For a moment, I looked round, with a puzzled sense of something unusual. There was a misty look about the room, giving a curious softness to each table and chair and furnishing.

"Gradually, the mistiness increased; growing, as it were, out of nothing. Then, slowly, a soft, white light began to glow in the room. The flames of the candles shone through it, palely. I looked from side

75

to side, and found that I could still see each piece of furniture; but in a strangely unreal way, more as though the ghost of each table and chair had taken the place of the solid article.

"Gradually, as I looked, I saw them fade and fade; until, slowly, they resolved into nothingness. Now, I looked again at the candles. They shone wanly, and, even as I watched, grew more unreal, and so vanished. The room was filled, now, with a soft, yet luminous, white twilight, like a gentle mist of light. Beyond this, I could see nothing. Even the walls had vanished.

"Presently, I became conscious that a faint, continuous sound, pulsed through the silence that wrapped me. I listened intently. It grew more distinct, until it appeared to me that I harked to the breathings of some great sea. I cannot tell how long a space passed thus; but, after a while, it seemed that I could see through the mistiness; and, slowly, I became aware that I was standing upon the shore of an immense and silent sea. This shore was smooth and long, vanishing to right and left of me, in extreme distances. In front, swam a still immensity of sleeping ocean. At times, it seemed to me that I caught a faint glimmer of light, under its surface; but of this, I could not be sure. Behind me, rose up, to an extraordinary height, gaunt, black cliffs. Overhead, the sky was of a uniform cold grey colour—the whole place being lit by a stupendous globe of pale fire, that swam a little above the far horizon, and shed a foam-like light above the quiet waters.

"Beyond the gentle murmur of the sea, an intense stillness prevailed. For a long while, I stayed there, looking out across its strangeness. Then, as I stared, it seemed that a bubble of white foam floated up out of the depths, and then, even now I know not how it was, I was looking upon, nay, looking *into* the face of Her—aye! into her face—into her soul; and she looked back at me, with such a commingling of joy and sadness, that I ran towards her, blindly; crying strangely to her, in a very agony of remembrance, of terror, and of hope, to come to me. Yet, spite of my crying, she stayed out there upon the sea, and only shook her head, sorrowfully; but, in her eyes was the old earth-light of tenderness, that I had come to know, before all things, ere we were parted.

"At her perverseness, I grew desperate, and essayed to wade out to her; yet, though I would, I could not. Something, some invisible barrier, held me back, and I was fain to stay where I was, and cry out to her in the fullness of my soul, 'O, my Darling, my Darling—' but could say no more, for very intensity. And, at that, she came over, swiftly, and touched me, and it was as though heaven had opened. Yet, when I reached out my hands to her, she put me from her with tenderly stern hands, and I was abashed—"

NOTE.—Here, the writing becomes undecipherable, owing to the damaged condition of this part of the MS. Below I print such fragments as are legible.—Ed.

THE FRAGMENTS
(The legible portions of the mutilated leaves.)

"... through tears... noise of eternity in my ears, we parted.... She whom I love. O, my God!...

"I was a great time dazed, and then I was alone in the blackness of the night. I knew that I journeyed back, once more, to the known universe. Presently, I emerged from that enormous darkness. I had come among the stars... vast time... the sun, far and remote.

"I entered into the gulf that separates our system from the outer suns. As I sped across the dividing dark, I watched, steadily, the ever growing brightness and size of our sun. Once, I glanced back to the stars, and saw them shift, as it were, in my wake, against the mighty background of night, so vast was the speed of my passing spirit.

"I drew nigher to our system, and now I could see the shine of Jupiter. Later, I distinguished the cold, blue gleam of the earth-light.... I had a moment of bewilderment. All about the sun there seemed to be bright, objects, moving in rapid orbits. Inward, nigh to the savage glory of the sun, there circled two darting points of light, and, further off, there flew a blue, shining speck, that I knew to be the earth. It circled the sun in a space that seemed to be no more than an earth-minute.

"... nearer with great speed. I saw the radiances of Jupiter and Saturn, spinning, with incredible swiftness, in huge orbits. And ever I drew more nigh, and looked out upon this strange sight—the visible circling of the planets about the mother sun. It was as though time had been annihilated for me; so that a year was no more to my unfleshed spirit, than is a moment to an earth-bound soul.

"The speed of the planets, appeared to increase; and, presently, I was watching the sun, all ringed about with hair-like circles of different coloured fire—the paths of the planets, hurtling at mighty speed, about the central flame....

"... the sun grew vast, as though it leapt to meet me.... And now I was within the circling of the outer planets, and flitting swiftly, towards the place where the earth, glimmering through the blue splendour of its orbit, as though a fiery mist, circled the sun at a monstrous speed...."

NOTE.—The severest scrutiny has not enabled me to decipher more of the damaged portion of the MS. It commences to be legible again with the chapter entitled "The Noise in the Night."—Ed.

XV
The Noise in the Night

"AND NOW, I COME to the strangest of all the strange happenings that have befallen me in this house of mysteries. It occurred quite lately—within the month; and I have little doubt, but that, what I saw, was, in reality, the end of all things. However, to my story.

"I do not know how it is; but, up to the present, I have never been able to write these things down, directly they happened. It is as though I have to wait a time, recovering my just balance, and digesting—as it were—the things I have heard or seen. No doubt, this is as it should be; for, by waiting, I see the incidents more truly, and write of them in a calmer and more judicial frame of mind. This by the way.

"It is now the end of November. My story relates to what happened in the first week of the month.

"It was night, about eleven o'clock. Pepper and I kept one another company in the study—that great, old room of mine, where I read and work. I was reading, curiously enough, the Bible. I have begun, in these later days, to take a growing interest in that great and ancient book. Suddenly, a distinct tremor shook the house, and there came a faint and distant, whirring buzz, that grew rapidly into a far, muffled screaming. It reminded me, in a queer, gigantic way, of the noise that a clock makes, when the catch is released, and it is allowed to run down. The sound appeared to come from some remote height—somewhere up in the night. There was no repetition of the shock. I looked across at Pepper. He was sleeping peacefully.

"Gradually, the whirring noise decreased, and there came a long silence.

"All at once, a glow lit up the end window, which protrudes far out from the side of the house, so that, from it, one may look both East and West. I felt puzzled, and, after a moment's hesitation, walked across the room, and pulled aside the blind. As I did so, I saw the Sun rise,

79

from behind the horizon. It rose with a steady, perceptible movement. I could see it travel upwards. In a minute, it seemed, it had reached the tops of the trees, through which I had watched it. Up, up— It was broad daylight now. Behind me, I was conscious of a sharp, mosquito-like buzzing. I glanced round, and knew that it came from the clock. Even as I looked, it marked off an hour. The minute-hand was moving round the dial, faster than an ordinary second-hand. The hour-hand moved quickly from space to space. I had a numb sense of astonishment. A moment later, so it seemed, the two candles went out, almost together. I turned swiftly back to the window; for I had seen the shadow of the window-frames, travelling along the floor towards me, as though a great lamp had been carried up past the window.

"I saw now, that the sun had risen high into the heavens, and was still visibly moving. It passed above the house, with an extraordinary sailing kind of motion. As the window came into shadow, I saw another extraordinary thing. The fine-weather clouds were not passing, easily, across the sky—they were scampering, as though a hundred-mile-an-hour wind blew. As they passed, they changed their shapes a thousand times a minute, as though writhing with a strange life; and so were gone. And, presently, others came, and whisked away likewise.

"To the West, I saw the sun drop with an incredible, smooth, swift motion. Eastward, the shadows of every seen thing crept towards the coming greyness. And the movement of the shadows was visible to me—a stealthy, writhing creep of the shadows of the wind-stirred trees. It was a strange sight.

"Quickly, the room began to darken. The sun slid down to the horizon, and seemed, as it were, to disappear from my sight, almost with a jerk. Through the greyness of the swift evening, I saw the silver crescent of the moon, falling out of the Southern sky, towards the West. The evening seemed to merge into an almost instant night. Above me, the many constellations passed in a strange, 'noiseless' circling, Westwards. The moon fell through that last thousand fathoms of the night-gulf, and there was only the starlight. . . .

"About this time, the buzzing in the corner ceased; telling me that the clock had run down. A few minutes passed, and I saw the Eastward sky lighten. A grey, sullen morning spread through all the darkness, and hid the march of the stars. Overhead, there moved, with a heavy, everlasting rolling, a vast, seamless sky of grey clouds—a cloud-sky that would have seemed motionless, through all the length of an ordinary earth-day. The sun was hidden from me; but, from moment to moment, the world would brighten and darken, brighten and darken, beneath waves of subtle light and shadow. . . .

"The light shifted ever Westward, and the night fell upon the earth. A vast rain seemed to come with it, and a wind of a most extraordinary loudness—as though the howling of a night-long gale, were packed into the space of no more than a minute.

"This noise passed, almost immediately, and the clouds broke; so that, once more, I could see the sky. The stars were flying Westward, with astounding speed. It came to me now, for the first time, that, though the noise of the wind had passed, yet a constant 'blurred' sound was in my ears. Now that I noticed it, I was aware that it had been with me all the time. It was the world-noise.

"And then, even as I grasped at so much comprehension, there came the Eastward light. No more than a few heartbeats, and the sun rose, swiftly. Through the trees, I saw it, and then it was above the trees. Up—up, it soared and all the world was light. It passed, with a swift, steady swing to its highest altitude, and fell thence, Westward. I saw the day roll visibly over my head. A few light clouds flittered Northward, and vanished. The sun went down with one swift, clear plunge, and there was about me, for a few seconds, the darker growing grey of the gloaming.

"Southward and Westward, the moon was sinking rapidly. The night had come, already. A minute it seemed, and the moon fell those remaining fathoms of dark sky. Another minute, or so, and the Eastward sky glowed with the coming dawn. The sun leapt upon me with a frightening abruptness, and soared ever more swiftly towards the zenith. Then, suddenly, a fresh thing came to my sight. A black thunder-cloud rushed up out of the South, and seemed to leap all the arc of the sky, in a single instant. As it came, I saw that its advancing edge flapped, like a monstrous black cloth in the heaven, twirling and undulating rapidly, with a horrid suggestiveness. In an instant, all the air was full of rain, and a hundred lightning flashes seemed to flood downwards, as it were in one great shower. In the same second of time, the world-noise was drowned in the roar of the wind, and then my ears ached, under the stunning impact of the thunder.

"And, in the midst of this storm, the night came; and then, within the space of another minute, the storm had passed, and there was only the constant 'blur' of the world-noise on my hearing. Overhead, the stars were sliding quickly Westward; and something, mayhaps the particular speed to which they had attained, brought home to me, for the first time, a keen realisation of the knowledge that it was the world that revolved. I seemed to see, suddenly, the world—a vast, dark mass—revolving visibly against the stars.

"The dawn and the sun seemed to come together, so greatly had the speed of the world-revolution increased. The sun drove up, in one long, steady curve; passed its highest point, and swept down into the Western sky, and disappeared. I was scarcely conscious of evening, so brief was it. Then I was watching the flying constellations, and the Westward hastening moon. In but a space of seconds, so it seemed, it was sliding swiftly downward through the night-blue, and then was gone. And, almost directly, came the morning.

"And now there seemed to come a strange acceleration. The sun made one clean, clear sweep through the sky, and disappeared behind the Westward horizon, and the night came and went with a like haste.

"As the succeeding day, opened and closed upon the world, I was aware of a sweat of snow, suddenly upon the earth. The night came, and, almost immediately, the day. In the brief leap of the sun, I saw that the snow had vanished; and then, once more, it was night.

"Thus matters were; and, even after the many incredible things that I have seen, I experienced all the time a most profound awe. To see the sun rise and set, within a space of time to be measured by seconds; to watch (after a little) the moon leap—a pale, and ever growing orb—up into the night sky, and glide, with a strange swiftness, through the vast arc of blue; and, presently, to see the sun follow, springing out of the Eastern sky, as though in chase; and then again the night, with the swift and ghostly passing of starry constellations, was all too much to view believingly. Yet, so it was—the day slipping from dawn to dusk, and the night sliding swiftly into day, ever rapidly and more rapidly.

"The last three passages of the sun had shown me a snow-covered earth, which, at night, had seemed, for a few seconds, incredibly weird under the fast-shifting light of the soaring and falling moon. Now, however, for a little space, the sky was hidden, by a sea of swaying, leaden-white clouds, which lightened and blackened, alternately, with the passage of day and night.

"The clouds rippled and vanished, and there was once more before me, the vision of the swiftly leaping sun, and nights that came and went like shadows.

"Faster and faster, spun the world. And now each day and night was completed within the space of but a few seconds; and still the speed increased.

"It was a little later, that I noticed that the sun had begun to have the suspicion of a trail of fire behind it. This was due, evidently, to the speed

---

[1] The Recluse uses this as an illustration, evidently in the sense of the popular conception of a comet.—Ed.

at which it, apparently, traversed the heavens. And, as the days sped, each one quicker than the last, the sun began to assume the appearance of a vast, flaming comet[1], flaring across the sky at short, periodic intervals. At night, the moon presented, with much greater truth, a comet-like aspect; a pale, and singularly clear, fast travelling shape of fire, trailing streaks of cold flame. The stars showed now, merely as fine hairs of fire against the dark.

"Once, I turned from the window, and glanced at Pepper. In the flash of a day, I saw that he slept, quietly, and I moved once more to my watching.

"The sun was now bursting up from the Eastern horizon, like a stupendous rocket, seeming to occupy no more than a second or two in hurling from East to West. I could no longer perceive the passage of clouds across the sky, which seemed to have darkened somewhat. The brief nights, appeared to have lost the proper darkness of night; so that the hair-like fire of the flying stars, showed but dimly. As the speed increased, the sun began to sway very slowly in the sky, from South to North, and then, slowly again, from North to South.

"So, amid a strange confusion of mind, the hours passed.

"All this while had Pepper slept. Presently, feeling lonely and distraught, I called to him, softly; but he took no notice. Again, I called, raising my voice slightly; still he moved not. I walked over to where he lay, and touched him with my foot, to rouse him. At the action, gentle though it was, he fell to pieces. That is what happened; he literally and actually crumbled into a mouldering heap of bones and dust.

"For the space of, perhaps a minute, I stared down at the shapeless heap, that had once been Pepper. I stood, feeling stunned. What can have happened? I asked myself; not at once grasping the grim significance of that little hill of ash. Then, as I stirred the heap with my foot, it occurred to me that this could only happen in a great space of time. Years—and years.

"Outside, the weaving, fluttering light held the world. Inside, I stood, trying to understand what it meant—what that little pile of dust and dry bones, on the carpet, meant. But I could not think, coherently.

"I glanced away, round the room, and now, for the first time, noticed how dusty and old the place looked. Dust and dirt everywhere; piled in little heaps in the corners, and spread about upon the furniture. The very carpet, itself, was invisible beneath a coating of the same, all-pervading, material. As I walked, little clouds of the stuff rose up from under my footsteps, and assailed my nostrils, with a dry, bitter odour that made me wheeze, huskily.

"Suddenly, as my glance fell again upon Pepper's remains, I stood still, and gave voice to my confusion—questioning, aloud, whether the years were, indeed, passing; whether this, which I had taken to be a form of vision, was, in truth, a reality. I paused. A new thought had struck me. Quickly, but with steps which, for the first time, I noticed, tottered, I went across the room to the great pier-glass, and looked in. It was too covered with grime, to give back any reflection, and, with trembling hands, I began to rub off the dirt. Presently, I could see myself. The thought that had come to me, was confirmed. Instead of the great, hale man, who scarcely looked fifty, I was looking at a bent, decrepit man, whose shoulders stooped, and whose face was wrinkled with the years of a century. The hair—which a few short hours ago had been nearly coal black—was now silvery white. Only the eyes were bright. Gradually, I traced, in that ancient man, a faint resemblance to my self of other days.

"I turned away, and tottered to the window. I knew, now, that I was old, and the knowledge seemed to confirm my trembling walk. For a little space, I stared moodily out into the blurred vista of changeful landscape. Even in that short time, a year passed, and, with a petulant gesture, I left the window. As I did so, I noticed that my hand shook with the palsy of old age; and a short sob choked its way through my lips.

"For a little while, I paced, tremulously, between the window and the table; my gaze wandering hither and thither, uneasily. How dilapidated the room was. Everywhere lay the thick dust—thick, sleepy and black. The fender was a shape of rust. The chains that held the brass clock-weights, had rusted through long ago, and now the weights lay on the floor beneath; themselves two cones of verdigris.

"As I glanced about, it seemed to me that I could see the very furniture of the room rotting and decaying before my eyes. Nor was this fancy, on my part; for, all at once, the bookshelf, along the side wall, collapsed, with a cracking and rending of rotten wood, precipitating its contents upon the floor, and filling the room with a smother of dusty atoms.

"How tired I felt. As I walked, it seemed that I could hear my dry joints, creak and crack at every step. I wondered about my sister. Was she dead, as well as Pepper? All had happened so quickly and suddenly. This must be, indeed, the beginning of the end of all things! It occurred to me, to go to look for her; but I felt too weary. And then, she had been so queer about these happenings, of late. Of late! I repeated the words, and laughed, feebly—mirthlessly, as the realisation was borne in upon me that I spoke of a time, half a century gone. Half a century! It might have been twice as long!

"I moved slowly to the window, and looked out once more across the world. I can best describe the passage of day and night, at this period, as a sort of gigantic, ponderous flicker. Moment by moment, the acceleration of time continued; so that, at nights now, I saw the moon, only as a swaying trail of palish fire, that varied from a mere line of light to a nebulous path, and then dwindled again, disappearing periodically.

"The flicker of the days and nights quickened. The days had grown perceptibly darker, and a queer quality of dusk lay, as it were, in the atmosphere. The nights were so much lighter, that the stars were scarcely to be seen, saving here and there an occasional hair-like line of fire, that seemed to sway a little, with the moon.

"Quicker, and ever quicker, ran the flicker of day and night; and, suddenly it seemed, I was aware that the flicker had died out, and, instead, there reigned a comparatively steady light, which was shed upon all the world, from an eternal river of flame that swung up and down, North and South, in stupendous, mighty swings.

"The sky was now grown very much darker, and there was in the blue of it a heavy gloom, as though a vast blackness peered through it upon the earth. Yet, there was in it, also, a strange and awful clearness, and emptiness. Periodically, I had glimpses of a ghostly track of fire that swayed thin and darkly towards the sun-stream; vanished and re-appeared. It was the scarcely visible moon-stream.

"Looking out at the landscape, I was conscious again, of a blurring sort of 'flitter', that came either from the light of the ponderous-swinging sun-stream, or was the result of the incredibly rapid changes of the earth's surface. And every few moments, so it seemed, the snow would lie suddenly upon the world, and vanish as abruptly, as though an invisible giant 'flitted' a white sheet off and on the earth.

"Time fled, and the weariness that was mine, grew insupportable. I turned from the window, and walked once across the room, the heavy dust deadening the sound of my footsteps. Each step that I took, seemed a greater effort than the one before. An intolerable ache, knew me in every joint and limb, as I trod my way, with a weary uncertainty.

"By the opposite wall, I came to a weak pause, and wondered, dimly, what was my intent. I looked to my left, and saw my old chair. The thought of sitting in it brought a faint sense of comfort to my bewildered wretchedness. Yet, because I was so weary and old and tired, I would scarcely brace my mind to do anything but stand, and wish myself past those few yards. I rocked, as I stood. The floor, even, seemed a place for rest; but the dust lay so thick and sleepy and black. I turned, with a great effort of will, and made towards my chair. I reached it, with a groan of thankfulness. I sat down.

"Everything about me appeared to be growing dim. It was all so strange and unthought of. Last night, I was a comparatively strong, though elderly man; and now, only a few hours later—! I looked at the little dust-heap that had once been Pepper. Hours! and I laughed, a feeble, bitter laugh; a shrill, cackling laugh, that shocked my dimming senses.

"For a while, I must have dozed. Then I opened my eyes, with a start. Somewhere across the room, there had been a muffled noise of something falling. I looked, and saw, vaguely, a cloud of dust hovering above a pile of *débris*. Nearer the door, something else tumbled, with a crash. It was one of the cupboards; but I was tired, and took little notice. I closed my eyes, and sat there in a state of drowsy, semi-unconsciousness. Once or twice—as though coming through thick mists—I heard noises, faintly. Then I must have slept.

XVI
The Awakening

"I AWOKE, WITH A start. For a moment, I wondered where I was. Then memory came to me. . . .

"The room was still lit with that strange light—half-sun, half-moon, light. I felt refreshed, and the tired, weary ache had left me. I went slowly across to the window, and looked out. Overhead, the river of flame drove up and down, North and South, in a dancing semi-circle of fire. As a mighty sley in the loom of time it seemed—in a sudden fancy of mine—to be beating home the picks of the years. For, so vastly had the passage of time been accelerated, that there was no longer any sense of the sun passing from East to West. The only apparent movement was the North and South beat of the sun-stream, that had become so swift now, as to be better described as a *quiver*.

"As I peered out, there came to me a sudden, inconsequent memory of that last journey among the Outer worlds[1]. I remembered the sudden vision that had come to me, as I neared the Solar System, of the fast whirling planets about the sun—as though the governing quality of time had been held in abeyance, and the Machine of a Universe allowed to run down an eternity, in a few moments or hours. The memory passed, along with a but partially comprehended suggestion that I had been permitted a glimpse into further time spaces. I stared out again, seemingly, at the quake of the sun-stream. The speed seemed to increase, even as I looked. Several life-times came and went, as I watched.

"Suddenly, it struck me, with a sort of grotesque seriousness, that I was still alive. I thought of Pepper, and wondered how it was that I had not followed his fate. He had reached the time of his dying, and

---

[1] Evidently referring to something set forth in the missing and multilated pages. See Fragments, p. 77.— Ed.

had passed, probably through sheer length of years. And here was I, alive, hundreds of thousands of centuries after my rightful period of years.

"For, a time, I mused, absently. 'Yesterday—' I stopped, suddenly. Yesterday! There was no yesterday. The yesterday, of which I spoke, had been swallowed up in the abyss of years, ages gone. I grew dazed with much thinking.

"Presently, I turned from the window, and glanced round the room. It seemed different—strangely, utterly different. Then, I knew what it was that made it appear so strange. It was bare: there was not a piece of furniture in the room; not even a solitary fitting of any sort. Gradually, my amazement went, as I remembered, that this was but the inevitable end of that process of decay, which I had witnessed commencing, before my sleep. Thousands of years! Millions of years!

"Over the floor was spread a deep layer of dust, that reached half way up to the window-seat. It had grown immeasurably, whilst I slept; and represented the dust of untold ages. Undoubtedly, atoms of the old, decayed furniture helped to swell its bulk; and, somewhere among it all, mouldered the long-ago-dead Pepper.

"All at once, it occurred to me, that I had no recollection of wading knee-deep through all that dust, after I awoke. True, an incredible age of years had passed, since I approached the window; but that was evidently as nothing, compared with the countless spaces of time that, I conceived, had vanished whilst I was sleeping. I remembered now, that I had fallen asleep, sitting in my old chair. Had it gone . . . ? I glanced towards where it had stood. Of course, there was no chair to be seen. I could not satisfy myself, whether it had disappeared, after my waking, or before. If it had mouldered under me, surely, I should have been waked by the collapse. Then I remembered that the thick dust, which covered the floor, would have been sufficient to soften my fall; so that it was quite possible, I had slept upon the dust for a million years or more.

"As these thoughts wandered through my brain, I glanced again, casually, to where the chair had stood. Then, for the first time, I noticed that there were no marks, in the dust, of my footprints, between it and the window. But then, ages of years had passed, since I had awaked—tens of thousands of years!

"My look rested thoughtfully, again upon the place where once had stood my chair. Suddenly, I passed from abstraction to intentness; for there, in its standing place, I made out a long undulation, rounded off with the heavy dust. Yet it was not so much hidden, but that I could tell what had caused it. I knew—and shivered at the knowledge—that it was a human body, ages-dead, lying there, beneath the place where I had slept. It was lying on its right side, its back turned towards me. I could make out and trace each curve and outline, softened, and moulded, as it were, in the black dust. In a vague sort of way, I tried to account for its presence there. Slowly, I began to grow bewildered, as the thought came to me that it lay just about where I must have fallen when the chair collapsed.

"Gradually, an idea began to form itself within my brain; a thought that shook my spirit. It seemed hideous and insupportable; yet it grew upon me, steadily, until it became a conviction. The body under that coating, that shroud of dust, was neither more nor less than my own dead shell. I did not attempt to prove it. I knew it now, and wondered I had not known it all along. I was a bodyless thing.

"Awhile, I stood, trying to adjust my thoughts to this new problem. In time—how many thousands of years, I know not—I attained to some degree of quietude—sufficient to enable me to pay attention to what was transpiring around me.

"Now, I saw that the elongated mound had sunk, collapsed, level with the rest of the spreading dust. And fresh atoms, impalpable, had settled above that mixture of grave-powder, which the aeons had ground. A long while, I stood, turned from the window. Gradually, I grew more collected, while the world slipped across the centuries into the future.

"Presently, I began a survey of the room. Now, I saw that time was beginning its destructive work, even on this strange old building. That it had stood through all the years was, it seemed to me, proof that it was something different from any other house. I do not think, somehow, that I had thought of its decaying. Though, why, I could not have said. It was not until I had meditated upon the matter, for some considerable time, that I fully realised that the extraordinary space of time through which it had stood, was sufficient to have utterly pulverised the very stones of which it was built, had they been taken from any earthly quarry. Yes, it was undoubtedly mouldering now. All the plaster had gone from the walls; even as the woodwork of the room had gone, many ages before.

"While I stood, in contemplation, a piece of glass, from one of the small, diamond-shaped panes, dropped, with a dull tap, amid the dust upon the sill behind me, and crumbled into a little heap of powder. As I turned from contemplating it, I saw light between a couple of the stones that formed the outer wall. Evidently, the mortar was falling away. . . .

"After awhile, I turned once more to the window, and peered out. I discovered, now, that the speed of time had become enormous. The lateral quiver of the sun-stream, had grown so swift as to cause the dancing semi-circle of flame to merge into, and disappear in, a sheet of fire that covered half the Southern sky from East to West.

"From the sky, I glanced down to the gardens. They were just a blur of a palish, dirty green. I had a feeling that they stood higher than in the old days; a feeling that they were nearer my window, as though they had risen, bodily. Yet, they were still a long way below me; for the rock, over the mouth of the pit, on which this house stands, arches up to a great height.

"It was later, that I noticed a change in the constant colour of the gardens. The pale, dirty green was growing ever paler and paler, towards white. At last, after a great space, they became greyish-white, and stayed thus for a very long time. Finally, however, the greyness began to fade, even as had the green, into a dead white. And this remained, constant and unchanged. And by this I knew that, at last, snow lay upon all the Northern world.

"And so, by millions of years, time winged onward through eternity, to the end—the end, of which, in the old-earth days, I had thought remotely, and in hazily speculative fashion. And now, it was approaching in a manner of which none had ever dreamed.

"I recollect that, about this time, I began to have a lively, though morbid, curiosity, as to what would happen when the end came—but I seemed strangely without imaginings.

"All this while, the steady process of decay was continuing. The few remaining pieces of glass, had long ago vanished; and, every now and then, a soft thud, and a little cloud of rising dust, would tell of some fragment of fallen mortar or stone.

"I looked up again, to the fiery sheet that quaked in the heavens above me and far down into the Southern sky. As I looked, the impression was borne in upon me, that it had lost some of its first brilliancy—that it was duller, deeper hued.

"I glanced down, once more, to the blurred white of the worldscape. Sometimes, my look returned to the burning sheet of dulling flame, that was, and yet hid, the sun. At times, I glanced behind me, into the growing dusk of the great, silent room, with its aeon-carpet of sleeping dust. . . .

"So, I watched through the fleeting ages, lost in soul-wearing thoughts and wonderings, and possessed with a new weariness."

XVII

The Slowing Rotation

"IT MIGHT HAVE BEEN a million years later, that I perceived, beyond possibility of doubt, that the fiery sheet that lit the world, was indeed darkening.

"Another vast space went by, and the whole enormous flame had sunk to a deep, copper colour. Gradually, it darkened, from copper to copper-red, and from this, at times, to a deep, heavy, purplish tint, with, in it, a strange loom of blood.

"Although the light was decreasing, I could perceive no diminishment in the apparent speed of the sun. It still spread itself in that dazzling veil of speed.

"The world, so much of it as I could see, had assumed a dreadful shade of gloom, as though, in very deed, the last day of the worlds approached.

"The sun was dying; of that there could be little doubt; and still the earth whirled onward, through space and all the aeons. At this time, I remember, an extraordinary sense of bewilderment took me. I found myself, later, wandering, mentally, amid an odd chaos of fragmentary modern theories and the old Biblical story of the world's ending.

"Then, for the first time, there flashed across me, the memory that the sun, with its system of planets, was, and had been, travelling through space at an incredible speed. Abruptly, the question rose— *Where?* For a very great time, I pondered this matter; but, finally, with a certain sense of the futility of my puzzlings, I let my thoughts wander to other things. I grew to wondering, how much longer the house would stand. Also, I queried, to myself, whether I should be doomed to stay, bodyless, upon the earth, through the dark-time that I knew was coming. From these thoughts, I fell again to speculations upon the possible direction of the sun's journey through space. . . . And so another great while passed.

"Gradually, as time fled, I began to feel the chill of a great winter. Then, I remembered that, with the sun dying, the cold must be, necessarily, extraordinarily intense. Slowly, slowly, as the aeons slipped into eternity, the earth sank into a heavier and redder gloom. The dull flame in the firmament took on a deeper tint, very sombre and turbid.

"Then, at last, it was borne upon me that there was a change. The fiery, gloomy curtain of flame that hung quaking overhead, and down away into the Southern sky, began to thin and contract; and, in it, as one sees the fast vibrations of a jarred harp-string, I saw once more the sun-stream quivering, giddily, North and South.

"Slowly, the likeness to a sheet of fire, disappeared, and I saw, plainly, the slowing beat of the sun-stream. Yet, even then, the speed of its swing was inconceivably swift. And all the time, the brightness of the fiery arc grew ever duller. Underneath, the world loomed dimly—an indistinct, ghostly region.

"Overhead, the river of flame swayed slower, and even slower; until, at last, it swung to the North and South in great, ponderous beats, that lasted through seconds. A long space went by, and now each sway of the great belt lasted nigh a minute; so that, after a great while, I ceased to distinguish it as a visible movement; and the streaming fire ran in a steady river of dull flame, across the deadly-looking sky.

"An indefinite period passed, and it seemed that the arc of fire became less sharply defined. It appeared to me to grow more attenuated, and I thought blackish streaks showed, occasionally. Presently, as I watched, the smooth onward-flow ceased; and I was able to perceive that there came a momentary, but regular, darkening of the world. This grew until, once more, night descended, in short, but periodic, intervals upon the wearying earth.

"Longer and longer became the nights, and the days equalled them; so that, at last, the day and the night grew to the duration of seconds in length, and the sun showed, once more, like an almost invisible, coppery-red coloured ball, within the glowing mistiness of its flight. Corresponding to the dark lines, showing at times in its trail, there were now distinctly to be seen on the half-visible sun itself, great, dark belts.

"Year after year flashed into the past, and the days and nights spread into minutes. The sun had ceased to have the appearance of a tail; and now rose and set—a tremendous globe of a glowing copper-bronze hue; in parts ringed with blood-red bands; in others, with the dusky ones, that I have already mentioned. These circles—both red and black—were of varying thicknesses. For a time, I was at a loss to account for their presence. Then it occurred to me, that it was scarcely likely that the sun would cool evenly all over; and that these markings were due, probably, to differences in temperature of the various areas; the red representing those parts where the heat was still fervent, and the black those portions which were already comparatively cool.

"It struck me, as a peculiar thing, that the sun should cool in evenly defined rings; until I remembered that, possibly, they were but isolated patches, to which the enormous rotatory speed of the sun had imparted a belt-like appeerance. The sun, itself, was very much greater than the sun I had known in the old-world days; and, from this, I argued that it was considerably nearer.

"At nights, the moon[1] still showed; but small and remote; and the light she reflected was so dull and weak that she seemed little more than the small, dim ghost of the olden moon, that I had known.

"Gradually, the days and nights lengthened out, until they equalled a space somewhat less than one of the old-earth hours; the sun rising and setting like a great, ruddy bronze disk, crossed with ink-black bars. About this time, I found myself, able once more, to see the gardens, with clearness. For the world had now grown very still, and changeless. Yet, I am not correct in saying, 'gardens'; for there were no gardens—nothing that I knew or recognised. In place thereof, I looked out upon a vast plain, stretching away into distance. A little to my left, there was a low range of hills. Everywhere, there was a uniform, white covering of snow, in places rising into hummocks and ridges.

"It was only now, that I recognised how really great had been the snowfall. In places it was vastly deep, as was witnessed by a great, upleaping, wave-shaped hill, away to my right; though it is not impossible, that this was due, in part, to some rise in the surface of the ground. Strangely enough, the range of low hills to my left—already mentioned—was not entirely covered with the universal snow; instead, I could see their bare, dark sides showing in several places. And everywhere and always there reigned an incredible death-silence and desolation. The immutable, awful quiet of a dying world.

"All this time, the days and nights were lengthening, perceptibly. Already, each day occupied, maybe, some two hours from dawn to dusk. At night, I had been surprised to find that there were very few

---

[1] No further mention is made of the moon. From what is said here, it is evident that our satellite had greatly increased its distance from the earth. Possibly, at a later age it may even have broken loose from our attraction. I cannot but regret that no light is shed on this point.—Ed.

stars overhead, and these small, though of an extraordinary brightness; which I attributed to the peculiar, but clear, blackness of the night-time.

"Away to the North, I could discern a nebulous sort of mistiness; not unlike, in appearance, a small portion of the Milky Way. It might have been an extremely remote star-cluster; or—the thought came to me suddenly—perhaps it was the sidereal universe that I had known, and now left far behind, for ever—a small, dimly glowing mist of stars, far in the depths of space.

"Still, the days and nights lengthened, slowly. Each time, the sun rose duller than it had set. And the dark belts increased in breadth.

"About this time, there happened a fresh thing. The sun, earth, and sky were suddenly darkened, and, apparently, blotted out for a brief space. I had a sense, a certain awareness (I could learn little by sight), that the earth was enduring a very great fall of snow. Then, in an instant, the veil that had obscured everything, vanished, and I looked out, once more. A marvellous sight met my gaze. The hollow in which this house, with its gardens, stands, was brimmed with snow.[2] It lipped over the sill of my window. Everywhere, it lay, a great level stretch of white, which caught and reflected, gloomily, the sombre coppery glows of the dying sun. The world had become a shadowless plain, from horizon to horizon.

"I glanced up at the sun. It shone with an extraordinary, dull clearness. I saw it, now, as one who, until then, had seen it, only through a partially obscuring medium. All about it, the sky had become black, with a clear, deep blackness, frightful in its nearness, and its unmeasured deep, and its utter unfriendliness. For a great time, I looked into it, newly, and shaken and fearful. It was so near. Had I been a child, I might have expressed some of my sensation and distress, by saying that the sky had lost its roof.

"Later, I turned, and peered about me, into the room. Everywhere, it was covered with a thin shroud of the all-pervading white. I could see it but dimly, by reason of the sombre light that now lit the world. It appeared to cling to the ruined walls; and the thick, soft dust of the years, that covered the floor knee-deep, was nowhere visible. The snow must have blown in through the open framework of the windows. Yet, in no place had it drifted; but lay everywhere about the great, old room, smooth and level. Moreover, there had

---

[2] Conceivably, frozen air.—Ed.

been no wind these many thousand years. But there was the snow,[3] as I have told.

"And all the earth was silent. And there was a cold, such as no living man can ever have known.

"The earth was now illuminated, by day, with a most doleful light, beyond my power to describe. It seemed as though I looked at the great plain, through the medium of a bronze-tinted sea.

"It was evident that the earth's rotatory movement was departing, steadily.

"The end came, all at once. The night had been the longest yet; and when the dying sun showed, at last, above the world's edge, I had grown so wearied of the dark, that I greeted it as a friend. It rose steadily, until about twenty degrees above the horizon. Then, it stopped suddenly, and, after a strange retrograde movement, hung motionless—a great shield in the sky.[4] Only the circular rim of the sun showed bright— only this, and one thin streak of light near the equator.

"Gradually, even this thread of light died out; and now, all that was left of our great and glorious sun, was a vast dead disk, rimmed with a thin circle of bronze-red light.

---

[3] See previous footnote. This would explain the snow (?) within the room.— Ed.

[4] I am confounded, that neither here, nor later on, does the Recluse make any further mention of the continued north and south movement (apparent, of course) of the sun from solstice to solstice.—Ed.

XVIII
The Green Star

"THE WORLD WAS HELD in a savage gloom—cold and in tolerable. Outside, all was quiet—quiet! From the dark room behind me, came the occasional, soft thud[1] of falling matter—fragments of rotting stone. So time passed, and night grasped the world, wrapping it in wrappings of impenetrable blackness.

"There was no night-sky, as we know it. Even the few straggling stars had vanished, conclusively. I might have been in a shuttered room, without a light; for all that I could see. Only, in the impalpableness of gloom, opposite, burnt that vast, encircling hair of dull fire. Beyond this, there was no ray in all the vastitude of night that surrounded me; save that, far in the North, that soft, mist-like glow still shone.

"Silently, years moved on. What period of time passed, I shall never know. It seemed to me, waiting there, that eternities came and went, stealthily; and still I watched. I could see only the glow of the sun's edge, at times; for now, it had commenced to come and go—lighting up a while, and again becoming extinguished.

"All at once, during one of these periods of life, a sudden flame cut across the night—a quick glare that lit up the dead earth, shortly; giving me a glimpse of its flat lonesomeness. The light appeared to come from the sun—shooting out from somewhere near its centre, diagonally. A moment, I gazed, startled. Then the leaping flame sank, and the gloom fell again. But now it was not so dark; and the sun was belted by a thin line of vivid, white light. I stared, intently. Had a

---

[1] At this time the sound-carrying atmosphere must have been either incredibly attenuated, or—more probably—nonexistent. In the light of this, it cannot be supposed that these, or any other, noises would have been apparent to living ears—to hearing, as we, in the material body, understand that sense.—Ed.

volcano broken out on the sun? Yet, I negatived the thought, as soon as formed. I felt that the light had been far too intensely white, and large, for such a cause.

"Another idea there was, that suggested itself to me. It was, that one of the inner planets had fallen into the sun—becoming incandescent, under that impact. This theory appealed to me, as being more plausible, and accounting more satisfactorily for the extraordinary size and brilliance of the blaze, that had lit up the dead world, so unexpectedly.

"Full of interest and emotion, I stared, across the darkness, at that line of white fire, cutting the night. One thing it told to me, unmistakably: the sun was yet rotating at an enormous speed.[2] Thus, I knew that the years were still fleeting at an incalculable rate; though so far as the earth was concerned, life, and light, and time, were things belonging to a period lost in the long gone ages.

"After that one burst of flame, the light had shown, only as an encircling band of bright fire. Now, however, as I watched, it began slowly to sink into a ruddy tint, and, later, to a dark, copper-red colour; much as the sun had done. Presently, it sank to a deeper hue; and, in a still further space of time, it began to fluctuate; having periods of glowing, and anon, dying. Thus, after a great while, it disappeared.

"Long before this, the smouldering edge of the sun had deadened into blackness. And so, in that supremely future time, the world, dark and intensely silent, rode on its gloomy orbit around the ponderous mass of the dead sun.

"My thoughts, at this period, can be scarcely described. At first, they were chaotic and wanting in coherence. But, later, as the ages came and went, my soul seemed to imbibe the very essence of the oppressive solitude and dreariness, that held the earth.

"With this feeling, there came a wonderful clearness of thought, and I realised, despairingly, that the world might wander forever, through that enormous night. For a while, the unwholesome idea filled me, with a sensation of overbearing desolation; so that I could have cried like a child. In time, however, this feeling grew, almost insensibly, less, and an unreasoning hope possessed me. Patiently, I waited.

"From time to time, the noise of dropping particles, behind in the room, came dully to my ears. Once, I heard a loud crash, and turned, instinctively, to look; forgetting, for the moment, the impenetrable night in which every detail was submerged. In a while, my gaze sought

---

[2] I can only suppose that the time of the earth's yearly journey had ceased to bear its present *relative* proportion to the period of the sun's rotation.—Ed.

the heavens; turning, unconsciously, towards the North. Yes, the nebulous glow still showed. Indeed, I could have almost imagined that it looked somewhat plainer. For a long time, I kept my gaze fixed upon it; feeling, in my lonely soul, that its soft haze was, in some way, a tie with the past. Strange, the trifles from which one can suck comfort! And yet, had I but known—But I shall come to that in its proper time.

"For a very long space, I watched, without experiencing any of the desire for sleep, that would so soon have visited me in the old-earth days. How I should have welcomed it; if only to have passed the time, away from my perplexities and thoughts.

"Several times, the comfortless sound of some great piece of masonry falling, disturbed my meditations; and, once, it seemed I could hear whispering in the room, behind me. Yet it was utterly useless to try to see anything. Such blackness, as existed, scarcely can be conceived. It was palpable, and hideously brutal to the sense; as though something dead, pressed up against me—something soft, and icily cold.

"Under all this, there grew up within my mind, a great and overwhelming distress of uneasiness, that left me, but to drop me into an uncomfortable brooding. I felt that I must fight against it; and, presently, hoping to distract my thoughts, I turned to the window, and looked up towards the North, in search of the nebulous whiteness, which, still, I believed to be the far and misty glowing of the universe we had left. Even as I raised my eyes, I was thrilled with a feeling of wonder; for, now, the hazy light had resolved into a single, great star, of vivid green.

"As I stared, astonished, the thought flashed into my mind; that the earth must be travelling towards the star; not away, as I had imagined. Next, that it could not be the universe the earth had left; but, possibly, an outlying star, belonging to some vast star-cluster, hidden in the enormous depths of space. With a sense of commingled awe and curiosity, I watched it, wondering what new thing was to be revealed to me.

"For a while, vague thoughts and speculations occupied me, during which my gaze dwelt insatiably upon that one spot of light, in the otherwise pit-like darkness. Hope grew up within me, banishing the oppression of despair, that had seemed to stifle me. Wherever the earth was travelling, it was, at least, going once more towards the realms of light. Light! One must spend an eternity wrapped in soundless night, to understand the full horror of being without it.

"Slowly, but surely, the star grew upon my vision, until, in time, it shone as brightly as had the planet Jupiter, in the old-earth days. With increased size, its colour became more impressive; reminding me of a huge emerald, scintillating rays of fire across the world.

"Years fled away in silence, and the green star grew into a great splash of flame in the sky. A little later, I saw a thing that filled me with amazement. It was the ghostly outline of a vast crescent, in the night; a gigantic new moon, seeming to be growing out of the surrounding gloom. Utterly bemused, I stared at it. It appeared to be quite close— comparatively; and I puzzled to understand how the earth had come so near to it, without my having seen it before.

"The light, thrown by the star, grew stronger; and, presently, I was aware that it was possible to see the earthscape again; though indistinctly. Awhile, I stared, trying to make out whether I could distinguish any detail of the world's surface, but I found the light insufficient. In a little, I gave up the attempt, and glanced once more towards the star. Even in the short space, that my attention had been diverted, it had increased considerably, and seemed now, to my bewildered sight, about a quarter of the size of the full moon. The light it threw, was extraordinarily powerful; yet its colour was so abominably unfamiliar, that such of the world as I could see, showed unreal; more as though I looked out upon a landscape of shadow, than aught else.

"All this time, the great crescent was increasing in brightness, and began, now, to shine with a perceptible shade of green. Steadily, the star increased in size and brilliancy, until it showed, fully as large as half a full moon; and, as it grew greater and brighter, so did the vast crescent throw out more and more light, though of an ever deepening hue of green. Under the combined blaze of their radiances, the wilderness that stretched before me, became steadily more visible. Soon, I seemed able to stare across the whole world, which now appeared, beneath the strange light, terrible in its cold and awful, flat dreariness.

"It was a little later, that my attention was drawn to the fact, that the great star of green flame, was slowly sinking out of the North, towards the East. At first, I could scarcely believe that I saw aright; but soon there could be no doubt that it was so. Gradually, it sank, and, as it fell, the vast crescent of glowing green, began to dwindle and dwindle, until it became a mere arc of light, against the livid coloured sky. Later it vanished, disappearing in the self-same spot from which I had seen it slowly emerge.

"By this time, the star had come to within some thirty degrees of the hidden horizon. In size it could now have rivalled the moon at its full; though, even yet, I could not distinguish its disk. This fact led me to conceive that it was, still, an extraordinary distance away; and, this being so, I knew that its size must be huge, beyond the conception of man to understand or imagine.

"Suddenly, as I watched, the lower edge of the star vanished—cut by a straight, dark line. A minute—or a century—passed, and it dipped lower, until the half of it had disappeared from sight. Far away out on the great plain, I saw a monstrous shadow blotting it out, and advancing swiftly. Only a third of the star was visible now. Then, like a flash, the solution of this extraordinary phenomenon revealed itself to me. The star was sinking behind the enormous mass of the dead sun. Or rather, the sun—obedient to its attraction—was rising towards it,[3] with the earth following in its trail. As these thoughts expanded in my mind, the star vanished; being completely hidden by the tremendous bulk of the sun. Over the earth there fell, once more, the brooding night.

"With the darkness, came an intolerable feeling of loneliness and dread. For the first time, I thought of the Pit, and its inmates. After that, there rose in my memory the still more terrible Thing, that had haunted the shores of the Sea of Sleep, and lurked in the shadows of this old building. Where were they? I wondered—and shivered with miserable thoughts. For a time, fear held me, and I prayed, wildly and incoherently, for some ray of light with which to dispel the cold blackness that enveloped the world.

"How long I waited, it is impossible to say—certainly for a very great period. Then, all at once, I saw a loom of light shine out ahead. Gradually, it became more distinct. Suddenly, a ray of vivid green, flashed across the darkness. At the same moment, I saw a thin line of livid flame, far in the night. An instant, it seemed, and it had grown into a great clot of fire; beneath which, the world lay bathed in a blaze of emerald green light. Steadily it grew, until, presently, the whole of the green star had come into sight again. But now, it could be scarcely called a star; for it had increased to vast proportions, being incomparably greater than the sun had been in the olden time.

"Then, as I stared, I became aware that I could see the edge of the lifeless sun, glowing like a great crescent-moon. Slowly, its lighted surface, broadened out to me, until half of its diameter was visible; and

---

[3] A careful reading of the MS. suggests that, either the sun is travelling on an orbit of great eccentricity, or else that it was approaching the green star on a lessening orbit. And at this moment, I conceive it to be finally torn directly from its oblique course, by the gravitational pull of the immense star.—Ed.

the star began to drop away on my right. Time passed, and the earth moved on, slowly traversing the tremendous face of the dead sun. [4]

"Gradually, as the earth travelled forward, the star fell still more to the right; until, at last, it shone on the back of the house, sending a flood of broken rays, in through the skeleton-like walls. Glancing upwards, I saw that much of the ceiling had vanished, enabling me to see that the upper storeys were even more decayed. The roof had, evidently, gone entirely; and I could see the green effulgence of the Star-light shining in, slantingly.

---

[4] It will be noticed here that the earth was "*slowly* traversing the tremendous face of the dead sun". No explanation is given of this, and we must conclude, either that the speed of time had slowed, or else that the earth was actually progressing on its orbit at a rate, slow, when measured by existing standards. A careful study of the MS. however, leads me to conclude that the speed of time had been steadily decreasing for a very considerable period.—Ed.

XIX

The End of the Solar System

"FROM THE ABUTMENT, WHERE once had been the windows, through which I had watched that first, fatal dawn, I could see that the sun was hugely greater, than it had been, when first the Star lit the world. So great was it, that its lower edge seemed almost to touch the far horizon. Even as I watched, I imagined that it drew closer. The radiance of green that lit the frozen earth, grew steadily brighter.

"Thus, for a long space, things were. Then, on a sudden, I saw that the sun was changing shape, and growing smaller, just as the moon would have done in past time. In a while, only a third of the illuminated part was turned towards the earth. The Star bore away on the left.

"Gradually, as the world moved on, the Star shone upon the front of the house, once more; while the sun showed, only as a great bow of green fire. An instant, it seemed, and the sun had vanished. The Star was still fully visible. Then the earth moved into the black shadow of the sun, and all was night—Night, black, starless, and intolerable.

"Filled with tumultuous thoughts, I watched across the night—waiting. Years, it may have been, and then, in the dark house behind me, the clotted stillness of the world was broken. I seemed to hear a soft padding of many feet, and a faint, inarticulate whisper of sound, grew on my sense. I looked round into the blackness, and saw a multitude of eyes. As I stared, they increased, and appeared to come towards me. For an instant, I stood, unable to move. Then a hideous swine-noise[1] rose up into the night; and, at that, I leapt from the window, out on to the frozen world. I have a confused notion of having run awhile; and, after that, I just waited—waited. Several times, I heard shrieks; but always as though from a distance. Except for these sounds, I had

---

[1] See first footnote, Chapter 18.

no idea of the whereabouts of the house. Time moved onward. I was conscious of little, save a sensation of cold and hopelessness and fear.

"An age, it seemed, and there came a glow, that told of the coming light. It grew, tardily. Then—with a loom of unearthly glory—the first ray from the Green Star, struck over the edge of the dark sun, and lit the world. It fell upon a great, ruined structure, some two hundred yards away. It was the house. Staring, I saw a fearsome sight—over its walls crawled a legion of unholy things, almost covering the old building, from tottering towers to base. I could see them, plainly; they were the Swine-creatures.

"The world moved out into the light of the Star, and I saw that, now, it seemed to stretch across a quarter of the heavens. The glory of its livid light was so tremendous, that it appeared to fill the sky with quivering flames. Then, I saw the sun. It was so close that half of its diameter lay below the horizon; and, as the world circled across its face, it seemed to tower right up into the sky, a stupendous dome of emerald-coloured fire. From time to time, I glanced towards the house; but the Swine-things seemed unaware of my proximity.

"Years appeared to pass, slowly. The earth had almost reached the centre of the sun's disk. The light from the Green *Sun*—as now it must be called—shone through the interstices, that gapped the mouldered walls of the old house, giving them the appearance of being wrapped in green flames. The Swine-creatures still crawled about the walls.

"Suddenly, there rose a loud roar of swine-voices, and, up from the centre of the roofless house, shot a vast column of blood-red flame. I saw the little, twisted towers and turrets flash into fire; yet still preserving their twisted crookedness. The beams of the Green Sun, beat upon the house, and intermingled with its lurid glows; so that it appeared a blazing furnace of red and green fire.

"Fascinated, I watched, until an overwhelming sense of coming danger, drew my attention. I glanced up, and, at once, it was borne upon me, that the sun was closer; so close, in fact, that it seemed to overhang the world. Then—I know not how—I was caught up into strange heights—floating like a bubble in the awful effulgence.

"Far below me, I saw the earth, with the burning house leaping into an ever-growing mountain of flame. Round about it, the ground appeared to be glowing; and, in places, heavy wreaths of yellow smoke ascended from the earth. It seemed as though the world were becoming ignited from that one plague-spot of fire. Faintly, I could see the Swine-things. They appeared quite unharmed. Then the ground seemed to cave in, suddenly, and the house, with its load of foul creatures, disappeared into the depths of the earth, sending a strange, blood-coloured cloud into the heights. I remembered the hell Pit under the house.

"In a while, I looked round. The huge bulk of the sun, rose high above me. The distance between it and the earth, grew rapidly less. Suddenly, the earth appeared to shoot forward. In a moment, it had traversed the space between it and the sun. I heard no sound; but, out from the sun's face, gushed an ever growing tongue of dazzling flame. It *seemed* to leap, almost to the distant Green Sun—shearing through the emerald light, a very cataract of blinding fire. It reached its limit, and sank; and, on the sun, glowed a vast splash of burning white—the grave of the earth.

"The sun was very close to me, now. Presently, I found that I was rising higher; until, at last, I rode above it, in the emptiness. The Green Sun was now so huge that its breadth seemed to fill up all the sky, ahead. I looked down, and noted that the sun was passing directly beneath me.

"A year may have gone by—or a century—and I was left, suspended, alone. The sun showed far in front—a black, circular mass, against the molten splendour of the great, Green Orb. Near one edge, I observed that a lurid glow had appeared, marking the place where the earth had fallen. By this, I knew that the long-dead sun was still revolving, though with great slowness.

"Afar to my right, I seemed to catch, at times, a faint glow of whitish light. For a great time, I was uncertain whether to put this down to fancy or not. Thus, for a while, I stared, with fresh wonderings; until, at last, I knew that it was no imaginary thing; but a reality. It grew brighter; and, presently, there slid out of the green, a pale globe of softest white. It came nearer, and I saw that it was apparently surrounded by a robe of gently glowing clouds. Time passed. . . .

"I glanced towards the diminishing sun. It showed, only as a dark blot on the face of the Green Sun. As I watched, I saw it grow smaller, steadily, as though rushing towards the superior orb, at an immense speed. Intently, I stared. What would happen? I was conscious of extraordinary emotions, as I realised that it would strike the Green Sun. It grew no bigger than a pea, and I looked, with my whole soul, to witness the final end of our System—that system which had borne the world through so many aeons, with its multitudinous sorrows and joys; and now—

"Suddenly, something crossed my vision, cutting from sight all vestige of the spectacle I watched with such soul-interest. What happened to the dead sun, I did not see; but I have no reason—in the light of that which I saw afterwards—to disbelieve that it fell into the strange fire of the Green Sun, and so perished.

"And then, suddenly, an extraordinary question rose in my mind, whether this stupendous globe of green fire might not be the vast *Central* Sun—the great sun, round which our universe and countless others revolve. I felt confused. I thought of the probable end of the dead sun, and another suggestion came, dumbly—Do the dead stars make the Green Sun their grave? The idea appealed to me with no sense of grotesqueness; but rather as something both possible and probable.

XX

The Celestial Globes

"FOR AWHILE, MANY THOUGHTS crowded my mind, so that I was unable to do aught, save stare, blindly, before me. I seemed whelmed in a sea of doubt and wonder and sorrowful remembrance.

"It was later, that I came out of my bewilderment. I looked about, dazedly. Thus, I saw so extraordinary a sight that, for a while, I could scarcely believe I was not still wrapped in the visionary tumult of my own thoughts. Out of the reigning green, had grown a boundless river of softly shimmering globes—each one enfolded in a wondrous fleece of pure cloud. They reached, both above and below me, to an unknown distance; and, not only hid the shining of the Green Sun; but supplied, in place thereof, a tender glow of light, that suffused itself around me, like unto nothing I have ever seen, before or since.

"In a little, I noticed that there was about these spheres, a sort of transparency, almost as though they were formed of clouded crystal, within which burned a radiance—gentle and subdued. They moved on, past me, continually, floating onward at no great speed; but rather as though they had eternity before them. A great while, I watched, and could perceive no end to them. At times, I seemed to distinguish faces, amid the cloudiness; but strangely indistinct, as though partly real, and partly formed of the mistiness through which they showed.

"For a long time, I waited, passively, with a sense of growing content. I had no longer that feeling of unutterable loneliness; but felt, rather, that I was less alone, than I had been for kalpas of years. This feeling of contentment, increased, so that I would have been satisfied to float in company with those celestial globules, for ever.

"Ages slipped by, and I saw the shadowy faces, with increased frequency, also with greater plainness. Whether this was due to my soul having become more attuned to its surroundings, I cannot tell— probably it was so. But, however this may be, I am assured now, only of the fact that I became steadily more conscious of a new mystery about me, telling me that I had, indeed, penetrated within the borderland of some unthought-of region—some subtle, intangible place, or form, of existence.

"The enormous stream of luminous spheres continued to pass me, at an unvarying rate—countless millions; and still they came, showing no signs of ending, nor even diminishing.

"Then, as I was borne, silently, upon the unbuoying ether, I felt a sudden, irresistible, forward movement, towards one of the passing globes. An instant, and I was beside it. Then, I slid through, into the interior, without experiencing the least resistance, of any description. For a short while, I could see nothing; and waited, curiously.

"All at once, I became aware that a sound broke the inconceivable stillness. It was like the murmur of a great sea at calm—a sea breathing in its sleep. Gradually, the mist that obscured my sight, began to thin away; and so, in time, my vision dwelt once again upon the silent surface of the Sea of Sleep.

"For a little, I gazed, and could scarcely believe I saw aright. I glanced round. There was the great globe of pale fire, swimming, as I had seen it before, a short distance above the dim horizon. To my left, far across the sea, I discovered, presently, a faint line, as of thin haze, which I guessed to be the shore, where my Love and I had met, during those wonderful periods of soul-wandering, that had been granted to me in the old earth days.

"Another, a troubled, memory came to me—of the Formless Thing that had haunted the shores of the Sea of Sleep. The guardian of that silent, echoless place. These, and other, details, I remembered, and knew, without doubt that I was looking out upon that same sea. With the assurance, I was filled with an overwhelming feeling of surprise, and joy, and shaken expectancy, conceiving it possible that I was about to see my Love, again. Intently, I gazed around; but could catch no sight of her. At that, for a little, I felt hopeless. Fervently, I prayed, and ever peered, anxiously. . . . How still was the sea!

"Down, far beneath me, I could see the many trails of changeful fire, that had drawn my attention, formerly. Vaguely, I wondered what caused them; also, I remembered that I had intended to ask my dear One about them, as well as many other matters—and I had been forced to leave her, before the half that I had wished to say, was said.

"My thoughts came back with a leap. I was conscious that something had touched me. I turned quickly. God, Thou wert indeed gracious—it was She! She looked up into my eyes, with an eager longing, and I looked down to her, with all my soul. I should like to have held her; but the glorious purity of her face, kept me afar. Then, out of the winding mist, she put her dear arms. Her whisper came to me, soft as the rustle of a passing cloud. 'Dearest!' she said. That was all; but I had heard, and, in a moment I held her to me—as I prayed—for ever.

"In a little, she spoke of many things, and I listened. Willingly, would I have done so through all the ages that are to come. At times, I whispered back, and my whispers brought to her spirit face, once more, an indescribably delicate tint—the bloom of love. Later, I spoke more freely, and to each word she listened, and made answer, delightfully; so that, already, I was in Paradise.

"She and I; and nothing, save the silent, spacious void to see us; and only the quiet waters of the Sea of Sleep to hear us.

"Long before, the floating multitude of cloud-enfolded spheres had vanished into nothingness. Thus, we looked upon the face of the slumberous deeps, and were alone. Alone, God, I would be thus alone in the hereafter, and yet be never lonely! I had her, and, greater than this, she had me. Aye, aeon-aged me; and on this thought, and some others, I hope to exist through the few remaining years that may yet lie between us.

XXI
The Dark Sun

"NOW LONG OUR SOULS lay in the arms of joy, I cannot say; but, all at once, I was waked from my happiness, by a diminution of the pale and gentle light that lit the Sea of Sleep. I turned towards the huge, white orb, with a premonition of coming trouble. One side of it was curving inward, as though a convex, black shadow were sweeping across it. My memory went back. It was thus, that the darkness had come, before our last parting. I turned towards my Love, inquiringly. With a sudden knowledge of woe, I noticed how wan and unreal she had grown, even in that brief space. Her voice seemed to come to me from a distance. The touch of her hands was no more than the gentle pressure of a summer wind, and grew less perceptible.

"Already, quite half of the immense globe was shrouded. A feeling of desperation seized me. Was she about to leave me? Would she have to go, as she had gone before? I questioned her, anxiously, frightenedly; and she, nestling closer, explained, in that strange, faraway voice, that it was imperative she should leave me, before the Sun of Darkness—as she termed it—blotted out the light. At this confirmation of my fears, I was overcome with despair; and could only look, voicelessly, across the quiet plains of the silent sea.

"How swiftly the darkness spread across the face of the White Orb. Yet, in reality, the time must have been long, beyond human comprehension.

"At last, only a crescent of pale fire, lit the, now dim, Sea of Sleep. All this while, she had held me; but, with so soft a caress, that I had been scarcely conscious of it. We waited there, together, she and I; speechless, for very sorrow. In the dimming light, her face showed, shadowy—blending into the dusky mistiness that encircled us.

"Then, when a thin, curved line of soft light was all that lit the sea, she released me—pushing me from her, tenderly. Her voice sounded in my ears, 'I may not stay longer, Dear One.' It ended in a sob.

"She seemed to float away from me, and became invisible. Her voice came to me, out of the shadows, faintly; apparently from a great distance:—

" 'A little while—' It died away, remotely. In a breath, the Sea of Sleep darkened into night. Far to my left, I seemed to see, for a brief instant, a soft glow. It vanished, and, in the same moment, I became aware that I was no longer above the still sea; but once more suspended in infinite space, with the Green Sun—now eclipsed by a vast, dark sphere—before me.

"Utterly bewildered, I stared, almost unseeingly, at the ring of green flames, leaping above the dark edge. Even in the chaos of my thoughts, I wondered, dully, at their extraordinary shapes. A multitude of questions assailed me. I thought more of her, I had so lately seen, than of the sight before me. My grief, and thoughts of the future, filled me. Was I doomed to be separated from her, always? Even in the old earth-days, she had been mine, only for a little while; then she had left me, as I thought, for ever. Since then, I had seen her but these times, upon the Sea of Sleep.

"A feeling of fierce resentment filled me, and miserable questionings. Why could I not have gone with my Love? What reason to keep us apart? Why had I to wait alone, while she slumbered through the years, on the still bosom of the Sea of Sleep? The Sea of Sleep! My thoughts turned, inconsequently, out of their channel of bitterness, to fresh, desperate questionings. Where was it? Where was it? I seemed to have but just parted from my Love, upon its quiet surface, and it had gone, utterly. It could not be far away! And the White Orb which I had seen hidden in the shadow of the Sun of Darkness! My sight dwelt upon the Green Sun—eclipsed. What had eclipsed it? Was there a vast, dead star circling it? Was the *Central* Sun—as I had come to regard it—a double star? The thought had come, almost unbidden; yet why should it not be so?

"My thoughts went back to the White Orb. Strange, that it should have been— I stopped. An idea had come, suddenly. The White Orb and the Green Sun! Were they one and the same? My imagination wandered backwards, and I remembered the luminous globe to which I had been so unaccountably attracted. It was curious that I should have forgotten it, even momentarily. Where were the others? I reverted again to the globe I had entered. I thought, for a time, and matters became clearer. I conceived that, by entering that impalpable globule, I had passed, at once, into some further, and, until then, invisible dimension; There, the Green Sun was still visible; but as a stupendous sphere of pale, white light—almost as though its ghost showed, and not its material part.

"A long time, I mused on the subject. I remembered how, on entering the sphere, I had, immediately, lost all sight of the others. For a still further period, I continued to revolve the different details in my mind.

"In a while, my thoughts turned to other things. I came more into the present, and began to look about me, seeingly. For the first time, I perceived that innumerable rays, of a subtle, violet hue, pierced the strange semi-darkness, in all directions. They radiated from the fiery rim of the Green Sun. They seemed to grow upon my vision, so that, in a little, I saw that they were countless. The night was filled with them—spreading outwards from the Green Sun, fan-wise. I concluded that I was enabled to see them, by reason of the Sun's glory being cut off by the eclipse. They reached right out into space, and vanished.

"Gradually, as I looked, I became aware that fine points of intensely brilliant light, traversed the rays. Many of them seemed to travel from the Green Sun, into distance. Others came out of the void, towards the Sun; but one and all, each kept strictly to the ray in which it travelled. Their speed was inconceivably great; and it was only when they neared the Green Sun, or as they left it, that I could see them as separate specks of light. Further from the sun, they became thin lines of vivid fire within the violet.

"The discovery of these rays, and the moving sparks, interested me, extraordinarily. To where did they lead, in such countless profusion? I thought of the worlds in space. . . . And those sparks! Messengers! Possibly, the idea was fantastic; but I was not conscious of its being so. Messengers! Messengers from the Central Sun!

"An idea evolved itself, slowly. Was the Green Sun the abode of some vast Intelligence? The thought was bewildering. Visions of the Unnamable rose, vaguely. Had I, indeed, come upon the dwelling-place of the Eternal? For a time, I repelled the thought, dumbly. It was too stupendous. Yet. . . .

"Huge, vague thoughts had birth within me. I felt, suddenly, terribly naked. And an awful Nearness, shook me.

"And Heaven! . . . Was that an illusion?

"My thoughts came and went, erratically. The Sea of Sleep—and she! Heaven. . . . I came back, with a bound, to the present. Somewhere, out of the void behind me, there rushed an immense, dark body—huge and silent. It was a dead star, hurling onwards to the burying place of the stars. It drove between me and the Central Suns—blotting them out from my vision, and plunging me into an impenetrable night.

"An age, and I saw again the violet rays. A great while later—aeons it must have been—a circular glow grew in the sky, ahead, and I saw the edge of the receding star, show darkly against it. Thus, I knew that it was nearing the Central Suns. Presently, I saw the bright ring of the Green Sun, show plainly against the night. The star had passed into the shadow of the Dead Sun. After that, I just waited. The strange years went slowly, and ever, I watched, intently.

"'The thing I had expected, came at last—suddenly, awfully. A vast flare of dazzling light. A streaming burst of white flame across the dark void. For an indefinite while, it soared outwards—a gigantic mushroom of fire. It ceased to grow. Then, as time went by, it began to sink backwards, slowly. I saw, now, that it came from a huge, glowing spot near the centre of the Dark Sun. Mighty flames, still soared outwards from this. Yet, spite of its size, the grave of the star was no more than the shining of Jupiter upon the face of an ocean, when compared with the inconceivable mass of the Dead Sun.

"I may remark here, once more, that no words will ever convey to the imagination, the enormous bulk of the two Central Suns.

XXII
The Dark Nebula

"YEARS MELTED INTO THE past, centuries, aeons. The light of the incandescent star sank to a furious red.

"It was later, that I saw the dark nebula—at first, an impalpable cloud, away to my right. It grew, steadily, to a clot of blackness in the night. How long I watched, it is impossible to say; for time, as we count it, was a thing of the past. It came closer, a shapeless monstrosity of darkness—tremendous. It seemed to slip across the night, sleepily—a very hell-fog. Slowly, it slid nearer, and passed into the void, between me and the Central Suns. It was as though a curtain had been drawn before my vision. A strange tremor of fear took me, and a fresh sense of wonder.

"The green twilight that had reigned for so many millions of years, had now given place to impenetrable gloom. Motionless, I peered about me. A century fled, and it seemed to me that I detected occasional dull glows of red, passing me at intervals.

"Earnestly, I gazed, and, presently, seemed to see circular masses, that showed muddily red, within the clouded blackness. They appeared to be growing out of the nebulous murk. Awhile, and they became plainer to my accustomed vision. I could see them, now, with a fair amount of distinctness—ruddy-tinged spheres, similar, in size, to the luminous globes that I had seen, so long previously.

"They floated past me, continually. Gradually, a peculiar uneasiness seized me. I became aware of a growing feeling of repugnance and dread. It was directed against those passing orbs, and seemed born of intuitive knowledge, rather than of any real cause or reason.

"Some of the passing globes were brighter than others; and, it was from one of these, that a face looked, suddenly. A face, human in its outline; but so tortured with woe, that I stared, aghast. I had not thought there was such sorrow, as I saw there. I was conscious

114

of an added sense of pain, on perceiving that the eyes, which glared so wildly, were sightless. A while longer, I saw it; then it had passed on, into the surrounding gloom. After this, I saw others—all wearing that look of hopeless sorrow; and blind.

"A long time went by, and I became aware that I was nearer to the orbs, than I had been. At this, I grew uneasy; though I was less in fear of those strange globules, than I had been, before seeing their sorrowful inhabitants; for sympathy had tempered my fear.

"Later, there was no doubt but that I was being carried closer to the red spheres, and, presently, I floated among them. In awhile, I perceived one bearing down upon me. I was helpless to move from its path. In a minute, it seemed, it was upon me, and I was submerged in a deep red mist. This cleared, and I stared, confusedly, across the immense breadth of the Plain of Silence. It appeared just as I had first seen it. I was moving forward, steadily, across its surface. Away ahead, shone the vast, blood-red ring[1] that lit the place. All around, was spread the extraordinary desolation of stillness, that had so impressed me during my previous wanderings across its starkness.

"Presently, I saw, rising up into the ruddy gloom, the distant peaks of the mighty amphitheatre of mountains, where, untold ages before, I had been shown my first glimpse of the terrors that underlie many things; and where, vast and silent, watched by a thousand mute gods, stands the replica of this house of mysteries—this house that I had seen swallowed up in that hell-fire, ere the earth had kissed the sun, and vanished for ever.

"Though I could see the crests of the mountain-amphitheatre, yet it was a great while before their lower portions became visible. Possibly, this was due to the strange, ruddy haze, that seemed to cling to the surface of the Plain. However, be this as it may, I saw them at last.

"In a still further space of time, I had come so close to the mountains, that they appeared to overhang me. Presently, I saw the great rift, open before me, and I drifted into it; without volition on my part.

"Later, I came out upon the breadth of the enormous arena. There, at an apparent distance of some five miles, stood the House, huge, monstrous and silent—lying in the very centre of that stupendous amphitheatre. So far as I could see, it had not altered in any way; but looked as though it were only yesterday that I had seen it. Around, the grim, dark mountains frowned down upon me from their lofty silences.

---

[1] Without doubt, the flame-edged mass of the Dead Central Sun, seen from another dimension.—Ed.

"Far to my right, away up among inaccessible peaks, loomed the enormous bulk of the great Beast-god. Higher, I saw the hideous form of the dread goddess, rising up through the red gloom, thousands of fathoms above me. To the left, I made out the monstrous Eyeless-Thing, grey and inscrutable. Further off, reclining on its lofty ledge, the livid Ghoul-Shape showed—a splash of sinister colour, among the dark mountains.

"Slowly, I moved out across the great arena—floating. As I went, I made out the dim forms of many of the other lurking Horrors that peopled those supreme heights.

"Gradually, I neared the House, and my thoughts flashed back across the abyss of years. I remembered the dread Spectre of the Place. A short while passed, and I saw that I was being wafted directly towards the enormous mass of that silent building.

"About this time, I became aware, in an indifferent sort of way, of a growing sense of numbness, that robbed me of the fear, which I should otherwise have felt, on approaching that awesome Pile. As it was, I viewed it, calmly—much as a man views calamity through the haze of his tobacco smoke.

"In a little while, I had come so close to the House, as to be able to distinguish many of the details about it. The longer I looked, the more was I confirmed in my long-ago impressions of its entire similitude to this strange house. Save in its enormous size, I could find nothing unlike.

"Suddenly, as I stared, a great feeling of amazement filled me. I had come opposite to that part, where the outer door, leading into the study, is situated. There, lying right across the threshold, lay a great length of coping stone, identical—save in size and colour—with the piece I had dislodged in my fight with the Pit-creatures.

"I floated nearer, and my astonishment increased, as I noted that the door was broken partly from its hinges, precisely in the manner that my study door had been forced inwards, by the assaults of the Swine-things. The sight started a train of thoughts, and I began to trace, dimly, that the attack on *this* house, might have a far deeper significance than I had, hitherto, imagined. I remembered how, long ago, in the old earth-days, I had half suspected that, in some unexplainable manner, this house, in which I live, was *en rapport*—to use a recognised term—with that other tremendous structure, away in the midst of that incomparable Plain.

"Now, however, it began to be borne upon me, that I had but vaguely conceived what the realisation of my suspicion meant. I began to understand, with a more than human clearness, that the attack I had repelled, was, in some extraordinary manner, connected with an attack upon that strange edifice.

"With a curious inconsequence, my thoughts abruptly left the matter; to dwell, wonderingly, upon the peculiar material, out of which the House was constructed. It was—as I have mentioned, earlier—of a deep, green colour. Yet, now that I had come so close to it, I perceived that it fluctuated at times, though slightly—glowing and fading, much as do the fumes of phosphorus, when rubbed upon the hand, in the dark.

"Presently, my attention was distracted from this, by coming to the great entrance. Here, for the first time, I was afraid; for, all in a moment, the huge doors swung back, and I drifted in between them, helplessly. Inside, all was blackness, impalpable. In an instant, I had crossed the threshold, and the great doors closed, silently, shutting me in that lightless place.

"For a while, I seemed to hang, motionless; suspended amid the darkness. Then, I became conscious that I was moving again; where, I could not tell. Suddenly, far down beneath me, I seemed to hear a murmurous noise of Swine-laughter. It sank away, and the succeeding silence appeared clogged with horror.

"Then a door opened somewhere ahead; a white haze of light filtered through, and I floated slowly into a room, that seemed strangely familiar. All at once, there came a bewildering, screaming noise, that deafened me. I saw a blurred vista of visions, flaming before my sight. My senses were dazed, through the space of an eternal moment. Then, my power of seeing, came back to me. The dizzy, hazy feeling passed, and I saw, clearly.

XXIII
Pepper

"I WAS SEATED IN my chair, back again in this old study. My glance wandered round the room. For a minute, it had a strange, quivery appearance—unreal and unsubstantial. This disappeared, and I saw that nothing was altered in any way. I looked towards the end window—the blind was up.

"I rose to my feet, shakily. As I did so, a slight noise, in the direction of the door, attracted my attention. I glanced towards it. For a short instant, it appeared to me that it was being closed, gently. I stared, and saw that I must have been mistaken—it seemed closely shut.

"With a succession of efforts, I trod my way to the window, and looked out. The sun was just rising, lighting up the tangled wilderness of gardens. For, perhaps, a minute, I stood, and stared. I passed my hand, confusedly, across my forehead.

"Presently, amid the chaos of my senses, a sudden thought came to me; I turned, quickly, and called to Pepper. There was no answer, and I stumbled across the room, in a quick access of fear. As I went, I tried to frame his name; but my lips were numb. I reached the table, and stooped down to him, with a catching at my heart. He was lying in the shadow of the table, and I had not been able to see him, distinctly, from the window. Now, as I stooped, I took my breath, shortly. There was no Pepper; instead, I was reaching towards an elongated, little heap of grey, ash-like dust. . . .

"I must have remained, in that half-stooped position, for some minutes. I was dazed—stunned. Pepper had really passed into the land of shadows.

XXIV
The Footsteps in the Garden

"PEPPER IS DEAD! EVEN now, at times, I seem scarcely able to realise that this is so. It is many weeks, since I came back from that strange and terrible journey through space and time. Sometimes, in my sleep, I dream about it, and go through, in imagination, the whole of that fearsome happening. When I wake, my thoughts dwell upon it. That Sun—those Suns, were they indeed the great Central Suns, round which the whole universe, of the unknown heavens, revolves? Who shall say? And the bright globules, floating forever in the light of the Green Sun! And the Sea of Sleep on which they float! How unbelievable it all is. If it were not for Pepper, I should, even after the many extraordinary things that I have witnessed, be inclined to imagine that it was but a gigantic dream. Then, there is that dreadful, dark nebula (with its multitudes of red spheres) moving always within the shadow of the Dark Sun, sweeping along on its stupendous orbit, wrapped eternally in gloom. And the faces that peered out at me! God, do they, and does such a thing really exist?.... There is still that little heap of grey ash, on my study floor. I will not have it touched.

"At times, when I am calmer, I have wondered what became of the outer planets of the Solar System. It has occurred to me, that they may have broken loose from the sun's attraction, and whirled away into space. This is, of course, only a surmise. There are so many things, about which I wonder.

"Now that I am writing, let me record that I am certain, there is something horrible about to happen. Last night, a thing occurred, which has filled me with an even greater terror, than did the Pit fear. I will write it down now, and, if anything more happens, endeavour to make a note of it, at once. I have a feeling, that there is more in this last affair, than in all those others. I am shaky and nervous, even now, as I write. Somehow, I think death is not very far away. Not that I fear death—as death is understood. Yet, there is that in the air, which bids me fear—an intangible, cold horror. I felt it last night. It was thus:—

"Last night, I was sitting here in my study, writing. The door, leading into the garden, was half open. At times, the metallic rattle of a dog's chain, sounded faintly. It belongs to the dog I have bought, since Pepper's death. I will not have him in the house—not after Pepper. Still, I have felt it better to have a dog about the place. They are wonderful creatures.

"I was much engrossed in my work, and the time passed, quickly. Suddenly, I heard a soft noise on the path, outside in the garden—pad, pad, pad, it went, with a stealthy, curious sound. I sat upright, with a quick movement, and looked out through the opened door. Again the noise came—pad, pad, pad. It appeared to be approaching. With a slight feeling of nervousness, I stared into the gardens; but the night hid everything.

"Then the dog gave a long howl, and I started. For a minute, perhaps, I peered, intently; but could hear nothing. After a little, I picked up the pen, which I had laid down, and recommenced my work. The nervous feeling had gone; for I imagined that the sound I had heard, was nothing more than the dog walking round his kennel, at the length of his chain.

"A quarter of an hour may have passed; then, all at once, the dog howled again, and with such a plaintively sorrowful note, that I jumped to my feet, dropping my pen, and inking the page on which I was at work.

"'Curse that dog!' I muttered, noting what I had done. Then, even as I said the words, there sounded again that queer—pad, pad, pad. It was horribly close—almost by the door, I thought. I knew, now, that it could not be the dog; his chain would not allow him to come so near.

"The dog's growl came again, and I noted, subconsciously, the taint of fear in it.

"Outside, on the window-sill, I could see Tip, my sister's pet cat. As I looked, it sprang to its feet, its tail swelling, visibly. For an instant it stood thus; seeming to stare, fixedly, at something, in the direction of the door. Then, quickly, it began to back along the sill; until, reaching the wall at the end, it could go no further. There it stood, rigid, as though frozen in an attitude of extraordinary terror.

"Frightened, and puzzled, I seized a stick from the corner, and went towards the door, silently; taking one of the candles with me. I had come to within a few paces of it, when, suddenly, a peculiar sense of fear thrilled through me—a fear, palpitant and real; whence, I knew not, nor why. So great was the feeling of terror, that I wasted no time; but retreated straightway—walking backwards, and keeping my gaze, fearfully, on the door. I would have given much, to rush at it, fling it to, and shoot the bolts; for I have had it repaired and strengthened, so that, now, it is far stronger than ever it has been. Like Tip, I continued my, almost unconscious, progress backwards, until the wall brought me up. At that, I started, nervously, and glanced round, apprehensively. As I did so, my eyes dwelt, momentarily, on the rack of firearms, and I took a step towards them; but stopped, with a curious feeling that they would be needless. Outside, in the gardens, the dog moaned, strangely.

"Suddenly, from the cat, there came a fierce, long screech. I glanced, jerkily, in its direction—Something, luminous and ghostly, encircled it, and grew upon my vision. It resolved into a glowing hand, transparent, with a lambent, greenish flame flickering over it. The cat gave a last, awful caterwaul, and I saw it smoke and blaze. My breath came with a gasp, and I leant against the wall. Over *that* part of the window there spread a smudge, green and fantastic. It hid the thing from me, though the glare of fire shone through, dully. A stench of burning, stole into the room.

"Pad, pad, pad—Something passed down the garden path, and a faint, mouldy odour seemed to come in through the open door, and mingle with the burnt smell.

"The dog had been silent for a few moments. Now, I heard him yowl, sharply, as though in pain. Then, he was quiet, save for an occasional, subdued whimper of fear.

"A minute went by; then the gate on the West side of the gardens, slammed, distantly. After that, nothing; not even the dog's whine.

"I must have stood there some minutes. Then a fragment of courage stole into my heart, and I made a frightened rush at the door, dashed it to, and bolted it. After that, for a full half-hour, I sat, helpless—staring before me, rigidly.

"Slowly, my life came back into me, and I made my way, shakily, up-stairs to bed.

"That is all.

XXV
The Thing From the Arena

"THIS MORNING, EARLY, I went through the gardens; but found everything as usual. Near the door, I examined the path, for footprints; yet, here again, there was nothing to tell me whether, or not, I dreamed last night.

"It was only when I came to speak to the dog, that I discovered tangible proof, that something did happen. When I went to his kennel, he kept inside, crouching up in one corner, and I had to coax him, to get him out. When, finally, he consented to come, it was in a strangely cowed and subdued manner. As I patted him, my attention was attracted to a greenish patch, on his left flank. On examining it, I found, that the fur and skin had been, apparently, burnt off; for the flesh showed, raw and scorched. The shape of the mark was curious, reminding me of the imprint of a large talon or hand.

"I stood up, thoughtful. My gaze wandered towards the study window. The rays of the rising sun, shimmered on the smoky patch in the lower corner, causing it to fluctuate from green to red, oddly. Ah! that was undoubtedly another proof; and, suddenly, the horrible Thing I saw last night, rose in my mind. I looked at the dog, again. I knew the cause, now, of that hateful looking wound on his side—I knew, also, that, what I had seen last night, had been a real happening. And a great discomfort filled me. Pepper! Tip! And now this poor animal! . . . I glanced at the dog again, and noticed that he was licking at his wound.

" 'Poor brute!' I muttered, and bent to pat his head. At that, he got upon his feet, nosing and licking my hand, wistfully.

"Presently, I left him, having other matters to which to attend.

"After dinner, I went to see him, again. He seemed quiet, and disinclined to leave his kennel. From my sister, I have learnt that he has refused all food to-day. She appeared a little puzzled, when she told me; though quite unsuspicious of anything of which to be afraid.

"The day has passed, uneventfully enough. After tea, I went, again, to have a look at the dog. He seemed moody, and somewhat restless; yet persisted in remaining in his kennel. Before locking up, for the night, I moved his kennel out, away from the wall, so that I shall be able to watch it from the small window, to-night. The thought came to me, to bring him into the house for the night; but consideration has decided me, to let him remain out. I cannot say that the house is, in any degree, less to be feared than the gardens. Pepper was in the house, and yet. . . .

"It is now two o'clock. Since eight, I have watched the kennel, from the small, side window in my study. Yet, nothing has occurred, and I am too tired to watch longer. I will go to bed. . . .

"During the night, I was restless. This is unusual for me; but, towards morning, I obtained a few hours' sleep.

"I rose early, and, after breakfast, visited the dog. He was quiet; but morose, and refused to leave his kennel. I wish there was some horse doctor near here; I would have the poor brute looked to. All day, he has taken no food; but has shown an evident desire for water—lapping it up, greedily. I was relieved to observe this.

"The evening has come, and I am in my study. I intend to follow my plan of last night, and watch the kennel. The door, leading into the garden, is bolted, securely. I am consciously glad there are bars to the windows. . . .

"Night:—Midnight has gone. The dog has been silent, up to the present. Through the side window, on my left, I can make out, dimly, the outlines of the kennel. For the first time, the dog moves, and I hear the rattle of his chain. I look out, quickly. As I stare, the dog moves again, restlessly, and I see a small patch of luminous light, shine from the interior of the kennel. It vanishes; then the dog stirs again, and, once more, the gleam comes. I am puzzled. The dog is quiet, and I can see the luminous thing, plainly. It shows distinctly. There is something familiar about the shape of it. For a moment, I wonder; then it comes to me, that it is not unlike the four fingers and thumb of a hand. Like a hand! And I remember the contour of that fearsome wound on the dog's side. It must be the wound I see. It is luminous at night—Why? The minutes pass. My mind is filled with this fresh thing. . . .

"Suddenly, I hear a sound, out in the gardens. How it thrills through me. It is approaching. Pad, pad, pad. A prickly sensation traverses my spine, and seems to creep across my scalp. The dog moves in his kennel, and whimpers, frightenedly. He must have turned round; for, now, I can no longer see the outline of his shining wound.

"Outside, the gardens are silent, once more, and I listen, fearfully. A minute passes, and another; then I hear the padding sound, again. It is quite close, and appears to be coming down the gravelled path. The noise is curiously measured and deliberate. It ceases outside the door; and I rise to my feet, and stand motionless. From the door, comes a slight sound—the latch is being slowly raised. A singing noise is in my ears, and I have a sense of pressure about the head—

"The latch drops, with a sharp click, into the catch. The noise startles me afresh; jarring, horribly, on my tense nerves. After that, I stand, for a long while, amid an ever growing quietness. All at once, my knees begin to tremble, and I have to sit, quickly.

"An uncertain period of time passes, and, gradually, I begin to shake off the feeling of terror, that has possessed me. Yet, still I sit. I seem to have lost the power of movement. I am strangely tired, and inclined to doze. My eyes open and close, and, presently, I find myself falling asleep, and waking, in fits and starts.

"It is some time later, that I am sleepily aware that one of the candles is guttering. When I wake again, it has gone out, and the room is very dim, under the light of the one remaining flame. The semi-darkness troubles me little. I have lost that awful sense of dread, and my only desire seems to be to sleep—sleep.

"Suddenly, although there is no noise, I am awake—wide awake. I am acutely conscious of the nearness of some mystery, of some overwhelming Presence. The very air seems pregnant with terror. I sit huddled, and just listen, intently. Still, there is no sound. Nature, herself, seems dead. Then, the oppressive stillness is broken by a little eldritch scream of wind, that sweeps round the house, and dies away, remotely.

"I let my gaze wander across the half-lighted room. By the great clock in the far corner, is a dark, tall shadow. For a short instant, I stare, frightenedly. Then, I see that it is nothing, and am, momentarily, relieved.

"In the time that follows, the thought flashes through my brain, why not leave this house—this house of mystery and terror? Then, as though in answer, there sweeps up, across my sight, a vision of the wondrous Sea of Sleep—the Sea of Sleep where she and I have been allowed to meet, after the years of separation and sorrow; and I know that I shall stay on here, whatever happens.

"Through the side window, I note the sombre blackness of the night. My glance wanders away, and round the room; resting on one shadowy object and another. Suddenly, I turn, and look at the window on my right; as I do so, I breathe quickly, and bend forward, with a frightened gaze at something outside the window, but close to the bars. I am looking at a vast, misty swine-face, over which fluctuates a flamboyant flame, of a greenish hue. It is the Thing from the arena. The quivering mouth seems to drip with a continual, phosphorescent slaver. The eyes are staring straight into the room, with an inscrutable expression. Thus, I sit rigidly—frozen.

"The Thing has begun to move. It is turning, slowly, in my direction. Its face is coming round towards me. It sees me. Two huge, inhumanly human, eyes are looking through the dimness at me. I am cold with fear; yet, even now, I am keenly conscious, and note, in an irrelevant way, that the distant stars are blotted out by the mass of the giant face.

"A fresh horror has come to me. I am rising from my chair, without the least intention. I am on my feet, and something is impelling me towards the door that leads out into the gardens. I wish to stop; but cannot. Some immutable power is opposed to my will, and I go slowly forward, unwilling and resistant. My glance flies round the room, helplessly, and stops at the window. The great swine-face has disappeared, and I hear, again, that stealthy pad, pad, pad. It stops outside the door—the door towards which I am being compelled. . . .

"There succeeds a short, intense silence; then there comes a sound. It is the rattle of the latch, being slowly lifted. At that, I am filled with desperation. I will not go forward another step. I make a vast effort to return; but it is, as though I press back, upon an invisible wall. I groan out loud, in the agony of my fear, and the sound of my voice is frightening. Again comes that rattle, and I shiver, clammily. I try—aye, fight and struggle, to hold back, *back*; but it is no use. . . .

"I am at the door, and, in a mechanical way, I watch my hand go forward, to undo the topmost bolt. It does so, entirely without my volition. Even as I reach up towards the bolt, the door is violently shaken, and I get a sickly whiff of mouldy air, which seems to drive in through the interstices of the doorway. I draw the bolt back, slowly, fighting, dumbly, the while. It comes out of its socket, with a click, and I begin to shake, aguishly. There are two more; one at the bottom of the door; the other, a massive affair, is placed about the middle.

"For, perhaps a minute, I stand, with my arms hanging slackly, by my sides. The influence to meddle with the fastenings of the door, seems to have gone. All at once, there comes the sudden rattle of iron, at my feet. I glance down, quickly, and realise, with an unspeakable terror, that my foot is pushing back the lower bolt. An awful sense of helplessness assails me. . . . The bolt comes out of its hold, with a slight, ringing sound and I stagger on my feet, grasping at the great, central bolt, for support. A minute passes, an eternity; then another. . . . My God, help me! I am being forced to work upon the last fastening. *I will not!* Better to die, than open to the Terror, that is on the other side of the door. Is there no escape? . . . God help me, I have jerked the bolt half out of its socket! My lips emit a hoarse scream of terror, the bolt is three parts drawn, now, and still my unconscious hands work towards my doom. Only a fraction of steel, between my soul and *That*. Twice, I scream out in the supreme agony of my fear; then, with a mad effort, I tear my hands away. My eyes seem blinded. A great blackness is falling upon me. Nature has come to my rescue. I feel my knees giving. There is a loud, quick thudding upon the door, and I am falling, falling. . . .

"I must have lain there, at least a couple of hours. As I recover, I am aware that the other candle has burnt out, and the room is in an almost total darkness. I cannot rise to my feet, for I am cold, and filled with a terrible cramp. Yet my brain is clear, and there is no longer the strain of that unholy influence.

"Cautiously, I get upon my knees, and feel for the central bolt. I find it, and push it securely back into its socket; then the one at the bottom of the door. By this time, I am able to rise to my feet, and so manage to secure the fastening at the top. After that, I go down upon my knees, again, and creep away among the furniture, in the direction of the stairs. By doing this, I am safe from observation from the window.

"I reach the opposite door, and, as I leave the study, cast one nervous glance over my shoulder, towards the window. Out in the night, I seem to catch a glimpse of something impalpable; but it may be only a fancy. Then, I am in the passage, and on the stairs.

"Reaching my bedroom, I clamber into bed, all clothed as I am, and pull the bedclothes over me. There, after a while, I begin to regain a little confidence. It is impossible to sleep; but I am grateful for the added warmth of the bedclothes. Presently, I try to think over the happenings of the past night; but, though I cannot sleep, I find that it is useless, to attempt consecutive thought. My brain seems curiously blank.

"Towards morning, I begin to toss, uneasily. I cannot rest, and, after a while, I get out of bed, and pace the floor. The wintry dawn is beginning to creep through the windows, and shows the bare discomfort of the old room. Strange, that, through all these years, it has never occurred to me how dismal the place really is. And so a time passes.

"From somewhere down stairs, a sound comes up to me. I go to the bedroom door, and listen. It is Mary, bustling about the great, old kitchen, getting the breakfast ready. I feel little interest. I am not hungry. My thoughts, however; continue to dwell upon her. How little the weird happenings in this house seem to trouble her. Except in the incident of the Pit creatures, she has seemed unconscious of anything unusual occurring. She is old, like myself; yet how little we have to do with one another. Is it because we have nothing in common; or only that, being old, we care less for society, than quietness? These and other matters pass through my mind, as I meditate; and help to distract my attention, for a while, from the oppressive thoughts of the night.

"After a time, I go to the window, and, opening it, look out. The sun is now above the horizon, and the air, though cold, is sweet and crisp. Gradually, my brain clears, and a sense of security, for the time being, comes to me. Somewhat happier, I go down stairs, and out into the garden, to have a look at the dog.

"As I approach the kennel, I am greeted by the same mouldy stench that assailed me at the door last night. Shaking off a momentary sense of fear, I call to the dog; but he takes no heed, and, after calling once more, I throw a small stone into the kennel. At this, he moves, uneasily, and I shout his name, again; but do not go closer. Presently, my sister comes out, and joins me, in trying to coax him from the kennel.

"In a little the poor beast rises, and shambles out lurching queerly. In the daylight he stands swaying from side to side, and blinking stupidly. I look and note that the horrid wound is larger, much larger, and seems to have a whitish, fungoid appearance. My sister moves to fondle him; but I detain her, and explain that I think it will be better not to go too near him for a few days; as it is impossible to tell what may be the matter with him; and it is well to be cautious.

"A minute later, she leaves me; coming back with a basin of odd scraps of food. This she places on the ground, near the dog, and I push it into his reach, with the aid of a branch, broken from one of the shrubs. Yet, though the meat should be tempting, he takes no notice of it; but retires to his kennel. There is still water in his drinking vessel, so, after a few moments' talk, we go back to the house. I can see that my sister is much puzzled as to what is the matter with the animal; yet it would be madness, even to hint the truth to her.

"The day slips away, uneventfully; and night comes on. I have de-

termined to repeat my experiment of last night. I cannot say that it is
wisdom; yet my mind is made up. Still, however, I have taken precautions; for I have driven stout nails in at the back of each of the three
bolts, that secure the door, opening from the study into the gardens.
This will, at least, prevent a recurrence of the danger I ran last night.

"From ten to about two-thirty, I watch; but nothing occcurs; and,
finally, I stumble off to bed, where I am soon asleep.

XXVI
The Luminous Speck

"I AWAKE SUDDENLY. IT is still dark. I turn over, once or twice, in my endeavours to sleep again; but I cannot sleep. My head is aching, slightly; and, by turns I am hot and cold. In a little, I give up the attempt, and stretch out my hand, for the matches. I will light my candle, and read, awhile; perhaps, I shall be able to sleep, after a time. For a few moments, I grope; then my hand touches the box; but, as I open it, I am startled, to see a phosphorescent speck of fire, shining amid the darkness. I put out my other hand, and touch it. It is on my wrist. With a feeling of vague alarm, I strike a light, hurriedly, and look; but can see nothing, save a tiny scratch.

" 'Fancy!' I mutter, with a half sigh of relief. Then the match burns my finger, and I drop it, quickly. As I fumble for another, the thing shines out again. I know, now, that it is no fancy. This time, I light the candle, and examine the place, more closely. There is a slight, greenish discoloration round the scratch. I am puzzled and worried. Then a thought comes to me. I remember the morning after the Thing appeared. I remember that the dog licked my hand. It was this one, with the scratch on it; though I have not been even conscious of the abrasement, until now. A horrible fear has come to me. It creeps into my brain—the dog's wound, shines at night. With a dazed feeling, I sit down on the side of the bed, and try to think; but cannot. My brain seems numbed with the sheer horror of this new fear.

"Time moves on, unheeded. Once, I rouse up, and try to persuade myself that I am mistaken; but it is no use. In my heart, I have no doubt.

"Hour after hour, I sit in the darkness and silence, and shiver, hopelessly....

"The day has come and gone, and it is night again.

"This morning, early, I shot the dog, and buried it, away among the bushes. My sister is startled and frightened; but I am desperate.

Besides, it is better so. The foul growth had almost hidden its left side. And I——the place on my wrist has enlarged, perceptibly. Several times, I have caught myself muttering prayers——little things learnt as a child. God, Almighty God, help me! I shall go mad.

* * * *

"Six days, and I have eaten nothing. It is night. I am sitting in my chair. Ah, God! I wonder have any ever felt the horror of life that I have come to know? I am swathed in terror. I feel ever the burning of this dread growth. It has covered all my right arm and side, and is beginning to creep up my neck. To-morrow, it will eat into my face. I shall become a terrible mass of living corruption. There is no escape. Yet, a thought has come to me, born of a sight of the gun-rack, on the other side of the room. I have looked again——with the strangest of feelings. The thought grows upon me. God, Thou knowest, Thou must know, that death is better, aye, better a thousand times than *This*. This! Jesus, forgive me, but I cannot live, cannot, cannot! I dare not! I am beyond *all* help——there is nothing else left. It will, at least, spare me that final horror....

"I think I must have been dozing. I am very weak, and oh! so miserable, so miserable and tired——tired. The rustle of the paper, tries my brain. My hearing seems preternaturally sharp. I will sit awhile and think....

"Hush! I hear something, down——down in the cellars. It is a creaking sound. My God, it is the opening of the great, oak trap. What can be doing that? The scratching of my pen deafens me.... I must listen.... There are steps on the stairs; strange padding steps, that come up and nearer.... Jesus, be merciful to me, an old man. There is something fumbling at the door-handle. O God, help me now! Jesus——The door is opening——slowly. Somethi——"

That is all.

NOTE.——From the unfinished word, it is possible, on the MS., to trace a faint line of ink, which suggests that the pen has trailed away over the paper; possibly, through fright and weakness.——Ed.

XXVII
Conclusion

I PUT DOWN THE Manuscript, and glanced across at Tonnison: he was sitting, staring out into the dark. I waited a minute; then I spoke.

"Well?" I said.

He turned, slowly, and looked at me. His thoughts seemed to have gone out of him into a great distance.

"Was he mad?" I asked, and indicated the MS., with a half nod.

Tonnison stared at me, unseeingly, a moment; then, his wits came back to him, and, suddenly, he comprehended my question.

"No!" he said.

I opened my lips, to offer a contradictory opinion; for my sense of the saneness of things, would not allow me to take the story literally; then I shut them again, without saying anything. Somehow, the certainty in Tonnison's voice affected my doubts. I felt, all at once, less assured; though I was by no means convinced as yet.

After a few moments' silence, Tonnison rose, stiffly, and began to undress. He seemed disinclined to talk; so I said nothing; but followed his example. I was weary; though still full of the story I had just read.

Somehow, as I rolled into my blankets, there crept into my mind a memory of the old gardens, as we had seen them. I remembered the odd fear that the place had conjured up in our hearts; and it grew upon me, with conviction, that Tonnison was right.

It was very late when we rose—nearly midday; for the greater part of the night had been spent in reading the MS.

Tonnison was grumpy, and I felt out of sorts. It was a somewhat dismal day, and there was a touch of chilliness in the air. There was no mention of going out fishing on either of our parts. We got dinner, and, after that, just sat and smoked in silence.

Presently, Tonnison asked for the Manuscript: I handed it to him, and he spent most of the afternoon in reading it through by himself.

It was while he was thus employed, that a thought came to me:—

"What do you say to having another look at——?" I nodded my head down stream.

Tonnison looked up. "Nothing!" he said, abruptly; and, somehow, I was less annoyed, than relieved, at his answer.

After that, I left him alone.

A little before tea-time, he looked up at me, curiously.

"Sorry, old chap, if I was a bit short with you just now;" (just now, indeed! he had not spoken for the last three hours) "but I would not go there again," and he indicated with his head, "for anything that you could offer me. Ugh!" and he put down that history of a man's terror and hope and despair.

The next morning, we rose early, and went for our accustomed swim: we had partly shaken off the depression of the previous day; and so, took our rods when we had finished breakfast, and spent the day at our favourite sport.

After that day, we enjoyed our holiday to the utmost; though both of us looked forward to the time when our driver should come; for we were tremendously anxious to inquire of him, and through him among the people of the tiny hamlet, whether any of them could give us information about that strange garden, lying away by itself in the heart of an almost unknown tract of country.

At last, the day came, on which we expected the driver to come across for us. He arrived early, while we were still abed; and, the first thing we knew, he was at the opening of the tent, inquiring whether we had had good sport. We replied in the affirmative; and then, both together, almost in the same breath, we asked the question that was uppermost in our minds:—Did he know anything about an old garden, and a great pit, and a lake, situated some miles away, down the river; also, had he ever heard of a great house thereabouts?

No, he did not, and had not; yet, stay, he had heard a rumour, once upon a time, of a great, old house standing alone out in the wilderness; but, if he remembered rightly it was a place given over to the fairies; or, if that had not been so, he was certain that there had been something "quare" about it; and, anyway, he had heard nothing of it for a very long while—not since he was quite a gossoon. No, he could not remember anything particular about it; indeed, he did not know he remembered anything "at all, at all" until we questioned him.

"Look here," said Tonnison, finding that this was about all that he could tell us, "just take a walk round the village, while we dress, and find out something, if you can."

With a nondescript salute, the man departed on his errand; while we made haste to get into our clothes; after which, we began to prepare breakfast.

We were just sitting down to it, when he returned.

"It's all in bed the lazy divvils is, sor," he said, with a repetition of the salute, and an appreciative eye to the good things spread out on our provision chest, which we utilised as a table.

"Oh, well, sit down," replied my friend, "and have something to eat with us." Which the man did without delay.

After breakfast, Tonnison sent him off again on the same errand, while we sat and smoked. He was away some three-quarters of an hour, and, when he returned, it was evident that he had found out something. It appeared that he had got into conversation with an ancient man of the village, who, probably, knew more—though it was little enough—of the strange house, than any other person living.

The substance of this knowledge was, that, in the "ancient man's" youth—and goodness knows how long back that was—there had stood a great house in the centre of the gardens, where now was left only that fragment of ruin. This house had been empty for a great while; years before his—the ancient man's—birth. It was a place shunned by the people of the village, as it had been shunned by their fathers before them. There were many things said about it, and all were of evil. No one ever went near it, either by day or night. In the village it was a synonym of all that is unholy and dreadful.

And then, one day, a man, a stranger, had ridden through the village, and turned off down the river, in the direction of the House, as it was always termed by the villagers. Some hours afterwards, he had ridden back, taking the track by which he had come, towards Ardrahan. Then, for three months or so, nothing was heard. At the end of that time, he reappeared; but now, he was accompanied by an elderly woman, and a large number of donkeys, laden with various articles. They had passed through the village without stopping, and gone straight down the bank of the river, in the direction of the House.

Since that time, no one, save the man whom they had chartered to bring over monthly supplies of necessaries from Ardrahan, had ever seen either of them: and him, none had ever induced to talk; evidently, he had been well paid for his trouble.

The years had moved onwards, uneventfully enough, in that little hamlet; the man making his monthly journeys, regularly.

One day, he had appeared as usual on his customary errand. He had passed through the village without exchanging more than a surly nod with the inhabitants and gone on towards the House. Usually, it was evening before he made the return journey. On this occasion, however, he had reappeared in the village, a few hours later, in an extraordinary state of excitement, and with the astounding information, that the House had disappeared bodily, and that a stupendous pit now yawned in the place where it had stood.

This news, it appears, so excited the curiosity of the villagers, that they overcame their fears, and marched *en masse* to the place. There, they found everything, just as described by the carrier.

This was all that we could learn. Of the author of the MS., who he was, and whence he came, we shall never know.

His identity is, as he seems to have desired, buried for ever.

That same day, we left the lonely village of Kraighten. We have never been there since.

Sometimes, in my dreams, I see that enormous pit, surrounded, as it is, on all sides by wild trees and bushes. And the noise of the water rises upwards, and blends—in my sleep—with other and lower noises; while, over all, hangs the eternal shroud of spray.

Carnacki the Ghost-Finder

Carnacki the Ghost-Finder

The Thing Invisible

CARNACKI HAD JUST RETURNED to Cheyne Walk, Chelsea. I was aware of this interesting fact by reason of the curt and quaintly worded postcard which I was re-reading, and by which I was requested to present myself at his house not later than seven o'clock on that evening.

Mr. Carnacki had, as I and the others of his strictly limited circle of friends knew, been away in Kent for the past three weeks; but beyond that, we had no knowledge. Carnacki was genially secretive and curt, and spoke only when he was ready to speak. When this stage arrived, I, and his three other friends, Jessop, Arkright, and Taylor, would receive a card or a wire, asking us to call. Not one of us ever willingly missed; for after a throughly sensible little dinner, Carnacki would snuggle down into his big armchair, light his pipe, and wait whilst we arranged ourselves comfortably in our accustomed seats and nooks. Then he would begin to talk.

Upon this particular night, I was the first to arrive, and found Carnacki sitting, quietly smoking, over a paper. He stood up; shook me firmly by the hand; pointed to a chair, and sat down again; never having uttered a word.

For my part, I said nothing, either. I knew the man too well to bother him with questions, or the weather; and so took a seat and a cigarette. Presently, the three others turned up, and after that we spent a comfortable and busy hour at dinner.

Dinner over, Carnacki snugged himself down into his great chair, as I have said was his habit; filled his pipe and puffed for a while, his gaze directed thoughtfully at the fire. The rest of us, if I may so express it, made ourselves cosy, each after his own particular manner. A minute or so later Carnacki began to speak, ignoring any preliminary remarks, and going straight to the subject of the story we knew he had to tell:—

"I have just come back from Sir Alfred Jarnock's place, at Burtontree, in South Kent," he began, without removing his gaze from the fire. "Most extraordinary things have been happening down there lately, and Mr. George Jarnock, the eldest son, wired to ask me to run over and see whether I could help to clear matters up a bit. I went.

"When I got there, I found that they have an old Chapel attached to the castle, which has had quite a distinguished reputation for being what is popularly termed 'haunted'. They have been rather proud of this, as I managed to discover, until quite lately, when something very disagreeable occurred, which served to remind them that family ghosts are not always content, as I might say, to remain purely ornamental.

"It sounds almost laughable, I know, to hear of a long respected supernatural phenomenon growing unexpectedly dangerous; and in this case, the tale of the haunting was considered as little more than an old myth except after night-fall, when possibly it became more plausible seeming.

"But however this may be, there is no doubt at all but that what I might term the Haunting Essence which lived in the place, had become suddenly dangerous—deadly dangerous too, the old butler being nearly stabbed to death one night in the Chapel, with a peculiar old dagger.

"It is, in fact, this dagger which is popularly supposed to 'haunt' the Chapel. At least, there has been always a story handed down in the family that this dagger would attack any enemy who should dare to venture into the Chapel, after night-fall. But, of course, this had been taken with just about the same amount of seriousness that people take most ghost-tales, and that is not usually of a worryingly *real* nature. I mean, that most people never quite know how much or how little they believe of matters ab-human or abnormal, and generally they never have an opportunity to learn. And, indeed, as you are all aware, I am as big a sceptic concerning the truth of ghost-tales as any man you are likely to meet; only I am what I might term an unprejudiced sceptic. I am not given to either believing or disbelieving things 'on principle', as I have found many idiots prone to be, and what is more, some of them not ashamed to boast of the insane fact. I view all reported 'hauntings' as un-proven until I have examined into them; and I am bound to admit that ninety-nine cases in a hundred turn out to be sheer bosh and fancy. But the hundredth!

Well, if it were not for the hundredth, I should have few stories to tell you—eh?

"Of course, after the attack on the butler, it became evident that there was at least 'something' in the old story concerning the dagger, and I found everyone in a half belief that the queer old weapon did really strike the butler, either by the aid of some inherent force, which I found them peculiarly unable to explain, or else in the hand of some invisible thing or monster of the Outer World!

"From considerable experience, I knew that it was much more likely that the butler had been 'knifed' by some vicious and quite material human!

"Naturally, the first thing to do, was to test this probability of human agency, and I set to work to make a pretty drastic examination of the people who knew most about the tragedy.

"The result of this examination, both pleased and surprised me; for it left me with very good reasons for belief that I had come upon one of those extraordinarily rare 'true manifestations' of the extrusion of a Force from the Outside. In more popular phraseology—a genuine case of haunting.

"These are the facts:— On the previous Sunday evening but one, Sir Alfred Jarnock's household had attended family service, as usual, in the Chapel. You see, the Rector goes over to officiate twice each Sunday, after concluding his duties, at the public Church, about three miles away.

"At the end of the service in the Chapel, Sir Alfred Jarnock, his son Mr. George Jarnock, and the Rector had stood for a couple of minutes, talking, whilst old Bellett the butler went round, putting out the candles.

"Suddenly, the Rector remembered that he had left his small prayer-book on the Communion table in the morning; he turned, and asked the butler to get it for him, before he blew out the chancel candles.

"Now, I have particularly called your attention to this, because it is important, in that it provided witnesses in a most fortunate manner at an extraordinary moment. You see, the Rector's turning to speak to Bellett had naturally caused both Sir Alfred Jarnock and his son to glance in the direction of the butler, and it was at this identical instant, and whilst all three were looking at him, that the old butler was stabbed—there, full in the candle-light, before their very eyes.

"I took the opportunity to call early upon the Rector, after I had questioned Mr. George Jarnock, who replied to my queries in place of Sir Alfred Jarnock, for the older man was in a nervous and shaken condition, as a result of the happening, and his son wished him to avoid dwelling upon the scene, as much as possible.

"The Rector's version was clear and vivid, and he had evidently received the astonishment of his life. He pictured to me the whole affair—Bellett, up at the chancel gate, going for the prayer-book, and absolutely alone; and then the BLOW, out of the Void, he described it; and the *force* prodigious—the old man being driven headlong into the body of the Chapel. Like the kick of a great horse, the Rector said, his benevolent old eyes bright and intense with the effort he made to make me see the thing that he had actually witnessed, in defiance of all that he had hitherto believed.

"When I left him, he went back to the writing which he had put aside, when I appeared. I feel sure that he was developing the first unorthodox sermon that he had ever evolved. He was a dear old chap, and I should certainly like to have heard it.

"The last man I visited, was the butler. He was, of course, in a frightfully weak and shaken condition; but he could tell me nothing that did not point to there being a Power abroad in the Chapel. He told the same tale, in every minute particle, that I had learned from the others. He had been just going up to put out the altar candles and fetch the Rector's book, when something struck him an enormous blow high up on the left breast, and he was driven headlong into the aisle.

"Examination had shown that he had been stabbed by the dagger—of which I will tell you more in a moment—that hung always above the altar. The weapon had entered, fortunately some inches above the heart, just under the collar-bone, which had been broken by the stupendous force of the blow, the dagger itself being driven clean through the body, and out through the scapula behind.

"The poor old fellow could not talk much, and I soon left him; but what he had told me was sufficient to make it unmistakable that no living person had been within yards of him, when he was attacked; and, as I knew, this fact was verified by three capable and responsible witnesses, independent of Bellett himself.

"The thing now, was to search the Chapel, which is small and extremely old. It is very massively built, and entered through only one door, which leads out of the castle itself, and the key of which is kept by Sir Alfred Jarnock, the butler having no duplicate.

"The shape of the Chapel is oblong, and the altar is railed off after the usual fashion. There are two tombs in the body of the place;

but none in the chancel, which is bare, except for the tall candlesticks, and the chancel rail, beyond which is the undraped altar of solid marble, upon which stand four small candlesticks, two at each end.

"Above the altar hangs the 'waeful dagger', as I had learned it was named. I fancy the term has been taken from an old vellum, which describes the dagger and its supposed abnormal properties. I took the dagger down, and examined it minutely and with method. The blade is ten inches long, two inches broad at the base, and tapering to a rounded but sharp point, rather peculiar. It is double-edged.

"The metal sheath is curious for having a cross-piece, which, taken with the fact that the sheath itself is continued three parts up the hilt of the dagger (in a most inconvenient fashion), gives it the appearance of a cross. That this is not unintentional is shown by an engraving of the Christ crucified upon one side, whilst upon the other, in Latin, is the inscription:— 'Vengeance is Mine, I will Repay.' A quaint and rather terrible conjunction of ideas. Upon the blade of the dagger is graven in old English capitals:— 'I Watch. I Strike.' On the butt of the hilt there is carved deeply a Pentacle.

"This is a pretty accurate description of the peculiar old weapon that has had the curious and uncomfortable reputation of being able (either of its own accord or in the hand of something invisible) to strike murderously any enemy of the Jarnock family who may chance to enter the Chapel after night-fall. I may tell you here and now, that, before I left, I had very good reason to put certain doubts behind me; for I tested the deadliness of the thing, myself.

"As you know, however, at this point of my investigation, I was still at that stage where I considered the existence of a supernatural Force unproven. In the meanwhile, I treated the Chapel drastically, sounding and scrutinising the walls and floor, dealing with them almost foot by foot, and particularly examining the two tombs.

"At the end of this search, I had in a ladder, and made a close survey of the groined roof. I passed three days in this fashion, and by the evening of the third day, I had proved to my entire satisfaction that there is no place in the whole of that Chapel where any living being could have hidden, and also that the only way of ingress and egress to and from the Chapel is through the doorway which leads into the castle, the door of which was always kept locked, and the key kept by Sir Alfred Jarnock himself, as I have told you. I mean, of course, that this doorway is the only entrance practicable to *material* people.

"Yet, as you will see, even had I discovered some other opening, secret or otherwise, it would not have helped at all to explain the mystery of the incredible attack, in a normal fashion. For the butler, as you know, was struck in full sight of the Rector, Sir Jarnock and his son. And old Bellett himself knew that no living person had touched him. . . . 'OUT OF THE VOID', the Rector had described the inhumanly brutal attack. 'Out of the Void!' A strange feeling it gives one—eh?

"And this is the thing that I had been called in to bottom!

"After considerable thought, I decided on a plan of action. I proposed to Sir Alfred Jarnock that I should spend a night in the Chapel, and keep a constant watch upon the dagger. But to this, the old knight—a little, weasened, nervous man—would not listen for a moment. He, at least, I felt assured had no doubt of the *reality* of some dangerous supernatural Force a-roam at night in the Chapel. He informed me that it had been his habit every evening to lock the Chapel door; so that no one might foolishly or heedlessly run the risk of any peril that it might hold at night; and that he could not allow me to attempt such a thing, after what had happened to the butler.

"I could see that Sir Alfred Jarnock was very much in earnest, and would evidently have held himself to blame, had he allowed me to make the experiment, and any harm come to me; so I said nothing in argument; and presently, pleading the fatigue of his years and health, he said good-night, and left me; having given me the impression of being a polite, but rather superstitious, old gentleman.

"That night, however, whilst I was undressing, I saw how I might achieve the thing I wished, and be able to enter the Chapel after dark, without making Sir Alfred Jarnock nervous. On the morrow, when I borrowed the key, I would take an impression, and have a duplicate made. Then, with my private key, I could do just what I liked.

"In the morning I carried out my idea. I borrowed the key, as I wanted to take a photograph of the chancel by daylight. When I had done this I locked up the Chapel and handed the key to Sir Alfred Jarnock, having first taken an impression in soap. I had brought out the exposed plate—in its slide—with me; but the camera I had left exactly as it was, as I wanted to take a second photograph of the chancel that night, from the same position.

"I took the dark-slide into Burtontree, also the cake of soap with the impress. The soap I left with the local ironmonger, who was something of a locksmith and promised to let me have my duplicate, finished, if I would call in two hours. This I did, having, in the meanwhile, found out a photographer, where I developed the plate, and left it to dry, telling him I would call next day. At the end of the two hours, I went for my key, and found it ready, much to my satisfaction. Then I returned to the castle.

"After dinner that evening, I played billiards with young Jarnock for a couple of hours. Then, I had a cup of coffee, and went off to my room, telling him I was feeling awfully tired. He nodded, and told me he felt the same way. I was glad; for I wanted the house to settle as soon as possible.

"I locked the door of my room; then from under the bed—where I had hidden them earlier in the evening—I drew out several fine pieces of plate-armour, which I had removed from the armoury. There was also a shirt of chain-mail, with a sort of quilted hood of mail to go over the head.

"I buckled on the plate-armour, and found it extraordinarily uncomfortable, and over all I drew on the chain-mail. I know nothing about armour; but, from what I have learned since, I must have put on parts of two suits. Anyway, I felt beastly, clamped and clumsy and unable to move my arms and legs naturally. But I knew that the thing I was thinking of doing, called for some sort of protection for my body. Over the armour, I pulled on my dressing-gown, and shoved my revolver into one of the side-pockets—and my repeating flashlight into the other. My dark lantern I carried in my hand.

"As soon as I was ready I went out into the passage, and listened. I had been some considerable time making my preparations, and I found that now the big hall and staircase were in darkness and all the house seemed quiet. I stepped back, and closed and locked my door. Then, very slowly and silently, I went downstairs to the hall, and turned into the passage that led to the Chapel.

"I reached the door, and tried my key. It fitted perfectly, and a moment later I was in the Chapel, with the door locked behind me, and all about me the utter dree silence of the place, with just the faint showings of the outlines of the stained, leaded windows, making the darkness and lonesomeness almost the more apparent.

"Now it would be silly to say I did not feel queer. I felt very queer indeed. You just try, any of you, to imagine yourself standing there in the dark silence, and remembering not only the legend that was attached to the place; but what had really happened to the old butler only a little while gone. I can tell you, as I stood there, I could believe that something invisible was coming towards me in the air of the

Chapel. Yet, I had got to go through with the business; and I just took hold of my little bit of courage and set to work.

"First of all, I switched on my light; then I began a careful tour of the place, examining every corner and nook. I found nothing unusual. At the chancel gate, I held up my lamp and flashed the light at the dagger. It hung there, right enough, above the altar; but I remember thinking of the word 'demure', as I looked at it. However, I pushed the thought away; for what I was doing needed no addition of uncomfortable thoughts.

"I completed the tour of the place, with a constantly growing awareness of its utter chill and unkind desolation—an atmosphere of cold dismalness seemed to be everywhere, and the quiet was abominable.

"At the conclusion of my search, I walked across to where I had left my camera focussed upon the chancel. From the satchel that I had put beneath the tripod, I took out a dark-slide and inserted it in the camera, drawing the shutter. After that, I uncapped the lens, pulled out my flashlight apparatus, and pressed the trigger. There was an intense, brilliant flash, that made the whole of the interior of the Chapel jump into sight, and disappear as quickly. Then, in the light from my lantern, I inserted the shutter into the slide, and reversed the slide, so as to have a fresh plate ready to expose at any time.

"After I had done this, I shut off my lantern and sat down in one of the pews near to my camera. I cannot say what I expected to happen; but I had an extraordinary feeling, almost a conviction, that something peculiar or horrible would soon occur. It was, you know, as if I *knew*.

"An hour passed, of absolute silence. The time I knew by the far-off, faint chime of a clock that had been erected over the stables. I was beastly cold; for the whole place is without any kind of heating pipes or furnace, as I had noticed during my search; so that the temperature was sufficiently uncomfortable to suit my frame of mind. I felt like a kind of human periwinkle encased in boilerplate and frozen with cold and funk. And, you know, somehow the dark about me seemed to press coldly against my face. I cannot say whether any of you have ever had the feeling; but if you have, you will know just how disgustingly unnerving it is. And then, all at once, I had a horrible sense that something was moving in the place. It was not that I could hear anything; but I had a kind of intuitive knowledge that something had stirred in the darkness. Can you imagine how I felt?

"Suddenly my courage went. I put up my mailed arms over my

face. I wanted to protect it. I had got a sudden sickening feeling that something was hovering over me in the dark. Talk about fright! I could have shouted, if I had not been afraid of the noise.... And then, abruptly, I heard something. Away up the aisle, there sounded a dull clang of metal, as it might be the tread of a mailed heel upon the stone of the aisle. I sat, immovable. I was fighting with all my strength to get back my courage. I could not take my arms down from over my face; but I knew that I was getting hold of the gritty part of me again. And suddenly I made a mighty effort and lowered my arms. I held my face up in the darkness. And, I tell you, I respect myself for the act, because I thought truly at that moment that I was going to die. But I think, just then, by the slow revulsion of feeling which had assisted my effort, I was less sick, in that instant, at the thought of having to die, than at the knowledge of the utter weak cowardice that had so unexpectedly shaken me all to bits, for a time.

"Do I make myself clear? You understand, I feel sure, that the sense of respect, which I spoke of, is not really unhealthy egotism; because, you see, I am not blind to the state of mind which helped me. I mean that if I had uncovered my face by a sheer effort of will, unhelped by any revulsion of feeling, I should have done a thing much more worthy of mention. But, even as it was, there were elements in the act, worthy of respect. You follow me, don't you?

"And, you know, nothing touched me, after all! So that, in a little while, I had got back a bit to my normal, and felt steady enough to go through with the business without any more funking.

"I daresay a couple of minutes passed; and then, away up near the chancel, there came again that clang, as though an armoured foot stepped cautiously. By Jove! but it made me stiffen. And suddenly the thought came that the sound I heard might be the rattle of the dagger above the altar. It was not a particularly sensible notion; for the sound was far too heavy and resonant for such a cause. Yet, as can be easily understood, my reason was bound to submit somewhat to my fancy at such a time. I remember now, that the idea of that insensate thing becoming animate, and attacking me, did not occur to me with any sense of possibility or reality. I thought rather, in a vague way, of some invisible monster of outer space fumbling at the dagger. I remembered the old Rector's description of the attack on the butler.... OUT OF THE VOID. And he had described the stupendous force of the blow as being 'like the kick of a great horse'. You can see how uncomfortably my thoughts were running.

"I felt round swiftly and cautiously for my lantern. I found it close to me, on the pew seat, and with a sudden, jerky movement, I switched on the light. I flashed it up the aisle, to and fro across the chancel; but I could see nothing to frighten me. I turned quickly, and sent the jet of light darting across and across the rear end of the Chapel; then on each side of me, before and behind, up at the roof and down at the marble floor; but nowhere was there any visible thing to put me in fear; not a thing that need have set my flesh thrilling; just the quiet Chapel, cold, and eternally silent. You know the feeling.

"I had been standing, whilst I sent the light about the Chapel; but now I pulled out my revolver, and then, with a tremendous effort of will, switched off the light, and sat down again in the darkness, to continue my constant watch.

"It seemed to me that quite half an hour, or even more, must have passed, after this, during which no sound had broken the intense stillness. I had grown less nervously tense; for the flashing of the light round the place had made me feel less out of all bounds of the normal—it had given me something of that unreasoned sense of safety that a nervous child obtains at night, by covering its head up with the bedclothes. This just about illustrates the completely human illogicalness of the workings of my feelings; for, as you know, whatever Creature, Thing, or Being it was that had made that extraordinary and horrible attack on the old butler, it had certainly not been *visible*.

"And so you must picture me sitting there in the dark; clumsy with armour, and with my revolver in one hand, and nursing my lantern, ready, with the other. And then it was, after this little time of partial relief from intense nervousness, that there came a fresh strain on me; for somewhere in the utter quiet of the Chapel, I thought I heard something. I listened, tense and rigid, my heart booming just a little in my ears for a moment; then I thought I heard it again. I felt sure that something had moved at the top of the aisle. I strained in the darkness, to hark; and my eyes showed me blackness within blackness, wherever I glanced, so that I took no heed of what they told me; for even if I looked at the dim loom of the stained window at the top of the chancel, my sight gave me the shapes of vague shadows passing noiseless and ghostly across, constantly. There was a time of almost peculiar silence, horrible to me, as I felt just then. And suddenly I seemed to hear a sound again, nearer to me, and repeated, infinitely stealthy. It was as if a vast, soft tread were coming slowly down the aisle.

"Can you imagine how I felt? I do not think you can. I did not move, any more than the stone effigies on the two tombs; but sat there, *stiffened*. I fancied now, that I heard the tread all about the Chapel. And then, you know, I was just as sure in a moment that I could not hear it—that I had never heard it.

"Some particularly long minutes passed, about this time; but I think my nerves must have quietened a bit; for I remember being sufficiently aware of my feelings, to realise that the muscles of my shoulders *ached*, with the way that they must have been contracted, as I sat there, hunching myself, rigid. Mind you, I was still in a disgusting funk; but what I might call the 'imminent sense of danger' seemed to have eased from around me; at any rate, I felt, in some curious fashion, that there was a respite—a temporary cessation of malignity from about me. It is impossible to word my feelings more clearly to you; for I cannot see them more clearly than this, myself.

"Yet, you must not picture me as sitting there, free from strain; for the nerve tension was so great that my heart action was a little out of normal control, the blood-beat making a dull booming at times in my ears, with the result that I had the sensation that I could not hear acutely. This is a simply beastly feeling, especially under such circumstances.

"I was sitting like this, listening, as I might say with body and soul, when suddenly I got that hideous conviction again that something was moving in the air of the place. The feeling seemed to stiffen me, as I sat, and my head appeared to tighten, as if all the scalp had grown *tense*. This was so real, that I suffered an actual pain, most peculiar and at the same time intense; the whole head pained. I had a fierce desire to cover my face again with my mailed arms; but I fought it off. If I had given way then to that, I should simply have bunked straight out of the place. I sat and sweated coldly (that's the bald truth), with the 'creep' busy at my spine....

"And then, abruptly, once more I thought I heard the sound of that huge, soft tread on the aisle; and this time closer to me. There was an awful little silence, during which I had the feeling that something enormous was bending over towards me, from the aisle.... And then, through the booming of the blood in my ears, there came a slight sound from the place where my camera stood—a disagreeable sort of slithering sound, and then a sharp tap. I had the lantern ready in my left hand, and now I snapped it on, desperately, and shone it straight above me; for I had a conviction that there was something there. But I *saw* nothing. Immediately, I flashed the light at the camera, and then along the aisle; but again there was nothing visible. I wheeled round, shooting the beam of light in a great circle about the place; to and fro I shone it, jerking it here and there; but it showed me nothing.

"I had stood up, the instant that I had seen that there was nothing in sight over me, and now I determined to visit the chancel, and see whether the dagger had been touched. I stepped out of the pew into the aisle; and here I came to an abrupt pause; for an almost invincible, sick repugnance was fighting me back from the upper part of the Chapel. A constant, queer prickling went up and down my spine, and a dull ache took me in the small of the back, as I fought with myself to conquer this sudden new feeling of terror and horror. I tell you, that no one, who has not been through these kinds of experiences, has any idea of the sheer, *actual physical pain* attendant upon, and resulting from, the intense nerve-strain that ghostly-fright sets up in the human system. I stood there, feeling positively ill. But I got myself in hand, as it were, in about half a minute, and then I went, walking, I expect, as jerky as a mechanical tin man, and switching the light from side to side, before and behind, and over my head continually. And the hand that held my revolver, sweated so much, that the thing fairly slipped in my fist. Does not sound very heroic, does it?

"I passed through the short chancel, and reached the step that led up to the small gate in the chancel-rail. I threw the beam from my lantern upon the dagger. Yes, I thought, it's all right. Abruptly, it seemed to me that there was something wanting, and I leaned forward over the chancel-gate to peer, holding the light high. My suspicion was hideously correct. *The dagger had gone.* Only the cross-shaped sheath hung there above the altar.

"In a sudden, frightened flash of imagination, I pictured the thing adrift in the Chapel, moving here and there, as though of its own volition; for whatever Force wielded it, was certainly beyond visibility. I turned my head stiffly over to the left, glancing frightenedly behind me, and flashing the light to help my eyes. In the same instant, I was struck a tremendous blow over the left breast, and hurled backward from the chancel-rail, into the aisle, my armour clanging loudly in the horrible silence. I landed on my back, and slithered along on the polished marble. My shoulder struck the corner of a pew front, and brought me up, half stunned. I scrambled to my feet, horribly sick and shaken; but the fear that was on me, making little of this at the moment. I was minus both revolver and lantern, and utterly bewildered as to just where I was standing. I bowed my head, and made a scrambling run in the complete darkness, and dashed into a pew. I jumped back, staggering, got my bearings a little, and raced down the centre of the aisle, putting my mailed arms over my face. I plunged into my camera, hurling it among the pews. I crashed into the font, and reeled back. Then I was at the exit. I fumbled madly in my dressing-gown pocket for the key. I found it and scraped at the door, feverishly, for the keyhole. I found the keyhole; turned the key; burst the door open, and was into the passage. I slammed the door, and leant hard against it, gasping, whilst I felt crazily again for the keyhole, this time to lock the door upon what was in the Chapel. I succeeded, and began to feel my way stupidly along the wall of the corridor. Presently, I had come to the big hall, and so in a little to my room.

"In my room, I sat for a while, until I had steadied down something to the normal. After a time I commenced to strip off the armour. I saw then that both the chain-mail and the plate-armour had been pierced over the breast. And, suddenly, it came home to me that the Thing had struck for my heart.

"Stripping rapidly, I found that the skin of the breast, over the heart, had just been cut sufficiently to allow a little blood to stain my shirt; nothing more. Only, the whole breast was badly bruised and intensely painful. You can imagine what would have happened, if I had not worn the armour. In any case, it is a marvel that I was not knocked senseless.

"I did not go to bed at all that night; but sat upon the edge, thinking, and waiting for the dawn; for I had to remove my litter, before Sir Alfred Jarnock should enter, if I were to hide from him the fact that I had managed a duplicate key.

"So soon as the pale light of the morning had strengthened sufficiently to show me the various details of my room, I made my way quietly down to the Chapel. Very silently, and with tense nerves, I opened the door. The chill light of the dawn made distinct the whole place—everything seeming instinct with a ghostly unearthly quiet. Can you get the feeling? I waited several minutes at the door, allowing the morning to grow, and likewise my courage, I suppose. Presently, the rising sun threw an odd beam right in through the big, East window, making coloured sunshine all the length of the Chapel. And then, with a tremendous effort, I forced myself to enter.

"I went up the aisle, to where I had overthrown my camera in the darkness. The legs of the tripod were sticking up from the interior of a pew, and I expected to find the machine smashed to pieces; yet, beyond that the ground glass was broken, there was no real damage done.

" I replaced the camera in the position from which I had taken the previous photographs; but the slide containing the plate I had exposed by flashlight, I removed and put into one of my side pockets, regretting that I had not taken a second flash-picture at the instant when I heard those strange sounds up in the chancel.

"Having tidied my photographic apparatus, I went into the chancel, to recover my lantern and revolver, which had both—as you know—been knocked from my hands when I was stabbed. I found the lantern lying, hopelessly bent, with smashed lens, just under the pulpit. My revolver I must have held, until my shoulder struck the pew; for it was lying there in the aisle, just about where I believe I cannoned into the pew-corner. It was quite undamaged.

"Having secured these two articles, I walked up to the chancel-rail, to see whether the dagger had returned, or been returned, to its sheath above the altar. Before, however, I reached the chancel-rail, I had a slight shock; for there, on the floor of the chancel, about a yard away from where I had been struck, lay the dagger, quiet and demure upon the polished marble pavement. I wonder whether you will, any of you, understand the nervousness that took me at the sight of the thing. With a sudden, unreasoned action, I jumped forward and put my foot on it, to hold it there. Can you understand? Do you? And, you know, I could not stoop down and pick it up with my hands, for quite a minute, I should think. Afterwards, when I had done so, however, and handled it a little, this feeling passed away, and my Reason (and also, I expect, the daylight) made me feel that I had been a little bit of an ass. Quite natural, though, I assure you! Yet it was a new kind of fear to me. I'm taking no notice of the cheap joke about the ass! I am talking about the curiousness of learning in that moment a new shade or quality of fear, that had hitherto been outside of my knowledge or imagination. Does it interest you?

"I examined the dagger, minutely, turning it over and over in my hands, and never—as I suddenly discovered—holding it loosely. It was as if I were subconsciously surprised that it lay quiet in my hands. Yet even this feeling passed, largely, after a short while. The curious weapon showed no signs of the blow, except that the dull colour of the blade was slightly brighter on the rounded point, that had cut through the armour.

"Presently, when I had made an end of staring at the dagger, I went up the chancel step, and in through the little gate. Then, kneeling upon the altar, I replaced the dagger in its sheath, and came outside of the rail, again, closing the gate after me, and feeling awaredly uncomfortable, because the horrible old weapon was back again in its accustomed place. I suppose, without analysing my feelings very deeply, I had an unreasoned and only half conscious belief that there was a greater probability of danger, when the dagger hung in its five-century resting place, than when it was out of it. Yet, somehow I don't think this is a very good explanation, when I remember the *demure* look the thing seemed to have, when I saw it lying on the floor of the chancel. Only I know this, that when I had replaced the dagger I had quite a touch of nerves, and I stopped only to pick up my lantern, from where I had placed it whilst I examined the weapon; after which I went down the quiet aisle at a pretty quick walk, and so got outside of the place.

"That the nerve tension had been considerable, I realised, when I had locked the door behind me. I felt no inclination now to think of old Sir Alfred as a hypochondriac because he had taken such hyper-seeming precautions regarding the Chapel. I had a sudden wonder as to whether he might not have some knowledge of a long prior tragedy, in which the dagger had been concerned.

"I returned to my room, washed, shaved and dressed; after which I read awhile. Then I went downstairs and got the acting butler to give me some sandwiches and a cup of coffee.

"Half an hour later, I was heading for Burtontree, as hard as I could walk; for a sudden idea had come to me, which I was anxious to test. I reached the town a little before eight-thirty, and found the local photographer with his shutters still up. I did not wait, but knocked until he appeared with his coat off, evidently in the act of dealing with his breakfast. In a few words, I made clear that I wanted the use of his dark room, immediately; and this, he at once placed at my disposal.

"I had brought with me the slide which contained the plate that I had used with the flashlight; and as soon as I was ready, I set to work to develop. Yet, it was not the plate which I had exposed, that I first put into the solution; but the second plate, which had been ready in the camera during all the time of my waiting in the darkness. You see, the lens had been uncapped all that while, so that the whole chancel had been, as it were, under observation.

"You all know something of my experiments in 'Lightless Photography', that is, 'Lightless' so far as our eyes are capable of appreciating light. It was X-ray work that started me in that direction. Yet, you must understand, though I was attempting to develop this 'unexposed' plate, I had no definite idea of results—nothing more than a vague hope that it might show me something.

"Yet, because of the possibilities, it was with the most intense and absorbing interest that I watched the plate, under the action of the developer. Presently, I saw a faint smudge of black appear in the upper part, and after that, others, indistinct and wavering of outline. I held the negative up to the light. The marks were rather small, and were almost entirely confined to one end of the plate; but, as I have said, lacked definiteness. Yet, such as they were, they were sufficient to make me very excited, and I shoved the thing quickly back into the solution.

"For some minutes further I watched it; lifting it out once or twice to make a more exact scrutiny; but could not imagine what the markings might represent, until, suddenly, it occurred to me that, in one or two places, they certainly had shapes suggestive of a cross-hilted dagger. Yet, the shapes were sufficiently indefinite to make me careful not to let myself be over-impressed by the uncomfortable resemblance; though, I must confess, the very thought was sufficient to set some odd thrills adrift in me.

"I carried development a little further; then put the negative into the hypo, and commenced work upon the other plate. This came up nicely, and very soon I had a really decent negative, that appeared similar in every respect (except for the difference of lighting) to the negative I had taken during the previous day. I fixed the plate; then, having washed both it and the 'unexposed' one for a few minutes under the tap, I put them into methylated spirits for fifteen minutes; after which I carried them into the photographer's kitchen, and dried them in the oven.

"Whilst the two plates were drying, the photographer and I made an enlargement from the negative I had taken by daylight. Then we did the same with the two that I had just developed, washing them as quickly as possible, for I was not troubling about the permanency of the prints, and drying them with spirits.

"When this was done, I took them to the window, and made a thorough examination, commencing with the one that appeared to show shadowy daggers in several places. Yet, though it was now enlarged, I was still unable to feel convinced that the marks truly represented anything abnormal; and because of this, I put it on one side, determined not to let my imagination play too large a part in constructing weapons out of the indefinite outlines.

"I took up the two other enlargements, both of the chancel, as you will remember, and commenced to compare them. For some minutes, I examined them, without being able to distinguish any difference in the scene they portrayed; and then, abruptly, I saw something in which they varied. In the second enlargement—the one made from the flashlight negative—the dagger was not in its sheath. Yet, I had felt sure it was there, but a few minutes before I took the photograph.

"After this discovery, I began to compare the two enlargements, in a very different manner from my previous scrutiny. I borrowed a pair of calipers from the photographer, and with these I carried out a most methodical and exact comparison of the details shown in the two photographs.

"Suddenly, I came upon something that set me all tingling with excitement. I threw the calipers down, paid the photographer, and walked out through the shop, into the street. The three enlargements, I took with me, making them into a roll, as I went. At the corner of the street, I had the luck to get a cab, and was soon back at the castle.

"I hurried up to my room, and put the photographs away; then I went down to see whether I could find Sir Alfred Jarnock; but Mr. George Jarnock, who met me, told me that his father was too unwell to rise, and would prefer that no one entered the Chapel, unless he were about.

"Young Jarnock made a half apologetic excuse for his father; remarking that Sir Alfred Jarnock was perhaps inclined to be a little over careful; but that, considering what had happened, we must agree that the need for his carefulness had been justified. He added, also, that even before the horrible attack on the butler, his father had been just as particular, always keeping the key, and never allowing the door to be unlocked, except when the place was in use for Divine Service, and for an hour each forenoon, when the cleaners were in.

"To all this, I nodded, understandingly; but when, presently, the young man left me, I took my duplicate key, and made for the door of the Chapel. I went in, and locked it behind me; after which I carried out some intensely interesting and rather weird experiments. These proved successful to such an extent, that I came out of the place in a perfect fever of excitement. I inquired for Mr. George Jarnock, and was told that he was in the morning room.

" 'Come along,' I said, when I had found him. 'Please give me a lift. I've something exceedingly strange to show you.'

"He was palpably very much puzzled; but came quickly. As we strode along, he asked me a score of questions, to all of which I just shook my head, asking him to wait a little.

"I led the way to the Armoury. Here, I suggested that he should take one side of a dummy, dressed in half-plate armour, whilst I took the other. He nodded, though obviously vastly bewildered, and together we carried the thing to the Chapel door. When he saw me take out my key, and open the way for us, he appeared even more astonished; but held himself in, evidently waiting for me to explain. We entered the Chapel, and I locked the door behind us, after which we carted the armoured dummy up the aisle to the gate in the chancel-rail, where we put it down upon its round, wooden stand.

" 'Stand back!' I shouted, suddenly, as young Jarnock made a movement to open the gate. 'My God, man! you mustn't do that!'

" 'Do what?' he asked, half startled and half irritated by my words and manner.

" 'One minute,' I said. 'Just stand to the side a moment, and watch.'

"He stepped to the left, whilst I took the dummy in my arms, and turned it to face the altar, so that it stood close to the gate. Then, standing well away on the right side, I pressed the back of the thing, so that it leant forward a little upon the gate, which flew open. In the same instant, the dummy was struck a tremendous blow, that hurled it into the aisle, the armour rattling and clanging upon the polished marble floor.

" 'Good God!' shouted young Jarnock, and ran back from the chancel-rail, his face very white.

" 'Come and look at the thing,' I said, and led the way to where the dummy lay, its armoured upper limbs all splayed adrift in queer contortions. I stooped over it, and pointed. There, driven right through the thick steel breastplate, was the 'waeful dagger'.

" 'Good God!' said young Jarnock, again. 'Good God! It's the dagger! The thing's been stabbed, same as Bellett!'

" 'Yes,' I replied, and saw him glance swiftly towards the entrance of the Chapel. But I will do him the justice to say that he never budged an inch.

" 'Come and see how it was done,' I said; and led the way back to the chancel-rail. From the wall to the left of the altar, I took down a long, curiously ornamented, iron instrument, not unlike a short spear. The sharp end of this I inserted in a hole in the left-hand gate-post of the chancel gateway. I lifted hard, and a section of the post, from the floor upwards, bent inwards towards the altar, as though hinged at the bottom. Down it went, leaving the remaining part of the post standing. As I bent the movable portion lower, there came a quick click, and a section of the floor slid to one side, showing a long, shallow cavity, sufficient to enclose the post. I put my weight to the lever, and hove the post down into the niche. Immediately, there was a sharp clang, as some catch snicked in, and held it against the powerful operating spring.

"I went over now to the dummy, and after a few minutes' work, managed to wrench the dagger loose out of the armour. I brought the old weapon, and placed its hilt in a hole near the top of the post, where it fitted loosely, the point upwards. After that, I went again to the lever and gave another strong heave, and the post descended about a foot, to the bottom of the cavity, catching there, with an-other clang. I withdrew the lever, and the narrow strip of floor slid back, covering post and dagger, and looking no different from the surrounding surface.

"Then I shut the chancel-gate, and we both stood well to one side. I took the spear-like lever, and gave the gate a little push, so that it opened. Instantly, there was a loud thud, and something sang through the air, striking the bottom wall of the Chapel. It was the dagger. I showed Jarnock then that the other half of the post had sprung back into place, making the whole post as thick as the one upon the right-hand side of the gate.

" 'There!' I said, turning to the young man, and tapping the divided post. 'There's the 'invisible' thing that uses the dagger; but who, the deuce, is the person who sets the trap?' I looked at him, keenly, as I spoke.

" 'My father is the only one who has a key,' he said. 'So it's prac-tically impossible for anyone to get in and meddle.'

"I looked at him, again; but it was obvious that he had not yet reached out to any conclusion.

" 'See here, Mr. Jarnock,' I said, perhaps rather curter than I should have done, considering what I had to say. 'Are you quite sure that Sir Alfred is quite balanced—mentally?'

"He looked at me, half-frightenedly, and flushing a little. I realised then how baldly I had put it.

" 'I—I don't know,' he replied, after a slight pause, and was then silent, except for one or two incoherent half-remarks.

" 'Tell the truth,' I said. 'Haven't you suspected something, now and again? You needn't be afraid to tell me.'

" 'Well,' he answered, slowly, 'I'll admit I've thought father a little—a little strange, perhaps, at times. But I've always tried to think I was mistaken. I've always hoped no one else would see it. You see, I'm very fond of the old guv'nor.'

"I nodded.

" 'Quite right, too,' I said. 'There's not the least need to make any kind of scandal about this. We must do something, though, but in a quiet way. No fuss, you know. I should go and have a chat with your father, and tell him we've found out about this thing.' I touched the divided post.

"Young Jarnock seemed very grateful for my advice, and after shaking my hand, pretty hard, took my key, and let himself out of the Chapel. He came back in about an hour, looking rather upset. He told me that my conclusions were perfectly correct. It was Sir Alfred Jarnock who had set the trap, both on the night that the butler was nearly killed, and on the past night. Indeed, it seemed that the old gentleman had set it every night for many years. He had learnt of its existence from an old MS.-book in the Castle library. It had been planned and used in an earlier age as a protection for the gold vessels of the Ritual, which were, it seemed, kept in a hidden recess at the back of the altar.

"This recess, Sir Alfred Jarnock had utilised, secretly, to store his wife's jewellery. She had died some twelve years back, and the young man told me that his father had never seemed quite himself, since.

"I mentioned to young Jarnock how puzzled I was that the trap had been set *before* the service, on the night that the butler was struck; for, if I understood him aright, his father had been in the habit of setting the trap late every night, and unsetting it each morning, before anyone entered the Chapel. He replied that his father, in a fit of temporary forgetfulness (natural enough in his neurotic condition), must have set it too early, and hence what had so nearly proved a tragedy.

"That is about all there is to tell. The old man is not (so far as I could learn), really insane in the popularly accepted sense of the word. He is extremely neurotic, and has developed into a hypochondriac; the whole condition probably brought about by the shock and sorrow resultant on the death of his wife, leading to years of sad broodings and to overmuch of his own company and thoughts. Indeed, young Jarnock told me that his father would sometimes pray for hours together, alone in the Chapel."

Carnacki made an end of speaking, and leant forward for a spill.

"But you've never told us just *how* you discovered the secret of the divided post, and all that," I said, speaking for the four of us.

"Oh, that!" replied Carnacki, puffing vigorously at his pipe. " I found on comparing the photos that the one taken in the daytime, showed a thicker left-hand gate-post, than the one taken at night by the flashlight. That put me on to the track. I saw at once that there might be some mechanical dodge at the back of the whole queer business, and nothing at all of an abnormal nature. I examined the post, and the rest was simple enough, you know.

"By the way," he continued, rising and going to the mantelpiece, "you may be interested to have a look at the so-called 'waeful dagger'. Young Jarnock was kind enough to present it to me, as a little memento of my adventure."

He handed it round to us, and whilst we examined it, stood silent before the fire, puffing meditatively at his pipe,

"Jarnock and I made the trap so that it won't work," he remarked, after a few moments. "*I've* got the dagger, as you see; and old Bellett's getting about again, so that the whole business can be hushed up, decently. All the same, I fancy the Chapel will never lose its reputation as a dangerous place. Should be pretty safe now to keep valuables in."

"There's two things you haven't explained yet," I said. "What do you think caused the two clangey sounds when you were in the Chapel in the dark? And do you believe the soft tready sounds were real, or only a fancy, with your being so worked up and tense?"

"Don't know, for certain, about the clangs," replied Carnacki. "I've puzzled quite a bit about them. I can only think that the spring, which worked the post, must have 'given' a trifle, slipped, you know, in the catch. If it did, under such a tension, it would make a bit of a ringing noise. And a little sound goes a long way, in the middle of the night, when you're thinking of 'ghostesses'. You can understand that—eh?"

"Yes," I agreed. "And the other sounds?"

"Well, the same thing—I mean the extraordinary quietness— may help to explain these a bit. They may have been some usual enough sound, that would never have been noticed under ordinary conditions; or they may have been only fancy. It is just impossible to say. They were disgustingly real to me. As for the slithery noise, I am pretty sure that one of the tripod legs of my camera must have slipped a few inches; if it did so, it may easily have jolted the lens-cap off the base-board, which would account for that queer little tap which I heard directly after."

"How do you account for the dagger being in its place above the altar, when you first examined it that night?" I asked. "How could it be there, when at that very moment it was set in the trap?"

"That was my mistake," replied Carnacki. "The dagger could not possibly have been in its sheath at the time; though I thought it was. You see, the curious cross-hilted sheath gave the appearance of the complete weapon, as you can understand. The hilt of the dagger protrudes very little above the continued portion of the sheath—a most inconvenient arrangement for drawing quickly!"

He nodded, sagely, at the lot of us, and yawned; then glanced at the clock.

"Out you go!" he said, in friendly fashion, using the recognised formula. "I want a sleep."

We rose, shook him by the hand, and went out presently into the night and the quiet of the Embankment; and so to our homes.

The Gateway of the Monster

I N RESPONSE TO CARNACKI'S usual card of invitation to have
dinner and listen to a story, I arrived promptly at Cheyne Walk,
to find the three others who were always invited to these happy
little times, there before me. Five minutes later, Carnacki, Arkright,
Jessop, Taylor and I were all engaged in the "pleasant occupation"
of dining.

"You've not been long away, this time," I remarked, as I finished
my soup; forgetting momentarily, Carnacki's dislike of being asked
even to skirt the borders of his story until such time as he was
ready. Then he would not stint words.

"No," he replied, with brevity; and I changed the subject, remarking that I had been buying a new gun, to which piece of news
he gave an intelligent nod, and a smile, which I think showed a
genuinely good-humoured appreciation of my intentional changing
of the conversation.

Later, when dinner was finished, Carnacki snugged himself
comfortably down in his big chair, along with his pipe, and began
his story, with very little circumlocution:—

"As Dodgson was remarking just now, I've only been away a
short time, and for a very good reason too—I've only been away a
short distance. The exact locality I am afraid I must not tell you; but
it is less than twenty miles from here; though, except for changing
a name, that won't spoil the story. And it *is* a story too! One of the
most extraordinary things I have ever run against.

"I received a letter a fortnight ago from a man I will call Anderson, asking for an appointment. I arranged a time, and when he
turned up, I found that he wished me to look into, and see whether
I could not clear up, a long-standing and well-authenticated case

159

of what he termed 'haunting'. He gave me very full particulars, and, finally, as the thing seemed to present something unique, I decided to take it up.

"Two days later, I drove up to the house, late in the afternoon, and discovered it a very old place, standing quite alone in its own grounds.

"Anderson had left a letter with the butler, I found, pleading excuses for his absence, and leaving the whole house at my disposal for my investigations.

"The butler evidently knew the object of my visit, and I questioned him pretty thoroughly during dinner, which I had in rather lonely state. He is an elderly and privileged servant, and had the history of the Grey Room exact in detail. From him I learned more particulars regarding two things that Anderson had mentioned in but a casual manner. The first was that the door of the Grey Room would be heard in the dead of night to open, and slam heavily, and this even though the butler knew it was locked, and the key on the bunch in his pantry. The second was that the bedclothes would always be found torn off the bed, and hurled in a heap into a corner.

"But it was the door slamming that chiefly bothered the old butler. Many and many a time, he told me, had he lain awake and just shivered with fright, listening; for, at times the door would be slammed time after time, thud! thud! thud! so that sleep was impossible.

"From Anderson, I knew already that the room had a history extending back over a hundred and fifty years. Three people had been strangled in it—an ancestor of his and his wife and child. This is authentic, as I had taken very great pains to make sure; so that you can imagine it was with a feeling that I had a striking case to investigate, that I went upstairs after dinner to have a look at the Grey Room.

"Peters, the butler, was in rather a state about my going, and assured me with much solemnity that in all the twenty years of his service, no one had ever entered that room after night-fall. He begged me, in quite a fatherly way, to wait till the morning, when there would be no danger, and then he could accompany me himself.

"Of course, I told him not to bother. I explained that I should do no more than look round a bit, and, perhaps, fix a few seals. He need not fear; I was used to that sort of thing. But he shook his head, when I said that.

"'There isn't many ghosts like ours, sir,' he assured me, with mournful pride. And, by Jove! he was right, as you will see.

"I took a couple of candles, and Peters followed, with his bunch of keys. He unlocked the door; but would not come inside with me. He was evidently in quite a fright, and renewed his request, that I would put off my examination, until daylight. Of course, I laughed at him, and told him he could stand sentry at the door, and catch anything that came out.

" 'It never comes outside, sir,' he said, in his funny, old, solemn manner. Somehow, he managed to make me feel as if I were going to have the creeps right away. Anyway, it was one to him, you know.

"I left him there, and examined the room. It is a big apartment, and well-furnished in the grand style, with a huge four-poster, which stands with its head to the end wall. There were two candles on the mantelpiece, and two on each of the three tables that were in the room. I lit the lot, and after that, the room felt a little less inhumanly dreary; though, mind you, it was quite fresh, and well kept, in every way.

"After I had taken a good look round, I sealed lengths of *bébé* ribbon across the windows, along the walls, over the pictures, and over the fireplace and the wall-closets.

All the time, as I worked, the butler stood just without the door, and I could not persuade him to enter; though I jested with him a little, as I stretched the ribbons, and went here and there about my work. Every now and again, he would say:— 'You'll excuse me, I'm sure, sir; but I do wish you would come out, sir. I'm fair in a quake for you.'

"I told him he need not wait; but he was loyal enough in his way to what he considered his duty. He said he could not go away and leave me all alone there. He apologised; but made it very clear that I did not realise the danger of the room; and I could see, generally, that he was getting into a really frightened state. All the same, I had to make the room so that I should know if anything material entered it; so I asked him not to bother me, unless he really heard or saw something. He was beginning to fret my nerves, and the 'feel' of the room was bad enough already, without making things any nastier.

"For a time further, I worked, stretching ribbons across, a little above the floor, and sealing them so that the merest touch would break the seals, were anyone to venture into the room in the dark, with the intention of playing the fool.

"All this, had taken me far longer than I had anticipated; and, suddenly, I heard a clock strike eleven. I had taken off my coat soon after commencing work; now, however, as I had practically made an end of all that I intended to do, I walked across to the settee, and picked it up. I was in the act of getting into it, when the old butler's voice (he had not said a word for the last hour) came sharp and frightened:— 'Come out, sir, quick! There's something going to happen!' Jove! but I jumped, and then, in the same moment, one of the candles on the table to the left of the bed went out. Now, whether it was the wind, or what, I do not know; but, just for a moment, I was enough startled to make a run for the door; though I am glad to say that I pulled up, before I reached it. I simply could not bunk out, with the butler standing there, after having, as it were, read him a sort of lesson on 'bein' brave, y'know.' So I just turned right round, picked up the two candles off the mantelpiece, and walked across to the table near the bed. Well, I saw nothing. I blew out the candle that was still alight; then I went to those on the two other tables, and blew them out. Then, outside of the door, the old man called again:— 'Oh! sir, do be told! Do be told!'

" 'All right, Peters,' I said, and, by Jove, my voice was not as steady as I should have liked! I made for the door, and had a bit of work, not to start running. I took some thundering long strides, though, as you can imagine. Near the entrance, I had a sudden feeling that there was a cold wind in the room. It was almost as if the window had been suddenly opened a little. I got to the door, and the old butler gave back a step, in a sort of instinctive way.

" 'Collar the candles, Peters!' I said, pretty sharply, and shoved them into his hands. I turned, and caught the handle, and slammed the door shut, with a crash. Somehow, do you know, as I did so, I thought I felt something pull back on it; but it must have been only fancy. I turned the key in the lock, and then again, double-locking the door.

"I felt easier then, and set-to and sealed the door. In addition, I put my card over the keyhole, and sealed it there; after which I pocketed the key, and went down-stairs—with Peters, who was nervous and silent, leading the way. Poor old beggar! It had not struck me until that moment that he had been enduring a considerable strain during the last two or three hours.

"About midnight, I went to bed. My room lay at the end of the

corridor upon which opens the door of the Grey Room. I counted the doors between it and mine, and found that five rooms lay
between. And I am sure you can understand that I was not sorry.

"Just as I was beginning to undress, an idea came to me, and
I took my candle and sealing-wax, and sealed the doors of all the
five rooms. If any door slammed in the night, I should know just
which one.

"I returned to my room, locked myself in, and went to bed. I
was waked suddenly from a deep sleep by a loud crash somewhere
out in the passage. I sat up in bed, and listened; but heard nothing. Then I lit my candle. I was in the very act of lighting it, when
there came the bang of a door being violently slammed, along the
corridor,

"I jumped out of bed, and got my revolver. I unlocked the
door, and went out into the passage, holding my candle high,
and keeping the pistol ready. Then a queer thing happened. I
could not go a step towards the Grey Room. You all know I
am not really a cowardly chap. I've gone into too many cases
connected with ghostly things, to be accused of that; but I
tell you I funked it; simply funked it, just like any blessed kid.
There was something precious unholy in the air that night. I
backed into my bedroom, and shut and locked the door. Then
I sat on the bed all night, and listened to the dismal thudding
of a door up the corridor. The sound seemed to echo through
all the house.

"Daylight came at last, and I washed and dressed. The door
had not slammed for about an hour, and I was getting back my
nerve again. I felt ashamed of myself; though, in some ways it was
silly; for when you're meddling with that sort of thing, your nerve
is bound to go, sometimes. And you just have to sit quiet and call
yourself a coward until the safety of the day comes. Sometimes it
is more than just cowardice, I fancy. I believe at times it is Something warning you, and fighting *for* you. But, all the same, I always
feel mean and miserable, after a time like that.

"When the day came properly, I opened my door, and, keeping
my revolver handy, went quietly along the passage. I had to pass
the head of the stairs, on the way; and who should I see coming
up, but the old butler, carrying a cup of coffee. He had merely
tucked his nightshirt into his trousers, and he'd an old pair of
carpet slippers on.

" 'Hullo, Peters!' I said, feeling suddenly cheerful; for I was as glad as any lost child to have a live human being close to me. 'Where are you off to with the refreshments?'

"The old man gave a start, and slopped some of the coffee. He stared up at me, and I could see that he looked white and done-up. He came on up the stairs, and held out the little tray to me.

'I'm very thankful indeed, sir, to see you safe and well,' he said. 'I feared, one time, you might risk going into the Grey Room, sir. I've lain awake all night, with the sound of the Door. And when it came light, I thought I'd make you a cup of coffee. I knew you would want to look at the seals, and somehow it seems safer if there's two, sir.'

" 'Peters,' I said, 'you're a brick. This is very thoughtful of you.' And I drank the coffee. 'Come along,' I told him, and handed him back the tray. 'I'm going to have a look at what the Brutes have been up to. I simply hadn't the pluck to in the night.'

" 'I'm very thankful, sir,' he replied. 'Flesh and blood can do nothing, sir, against devils; and that's what's in the Grey Room after dark.'

"I examined the seals on all the doors, as I went along, and found them right; but when I got to the Grey Room, the seal was broken; though the visiting-card, over the keyhole, was untouched. I ripped it off, and unlocked the door, and went in, rather cautiously, as you can imagine; but the whole room was empty of anything to frighten one; and there was heaps of light. I examined all my seals, and not a single one was disturbed. The old butler had followed me in, and, suddenly, he said, 'The bedclothes, sir!'

"I ran up to the bed, and looked over; and, surely, they were lying in the corner to the left of the bed. Jove! you can imagine how queer I felt. Something *had* been in the room. I stared for a while, from the bed to the clothes on the floor. I had a feeling that I did not want to touch either. Old Peters, though, did not seem to be affected that way. He went over to the bed-coverings, and was going to pick them up, as, doubtless, he had done every day these twenty years back; but I stopped him. I wanted nothing touched, until I had finished my examination. This, I must have spent a full hour over, and then I let Peters straighten up the bed; after which we went out, and I locked the door; for the room was getting on my nerves.

"I had a short walk, and then breakfast; which made me feel more my own man. Then to the Grey Room again; and, with Peters' help, and one of the maids, I had everything taken out except the bed, even the very pictures.

"I examined the walls, floor and ceiling then, with probe, hammer and magnifying-glass; but found nothing unusual. I can assure you, I began to realise, in very truth, that some incredible thing had been loose in the room during the past night.

"I sealed up everything again, and went out, locking and sealing the door as before.

"After dinner that night, Peters and I unpacked some of my stuff, and I fixed up my camera and flashlight opposite to the door of the Grey Room, with a string from the trigger of the flashlight to the door. You see, if the door were really opened, the flashlight would blare out, and there would be, possibly, a very queer picture to examine in the morning.

"The last thing I did, before leaving, was to uncap the lens; and after that I went off to my bedroom, and to bed; for I intended to be up at midnight; and to insure this, I set my little alarm to call me; also I left my candle burning.

"The clock woke me at twelve, and I got up and into my dressing-gown and slippers. I shoved my revolver into my right side-pocket, and opened my door. Then, I lit my dark-room lamp, and withdrew the slide, so that it would give a clear light. I carried it up the corridor, about thirty feet, and put it down on the floor, with the open side away from me; so that it would show me anything that might approach along the dark passage. Then I went back, and sat in the doorway of my room, with my revolver handy, staring up the passage towards the place where I knew my camera stood outside of the door of the Grey Room.

"I should think I had watched for about an hour and a half, when, suddenly, I heard a faint noise, away up the corridor. I was immediately conscious of a queer prickling sensation about the back of my head, and my hands began to sweat a little. The following instant the whole end of the passage flicked into sight in the abrupt glare of the flashlight. Then came the succeeding darkness, and I peered nervously up the corridor, listening tensely, and trying to find what lay beyond the faint, red glow of my dark-lamp, which now seemed ridiculously dim, by contrast with the tremendous blaze of the flash-powder.... And then, as I stooped forward, staring and listening, there came the crashing thud of the door of the Grey Room. The sound seemed to fill the whole of the large corridor, and go echoing hollowly through the house. I tell you, I felt horrible—as if my bones were water. Simply beastly. Jove! how I did stare, and how I listened. And then it came again, thud, thud, thud, and then a silence that was almost worse than the noise of the door; for I kept fancying that some brutal thing was stealing upon me along the corridor.

'Suddenly, my lamp was put out, and I could not see a yard before me. I realised all at once that I was doing a very silly thing, sitting there, and I jumped up. Even as I did so, I *thought* I heard a sound in the passage, quite *near* to me. I made one backward spring into my room, and slammed and locked the door.

"I sat on my bed, and stared at the door. I had my revolver in my hand; but it seemed an abominably useless thing. Can you understand? I felt that there was something the other side of my door. For some unknown reason, I *knew* it was pressed up against the door, and it was soft. That was just what I thought. Most extraordinary thing to imagine, when you come to think of it!

"Presently, I got hold of myself a bit, and marked out a pentacle hurriedly with chalk on the polished floor; and there I sat in it until it was almost dawn. And all the time, away up the corridor, the door of the Grey Room thudded at solemn and horrid intervals. It was a miserable, brutal night.

"When the day began to break, the thudding of the door came gradually to an end, and at last, I grabbed together my courage, and went along the corridor, in the half light, to cap the lens of my camera. I can tell you, it took some doing; but if I had not gone, my photograph would have been spoilt, and I was tremendously keen to save it. I got back to my room, and then set-to and rubbed out the five-pointed star in which I had been sitting.

"Half an hour later there was a tap at my door. It was Peters, with my coffee. When I had drunk it, we both walked along to the Grey Room. As we went, I had a look at the seals on the other doors; but they were untouched. The seal on the door of the Grey Room was broken, as also was the string from the trigger of the flashlight; but the visiting-card over the keyhole was still there. I ripped it off, and opened the door.

"Nothing unusual was to be seen, until we came to the bed; then I saw that, as on the previous day, the bedclothes had been torn off, and hurled into the left-hand corner, exactly where I had seen them before. I felt very queer; but I did not forget to look at all the seals, only to find that not one had been broken.

"Then I turned and looked at old Peters, and he looked at me, nodding his head.

" 'Let's get out of here!' I said. ' It's no place for any living human to enter, without proper protection.'

"We went out then, and I locked and sealed the door, again.

"After breakfast, I developed the negative; but it showed only the door of the Grey Room, half opened. Then I left the house, as I wanted to get certain matters and implements that might be necessary to life; perhaps to the spirit; for I intended to spend the coming night in the Grey Room.

"I got back in a cab, about half past five, with my apparatus, and this, Peters and I carried up to the Grey Room, where I piled it carefully in the centre of the floor. When everything was in the room, including a cat which I had brought, I locked and sealed the door, and went towards my bedroom, telling Peters I should not be down to dinner. He said 'Yes, sir,' and went downstairs, thinking that I was going to turn-in; which was what I wanted him to believe, as I knew he would have worried both himself and me, if he had known what I intended.

" 'But I merely got my camera and flashlight from my bedroom, and hurried back to the Grey Room. I entered, and locked and sealed myself in, and set to work; for I had a lot to do before it got dark.

"First, I cleared away all the ribbons across the floor; then I carried the cat—still fastened in its basket—over towards the far wall, and left it. I returned then to the centre of the room, and measured out a space twenty-one feet in diameter, which I swept with a 'broom of hyssop'. About this, I drew a circle of chalk, taking care never to step over the circle.

"Beyond this, I smudged, with a bunch of garlic, a broad belt right around the chalked circle, and when this was complete, I took from among my stores in the centre a small jar of a certain water. I broke away the parchment, and withdrew the stopper. Then, dipping my left forefinger in the little jar, I went round the circle again, making upon the floor, just within the line of chalk, the Second Sign of the Saaamaaa Ritual, and joining each Sign most carefully with the left-handed crescent. I can tell you, I felt easier when this was done, and the 'water-circle' complete.

"Then, I unpacked some more of the stuff that I had brought, and placed a lighted candle in the 'valley' of each Crescent. After that, I drew a Pentacle, so that each of the five points of the defensive star touched the chalk circle. In the five points of the star, I placed five portions of a certain bread, each wrapped in linen; and in the five 'vales', five opened jars of the water I had used to make the 'water-circle.' And now I had my first protective barrier complete.

"Now, anyone, except you who know something of my methods of investigation, might consider all this a piece of useless and foolish superstition; but you all remember the Black Veil case, in which I believe my life was saved by a very similar form of protection; whilst Aster, who sneered at it, and would not come inside, died.

"I got the idea from the Sigsand MS., written, so far as I can make out, in the fourteenth century. At first, naturally, I imagined it was just an expression of the superstition of his time; and it was not until long after my first reading that it occurred to me to test his 'Defense', which I did, as I've just said, in that horrible Black Veil business. You know how *that* turned out. Later, I used it several times, and always I came through safe, until that Moving Fur case. It was only a partial 'Defense' there, and I nearly died in the pentacle. After that, I came across Professor Garder's 'Experiments with a Medium'. When they surrounded the Medium with a current of a certain number of vibrations, in vacuum, he lost his power—almost as if it cut him off from the Immaterial.

"That made me think; and led eventually to the Electric Pentacle, which is a most marvellous 'Defense' against certain manifestations. I used the shape of the defensive star for this protection, because I have, personally, no doubt at all but that there is some extraordinary virtue in the old magic figure. Curious thing for a Twentieth Century man to admit, is it not? But then, as you all know, I never did, and never will, allow myself to be blinded by a little cheap laughter. I ask questions, and keep my eyes open!

"In this last case, I had little doubt that I had run up against an ab-natural monster, and I meant to take every possible care; for the danger is abominable.

"I turned-to now to fit the Electric Pentacle, setting it so that each of its 'points' and 'vales' coincided exactly with the 'points' and 'vales' of the drawn pentagram upon the floor. Then I connected up the battery, and the next instant the pale blue glare from the intertwining vacuum tubes shone out.

"I glanced about me then, with something of a sigh of relief, and realised suddenly that the dusk was upon me; for the window was grey and unfriendly. Then I stared round at the big, empty room, over the double-barrier of electric and candle light; and had an abrupt, extraordinary sense of weirdness thrust upon me—in the air, you know, it seemed; as it were a sense of something in-human impending. The room was full of the stench of bruised garlic, a smell I hate.

"I turned now to my camera, and saw that it and the flashlight were in order. Then I tested the action of my revolver, carefully; though I had little thought that it would be needed. Yet, to what extent materialisation of an ab-natural creature is possible, given favourable conditions, no one can say; and I had no idea what horrible thing I was going to see, or feel the presence of. I might, in the end, have to fight with a material thing. I did not know, and could only be prepared. You see, I never forgot that three people had been strangled in the bed close to me; and the fierce slamming of the door, I had heard myself. I had no doubt that I was inves-tigating a dangerous and ugly case.

"By this time, the night had come (though the room was very light with the burning candles), and I found myself glancing behind me, constantly, and then all round the room. It was nervy work waiting for that thing to come into the room.

"Suddenly, I was aware of a little, cold wind sweeping over me, coming from behind. I gave one great nerve-thrill, and a prickly feeling went all over the back of my head. Then I hove myself round with a sort of stiff jerk, and stared straight against that queer wind. It seemed to come from the corner of the room to the left of the bed—the place where both times I had found the heap of tossed bedclothes. Yet I could see nothing unusual; no opening— Nothing!...

"Abruptly, I was aware that the candles were all a-flicker in that unnatural wind.... I believe I just squatted there and stared in a horribly frightened, wooden way for some minutes. I shall never be able to let you know how disgustingly horrible it was sitting in that vile, cold wind! And then, flick! flick! flick! all the candles round the outer barrier went out; and there was I, locked and sealed in that room, and with no light beyond the weakish blue glare of the Electric Pentacle.

"A time of abominable tenseness passed, and still that wind blew upon me; and then, suddenly, I knew that something stirred in the corner to the left of the bed. I was made conscious of it, rather by some inward, unused sense, than by either sight or sound; for the pale, short-radius glare of the Pentacle gave but a very poor light for seeing by. Yet, as I stared, something began slowly to grow upon my sight—a moving shadow, a little darker than the surrounding shadows. I lost the thing amid the vagueness, and for a moment or two I glanced swiftly from side to side, with a fresh, new-sense of impending danger. Then my attention was directed to the bed. All the coverings were being drawn steadily off, with a hateful, stealthy sort of motion. I heard the slow, dragging slither of the clothes, but I could see nothing of the thing that pulled. I was aware in a funny, subconscious, introspective fashion that the 'creep' had come upon me, prickling all over my head, yet that I was cooler mentally than I had been for some minutes; sufficiently so to feel that my hands were sweating coldly, and to shift my revolver, half-consciously, whilst I rubbed my right hand dry upon my knee; though never, for an instant, taking my gaze or my attention from those moving clothes.

"The faint noises from the bed ceased once, and there was a most intense silence, with only the dull thudding of the blood beating in my head. Yet, immediately afterwards, I heard again the slurring sound of the bedclothes being dragged off the bed. In the midst of my nervous tension I remembered the camera, and reached round for it; but without looking away from the bed. And then, you know, all in a moment, the whole of the bed-coverings were torn off with extraordinary violence, and I heard the flump they made as they were hurled into the corner.

"There was a time of absolute quietness then, for perhaps a couple of minutes; and you can imagine how horrible I felt. The bedclothes had been thrown with such savageness! And, then again, the abominable unnaturalness of the thing that had just been done before me!

"Suddenly, over by the door, I heard a faint noise—a sort of crickling sound, and then a pitter or two upon the floor. A great, nervous thrill swept over me, seeming to run up my spine and over the back of my head; for the seal that secured the door had just been broken. Something was there. I could not see the door; at least, I mean to say that it was impossible to say how much I actually saw, and how much my imagination supplied. I made it out only as a continuation of the grey walls.... And then it seemed to me that something dark and indistinct moved and wavered there among the shadows.

"Abruptly, I was aware that the door was opening, and with an effort I reached again for my camera; but before I could aim it, the door was slammed with a terrific crash that filled the whole room with a sort of hollow thunder. I jumped, like a frightened child. There seemed such a power behind the noise; as if a vast, wanton Force were 'out'. Can you understand?

"The door was not touched again; but, directly afterwards, I heard the basket, in which the cat lay, creak. I tell you, I fairly pringled all along my back. I knew that I was going to learn definitely whether whatever was abroad was dangerous to Life. From the cat there rose suddenly a hideous catterwaul, that ceased abruptly; and then—too late—I snapped off the flashlight. In the great glare, I saw that the basket had been overturned, and the lid was wrenched open, with the cat lying half in, and half out upon the floor. I saw nothing else; but I was full of the knowledge that I was in the presence of some Being or Thing that had power to destroy.

"During the next two or three minutes, there was an odd, noticeable quietness in the room, and you must remember I was half-blinded, for the time, because of the flashlight; so that the whole place seemed to be pitchy dark just beyond the shine of the pentacle. I tell you it was most horrible. I just knelt there in the star, and whirled round on my knees, trying to see whether anything was coming at me.

"My power of sight came gradually, and I got a little hold of myself; and abruptly I saw the thing I was looking for, close to the 'water-circle'. It was big and indistinct, and wavered curiously, as though the shadow of a vast spider hung suspended in the air, just beyond the barrier. It passed swiftly round the circle, and seemed to probe ever towards me; but only to draw back with extraordinary jerky movements, as might a living person who touched the hot bar of a grate.

"Round and round it moved, and round and round I turned. Then, just opposite to one of the 'vales' in the pentacles, it seemed to pause, as though preliminary to a tremendous effort. It retired almost beyond the glow of the vacuum light, and then came straight towards me, appearing to gather form and solidity as it came. There seemed a vast, malign determination behind the movement, that must succeed. I was on my knees, and I jerked back, falling onto my left hand and hip, in a wild endeavour to get back from the advancing thing. With my right hand I was grabbing madly for my revolver, which I had let slip. The brutal thing came with one great sweep straight over the garlic and the 'water-circle', almost to the vale of the pentacle. I believe I yelled. Then, just as suddenly as it had swept over, it seemed to be hurled back by some mighty, invisible force.

"It must have been some moments before I realised that I was safe; and then I got myself together in the middle of the pentacles, feeling horribly gone and shaken, and glancing round and round the barrier; but the thing had vanished. Yet I had learnt something; for I knew now that the Grey Room was haunted by a monstrous hand.

"Suddenly, as I crouched there, I saw what had so nearly given the monster an opening through the barrier. In my movements within the pentacle, I must have touched one of the jars of water; for just where the thing had made its attack, the jar that guarded the 'deep' of the 'vale' had been moved to one side, and this had left one of the 'five doorways' unguarded. I put it back, quickly, and felt almost safe again; for I had found the cause, and the 'Defense' was still good. I began to hope again that I should see the morning come in. When I saw that thing so nearly succeed, I'd had an awful, weak, overwhelming feeling that the 'barriers' could never bring me safe through the night, against such a Force. You can understand?

"For a long time I could not see the hand; but, presently, I thought I saw, once or twice, an odd wavering, over among the shadows near the door. A little later, as though in a sudden fit of malignant rage, the dead body of the cat was picked up, and beaten with dull, sickening blows against the solid floor. That made me feel rather queer.

"A minute afterwards, the door was opened and slammed twice with tremendous force. The next instant, the thing made one swift, vicious dart at me, from out of the shadows. Instinctively, I started sideways from it, and so plucked my hand from upon the Electric Pentacle, where—for a wickedly careless moment—I had placed it. The monster was hurled off from the neighbourhood of the pentacles; though—owing to my inconceivable foolishness—it had been enabled for a second time to pass the outer barriers. I can tell you, I shook for a time, with sheer funk. I moved right to the centre of the pentacles again, and knelt there, making myself as small and compact as possible.

"As I knelt, I began to have presently, a vague wonder at the two 'accidents' which had so nearly allowed the brute to get at me. Was I being *influenced* to unconscious voluntary actions that endangered me? The thought took hold of me; and I watched my every movement. Abruptly, I stretched a tired leg, and knocked over one of the jars of water. Some was spilled; but because of my suspicious watchfulness, I had it upright and back within the vale, while yet some of the water remained. Even as I did so, the vast, black half-materialised hand beat up at me out of the shadows, and seemed to leap almost into my face; so nearly did it approach; but for the third time it was thrown back by some altogether enormous, overmastering force. Yet, apart from the dazed fright in which it left me, I had for a moment that feeling of spiritual sickness, as if some delicate, beautiful, inward grace had suffered, which is felt only upon the too near approach of the ab-human, and is more dreadful in a strange way, than any physical pain that can be suffered. I knew by this, more of the extent and closeness of the danger; and for a long time I was simply cowed by the butt-headed brutality of that Force upon my spirit. I can put it no other way.

"I knelt again in the centre of the pentacles, watching myself with as much fear, almost, as the monster; for I knew now that, unless I guarded myself from every sudden impulse that came to me, I might simply work my own destruction. Do you see how horrible it all was?

"I spent the rest of the night in a haze of sick fright, and so tense that I could not make a single movement naturally. I was in such fear that any desire for action that came to me might be prompted by the Influence that I knew was at work on me. And outside of the barrier, that ghastly thing went round and round, grabbing and grabbing in the air at me. Twice more was the body of the dead cat molested. The second time, I heard every bone in its body scrunch and crack. And all the time the horrible wind was blowing upon me from the corner of the room to the left of the bed.

"Then, just as the first touch of dawn came into the sky, the unnatural wind ceased, in a single moment; and I could see no sign of the hand. The dawn came slowly, and presently the wan light filled all the room, and made the pale glare of the Electric Pentacle look more unearthly. Yet, it was not until the day had fully come, that I made any attempt to leave the barrier; for I did not know but that there was some method abroad, in the sudden stopping of that wind, to entice me from the pentacles.

"At last, when the dawn was strong and bright, I took one last look round, and ran for the door. I got it unlocked, in a nervous, clumsy fashion; then locked it hurriedly, and went to my bedroom, where I lay on the bed, and tried to steady my nerves. Peters came, presently, with the coffee, and when I had drunk it, I told him I meant to have a sleep, as I had been up all night. He took the tray, and went out quietly; and after I had locked my door, I turned in properly, and at last got to sleep.

"I woke about midday, and after some lunch, went up to the Grey Room. I switched off the current from the Pentacle, which I had left on, in my hurry; also, I removed the body of the cat. You can understand, I did not want anyone to see the poor brute.

"After that, I made a very careful search of the corner where the bedclothes had been thrown. I made several holes through the woodwork, and probed; but found nothing. Then it occurred to me to try with my instrument under the skirting. I did so, and heard my wire ring on metal. I turned the hook-end of the probe that way, and fished for the thing. At the second go, I got it. It was a small object, and I took it to the window. I found it to be a curious ring, made of some greyish metal. The curious thing about it was that it was made in the form of a pentagon; that is, the same shape as the inside of the magic pentacle; but without the 'mounts' which form the points of the defensive star. It was free from all chasing or engraving.

"You will understand that I was excited, when I tell you that I felt sure I held in my hand the famous Luck Ring of the Anderson family; which, indeed, was of all things the one most intimately connected with the history of the haunting. This ring had been handed on from father to son, through generations; and always— in obedience to some ancient family traditions—each son had to promise never to wear the ring. The ring, I may say, was brought home by one of the Crusaders, under very peculiar circumstances; but the story is too long to go into here.

"It appears that young Sir Hulbert, an ancestor of Anderson's, made a bet one evening, in drink, you know, that he would wear the ring that night. He did so, and in the morning his wife and child were found strangled in the bed, in the very room in which

I stood. Many people, it would seem, thought young Sir Hulbert was guilty of having done the thing in drunken anger; and he, in an attempt to prove his innocence, slept a second night in the room. He also was strangled.

"Since then, no one has spent a night in the Grey Room, until I did so. The ring had been lost so long, that its very existence had become almost a myth; and it was most extraordinary to stand there, with the actual thing in my hand, as you can understand.

"It was whilst I stood there, looking at the ring, that I got an idea. Supposing that it were, in a way, a doorway— You see what I mean? A sort of gap in the world-hedge, if I may so phrase my idea. It was a queer thought, I know, and possibly was not my own; but one of those mental nudgings from the Outside.

"You see, the wind had come from that part of the room where the ring lay. I pondered the thought a lot. Then the shape—the inside of a pentacle. It had no 'mounts', and without mounts, as the Sigsand MS. has it:— 'Thee mownts wych are thee Five Hills of safetie. To lack is to gyve pow'r to thee daemon; and surelie to fayvor thee Evill Thynge.' You see, the very shape of the ring was significant. I determined to test it.

"I unmade my pentacle; for it must be 'made' afresh *and around* the one to be protected. Then I went out and locked the door; after which I left the house, to get certain matters, for neither 'yarbs nor fyre nor water' must be used a second time. I returned about seven-thirty; and as soon as the things I had brought had been carried up to the Grey Room, I dismissed Peters for the night, just as I had done the evening before. When he had gone downstairs, I let myself into the room, and locked and sealed the door. I went to the place in the centre of the room where all the stuff had been packed, and set to work with all my speed to construct a barrier about me and the ring.

"I do not remember whether I explained to you. But I had reasoned that, if the ring were in any way a 'medium of admission', and it were enclosed with me in the Electric pentacle, it would be, to express it loosely, insulated. Do you see? The Force which had visible expression as a Hand, would have to stay beyond the Barrier which separates the Ab from the Normal; for the 'gateway' would be removed from accessibility.

"As I was saying, I worked with all my speed to get the barrier completed about me and the ring; for it was already later than I cared to be in that room 'unprotected'. Also, I had a feeling that there would be a vast effort made that night to regain the use of the ring. For I had the strongest conviction that the ring was a necessity to materialisation. You will see whether I was right.

"I completed the barriers in about an hour, and you can imagine something of the relief I felt when I saw the pale glare of the Electric Pentacle once more all about me. From then, onwards, for about two hours, I sat quietly, facing the corner from which the wind came.

"About eleven o'clock I had a queer knowledge that something was near to me; yet nothing happened for a whole hour after that. Then, suddenly, I felt the cold, queer wind begin to blow upon me. To my astonishment, it seemed now to come from behind me, and I whipped round, with a hideous quake of fear. The wind met me in the face. It was blowing up from the floor close to me. I stared down, in a sickening maze of new frights. What on earth had I done now! The ring was there, close beside me, where I had put it. Suddenly, as I stared, bewildered, I was aware that there was something queer about the ring—funny shadowy movements and convolutions. I look at them, stupidly. And then, abruptly, I knew that the wind was blowing up at me from the ring. A queer indistinct smoke became visible to me, seeming to pour upwards through the ring, and mix with the moving shadows. Suddenly, I realised that I was in more than any mortal danger; for the convoluting shadows about the ring were taking shape, and the death-hand was forming *within* the Pentacle. My Goodness! do you realise it! I had brought the 'gateway' into the pentacles, and the brute was coming through—pouring into the material world, as gas might pour out from the mouth of a pipe.

"I should think that I knelt for a couple of moments in a sort of stunned fright. Then, with a mad, awkward movement, I snatched at the ring, intending to hurl it out of the Pentacle. Yet, it eluded me, as though some invisible, living thing jerked it hither and thither. At last, I gripped it; but, in the same instant, it was torn from my grasp with incredible and brutal force. A great, black shadow covered it, and rose into the air, and came at me. I saw that it was the Hand, vast and nearly perfect in form. I gave one crazy yell, and jumped over the Pentacle and the ring of burning candles, and ran despairingly for the door. I fumbled idiotically and ineffectually with the key, and all the time I stared, with a fear that was like insanity, towards the Barriers. The hand was plunging towards me; yet, even as it had been unable to pass into the pentacle when the ring was without; so, now that the ring was within, it had no power to pass out. The monster was chained, as surely as any beast would be, were chains rivetted upon it.

"Even then, in that moment, I got a flash of this knowledge; but I was too utterly shaken with fright, to reason; and the instant I managed to get the key turned, I sprang into the passage, and slammed the door, with a crash. I locked it, and got to my room, somehow; for I was trembling so that I could hardly stand, as you can imagine. I locked myself in, and managed to get the candle lit; then I lay down on the bed, and kept quiet for an hour or two, and so I grew steadier.

"I got a little sleep, later; but woke when Peters brought my coffee. When I had drunk it, I felt altogether better, and took the old man along with me whilst I had a look into the Grey Room. I opened the door and peeped in. The candles were still burning, wan against the daylight; and behind them was the pale, glowing star of the Electric Pentacle. And there, in the middle, was the ring—the gateway of the monster, lying demure and ordinary.

"Nothing in the room was touched, and I knew that the brute had never managed to cross the Pentacles. Then I went out, and locked the door.

"After a further sleep of some hours, I left the house. I returned in the afternoon, in a cab. I had with me an oxy-hydrogen jet, and two cylinders, containing the gases. I carried the things to the Grey Room; and there, in the centre of the Electric Pentacle, I erected the little furnace. Five minutes later, the Luck Ring, once the 'luck' but now the 'bane' of the Anderson family, was no more than a little splash of hot metal."

Carnacki felt in his pocket, and pulled out som/,ething wrapped in tissue paper. He passed it to me. I opened it, and found a small circle of greyish metal, something like lead, only harder and rather brighter.

"Well?" I asked, at length, after examining it and handing it round to the others. "Did that stop the haunting?"

Carnacki nodded. "Yes," he said. "I slept three nights in the Grey Room, before I left. Old Peters nearly fainted when he knew that I meant to; but by the third night he seemed to realise that the house was just safe and ordinary. And, you know, I believe, in his heart, he hardly approved.

Carnacki stood up, and began to shake hands. "Out you go!" he said, genially.

And, presently, we went pondering to our various homes.

The House Among the Laurels

"THIS IS A CURIOUS yarn that I am going to tell you," said Carnacki, as after a quiet little dinner we made ourselves comfortable in his cosy dining room.

"I have just got back from the West of Ireland," he continued. "Wentworth, a friend of mine, has lately had rather an unexpected legacy, in the shape of a large estate and manor, about a mile and a half outside of the village of Korunton. The place is named Gannington Manor, and has been empty a great number of years; as you will find is so often the case with houses reputed to be haunted.

"It seems that when Wentworth went over to take possession, he found the place in very poor repair, and the estate totally uncared for, and, as I know, looking very desolate and lonesome generally. He went through the big house by himself, and he admitted to me that it had an uncomfortable feeling about it; but, of course, that might be nothing more than the natural dismalness of a big, empty house, which has been long uninhabited, and through which one is wandering alone.

"When he had finished his look round, he went down to the village, meaning to see the one-time Agent of the Estate, and arrange for someone to go in as caretaker. The Agent, who proved, by the way, to be a Scotchman, was very willing to take up the management of the Estate once more; but he assured Wentworth that they would get no one to go in as caretaker; and that his—the Agent's—advice was to have the house pulled down, and a new one built.

"This, naturally, astonished my friend, and, as they went down to the village, he managed to get a kind of explanation from the man. It seems that there had been always curious stories told about the place, which in the early days was called Landru Castle, and

179

that within the last seven years there had been two extraordinary deaths there. In each case they had been tramps, who were ignorant of the reputation of the house, and had probably thought the big empty place suitable for a night's free lodging. There had been absolutely no signs of violence to indicate the method by which death was caused, and on each occasion the body had been found in the great entrance hall.

"By this time they had reached the inn where Wentworth had put up, and he told the Agent that he would prove that it was all rubbish about the haunting, by staying a night or two in the Manor himself. The death of the tramps was certainly curious; but did not prove that any supernatural agency had been at work. They were but isolated accidents, spread over a large number of years by the memory of the villagers, which was natural enough in a little place like Korunton. Tramps had to die some time, and in some place, and it proved nothing that two, out of possibly hundreds who had slept in the empty house, had happened to take the opportunity to die under its shelter.

"But the Agent took his remark very seriously, and both he and Dennis, the Landlord of the inn, tried their best to persuade him not to go. For his 'sowl's sake', Irish Dennis begged him to do no such thing; and because of his 'life's sake', the Scotchman was equally in earnest.

"It was late afternoon at the time, and as Wentworth told me, it was warm and bright, and it seemed such utter rot to hear those two talking seriously about the Impossible. He felt full of pluck, and he made up his mind he would smash the story of the haunting, at once, by staying that very night in the Manor. He made this quite clear to them, and told them that it would be more to the point and to their credit, if they offered to come up along with him, and keep him company. But poor old Dennis was quite shocked, I believe, at the suggestion; and though Tabbit, the Agent, took it more quietly, he was very solemn about it.

"It appears that Wentworth did go; though, as he said to me, when the evening began to come on, it seemed a very different sort of thing to tackle.

"A whole crowd of the villagers assembled to see him off; for by this time they all knew of his intention. Wentworth had his gun with him, and a big packet of candles; and he made it clear to them all that it would not be wise for anyone to play any tricks; as he intended to shoot 'at sight'. And then, you know, he got a hint of how serious they considered the whole thing; for one of them came up to him, leading a great bull-mastiff, and offered it to him, to take to keep him company. Wentworth patted his gun; but the old man who owned the dog, shook his head and explained that the brute might warn him in sufficient time for him to get away from the castle. For it was obvious that he did not consider the gun would prove of any use.

"Wentworth took the dog, and thanked the man. He told me that, already, he was beginning to wish that he had not said definitely that he would go; but, as it was, he was simply forced to. "He went through the crowd of men, and found suddenly that they had all turned in a body and were keeping him company. They stayed with him all the way to the Manor, and then went right over the whole place with him.

"It was still daylight when this was finished, though turning to dusk; and, for a little, the men stood about, hesitating, as if they felt ashamed to go away and leave Wentworth there all alone. He told me that, by this time, he would gladly have given fifty pounds to be going back with them. And then, abruptly, an idea came to him. He suggested that they should stay with him, and keep him company through the night. For a time they refused, and tried to persuade him to go back with them; but finally he made a proposition that got home to them all. He planned that they should all go back to the inn, and there get a couple of dozen bottles of whisky, a donkey-load of turf and wood, and some more candles. Then they would come back, and make a great fire in the big fire-place, light all the candles, and put them round the place, open the whisky and make a night of it. And, by Jove! he got them to agree.

"They set off back, and were soon at the inn, and here, whilst the donkey was being loaded, and the candles and whisky distributed, Dennis was doing his best to keep Wentworth from going back; but he was a sensible man in his way; for when he found that it was no use, he stopped. I believe, he did not want to frighten the others from accompanying Wentworth.

"'I tell ye, sorr,' he told him, ' 'tis no use at all at all thryin' to reclaim ther castle. 'Tis curst with innocent blood, an' ye'll be betther pullin' it down, an' buildin' a fine new wan. But if ye be intendin' to shtay this night, kape the big dhoor open whide, an' watch for the bhlood-dhrip. If so much as a single dhrip falls, don't shtay though all the gold in the worrld was offered ye.'

"Wentworth asked him what he meant by the blood-drip.

" 'Shure,' he said, ' 'tis the bhlood av thim as ould Black Mick, 'way back in the ould days, kilt in their shlape. 'Twas a feud as he pretendid to patch up, an' he invited thim—the O'Haras they was—sivinty av thim. An' he fed thim, an' shpoke soft to thim, an' thim thrustin' him, shtayed to shlape with him. Thin, he an' thim with him, stharted in an' mhurdered thim wan an' all as they slep'. 'Tis from me father's grandfather ye have the sthory. An' sence thin 'tis death to any, so they say, to pass the night in the castle whin the bhlood-drip comes. 'Twill put out candle an' fire, an' thin in the darkness the Virgin Herself would be powerless to protect ye.'

"Wentworth told me he laughed at this; chiefly because, as he put it:— One always must laugh at that sort of yarn, however it makes you feel inside. He asked old Dennis whether he expected him to believe it.

" 'Yes, Sorr,' said Dennis, 'I do mane ye to b'lieve it; an', please God, if ye'll b'lieve, ye may be back safe befor' mornin'.' The man's serious simplicity took hold of Wentworth, and he held out his hand. But, for all that, he went; and I must admire his pluck.

"There were now about forty men, and when they got back to the Manor—or castle as the villagers always call it—they were not long in getting a big fire going, and lighted candles all round the great hall. They had all brought sticks; so that they would have been a pretty formidable lot to tackle by anything simply physical; and, of course, Wentworth had his gun. He kept the whisky in his own charge; for he intended to keep them sober; but he gave them a good strong tot all round first, so as to make things cheerful; and to get them yarning. If you once let a crowd of men like that grow silent, they begin to think, and then to fancy things.

"The big entrance door had been left wide open, by his orders; which shows that he had taken some notice of Dennis. It was a quiet night, so this did not matter, for the lights kept steady, and all went on in a jolly sort of fashion for about three hours. He had opened a second lot of bottles, and everyone was feeling cheerful; so much so that one of the men called out aloud to the ghosts to come out and show themselves. And then, you know, a very extraordinary thing happened; for the ponderous main door swung quietly and steadily to, as if pushed by an invisible hand, and shut with a sharp click.

"Wentworth stared, feeling suddenly rather chilly. Then he remembered the men, and looked round at them. Several had ceased their talk, and were staring in a frightened way at the big door; but the greater number had never noticed, and were talking and yarning. He reached for his gun, and the following instant the great bull-mastiff set up a tremendous barking, which drew the attention of the whole company.

"The hall I should tell you is oblong. The South wall is all windows; but the North and the East have rows of doors leading into the house, whilst the West wall is occupied by the great entrance. The rows of doors leading into the house were all closed, and it was towards one of these in the North wall that the big dog ran; yet he would not go very close; and suddenly the door began to move slowly open, until the blackness of the passage beyond was shown. The dog came back among the men, whimpering, and for perhaps a minute there was an absolute silence.

"Then Wentworth went out from the men a little, and aimed his gun at the doorway.

" 'Whoever is there, come out, or I shall fire,' he shouted; but nothing came, and he blazed both barrels into the dark. As though the report had been a signal, all the doors along the North and East walls moved slowly open, and Wentworth and his men were staring, frightened, into the black shapes of the empty doorways.

"Wentworth loaded his gun quickly, and called to the dog; but the brute was burrowing away in among the men; and this fear on the dog's part frightened Wentworth more, he told me, than anything. Then something else happened. Three of the candles over in the corner of the hall went out; and immediately about half a dozen in different parts of the place. More candles were put out, and the hall had become quite dark in the corners.

"The men were all standing now, holding their clubs, and crowded together. And no one said a word. Wentworth told me he felt positively ill with fright. I know the feeling. Then, suddenly, something splashed on to the back of his left hand. He lifted it, and looked. It was covered with a great splash of red that dripped through his fingers. An old Irishman near to him, saw it, and croaked out in a quavering voice:— 'The bhlood-dhrip!' When the old man called out, they all looked, and in the same instant others felt it upon them. There were frightened cries of:— 'The bhlood-dhrip! The bhlood-dhrip!' And then, about a dozen candles went out simultaneously, and the hall was suddenly almost dark. The dog let out a great, mournful howl, and there was a horrible little silence, with everyone standing rigid. Then the tension broke, and there was a mad rush for the main door. They wrenched it open, and tumbled out into the dark; but something slammed it with a crash after them, and shut the dog in; for Wentworth heard it howling as they raced down the drive. Yet no one had the pluck to go back to let it out, which does not surprise me.

"Wentworth sent for me the following day. He had heard of me in connection with that Steeple Monster Case. I arrived by the night mail, and put up with him at the inn. The next day we went up to the old manor, which certainly lies in rather a wilderness; though what struck me most was the extraordinary number of laurel bushes about the house. The place was smothered with them; so that the house seemed to be growing up out of a sea of green laurel. These, and the grim, ancient look of the old building, made the place look a bit dank and ghostly, even by daylight.

"The hall was a big place, and well lit by daylight; for which I was not sorry. You see, I had been rather wound-up by Wentworth's yarn. We found one rather funny thing, and that was the great bull-mastiff, lying stiff with its neck broken. This made me feel very serious; for it showed that whether the cause was supernatural or not, there was present in the house some force dangerous to life.

"Later, whilst Wentworth stood guard with his shot-gun, I made an examination of the hall. The bottles and mugs from which the men had drunk their whisky were scattered about; and all over the place were the candles, stuck upright in their own grease. But in that somewhat brief and general search, I found nothing; and decided to begin my usual exact examination of every square foot of the place—not only of the hall, in this case, but of the whole interior of the castle.

"I spent three uncomfortable weeks, searching; but without result of any kind. And, you know, the care I take at this period is extreme; for I have solved hundreds of cases of so-called 'hauntings' at this early stage, simply by the most minute investigation, and the keeping of a perfectly open mind. But, as I have said, I found nothing. During the whole of the examination, I got Wentworth to stand guard with his loaded shot-gun; and I was very particular that we were never caught there after dusk.

"I decided now to make the experiment of staying a night in the great hall, of course 'protected'. I spoke about it to Wentworth; but his own attempt had made him so nervous that he begged me to do no such thing. However, I thought it well worth the risk, and I managed in the end to persuade him to be present.

"With this in view, I went to the neighbouring town of Gaunt, and by an arrangement with the Chief Constable I obtained the services of six policemen with their rifles. The arrangement was unofficial, of course, and the men were allowed to volunteer, with a promise of payment.

"When the constables arrived early that evening at the inn, I gave them a good feed; and after that we all set out for the manor. We had four donkeys with us, loaded with fuel and other matters; also two great boar-hounds, which one of the police led. When we reached the house, I set the men to unload the donkeys; whilst Wentworth and I set-to and sealed all the doors, except the main entrance, with tape and wax; for if the doors were really opened, I was going to be sure of the fact. I was going to run no risk of being deceived either by ghostly hallucination, or mesmeric influence.

"By the time that we had sealed the doors, the policemen had unloaded the donkeys, and were waiting, looking about them, curiously. I set two of them to lay a fire in the big grate, and the others I used as I required them. I took one of the boar hounds to the end of the hall furthest from the entrance, and there I drove a staple into the floor, to which I tied the dog with a short tether. Then, round him, I drew upon the floor the figure of a pentacle, in chalk. Outside of the pentacle, I made a circle with garlic. I did exactly the same thing with the other hound; but over in the North-East corner of the big hall, where the two rows of doors make the angle.

"When this was done, I cleared the whole centre of the hall, and put one of the policemen to sweep it; after which I had all my apparatus carried into the cleared space. Then I went over to the main door, and hooked it open, so that the hook would have to be lifted out of the hasp, before the door could be closed.

"After that, I placed lighted candles before each of the sealed doors, and one in each corner of the big room; and then I lit the fire. When I saw that it was properly alight, I got all the men together, by the pile of things in the centre of the room, and took their pipes from them; for, as the Sigsand MS. has it:— 'Theyre must noe lyght come from wythin the barryier.' And I was going to make sure.

"I got my tape-measure then, and measured out a circle ninety-nine feet in circumference, and immediately began to chalk it out. The police and Wentworth were tremendously interested, and I took the opportunity to warn them that this was no piece of silly mumming on my part, but done with a definite intention of erecting a barrier between us and any ab-human thing that the night might show to us. I warned them that, as they valued their lives (and more than their lives, it might be), no one must on any account whatever pass beyond the limits of the barrier that I was making.

"After I had drawn the circle, I took a bunch of the garlic, and smudged it right round the chalk circle, a little outside of it. When this was complete, I called for candles from my stock of material. I set the police to lighting them, and as they were lit I took them and sealed them down on to the floor, just along the chalk circle, five inches apart. Each candle measured one inch in diameter, and it took one hundred and ninety-eight candles to complete the circle. I need hardly say that every number and measurement has a significance.

"Then, from candle to candle I took a 'gayrd' of human hair, entwining it alternately to the left and to the right, until the circle was completed, and the ends of the final hairs shod with silver, were pressed into the wax of the one hundredth and ninety-eighth candle.

"It had now been dark some time, and I made haste to get the 'Defense' complete. To this end I got the men well together, and began to fit the Electric Pentacle right around us, so that the five points of the Defensive Star came just within the Hair-Circle. This did not take me long, and a few minutes later I had connected up the batteries, and the weak blue glare of the intertwining vacuum tubes shone all round us.

"I felt happier then; for this Pentacle is, as you all know, a wonderful 'Defense'. I have told you before how the idea came to me, after reading Professor Garder's 'Experiments with a Medium'. He found that a current, of a certain number of vibrations, *in vacua,* 'insulated' the Medium. It is difficult to suggest an explanation non-technically, and if you are really interested you should read Carder's Lecture on 'Astarral Vibrations Compared with Matero-involuted Vibrations Below The Six-Billion Limit'.

"As I stood up from my work, I could hear outside in the night a constant drip from the laurels, which, as I have said, come right up around the house very thick. By the sound, I knew that a 'soft' rain had set in, and there was absolutely no wind, as I could tell by the steady flames of the candles.

"I stood a moment or two, listening, and then one of the men touched my arm, and asked me in a low voice what they should do. By his tone I could tell that he was feeling something of the strangeness of it all; and the other men, including Wentworth, were so quiet that I was afraid they were beginning to get nervy.

"I set-to, then, and arranged them with their backs to one common centre, so that they were sitting flat upon the floor, with their feet radiating outwards. Then, by compass, I laid their legs to the eight chief points, and afterwards I drew a 'circle' with chalk round them; and opposite to their feet, I made the Eight Signs of the Saaamaaa Ritual. The eighth place was, of course, empty; but ready for me to occupy at any moment; for I had omitted to make the Sealing Sign to that point, until I had finished all my preparations, and could enter the 'Inner Star'.

"I took a last look round the great hall, and saw that the two big hounds were lying quietly, with their noses between their paws. The fire was big and cheerful, and the candles before the two rows of doors, burnt steadily, as well as the solitary ones in the corners. Then I went round the little star of men, and warned them not to be frightened whatever happened; but to trust to the 'Defense', and to let *nothing* tempt or drive them to cross the Barriers. Also, I told them to watch their movements, and to keep their feet strictly to their places. For the rest, there was to be no shooting, unless I gave the word.

"And now at last, I went to my place, and, sitting down, made the Eighth Sign just beyond my feet. Then I arranged my camera and flashlight handy, and examined my revolver.

"Wentworth sat behind the First Sign, and as the numbering went round reversed, that put him next to me on my left. I asked him, in a low voice, how he felt; and he told me, rather nervous; but that he had confidence in my knowledge, and was resolved to go through with the matter, whatever happened.

"We settled down then to wait. There was no talking, except that, once or twice, the police bent towards one another, and whispered odd remarks concerning the hall... their whispers being queerly audible in the intense silence. But in a while there was not even a word from anyone, and only the monotonous drip, drip of the quiet rain without the great entrance, and the low, dull sound of the fire in the big fireplace.

"It was a queer group that we made sitting there, back to back, with our legs starred outwards; and all around us the strange, weak blue glow of the intertwining Pentacle, and beyond that the brilliant shining of the great ring of lighted candles. Outside of the glare of the candles, the large empty hall looked a little gloomy, by contrast, except where the lights shone before the sealed doors and in the corners; whilst the blaze of the big fire made a good honest mass of flame on the monster hearth. And the feeling of mystery! Can you picture it all?

"It might have been an hour later that it came to me suddenly that I was aware of an extraordinary sense of dreeness, as it were, come into the air of the place. Not the nervous feeling of mystery that had been with us all the time; but a new feeling, as if there were something going to happen any moment.

"Abruptly, there came a slight noise from the East end of the hall, and I felt the star of men move suddenly. 'Steady! Keep steady!' I said sharply, and they quietened. I looked up the hall, and saw that the dogs were upon their feet, and staring in an extraordinary fashion towards the great entrance. I turned and stared, also, and felt the men move as they craned their heads to look. Suddenly, the dogs set up a tremendous barking, and I glanced across to them, and found they were still 'pointing' for the big door way. They ceased their noise just as quickly, and seemed to be listening. In the same instant, I heard a faint chink of metal to my left, that set me staring at the hook which held the great door wide. It moved, even as I looked. Some invisible thing was meddling with it. A queer, sickening thrill went through me, and I felt all the men about me, stiffen and go rigid with intensity. I had a certainty of something impending; as it might be the impression of an invisible, but overwhelming, Presence. The hall was full of a queer silence, and not a sound came from the dogs. *Then, I saw the hook slowly raised from out of its hasp, without any visible thing touching it.* A sudden power of movement came to me. I raised my camera, with the flashlight fixed, and snapped it at the door. There came the great blare of the flashlight, and a simultaneous roar of barking from the two dogs.

"The intensity of the flash made all the place seem dark for some moments after, and in that time of darkness, I heard a jingle in the direction of the door, that made me strain to look. The effect of the bright light passed, and I could see clearly again. The great entrance door was being slowly closed. It shut with a sharp snick, and there followed a long silence, broken only by the whimpering of the dogs.

"I turned suddenly, and looked at Wentworth. He was looking at me.

" 'Just as it did before,' he whispered.

" 'Most extraordinary,' I said, and he nodded and looked round, nervously.

"The policemen were pretty quiet, and I judged that they were feeling rather worse than Wentworth; though, for that matter, you must not think that I was altogether natural; yet I have seen so much that is extraordinary, that I daresay I can keep my nerves steady longer than most people; at any rate, in that kind of thing.

"I looked over my shoulder at the men, and cautioned them, in a low voice, not to move outside of the Barriers, *whatever happened*; not even though the house should seem to be rocking and about to tumble on to them; for I knew well enough what some of the great Forces are capable of doing. Yet, unless it should prove to be one of the cases of the more terrible Saiitii Manifestations, we were almost certain of safety, so long as we kept to our order within the Pentacle.

"Perhaps an hour and a half passed, quietly, except when, once in a way, the dogs would whine distressfully. Presently, however, they ceased even from this, and I could see them lying on the floor with their paws over their noses, in a most peculiar fashion, and shivering visibly. The sight made me feel more serious, as you can understand.

"Suddenly, the candle in the corner furthest from the main door, went out. An instant later, Wentworth jerked my arm, and I saw that a candle before one of the sealed doors had been put out. I held my camera ready. Then, one after another, every candle about the hall was put out, and with such speed and irregularity, that I could never catch one in the actual act of being extinguished. Yet, for all that, I took a flashlight of the hall in general.

"There was a time in which I sat half-blinded by the great glare of the flash, and I blamed myself for not having remembered to bring a pair of smoked goggles, which I have sometimes used at these times. I had felt the men jump, at the sudden light, and I called out loud to them to sit quiet, and to keep their feet exactly to their proper places. My voice, as you can imagine, sounded rather horrid and frightening in the great, empty room, and altogether it was a beastly moment.

"Then, I was able to see again, and I stared round and round the hall; but there was nothing showing unusual; only, of course, it was dark now over in the corners.

"Suddenly, I saw that the great fire was blackening. It was going out visibly, as I looked. If I said that some monstrous, invisible, impossible Force sucked the life from it, I could best explain my impression of the way the light and flame went out of it. It was most extraordinary to watch. In the time that I stared at it, every vestige of fire disappeared, and there was no light outside of the ring of candles around the Pentacle.

"The deliberateness of the thing troubled me more than I can make clear to you. It conveyed to me such a sense of a calm, Deliberate Force present in the hall. The steadfast intention to 'make a darkness' was horrible. The *extent* of the Power to affect the Material was now the one constant, anxious questioning in my brain. You can understand?

"Behind me, I heard the policemen moving again, and I knew that they were getting thoroughly frightened. I turned half round, and told them, quietly but plainly, that they were safe only so long as they stayed within the Pentacle, in the position in which I had put them. If they once broke, and went outside of the Barrier, no knowledge of mine could state the full extent or dreadfulness of the danger.

"I steadied them up, by this quiet, straight reminder; but if they had known, as I knew, that there is no *certainty* in any 'Protection', they would have suffered a great deal more, and probably have broken the 'Defense' and made a mad, foolish run for an impossible safety.

"Another hour passed, after this, in an absolute quietness. I had a sense of awful strain and oppression, as if I were an infinitely insignificant spirit in the company of some invisible, brooding monster of the unseen world, who, as yet, was scarcely conscious of us. I leant across to Wentworth, and asked him in a whisper whether he had a feeling as if Something were in the room. He looked very pale, and his eyes kept always on the move. He glanced just once at me, and nodded; then stared away round the hall again.

"Abruptly, as though a hundred unseen hands had snuffed them, every candle in the barrier went dead out, and we were left in a darkness that seemed, for a little, absolute; for the light from the Pentacle was too weak and pale to penetrate far across the great hall.

"I tell you, for a moment, I just sat there as though I had been frozen solid. I felt the 'creep' go all over me, and seem to stop in my brain. I felt all at once to be given a power of hearing that was far beyond the normal. I could hear my own heart thudding most extraordinarily loud. I began, however, to feel better, after a little; but I simply had not the pluck to move. You can understand?

"Presently, I began to get my courage back. I gripped at my camera and flashlight, and waited. My hands were simply soaked with sweat. I glanced once at Wentworth. I could see him only dimly. His shoulders were hunched a little, his head forward; but though it was motionless, I knew that his eyes were not. It is queer how one knows that sort of thing at times. The police were just as silent. And in this way a while passed.

"A sound broke across the silence. From two sides of the room there came faint noises. I recognised them at once, as the breaking of the sealing-wax. *The sealed doors were opening.* I raised the camera and flashlight, and it was a peculiar mixture of fear and courage that helped me to press the button. As the great belch of light lit up the hall, I felt the men all about me, jump. The darkness fell like a clap of thunder, if you can understand, and seemed tenfold. Yet, in the moment of brightness, I had seen that all the sealed doors were wide open.

"Suddenly, all around us, there sounded a drip, drip drip, upon the floor of the great hall. I thrilled with a queer, realising emotion, and a sense of a very real and present danger—*imminent.* The 'blood-drip' had commenced. And the grim question was now whether the Barriers could save us from whatever had come into the huge room.

"Through some awful minutes the 'blood-drip' continued to fall in an increasing rain, and presently some began to fall within the Barriers. I saw several great drops splash and star upon the pale glowing intertwining tubes of the Electric Pentacle; but, strangely enough, I could not trace that any fell among us.

"Beyond the strange horrible noise of the 'drip', there was no other sound. And then, abruptly, from the boarhound over in the far corner, there came a terrible yelling howl of agony, followed instantly by a sickening, breaking noise, and an immediate silence. If you have ever, when out shooting, broken a rabbit's neck, you will know the sound that I mean—in miniature! Like lightning, the thought sprang into my brain:— IT *has crossed the pentacle.* For you will remember that I had made one about each of the dogs. I thought instantly, with a sick apprehension, of our own Barriers. There was something in the hall with us that had passed the barrier of the pentacle about one of the dogs. In the awful succeeding silence, I positively quivered. And suddenly, one of the men behind me, gave out a scream, like any woman, and bolted for the door. He fumbled, and had it open in a moment. I yelled to the others not to move; but they followed like sheep, and I heard them kick the candles flying, in their panic. One of them stepped on the Electric Pentacle and smashed it, and there was an utter darkness. In an instant, I realised that I was defenceless against the powers of the Unknown World, and with one savage leap I was out of the useless Barriers, and instantly through the great doorway, and into the night. I believe I yelled with sheer funk.

"The men were a little ahead of me, and I never ceased running, and neither did they. Sometimes, I glanced back over my shoulder; and I kept glancing into the laurels which grew all along the drive. The beastly things kept rustling, rustling in a hollow sort of way, as though something were keeping parallel with me, among them. The rain had stopped, and a dismal little wind kept moaning through the grounds. It was disgusting.

"I caught Wentworth and the police at the lodge gate. We got outside, and ran all the way to the village. We found old Dennis up, waiting for us, and half the Villagers to keep him company. He told us that he had known in his 'sowl' that we should come back—that is, if we came back at all; which is not a bad rendering of his remark.

"Fortunately, I had brought my camera away from the House— possibly because the strap had happened to be over my head. Yet, I did not go straight away to develop; but sat with the rest in the bar, where we talked for some hours, trying to be coherent about the whole horrible business.

"Later, however, I went up to my room, and proceeded with my photography. I was steadier now, and it was just possible, so I hoped, that the negatives might show something.

"On two of the plates, I found nothing unusual; but on the third, which was the first one that I snapped, I saw something that made me quite excited. I examined it very carefully with a magnifying-glass; then I put it to wash, and slipped a pair of rubber half shoes over my boots.

"The negative had shown me something very extraordinary, and I had made up my mind to test the truth of what it seemed to indicate, without losing another moment. It was no use telling anything to Wentworth and the police, until I was certain; and, also, I believed that I stood a greater chance to succeed by myself; though, for that matter, I do not suppose anything would have got them up to the Manor again that night.

"I took my revolver, and went quietly downstairs, and into the dark. The rain had commenced again; but that did not bother me. I walked hard. When I came to the lodge gates, a sudden, queer instinct stopped me from going through, and I climbed the wall into the park. I kept away from the drive, and approached the building through the dismal, dripping laurels. You can imagine how beastly it was. Every time a leaf rustled, I jumped.

"I made my way round to the back of the big House, and got in through a little window which I had taken note of during my search; for, of course, I knew the whole place now from roof to cellars. I went silently up the kitchen stairs, fairly quivering with funk; and at the top, I stepped to the left, and then into a long corridor that opened, through one of the doorways we had sealed, into the big hall. I looked up it, and saw a faint flicker of light away at the end; and I tip-toed silently towards it, holding my revolver ready. As I came near to the open door, I heard men's voices, and then a burst of laughing. I went on, until I could see into the hall. There were several men there, all in a group. They were well dressed, and one, at least, I saw was armed. They were examining my 'barriers' against the Supernatural, with a good deal of unkind laughter. I never felt such a fool in my life.

"It was plain to me that they were a gang of men who had made use of the empty Manor, perhaps for years, for some purpose of their own; and now that Wentworth was attempting to take possession, they were acting up to the traditions of the Place, with the view of driving him away, and keeping so useful a place still at their disposal. But what they were, I mean whether Coiners, Thieves, Inventors, or what—I could not imagine.

"Presently, they left the Pentacle, and gathered round the living boarhound, which seemed curiously quiet, as if it were half-drugged. There was some talk as to whether to let the poor brute live, or not; but finally they decided it would be good policy to kill it. I saw two of them force a twisted loop of rope into its mouth, and the two bights of the loop were brought together at the back of the hound's neck. Then a third man thrust a thick walking-stick through the two loops. The two men with the rope, stooped to hold the dog, so that I could not see what was done; but the poor beast gave a sudden awful howl, and immediately there was a repetition of the uncomfortable breaking sound, I had heard earlier in the night, as you will remember.

"The men stood up, and left the dog lying there—quiet enough now, as you may suppose. For my part, I fully appreciated the calculated remorselessness which had decided upon the animal's death, and the cold determination with which it had been afterwards executed so neatly. I guessed that a man who might get into the 'light' of these particular men, would be likely to come to quite as uncomfortable an ending.

"A minute later, one of them called out to the rest that they should 'shift the wires'. One of the men came towards the door-way of the corridor in which I stood, and I ran quickly back into the darkness of the upper end. I saw the man reach up, and take something from the top of the door, and I heard the slight, ringing jangle of steel-wire.

"When he had gone, I ran back again, and saw the men passing, one after another, through an opening in the stairs, formed by one of the marble steps being raised. When the last man had vanished, the slab that made the step was shut down, and there was not a sign of the secret door. It was the seventh step from the bottom, as I took care to count; and a splendid idea, for it was so solid that it did not ring hollow, even to a fairly heavy hammer, as I found later.

"There is little more to tell. I got out of the House as quickly and quietly as possible, and back to the inn. The Police came without any coaxing, when they knew the 'ghosts' were normal flesh and blood. We entered the Park and the Manor in the same way that I had done. Yet, when we tried to open the step, we failed, and had finally to smash it. This must have warned the haunters; for when we descended to a secret room which we found at the end of a long and narrow passage in the thickness of the walls, we found no one.

"The Police were horribly disgusted, as you can imagine; for they seemed tolerably certain that I had dropped on the meet-ing-place of a certain 'political' club much wanted by the author-ities; but for my part, I did not care either way. I had 'laid the ghost', as you might say, and that was what I set out to do. I was not particularly afraid of being laughed at by the others; for they had all been thoroughly 'taken in'; and in the end, I had scored, without their help.

"We searched right through the secret ways, and found that there was an exit, at the end of a long tunnel, which opened in the side of a well, out in the grounds. The ceiling of the hall was hollow, and reached by a little secret stairway inside of the big staircase. The 'blood-drip' was merely coloured water, dropped through the minute crevices of the ornamented ceiling. How the candles and the fire were put out, I do not know; for the haunters certainly did not act quite up to tradition, which held that the lights were put out by the 'blood-drip.' Perhaps it was too difficult to direct the fluid, without positively squirting it, which might have given the whole thing away. The candles and the fire may possibly have been extinguished by the agency of carbonic acid gas; but how suspended, I have no idea.

"The secret hiding places were, of course, ancient. There was also (did I tell you?) a bell which they had rigged up to ring, when anyone entered the gates at the end of the drive. If I had not climbed the wall, I should have found nothing for my pains; for the bell would have warned them, had I gone in through the gateway."

"What was on the negative?" I asked, with much curiosity.

"A picture of the fine wire with which they were grappling for the hook that held the entrance door open. They were doing it from one of the crevices in the ceiling. They had evidently made no preparations for lifting the hook. I suppose they never thought that anyone would make use of it, and so they had to improvise a grapple. The wire was too fine to be seen by the amount of light we had in the hall; but the flashlight 'picked it out'. Do you see?

"The opening of the inner doors was managed by wires, as you will have guessed, which they unshipped after use, or else I should soon have found them, when I made my search.

"I think I have now explained everything. The hound was killed, of course, by the men direct. You see, they made the place as dark as possible, first. Of course, if I had managed to take a flashlight just at that instant, the whole secret of the haunting would have been exposed. But Fate just ordered it the other way."

"And the tramps?" I asked.

"O, you mean the two tramps who were found dead in the Manor," said Carnacki. " Well, of course it is impossible to be sure, one way or the other. Perhaps they happened to find out something, and were given a hypodermic. Or it is quite as probable that they had come to the time of their dying, and just died naturally. It is conceivable that a great many tramps had slept in the old house, at one time or another."

Carnacki stood up, and knocked out his pipe. We rose also, and went for our coats and hats.

"Out you go!" said Carnacki, genially, using the recognised formula. And we went out on to the Embankment, and presently through the darkness to our various houses.

The Whistling Room

CARNACKI SHOOK A FRIENDLY fist at me, as I entered, late. Then, he opened the door into the dining room, and ushered the four of us—Jessop, Arkright, Taylor and myself—in to dinner.

We dined well, as usual, and, equally as usual, Carnacki was pretty silent during the meal. At the end, we took our wine and cigars to our accustomed positions, and Carnacki—having got himself comfortable in his big chair—began without any preliminary:—

"I have just got back from Ireland, again," he said. "And I thought you chaps would be interested to hear my news. Besides, I fancy I shall see the thing clearer, after I have told it all out straight. I must tell you this, though, at the beginning—up to the present moment, I have been utterly and completely 'stumped'. I have tumbled upon one of the most peculiar cases of 'haunting'—or devilment of some sort—that I have come against. Now listen.

"I have been spending the last few weeks at Iastrae Castle, about twenty miles North-East of Galway. I got a letter about a month ago from a Mr. Sid K. Tassoc, who it seemed had bought the place lately, and moved in, only to find that he had got a very peculiar piece of property.

"When I reached there, he met me at the station, driving a jaunting-car, and drove me up to the castle, which, by the way, he called a 'house-shanty'. I found that he was 'pigging it' there with his boy brother and another American, who seemed to be half-servant and half-companion. It appears that all the servants had left the place, in a body, as you might say; and now they were managing among themselves, assisted by some day-help.

"The three of them got together a scratch feed, and Tassoc told me all about the trouble, whilst we were at table. It is most

197

extraordinary, and different from anything that I have had to do with; though that Buzzing Case was very queer, too.

"Tassoc began right in the middle of his story. 'We've got a room in this shanty,' he said, 'which has got a most infernal whistling in it; sort of haunting it. The thing starts any time; you never know when, and it goes on until it frightens you. All the servants have gone, as I've told you. It's not ordinary whistling, and it isn't the wind. Wait till you hear it.'

" 'We're all carrying guns,' said the boy; and slapped his coat pocket.

" 'As bad as that?' I said; and the older brother nodded. 'I may be soft,' he replied; 'but wait till you've heard it. Sometimes I think it's some infernal thing, and the next moment, I'm just as sure that someone's playing a trick on us.'

" 'Why?' I asked. 'What is to be gained?'

" 'You mean,' he said, 'that people usually have some good reason for playing tricks as elaborate as this. Well, I'll tell you. There's a lady in this province, by the name of Miss Donnehue, who's going to be my wife, this day two months. She's more beautiful than they make them, and so far as I can see, I've just stuck my head into an Irish hornet's nest. There's about a score of hot young Irishmen been courting her these two years gone, and now that I've come along and cut them out, they feel raw against me. Do you begin to understand the possibilities?'

" 'Yes,' I said. 'Perhaps I do in a vague sort of way; but I don't see how all this affects the room?'

" 'Like this,' he said. 'When I'd fixed it up with Miss Donnehue, I looked out for a place, and bought this little house-shanty. Afterwards, I told her—one evening during dinner, that I'd decided to tie up here. And then she asked me whether I wasn't afraid of the whistling room. I told her it must have been thrown in gratis, as I'd heard nothing about it. There were some of her men friends present, and I saw a smile go round. I found out, after a bit of questioning, that several people have bought this place during the last twenty odd years. And it was always on the market again, after a trial.

" 'Well, the chaps started to bait me a bit, and offered to take bets after dinner that I'd not stay six months in this shanty. I looked once or twice to Miss Donnehue, so as to be sure I was "getting the note" of the talkee-talkee; but I could see that she didn't take it as a joke, at all. Partly, I think, because there was a bit of a sneer in the way the men were tackling me, and partly because she really believes there is something in this yarn of the whistling room.

" 'However, after dinner, I did what I could to even things up with the others. I nailed all their bets, and screwed them down good and safe. I guess some of them are going to be hard hit, unless I lose; which I don't mean to. Well, there you have practically the whole yarn.'

" 'Not quite,' I told him. 'All that I know, is that you have bought a castle, with a room in it that is in some way "queer", and that you've been doing some betting. Also, I know that your servants have got frightened, and run away. Tell me something about the whistling?'

" 'O, that!' said Tassoc; 'that started the second night we were in. I'd had a good look round the room in the daytime, as you can understand; for the talk up at Arlestrae—Miss Donnehue's place— had made me wonder a bit. But it seems just as usual as some of the other rooms in the old wing, only perhaps a bit more lonesome feeling. But that may be only because of the talk about it, you know.

" 'The whistling started about ten o'clock, on the second night, as I said. Tom and I were in the library, when we heard an awfully queer whistling, coming along the East Corridor— The room is in the East Wing, you know.

" 'That's that blessed ghost!' I said to Tom, and we collared the lamps off the table, and went up to have a look. I tell you, even as we dug along the corridor, it took me a bit in the throat, it was so beastly queer. It was a sort of tune, in a way; but more as if a devil or some rotten thing were laughing at you, and going to get round at your back. That's how it makes you feel.

" 'When we got to the door, we didn't wait; but rushed it open; and then I tell you the sound of the thing fairly hit me in the face. Tom said he got it the same way— Sort of felt stunned and bewildered. We looked all round, and soon got so nervous, we just cleared out, and I locked the door.

" 'We came down here, and had a stiff peg each. Then we landed fit again, and began to feel we'd been nicely had. So we took sticks, and went out into the grounds, thinking after all it must be some of these confounded Irishmen working the ghost-trick on us. But there was not a leg stirring.

" 'We went back into the house, and walked over it, and then paid another visit to the room. But we simply couldn't stand it. We fairly ran out, and locked the door again. I don't know how to put it into words; but I had a feeling of being up against something that was rottenly dangerous. You know! We've carried our guns ever since.

" 'Of course, we had a real turn-out of the room next day, and the whole house-place; and we even hunted round the grounds; but there was nothing queer. And now I don't know what to think; except that the sensible part of me tells me that it's some plan of these Wild Irishmen to try to take a rise out of me.'

" 'Done anything since?' I asked him.

" 'Yes,' he said— 'Watched outside of the door of the room at nights, and chased round the grounds, and sounded the walls and floor of the room. We've done everything we could think of; and it's beginning to get on our nerves; so we sent for you.'

"By this, we had finished eating. As we rose from the table, Tassoc suddenly called out:— 'Ssh! Hark!'

"We were instantly silent, listening. Then I heard it, an extraordinary hooning whistle, monstrous and inhuman, coming from far away through corridors to my right.

" 'By God! said Tassoc; 'and it's scarcely dark yet! Collar those candles, both of you, and come along.'

"In a few moments, we were all out of the door and racing up the stairs. Tassoc turned into a long corridor, and we followed, shielding our candles as we ran. The sound seemed to fill all the passage as we drew near, until I had the feeling that the whole air throbbed under the power of some wanton Immense Force—a sense of an actual taint, as you might say, of monstrosity all about us.

"Tassoc unlocked the door; then, giving it a push with his foot, jumped back, and drew his revolver. As the door flew open, the sound beat out at us, with an effect impossible to explain to one who has not heard it—with a certain, horrible personal note in it; as if in there in the darkness you could picture the room rocking and creaking in a mad, vile glee to its own filthy piping and whistling and hooning; and yet all the time aware of you in particular. To stand there and listen, was to be stunned by Realisation. It was as if someone showed you the mouth of a vast pit suddenly, and said:— That's Hell. And you *knew* that they had spoken the truth. Do you get it, even a little bit?

"I stepped a pace into the room, and held the candle over my head, and looked quickly round. Tassoc and his brother joined me, and the man came up at the back, and we all held our candles high.

I was deafened with the shrill, piping hoon of the whistling; and then, clear in my ear, something seemed to be saying to me:— 'Get out of here—quick! Quick! Quick!'

"As you chaps know, I never neglect that sort of thing. Sometimes it may be nothing but nerves; but as you will remember, it was just such a warning that saved me in the 'Grey Dog' Case, and in the 'Yellow Finger' Experiments; as well as other times. Well, I turned sharp round to the others: 'Out!' I said. 'For God's sake, *out* quick!' And in an instant I had them into the passage.

"There came an extraordinary yelling scream into the hideous whistling, and then, like a clap of thunder, an utter silence. I slammed the door, and locked it. Then, taking the key, I looked round at the others.

"They were pretty white, and I imagine I must have looked that way too. And there we stood a moment, silent.

" 'Come down out of this, and have some whisky,' said Tassoc, at last, in a voice he tried to make ordinary; and he led the way. I was the back man, and I knew we all kept looking over our shoulders. When we got down-stairs, Tassoc passed the bottle round. He took a drink, himself, and slapped his glass on to the table. Then sat down with a thud.

" 'That's a lovely thing to have in the house with you, isn't it!' he said. And directly afterwards:— 'What on earth made you hustle us all out like that, Carnacki?'

" 'Something seemed to be telling me to get out, *quick*,' I said. 'Sounds a bit silly-superstitious, I know; but when you are meddling with this sort of thing, you've got to take notice of queer fancies, and risk being laughed at.'

"I told him then about the 'Grey Dog' business, and he nodded a lot to that. 'Of course,' I said, 'this may be nothing more than those would-be rivals of yours playing some funny game; but, personally, though I'm going to keep an open mind, I feel that there is something beastly and dangerous about this thing.'

"We talked for a while longer, and then Tassoc suggested billiards, which we played in a pretty half-hearted fashion, and all the time cocking an ear to the door, as you might say, for sounds; but none came, and later, after coffee, he suggested early bed, and a thorough overhaul of the room on the morrow.

"My bedroom was in the newer part of the castle, and the door opened into the picture gallery. At the East end of the gallery was the entrance to the corridor of the East Wing; this was shut off from the gallery by two old and heavy oak doors, which looked rather odd and quaint beside the more modern doors of the various rooms.

"When I reached my room, I did not go to bed; but began to unpack my instrument-trunk, of which I had retained the key. I intended to take one or two preliminary steps at once, in my investigation of the extraordinary whistling.

"Presently, when the castle had settled into quietness, I slipped out of my room, and across to the entrance of the great corridor. I opened one of the low, squat doors, and threw the beam of my pocket search-light down the passage. It was empty, and I went through the doorway, and pushed-to the oak behind me. Then along the great passageway, throwing my light before and behind, and keeping my revolver handy.

"I had hung a 'protection belt' of garlic round my neck, and the smell of it seemed to fill the corridor and give me assurance; for, as you all know, it is a wonderful 'protection' against the more usual Aeiirii forms of semi-materialisation, by which I supposed the whistling might be produced; though, at that period of my investigation, I was still quite prepared to find it due to some perfectly natural cause; for it is astonishing the enormous number of cases that prove to have nothing abnormal in them.

"In addition to wearing the necklet, I had plugged my ears loosely with garlic, and as I did not intend to stay more than a few minutes in the room, I hoped to be safe.

"When I reached the door, and put my hand into my pocket for the key, I had a sudden feeling of sickening funk. But I was not going to back out, if I could help it. I unlocked the door and turned the handle. Then I gave the door a sharp push with my foot, as Tassoc had done, and drew my revolver, though I did not expect to have any use for it, really.

"I shone the searchlight all round the room, and then stepped inside, with a disgustingly horrible feeling of walking slap into a waiting Danger. I stood a few seconds, expectant, and nothing happened, and the empty room showed bare from corner to corner. And then, you know, I realised that the room was full of an abominable silence; can you understand that? A sort of purposeful silence, just as sickening as any of the filthy noises the Things have power to make. Do you remember what I told you about that 'Silent Garden' business? Well, this room had just that same *malevolent* silence—the beastly quietness of a thing that is looking at you and not seeable itself, and thinks that it has got you. O, I recognised it instantly, and I whipped the top off my lantern, so as to have light over the *whole* room.

"Then I set-to, working like fury, and keeping my glance all about me. I sealed the two windows with lengths of human hair, right across, and sealed them at every frame. As I worked, a queer, scarcely perceptible tenseness stole into the air of the place, and the silence seemed, if you can understand me, to grow more solid. I knew then that I had no business there without 'full protection'; for I was practically certain that this was no mere Aeiirii development; but one of the worse forms, as the Saiitii; like that 'Grunting Man' case—you know.

"I finished the window, and hurried over to the great fire-place. This is a huge affair, and has a queer gallows-iron, I think they are called, projecting from the back of the arch. I sealed the opening with seven human hairs—the seventh crossing the six others.

"Then, just as I was making an end, a low, mocking whistle grew in the room. A cold, nervous prickling went up my spine, and round my forehead from the back. The hideous sound filled all the room with an extraordinary, grotesque parody of human whistling, too gigantic to be human—as if something gargantuan and monstrous made the sounds softly. As I stood there a last moment, pressing down the final seal, I had little doubt but that I had come across one of those rare and horrible cases of the *Inanimate* reproducing the functions of the *Animate*. I made a grab for my lamp, and went quickly to the door, looking over my shoulder, and listening for the thing that I expected. It came, just as I got my hand upon the handle—a squeal of incredible, malevolent anger, piercing through the low hooning of the whistling. I dashed out, slamming the door and locking it.

"I leant a little against the opposite wall of the corridor, feeling rather funny; for it had been a hideously narrow squeak.... 'Theyr be noe sayfetie to be gained bye gayrds of holiness when the monyster hath pow'r to speak throe woode and stoene.' So runs the passage in the Sigsand MS., and I proved it in that 'Nodding Door' business. There is no protection against this particular form of monster, except, possibly, for a fractional period of time; for it can reproduce itself in, or take to its purposes, the very protective material which you may use, and has power to '*forme* wythine the pentycle'; though not immediately. There is, of course, the possibility of the Unknown Last Line of the Saaamaaa Ritual being uttered; but it is too uncertain to count upon, and the danger is too hideous; and even then it has no power to protect for more than 'maybee fyve beats of the harte', as the Sigsand has it.

"Inside of the room, there was now a constant, meditative, hooning whistling; but presently this ceased, and the silence seemed worse; for there is such a sense of hidden mischief in a silence.

"After a little, I sealed the door with crossed hairs, and then cleared off down the great passage, and so to bed.

"For a long time I lay awake; but managed eventually to get some sleep. Yet, about two o'clock I was waked by the hooning whistling of the room coming to me, even through the closed doors. The sound was tremendous, and seemed to beat through the whole house with a presiding sense of terror. As if (I remember thinking) some monstrous giant had been holding mad carnival with itself at the end of that great passage.

"I got up and sat on the edge of the bed, wondering whether to go along and have a look at the seal; and suddenly there came a thump on my door, and Tassoc walked in, with his dressing-gown over his pyjamas.

" 'I thought it would have waked you, so I came along to have a talk,' he said. 'I can't sleep. Beautiful! Isn't it!'

" 'Extraordinary!' I said, and tossed him my case.

"He lit a cigarette, and we sat and talked for about an hour; and all the time that noise went on, down at the end of the big corridor.

"Suddenly, Tassoc stood up:—

" 'Let's take our guns, and go and examine the brute,' he said, and turned towards the door.

" 'No!' I said. 'By Jove—NO! I can't say anything definite, yet; but I believe that room is about as dangerous as it well can be.'

" 'Haunted—*really* haunted?' he asked, keenly and without any of his frequent banter.

"I told him, of course, that I could not say a definite *yes* or *no* to such a question; but that I hoped to be able to make a statement, soon. Then I gave him a little lecture on the False Re-Materialisation of the Animate-Force through the Inanimate-Inert. He began then to understand the particular way in which the room might be dangerous, if it were really the subject of a manifestation.

"About an hour later, the whistling ceased quite suddenly, and Tassoc went off again to bed. I went back to mine, also, and eventually got another spell of sleep.

"In the morning, I walked along to the room. I found the seals on the door intact. Then I went in. The window seals and the hair were all right; but the seventh hair across the great fireplace was broken. This set me thinking. I knew that it might, very possibly, have snapped, through my having tensioned it too highly; but then, again, it might have been broken by something else. Yet, it was scarcely possible that a man, for instance, could have passed between the six unbroken hairs; for no one would ever have noticed them, entering the room that way, you see; but just walked through them, ignorant of their very existence.

"I removed the other hairs, and the seals. Then I looked up the chimney. It went up straight, and I could see blue sky at the top. It was a big, open flue, and free from any suggestion of hiding places, or corners. Yet, of course, I did not trust to any such casual examination, and after breakfast, I put on my overalls, and climbed to the very top, sounding all the way; but I found nothing.

"Then I came down, and went over the whole of the room—floor, ceiling, and walls, mapping them out in six-inch squares, and sounding with both hammer and probe. But there was nothing unusual.

"Afterwards, I made a three-weeks' search of the whole castle, in the same thorough way; but found nothing. I went even further, then; for at night, when the whistling commenced, I made a microphone test. You see, if the whistling were mechanically produced, this test would have made evident to me the working of the machinery, if there were any such concealed within the walls. It certainly was an up-to-date method of examination, as you must allow.

"Of course, I did not think that any of Tassoc's rivals had fixed up any mechanical contrivance; but I thought it just possible that there had been some such thing for producing the whistling, made away back in the years, perhaps with the intention of giving the room a reputation that would insure its being free of inquisitive folk. You see what I mean? Well, of course, it was just possible, if this were the case, that someone knew the secret of the machinery, and was utilizing the knowledge to play this devil of a prank on Tassoc. The microphone test of the walls would certainly have made this known to me, as I have said; but there was nothing of the sort in the castle; so that I had practically no doubt at all now, but that it was a genuine case of what is popularly termed 'haunting'.

"All this time, every night, and sometimes most of each night, the hooning whistling of the Room was intolerable. It was as if an

Intelligence there, knew that steps were being taken against it, and piped and hooned in a sort of mad, mocking contempt. I tell you, it was as extraordinary as it was horrible. Time after time, I went along—tip-toeing noiselessly on stockinged feet—to the sealed door (for I always kept the Room sealed). I went at all hours of the night, and often the whistling, inside, would seem to change to a brutally jeering note, as though the half-animate monster saw me plainly through the shut door. And all the time, as I would stand, watching, the hooning of the whistling would seem to fill the whole corridor, so that I used to feel a precious lonely chap, messing about there with one of Hell's mysteries.

"And every morning, I would enter the room, and examine the different hairs and seals. You see, after the first week, I had stretched parallel hairs all along the walls of the room, and along the ceiling; but over the floor, which was of polished stone, I had set out little, colourless wafers, tacky-side uppermost. Each wafer was numbered, and they were arranged after a definite plan, so that I should be able to trace the exact movements of any living thing that went across.

"You will see that no material being or creature could possibly have entered that room, without leaving many signs to tell me about it. But nothing was ever disturbed, and I began to think that I should have to risk an attempt to stay a night in the room, in the Electric Pentacle. Mind you, I *knew* that it would be a crazy thing to do; but I was getting stumped, and ready to try anything.

"Once, about midnight, I did break the seal on the door, and have a quick look in; but, I tell you, the whole Room gave one mad yell, and seemed to come towards me in a great belly of shadows, as if the walls had bellied in towards me. Of course, that must have been fancy. Anyway, the yell was sufficient, and I slammed the door, and locked it, feeling a bit weak down my spine. I wonder whether you know the feeling.

"And then, when I had got to that state of readiness for anything, I made what, at first, I thought was something of a discovery:—

"It was about one in the morning, and I was walking slowly round the castle, keeping in the soft grass. I had come under the shadow of the East Front, and far above me, I could hear the vile, hooning whistling of the Room, up in the darkness of the unlit wing. Then, suddenly, a little in front of me, I heard a man's voice, speaking low, but evidently in glee:—

" 'By George! You Chaps; but I wouldn't care to bring a wife home to that!' it said, in the tone of the cultured Irish.

"Someone started to reply; but there came a sharp exclamation, and then a rush, and I heard footsteps running in all directions. Evidently, the men had spotted me.

"For a few seconds, I stood there, feeling an awful ass. After all, *they* were at the bottom of the haunting! Do you see what a big fool it made me seem? I had no doubt but that they were some of Tassoc's rivals; and here I had been feeling in every bone that I had hit a genuine Case! And then, you know, there came the memory of hundreds of details, that made me just as much in doubt, again. Anyway, whether it was natural, or ab-natural, there was a great deal yet to be cleared up.

"I told Tassoc, next morning, what I had discovered, and through the whole of every night, for five nights, we kept a close watch round the East Wing; but there was never a sign of anyone prowling about; and all the time, almost from evening to dawn, that grotesque whistling would hoon incredibly, far above us in the darkness.

"On the morning after the fifth night, I received a wire from here, which brought me home by the next boat. I explained to Tassoc that I was simply bound to come away for a few days; but told him to keep up the watch round the castle. One thing I was very careful to do, and that was to make him absolutely promise never to go into the Room, between sunset and sunrise. I made it clear to him that we knew nothing definite yet, one way or the other; and if the room were what I had first thought it to be, it might be a lot better for him to die first, than enter it after dark.

"When I got here, and had finished my business, I thought you chaps would be interested; and also I wanted to get it all spread out clear in my mind; so I rang you up. I am going over again to-morrow, and when I get back, I ought to have something pretty extraordinary to tell you. By the way, there is a curious thing I forgot to tell you. I tried to get a phonographic record of the whistling; but it simply produced no impression on the wax at all. That is one of the things that has made me feel queer.

"Another extraordinary thing is that the microphone will not magnify the sound—will not even transmit it; seems to take no account of it, and acts as if it were nonexistent. I am absolutely and utterly stumped, up to the present. I am a wee bit curious to see whether any of your dear clever heads can make daylight of it. *I* cannot—not yet."

He rose to his feet.

"Good-night, all," he said, and began to usher us out abruptly, but without offence, into the night.

A fortnight later, he dropped us each a card, and you can imagine that I was not late this time. When we arrived, Carnacki took us straight into dinner, and when we had finished, and all made ourselves comfortable, he began again, where he had left off:—

"Now just listen quietly; for I have got something very queer to tell you. I got back late at night, and I had to walk up to the castle, as I had not warned them that I was coming. It was bright moonlight; so that the walk was rather a pleasure, than otherwise. When I got there, the whole place was in darkness, and I thought I would go round outside, to see whether Tassoc or his brother was keeping watch. But I could not find them anywhere, and concluded that they had got tired of it, and gone off to bed.

"As I returned across the lawn that lies below the front of the East Wing, I caught the hooning whistling of the Room, coming down strangely clear through the stillness of the night. It had a peculiar note in it, I remember—low and constant, queerly meditative. I looked up at the window, bright in the moonlight, and got a sudden thought to bring a ladder from the stable-yard, and try to get a look into the Room, from the outside.

"With this notion, I hunted round at the back of the castle, among the straggle of offices, and presently found a long, fairly light ladder; though it was heavy enough for one, goodness knows! I thought at first that I should never get it reared. I managed at last, and let the ends rest very quietly against the wall, a little below the sill of the larger window. Then, going silently, I went up the ladder. Presently, I had my face above the sill, and was looking in, alone with the moonlight.

"Of course, the queer whistling sounded louder up there; but it still conveyed that peculiar sense of something whistling quietly to itself—can you understand? Though, for all the meditative lowness of the note, the horrible, gargantuan quality was distinct—a mighty parody of the human; as if I stood there and listened to the whistling from the lips of a monster with a man's soul.

"And then, you know, I saw something. The floor in the middle of the huge, empty room, was puckered upwards in the centre into a strange, soft-looking mound, parted at the top into an everchanging hole, that pulsated to that great, gentle hooning. At times, as I watched, I saw the heaving of the indented mound, gap across with a queer, inward suction, as with the drawing of an enormous breath; then the thing would dilate and pout once more to the incredible melody. And suddenly, as I stared, dumb, it came to me that the thing was living. I was looking at two enormous, blackened lips, blistered and brutal, there in the pale moonlight....

"Abruptly, they bulged out to a vast, pouting mound of force and sound, stiffened and swollen, and hugely massive and clean-cut in the moonbeams. And a great sweat lay heavy on the vast upper-lip. In the same moment of time, the whistling had burst into a mad screaming note, that seemed to stun me, even where I stood, outside of the window. And then, the following moment, I was staring blankly at the solid, undisturbed floor of the room—smooth, polished stone flooring, from wall to wall. And there was an absolute silence.

"You can picture me staring into the quiet Room, and knowing what I knew. I felt like a sick, frightened child, and I wanted to slide *quietly* down the ladder, and run away. But in that very instant, I heard Tassoc's voice calling to me from within the Room, for help, *help*. My God! but I got such an awful dazed feeling; and I had a vague, bewildered notion that, after all, it was the Irishmen who had got him in there, and were taking it out of him. And then the call came again, and I burst the window, and jumped in to help him. I had a confused idea that the call had come from within the shadow of the great fireplace, and I raced across to it; but there was no one there.

" 'Tassoc!' I shouted, and my voice went empty-sounding round the great apartment; and then, in a flash, *I knew that Tassoc had never called*. I whirled round, sick with fear, towards the window, and as I did so, a frightful, exultant whistling scream burst through the Room. On my left, the end wall had bellied-in towards me, in a pair of gargantuan lips, black and utterly monstrous, to within a yard of my face. I fumbled for a mad instant at my revolver; not for *it*, but myself; for the danger was a thousand times worse than death. And then, suddenly, the Unknown Last Line of the Saaamaaa Ritual was whispered quite audibly in the room. Instantly, the thing happened that I have known once before. There came a sense as of dust falling continually and monotonously, and I knew that my life hung uncertain and suspended for a flash, in a brief, reeling vertigo of unseeable things. Then *that* ended, and I knew that I might live. My soul and body blended again, and life and power came to me. I dashed furiously at the window, and hurled myself out head-foremost; for I can tell you that I had stopped being afraid of death. I crashed down on to the ladder, and slithered, grabbing and grabbing; and so came some way or other alive to the bottom. And there I sat in the soft, wet grass, with the moonlight all about me; and far above, through the broken window of the Room, there was a low whistling.

"That is the chief of it. I was not hurt, and I went round to the front, and knocked Tassoc up. When they let me in, we had a long yarn, over some good whisky—for I was shaken to pieces—and I explained things as much as I could. I told Tassoc that the room would have to come down, and every fragment of it be burned in a blast-furnace, erected within a pentacle. He nodded. There was nothing to say. Then I went to bed.

"We turned a small army on to the work, and within ten days, that lovely thing had gone up in smoke, and what was left was calcined, and clean.

"It was when the workmen were stripping the panelling, that I got hold of a sound notion of the beginnings of that beastly development. Over the great fireplace, after the great oak panels had been torn down, I found that there was let into the masonry a scrollwork of stone, with on it an old inscription, in ancient Celtic, that here in this room was burned Dian Tiansay, Jester of King Alzof, who made the Song of Foolishness upon King Ernore of the Seventh Castle.

"When I got the translation clear, I gave it to Tassoc. He was tremendously excited; for he knew the old tale, and took me down to the library to look at an old parchment that gave the story in detail. Afterwards, I found that the incident was well-known about the countryside; but always regarded more as a legend, than as history. And no one seemed ever to have dreamt that the old East Wing of Iastrae Castle was the remains of the ancient Seventh Castle.

"From the old parchment, I gathered that there had been a pretty dirty job done, away back in the years. It seems that King Alzof and King Ernore had been enemies by birthright, as you might say truly; but that nothing more than a little raiding had occurred on either side for years, until Dian Tiansay made the Song of Foolishness upon King Ernore, and sang it before King Alzof; and so greatly was it appreciated that King Alzof gave the jester one of his ladies, to wife.

"Presently, all the people of the land had come to know the song, and so it came at last to King Ernore, who was so angered that he made war upon his old enemy, and took and burned him and his castle; but Dian Tiansay, the jester, he brought with him to his own place, and having torn his tongue out because of the song which he had made and sung, he imprisoned him in the Room in the East Wing (which was evidently used for unpleasant purposes), and the jester's wife, he kept for himself, having a fancy for her prettiness.

"But one night, Dian Tiansay's wife was not to be found, and in the morning they discovered her lying dead in her husband's arms, and he sitting, whistling the Song of Foolishness, for he had no longer the power to sing it.

"Then they roasted Dian Tiansay, in the great fireplace—probably from that selfsame 'gallows-iron' which I have already mentioned. And until he died, Dian Tiansay 'ceased not to whistle' the Song of Foolishness, which he could no longer sing. But afterwards, 'in that room' there was often heard at night the sound of something whistling; and there 'grew a power in that room', so that none dared to sleep in it.

And presently, it would seem, the King went to another castle; for the whistling troubled him.

"There you have it all. Of course, that is only a rough rendering of the translation from the parchment. It's a bit quaint! Don't you think so?"

"Yes," I said, answering for the lot. "But how did the thing grow to such a tremendous manifestation?"

"One of those cases of continuity of thought producing a positive action upon the immediate surrounding material," replied Carnacki. "The development must have been going forward through centuries, to have produced such a monstrosity. It was a true instance of Saiitii manifestation, which I can best explain by likening it to a living spiritual fungus, which involves the very structure of the aether-fibre itself, and, of course, in so doing, acquires an essential control over the 'material-substance' involved in it. It is impossible to make it plainer in a few words."

"What broke the seventh hair?" asked Taylor.

But Carnacki did not know. He thought it was probably nothing but being too severely tensioned. He also explained that they found out that the men who had run away, had not been up to mischief; but had come over secretly, merely to hear the whistling, which, indeed, had suddenly become the talk of the whole countryside.

"One other thing," said Arkright, "have you any idea what governs the use of the Unknown Last Line of the Saaamaaa Ritual? I know, of course, that it was used by the Ab-human Priests in the Incantation of Raaaee; but what used it on your behalf, and what made it?"

"You had better read Harzam's Monograph, and my Addenda to it, on Astral and 'Astarral' Co-ordination and Interference," said Carnacki. "It is an extraordinary subject, and I can only say here that the human-vibration may not be insulated from the 'astarral' (as is always believed to be the case, in interferences by the Ab-human), without immediate action being taken by those Forces which govern the spinning of the outer circle. In other words, it is being proved, time after time, that there is some inscrutable Protective Force constantly intervening between the human-soul (not the body, mind you), and the Outer Monstrosities. Am I clear?"

"Yes, I think so," I replied. "And you believe that the Room had become the material expression of the ancient Jester—that his soul, rotted with hatred, had bred into a monster—eh?" I asked.

"Yes," said Carnacki, nodding. "I think you've put my thought rather neatly. It is a queer coincidence that Miss Donnehue is supposed to be descended (so I have heard since) from the same King Ernore. It makes one think some rather curious thoughts, doesn't it? The marriage coming on, and the Room waking to fresh life. If she had gone into that room, ever... eh? IT had waited a long time. Sins of the fathers. Yes, I've thought of that. They're to be married next week, and I am to be best man, which is a thing I hate. And he won his bets, rather! Just think, *if* ever she had gone into that room. Pretty horrible, eh?"

He nodded his head, grimly, and we four nodded back. Then he rose and took us collectively to the door, and presently thrust us forth in friendly fashion on to the Embankment, and into the fresh night air.

"Good night," we all called back, and went to our various homes.

If she had, eh? If she had? That is what I kept thinking.

The Searcher of the End House

I T WAS STILL EVENING, as I remember, and the four of us, Jessop, Arkright, Taylor and I, looked disappointedly at Carnacki, where he sat silent in his great chair.

We had come in response to the usual card of invitation, which—as you know—we have come to consider as a sure prelude to a good story; and now, after telling us the short incident of the Three Straw Platters, he had lapsed into a contented silence, and the night not half gone, as I have hinted.

However, as it chanced, some pitying fate jogged Carnacki's elbow, or his memory, and he began again, in his queer level way:—

"This 'Straw Platters' business reminds me, you know, of the 'Searcher' Case, which I have sometimes thought might interest you.

It was some time ago, in fact a deuce of a long time ago, that the thing happened; and my experience of what I might term 'curious' things was very small indeed.

"I was living with my Mother, when it occurred, in a small house just outside of Appledorn, on the South Coast. The house was the last of a row of detached cottage-villas, I might call them, each house standing in its own garden; and very dainty little places they were, exceedingly old, and most of them smothered in roses; and all, you know, with those quaint, leaded windows, and the doors built of genuine oak. You must just try to picture them for the sake of their complete niceness.

"Now I must remind you at the beginning, that my Mother and I had lived in that little house for two years, and in the whole of that time there had not been a single thing peculiar to worry us.

213

"And then, you know, something happened.

"It was about two o'clock one morning, just as I was finishing some letters, that I heard the door of my Mother's bedroom open, and she came to the top of the stairs, and knocked on the banisters.

" 'All right, dear,' I called; for I supposed that she was merely reminding me that I should have been in bed long ago; then I heard her go back to her room, and I hurried my work, for fear that she should lie awake, until she had heard me safe up to my room.

"When I was finished, I lit my candle, put out the lamp, and went upstairs. As I came opposite to the door of my Mother's room, I saw that it was open, and called good-night to her, very softly, and asked whether I should close the door.

"As there was no answer, I knew that she had dropped over again to sleep, and I closed the door very gently, and turned into my room, just across the passage. As I did so, I had a momentary, half-aware sense that there was a faint, peculiar, disagreeable odour in the passage; but it was not until the following night that I *realised* that I had seemed to smell something that offended me. You follow me, don't you? I mean, it is so often like that—one suddenly knows about a thing that really recorded itself on one's consciousness, perhaps a year before.

"The next morning at breakfast, I mentioned casually to my Mother that she had 'dropped-off', and that I had shut her door for her. But, to my surprise, she assured me that she had never been out of her room. I reminded her about the two raps that she had given upon the banister; but she was still certain that I must be mistaken; and in the end I teased her that she had got so accustomed to my bad habit of sitting up late, that she had come to call me in her sleep. Of course, she denied this, and I let the matter drop; but I was more than a little puzzled, and did not know whether to believe my own explanation, or to take the Mater's, which was to put the noises to the blame of mice, and the open door to the fact that she may not have properly latched it when she went to bed. I suppose, away in the subconscious part of me, I had a stirring of less reasonable-seeming thoughts; but certainly, I had no knowledge of real uneasiness at that time.

"Then, the next night there came a further development, for about two-thirty a.m., I heard my Mother's door open, exactly as on the previous night, and immediately afterward she rapped sharply, on the banister, as it seemed to me. I stopped my work a moment, and called up to her that I would not be long; but as she made no reply, and I did not hear her go back to bed, I had a quick wonder whether she might not be doing it in her sleep, after all, just as I had said.

"With the thought, I stood up, and taking the lamp from the table, began to go towards the door, which was open into the passage. And then, you know, I got a sudden nasty sort of thrill; for it came to me, all at once, that my Mother never knocked, when I had sat up too late, but called. But you will understand that I was not really frightened in any way; only vaguely uneasy, and pretty sure that she must be really doing the thing in her sleep.

"I went up the stairs quickly, and when I had come to the top, my Mother was not there; but her door was open. I had a little bewildered sense that she must have gone quietly back to bed, after all, without my hearing her; but, for all that I thought I believed this, I was pretty quick into her room. Yet, when I got there, she was sleeping quietly and naturally; for the vague sense of trouble in me was sufficiently strong to make me go over to look at her, to make certain.

"When I was sure that she was perfectly right in every way, I was still a little bothered; but much more inclined to believe that my suspicion was right and that she had got quietly back to bed in her sleep, without waking to know what she had been doing. This was the most reasonable thing to think, as you must see.

"And then, it came to me, suddenly, that there was a vague, queer, mildewy smell in the room; and it was in that instant that I became aware that I had smelt the same strange, uncertain smell the night before, in the passage, as you remember.

"I was definitely uneasy now, and began quietly to search my Mother's room; though with no aim or clear thought of anything, except to assure myself that there was nothing in the room. And all the time, you know, I never *expected really* to find anything; only that my uneasiness had to be reassured.

"In the middle of my search round, my Mother woke up, and of course I had to explain. I told her about her door opening, and then the knocks on the banister, and that I had come up and found her asleep. I said nothing about the smell, which was not very distinct; but told her that the thing happening twice had made me a bit nervous, and possibly fanciful, and that I thought I would take a look about, just to feel satisfied.

"I have thought since then that the reason I made no mention of the smell, was not only that I did not want to make my Mother feel frightened—for I was scarcely that way myself—but because I had a vague half-knowledge that I associated the smell with fancies too indefinite and peculiar to bear talking about. You will understand that I am able *now* to analyse and put the thing into words; but *then* I did not even know my chief reason for saying nothing; let alone appreciate its possible significance. You follow me?

"It was my Mother, after all, who put part of my vague sensations into words:—

" 'What a disagreeable smell,' she exclaimed, and was silent a moment, looking at me. Then:— 'You feel that there's something wrong,' still looking at me, very quiet, you know; but with a little, questioning, nervous note of expectancy.

" 'I don't know,' I said. 'I can't understand it, unless you've really been walking about in your sleep.'

" 'But the smell,' she said.

" 'Yes,' I replied. 'That's what puzzles me, too. I'll have a walk through the house; though I don't suppose it's anything.'

"I lit her candle, and then taking the lamp, I went through the two other bedrooms, and afterwards all over the house, including the three underground cellars, which I found a little trying to the nerves.

"Then I went back to my Mother, and told her that there was really nothing to bother about; and, you know, in the end, we talked ourselves into believing that it was nothing. My Mother would not agree that she might have been sleep-walking; but she was ready to put the door opening, down to the fault of the latch, which certainly snicked very lightly. As for the knocks, they might be the old warped woodwork of the house, cracking a bit, or a mouse rattling a piece of loose plaster. The smell was a little more difficult to explain; but finally we agreed that it might easily be the queer night-smell of the moist earth, coming in through the window of my Mother's room, from the back garden, or—for that matter—from the little church-yard beyond the big wall at the bottom of the garden.

"And so, at last, we quietened down, and finally I went off to bed, and had some sleep.

"I think this is certainly a good lesson on the way in which we humans can delude ourselves; for there was not one of these explanations that my reason could really accept. You just try to imagine yourselves in the same circumstances, and you will see how absurd our attempts to explain the happenings really were.

"In the morning, when I came down to breakfast, we talked it all over again, and whilst we agreed that it was strange, we also agreed that we had begun to imagine queer things in the backs of our minds, which now we felt half ashamed to admit. I think this is very funny, when you come to look into it; but it's absurdly human.

"And then, you know, that night, my Mother's door was slammed once violently, just after midnight.

"I caught up the lamp, and when I reached her door, I found it shut. I opened it quickly and went in, to find my Mother lying with her eyes open, and rather nervous; having been waked by the slam of the door. But what upset me more than anything, was the fact that there was a simply brutal smell in the passage and in her room.

"Whilst I was asking her whether she was all right, a door slammed twice downstairs; and you can imagine how it made me feel. My Mother and I looked at one another; and then I lit her candle, and taking the poker from the fender, went downstairs with the lamp, feeling really horribly nervous. The culminative effect of so many queer little things was getting hold of me; and all the *apparently* reasonable explanations seemed abjectly futile.

"The horrible smell seemed to be very strong in the downstairs passage; also in the front room and the cellars; but chiefly in the passage. However, I made a very thorough search of the house, and when I had finished, I knew that all the lower windows and doors had been properly shut and fastened, and that there was certainly no living thing in the house, beyond our two selves.

"Then I went upstairs again to my Mother's room, and we talked the thing over for an hour or more, and in the end came to the conclusion that we might, after all, be reading too much into a number of little things; but, you know, inside of us, we did not believe this. You just think!

"Later, when we had talked ourselves into a more comfortable state of mind, I said good night, and went off to bed; and presently managed to get to sleep.

"Then, in the early hours of the morning, whilst it was still dark, I was waked by a loud noise. You can imagine that it made me feel rather queer, after the little unexplained things that had been happening; and I sat up pretty quick in bed, and listened. And then, downstairs, I heard:—bang, bang, bang, one door after another being slammed; at least, that is the impression that the sounds gave me.

"I jumped out of bed, with a tingle and shiver of sudden fright on me; and at the same moment, as I lit my candle, my door was pushed slowly open; you see, I had not latched it, so as to feel that my Mother was not shut off from me in any way.

" 'Who's there!' I shouted out, in a voice about twice as deep as natural, and with that queer breathlessness, that a sudden fright so often gives one. 'Who's there!'

"Then I heard my Mother saying:—

" 'It's me, Thomas. Whatever *is* happening downstairs?'

"She was in the room, by this, and I saw that she had her bedroom poker in one hand, and her candle in the other. I could have smiled at her, if it had not been for the extraordinary sounds downstairs; for, you know, she was such a little woman; but with heaps of pluck.

"I got into my slippers, and reached down an old sword-bayonet from the wall. Then I picked up my candle, and begged my Mother not to come; but I knew it would be little use, if she had made up her mind; and she had, with the result that she acted as a sort of rearguard for me, during our search. I know, in some ways, selfishly, I was very glad to have her with me.

"By this time, the door-slamming had ceased, and there seemed, probably because of the sheer contrast, to be a simply beastly silence in the house. However, I led the way, holding my candle high, and keeping the sword-bayonet handy.

"When we got downstairs, I saw that all the room doors were wide open; and when we had made a thorough search, and found the outer doors and the windows all secured, I tell you, I wondered whether the noises had been made by the doors at all. Of one thing only we were able to make sure, and that was that there was no living thing in the house, beside ourselves. But everywhere, in the whole house, there seemed the taint of that extraordinarily horrible smell.

"Of course, it was absurd to try to 'make-believe' any longer.

There was something strange about the house; and as soon as it was daylight, I set my Mother to packing. After breakfast, I saw her off by train to one of my aunts, with a wire in advance, to prepare them.

"Then I set to work to try to clear up this mystery. I went first to the landlord, and told him all the circumstances. From him, I found that twelve or fifteen years back, the house had got rather a curious name from three or four tenants; with the result that it had remained empty for a long while; and in the end he had let it at a low rent to a Captain Tobias, on the one condition that the Captain should hold his tongue, if he saw anything peculiar. The Landlord's idea—as he told me frankly—was to free the house from these tales of 'something queer', by keeping a tenant in it, and then to sell it for the best price he could get.

"However, when Captain Tobias left, after a ten years' tenancy, there was no longer any 'talk' about the house; so that when we came and offered to take it on a five years' lease, he had jumped at the chance. This was the whole story; at least, so he gave me to understand. When I pressed him for details of the supposed peculiar happenings in the house, all those years back, he said that the tenants had talked about a woman who was always going about the house at night. Some tenants never saw anything; but others would not stay the first month's tenancy.

"One thing the landlord was particular to point out, that no tenant had ever complained about knockings, or doors slamming. As for the smell, he seemed positively indignant about it; but why, I don't suppose he quite knew himself, except that he probably had some vague feeling that it was an indirect accusation on my part that the drains were not right.

"In the end, I suggested that he should come down that evening and spend the night with me. He agreed at once, especially as I told him that I intended to keep the whole business quiet, and try to get really to the bottom of the curious happenings; for he was very anxious to keep the rumour of the haunting from getting about again.

"About three o'clock that afternoon, he came down, and we made a thorough search of the house, which, however, showed us nothing unusual. Afterwards, the Landlord made one or two tests, which showed him that the drainage was in perfect order; and after that, we made our preparations for sitting up all night.

"First, we borrowed two policemen's dark lanterns from the station near by, where the Superintendent and I were very friendly; and as soon as it was really dusk, the Landlord went up to his house for his gun. I had the sword-bayonet that I have told you about; and when the Landlord got back, we sat talking in my study until nearly midnight.

"Then we lit the lanterns and went upstairs on to the landing, where I brought a small table and a couple of chairs out of one of the bedrooms. We put the lanterns and the gun and bayonet handy on the table; then I shut and sealed the bedroom-doors; after which we took our seats, and turned off the lights.

"From then, until two o'clock, nothing happened; but a little after two, as I found by holding my watch near to the faint glow of the closed lanterns, I had a time of quite extraordinary nervousness. At last I bent towards the Landlord, and whispered to him that I had a queer feeling that something was about to happen, and to be ready with his lantern. At the same time, I reached out towards mine. In the very instant that I made this movement, the night which filled the passage seemed to become suddenly of a dull violet colour; not, mind you, as if a light had been shone; but as if the natural blackness of the night had changed colour, as I might say from the inside. Do you understand what I am trying to tell you? And then, coming through this violet night, through this violet-coloured gloom, came a little naked child, running. In an extraordinary way, the child seemed not to be distinct from the surrounding gloom; but almost as if it were a concentration of that extraordinary atmosphere; almost—can you understand?—as if that gloomy colour which had changed the night, came from the child. It seems impossible to make clear to you; but try to take hold of what I'm saying.

"The child went past me, running, quite naturally, as a chubby human child might run; only in an absolute and inconceivable silence. I remember that it was a very small child, and must have passed under the table; but I saw it through the table, as if the table had been only a slightly darker shadow than the coloured gloom. In the same instant, I saw that a fluctuating shimmer of violet light outlined the metal of the gun-barrels and the blade of the sword-bayonet, making them seem like faint shapes of glimmering light, floating unsupported where the table-top should have shown solid.

"Now, curiously, as I saw these things, I was subconsciously aware that I heard the anxious breathing of the Landlord, quite clear and laboured, close to my elbow, where he waited nervously with his hands on the lantern. And, you know, I realised in that moment that he saw nothing; but waited in the darkness, for my warning to come true.

"Even as I took heed of these minor things, I saw the child jump to one side, and hide behind some half-seen object, that was certainly nothing belonging to the passage. I stared, intently, with a most extraordinary thrill of expectant wonder, and fright making goose-flesh of my back. And even as I stared, I solved for myself the less important problem of what two black clouds were that hung over a part of the table. I think it is very curious and interesting, that double working of the mind, often so much more apparent during times of stress. The two black clouds came from two faintly shining shapes, which I knew must be the metal of the lanterns; and the things that looked black to the sight with which I was then seeing; could be nothing else but what to normal human sight is known as light. This phenomenon I have always remembered. I have twice seen a somewhat similar thing, in that Dark Light Case, and in that trouble of Maaetheson's, which you know about.

"Even as I understood this matter of the lights, I was looking to my left, to understand why the child was hiding. And suddenly, I heard the Landlord shout out:— 'The woman!' But I saw nothing. I had a vague, disagreeable sense that something repugnant was near to me, and I was aware in the same moment that the Landlord was gripping my arm in a hard, frightened grip. Then I was staring back to where the child had hidden. I saw the child peeping out from behind its hiding-place, seeming to be looking up the passage; but whether in fear or not, I could not tell. Then it came out, and ran headlong away, through the place where should have been the wall of my Mother's bedroom; but the sense with which I was seeing these things, showed me the wall only as a vague, upright shadow, unsubstantial. And immediately the child was lost to me, in the dull violet gloom. At the same time, I felt the Landlord press back against me, as if something passed too close to him; and he gave out again a hoarse little cry:— 'The Woman! The Woman!' and turned the shade clumsily from off his lantern, which seemed to let loose instantly a great fan-shaped jet of blackness across the violet-coloured gloom. But I had seen no Woman. Abruptly, the violet tint went out of the night, and the fan-shaped jet of blackness became plain to me as the funnel of light from the landlord's lantern. I saw that the passage showed empty, as he shone the beam of his light jerkily to and fro; but chiefly in the direction of the doorway of my Mother's room.

"He was still clutching my arm, and had risen to his feet; and now, mechanically and almost slowly, I picked up my own lantern and turned on the light. I shone it, a little dazedly, at the seals upon the doors; but none was broken; then I sent the light to and fro, up and down the passage; but there was nothing there; and I looked at the Landlord, who was saying something in a rather incoherent fashion. As my light passed over his face, I noted, in a stupid sort of way, that it was drenched with sweat.

"Then my wits became more handleable, and I began to catch the drift of his words:— 'Did you see her? Did you see her?' he was saying, over and over again. I found myself telling him, in quite a level voice, that I had not seen any woman. He became more coherent then, and told me that he had seen a Woman come from the end of the passage, and go right past us; but he could not describe her, except that she kept stopping and looking about her, and had even peered at the wall, close beside him, as if looking for something. But what seemed to trouble him most, was that she had not seemed to see him, at all. He repeated this so often, that in the end I told him, in an absurd sort of way, that he ought to be very glad that she had not. You can imagine what my nerves felt like. What did it all mean? was the one question; and somehow I was not so frightened, as utterly bewildered. I had seen less then, than since; and knew less of possible and actual dangers. The chief effect of what I had seen, was to make me feel adrift from all my anchorages of Reason.

"What did it mean? He had seen a Woman, searching for something. I had not seen this Woman. I had seen a Child, running away, and hiding from Something or Someone. He had not seen this Child, or the other things—only the Woman. And I had not seen her. What did it all mean?

"I had said nothing yet to the Landlord about the Child. I had been too bewildered in the first few moments; and afterwards, I realised immediately that it would be futile to attempt to explain it to him. He was already frightened and stupid, with the thing that he had seen; and not the kind of man to understand.

All this went through my mind very quickly, as we stood there, shining the lanterns to and fro; and as a result, I said nothing of what I had seen. And all the time, intermingled with this streak of practical reasoning, I was questioning to myself, what did it all mean; what was the Woman searching for, and what was the Child running from? You can understand the multitude of vague minor questions that kept rising.

"And suddenly, as I stood there, bewildered and nervous, and making random answers to the Landlord, a door was violently slammed downstairs; and directly I caught the horrible reek of which I have told you before.

" 'There!' I said to the Landlord, and caught his arm, in my turn. 'And the Smell! The Smell, do *you* smell it?'

"He looked at me, stupidly, so that I shook him, with a sort of nervous anger.

" 'Yes,' he said, at last, in a queer voice, and trying to shine the light from his shaking lantern at the stair-head.

" 'Come on!' I said, and picked up my bayonet; and he came, carrying his gun awkwardly. I think he came, more because he was afraid to be left alone, than because he had any pluck left, poor beggar. I never sneer at that kind of funk, at least very seldom; for when it takes hold of you, it makes rags of your courage, as I know.

"I began to go downstairs, shining my light over the banisters into the lower passage, and afterwards at the doors to see whether they were shut; for I had closed and latched them, leaning a corner of a mat up against each door, so that I should know which had been opened, in the event of anything happening.

"I saw at once that none of the doors had been opened; then I paused and threw the beam of my light down alongside of the stairway, so as to see the mat that I had leaned against the door at the top of the cellar stairs. In a moment, I got a horrid thrill; for the mat was flat. I waited a couple of seconds, shining my light to and fro in the passage. Then, holding pretty solid on to my courage, I went down the remainder of the stairs.

"As I came to the bottom step, I saw suddenly that there were wet patches all up and down the passage. I shone my lantern on to one of them. It was the imprint of a wet foot on the black oak floor; not an ordinary footprint, but a queer, soft, flabby, spreading imprint, that gave me an extraordinary feeling of horror.

"Backward and forward I flashed the light over the impossible footprints, and saw them everywhere. And suddenly I saw that they led to each of the closed doors. I felt something touch my back, and glanced round swiftly, to find that the Landlord had come down close to me, almost pressing against me, in his fear.

" 'It's all right,' I said, but in a rather breathless whisper, meaning to put a little courage into him; for I could feel that he was shaking through all his body. And then, you know, even as I tried to get him steadied enough to be of some use, his gun went off with a tremendous bang and knocked the seat clean out of one of the hall chairs. He jumped, and yelled with sheer terror; and I swore at the top of my voice, because of the shock.

" 'For God's sake give it to me!' I said, and slipped the gun from his hand; in the same instant there was a sound of running footsteps up the garden path, and immediately the flash of a bull's-eye lantern upon the fanlight over the front door. Then the door was tried, and directly afterwards there came a thundering knocking, which told me that the policeman on the beat had heard the shot, and run up to see what was wrong.

"I went quickly to the door, and opened it. Fortunately the Constable knew me well, and when I had beckoned him in, I was able to explain matters in a very short time.

"Whilst I was doing this, Inspector Johnstone, whose round lay that way, came up the path, having missed the officer, and seen the lights and the open door. I told him as briefly as possible what had happened; but nothing about the Child or the Woman; for it would have seemed too fantastic for him to notice seriously. Then I showed him the queer, wet footprints and how they went towards the closed doors. I explained quickly about the mats, and how that the one against the cellar door was flat, which showed that the door must have been opened.

"The Inspector nodded, and told the Constable to draw his staff and guard the door. He asked then for the hall lamp to be lit; after which he took the policeman's lantern, and led the way into the front room. He paused with the door wide open, and threw the light all round; then jumped into the room, and looked behind the door; there was no one there; nor had I expected that there would be anyone; but all over the polished oak floor, between the scattered rugs, went the marks of those horrible spreading footprints; and the whole room was tainted with the disgusting smell.

"The Inspector searched carefully but quickly, and then came out and went into the middle room, using the same precautions. You can imagine just how beastly it was going into those rooms. There was nothing, of course, in the middle one, or in the kitchen and pantry; but everywhere went the wet footmarks about all the rooms, showing plain wherever there was clear woodwork or oilcloth; and always wherever we went there was the smell.

"The Inspector ceased from his search, and spent a minute in trying whether the mats would really fall flat when the doors were open, or merely ruckle upward again, in such a way as to appear that they had been untouched. But in each case, the mats fell flat, and remained so.

" 'Most extraordinary!' I heard Inspector Johnstone mutter to himself. Then he went towards the cellar door. He had inquired at first whether there were any windows to the cellars, and when he knew there was no way out, except by the door, he had left this part of the search to the last.

"As Johnstone came up to the door, the policeman made a motion of salute, and said something in a low voice; and something in the tone made me flick my light across him. I saw then that the man was very white, and he looked scared and bewildered.

" 'What?' said Johnstone, impatiently. 'Speak up!'

" 'A woman come along 'ere, sir, and went through this 'ere door,' said the Constable, clearly, but with that curious monotonous intonation that you sometimes get from an unintelligent human who is badly frightened.

" 'What!' shouted the Inspector.

" 'A woman come along 'ere, sir, and went through this 'ere door,' said the man, monotonously.

"The Inspector caught the man by the shoulder, and deliberately smelt his breath.

" 'No!' he said. And then sarcastically:— 'I hope you held the door open politely for the lady.'

" 'The door weren't opened, sir,' said the man, simply.

" 'Are you mad—' began Johnstone.

" 'No,' said the Landlord's voice from the back, and speaking steadily enough. 'I saw the woman upstairs.' It was evident that he had got back his control again.

" 'I'm afraid, Inspector Johnstone,' I said, 'that there's more in this than you think. I certainly saw something very extraordinary upstairs.'

"The Inspector seemed about to say something; but, instead, he turned again to the door, and flashed his light down and round about the mat. I saw then that the strangely horrible footmarks came straight up to the cellar door; and the last print showed *under* the door; yet the policeman said the door had not been opened.

"And suddenly, without any intention, or realisation of what I was saying, I said to the Landlord:—

" 'What were the feet like?'

"I received no answer; for the Inspector was ordering the Constable to open the cellar door, and the man was not obeying. Johnstone repeated the order, and at last, in a queer automatic way, the man obeyed, and pushed the door open. The disgusting smell beat up at us, in a great wave of horror, and the Inspector came backward a step.

" 'My God!' he said, and went forward again, and shone his light down the steps; but there was nothing visible, only that on each step showed the unnatural footprints.

" 'The Inspector brought the beam of the light vividly on to the top step; and there, clear in the light, there was something small, moving. The Inspector bent to look, and the policeman and I with him. Now I don't want to disgust you; but the thing was a maggot. The Policeman backed suddenly out of the doorway.

" 'The churchyard,' he said, '…at the back of the 'ouse.'

" 'Si-lence !' said Johnstone, with a queer break in the word, and I knew that at last he was frightened. He put his lantern into the doorway, and shone it from step to step, following the footprints down into the darkness; then he stepped back from the open doorway, and we all gave back with him. He looked round, and I had a feeling that he was looking for a weapon of some kind.

" 'Your gun,' I said to the Landlord, and he brought it from the front hall, and passed it over to the Inspector, who took it and ejected the empty shell from the right barrel. He held out his hand for a live cartridge, which the Landlord brought from his pocket. Then he loaded the gun and snapped the breech. He turned to the Constable:—

" 'Come on,' he said, and moved towards the cellar doorway.

" 'I ain't comin', sir,' said the policeman, very white in the face.

"With a sudden blaze of passion, the Inspector took the man by the scruff, and hove him bodily down into the darkness, and he went downward, screaming. The Inspector followed him instantly, with his lantern and the gun; and I after the Inspector, with the bayonet ready. Behind me, I heard the Landlord come, stumbling nervously.

At the bottom of the stairs, the Inspector was helping the policeman to his feet, where he stood swaying a moment, in a bewildered manner; then the Inspector went into the front cellar, and his man followed him in a quiet, stupid fashion; but evidently no longer with any thought of running away from anything we might find dangerous or horrible.

"We all crowded into the front cellar, flashing our lights to and fro, over the place. Inspector Johnstone was examining the floor, and I saw that the footmarks went round the cellar, into each of the corners, and across and across the floor. And I thought suddenly of the Child that was running away from Something. Do you realise the thing that I was seeing vaguely?

"We went out of the front cellar, in a body, for there was nothing to be found. In the next, the footprints went everywhere in that same queer erratic fashion, as of something or someone searching for something, or following some blind scent.

"In the third cellar the prints ended at the shallow well that had been the old water-supply of the little house. The well was full to the brim, and the water so clear that the pebbly bottom was plain to be seen, as we shone the lights into the water. The search came to an abrupt *end,* and we stood about the well, looking at one another, in an absolute, horrible quiet.

"Johnstone made another examination of the footprints; then he shone his light again into the clear shallow water, searching each inch of the plainly-seen bottom; but there was nothing there. The cellar was heavy with the dreadful smell; and we all stood silent, turning the beams of our lamps constantly to and fro around the cellar.

"The Inspector looked up from his search of the well; and nodded quietly across at me; and with his sudden, dumb acknowledgment that our belief was now his belief, the smell in the cellar seemed to grow more dreadful, and to be, as it were, a menace—the material evidence that some monstrous thing was there with us, invisible.

" 'I think—' began the Inspector, and shone his light towards the stairway. With the hint, the Constable's restraint went utterly, and he ran for the stairs, making a queer sound in his throat.

"The Landlord followed, at a quick walk, and then the Inspector and I. He waited a single instant for me, and we went up together, treading on the same steps, and with our lights held backwards. At the top, I slammed and locked the stair door, and wiped my forehead. By Jove! my hands were shaking.

"The Inspector asked me to give his man a glass of whisky, and then he shunted him out on to his beat. He stayed a short while with the Landlord and me, and it was arranged that he would join us the following night, and watch the Well with us from midnight until daylight. When he left us, the dawn was just coming in; and the Landlord and I locked up the house and went over to his own place for a sleep.

"In the afternoon, the Landlord and I returned to the house, to make arrangements for the night. He was very quiet, and I felt that he was to be relied on, now that he had been 'salted', as it were, with his fright of the previous night.

"We opened all the doors and windows, and blew the house through thoroughly; and in the meanwhile, we lit all the lamps we could find, and took them down into the cellars, where we set them all about, so as to have light everywhere. Then we carried down three chairs and a table, and put them in the cellar where the well was sunk. After that, we stretched thin piano wire across the cellar floor, at such a height that it should trip anything moving about in the dark.

"When this was done, I went through the house with the Landlord, and sealed every window and door in the place, excepting only the front-door and the door at the top of the cellar stairs.

"In the meanwhile, a local wire-smith was making something to my order; and when the Landlord and I had finished tea at his house, we went down to see how the smith was getting on.

"We found the thing completed. It looked rather like a huge parrot's cage, without any bottom, made of heavy-gauge wire, and about seven feet high. It was exactly three feet in diameter. Fortunately, I had remembered to have it made longitudinally in two halves, or else we should never have got it through the doorways and down the cellar stairs.

I told the wire-smith to bring the cage up to the house right away, so that he could fit the two halves rigidly together for me; and as we returned, I called in at an ironmongers, where I bought some thin hemp rope and an iron rack-pulley, like those used in Lancashire for hauling up the ceiling clothes-racks, which you find in every house and cottage. I bought also a couple of pitchforks.

" 'We shan't want to touch it,' I said to the Landlord; and he nodded, looking rather white all at once, but saying nothing.

"As soon as the cage had arrived, and been fitted together rigidly in the cellar, I sent away the smith; and the Landlord and I suspended it exactly over the well, into which it just fitted easily. In the end, and after a lot of trouble, we managed to hang it so perfectly central from the rope over the iron pulley, that when hoisted to the ceiling, and dropped, it went every time plunk into the well, like a candle-extinguisher. When we had got this finally arranged, I hoisted it up once more, to the ready position, and made the rope fast to a heavy wooden pillar, which stood in the middle of the cellar, near to the table.

"By ten o'clock I had everything arranged, with the two pitchforks and the two police lanterns; also some whisky and sandwiches on the table; and underneath, I had several buckets full of disinfectant.

"A little after eleven o'clock, there was a knock at the front door, and when I went, I found that Inspector Johnstone had arrived, and brought with him one of his plain-clothes men. You will understand how pleased I was to see that there would be this addition to our watch; for he looked a tough, nerveless man, brainy and collected; just the man I should have picked to help us with the horrible job I felt pretty sure we should have to do that night.

"When the inspector and the detective had entered, I shut and locked the front door; then, while the Inspector held the light, I sealed the door carefully, with tape and wax. At the head of the cellar stairs, I shut and locked that door also, behind us, and sealed it in the same way.

"As we entered the cellar, I warned Johnstone and his man to be careful not to trip over the wires; and then, as I saw his surprise at my arrangements, I began to explain my ideas and intentions, to all of which he listened with a very strong approval. I was pleased to see also that the detective was nodding his head, as I talked, in a way that showed he appreciated all my precautions.

"Both Johnstone and his man had brought police lanterns with them, and these they put on the table, by the two that we had borrowed from the station. As he put his lantern down, the inspector picked up one of the pitch-forks, and balanced it in his hand; then looked at me, and nodded.

" 'The best thing,' he said. 'I only wish you'd got two more.'

"Then we all took our seats, the detective getting a washing-stool from the corner of the cellar, as we had brought down only three chairs. From then, until a quarter to twelve, we talked quietly, whilst we made a light supper of whisky and sandwiches; after which, we cleared everything off the table, excepting the lanterns and the pitch-forks. One of the latter, I handed to the Inspector; the other I took myself, and, then, having set my chair so as to be handy to the rope which lowered the cage into the well, I went round the cellar and put out every lamp.

"I groped my way back to my chair, and arranged the pitch-fork and the dark lantern ready to my hand; after which I suggested that everyone should keep an absolute silence throughout the watch. I asked, also, that no lantern should be turned on, until I gave the word.

"I put my watch on the table, where a faint glow from my lantern made me able to see the time. For an hour nothing happened, and everyone kept an absolute silence, except for an occasional uneasy movement.

"About half-past one, however, I was conscious again of the same extraordinary and peculiar nervousness, which I had felt on the previous night. I put my hand out quickly, and eased the hitched rope from around the pillar. The Inspector seemed aware of the movement; for I saw the faint light from his lantern, move a little, as if he had suddenly taken hold of it, in readiness.

"About a minute later, I became aware that there was a change in the colour of the night in the cellar, and it grew slowly violet-tinged upon my eyes. I glanced to and fro, quickly, in the new darkness, and even as I looked, I was conscious that the violet colour of the night deepened. In the direction of the well, but seeming to be at a great distance beyond, there was, as it were, a nucleus to the night; and the nucleus came swiftly towards us, appearing to come through a great space, almost in a single moment. It came near, and I saw again, as on the previous occasion, that it was a little naked child, running, and seeming to be *of* the violet night in which it ran.

"The child came with a natural running movement, exactly as I have already described it; but in a silence so peculiarly intense, that it was as if it brought the silence with it. I don't suppose you understand what I am trying to tell you; but I cannot make it clearer. Seemingly, about half-way between the well and the table, the child turned swiftly, and looked back at something invisible to me; and suddenly it went down into a crouching attitude, and seemed to be hiding behind something shadowy that showed vaguely; but, you know, there was nothing there, except the bare floor of the cellar; nothing, I mean, in our world.

"About this time I remember thinking to myself in a queerly collected way that I could hear the breathing of the three other men, with a wonderful distinctness; and also the tick of my watch upon the table seemed to sound as loud and as slow as the tick of one of those old grandfather's clocks. And, you know, I knew that none of the others saw what I was seeing.

"Abruptly, the Landlord, who was next to me, let out his breath with a little hissing sound; and I knew that something was visible to him. There came a creak from the table, and I had a feeling that the Inspector was leaning forward, looking at something that I could not see. The Landlord reached out his hand through the darkness, and fumbled a moment to catch my arm:—

" 'The Woman!' he whispered, close to my ear. 'Over by the well.'

"I stared hard in that direction; but saw nothing, except that perhaps the violet colour of the night seemed a little duller just there.

'I looked back quickly to the shadow where the child was hiding. I saw that it was peering backward from the hiding-place. And suddenly it rose and ran straight for the middle of the table, which showed only as a vague shadow half-way between my eyes and the unseen floor. As the child ran under the table, I saw that the steel prongs of my pitch-fork were glimmering with a violet, fluctuating light. A little way off, there showed high up in the gloom, the vaguely shining outline of the other fork, so that I knew the Inspector had it raised in his hand, ready. There was no doubt but that he saw something. On the table, the metal of the five lanterns shone with the same strange glowing; and about each lantern there was a little cloud of absolute blackness, where the phenomenon that is light to our natural eyes, came through the fittings; and through each complete blackness, the metal of each lantern showed plain, as might a cat's-eye stone in a nest of black cotton-wool.

"Just beyond the table, the Child paused again, and stood, seeming to oscillate a little upon its feet, which gave me a queer impression that it was lighter and vaguer than a cloud; and yet, in the same moment, another part of me seemed to know that it was to me, as something that might be beyond thick, invisible glass, and subject to conditions and forces that I was vacant to comprehend. In some ways, I might say that the impression left, was as if I had looked through thick, plate-glass windows at someone out in a strong wind; and all the time I could not hear or know of the wind, except by seeing the person rocked by it. Do I get the thing in any way clear to you ?

"The Child was looking back again, and my gaze went the same way. I stared across the cellar, and saw the cage hanging clear in the violet light, every wire and tie outlined with a glimmering of strange light; above it there was a little space of gloom, and then the dull shining of the iron pulley which I had screwed into the ceiling.

"I stared in a bewildered, abnormal sort of way, round the cellar; there were thin lines of vague fire crossing the floor in all directions; and suddenly I remembered the piano-wire that the Landlord and I had stretched. But there was nothing else to be seen, except that near the table there were indistinct glimmerings of light, and at the far end the outline of a dull-glowing revolver, evidently in the detective's pocket. I remember having felt a subconscious satisfaction, as my brain reasoned out this trifle in a queer automatic fashion. On the table, near to me, there was a little shapeless collection of the light; and this I knew, after an instant's uninterested consideration, to be the steel portions of the works of my watch.

"I had looked several times round the lost confines of the cellar, and at the child, whilst I was deciding these trifles; and had found it still in that attitude of looking at something. But now, suddenly, it ran clear away to my right into a great distance, and was nothing more than a slightly deeper coloured nucleus far off in the strange coloured night.

"Beside me, the Landlord gave out a queer little cry, and twisted over against me, as if to avoid something. From the Inspector there came a sharp breathing sound, as if he had been suddenly drenched with cold water. And abruptly the violet colour went out of the night, and the sense of distance and space; and I was conscious of the nearness of something monstrous and repugnant, that made me sweat.

"There was a tense silence, and the blackness of the cellar seemed absolute, with only the faint glow about each of the lanterns on the table. Then, in the dark and the silence, there sounded a faint tinkle of water from the well, as if something were rising noiselessly out of it, and the water running back off it with a gentle tinkling. In the same instant, there came to me a sudden waft of the disgusting smell.

"I gave a sharp cry of warning to the Inspector, and loosed the rope. There came instantly the sharp splash of the cage entering the water; and then, with a quick, stiff, frightened movement, I opened the shutter of my lantern, and shone the light at the cage, shouting to the others to do the same.

"As my light struck the cage, I saw that about two feet of it projected from the top of the well, and there was something protruded up out of the water, into the cage. I stared, with a feeling that I recognised the thing; and then, as the other lanterns were opened, I saw that it was a leg of mutton. The thing was held by a brawny fist and arm, which were rising out of the water; and I stood there, utterly stiff and bewildered, to see what was coming. In a moment there rose into view a great bearded face, that I felt sure in that grim instant was the face of a drowned man, long dead. Then the face opened at the mouth-part, and spluttered and coughed. Another big hand came into view, and wiped the water from the eyes, which were blinked rapidly, and then fixed themselves into a stare at the lights.

"From the Detective there came a sudden shout:—

" 'Captain Tobias!' he shouted, and the Inspector echoed him, and instantly they burst into loud roars of laughter.

"The Inspector and the Detective ran across the cellar to the cage; and I followed, still bewildered. The man in the cage was keeping the leg of mutton as far away from him, as possible, and holding his nose.

" 'Lift thig dam trap, quig!' he shouted in a stifled voice; but the Inspector and the Detective simply doubled before him, and tried to hold their noses, whilst they laughed, and the light from their lanterns went dancing all over the place.

" 'Quig! Quig!' said the man in the cage, still holding his nose, and trying to speak plainly.

"Then Johnstone and the Detective stopped laughing, and lifted the cage. The man in the well threw the leg across the cellar and turned swiftly to go down into the well; but the two officers were too quick for him, and had him out in a twinkling; then whilst they held him, dripping upon the floor, the Inspector jerked his thumb in the direction of the offending leg, and the Landlord, having got the keys from me, harpooned it with one of the pitch-forks, ran it upstairs and so into the open air.

"In the meanwhile, I had given the man from the well a stiff tot of whisky; for which he thanked me with a cheerful nod, and having emptied the glass at a draught, held out his hand for the bottle, which he finished, as if it had been so much water.

"Now, as you will be guessing, this Captain Tobias who had appeared from the well, was the very man who had been the previous tenant. In the course of the talk that followed, I learned the reason why Captain Tobias had been forced to leave the house. He had been wanted by the police for certain smuggling, and had undergone imprisonment; having been released only a couple of weeks earlier.

"He had returned home, to find us tenants of his old home. He had then entered the house through the well, the walls of which were not continued right to the bottom (this I will deal with later); and gone upstairs by a little stairway in my cellar wall, which opened at the top through a panel beside my Mother's bedroom. This panel was opened, by revolving the left doorpost of the bedroom door, with the result that the bedroom door always became unlatched, in the process of opening the panel.

"The Captain complained, without any bitterness, that the panel had warped, and that each time he opened it, it made a loud cracking noise. This had been evidently what I mistook for raps. He would not give his reason for entering the house; but it was pretty obvious that he had hidden something, which he wanted to get. However, as he found it impossible to enter the house, without the risk of being caught, he decided to try to drive us out, relying on the bad reputation of the place, and his own artistic efforts as a ghost. I must say he succeeded.

"He intended then to rent the house again, as before; when

he would, of course, have plenty of time to get whatever he had hidden. Moreover, no doubt the house suited him admirably; for there was a passage—as he showed me afterwards—connecting the dummy well with the crypt of the church beyond the garden wall; and these, in turn, were connected with certain caves in the cliffs, which went down to the beach beyond the church.

"In the course of his talk, Captain Tobias offered to take the house off my hands; and as this suited me perfectly, for I was just about 'stalled' with it, and also satisfied the Landlord, it was decided that no steps should be taken against him; and that the whole business be hushed up.

"I asked the Captain whether there was really anything queer about the house; whether he had ever seen anything. He said yes, that he had twice seen a woman going about the house at night. You can imagine how we all looked at one another, when he said that. The Captain told us that she never bothered him, and that he had only seen her the two times; and on each occasion it had been just after a narrow escape from the Revenue People, and when he had been rather badly frightened; that is, I ought to add, so far as a man of his type was capable of feeling fright.

"Captain Tobias was a cute man; for he had seen how I had leaned the mats up against the doors; and after entering the rooms, and walking all about them, so as to leave the foot-marks of an old pair of wet woollen slippers everywhere, he had deliberately put the mats back as he found them, as he left each room.

"The maggot which had dropped from his infernal leg-of-mutton, had been an accident, and beyond even his horrific planning; but he was hugely delighted to learn how it had affected us.

"The faint, mouldy smell which I had smelled, before the leg-abomination, was probably from the little, closed stairway, when the Captain had opened the panel; at least, this was the conclusion I came to when he took me through, to show it to me. The door-slamming was also another of his contributions.

"Now I come to the end of the Captain's ghost-play; and to the difficulty of trying to explain the other peculiar things. In the first place, it is obvious to you that there was something genuinely strange in the house; which made itself manifest as a Woman. So many people had seen this Woman, under different circumstances, that it is impossible to put the thing down to fancy; at the same time it must seem extraordinary that people should live years in the house, and see nothing; whilst the policeman saw the

Woman, before he had been twenty minutes in the place; also the Landlord, the Detective, and the Inspector all saw her.

"I have thought a great deal about this, and I can only suppose that *fear* was in every case the key, as I might say, which opened the senses to an awareness of the presence of the Woman. The policeman was a nervy, highly-strung man, and he got frightened. When he became frightened, he was able to see the Woman. The same reasoning applies all round. *I* saw nothing, until I became really frightened; then I saw, not the Woman, but a Child, running away from Something or Someone. However, I will touch on that later. In short, until a very strong degree of fear was present, the person was not capable of being affected by the Force which made Itself evident, as a Woman. I don't think I can put it clearer than this. I think my theory explains why some Tenants were never aware of anything strange in the house, whilst others left immediately. The more sensitive they were, the less would be the degree of fear necessary to make them aware of the Force present in the house. This is a peculiar and interesting point.

"The curious shining of all the metal objects in the cellar, had been visible only to me. The cause, naturally, I do not know; neither do I know why I alone was able to see the shining."

"The Child," I said. "Can you explain that part at all, Carnacki... why *you* didn't see the Woman, and why *they* didn't see the Child. Was it merely the same Force, appearing differently to different people?"

"No," said Carnacki. "I can't explain that. But I am quite sure in my own mind that the Woman and the Child were not only two complete and different entities; but also that they were not even in quite the same planes of Existence.

"It is impossible to put the thing into words, because language is not enough developed yet, to have produced words with sufficiently exact shades of meaning to enable me to tell you just what I do know. At the time that the thing occurred, I was quite unable to understand it, even slightly. Yet, later I gained a vague insight into certain possibilities.

"To give you the root-idea of the matter, it is held in the Sigsand MS. that a child 'still-born' is 'snayched bacyk bye thee Haggs'. This is crude; but may yet contain an elemental truth.

But, before I attempt to make this clearer, let me tell you a thought that has often been mine. It may be that physical birth is but a secondary process; and that, prior to the possibility, the Mother Spirit searches for, until it finds, the small Element—the primal Ego or Child's soul. It may be that a certain waywardness would cause Such to strive to evade capture by the Mother-Spirit. It may have been such a thing as this, that I saw. I have always tried to think so; but it is impossible to ignore the sense of repulsion that I felt when the unseen Woman went past me. This repulsion carries forward the idea suggested in the Sigsand MS., that primarily a *still-born* child is thus (eliminating obvious physical causes) because its ego or spirit has been snatched back, by the 'Haggs'. In other words, by certain of the Monstrosities of the Outer Circle. The thought is inconceivably terrible, and probably the more so because it is so fragmentary. It leaves us with the conception of a child's soul adrift half-way between two lives, and running through bye-ways of Eternity from Something incredible and inconceivable (because not understood) to our senses.

"The thing is beyond further discussion; for it is futile to attempt to discuss a thing, to any purpose, of which one has a conception so fragmentary as this. There is one thought, which is often mine. Perhaps there is a Mother-Spirit— No, it's no use trying to get that into words."

"And the well?" said Arkright. "How did the Captain get in from the other side?"

"As I said before," answered Carnacki. "The side-walls of the well did not reach to the bottom; so that you had only to dip down into the water, and come up again on the other side of the wall, under the cellar floor, and so climb into the hidden passage. Of course, the water was the same height on both sides of the walls. Don't ask me who made the well-entrance or the little stairway; for I don't know. The house was very old, as I have told you; and that sort of thing was useful in the wild old days."

"And the Child," I said, coming back to the thing which chiefly interested me. "You would say that the birth must have occurred in that house; and in this way, one might suppose the house to have become *en rapport*, if I can use the word in that way, with the Forces that produced the tragedy?"

"Yes," replied Carnacki. "That is, supposing we take the suggestion of the Sigsand MS., to account for the phenomenon."

"There may be other houses—" I began.

"There are," said Carnacki, and stood up.

"Out you go," he said, genially, using the familiar formula. And in five minutes we were on the Embankment, going thoughtfully to our various homes.

The Horse of the Invisible

I HAD THAT AFTERNOON received an invitation from Carnacki. When I reached his place, I found him sitting alone. As I came into the room, he rose with a perceptibly stiff movement, and extended his left hand. His face seemed to be badly scarred and bruised, and his right hand was bandaged. He shook hands, and offered me his paper, which I refused. Then he passed me a handful of photographs, and returned to his reading.

Now, that is just Carnacki. Not a word had come from him, and not a question from me. He would tell us all about it later. I spent about half an hour, looking at the photographs, which were chiefly 'snaps' (some by flash-light) of an extraordinarily pretty girl; though, in some of the photographs it was wonderful that her prettiness was so evident; for so frightened and startled was her expression, that it was difficult not to believe that she had been photographed in the presence of some imminent and overwhelming danger.

The bulk of the photographs were of interiors of different rooms and passages, and in every one the girl might be seen, either full length in the distance, or closer, with perhaps little more than a hand or arm, or portion of the head or dress included in the photograph. All of these had evidently been taken with some definite aim, that did not have for its first purpose the picturing of the girl, but obviously of her surroundings; and they made me very curious, as you can imagine.

Near the bottom of the pile, however, I came upon something *definitely* extraordinary. It was a photograph of the girl, standing abrupt and clear in the great blaze of a flash-light, as was plain to be seen. Her face was turned a little upward, as if she had been frightened suddenly by some noise. Directly above her, as though half-formed and coming down out of the shadows, was the shape of a single, enormous hoof.

I examined this photograph for a long time, without understanding it more than that it had probably to do with some queer Case in which Carnacki was interested.

When Jessop, Arkright, and Taylor came in, Carnacki quietly held out his hand for the photographs, which I returned in the same spirit, and afterwards we all went in to dinner. When we had spent a quiet hour at the table, we pulled our chairs round, and made ourselves snug; and Carnacki began:—

"I've been North," he said, speaking slowly and painfully, between puffs at his pipe. "Up to Hisgins of East Lancashire. It has been a pretty strange business all round, as I fancy you chaps will think, when I have finished. I knew, before I went, something about the 'horse story', as I have heard it called; but I had never thought of it as coming my way, somehow. Also, I know *now* that I had never considered it seriously—in spite of my rule always to keep an open mind. Funny creatures, we humans!

"Well, I got a wire, asking for an appointment, which of course told me that there was some trouble. On the date I fixed, old Captain Hisgins himself came up to see me. He told me a great many new details about the horse story; though, naturally, I had always known the main points, and understood that if the first child were a girl, that girl would be haunted by the Horse, during her courtship.

"It is, as you can see already, an extraordinary story; and though I have always known about it, I have never thought it to be anything more than an old-time legend, as I have already hinted. You see, for seven generations the Hisgin Family have had men-children for their first-born, and even the Hisgins themselves have long considered the tale to be little more than a myth.

"To come to the present, the eldest child of the reigning family is a girl, and she has been often teased and warned in jest by her friends and relations that she is the first girl to be the eldest for seven generations, and that she would have to keep her men friends at arm's length, or go into a nunnery, if she hoped to escape the haunting. And this, I think, shows us how thoroughly the tale had grown to be considered as nothing worthy of the least serious thought. Don't you think so?

"Two months ago, Miss Hisgins became engaged to Beaumont, a young Naval Officer, and on the evening of the very day of the engagement, before it was even formally announced, a most extraordinary thing happened, which resulted in Captain Hisgins making the appointment, and my ultimately going down to their place to look into the thing.

"From the old family records and papers that were entrusted to me, I found that there could be no possible doubt but that prior to something like a hundred and fifty years ago there were some very extraordinary and disagreeable coincidences, to put the thing in the least emotional way. In the whole of the two centuries prior to that date, there were five first-born girls, out of a total of seven generations of the family. Each of these girls grew up to Maidenhood, and each became engaged, and each one died during the period of the engagement, two by suicide, one by falling from a window, one from a 'broken-heart' (presumably heart-failure, owing to sudden shock through fright). The fifth girl was killed one evening in the park round the house; but just how, there seemed to be no *exact* knowledge; only that there was an impression that she had been kicked by a horse. She was dead, when found.

"Now, you see, all of these deaths might be attributed, in a way—even the suicides—to natural causes, I mean, as distinct from supernatural. You see? Yet, in every case, the Maidens had undoubtedly suffered some extraordinary and terrifying experiences during their various courtships; for in all of the records there was mention either of the neighing of an unseen horse, or of the sounds of an invisible horse galloping, as well as many other peculiar and quite inexplicable manifestations. You begin to understand now, I think, just how extraordinary a business it was that I was asked to look into.

"I gathered from one account that the haunting of the girls was so constant and horrible that two of the girls' lovers fairly ran away from their lady-loves. And I think it was this, more than anything else, that made me feel that there had been something more in it, than a mere succession of uncomfortable coincidences.

"I got hold of these facts, before I had been many hours in the house; and after this, I went pretty carefully into the details of the thing that happened on the night of Miss Hisgin's engagement to Beaumont. It seems that as the two of them were going through the big lower corridor, just after dusk and before the lamps had been lighted, there had been a sudden, horrible neighing in the corridor, close to them. Immediately afterward, Beaumont received a tremendous blow or kick, which broke his right forearm. Then the rest of the family and the servants came running, to know what was wrong. Lights were brought, and the corridor and, afterwards, the whole house searched; but nothing unusual was found.

"You can imagine the excitement in the house, and the half incredulous, half believing talk about the old legend. Then, later, in the middle of the night, the old Captain was waked by the sound of a great horse galloping round and round the house.

"Several times after this, both Beaumont and the girl said that they had heard the sounds of hoofs near to them, after dusk, in several of the rooms and corridors.

"Three nights later, Beaumont was waked by a strange neighing in the night-time, seeming to come from the direction of his sweetheart's bedroom. He ran hurriedly for her father, and the two of them raced to her room. They found her awake, and ill with sheer terror, having been awakened by the neighing, seemingly close to her bed.

The night before I arrived, there had been a fresh happening, and they were all in a frightfully nervy state, as you can imagine.

"I spent most of the first day, as I have hinted, in getting hold of details; but after dinner, I slacked off, and played billiards all the evening with Beaumont and Miss Hisgins. We stopped about ten o'clock, and had coffee, and I got Beaumont to give me full particulars about the thing that had happened the evening before.

"He and Miss Hisgins had been sitting quietly in her aunt's boudoir, whilst the old lady chaperoned them, behind a book. It was growing dusk, and the lamp was at her end of the table. The rest of the house was not yet lit, as the evening had come earlier than usual.

"Well, it seems that the door into the hall was open, and suddenly, the girl said:— 'S'ush! what's that?'

"They both listened, and then Beaumont heard it—the sound of a horse, outside of the front door.

" 'Your father?' he suggested; but she reminded him that her father was not riding.

"Of course, they were both ready to feel queer, as you can suppose; but Beaumont made an effort to shake this off, and went into the hall to see whether anyone was at the entrance. It was pretty dark in the hall, and he could see the glass panels of the inner draught-door, clear-cut in the darkness of the hall. He walked over to the glass, and looked through into the drive beyond; but there was nothing in sight.

"He felt nervous and puzzled, and opened the inner door and went out on to the carriage-circle. Almost directly afterward, the great hall door swung-to with a crash behind him. He told me that he had a sudden awful feeling of having been trapped in some way—that is how *he* put it. He whirled round, and gripped the door-handle; but something seemed to be holding it with a vast grip on the other side. Then, before he could be fixed in his mind that this was so, he was able to turn the handle, and open the door.

"He paused a moment in the doorway, and peered into the hall; for he had hardly steadied his mind sufficiently to know whether he was really frightened or not. Then he heard his sweetheart blow him a kiss out of the greyness of the big, unlit hall, and he knew that she had followed him, from the boudoir. He blew her a kiss back, and stepped inside the doorway, meaning to go to her. And then, suddenly, in a flash of sickening knowledge, he knew that it was not his sweetheart who had blown him that kiss. He knew that something was trying to tempt him alone into the darkness, and that the girl had never left the boudoir. He jumped back, and in the same instant of time, he heard the kiss again, nearer to him. He called out at the top of his voice:— 'Mary, stay in the boudoir. Don't move out of the boudoir until I come to you.' He heard her call something in reply, from the boudoir, and then he had struck a clump of a dozen, or so, matches, and was holding them above his head, and looking round the hall. There was no one in it; but even as the matches burned out, there came the sounds of a great horse galloping down the empty drive.

"Now, you see, both he and the girl had heard the sounds of the horse galloping; but when I questioned more closely, I found that the aunt had heard nothing; though, it is true, she is a bit deaf, and she was further back in the room. Of course, both he and Miss Hisgins had been in an extremely nervous state, and ready to hear anything. The door might have been slammed by a sudden puff of wind, owing to some inner door being opened; and as for the grip on the handle, that may have been nothing more than the sneck catching.

"With regard to the kisses and the sounds of the horse galloping, I pointed out that these might have seemed ordinary enough
sounds, if they had been only cool enough to reason. As I told him,
and as he knew, the sounds of a horse galloping, carry a long way
on the wind; so that what he had heard might have been nothing
more than a horse being ridden, some distance away. And as for the
kiss, plenty of quiet noises—the rustle of a paper or a leaf—have
a somewhat similar sound, especially if one is in an over-strung
condition, and imagining things.

"I finished preaching this little sermon on common-sense,
versus hysteria, as we put out the lights and left the billiard room.
But neither Beaumont nor Miss Hisgins would agree that there had
been any fancy on their parts.

"We had come out of the billiard-room, by this, and were going
along the passage; and I was still doing my best to make both of
them see the ordinary, commonplace possibilities of the happening,
when what killed my pig, as the saying goes, was the sound of a
hoof in the dark billiard room, we had just left.

"I felt the 'creep' come on me in a flash, up my spine and over
the back of my head. Miss Hisgins whooped like a child with the
whooping-cough, and ran up the passage, giving little gasping
screams. Beaumont, however, ripped round on his heels, and
jumped back a couple of yards. I gave back too, a bit, as you can
understand.

" 'There it is,' he said, in a low, breathless voice. 'Perhaps you'll
believe now.'

" 'There's certainly something,' I whispered, never taking my
gaze off the closed door of the billiard-room.

" 'H'sh!' he muttered. 'There it is again.'

"There was a sound like a great horse pacing round and round
the billiard-room, with slow, deliberate steps. A horrible cold
fright took me, so that it seemed impossible to take a full breath,
you know the feeling; and then I saw we must have been walking
backwards, for we found ourselves suddenly at the opening of the
long passage.

"We stopped there, and listened. The sounds went on steadily, with a horrible sort of deliberateness; as if the brute were
taking a sort of malicious gusto in walking about all over the
room which we had just occupied. Do you understand just what
I mean?

"Then there was a pause, and a long time of absolute quiet,

except for an excited whispering from some of the people down in the big hall. The sound came plainly up the wide stair-way. I fancy they were gathered round Miss Hisgins, with some notion of protecting her.

"I should think Beaumont and I stood there, at the end of the passage, for about five minutes, listening for any noise in the billiard-room. Then I realised what a horrible funk I was in, and I said to him:— 'I'm going to see what's there.'

" 'So'm I,' he answered. He was pretty white; but he had heaps of pluck. I told him to wait one instant, and I made a dash into my bedroom, and got my camera and flash-light. I slipped my revolver into my right-hand pocket, and a knuckle-duster over my left fist, where it was ready, and yet would not stop me from being able to work my flash-light.

"Then I ran back to Beaumont. He held out his hand, to show me that he had his pistol, and I nodded; but whispered to him not to be too quick to shoot, as there might be some silly practical-joking at work, after all. He had got a lamp from a bracket in the upper hall, which he was holding in the crook of his damaged arm, so that we had a good light. Then we went down the passage, towards the billiard-room; and you can imagine that we were a pretty nervous couple.

"All this time, there had not been a sound; but, abruptly when we were within perhaps a couple of yards of the door, we heard the sudden clumping of a hoof on the solid *parquet*-floor of the billiard-room. In the instant afterward, it seemed to me that the whole place shook beneath the ponderous hoof-falls of some huge thing, *coming towards the door*. Both Beaumont and I gave back a pace or two, and then realised, and hung on to our courage, as you might say, and waited. The great tread came right up to the door, and then stopped, and there was an instant of absolute silence, except that, so far as I was concerned, the pulsing in my throat and temples almost deafened me.

"I daresay we waited quite half a minute, and then came the further restless clumping of a great hoof. Immediately afterward, the sounds came right on, as if some invisible thing passed through the closed door, and the ponderous tread was upon us. We jumped, each of us, to our side of the passage, and I know that I spread myself stiff against the wall. The clungk clunck, clungk clunck, of the great hoof-falls passed right between us, and slowly and with deadly deliberateness, down the passage. I heard them through a haze of blood-beats in my ears and temples, and my body extraordinarily rigid and pringling, and I was horribly breathless. I stood for a little time like this, my head turned, so that I could see up the passage. I was conscious only that there was a hideous danger abroad. Do you understand?

"And then, suddenly, my pluck came back to me. I was aware that the noise of the hoof-beats sounded near the other end of the passage. I twisted quickly, and got my camera to bear, and snapped off the flash-light. Immediately afterward, Beaumont let fly a storm of shots down the passage, and began to run, shouting:— 'It's after Mary. Run! Run!'

"He rushed down the passage, and I after him. We came out on to the main landing and heard the sound of a hoof on the stairs, and after that, nothing. And from thence, onward, nothing.

"Down, below us in the big hall, I could see a number of the household round Miss Hisgins, who seemed to have fainted; and there were several of the servants clumped together a little way off, staring up at the main landing, and no one saying a single word. And about some twenty steps up the stairs was old Captain Hisgins with a drawn sword in his hand, where he had halted just below the last hoof-sound. I think I never saw anything finer than the old man standing there between his daughter and that infernal thing.

"I daresay you can understand the queer feeling of horror I had at passing that place on the stairs where the sounds had ceased. It was as if the monster were still standing there, invisible. And the peculiar thing was that we never heard another sound of the hoof, either up or down the stairs.

"After they had taken Miss Hisgins to her room, I sent word that I should follow, so soon as they were ready for me. And, presently, when a message came to tell me that I could come any time, I asked her father to give me a hand with my instrument-box, and between us we carried it into the girl's bedroom. I had the bed pulled well out into the middle of the room; after which, I erected the electric pentacle round the bed.

"Then I directed that lamps should be placed round the room, but that on no account must any light be made within the pentacle, neither must anyone pass in or out. The girl's mother, I had placed within the pentacle, and directed that her maid should sit without, ready to carry any message, so as to make sure that Mrs. Hisgins did not have to leave the pentacle. I suggested also, that the girl's father should stay the night in the room, and that he had better be armed.

"When I left the bedroom, I found Beaumont waiting outside the door, in a miserable state of anxiety. I told him what I had done, and explained to him that Miss Hisgins was probably perfectly safe within the 'protection'; but that, in addition to her father remaining the night in the room, I intended to stand guard at the door. I told him that I should like him to keep me company, for I knew that he could never sleep, feeling as he did, and I should not be sorry to have a companion. Also, I wanted to have him under my own observation; for there was no doubt but that he was actually in greater danger in some ways than the girl. At least, that was my opinion; and is still, as I think you will agree later.

"I asked him whether he would object to my drawing a pentacle round him for the night, and got him to agree; but I saw that he did not know whether to be superstitious about it, or to regard it more as a piece of foolish mumming; but he took it seriously enough, when I gave him some particulars about the Black Veil case, when young Aster died. You remember, he said it was a piece of silly superstition, and stayed outside. Poor devil!

"The night passed quietly enough, until a little while before dawn, when we both heard the sounds of a great horse galloping round and round the house, just as old Captain Hisgins had described it. You can imagine how queer it made me feel, and directly afterward, I heard someone stir within the bedroom. I knocked at the door; for I was uneasy, and the Captain came. I asked whether everything was right; to which he replied, yes; and immediately asked me whether I had heard the sounds of the galloping; so that I knew he had heard them also. I suggested that it might be as well to leave the bedroom door open a little, until the dawn came in, as there was certainly something abroad. This was done, and he went back into the room, to be near his wife and daughter.

"I had better say here, that I was doubtful whether there was any value in the 'Defense' about Miss Hisgins; for what I term the 'personal-sounds' of the manifestation were so extraordinarily material, that I was inclined to parallel the case with that one of Harford's, where the hand of the child kept materialising within the pentacle, and patting the floor. As you will remember, that was a hideous business.

"Yet, as it chanced, nothing further happened; and so soon as daylight had fully come, we all went off to bed.

"Beaumont knocked me up about midday, and I went down and made breakfast into lunch. Miss Hisgins was there, and seemed in very fair spirits, considering. She told me that I had made her feel almost safe, for the first time for days. She told me also that her cousin, Harry Parsket, was coming down from London, and she knew that he would do anything to help fight the ghost. And after that, she and Beaumont went out into the grounds, to have a little time together.

"I had a walk in the grounds myself, and went round the house; but saw no traces of hoof-marks; and after that, I spent the rest of the day, making an examination of the house; but found nothing.

"I made an end of my search, before dark, and went to my room to dress for dinner. When I got down, the cousin had just arrived; and I found him one of the nicest men I have met for a long time. A chap with a tremendous amount of pluck, and the particular kind of man I like to have with me, in a bad case like the one I was on.

"I could see that what puzzled him most was our belief in the genuineness of the haunting; and I found myself almost wanting something to happen, just to show him how true it was. As it chanced, something did happen, with a vengeance.

"Beaumont and Miss Hisgins had gone out for a stroll just before the dusk, and Captain Hisgins asked me to come into his study for a short chat whilst Parsket went upstairs with his traps, for he had no man with him.

"I had a long conversation with the old Captain, in which I pointed out that the 'haunting' had evidently no particular connection with the house, but only with the girl herself, and that the sooner she was married, the better, as it would give Beaumont a right to be with her at all times; and further than this, it might be that the manifestations would cease, if the marriage were actually performed.

"The old man nodded agreement to this, especially to the first part, and reminded me that three of the girls who were said to have been 'haunted', had been sent away from home, and met their deaths whilst away. And then in the midst of our talk there came a pretty frightening interruption; for all at once the old butler rushed into the room, most extraordinarily pale—

" 'Miss Mary, Sir! Miss Mary, Sir!' he gasped. 'She's screaming…
out in the Park, Sir! And they say they can hear the Horse—'

"The Captain made one dive for a rack of arms, and snatched
down his old sword, and ran out, drawing it as he ran. I dashed
out and up the stairs, snatched my camera-flashlight and a heavy
revolver, gave one yell at Parsket's door:— 'The Horse!' and was
down and into the grounds.

"Away in the darkness there was a confused shouting, and I
caught the sounds of shooting, out among the scattered trees. And
then, from a patch of blackness to my left, there burst suddenly
an infernal gobbling sort of neighing. Instantly I whipped round
and snapped off the flashlight. The great light blazed out momentarily, showing me the leaves of a big tree close at hand, quivering
in the night breeze; but I saw nothing else; and then the ten-fold
blackness came down upon me, and I heard Parsket shouting a
little way back to know whether I had seen anything.

"The next instant he was beside me, and I felt safer for his
company; for there was some incredible thing near to us, and I
was momentarily blind, because of the brightness of the flashlight.
'What was it? What was it?' he kept repeating in an excited voice.
And all the time I was staring into the darkness and answering,
mechanically, 'I don't know. I don't know.'

"There was a burst of shouting somewhere ahead, and then
a shot. We ran towards the sounds, yelling to the people not to
shoot; for in the darkness and panic there was this danger also.
Then there came two of the game-keepers, racing hard up the
drive, with lanterns and their guns; and immediately afterward a
row of lights dancing towards us from the house, carried by some
of the men-servants.

"As the lights came up, I saw that we had come close to Beaumont. He was standing over Miss Hisgins, and he had his revolver
in his hand. Then I saw his face, and there was a great wound across
his forehead. By him, was the Captain, turning his naked sword
this way and that, and peering into the darkness; a little behind
him stood the old butler, a battle-axe, from one of the arm-stands
in the hall, in his hands. Yet there was nothing strange to be seen
anywhere.

"We got the girl into the house, and left her with her mother and Beaumont, whilst a groom rode for a doctor. And then
the rest of us, with four other keepers, all armed with guns and

carrying lanterns, searched round the home-park. But we found nothing.

"When we got back, we found that the Doctor had been. He had bound up Beaumont's wound, which, luckily was not deep, and ordered Miss Hisgins straight to bed. I went upstairs with the Captain, and found Beaumont on guard outside of the girl's door. I asked him how he felt; and then, so soon as the girl and her mother were ready for us, Captain Hisgins and I went into the bedroom, and fixed the pentacle again round the bed. They had already got lamps about the room; and after I had set the same order of watching, as on the previous night, I joined Beaumont, outside of the door.

"Parsket had come up, while I had been in the bedroom, and between us, we got some idea from Beaumont as to what had happened out in the Park. It seems that they were coming home after their stroll, from the direction of the West Lodge. It had got quite dark; and, suddenly, Miss Hisgins said 'Hush!' and came to a standstill. He stopped, and listened; but heard nothing for a little. Then he caught it—the sound of a horse, seemingly a long way off, galloping towards them over the grass. He told the girl that it was nothing, and started to hurry her towards the house; but she was not deceived, of course. In less than a minute, they heard it quite close to them in the darkness, and they started running. Then Miss Hisgins caught her foot, and fell. She began to scream, and that is what the butler heard. As Beaumont lifted the girl, he heard the hoofs come thudding right at him. He stood over her, and fired all five chambers of his revolver right at the sounds. He told us that he was sure he saw something that looked like an enormous horse's head, right upon him, in the light of the last flash of his pistol. Immediately afterwards, he was struck a tremendous blow, which knocked him down; and then the Captain and the butler came running up, shouting. The rest, of course, we knew.

"About ten o'clock, the butler brought us up a tray; for which I was very glad; as the night before I had got rather hungry. I warned Beaumont, however, to be very particular not to drink any spirits, and I also made him give me his pipe and matches. At midnight I drew a pentacle round him; and Parsket and I sat one on each side of him; but outside of the pentacle; for I had no fear that there would be any manifestation made against anyone, except Beaumont or Miss Hisgins.

"After that, we kept pretty quiet. The passage was lit by a big lamp at each end; so that we had plenty of light; and we were all armed, Beaumont and I with revolvers, and Parsket with a shotgun. In addition to my weapon, I had my camera and flashlight.

"Now and again we talked in whispers; and twice the Captain came out of the bedroom to have a word with us. About half past one, we had all grown very silent; and suddenly, about twenty minutes later, I held up my hand, silently; for there seemed to me to be a sound of galloping, out in the night. I knocked on the bedroom door, for the Captain to open it, and when he came, I whispered to him that we thought we heard the Horse. For some time, we stayed, listening, and both Parsket and the Captain thought they heard it; but now I was not so sure, neither was Beaumont. Yet afterwards, I thought I heard it again.

"I told Captain Hisgins I thought he had better go back into the bedroom, and leave the door a little open, and this he did. But from that time onward, we heard nothing; and presently the dawn came in, and we all went very thankfully to bed.

"When I was called at lunch-time, I had a little surprise; for Captain Hisgins told me that they had held a family council, and had decided to take my advice, and have the marriage without a day's more delay than possible. Beaumont was already on his way to London to get a special licence, and they hoped to have the wedding next day.

"This pleased me; for it seemed the sanest thing to be done, in the extraordinary circumstances; and meanwhile I should continue my investigations; but until the marriage was accomplished, my chief thought was to keep Miss Hisgins near to me.

"After lunch, I thought I would take a few experimental photographs of Miss Hisgins and her *surroundings*. Sometimes the camera sees things that would seem very strange to normal human eyesight.

"With this intention, and partly to make an excuse to keep her in my company as much as possible, I asked Miss Hisgins to join me in my experiments. She seemed glad to do this, and I spent several hours with her, wandering all over the house, from room to room; and whenever the impulse came, I took a flashlight of her and the room or corridor in which we chanced to be at the moment.

"After we had gone right through the house in this fashion, I asked her whether she felt sufficiently brave to repeat the experiments in the cellars. She said, yes; and so I rooted out Captain

Hisgins and Parsket; for I was not going to take her even into what you might call artificial darkness, without help and companionship at hand.

"When we were ready, we went down into the wine-cellar, Captain Hisgins carrying a shot-gun, and Parsket a specially prepared background and a lantern. I got the girl to stand in the middle of the cellar, whilst Parsket and the Captain held out the background behind her. Then I fired off the flashlight, and we went into the next cellar, where we repeated the experiment.

"Then, in the third cellar, a tremendous, pitch-dark place, something extraordinary and horrible manifested itself. I had stationed Miss Hisgins in the centre of the place, with her father and Parsket holding the background, as before. When all was ready, and just as I pressed the trigger of the 'flash', there came in the cellar that dreadful, gobbling neighing, that I had heard out in the Park. It seemed to come from somewhere above the girl; and in the glare of the sudden light, I saw that she was staring tensely upward, but at no visible thing. And then in the succeeding comparative darkness, I was shouting to the Captain and Parsket to run Miss Hisgins out into the daylight.

"This was done, instantly; and I shut and locked the door afterwards making the First and Eighth signs of the Saaamaaa Ritual opposite to each post, and connecting them across the threshold with a triple line.

"In the meanwhile, Parsket and Captain Hisgins carried the girl to her Mother, and left her there, in a half-fainting condition; whilst I stayed on guard outside of the cellar door, feeling pretty horrible, for I knew that there was some disgusting thing inside; and along with this feeling there was a sense of half-ashamedness, rather miserable, you know, because I had exposed Miss Hisgins to the danger.

"I had got the Captain's shot-gun, and when he and Parsket came down again, they were each carrying guns and lanterns. I could not possibly tell you the utter relief of spirit and body that came to me, when I heard them coming; but just try to imagine what it was like, standing outside of that cellar. Can you?

"I remember noticing, just before I went to unlock the door, how white and ghastly Parsket looked, and the old Captain was grey-looking; and I wondered whether my face was like theirs. And this, you know, had its own distinct effect upon my nerves; for it seemed to bring the beastliness of the thing bash down on to me in a fresh way. I know it was only sheer will-power that carried me up to the door and made me turn the key.

"I paused one little moment, and then with a nervy jerk, sent the door wide open, and held my lantern over my head. Parsket and the Captain came one on each side of me, and held up their lanterns; but the place was absolutely empty. Of course, I did not trust to a casual look of this kind; but spent several hours with the help of the two others in sounding every square foot of the floor, ceiling and walls.

"Yet, in the end, I had to admit that the place itself was absolutely normal; and so we came away. But I sealed the door, and outside, opposite each door-post, I made the First and Last signs of the Saaamaaa Ritual, joining them as before, with a triple-line. Can you imagine what it was like, searching that cellar?

"When we got upstairs, I inquired very anxiously how Miss Hisgins was, and the girl came out herself to tell me that she was all right and that I was not to trouble about her, or blame myself, as I told her I had been doing.

"I felt happier then, and went off to dress for dinner; and after that was done, Parsket and I took one of the bathrooms, to develop the negatives that I had been taking. Yet none of the plates had anything to tell us, until we came to the one that was taken in the cellar. Parsket was developing, and I had taken a batch of the fixed plates out into the lamplight, to examine them.

"I had just gone carefully through the lot, when I heard a shout from Parskett, and when I ran to him, he was looking at a partly-developed negative, which he was holding up to the red-lamp. It showed the girl plainly, looking upward, as I had seen her; but the thing that astonished me, was the shadow of an enormous hoof, right above her, as if it were coming down upon her out of the shadows. And, you know, I had run her bang into that danger. That was the thought that was chief in my mind.

"As soon as the developing was complete, I fixed the plate, and examined it carefully in a good light. There was no doubt about it at all; the thing above Miss Hisgins was an enormous, shadowy hoof. Yet I was no nearer to coming to any definite knowledge; and the only thing I could do was to warn Parsket to say nothing about it to the girl; for it would only increase her fright; but I showed the thing to her father, for I considered it right that he should know.

"That night, we took the same precautions for Miss Hisgins' safety, as on the two previous nights; and Parsket kept me company;

yet the dawn came in, without anything unusual having happened, and I went off to bed.

"When I got down to lunch, I learnt that Beaumont had wired to say that he would be in soon after four; also that a message had been sent to the Rector. And it was generally plain that the ladies of the house were in a tremendous fluster.

"Beaumont's train was late, and he did not get home until five; but even then the Rector had not put in an appearance; and the butler came in to say that the coachman had returned without him, as he had been called away unexpectedly. Twice more during the evening the carriage was sent down; but the clergyman had not returned; and we had to delay the marriage until the next day.

"That night, I arranged the 'Defense' round the girl's bed, and the Captain and his wife sat up with her, as before. Beaumont, as I expected, insisted on keeping watch with me, and he seemed in a curiously frightened mood; not for himself, you know; but for Miss Hisgins. He had a horrible feeling, he told me, that there would be a final, dreadful attempt on his sweetheart that night.

"This, of course, I told him was nothing but nerves; yet, really, it made me feel very anxious; for I have seen too much, not to know that, under such circumstances, a premonitory *conviction* of impending danger, is not necessarily to be put down entirely to nerves. In fact, Beaumont was so simply and earnestly convinced that the night would bring some extraordinary manifestation, that I got Parsket to rig up a long cord from the wire of the butler's bell, to come along the passage handy.

"To the butler himself, I gave directions not to undress, and to give the same order to two of the footmen. If I rang, he was to come instantly, with the footmen, carrying lanterns; and the lanterns were to be kept ready lit all night. If, for any reason, the bell did not ring, and I blew my whistle, he was to take that as a signal in place of the bell.

"After I had arranged all these minor details, I drew a pentacle about Beaumont, and warned him very particularly to stay within it, whatever happened. And when this was done, there was nothing to do but wait, and pray that the night would go as quietly as the night before.

"We scarcely talked at all, and by about one a.m., we were all very tense and nervous; so that, at last, Parsket got up and began to walk up and down the corridor, to steady himself a bit. Presently,

I slipped off my pumps, and joined him; and we walked up and down, whispering occasionally, for something over an hour, until in turning I caught my foot in the bell-cord, and went down on my face; but without hurting myself, or making a noise.

"When I got up, Parsket nudged me.

" 'Did you notice that the bell never rang,' he whispered.

" 'Jove!' I said, you're right.'

" 'Wait a minute,' he answered. 'I'll bet it's only a kink somewhere in the cord. He left his gun, and slipped along the passage, and taking the top lamp, tiptoed away into the house, carrying Beaumont's revolver ready in his right-hand. He was a plucky chap, as I remember thinking then, and again, later.

"Just then, Beaumont motioned to me for absolute quiet. Directly afterwards, I heard the thing for which he listened—the sound of a horse galloping, out in the night. I think that I may say, I fairly shivered. The sound died away, and left a horrible, desolate, eerie feeling in the air, you know. I put my hand out to the bell-cord, hoping that Parsket had got it clear. Then I waited, glancing before and behind.

"Perhaps two minutes passed, full of what seemed like an almost unearthly quiet. And then, suddenly, down the corridor, at the lighted end, there sounded the clumping of a great hoof; and instantly the lamp was thrown down with a tremendous crash, and we were in the dark. I tugged hard on the cord, and blew the whistle; then I raised my snapshot, and fired the flashlight. The corridor blazed into brilliant light; but there was nothing; and then the darkness fell like thunder. I heard the Captain at the bedroom-door, and shouted to him to bring out a lamp, *quick*; but instead, something started to kick the door, and I heard the Captain shouting within the bedroom, and then the screaming of the women. I had a sudden horrible fear that the monster had got into the bedroom; but in the same instant, from up the corridor, there came abruptly the vile, gobbling neighing that we had heard in the park and the cellar. I blew the whistle again, and groped blindly for the bell-cord, shouting to Beaumont to stay in the Pentacle, whatever happened. I yelled again to the Captain to bring out a lamp, and there came a smashing sound against the bedroom door. Then I had my matches in my hand, to get some light, before that incredible, unseen Monster was upon us.

"The match scraped on the box, and flared up, dully; and in the same instant, I heard a faint sound behind me. I whipped round, in a kind of mad terror, and saw something, in the light of the match—a monstrous horse-head, close to Beaumont.

" 'Look out, Beaumont!' I shouted in a sort of scream. 'It's behind you!'

"The match went out, abruptly, and instantly there came the huge bang of Parsket's double-barrel (both barrels at once), fired evidently single-handed by Beaumont close to my ear, as it seemed. I caught a momentary glimpse of the great head, in the flash, and of an enormous hoof amid the belch of fire and smoke, seeming to be descending upon Beaumont. In the same instant, I fired three chambers of my revolver. There was the sound of a dull blow, and then that horrible, gobbling neigh, broke out close to me. I fired twice at the sound. Immediately afterward, Something struck me, and I was knocked backwards. I got on to my knees, and shouted for help, at the top of my voice. I heard the women screaming behind the closed door of the bedroom, and was dully aware that the door was being smashed from the inside; and directly afterwards I knew that Beaumont was struggling with some hideous thing, near to me. For an instant, I held back, stupidly, paralysed with funk; and then, blindly and in a sort of rigid chill of goose-flesh, I went to help him, shouting his name. I can tell you, I was nearly sick, with the naked fear I had on me. There came a little, choking scream, out of the darkness; and, at that, I jumped forward into the dark. I gripped a vast, furry ear. Then something struck me another great blow, knocking me sick. I hit back, weak and blind, and gripped with my other hand at the incredible thing. Abruptly, I was dimly aware of a tremendous crash behind me, and a great burst of light. There were other lights in the passage, and a noise of feet and shouting. My hand-grips were torn from the thing they held; I shut my eyes stupidly, and heard a loud yell above me; and then a heavy blow, like a butcher chopping meat; and then something fell upon me.

"I was helped to my knees by the Captain and the butler. On the floor lay an enormous horse-head, out of which protruded a man's trunk and legs. On the wrists were fixed great hoofs. It was the monster. The Captain cut something with the sword that he held in his hand, and stooped, and lifted off the mask; for that is what it was. I saw the face then of the man who had worn it. It was Parsket. He had a bad wound across the forehead, where the

Captain's sword had bit through the mask. I looked bewilderedly from him to Beaumont, who was sitting up, leaning against the wall of the corridor. Then I stared at Parsket, again.

" 'By Jove!' I said, at last; and then I was quiet; for I was so ashamed for the man. You can understand, can't you? And he was opening his eyes. And, you know, I had grown so to like him.

"And then, you know, just as Parsket was getting back his wits, and looking from one to the other of us, and beginning to remember, there happened a strange and incredible thing. For from the end of the corridor, there sounded, suddenly, the clumping of a great hoof. I looked that way, and then instantly at Parsket, and saw a horrible fear in his face and eyes. He wrenched himself round, weakly, and stared in mad terror up the corridor to where the sound had been; and the rest of us stared, in a frozen group. I remember hearing vaguely, half sobs and whispers from Miss Hisgins' bedroom, all the while that I stared frightenedly, up the corridor.

"The silence lasted several seconds; and then, abruptly, there came again the clumping of the great hoof, away at the end of the corridor. And immediately afterward, the clungk, clunk—clungk, clunk, of mighty hoofs coming down the passage, towards us.

"Even then, you know, most of us thought it was some mechanism of Parsket's still at work; and we were in the queerest mixture of fright and doubt. I think everyone looked at Parsket. And suddenly the Captain shouted out:—

" 'Stop this damned fooling at once. Haven't you done enough!'

"For my part, I was now frightened; for I had a *sense* that there was something horrible and wrong. And then Parsket managed to gasp out:—

" 'It's not me! My God! It's not me! My God! It's not me!'

"And then, you know, it seemed to come home to everyone in an instant that there was really some dreadful thing coming down the passage. There was a mad rush to get away, and even old Captain Hisgins gave back with the butler and the footmen. Beaumont fainted outright, as I found afterwards; for he had been badly mauled. I just flattened back against the wall, kneeling, as I was, too stupid and dazed even to run. And almost in the same instant the ponderous hoof-falls sounded close to me, and seeming to shake the solid floor, as they passed. Abruptly the great sounds ceased, and I knew in a sort of sick fashion that the thing had halted opposite to the open door of the girl's bedroom. And then I was aware that Parsket was standing rocking in the doorway, with his arms spread across, so as to fill the doorway with his body. I saw with less bewilderment. Parsket was extraordinarily pale, and the blood was running down his face from the wound in his forehead; and then I noticed that he seemed to be looking at something in the passage, with a peculiar, desperate, fixed, incredibly masterful gaze. But, there was really nothing to be seen. And suddenly, the clungk, clunk—clungk, clunk, recommenced, and passed onward down the passage. In the same moment, Parskett pitched forward out of the doorway on to his face.

"There were shouts from the huddle of men down the passage, and the two footmen and the butler simply ran, carrying their lanterns; but the Captain went against the side-wall with his back, and put the lamp he was carrying over his head. The dull tread of the Horse went past him, and left him unharmed; and I heard the monstrous hoof-falls going away and away through the quiet house; and after that a dead silence.

"Then the Captain moved, and came towards us, very slow and shaky, and with an extraordinarily grey face.

"I crept towards Parsket, and the Captain came to help me. We turned him over; and, you know, I knew in a moment that he was dead; but you can imagine what a feeling it sent through me.

"I looked up at the Captain; and suddenly he said:—

" 'That— That— That—' and I know that he was trying to tell me that Parsket had stood between his daughter and whatever it was that had gone down the passage. I stood up, and steadied him; though I was not very steady myself. And suddenly, his face began to work, and he went down on to his knees by Parsket, and cried like some shaken child. Then the women came out of the doorway of the bedroom; and I turned away and left him to them, whilst I went over to Beaumont.

"That is practically the whole story; and the only thing that is left to me is to try to explain some of the puzzling parts, here and there.

"Perhaps you have seen that Parsket was in love with Miss Hisgins; and this fact is the key to a good deal that was extraordinary. He was doubtless responsible for some portions of the 'haunting'; in fact, I think for nearly everything; but, you know, I can prove nothing, and what I have to tell you is chiefly the result of deduction.

"In the first place, it is obvious that Parsket's intention was to frighten Beaumont away; and when he found that he could not do this, I think he grew so desperate that he really intended to kill him. I hate to say this; but the facts force me to think so.

"I am quite certain that it was Parsket who broke Beaumont's arm. He knew all the details of the so-called 'Horse Legend', and got the idea to work upon the old story, for his own end. He evidently had some method of slipping in and out of the house, probably through one of the many French windows, or possibly he had a key to one or two of the garden doors; and when he was supposed to be away, he was really coming down, on the quiet, and hiding somewhere in the neighbourhood.

"The incident of the kiss in the dark hall, I put down to sheer nervous imaginings on the part of Beaumont and Miss Hisgins; yet, I must say that the sound of the horse outside of the front door, is a little difficult to explain away. But I am still inclined to keep to my first idea on this point, that there was nothing really unnatural about it.

"The hoof-sounds in the billiard-room and down the passage, were done by Parsket, from the floor below, by pomping up against the panelled ceiling, with a block of wood tied to one of the window-hooks. I proved this, by an examination, which showed the dints in the woodwork.

"The sounds of the horse galloping round the house, were possibly made also by Parsket, who must have had a horse tied up in the plantation, near by, unless, indeed, he made the sounds himself; but I do not see how he could have gone fast enough to produce the illusion. In any case, I don't feel perfect certainty on this point. I failed to find any hoof-marks, as you remember.

"The gobbling neighing in the park was a ventriloquial achievement on the part of Parsket; and the attack out there on Beaumont was also by him, so that when I thought he was in his bedroom, he must have been outside all the time, and joined me after I ran out of the front-door. This is almost probable; I mean that Parsket was the cause; for if it had been something more serious, he would certainly have given up his foolishness, knowing that there was no longer any need for it. I cannot imagine how he escaped being shot, both then, and in the last mad action, of which I have just told you. He was enormously without fear of any kind for himself, as you can see.

"The time when Parsket was with us, when we thought we

heard the Horse galloping round the house, we must have been deceived. No one was *very* sure, except, of course, Parsket, who would naturally encourage the belief.

"The neighing in the cellar, is where I consider there came the first suspicion into Parsket's mind that there was something more at work than his sham-haunting. The neighing was done by him, in the same way that he did it in the park; but when I remember how ghastly he looked, I feel sure that the sounds must have had some infernal quality added to them, which frightened the man himself. Yet, later, he would persuade himself that he had been getting fanciful. Of course, I must not forget that the effect upon Miss Hisgins must have made him feel pretty miserable.

"Then, about the clergyman being called away, we found afterwards that it was a bogus errand, or rather, call; and it is apparent that Parsket was at the bottom of this, so as to get a few more hours in which to achieve his end; and what that was, a very little imagination will show you; for he had found that Beaumont would not be frightened away. I hate to think this; but I'm bound to. Anyway, it is obvious that the man was temporarily a bit off his normal balance. Love's a queer disease!

"Then, there is no doubt at all but that Parsket left the cord to the butler's bell hitched somewhere, so as to give him an excuse to slip away naturally to clear it. This also gave him the opportunity to remove one of the passage lamps. Then he had only to smash the other, and the passage was in utter darkness, for him to make the attempt on Beaumont.

"In the same way, it was he who locked the door of the bedroom, and took the key (it was in his pocket). This prevented the Captain from bringing a light, and coming to the rescue. But Captain Hisgins broke down the door, with the heavy fender-curb; and it was his smashing the door that sounded so confusing and frightening in the darkness of the passage.

"The photograph of the monstrous hoof above Miss Hisgins in the cellar, is one of the things that I am less sure about. It might have been faked by Parsket, whilst I was out of the room, and this would have been easy enough, to anyone who knew how. But, you know, it does not look like a fake. Yet, there is as much evidence of probability that it was faked, as against; and the thing is too vague for an examination to help to a definite decision; so that I will express no opinion, one way or the other. It is certainly a horrible photograph.

"And now I come to that last, dreadful thing. There has been no further manifestation of anything abnormal; so that there is an extraordinary uncertainty in my conclusions. IF we had not heard those last sounds, and if Parsket had not shown that enormous sense of fear, the whole of this case could be explained in the way in which I have shown. And, in fact, as you have seen, I am of the opinion that almost all of it can be cleared up; but I see no way of going past the thing we heard at the last, and the fear that Parsket showed.

"His death— No, that proves nothing. At the inquest it was described somewhat untechnically as due to heart-spasm. That is normal enough, and leaves us quite in the dark as to whether he died because he stood between the girl and some incredible thing of monstrosity.

"The look on Parsket's face, and the thing he called out, when he heard the great hoof-sounds coming down the passage, seem to show that he had the sudden realisation of what before then may have been nothing more than a horrible suspicion. And his fear and appreciation of some tremendous danger approaching was probably more keenly real even than mine. And then he did the one fine, great thing!"

"And the cause?" I said. "What caused it?"

Carnacki shook his head.

"God knows," he answered, with a peculiar, sincere reverence. "IF that thing was what it seemed to be, one might suggest an explanation, which would not offend one's reason, but which may be utterly wrong. Yet I have thought, though it would take a long lecture on Thought Induction to get you to appreciate my reasons, that Parsket had produced what I might term a kind of 'induced haunting', a kind of induced simulation of his mental conceptions, due to his desperate thoughts and broodings. It *is* impossible to make it clearer, in a few words."

"But the old story!" I said. "Why may not there have been something in *that* ?"

"There may have been something in it," said Carnacki. "But I do not think it had anything to do with *this*. I have not clearly thought out my reasons, yet; but later I may be able to tell you why I think so."

"And the marriage. And the cellar—was there anything found there?" asked Taylor.

"Yes, the marriage was performed that day, in spite of the tragedy." Carnacki told us. "It was the wisest thing to do—considering the things that I cannot explain. Yes, I had the floor of that big cellar up; for I had a feeling I might find something there to give me some light. But there was nothing.

"You know, the whole thing is tremendous and extraordinary. I shall never forget the look on Parsket's face. And afterwards the disgusting sounds of those great hoofs going away through the quiet house."

Carnacki stood up:—

"Out you go!" he said, in friendly fashion, using the recognised formula.

And we went presently out into the quiet of the Embankment, and so to our homes.

The Haunted Jarvee

"SEEN ANYTHING OF CARNACKI lately?" I asked Arkright when we met in the City.

"No," he replied. "He's probably off on one of his jaunts. We'll be having a card one of these days inviting us to No. 472, Cheyne Walk, and then we'll hear all about it. Queer chap that."

He nodded, and went on his way. It was some months now since we four—Jessop, Arkright, Taylor and myself—had received the usual summons to drop in at No. 472 and hear Carnacki's story of his latest case. What talks they were! Stories of all kinds and true in every word, yet full of weird and extraordinary incidents that held one silent and awed until he had finished.

Strangely enough, the following morning brought me a curtly worded card telling me to be at No. 472 at seven o'clock promptly. I was the first to arrive, Jessop and Taylor soon followed and just before dinner was announced Arkright came in.

Dinner over, Carnacki as usual passed round his smokes, snuggled himself down luxuriously in his favourite armchair and went straight to the story we knew he had invited us to hear.

"I've been on a trip in one of the real old-time sailing ships," he said without any preliminary remarks. "The *Jarvee*, owned by my old friend Captain Thompson. I went on the voyage primarily for my health, but I picked on the old *Jarvee* because Captain Thompson had often told me there was something queer about her. I used to ask him up here whenever he came ashore and try to get him to tell me more about it, you know; but the funny thing was he never could tell me anything definite concerning her queerness. He seemed always to *know* but when it came to putting his knowledge into words it was as if he found that the reality melted out of it. He would end up usually by saying that you saw things and then

263

he would wave his hands vaguely, but further than that he never seemed able to pass on the knowledge of something strange which he had noticed about the ship, except odd outside details.

" 'Can't keep men in her no-how,' he often told me. 'They get frightened and they see things and they feel things. An' I've lost a power o' men out of her. Fallen from aloft, you know. She's getting a bad name.' And then he'd shake his head very solemnly.

"Old Thompson was a brick in every way. When I got aboard I found that he had given me the use of a whole empty cabin opening off my own as my laboratory and workshop. He gave the carpenter orders to fit up the empty cabin with shelves and other conveniences according to my directions and in a couple of days I had all the apparatus, both mechanical and electric with which I had conducted my other ghost-hunts, neatly and safely stowed away, for I took a great deal of gear with me as I intended to interest myself by examining thoroughly into the mystery about which the captain was at once so positive and so vague.

"During the first fortnight out I followed my usual methods of making a thorough and exhaustive search. This I did with the most scrupulous care, but found nothing abnormal of any kind in the whole vessel. She was an old wooden ship and I took care to sound and measure every casement and bulkhead, to examine every exit from the holds and to seal all the hatches. These and many other precautions I took, but at the end of the fortnight I had neither seen anything nor found anything.

"The old barque was just, to all seeming, a healthy, average old-timer jogging along comfortably from one port to another. And save for an indefinable sense of what I could now describe as 'abnormal peace' about the ship I could find nothing to justify the old captain's solemn and frequent assurances that I would see soon enough for myself. This he would say often as we walked the poop together; afterwards stopping to take a long, expectant, half-fearful look at the immensity of the sea around.

"Then on the eighteenth day something truly happened. I had been pacing the poop as usual with old Thompson when suddenly he stopped and looked up at the mizzen royal which had just begun to flap against the mast. He glanced at the wind-vane near him, then ruffled his hat back and stared at the sea.

" 'Wind's droppin', mister. There'll be trouble tonight,' he said. 'D'you see yon?' And he pointed away to windward.

" 'What?' I asked, staring with a curious little thrill that was due to more than curiosity. 'Where?'

" 'Right off the beam,' he said. 'Comin' from under the sun.'

" 'I don't see anything,' I explained after a long stare at the wide-spreading silence of the sea that was already glassing into a dead calm surface now that the wind had died.

" 'Yon shadow fixin',' said the old man, reaching for his glasses.

"He focussed them and took a long look, then passed them across to me and pointed with his finger. 'Just under the sun,' he repeated. 'Comin' towards us at the rate o' knots.' He was curiously calm and matter-of-fact and yet I felt that a certain excitement had him in the throat; so that I took the glasses eagerly and stared according to his directions.

"After a minute I saw it—a vague shadow upon the still surface of the sea that seemed to move towards us as I stared. For a moment I gazed fascinated, yet ready every moment to swear that I saw nothing and in the same instant to be assured that there was truly *something* out there upon the water, apparently coming towards the ship.

" 'It's only a shadow, captain,' I said at length.

" 'Just so, mister,' he replied simply. 'Have a look over the stern to the norrard.' He spoke in the quietest way, as a man speaks who is sure of all his facts and who is facing an experience he has faced before, yet who salts his natural matter-of-factness with a deep and constant excitement.

"At the captain's hint I turned about and directed the glasses to the northward. For a while I searched, sweeping my aided vision to and fro over the greying arc of the sea.

"Then I saw the thing plain in the field of the glass—a vague something, a shadow upon the water and the shadow seemed to be moving towards the ship.

" 'That's queer,' I muttered with a funny little stirring at the back of my throat.

" 'Now to the west'ard, mister,' said the captain, still speaking in his peculiar level way.

"I looked to the westward and in a minute I picked up the thing—a third shadow that seemed to move across the sea as I watched it.

" 'My God, captain,' I exclaimed, 'what does it mean?'

" 'That's just what I want to know, mister,' said the captain.

'I've seen 'em before and thought sometimes I must be going mad. Sometimes they're plain an' sometimes they're scarce to be seen, an' sometimes they're like livin' things, an' sometimes they're like nought at all but silly fancies. D'you wonder I couldn't name 'em proper to you?'

"I did not answer for I was staring now expectantly towards the south along the length of the barque. Afar off on the horizon my glasses picked up something dark and vague upon the surface of the sea, a shadow it seemed which grew plainer.

" 'My God!' I muttered again. 'This is real. This—' I turned again to the eastward.

" 'Comin' in from the four points, ain't they,' said Captain Thompson and he blew his whistle.

" 'Take them three r'yals off her,' he told the mate, 'an' tell one of the boys to shove lanterns up on the sherpoles. Get the men down smart before dark,' he concluded as the mate moved off to see the orders carried out.

" 'I'm sendin' no men aloft to-night,' he said to me. 'I've lost enough that way.'

" 'They may be only shadows, captain, after all,' I said, still looking earnestly at that far-off grey vagueness on the eastward sea. 'Bit of mist or cloud floating low.' Yet though I said this I had no belief that it was so. And as for old Captain Thompson, he never took the trouble to answer, but reached for his glasses which I passed to him.

" 'Gettin' thin an' disappearin' as they come near,' he said presently. 'I know, I've seen 'em do that oft an' plenty before. They'll be close round the ship soon but you nor me won't see them, nor no one else, but they'll be there. I wish 'twas mornin'. I do that!'

"He had handed the glasses back to me and I had been staring at each of the oncoming shadows in turn. It was as Captain Thompson had said. As they drew nearer they seemed to spread and thin out and presently to become dissipated into the grey of the gloaming so that I could easily have imagined that I watched merely four little portions of grey cloud, expanding naturally into impalpableness and invisibility.

" 'Wish I'd took them t'gallants off her while I was about it,' remarked the old man presently. 'Can't think to send no one off the decks to-night, not unless there's real need.' He slipped away from me and peered at the aneroid in the skylight. 'Glass steady, anyhow,' he muttered as he came away, seeming more satisfied.

"By this time the men had all returned to the decks and the night was down upon us so that I could watch the queer, dissolving shadows which approached the ship.

"Yet as I walked the poop with old Captain Thompson, you can imagine how I grew to feel. Often I found myself looking over my shoulder with quick, jerky glances; for it seemed to me that in the curtains of gloom that hung just beyond the rails there must be a vague, incredible thing looking inboard.

"I questioned the captain in a thousand ways, but could get little out of him beyond what I knew. It was as if he had no power to convey to another the knowledge which he possessed and I could ask no one else, for every other man in the ship was newly signed on, including the mates, which was in itself a significant fact.

"'You'll see for yourself, mister,' was the refrain with which the captain parried my questions, so that it began to seem as if he almost *feared* to put anything he knew into words. Yet once, when I had jerked round with a nervous feeling that something was at my back, he said calmly enough: 'Naught to fear, mister, whilst you're in the light and on the decks.' His attitude was extraordinary in the way in which he *accepted* the situation. He appeared to have no personal fear.

"The night passed quietly until about eleven o'clock when suddenly and without one atom of warning a furious squall burst on the vessel. There was something monstrous and abnormal in the wind; it was as if some power were using the elements to an infernal purpose. Yet the captain met the situation calmly. The helm was put down and the sails shaken while the three t'gallants were lowered. Then the three upper topsails. Yet still the breeze roared over us, almost drowning the thunder which the sails were making in the night.

"'Split 'em to ribbons!' the captain yelled in my ear above the noise of the wind. 'Can't help it. I ain't sendin' no men aloft to-night unless she seems like to shake the sticks out of her. That's what bothers me.'

"For nearly an hour after that, until eight bells went at midnight, the wind showed no signs of easing but breezed up harder than ever. And all the while the skipper and I walked the poop, he ever and again peering up anxiously through the darkness at the banging and thrashing sails.

"For my part I could do nothing except stare round and round at the extraordinarily dark night in which the ship seemed to be embedded solidly. The very feel and sound of the wind gave me a sort of constant horror, for there seemed to be an unnaturalness rampant in the atmosphere. But how much this was the effect of my over-strung nerves and excited imagination, I cannot say. Certainly, in all my experience I had never come across anything just like what I felt and endured through that peculiar squall.

"At eight bells when the other watch came on deck the captain was forced to send all hands aloft to make the canvas fast, as he had begun to fear that he would actually lose his masts if he delayed longer. This was done and the barque snugged right down.

"Yet, though the work was done successfully, the captain's fears were justified in a sufficiently horrible way, for as the men were beginning to make their way in off the wards there was a loud crying and shouting aloft and immediately afterwards a crash down on the main deck, followed instantly by a second crash.

" 'My God! Two of 'em!' shouted the skipper as he snatched a lamp from the forrard binnacle. Then down on to the main deck. It was as he had said. Two of the men had fallen, or—as the thought came to me—been thrown from aloft and were lying silent on the deck. Above us in the darkness I heard a few vague shouts followed by a curious quiet, save for the constant blast of the wind whose whistling and howling in the rigging seemed but to accentuate the complete and frightened silence of the men aloft. Then I was aware that the men were coming down swiftly and presently one after the other came with a quick leap out of the rigging and stood about the two fallen men with odd exclamations and questions which always merged off instantly into new silence.

"And all the time I was conscious of a most extraordinary sense of oppression and frightened distress and fearful expectation, for it seemed to me, standing there near the dead in that unnatural wind that a power of evil filled all the night about the ship and that some fresh horror was imminent.

"The following morning there was a solemn little service, very rough and crude, but undertaken with a nice reverence and the two men who had fallen were tilted off from a hatch-cover and plunged suddenly out of sight. As I watched them vanish in the deep blue of the water an idea came to me and I spent part of the afternoon talking it over with the captain, after which I passed the rest of the time until sunset was upon us in arranging and fitting up a part of my electrical apparatus. Then I went on deck and had a good look round. The evening was beautifully calm and ideal for the experiment which I had in mind, for the wind had died away with a peculiar suddenness after the death of the two men and all that day the sea had been like glass.

"To a certain extent I believed that I comprehended the primary cause of the vague but peculiar manifestations which I had witnessed the previous evening and which Captain Thompson believed implicitly to be intimately connected with the death of the two sailormen.

"I believed the origin of the happenings to lie in a strange but perfectly understandable cause, *i.e.*, in that phenomenon known technically as 'attractive vibrations'. Harzam, in his monograph on 'Induced Hauntings', points out that such are invariably produced by 'induced vibrations', that is, by temporary vibrations set up by some outside cause.

"This is somewhat abstruse to follow out in a story of this kind, but it was on a long consideration of these points that I had resolved to make experiments to see whether I could not produce a counter or 'repellent' vibration, a thing which Harzam had succeeded in producing on three occasions and in which I have had a partial success once, failing only because of the imperfectness of the apparatus I had aboard.

"As I have said, I can scarcely follow the reasoning further in a brief record such as this, neither do I think it would be of interest to you who are interested only in the startling and weird side of my investigations. Yet I have told you sufficient to show you the germ of my reasonings and to enable you to follow intelligently my hopes and expectations in sending out what I hoped would prove 'repellent' vibrations.

"Therefore it was that when the sun had descended to within ten degrees of the visible horizon the captain and I began to watch for the appearance of the shadows. Presently, under the sun, I discovered the same peculiar appearance of a moving greyness which I had seen on the preceding night and almost immediately Captain Thompson told me that he saw the same to the south.

"To the north and east we perceived the same extraordinary thing and I at once set my electric apparatus at work, sending out the strange repelling force to the dim, far shadows of mystery which moved steadily out of the distance towards the vessel.

"Earlier in the evening the captain had snugged the barque right down to her topsails, for as he said, until the calm went he would risk nothing. According to him it was always during calm weather that the extraordinary manifestations occurred. In this case he was certainly justified, for a most tremendous squall struck the ship in the middle watch, taking the fore upper topsail right out of the ropes.

"At the time when it came I was lying down on a locker in the saloon, but I ran up on to the poop as the vessel canted under the enormous force of the wind. Here I found the air pressure tremendous and the noise of the squall stunning. And over it all and through it all I was conscious of something abnormal and threatening that set my nerves uncomfortably acute. The thing was not natural.

"Yet, despite the carrying away of the topsail, not a man was sent aloft.

" 'Let 'em all go!' said old Captain Thompson. 'I'd have shortened her down to the bare sticks if I'd done all I wanted!'

"About two a.m. the squall passed with astonishing suddenness and the night showed clear above the vessel. From then onward I paced the poop with the skipper, often pausing at the break to look along the lighted main deck. It was on one of these occasions that I saw something peculiar. It was like a vague flitting of an impossible shadow between me and the whiteness of the well-scrubbed decks. Yet, even as I stared, the thing was gone and I could not say with surety that I had seen anything.

" 'Pretty plain to see, mister,' said the captain's voice at my elbow. 'I've only seen that once before an' we lost half of the hands that trip. We'd better be at 'ome, I'm thinkin'. It'll end in scrappin' her, sure.'

"The old man's calmness bewildered me almost as much as the confirmation his remark gave that I had really seen something abnormal floating between me and the deck eight feet below us.

" 'Good lord, Captain Thompson,' I exclaimed, 'this is simply infernal!'

" 'Just that,' he agreed. 'I said, mister, you'd see if you'd wait. And this ain't the half. You wait till you sees 'em looking like little black clouds all over the sea round the ship and movin' steady with the ship. All the same, I ain't seen 'em aboard but the once. Guess we're in for it.'

" 'How do you mean?' I asked. But though I questioned him in every way I could get nothing satisfactory out of him.

" 'You'll see, mister. You wait an' see. She's a queer un.' And that was about the extent of his further efforts and methods of enlightening me.

"From then on through the rest of the watch I leaned over the break of the poop, staring down at the main deck and odd whiles taking quick glances to the rear. The skipper had resumed his steady pacing of the poop, but now and again he would come to a pause beside me and ask calmly enough whether I had seen any more of 'them there.'

"Several times I saw the vagueness of something drifting in the lights of the lanterns and a sort of wavering in the air in this place and that, as if it might be an attenuated something having movement, that was half-seen for a moment and then gone before my brain could record anything definite.

"Towards the end of the watch, however, both the captain and I saw something very extraordinary. He had just come beside me and was leaning over the rail across the break. 'Another of 'em there,' he remarked in his calm way, giving me a gentle nudge and nodding his head towards the port side of the maindeck, a yard or two to our left.

"In the place he had indicated there was a faint, dull shadowy spot seeming suspended about a foot above the deck. This grew more visible and there was movement in it and a constant, oily-seeming whirling from the centre outwards. The thing expanded to several feet across, with the lighted planks of the deck showing vaguely through. The movement from the centre outwards was now becoming very distinct, till the whole strange shape blackened and grew more dense, so that the deck below was hidden.

"Then as I stared with the most intense interest there went a thinning movement over the thing and almost directly it had dissolved so that there was nothing more to be seen than a vague rounded shape of shadow, hovering and convoluting dimly between us and the deck below. This gradually thinned out and vanished and we were both of us left staring down at a piece of the deck where the planking and pitched seams showed plain and distinct in the light from the lamps that were now hung nightly on the sherpoles.

" 'Mighty queer that, mister,' said the captain meditatively as he fumbled for his pipe. 'Mighty queer.' Then he lit his pipe and began again his pacing of the poop.

"The calm lasted for a week with the sea like glass and every night without warning there was a repetition of the extraordinary squall, so that the captain had everything made fast at dusk and waited patiently for a trade wind.

"Each evening I experimented further with my attempts to set up 'repellent' vibrations, but without result. I am not sure whether I ought to say that my meddling produced no result; for the calm gradually assumed a more unnatural permanent aspect whilst the sea looked more than ever like a plain of glass, bulged anon with the low oily roll of some deep swell. For the rest, there was by day a silence so profound as to give a sense of unrealness, for never a sea-bird hove in sight whilst the movement of the vessel was so slight as scarce to keep up the constant creak, creak of spars and gear, which is the ordinary accompaniment of a calm.

"The sea appeared to have become an emblem of desolation and freeness, so that it seemed to me at last that there was no more any known world, but just one great ocean going on forever into the far distances in every direction. At night the strange squalls assumed a far greater violence so that sometimes it seemed as if the very spars would be ripped and twisted out of the vessel, yet fortunately no harm came in that wise.

"As the days passed I became convinced at last that my experiments were producing very distinct results, though the opposite to those which I hoped to produce, for now at each sunset a sort of grey cloud resembling light smoke would appear far away in every quarter almost immediately upon the commencement of the vibrations, with the effect that I desisted from any prolonged attempt and became more tentative in my experiments.

"At last, however, when we had endured this condition of affairs for a week, I had a long talk with old Captain Thompson and he agreed to let me carry out a bold experiment to its conclusion. It was to keep the vibrations going steadily at full power from a little before sunset until the dawn and to take careful notes of the results.

"With this in view, all was made ready. The royal and t'gallant yards were sent down, all the sails stowed and everything about the decks made fast. A sea anchor was rigged out over the bows and a long line of cable veered away. This was to ensure the vessel coming head to wind should one of those strange squalls strike us from any quarter during the night.

"Late in the afternoon the men were sent into the fo'c'sle and told that they might please themselves and turn in or do anything they liked, but that they were not to come on deck during the night whatever happened. To ensure this the port and starboard doors were padlocked. Afterwards I made the first and the eighth signs of the Saaamaaa Ritual opposite each door-post, connecting them with triple lines crossed at every seventh inch. You've dipped deeper into the science of magic than I have, Arkright, and you will know what that means. Following this I ran a wire entirely around the outside of the fo'c'sle and connected it up with my machinery, which I had erected in the sail-locker aft.

" 'In any case,' I explained to the captain, 'they run practically no risk other than the general risk which we may expect in the form of a terrific storm-burst. The real danger will be to those who are 'meddling'. The 'path of the vibrations' will make a kind of 'halo' round the apparatus. I shall have to be there to control and I'm willing to risk it, but you'd better get into your cabin and the three mates must do the same.'

"This the old captain refused to do and the three mates begged to be allowed to stay and 'see the fun'. I warned them very seriously that there might be a very disagreeable and unavoidable danger, but they agreed to risk it and I can tell you I was not sorry to have their companionship.

"I set to work then, making them help where I needed help, and so presently I had all my gear in order. Then I led my wires up through the skylight from the cabin and set the vibrator dial and trembler-box level, screwing them solidly down to the poop-deck, in the clear space that lay between the foreside of the skylight and the lid of the sail locker.

"I got the three mates and the captain to take their places close together and I warned them not to move whatever happened. I set to work then, alone, and chalked a temporary pentacle about the whole lot of us, including the apparatus. Afterwards I made haste to get the tubes of my electric pentacle fitted all about us, for it was getting on to dusk. As soon as this was done I switched on the current into the vacuum tubes and immediately the pale sickly glare shone dull all about us, seeming cold and unreal in the last light of the evening.

"Immediately afterwards I set the vibrations beating out into all space and then I took my seat beside the control board. Here I had a few words with the others, warning them again whatever they might hear or see not to leave the pentacle, if they valued their lives. They nodded to this and I knew that they were fully impressed with the possibility of the unknown danger that we were meddling with.

"Then we settled down to watch. We were all in our oilskins, for I expected the experiment to include some very peculiar behaviour on the part of the elements and so we were ready to face the night. One other thing I was careful to do and that was to confiscate all matches so that no one should forgetfully light his pipe, for the light rays are 'paths' to certain of the Forces.

"With a pair of marine glasses I was staring round at the horizon. All around, but miles away in the greying of the evening, there seemed to be a strange, vague darkening of the surface of the sea. This became more distinct and it seemed to me presently that it might be a slight, low-lying mist far away about the ship. I watched it very intently and the captain and the three mates were doing likewise through their glasses.

" 'Coming in on us at the rate o' knots, mister,' said the old man in a low voice. 'This is what I call playin' with 'ell. I only hope it'll all come right.' That was all he said and afterwards there was absolute silence from him and the others through the strange hours that followed.

"As the night stole down upon the sea we lost sight of the peculiar incoming circle of mist and there was a period of the most intense and oppressive silence to the five of us, sitting there watchful and quiet within the pale glow of the electric pentacle.

"Awhile later there came a sort of strange, noiseless lightning. By noiseless I mean that while the flashes appeared to be near at hand and lit up all the vague sea around, yet there was no thunder; neither, so it appeared to me, did there seem to be any *reality* in the flashes. This is a queer thing to say but it describes my impressions. It was as if I saw a representation of lightning rather than the physical electricity itself. No, of course, I am not pretending to use the word in its technical sense.

"Abruptly a strange quivering went through the vessel from end to end and died away. I looked fore and aft and then glanced at the four men who stared back at me with a sort of dumb and half-frightened wonder, but no one said anything. About five minutes passed with no sound anywhere except the faint buzz of the apparatus and nothing visible anywhere except the noiseless lightning which came down, flash after flash, lighting the sea all around the vessel.

"Then a most extraordinary thing happened. The peculiar quivering passed again through the ship and died away. It was followed immediately by a kind of undulation of the vessel, first fore and aft and then from side to side. I can give you no better illustration of the strangeness of the movement on that glass-like sea than to say that it was just such a movement as might have been given her had an invisible giant hand lifted her and toyed with her, canting her this way and that with a certain curious and rather sickening rhythm of movement. This appeared to last about two minutes, so far as I can guess, and ended with the ship being shaken up and down several times, after which there came again the quivering and then quietness.

"A full hour must have passed during which I observed nothing except that twice the vessel was faintly shaken and the second time this was followed by a slight repetition of the curious undulations. This, however, lasted but a few seconds and afterwards there was only the abnormal and oppressive silence of the night, punctured time after time by these noiseless flashes of lightning. All the time I did my best to study the appearance of the sea and atmosphere around the ship.

"One thing was apparent, that the surrounding wall of vagueness had drawn in more upon the ship, so that the brightest flashes now showed me no more than about a clear quarter of a mile of ocean around us, after which the sight was just lost in trying to penetrate a kind of shadowy distance that yet had no depth in it, but which still lacked any power to arrest the vision at any particular point so that one could not know definitely whether there was anything there or not, but only that one's sight was limited by some phenomenon which hid all the distant sea. Do I make this clear?

"The strange, noiseless lightning increased in vividness and the flashes began to come more frequently. This went on till they were almost continuous, so that all the near sea could be watched with scarce an intermission. Yet the brightness of the flashes seemed to have no power to dull the pale light of the curious detached glows that circled in silent multitudes about us.

"About this time I became aware of a strange sense of breathlessness. Each breath seemed to be drawn with difficulty and presently with a sense of positive distress. The three mates and the captain were breathing with curious little gasps and the faint buzz of the vibrator seemed to come from a great distance away. For the rest there was such a silence as made itself known like a dull, numbing ache upon the brain.

"The minutes passed slowly and then, abruptly, I saw something new. There were grey things floating in the air about the ship which were so vague and attenuated that at first I could not be sure that I saw anything, but in a while there could be no doubt that they were there.

"They began to show plainer in the constant glare of the quiet lightning and growing darker and darker they increased visibly in size. They appeared to be but a few feet above the level of the sea and they began to assume humped shapes.

"For quite half an hour, which seemed indefinitely longer, I watched those strange humps like little hills of blackness floating just above the surface of the water and moving round and round the vessel with a slow, everlasting circling that produced on my eyes the feeling that it was all a dream.

"It was later still that I discovered still another thing. Each of those great vague mounds had begun to oscillate as it circled round about us. I was conscious at the same time that there was communicated to the vessel the beginning of a similar oscillating movement, so very slight at first that I could scarcely be sure she so much as moved.

"The movement of the ship grew with a steady oscillation, the bows lifting first and then the stern, as if she were pivoted amidships. This ceased and she settled down on to a level keel with a series of queer jerks as if her weight were being slowly lowered again to the buoying of the water.

"Suddenly there came a cessation of the extraordinary lightning and we were in an absolute blackness with only the pale sickly glow of the electric pentacle above us and the faint buzz of the apparatus seeming far away in the night. Can you picture it all? The five of us there, tense and watchful and wondering what was going to happen.

"The thing began gently—a little jerk upward of the starboard side of the vessel, then a second jerk, then a third and the whole ship was canted distinctly to port. It continued in a kind of slow rhythmic tilting with curious timed pauses between the jerks and suddenly, you know, I saw that we were in absolute danger, for the vessel was being capsized by some enormous Force in the utter silence and blackness of that night.

" 'My God, mister, stop it!' came the captain's voice, quick and very hoarse. 'She'll be gone in a moment! She'll be gone!'

"He had got on to his knees and was staring round and gripping at the deck. The three mates were also gripping at the deck with their palms to stop them from sliding down the violent slope.

In that moment came a final tilting of the side of the vessel and the deck rose up almost like a wall. I snatched at the lever of the vibrator and switched it over.

"Instantly the angle of the deck decreased as the vessel righted several feet with a jerk. The righting movement continued with little rhythmic jerks until the ship was once more on an even keel.

"And even as she righted I was aware of an alteration in the tenseness of the atmosphere and a great noise far off to starboard. It was the roaring of wind. A huge flash of lightning was followed by others and the thunder crashed continually overhead. The noise of the wind to starboard rose to a loud screaming and drove towards us through the night. Then the lightning ceased and the deep roll of the thunder was lost in the nearer sound of the wind which was now within a mile of us and making a most hideous, bellowing scream. The shrill howling came at us out of the dark and covered every other sound. It was as if all the night on that side were a vast cliff, sending down high and monstrous echoes upon us. This is a queer thing to say, I know, but it may help you to get the feeling of the thing; for that just describes exactly how it felt to me at the time—that queer, echoing, empty sense above us in the night, yet all the emptiness filled with sound on high. Do you get it? It was most extraordinary and there was a grand something about it all as if one had come suddenly upon the steeps of some monstrous lost world.

"Then the wind rushed out at us and stunned us with its sound and force and fury. We were smothered and half-stunned. The vessel went over on to her port side merely from pressure of the wind on her naked spars and side. The whole night seemed one yell and the foam roared and snowed over us in countless tons. I have never known anything like it. We were all splayed about the poop, holding on to anything we could, while the pentacle was smashed to atoms so that we were in complete darkness. The storm-burst had come down on us.

"Towards morning the storm calmed and by evening we were running before a fine breeze; yet the pumps had to be kept going steadily for we had sprung a pretty bad leak, which proved so serious that we had to take to the boats two days later. However, we were picked up that night so that we had only a short time of it. As for the *Jarvee*, she is now safely at the bottom of the Atlantic, where she had better remain for ever."

Carnacki came to an end and tapped out his pipe.

"But you haven't explained," I remonstrated. "What made her like that? What made her different from other ships? Why did those shadows and things come to her? What's your idea?"

"Well," replied Carnacki, "in my opinion she was a focus. That is a technical term which I can best explain by saying that she possessed the 'attractive vibration' that is the power to draw to her any psychic waves in the vicinity, much in the way of a medium. The way in which the 'vibration' is acquired—to use a technical term again—is, of course, purely a matter for supposition. She may have developed it during the years, owing to a suitability of conditions, or it may have been in her ('of her' is a better term) from the very day her keel was laid. I mean the direction in which she lay the condition of the atmosphere, the state of the 'electric tensions', the very blows of the hammers and the accidental combining of materials suited to such an end—all might tend to such a thing. And this is only to speak of the *known*. The vast *unknown* it is vain to speculate upon in a brief chatter like this.

"I would like to remind you here of that idea of mine that certain forms of so-called 'hauntings' may have their cause in the 'attractive vibrations'. A building or a ship—just as I have indicated—may develop 'vibrations', even as certain materials in combination under the proper conditions will certainly develop an electric current.

"To say more in a talk of this scope is useless. I am more inclined to remind you of the glass which will vibrate to a certain note struck upon a piano and to silence all your worrying questions with that simple little unanswered one: What is electricity? When we've got that clear it will be time to take the next step in a more dogmatic fashion. We are but speculating on the coasts of a strange country of mystery. In this case, I think the next best step for you all will be home and bed."

And with this terse ending, in the most genial way possible, Carnacki ushered us out presently on to the quiet chill of the Embankment, replying heartily to our various good-nights.

The Find

IN RESPONSE TO CARNACKI'S usual card of invitation to dinner I arrived in good time at Cheyne Walk to find Arkright, Taylor and Jessop already there, and a few minutes later we were seated round the dining table.

We dined well as usual, and as nearly always happened at these gatherings Carnacki talked on every subject under the sun but the one on which we had all expectations. It was not until we were all seated comfortably in our respective armchairs that he began.

"A very simple case," he told us, puffing at his pipe. "Quite a simple bit of mental analysis. I had been talking one day to Jones of Malbrey and Jones, the editors of the *Bibliophile and Book Table*, and he mentioned having come across a book called the *Dumpley's Acrostics*. Now the only known copy of this book is in the Caylen Museum. This second copy which had been picked up by a Mr. Ludwig appeared to be genuine. Both Malbrey and Jones pronounced it to be so, and that, to anyone knowing their reputation, would pretty well settle it.

"I heard all about the book from my old friend Van Dyll, the Dutchman who happened to be at the Club for lunch.

" 'What do you know about a book called *Dumpley's Acrostics*?' I asked him.

" 'You might as well ask me what I know of your city of London, my friend,' he replied. 'I know all there is to know which is very little. There was but one copy of that extraordinary book printed, and that copy is now in the Caylen Museum.'

" 'Exactly what I had thought,' I told him.

" 'The book was written by John Dumpley,' he continued, 'and presented to Queen Elizabeth on her fortieth birthday. She had a passion for word-play of that kind—which is merely literary gymnastics but was raised by Dumpley to an extraordinary height of involved and scandalous punning in which those unsavoury tales of those at Court are told with a wit and pretended innocence that is incredible in its malicious skill.

" 'The type was distributed and the manuscript burnt immediately after printing that one copy which was for the Queen. The book was presented to her by Lord Welbeck who paid John Dumpley twenty English guineas and twelve sheep each year with twelve firkins of Miller Abbott's ale to hold his tongue. Lord Welbeck wished to be thought the author of the book, and undoubtedly he had supplied Dumpley with the very scandalous and intimate details of famous Court personages about whom the book is written.

" 'He had his own name put in the place of Dumpley's; for though it was not a matter for much pride for a well-born man to write well in those days, still a good wit such as the *Acrostics* was deemed to be was a thing for high praise at the Court.'

" 'I'd no idea it was as famous as you say,' I told him.

" 'It has a great fame among a few,' replied Van Dyll, 'because it is at the same time unique and of a value both historic and intrinsic. There are collectors today who would give their souls if a second copy might be discovered. But that's impossible.'

" 'The impossible seems to have been achieved,' I said. 'A second copy is being offered for sale by a Mr. Ludwig. I have been asked to make a few investigations. Hence my inquiries.'

"Van Dyll almost exploded.

" 'Impossible!' he roared. 'It's another fraud!'

"Then I fired my shell.

" 'Messrs. Malbrey and Jones have pronounced it unmistakably genuine,' I said, 'and they are, as you know, above suspicion. Also Mr. Ludwig's account of how he bought the book at a 'dump' sale in the Charing Cross Road seems quite straight and above-board. He got it at Bentloes, and I've just been up there. Mr. Bentloes says it is quite possible though not probable. And anyway, he's mighty sick about it. I don't wonder, either!'

"Van Dyll got to his feet.

" 'Come on round to Malbrey and Jones,' he said excitedly, and we went straight off to the offices of the *Bibliophile* where Dyll is well-known.

" 'What's all this about?' he called out almost before he got into the Editors' private room. 'What's all this about the *Dumpley's Acrostics*, eh? Show it to me. Where is it?'

" 'It's that newly discovered copy of the *Acrostics* the Professor is asking for,' I explained to Mr. Malbrey, who was at his desk. 'He's somewhat upset at the news I've just given him.'

" 'Probably to no other men in England, except its lawful owner, would Malbrey have handed the discovered volume on so brief a notice. But Van Dyll is among the great ones when it comes to bibliology, and Malbrey merely wheeled round in his office chair and opened a large safe. From this he took a volume wrapped about with tissue paper, and standing up he handed it ceremoniously to Professor Dyll.

"Van Dyll literally snatched it from him, tore off the paper and ran to the window to have a better light. There, for nearly an hour, while we watched in silence, he examined the book, using a magnifying glass as he studied type, paper, and binding.

"At last he sat back and brushed his hand across his forehead.

" 'Well?' we all asked.

" 'It appears to be genuine,' he said. 'Before pronouncing finally upon it, however, I should like to have the opportunity of comparing it with the authentic copy in the Caylen Museum.'

"Mr. Malbrey rose from his seat and closed his desk.

" 'I shall be delighted to come with you now, Professor,' he said. 'We shall be only too pleased to have your opinion in the next issue of the *Bibliophile* which we are making a special Dumpley number, for the interest aroused by this find will be enormous among collectors.'

"When we all arrived at the Museum, Van Dyll sent in his name to the chief librarian and we were all invited into his private room. Here the Professor stated the facts and showed him the book he had brought along with him.

"The librarian was tremendously interested, and after a brief examination of the copy expressed his opinion that it was apparently genuine, but he would like to compare it with the authentic copy.

"This he did and the three experts compared the book with the Museum copy for considerably over an hour, during which time I listened keenly and jotted down from time to time in my notebook my own conclusions.

"The verdict of all three was finally unanimous that the newly found copy of the *Acrostics* was undoubtedly genuine and printed at the same time and from the same type as the Museum copy.

" 'Gentlemen,' I said, 'as I am working in the interests of Messrs. Malbrey and Jones, may I ask two questions? First, I should like to ask the librarian whether the Museum copy has ever been lent out of the Museum.'

" 'Certainly not,' replied the librarian. 'Rare editions are never loaned, and are rarely even handled except in the presence of an attendant.'

" 'Thanks,' I said. 'That ought to settle things pretty well. The other question I wish to ask is why were you all so convinced before that there was but one copy in existence?'

" 'Because," said the librarian, 'as both Mr. Malbrey and Professor Dyll could tell you, Lord Welbeck states in his private *Memoirs* that only one copy was printed. He appears to have been determined upon this, apparently to enhance the value of his gift to the Queen. He states clearly that he had the one copy printed, and that the printing was done entirely in his presence at the House of Pennywell, Printers of Lamprey Court. You can see the name at the beginning of the book. He also personally superintended the distribution of the type and burnt the manuscript and even the proof-pulls, as he says. Indeed, so precise and unmistakable are his statements on these points that I should always refuse to consider the authenticity of any 'found' copy unless it could stand such a drastic test as this one has been put through. But here is the copy,' he went on, 'unmistakably genuine, and we have to take the evidence of our senses rather than the evidence of Lord Welbeck's statement. The finding of this book is a kind of literary thunderbolt. It will make some commotion in the collecting dove-cotes if I'm not mistaken!'

" 'What should you estimate its possible value at?' I asked him.

"He shrugged his shoulders.

" 'Impossible to say,' he answered. 'If I were a rich man I would gladly give a thousand pounds to possess it. Professor Dyll there, being more fortunately endowed with worldly wealth, would probably outbid me unmercifully! I expect if Messrs. Malbrey and Jones do not buy it, soon it will go across to America in the wake of half the treasures of the earth.'

"We separated then and went our various ways. I returned here, had a cup of tea and sat down for a good long think, for I wasn't at all satisfied in my mind that everything was as plain and aboveboard as it seemed.

" 'Now,' I said to myself, 'let's have a little plain and unbiased reasoning applied, and see what comes of the test.'

" 'First of all there is the apparently incontrovertible statement in Lord Welbeck's *Memoirs* that there was only one copy of the *Acrostics* printed. That titled gentleman evidently took extraordinary pains to see that no second copy of the book was printed, and the very proofs he burned. Also this copy is no conglomeration of collected printer's proofs, for the examination the three experts have given it quite preclude that idea. All this points then to what I might term "Certainty Number One", that only one copy was printed.

" 'But now—come to the next step, a second copy has been proved today to exist. That is Certainty Number Two. And the two make that impossibility—a paradox. Therefore, though of the two certainties I may be bound in the end to accept the second, yet equally I cannot accept the complete smashing of the plain statement made in Lord Welbeck's private *Memoirs*. There seems to be more in this than meets the eye.'

Carnacki puffed thoughtfully at his pipe for a few minutes before he resumed his story.

"In the next few days," he continued, "by simple methods of deduction and a matter-of-fact following of the dues that were thereby indicated, I had laid bare as cunningly planned a little drama of clever crime as I have ever met with.

"I got into communication with Scotland Yard, my clients Messrs. Malbrey and Jones, Ralph Ludwig the owner of the find, and Mr. Notts the librarian. I arranged for a detective from the Yard to meet us all at the offices of the *Bibliophile and Book Table*, and I managed to persuade Notts to bring along with him the Museum copy of the *Acrostics*.

"In this way I had my stage set, with all the characters involved, in that little bookish office of the hundred-year-old *Collectors' Weekly*.

"The meeting was for three in the afternoon, and when they had all arrived I asked them to listen to me for a few minutes.

" 'Gentlemen,' I said, 'I should like you to follow me a little in a line of reasoning which I wish to indicate to you. Two days ago Mr. Ludwig brought to this office a copy of a book of which only one copy was supposed to be extant. An examination of his find by three experts, perhaps the three greatest experts in England, proved it to be undoubtedly genuine. That is fact number one. Fact number two is that there were the very best reasons for supposing there could *not* be two original copies of this particular book in existence.

" 'Now we were forced, by the experts' opinion, into accepting the first fact as indubitable. But there still remained to explain away the second fact; that is, the good reason for supposing that only one copy of this book was originally printed.

" 'I found that although I was forced to accept the fact of the finding of the second copy, yet I could not see how to explain away the good reason I have mentioned. Therefore, not feeling that my reason was satisfied I followed the line of investigation which unsatisfied reason indicated. I went to the Caylen Museum and asked questions.

" 'I had already learned from Mr. Notts that rare editions were never loaned. And an examination of the registers showed that the *Acrostics* had been referred to only three times by three different people in the last two years, and then, as I knew, always in the presence of an attendant. This seemed proof enough that I was hunting a mare's nest; but reason still asserted that there were more things not explained. So I went home and thought it all out again.

" 'One deduction remained from all my hours of thinking. That was that the three different men who had examined the book within the last two years could be the only line of explanation left to me. I had found out their names—Charles, Noble and Waterfield. My meditations suggested a handwriting expert, and the two of us visited the Museum register with the result that I found my reason had not led me astray. The expert pronounced the handwriting of the three men to be the handwriting of one and the same person.

" 'My next step was simple. I came here to the office with the expert and asked if I could be shown any handwriting of Mr. Ralph Ludwig. I could, and the expert assured me that Mr. Ludwig was the man who had written the three different signatures in the register of the Museum.

" 'The next step is deduction on my part and is indicated by reasoning as the only possible lines on which Mr. Ludwig could have worked. I can only suppose that he must have come across a dummy copy of the *Acrostics* in some way or other, possibly in the bundle of books he says he picked up at Bentloes' sale. This blank-paper dummy of the book would be made up by the printers and bookbinders so as to enable Lord Welbeck to see how the *Acrostics* would bind up and bulk. The method is common in the publishing trade, as you know. The binding may be exactly a duplicate of what the finished article will be but the inside is nothing but blank paper of the same thickness and quality as that on which the book will be printed. In this way a publisher can see beforehand just how the book will look.

" 'I am quite convinced that I have described the first step in Mr. Ludwig's ingenious little plot. He made only three visits to the Museum and as you will see in a minute, if he had not been provided with a facsimile in binding of the *Acrostics* on his first visit, he could not have carried out his plot under four. Moreover, unless I am mistaken in my psychology of the incident it was through becoming possessed of this particular dummy copy that he thought out this scheme. Is that not so, Mr. Ludwig?' I asked him. But he refused to reply to my question, and sat there looking very crestfallen.

" 'Well, gentlemen,' I went on, 'the rest is plain sailing. He went the first time to the Museum to study their copy, after which he deftly replaced it with the dummy one he had brought in with him. The attendant took the copy—which was externally identical with the original and replaced it in its case. This was, of course, the one big risk in Mr. Ludwig's little adventure. A smaller risk was that someone should call and ask for the *Acrostics* before he could replace it with the original, for this was what he meant to do, and which he did after he had photographed each page. Isn't that so, Mr. Ludwig?' I asked him; but he still refused to open his mouth.

" 'This,' I resumed, 'accounts for his second visit when he returned the original and started to print on a handpress the photographic blocks which he had prepared. Once the pages were bound up in the dummy he went back to the Museum and exchanged the copies, this time taking away for keeps the Museum copy and leaving the very excellently printed dummy in its place. Each time, as you know, he used a new name and a new handwriting, and probably disguises of some kind; for he had no wish to be connected with the Museum copy. That is all I have to tell you; but I hardly think Mr. Ludwig will care to deny my story, eh, Mr. Ludwig?' "

Carnacki knocked out the ashes of his, pipe as he finished.

"I can't imagine what he stole it for," said Arkright. "He could surely never have hoped to sell it."

"No, that's true," Carnacki replied. "Certainly not in the open market. He would have to sell it to some unscrupulous collector who would, of course, knowing it was stolen, give him next to nothing for it, and might in the end hand him over to the police. But don't you see if he could so arrange that the Museum still had its copy he might sell his own without fear in the open market to the highest bidder, as an authentic second copy which had come to light. He had sense to know that *his* copy would be mercilessly challenged and examined, and that is why he made his third exchange, and finally left his dummy, printed as exactly like the original as was possible, and took away with him the authentic copy."

"But the two books were bound to be compared," I argued.

"Quite true, but the copy at the Museum would not be so suspiciously examined. Everyone considered that book beyond suspicion. If the three experts had given the same attention to the false copy in the Museum which they thought all the time was the original, I don't suppose for a moment this little story would have been told. It's a very good example of the way people take things for granted. Out you go!" he said, genially, which was his usual method of dismissing us. And a few minutes later we were out on the Embankment.

The Hog

"I saw something was rising up through the middle of the defense. It rose with a steady movement. I saw it pale and huge through the whirling funnel of cloud—a monstrous pallid snout rising out of that unknowable abyss. It rose higher and higher. Through a thinning of the cloud curtain I saw one small eye—I shall never see a pig's eye again without feeling something of what I felt then. A pig's eye with a sort of vile understanding shining at the back of it...."

WE HAD FINISHED DINNER and Carnacki had drawn his big chair up to the fire, and started his pipe.

Jessop, Arkright, Taylor and I had each of us taken up our favourite positions, and waited for Carnacki to begin.

"What I'm going to tell you about happened in the next room," he said, after drawing at his pipe for a while. "It has been a terrible experience. Doctor Witton first brought the case to my notice. We'd been chatting over a pipe at the Club one night about an article in the *Lancet*, and Witton mentioned having just such a similar case in a man called Bains. I was interested at once. It was one of those cases of a gap or flaw in a man's protection barrier, I call it. A failure to be what I might term efficiently insulated—spiritually—from the outer monstrosities.

"From what I knew of Witton, I knew he'd be no use. You all know Witton. A decent sort, hard-headed, practical, stand-no-kind-of-nonsense sort of man, all right at his own job when that job's a fractured leg or a broken collarbone; but he'd never have made anything of the Bains case."

For a space Carnacki puffed meditatively at his pipe, and we waited for him to go on with his tale.

"I told Witton to send Bains to me," he resumed, "and the following Saturday he came up. A little sensitive man. I liked him as soon as I set eyes on him. After a bit, I got him to explain what was troubling him, and questioned him about what Doctor Witton had called his 'dreams'.

" 'They're more than dreams,' he said, 'they're so real that they're actual experiences to me. They're simply horrible. And yet there's nothing very definite in them to tell you about. They generally come just as I am going off to sleep. I'm hardly over before suddenly I seem to have got down into some deep, vague place with some inexplicable and frightful horror all about me. I can never understand what it is, for I never see anything, only I always get a sudden knowledge like a warning that I have got down into some terrible place—a sort of hellplace I might call it, where I've no business ever to have wandered; and the warning is always insistent—even imperative—that I must get out, get out, or some enormous horror will come at me.'

" 'Can't you pull yourself back?' I asked him. 'Can't you wake up?'

" 'No,' he told me. 'That's just what I can't do, try as I will. I can't stop going along this labyrinth-of-hell as I call it to myself, towards some dreadful unknown Horror. The warning is repeated, ever so strongly—almost as if the live me of my waking moments was awake and aware. Something seems to warn me to wake up, that whatever I do I must wake, wake, and then my consciousness comes suddenly alive and I know that my body is there in the bed, but my essence or spirit is still down there in that hell, wherever it is, in a danger that is both unknown and inexpressible; but so overwhelming that my whole spirit seems sick with terror.

" 'I keep saying to myself all the time that I must wake up,' he continued, 'but it is as if my spirit is still down there, and as if my consciousness knows that some tremendous invisible Power is fighting against me. I know that if I do not wake then, I shall never wake up again, but go down deeper and deeper into some stupendous horror of soul destruction. So then I fight. My body lies in the bed there, and pulls. And the power down there in that labyrinth exerts itself too so that a feeling of despair, greater than any I have ever known on this earth, comes on me. I know that if I give way and cease to fight, and do not wake, then I shall pass out—out to that monstrous Horror which seems to be silently calling my soul to destruction.

" 'Then I make a final stupendous effort,' he continued, 'and my brain seems to fill my body like the ghost of my soul. I can even open my eyes and see with my brain, or consciousness, out of my own eyes. I can see the bedclothes, and I know just how I am lying in the bed; yet the real me is down in that hell in terrible danger. Can you get me?' he asked.

" 'Perfectly,' I replied.

" 'Well, you know,' he went on, 'I fight and fight. Down there in that great pit my very soul seems to shrink back from the call of some brooding horror that impels it silently a little further, always a little further round a visible corner, which if I once pass I know I shall never return again to this world. Desperately I fight; brain and consciousness fighting together to help it. The agony is so great that I could scream were it not that I am rigid and frozen in the bed with fear.

" 'Then, just when my strength seems almost gone, soul and body win, and blend slowly. And I lie there worn out with this terrible extraordinary fight. I have still a sense of a dreadful horror all about me, as if out of that horrible place some brooding monstrosity had followed me up, and hangs still and silent and invisible over me, threatening me there in my bed. Do I make it clear to you?' he asked. 'It's like some monstrous Presence.'

" 'Yes,' I said. 'I follow you.'

"The man's forehead was actually covered with sweat, so keenly did he live again through the horrors he had experienced.

"After a while he continued:

" 'Now comes the most curious part of the dream or whatever it is,' he said. 'There's always a sound I hear as I lie there exhausted in the bed. It comes while the bedroom is still full of the sort of atmosphere of monstrosity that seems to come up with me when I get out of that place. I hear the sound coming up out of that enormous depth, and it is always the noise of pigs—pigs grunting, you know. It's just simply dreadful. The dream is always the same. Sometimes I've had it every single night for a week, until I fight not to go to sleep; but, of course, I have to sleep sometimes. I think that's how a person might go mad, don't you?' he finished.

"I nodded, and looked at his sensitive face. Poor beggar! He had been through it, and no mistake.

" 'Tell me some more,' I said. 'The grunting—what does it sound like exactly?'

" 'It's just like pigs grunting,' he told me again. 'Only much more awful. There are grunts, and squeals and pighowls, like you hear when their food is being brought to them at a pig farm. You know those large pig farms where they keep hundreds of pigs. All the grunts, squeals and howls blend into one brutal chaos of sound—only it isn't a chaos. It all blends in a queer horrible way. I've heard it. A sort of swinish, clamouring melody that grunts and roars and shrieks in chunks of grunting sounds, all tied together with squealings and shot through with pig howls. I've sometimes thought there was a definite beat in it; for every now and again there comes a gargantuan GRUNT, breaking through the million pig-voiced roaring—a stupendous GRUNT that comes in with a beat. Can you understand me? It seems to shake everything.... It's like a spiritual earthquake. The howling, squealing, grunting, rolling clamour of swinish noise coming up out of that place, and then the monstrous GRUNT rising up through it all, an ever-recurring beat out of the depth—the voice of the swine-mother of monstrosity beating up from below through that chorus of mad swine-hunger.... It's no use! I can't explain it. No one ever could. It's just terrible! And I'm afraid you're saying to yourself that I'm in a bad way; that I want a change or a tonic; that I must buck up or I'll land myself in a madhouse. If only you could understand! Doctor Witton seemed to half understand, I thought; but I know he's only sent me to you as a sort of last hope. He thinks I'm booked for the asylum. I could tell it.'

" 'Nonsense!' I said. 'Don't talk such rubbish. You're as sane as I am. Your ability to think clearly what you want to tell me, and then to transmit it to me so well that you compel my mental retina to see something of what you have seen, stands sponsor for your mental balance.

" 'I am going to investigate your case, and if it is what I suspect, one of those rare instances of a "flaw" or "gap" in your protective barrier (what I might call your spiritual insulation from the Outer Monstrosities) I've no doubt we can end the trouble. But we've got to go properly into the matter first, and there will certainly be danger in doing so.'

" 'I'll risk it,' replied Bains. 'I can't go on like this any longer.'

" 'Very well,' I told him. 'Go out now, and come back at five o'clock. I shall be ready for you then. And don't worry about your sanity. You're all right, and we'll soon make things safe for you again. Just keep cheerful and don't brood about it.' "

2

"I put in the whole afternoon preparing my experimenting room, across the landing there, for his case. When he returned at five o'clock I was ready for him and took him straight into the room.

"It gets dark now about six-thirty, as you know, and I had just enough time before it grew dusk to finish my arrangements. I prefer always to be ready before the dark comes.

"Bains touched my elbow as we walked into the room.

" 'There's something I ought to have told you,' he said, looking rather sheepish. 'I've somehow felt a bit ashamed of it.'

" 'Out with it,' I replied.

"He hesitated a moment, then it came out with a jerk.

" 'I told you about the grunting of the pigs,' he said. 'Well, I grunt too. I know it's horrible. When I lie there in bed and hear those sounds after I've come up, I just grunt back as if in reply. I can't stop myself. I just do it. Something makes me. I never told Doctor Witton that. I couldn't. I'm sure now you think me mad,' he concluded.

"He looked into my face, anxious and queerly ashamed.

" 'It's only the natural sequence of the abnormal events, and I'm glad you told me,' I said, slapping him on the back. 'It follows logically on what you had already told me. I have had two cases that in some way resembled yours.'

" 'What happened?' he asked me. 'Did they get better?'

" 'One of them is alive and well today, Mr. Bains,' I replied. 'The other man lost his nerve, and fortunately for all concerned, he is dead.'

"I shut the door and locked it as I spoke, and Bains stared round, rather alarmed, I fancy, at my apparatus.

" 'What are you going to do?' he asked. 'Will it be a dangerous experiment?'

" 'Dangerous enough,' I answered, 'if you fail to follow my instructions absolutely in everything. We both run the risk of never leaving this room alive. Have I your word that I can depend on you to obey me whatever happens?'

"He stared round the room and then back at me.

" 'Yes,' he replied. And, you know, I felt he would prove the right kind of stuff when the moment came.

"I began now to get things finally in train for the night's work. I told Bains to take off his coat and his boots. Then I dressed him entirely from head to foot in a single thick rubber combination-overall, with rubber gloves, and a helmet with ear-flaps of the same material attached.

"I dressed myself in a similar suit. Then I began on the next stage of the night's preparations.

"First I must tell you that the room measures thirty-nine feet by thirty-seven, and has a plain board floor over which is fitted a heavy, half-inch rubber covering.

"I had cleared the floor entirely, all but the exact centre where I had placed a glass-legged, upholstered table, a pile of vacuum tubes and batteries, and three pieces of special apparatus which my experiment required.

" 'Now Bains,' I called, 'come and stand over here by this table. Don't move about. I've got to erect a protective "barrier" round us, and on no account must either of us cross over it by even so much as a hand or foot, once it is built.'

"We went over to the middle of the room, and he stood by the glass-legged table while I began to fit the vacuum tubing together round us.

"I intended to use the new spectrum 'defense' which I have been perfecting lately. This, I must tell you, consists of seven glass vacuum circles with the red on the outside, and the colour circles lying inside it, in the order of orange, yellow, green, blue, indigo and violet.

"The room was still fairly light, but a slight quantity of dusk seemed to be already in the atmosphere, and I worked quickly.

"Suddenly, as I fitted the glass tubes together I was aware of some vague sense of nerve-strain, and glancing round at Bains, who was standing there by the table, I noticed him staring fixedly before him. He looked absolutely drowned in uncomfortable memories.

" 'For goodness' sake stop thinking of those horrors,' I called out to him. 'I shall want you to think hard enough about them later; but in this specially constructed room it is better not to dwell on things of that kind till the barriers are up. Keep your mind on anything normal or superficial—the theatre will do—think about that last piece you saw at the Gaiety. I'll talk to you in a moment.'

"Twenty minutes later the 'barrier' was completed all round us, and I connected up the batteries. The room by this time was greying with the coming dusk, and the seven differently coloured circles shone out with extraordinary effect, sending out a cold glare.

" 'By Jove!' cried Bains, 'that's very wonderful—very wonderful!'

"My other apparatus which I now began to arrange consisted of a specially made camera, a modified form of phonograph with ear-pieces instead of a horn, and a glass disk composed of many fathoms of glass vacuum tubes arranged in a special way. It had two wires leading to an electrode constructed to fit round the head.

"By the time I had looked over and fixed up these three things, night had practically come, and the darkened room shone most strangely in the curious upward glare of the seven vacuum tubes.

" 'Now, Bains,' I said, 'I want you to lie on this table. Now put your hands down by your sides and lie quiet and think. You've just got two things to do,' I told him. 'One is to lie there and concentrate your thoughts on the details of the dream you are always having, and the other is not to move off this table whatever you see or hear, or whatever happens, unless I tell you. You understand, don't you?'

" 'Yes,' he answered, 'I think you may rely on me not to make a fool of myself. I feel curiously safe with you somehow.'

" 'I'm glad of that,' I replied. 'But I don't want you to minimise the possible danger too much. There may be horrible danger. Now, just let me fix this band on your head,' I added, as I adjusted the electrode. I gave him a few more instructions, telling him to concentrate his thoughts particularly upon the noises he heard just as he was waking, and I warned him again not to let himself fall asleep. 'Don't talk,' I said, 'and don't take any notice of me. If you find I disturb your concentration keep your eyes closed.'

"He lay back and I walked over to the glass disk arranging the camera in front of it on its stand in such a way that the lens was opposite the centre of the disk.

"I had scarcely done this when a ripple of greenish light ran across the vacuum tubes of the disk. This vanished, and for maybe a minute there was complete darkness. Then the green light rippled once more across it—rippled and swung round, and began to dance in varying shades from a deep heavy green to a rank ugly shade; back and forward, back and forward.

"Every half second or so there shot across the varying greens a flicker of yellow, an ugly, heavy repulsive yellow, and then abruptly there came sweeping across the disk a great beat of muddy red. This died as quickly as it came, and gave place to the changing greens shot through by the unpleasant and ugly yellow hues. About every seventh second the disk was submerged, and the other colours momentarily blotted out by the great beat of heavy, muddy red which swept over everything.

" 'He's concentrating on those sounds,' I said to myself, and I felt queerly excited as I hurried on with my operations. I threw a word over my shoulder to Bains.

" 'Don't get scared, whatever happens,' I said. 'You're all right!'

"I proceeded now to operate my camera. It had a long roll of specially prepared paper ribbon in place of a film or plates. By turning the handle the roll passed through the machine, exposing the ribbon.

"It took about five minutes to finish the roll, and during all that time the green lights predominated; but the dull heavy beat of muddy red never ceased to flow across the vacuum tubes of the disk at every seventh second. It was like a recurrent beat in some unheard and somehow displeasing melody.

"Lifting the exposed spool of paper ribbon out of the camera I laid it horizontally in the two 'rests' that I had arranged for it on my modified gramaphone. Where the paper had been acted upon by the varying coloured lights which had appeared on the disk, the prepared surface had risen in curious, irregular little waves.

"I unrolled about a foot of the ribbon and attached the loose end to an empty spool-roller (on the opposite side of the machine) which I had geared to the driving clockwork mechanism of the gramophone. Then I took the diaphragm and lowered it gently into place above the ribbon. Instead of the usual needle, the diaphragm was fitted with a beautifully made metal-filament brush, about an inch broad, which just covered the whole breadth of the ribbon. This fine and fragile brush rested lightly on the prepared surface of the paper, and when I started the machine the ribbon began to pass under the brush; and as it passed, the delicate metal-filament 'bristles' followed every minute inequality of those tiny, irregular wave-like excrescences on the surface.

"I put the ear-pieces to my ears, and instantly I knew that I had succeeded in actually recording what Bains had heard in his sleep. In fact, I was even then hearing 'mentally' by means of his effort of memory. I was listening to what appeared to be the faint, far-off squealing and grunting of countless swine. It was extraordinary, and at the same time exquisitely horrible and vile. It frightened me, with a sense of my having come suddenly and unexpectedly too near to something foul and most abominably dangerous.

"So strong and imperative was this feeling that I twitched the ear-pieces out of my ears, and sat awhile staring round the room trying to steady my sensations back to normality.

"The room looked strange and vague in the dull glow of light from the circles, and I had a feeling that a taint of monstrosity was all about me in the air. I remembered what Bains had told me of the feeling he'd always had after coming up out of 'that place'—as if some horrible atmosphere had followed him up and filled his bedroom. I understood him perfectly now—so much so that I had mentally used almost his exact phrase in explaining to myself what I felt.

"Turning round to speak to him I saw there was something curious about the centre of the 'defense'.

"Now, before I tell you fellows any more I must explain that there are certain, what I call 'focussing', qualities about this new 'defense' I've been trying.

"The Sigsand manuscript puts it something like this: 'Avoid diversities of colour; nor stand ye within the barrier of the colour lights; for in colour hath Satan a delight. Nor can he abide in the Deep if ye adventure against him armed with red purple. So be warned. Neither forget that in blue, which is God's colour in the Heavens, ye have safety.'

"You see, from that statement in the Sigsand manuscript I got my first notion for this new 'defense' of mine. I have aimed to make it a 'defense' and yet have 'focussing' or 'drawing' qualities such as the Sigsand hints at. I have experimented enormously, and I've proved that reds and purples—the two extreme colours of the spectrum—are fairly dangerous; so much so that I suspect they actually 'draw' or 'focus' the outside forces. Any action or 'meddling' on the part of the experimentalist is tremendously enhanced in its effect if the action is taken within barriers composed of these colours, in certain proportions and tints.

"In the same way blue is distinctly a 'general defense'. Yellow appears to be neutral, and green a wonderful protection within limits. Orange, as far as I can tell, is slightly attractive and indigo is dangerous by itself in a limited way, but in certain combinations with the other colours it becomes a very powerful 'defense'. I've not yet discovered a tenth of the possibilities of these circles of mine. It's a kind of colour organ upon which I seem to play a tune of colour combinations that can be either safe or infernal in its effects. You know I have a keyboard with a separate switch to each of the colour circles.

"Well, you fellows will understand now what I felt when I saw the curious appearance of the floor in the middle of the 'defense'. It looked exactly as if a circular shadow lay, not just on the floor, but a few inches above it. The shadow seemed to deepen and blacken at the centre even while I watched it. It appeared to be spreading from the centre outwardly, and all the time it grew darker.

"I was watchful, and not a little puzzled; for the combination of lights that I had switched on approximated a moderately safe 'general defense'. Understand, I had no intention of making a focus until I had learnt more. In fact, I meant that first investigation not to go beyond a tentative inquiry into the kind of thing I had got to deal with.

"I knelt down quickly and felt the floor with the palm of my hand, but it was quite normal to the feel, and that reassured me that there was no Saaaiti mischief abroad; for that is a form of danger which can involve, and make use of, the very material of the 'defense' itself. It can materialise out of everything except fire.

"As I knelt there I realised all at once that the legs of the table on which Bains lay were partly hidden in the ever-blackening shadow, and my hands seemed to grow vague as I felt at the floor.

"I got up and stood away a couple of feet so as to see the phenomenon from a little distance. It struck me then that there was something different about the table itself. It seemed unaccountably lower.

" 'It's the shadow hiding the legs,' I thought to myself. 'This promises to be interesting; but I'd better not let things go too far.'

"I called out to Bains to stop thinking so hard. 'Stop concentrating for a bit,' I said; but he never answered, and it occurred to me suddenly that the table appeared to be still lower.

" 'Bains,' I shouted, 'stop thinking a moment.' Then in a flash I realised it. 'Wake up, man! Wake up!' I cried.

"He had fallen over asleep—the very last thing he should have done; for it increased the danger twofold. No wonder I had been getting such good results! The poor beggar was worn out with his sleepless nights. He neither moved nor spoke as I strode across to him.

" 'Wake up!' I shouted again, shaking him by the shoulder.

"My voice echoed uncomfortably round the big empty room; and Bains lay like a dead man.

"As I shook him again I noticed that I appeared to be standing up to my knees in the circular shadow. It looked like the mouth of a pit. My legs, from the knees downwards, were vague. The floor under my feet felt solid and firm when I stamped on it; but all the same I had a feeling that things were going a bit too far, so striding across to the switchboard I switched on the 'full defense'.

"Stepping back quickly to the table I had a horrible and sickening shock. The table had sunk quite unmistakably. Its top was within a couple of feet of the floor, and the legs had that fore-shortened appearance that one sees when a stick is thrust into water. They looked vague and shadowy in the peculiar circle of dark shadows which had such an extraordinary resemblance to the black mouth of a pit. I could see only the top of the table plainly with Bains lying motionless on it; and the whole thing was going down, as I stared, into that black circle."

3

"There was not a moment to lose, and like a flash I caught Bains round his neck and body and lifted him clean up into my arms off the table. And as I lifted him he grunted like a great swine in my ear.

"The sound sent a thrill of horrible funk through me. It was just as though I held a hog in my arms instead of a human. I nearly dropped him. Then I held his face to the light and stared down at him. His eyes were half opened, and he was looking at me apparently as if he saw me perfectly.

"Then he grunted again. I could feel his small body quiver with the sound.

"I called out to him. 'Bains,' I said, 'can you hear me?'

"His eyes still gazed at me; and then, as we looked at each other, he grunted like a swine again.

"I let go one hand, and hit him across the cheek, a stinging slap.

" 'Wake up, Bains!' I shouted. 'Wake up!' But I might have hit a corpse. He just stared up at me. And suddenly I bent lower and looked into his eyes more closely. I never saw such a fixed, intelligent, mad horror as I saw there. It knocked out all my sudden disgust. Can you understand?

"I glanced round quickly at the table. It stood there at its normal height; and, indeed, it was in every way normal. The curious shadow that had somehow suggested to me the black mouth of the pit had vanished. I felt relieved; for it seemed to me that I had entirely broken up any possibility of a partial 'focus' by means of the full 'defense' which I had switched on.

"I laid Bains on the floor, and stood up to look round and consider what was best to do. I dared not step outside of the barriers, until any 'dangerous tensions' there might be in the room had been dissipated. Nor was it wise, even inside the full 'defense', to have him sleeping the kind of sleep he was in; not without certain preparations having been made first, which I had not made.

"I can tell you, I felt beastly anxious. I glanced down at Bains, and had a sudden fresh shock; for the peculiar circular shadow was forming all round him again, where he lay on the floor. His hands and face showed curiously vague, and distorted, as they might have looked through a few inches of faintly stained water. But his eyes were somehow clear to see. They were staring up, mute and terrible, at me, through that horrible darkening shadow.

"I stopped, and with one quick lift, tore him up off the floor into my arms, and for the third time he grunted like a swine, there in my arms. It was damnable.

"I stood up, in the barrier, holding Bains, and looked about the room again; then back at the floor. The shadow was still thick round about my feet, and I stepped quickly across to the other side of the table. I stared at the shadow, and saw that it had vanished; then I glanced down again at my feet, and had another shock; for the shadow was showing faintly again, all round where I stood.

"I moved a pace, and watched the shadow become invisible; and then, once more, like a slow stain, it began to grow about my feet.

"I moved again, a pace, and stared round the room, meditating a break for the door. And then, in that instant, I saw that this would be certainly impossible; for there was something indefinite in the atmosphere of the room—something that moved, circling slowly about the barrier.

"I glanced down at my feet, and saw that the shadow had grown thick about them. I stepped a pace to the right, and as it disappeared, I stared again round the big room and somehow it seemed tremendously big and unfamiliar. I wonder whether you can understand.

"As I stared I saw again the indefinite something that floated in the air of the room. I watched it steadily for maybe a minute. It went twice completely round the barrier in that time. And, suddenly, I saw it more distinctly. It looked like a small puff of black smoke.

"And then I had something else to think about; for all at once I was aware of an extraordinary feeling of vertigo, and in the same moment, a sense of sinking—I was sinking bodily. I literally sickened as I glanced down, for I saw in that moment that I had gone down, almost up to my thighs, into what appeared to be actually the shadowy, but quite unmistakable, mouth of a pit. Do you understand? I was sinking down into this thing, with Bains in my arms.

"A feeling of furious anger came over me, and I swung my right boot forward with a fierce kick. I kicked nothing tangible, for I went clean through the side of the shadowy thing, and fetched up against the table, with a crash. I had come through something that made all my skin creep and tingle—an invisible, vague something which resembled an electric tension. I felt that if it had been stronger, I might not have been able to charge through as I had. I wonder if I make it clear to you?

"I whirled round, but the beastly thing had gone; yet even as I stood there by the table, the slow greying of a circular shadow began to form again about my feet.

"I stepped to the other side of the table, and leaned against it for a moment: for I was shaking from head to foot with a feeling of extraordinary horror upon me, that was in some way, different from any kind of horror I have ever felt. It was as if I had in that one moment been near something no human has any right to be near, for his soul's sake. And abruptly, I wondered whether I had not felt just one brief touch of the horror that the rigid Bains was even then enduring as I held him in my arms.

"Outside of the barrier there were now several of the curious little clouds. Each one looked exactly like a little puff of black smoke. They increased as I watched them, which I did for several minutes; but all the time as I watched, I kept moving from one part to another of the 'defense', so as to prevent the shadow forming round my feet again.

"Presently, I found that my constant changing of position had resolved into a slow monotonous walk round and round, inside the 'defense'; and all the time I had to carry the unnaturally rigid body of poor Bains.

"It began to tire me; for though he was small, his rigidity made him dreadfully awkward and tiring to hold, as you can understand; yet I could not think what else to do; for I had stopped shaking him, or trying to wake him, for the simple reason that he was as wide awake as I was mentally; though but physically inanimate, through one of those partial spiritual disassociations which he had tried to explain to me.

"Now I had previously switched out the red, orange, yellow and green circles, and had on the full defense of the blue end of the spectrum—I knew that one of the repelling vibrations of each of the three colours: blue, indigo and violet were beating out protectingly into space; yet they were proving insufficient, and I was in the position of having either to take some desperate action to stimulate Bains to an even greater effort of will than I judged him to be making, or else to risk experimenting with fresh combinations of the defensive colours.

"You see, as things were at that moment, the danger was increasing steadily; for plainly, from the appearance of the air of the room outside the barrier, there were some mighty dangerous tensions generating. While inside the danger was also increasing; the steady recurrence of the shadow proving that the 'defense' was insufficient.

"In short, I feared that Bains in his peculiar condition was literally a 'doorway' into the 'defense'; and unless I could wake him or find out the correct combinations of circles necessary to set up stronger repelling vibrations against that particular danger, there were very ugly possibilities ahead. I felt I had been incredibly rash not to have foreseen the possibility of Bains falling asleep under the hypnotic effect of deliberately paralleling the associations of sleep.

"Unless I could increase the repulsion of the barriers or wake him there was every likelihood of having to chose between a rush for the door—which the condition of the atmosphere outside the barrier showed to be practically impossible—or of throwing him outside the barrier, which, of course, was equally not possible.

"All this time I was walking round and round inside the barrier, when suddenly I saw a new development of the danger which threatened us. Right in the centre of the 'defense' the shadow had formed into an intensely black circle, about a foot wide.

"This increased as I looked at it. It was horrible to see it grow. It crept out in an ever-widening circle till it was quite a yard across.

"Quickly I put Bains on the floor. A tremendous attempt was evidently going to be made by some outside force to enter the 'defense', and it was up to me to make a final effort to help Bains to 'wake up'. I took out my lancet, and pushed up his left coat sleeve.

"What I was going to do was a terrible risk, I knew, for there is no doubt that in some extraordinary fashion blood attracts.

"The Sigsand mentions it particularly in one passage which runs something like this: 'In blood there is the Voice which calleth through all space. Ye Monsters in ye Deep hear, and hearing, they lust. Likewise hath it a greater power to reclaim backward ye soul that doth wander foolish adrift from ye body in which it doth have natural abiding. But woe unto him that doth spill ye blood in ye deadly hour; for there will be surely Monsters that shall hear ye Blood Cry.'

"That risk I had to run. I knew that the blood would call to the outer forces; but equally I knew that it should call even more loudly to that portion of Bains' 'Essence' that was adrift from him, down in those depths.

"Before lancing him, I glanced at the shadow. It had spread out until the nearest edge was not more than two feet away from Bains' right shoulder; and the edge was creeping nearer, like the blackening edge of burning paper, even while I stared. The whole thing had a less shadowy, less ghostly appearance than at any time before. And it looked simply and literally like the black mouth of a pit.

" 'Now, Bains,' I said, 'pull yourself together, man. Wake up!' And at the same time as I spoke to him, I used my lancet quickly but superficially.

"I watched the little red spot of blood well up, then trickle round his wrist and fall to the floor of the 'defense'. And in the moment that it fell the thing that I had feared happened. There was a sound like a low peal of thunder in the room, and curious deadly-looking flashes of light rippled here and there along the floor outside the barrier.

"Once more I called to him, trying to speak firmly and steadily as I saw that the horrible shadowy circle had spread across every inch of the floor space of the centre of the 'defense', making it appear as if both Bains and I were suspended above an unutterable black void—the black void that stared up at me out of the throat of that shadowy pit. And yet, all the time I could feel the floor solid under my knees as I knelt beside Bains holding his wrist.

" 'Bains!' I called once more, trying not to shout madly at him. 'Bains, wake up! Wake up, man! Wake up!'

"But he never moved, only stared up at me with eyes of quiet horror that seemed to be looking at me out of some dreadful eternity."

4

"By this time the shadow had blackened all around us, and I felt that strangely terrible vertigo coming over me again. Jumping to my feet I caught up Bains in my arms and stepped over the first of the protective circles—the violet, and stood between it and the indigo circle, holding Bains as close to me as possible so as to prevent any portion of his helpless body from protruding outside the indigo and blue circles.

"From the black shadowy mouth which now filled the whole of the centre of the 'defense' there came a faint sound—not near but seeming to come up at me out of unknown abysses. Very, very faint and lost it sounded, but I recognised it as unmistakably the infinitely remote murmur of countless swine.

"And that same moment Bains, as if answering the sound, grunted like a swine in my arms.

"There I stood between the glass vacuum tubes of the circles, gazing dizzily into that black shadowy pit-mouth, which seemed to drop sheer into hell from below my left elbow.

"Things had gone so utterly beyond all that I had thought of, and it had all somehow come about so gradually and yet so suddenly, that I was really a bit below my natural self. I felt mentally paralysed, and could think of nothing except that not twenty feet away was the door and the outer natural world; and here was I face to face with some unthought-of danger, and all adrift, what to do to avoid it.

"You fellows will understand this better when I tell you that the bluish glare from the three circles showed me that there were now hundreds and hundreds of those small smoke-like puffs of black cloud circling round and round outside the barrier in an unvarying, unending procession.

"And all the time I was holding the rigid body of Bains in my arms, trying not to give way to the loathing that got me each time he grunted. Every twenty or thirty seconds he grunted, as if in answer to the sounds which were almost too faint for my normal hearing. I can tell you, it was like holding something worse than a corpse in my arms, standing there balanced between physical death on the one side and soul destruction on the other.

"Abruptly, from out of the deep that lay so close that my elbow and shoulder overhung it, there came again a faint, marvellously faint murmur of swine, so utterly far away that the sound was as remote as a lost echo.

"Bains answered it with a pig-like squeal that set every fibre in me protesting in sheer human revolt, and I sweated coldly from head to foot. Pulling myself together I tried to pierce down into the mouth of the great shadow when, for the second time, a low peel of thunder sounded in the room, and every joint in my body seemed to jolt and burn.

"In turning to look down the pit I had allowed one of Bains' heels to protrude for a moment slightly beyond the blue circle, and a fraction of the 'tension' outside the barrier had evidently discharged through Bains and me. Had I been standing directly inside the 'defense' instead of being 'insulated' from it by the violet circle, then no doubt things might have been much more serious.

As it was, I had, psychically, that dreadful soiled feeling which the healthy human always experiences when he comes too closely in contact with certain Outer Monstrosities. Do you fellows remember how I had just the same feeling when the Hand came too near me in the 'Gateway' case?

"The physical effects were sufficiently interesting to mention; for Bains' left boot had been ripped open, and the leg of his trousers was charred to the knee, while all around the leg were numbers of bluish marks in the form of irregular spirals.

"I stood there holding Bains, and shaking from head to foot. My head ached and each joint had a queer numbish feeling; but my physical pains were nothing compared with my mental distress. I felt that we were done! I had no room to turn or move for the space between the violet circle which was the innermost, and the blue circle which was the outermost of those in use was thirty-one inches, including the one inch of the indigo circle. So you see I was forced to stand there like an image, fearing each moment lest I should get another shock, and quite unable to think what to do.

"I daresay five minutes passed in this fashion. Bains had not grunted once since the 'tension' caught him, and for this I was just simply thankful; though at first I must confess I had feared for a moment that he was dead.

"No further sounds had come up out of the black mouth to my left, and I grew steady enough again to begin to look about me, and think a bit. I leant again so as to look directly down into the shadowy pit. The edge of the circular mouth was now quite defined, and had a curious solid look, as if it were formed out of some substance like black glass.

"Below the edge, I could trace the appearance of solidity for a considerable distance, though in a vague sort of way. The centre of this extraordinary phenomenon was simple and unmitigated blackness—an utter velvety blackness that seemed to soak the very light out of the room down into it. I could see nothing else, and if anything else came out of it except a complete silence, it was the atmosphere of frightening suggestion that was affecting me more and more every minute.

"I turned away slowly and carefully, so as not to run any risks of allowing either Bains or myself to expose any part of us over the blue circle. Then I saw that things outside of the blue circle had developed considerably; for the odd, black puffs of smoke-like cloud had increased enormously and blent into a great, gloomy, circular wall of tufted cloud, going round and round and round eternally, and hiding the rest of the room entirely from me.

"Perhaps a minute passed, while I stared at this thing; and then, you know, the room was shaken slightly. This shaking lasted for three or four seconds, and then passed; but it came again in about half a minute, and was repeated from time to time. There was a queer oscillating quality in the shaking, that made me think suddenly of that *Jarvee* Haunting case. You remember it?

"There came again the shaking, and a ripple of deadly light seemed to play round the outside of the barrier; and then, abruptly, the room was full of a strange roaring—a brutish enormous yelling, grunting storm of swine-sounds.

"They fell away into a complete silence, and the rigid Bains grunted twice in my arms, as if answering. Then the storm of swine noise came again, beating up in a gigantic riot of brute sound that roared through the room, piping, squealing, grunting, and howling. And as it sank with a steady declination, there came a single gargantuan grunt out of some dreadful throat of monstrousness, and in one beat, the crashing chorus of unknown millions of swine came thundering and raging through the room again.

"There was more in that sound than mere chaos—there was a mighty devilish rhythm in it. Suddenly, it swept down again into a multitudinous swinish whispering and minor gruntings of unthinkable millions; and then with a rolling, deafening bellow of sound came the single vast grunt. And, as if lifted upon it, the swine roar of the millions of the beasts beat up through the room again; and at every seventh second, as I knew well enough without the need of the watch on my wrist, came the single storm beat of the great grunt out of the throat of unknowable monstrosity—and in my arms, Bains, the human, grunted in time to the swine melody—a rigid grunting monster there in my two arms.

"I tell you from head to foot I shook and sweated. I believe I prayed; but if I did I don't know what I prayed. I have never before felt or endured just what I felt, standing there in that thirty-one-inch space, with that grunting thing in my arms, and the hell melody beating up out of the great Deeps: and to my right, 'tensions' that would have torn me into a bundle of blazing tattered flesh, if I had jumped out over the barriers.

"And then, with an effect like a clap of unexpected thunder, the vast storm of sound ceased; and the room was full of silence and an unimaginable horror.

"This silence continued. I want to say something which may sound a bit silly; but the silence seemed to *trickle* round the room. I don't know why I felt it like that; but my words give you just what I seemed to feel, as I stood there holding the softly grunting body of Bains.

"The circular, gloomy wall of dense black cloud enclosed the barrier as completely as ever, and moved round and round and round, with a slow, 'eternal' movement. And at the back of that black wall of circling cloud, a dead silence went trickling round the room, out of my sight. Do you understand at all?...

"It seemed to me to show very clearly the state of almost insane mental and psychic tension I was enduring.... The way in which my brain insisted that the silence was *trickling* round the room, interests me enormously; for I was either in a state approximating a phase of madness, or else I was, psychically, tuned to some abnormal pitch of awaredness and sensitiveness in which silence had ceased to be an abstract quality, and had become to me a definite concrete element, much as (to use a stupidly crude illustration), the invisible moisture of the atmosphere becomes a visible and concrete element when it becomes deposited as water. I wonder whether this thought attracts you as it does me?

"And then, you know, a slow awareness grew in me of some further horror to come. This sensation or knowledge or whatever it should be named, was so strong that I had a sudden feeling of suffocation.... I felt that I could bear no more; and that if anything else happened, I should just pull out my revolver and shoot Bains through the head, and then myself, and so end the whole dreadful business.

"This feeling, however, soon passed; and I felt stronger and more ready to face things again. Also, I had the first, though still indefinite, idea of a way in which to make things a bit safer; but I was too dazed to see how to 'shape' to help myself efficiently.

"And then a low, far-off whining stole up into the room, and I knew that the danger was coming. I leant slowly to my left, taking care not to let Bains' feet stick over the blue circle, and stared down into the blackness of the pit that dropped sheer into some Unknown, from under my left elbow.

"The whining died; but far down in the blackness, there was

something—just a remote luminous spot. I stood in a grim silence for maybe ten long minutes, and looked down at the thing. It was increasing in size all the time, and had become much plainer to see; yet it was still lost in the far, tremendous Deep.

"Then, as I stood and looked, the low whining sound crept up to me again, and Bains, who had lain like a log in my arms all the time, answered it with a long animal-like whine, that was somehow newly abominable.

"A very curious thing happened then; for all around the edge of the pit, that looked so peculiarly like black glass, there came a sudden, luminous glowing. It came and went oddly, smouldering queerly round and round the edge in an opposite direction to the circling of the wall of black, tufted cloud on the outside of the barrier.

"This peculiar glowing finally disappeared, and, abruptly, out of the tremendous Deep, I was conscious of a dreadful quality or 'atmosphere' of monstrousness that was coming up out of the pit. If I said there had been a sudden waft of it, this would very well describe the actuality of it; but the spiritual sickness of distress that it caused me to feel, I am simply stumped to explain to you. It was something that made me feel I should be soiled to the very core of me, if I did not beat it off from me with my will.

"I leant sharply away from the pit towards the outer of the burning circles. I meant to see that no part of my body should overhang the pit whilst that disgusting power was beating up out of the unknown depths.

"And thus it was, facing so rigidly away from the centre of the 'defense', I saw presently a fresh thing; for there was something, many things, I began to think, on the other side of the gloomy wall that moved everlastingly around the outside of the barrier.

"The first thing I noticed was a queer disturbance of the ever circling cloud-wall. This disturbance was within eighteen inches of the floor, and directly before me. There was a curious, 'puddling' action in the misty wall; as if something were meddling with it. The area of this peculiar little disturbance could not have been more than a foot across, and it did not remain opposite to me; but was taken round by the circling of the wall.

"When it came past me again, I noticed that it was bulging slightly inwards towards me; and as it moved away from me once more, I saw another similar disturbance, and then a third and a fourth, all in different parts of the slowly whirling black wall; and all of them were no more than about eighteen inches from the floor.

"When the first one came opposite me again, I saw that the slight bulge had grown into a very distinct protuberance towards me.

"All around the moving wall, there had now come these curious swellings. They continued to reach inwards, and to elongate; and all the time they kept in a constant movement.

"Suddenly, one of them broke, or opened, at the apex, and there protruded through, for an instant, the tip of a pallid, but unmistakable *snout*. It was gone at once, but I had seen the thing distinctly; and within a minute, I saw another one poke suddenly through the wall, to my right, and withdraw as quickly. I could not look at the base of the strange, black, moving circle about the barrier without seeing a swinish snout peep through momentarily, in this place or that.

"I stared at these things in a very peculiar state of mind. There was so great a weight of the abnormal about me, before and behind and every way, that to a certain extent it bred in me a sort of antidote to fear. Can you understand? It produced in me a temporary dazedness in which things and the horror of things became less real. I stared at them, as a child stares out from a fast train at a quickly passing night-landscape, oddly hit by the furnaces of unknown industries. I want you to try to understand.

"In my arms Bains lay quiet and rigid; and my arms and back ached until I was one dull ache in all my body; but I was only partly conscious of this when I roused momentarily from my psychic to my physical awareness, to shift him to another position, less intolerable temporarily to my tired arms and back.

"There was suddenly a fresh thing—a low but enormous, solitary grunt came rolling, vast and brutal, into the room. It made the still body of Bains quiver against me, and he grunted thrice in return, with the voice of a young pig.

"High up in the moving wall of the barrier, I saw a fluffing out of the black tufted clouds; and a pig's hoof and leg, as far as the knuckle, came through and pawed a moment. This was about nine or ten feet above the floor. As it gradually disappeared I heard a low grunting from the other side of the veil of clouds, which broke out suddenly into a diafaeon of brute-sound, grunting, squealing and swine-howling; all formed into a sound that was the essential melody of the brute—a grunting, squealing, howling roar that rose, roar by roar, howl by howl, and squeal by squeal to a crescendo of horrors—the bestial growths, longings, zests and acts of some grotto of hell.... It is no use, I can't give it to you. I get dumb with the failure of my command over speech to tell you what that grunting, howling, roaring melody conveyed to me. It had in it something so inexplicably *below* the horizons of the soul in its monstrousness and fearfulness that the ordinary simple fear of death itself, with all its attendant agonies and terrors and sorrows, seemed like a thought of something peaceful and infinitely holy compared with the fear of those unknown elements in that dreadful roaring melody. And the sound was with me *inside* the room—there right in the room with me. Yet I seemed not to be aware of confining walls, but of echoing spaces of gargantuan corridors. Curious! I had in my mind those two words—gargantuan corridors.

As the rolling chaos of swine melody beat itself away on every side, there came booming through it a single grunt, the single recurring grunt of the HOG; for I knew now that I was actually and without any doubt hearing the beat of monstrosity, the HOG.

"In the Sigsand the thing is described something like this: 'Ye Hogge which ye Almighty alone hath power upon. If in sleep or in ye hour of danger ye hear the voice of ye Hogge, cease ye to meddle. For ye Hogge doth be of ye outer Monstrous Ones, nor shall any human come nigh him nor continue meddling when ye hear his voice, for in ye earlier life upon the world did the Hogge have power, and shall again in ye end. And in that ye Hogge had once a power upon ye earth, so doth he crave sore to come again. And dreadful shall be ye harm to ye soul if ye continue to meddle, and to let ye beast come nigh. And I say unto all, if ye have brought this dire danger upon ye, have memory of ye cross, for of all sign hath ye Hogge a horror.'

"There's a lot more, but I can't remember it all and that is about the substance of it.

"There was I holding Bains, who was all the time howling that dreadful grunt out with the voice of a swine. I wonder I didn't go mad. It was, I believe, the antidote of dazedness produced by the strain which helped me through each moment.

"A minute later, or perhaps five minutes, I had a sudden new sensation, like a warning cutting through my dulled feelings. I turned my head; but there was nothing behind me, and bending over to my left I seemed to be looking down into that black depth which fell away sheer under my left elbow. At that moment the roaring bellow of swine-noise ceased and I seemed to be staring down into miles of black aether at something that hung there—a pallid face floating far down and remote—a great swine face.

"And as I gazed I saw it grow bigger. A seemingly motionless, pallid swine-face rising upward out of the depth. And suddenly I realised that I was actually looking at the Hog."

5

"For perhaps a full minute I stared down through the darkness at that thing swimming like some far-off, dead-white planet in the stupendous void. And then I simply woke up bang, as you might say, to the possession of my faculties. For just a certain over-degree of strain had brought about the dumbly helpful anaesthesia of dazedness, so this sudden overwhelming supreme fact of horror produced, in turn, its reaction from inertness to action. I passed in one moment from listlessness to a fierce efficiency.

"I knew that I had, through some accident, penetrated beyond all previous 'bounds', and that I stood where no human soul had any right to be, and that in but a few of the puny minutes of earth's time I might be dead.

"Whether Bains had passed beyond the 'lines of retraction' or not, I could not tell. I put him down carefully but quickly on his side, between the inner circles—that is, the violet circle and the indigo circle—where he lay grunting slowly. Feeling that the dreadful moment had come I drew out my automatic. It seemed best to make sure of our end before that thing in the depth came any nearer: for once Bains in his present condition came within what I might term the 'inductive forces' of the monster, he would cease to be human. There would happen, as in that case of Aster who stayed outside the pentacles in the Black Veil Case, what can only be described as a pathological, spiritual change—literally in other words, soul destruction.

"And then something seemed to be telling me not to shoot. This sounds perhaps a bit superstitious; but I meant to kill Bains in that moment, and what stopped me was a distinct message from the outside.

"I tell you, it sent a great thrill of hope through me, for I knew that the forces which govern the spinning of the outer circle were intervening. But the very fact of the intervention proved to me afresh the enormous spiritual peril into which we had stumbled;

for that inscrutable Protective Force only intervenes between the human soul and the Outer Monstrosities.

"The moment I received that message I stood up like a flash and turned towards the pit, stepping over the violet circle slap into the mouth of darkness. I had to take the risk in order to get at the switch board which lay on the glass shelf under the table top in the centre. I could not shake free from the horror of the idea that I might fall down through that awful blackness. The floor felt solid enough under me; but I seemed to be walking on nothing above a black void, like an inverted starless night, with the face of the approaching Hog rising up from far down under my feet—a silent, incredible thing out of the abyss—a pallid, floating swine-face, framed in enormous blackness.

"Two quick, nervous strides took me to the table standing there in the centre with its glass legs apparently resting on nothing. I grabbed out the switch board, sliding out the vulcanite plate which carried the switch-control of the blue circle. The battery which fed this circle was the right-hand one of the row of seven, and each battery was marked with the letter of its circle painted on it, so that in an emergency I could select any particular battery in a moment.

"As I snatched up the B switch I had a grim enough warning of the unknown dangers that I was risking in that short journey of two steps; for that dreadful sense of vertigo returned suddenly and for one horrible moment I saw everything through a blurred medium as if I were trying to look through water.

"Below me, far away down between my feet, I could see the Hog; which, in some peculiar way, looked different dearer and much nearer, and enormous. I felt it had got nearer to me all in a moment. And suddenly I had the impression I was descending bodily.

"I had a sense of a tremendous force being used to push me over the side of that pit, but with every shred of will power I had in me I hurled myself into the smoky appearance that hid everything, and reached the violet circle where Bains lay in front of me.

"Here I crouched down on my heels, and with my two arms out before me I slipped the nails of each forefinger under the vulcanite base of the blue circle, which I lifted very gently so that when the base was far enough from the floor I could push the tips of my fingers underneath. I took care to keep from reaching farther under than the inner edge of the glowing tube which rested on the two-inch-broad foundation of vulcanite.

"Very slowly I stood upright, lifting the side of the blue circle with me. My feet were between the indigo and the violet circles, and only the blue circle between me and sudden death; for if it had snapped with the unusual strain I was putting upon it by lifting it like that, I knew that I should in all probability go west pretty quickly.

"So you fellows can imagine what I felt like. I was conscious of a disagreeable faint prickling that was strongest in the tips of my fingers and wrists, and the blue circle seemed to vibrate strangely as if minute particles of something were impinging upon it in countless millions. Along the shining glass tubes for a couple of feet on each side of my hands, a queer haze of tiny sparks boiled and whirled in the form of an extraordinary halo.

"Stepping forward over the indigo circle I pushed the blue circle out against the slowly moving wall of black cloud, causing a ripple of tiny pale flashes to curl in over the circle. These flashes ran along the vacuum tube until they came to the place where the blue circle crossed the indigo, and there they flicked off into space with sharp cracks of sound.

"As I advanced slowly and carefully with the blue circle a most extraordinary thing happened, for the moving wall of cloud gave from it in a great belly of shadow, and appeared to thin away from before it. Lowering my edge of the circle to the floor I stepped over Bains and right into the mouth of the pit, lifting the other side of the circle over the table. It creaked as if it were about to break in half as I lifted it, but eventually it came over safely.

"When I looked again into the depth of that shadow, I saw below me the dreadful pallid head of the Hog floating in a circle of night. It struck me that it glowed very slightly—just a vague luminosity. And quite near—comparatively. No one could have judged distances in that black void.

"Picking up the edge of the blue circle again as I had done before, I took it out further till it was half clear of the indigo circle. Then I picked up Bains and carried him to that portion of the floor guarded by the part of the blue circle which was clear of the 'defense'. Then I lifted the circle and started to move it forward as quickly as I dared, shivering each time the joints squeaked as the whole fabric of it groaned with the strain I was putting upon it. And all the time the moving wall of tufted clouds gave from the edge of the blue circle, bellying away from it in a marvellous fashion as if blown by an unheard wind.

"From time to time little flashes of light had begun to flick in over the blue circle, and I began to wonder whether it would be able to hold out the 'tension' until I had dragged it clear of the 'defense'.

"Once it was clear I hoped the abnormal stress would cease from about us, and concentrate chiefly around the 'defense' again, and the attractions of the negative 'tension'.

"Just then I heard a sharp tap behind me, and the blue circle jarred somewhat, having now ridden completely over the violet and indigo circles, and dropped clear on to the floor. The same instant there came a low rolling noise as of thunder, and a curious roaring. The black circling wall had thinned away from around us and the room showed clearly once more, yet nothing was to be seen, except that now and then a peculiar bluish flicker of light would ripple across the floor.

"Turning to look at the 'defense' I noticed it was surrounded by the circling wall of black cloud, and looked strangely extraordinary seen from the outside. It resembled a slightly swaying squat funnel of whirling black mist reaching from the floor to the ceiling, and through it I could see glowing, sometimes vague and sometimes plain, the indigo and violet circles. And then as I watched, the whole room seemed suddenly filled with an awful presence which pressed upon me with a weight of horror that was the very essence of spiritual deathliness.

"Kneeling there in the blue circle by Bains, my initiative faculties stupefied and temporarily paralysed, I could form no further plan of escape, and indeed I seemed to care for nothing at the moment. I felt I had already escaped from immediate destruction and I was strung up to an amazing pitch of indifference to any minor horrors.

"Bains all this while had been quietly lying on his side. I rolled him over and looked closely at his eyes, taking care on account of his condition not to gaze *into* them; for if he had passed beyond the 'line of retraction' he would be dangerous. I mean, if the 'wandering' part of his essence had been assimilated by the Hog, then Bains would be spiritually accessible and might be even then no more than the outer form of the man, charged with radiation of the monstrous ego of the Hog, and therefore capable of what I might term for want of a more exact phrase, a psychically *infective* force; such force being more readily transmitted through the eyes than any other way, and capable of producing a brain storm of an extremely dangerous character.

"I found Bains, however, with both eyes with an extraordinary distressed, interned quality; not the eyeballs, remember, but a reflex action transmitted from the 'mental eye' to the physical eye, and giving to the physical eye an expression of thought instead of sight. I wonder whether I make this clear to you?

"Abruptly, from every part of the room there broke out the noise of those hoofs again, making the place echo with the sound as if a thousand swine had started suddenly from an absolute immobility into a mad charge. The whole riot of animal sound seemed to heave itself in one wave towards the oddly swaying and circling funnel of black cloud which rose from floor to ceiling around the violet and indigo circles.

"As the sounds ceased I saw something was rising up through the middle of the 'defense'. It rose with a slow steady movement. I saw it pale and huge through the swaying, whirling funnel of cloud—a monstrous, pallid snout rising out of that unknowable abyss.... It rose higher like a huge pale mound. Through a thinning of the cloud curtain I saw one small eye.... I shall never see a pig's eye again without feeling something of what I felt then. A pig's eye with a sort of hell-light of vile understanding shining at the back of it."

6

"And then suddenly a dreadful terror came over me, for I saw the beginning of the end that I had been dreading all along—I saw through the slow whirl of the cloud curtains that the violet circle had begun to leave the floor. It was being taken up on the spread of the vast snout.

"Straining my eyes to see through the swaying funnel of clouds I saw that the violet circle had melted and was running down the pale sides of the snout in streams of violet-coloured fire. And as it melted there came a change in the atmosphere of the room. The black funnel shone with a dull gloomy red, and a heavy red glow filled the room.

"The change was such as one might experience if one had been looking through a protective glass at some light and the glass had been suddenly removed. But there was a further change that I realised directly through my feelings. It was as if the horrible presence in the room had come closer to my own soul. I wonder if I am making it at all clear to you. Before, it had oppressed me somewhat as a death on a very gloomy and dreary day beats down upon one's spirit. But now there was a savage menace, and the actual feeling of a foul thing close up against me. It was horrible, simply horrible.

"And then Bains moved. For the first time since he went to sleep the rigidity went out of him, and rolling suddenly over on to his stomach he fumbled up in a curious animal-like fashion, on to his hands and feet. Then he charged straight across the blue circle towards the thing in the 'defense'.

"With a shriek I jumped to pull him back; but it was not my voice that stopped him. It was the blue circle. It made him give back from it as though some invisible hand had jerked him backwards. He threw up his head like a hog, squealing with the voice of a swine, and started off round the inside of the blue circle. Round and round it he went, twice attempting to bolt across it to the horror in that swaying funnel of cloud. Each time he was thrown back, and each time he squealed like a great swine, the sounds echoing round the room in a horrible fashion as though they came from somewhere a long way off.

"By this time I was fairly sure that Bains had indeed passed the 'line of retraction', and the knowledge brought a fresh and more hopeless horror and pity to me, and a grimmer fear for myself. I knew that if it were so, it was not Bains I had with me in the circle but a monster, and that for my own last chance of safety I should have to get him outside of the circle.

"He had ceased his tireless running round and round, and now lay on his side grunting continually and softly in a dismal kind of way. As the slowly whirling clouds thinned a little I saw again that pallid face with some clearness. It was still rising, but slowly, very slowly, and again a hope grew in me that it might be checked by the 'defense'. Quite plainly I saw that the horror was looking at Bains, and at that moment I saved my own life and soul by looking down. There, close to me on the floor was the thing that looked like Bains, its hands stretched out to grip my ankles. Another second, and I should have been tripped outwards. Do you realise what that would have meant?

"It was no time to hesitate. I simply jumped and came down crash with my knees on top of Bains. He lay quiet enough after a short struggle; but I took off my braces and lashed his hands up behind him. And I shivered with the very touch of him, as though I was touching something monstrous.

"By the time I had finished I noticed that the reddish glow in the room had deepened quite considerably, and the whole room was darker. The destruction of the violet circle had reduced the light perceptibly; but the darkness that I am speaking of was something more than that. It seemed as if something now had come into the atmosphere of the room—a sort of gloom; and in spite of the shining of the blue circle and the indigo circle inside the funnel of cloud, there was now more red light than anything else.

"Opposite me the huge, cloud-shrouded monster in the indigo circle appeared to be motionless. I could see its outline vaguely all the time, and only when the cloud funnel thinned could I see it plainly—a vast, snouted mound, faintly and whitely luminous, one gargantuan side turned towards me, and near the base of the slope a minute slit out of which shone one whitish eye.

"Presently through the thin gloomy red vapour I saw something that killed the hope in me, and gave me a horrible despair; for the indigo circle, the final barrier of the defense, was being slowly lifted into the air—the Hog had begun to rise higher. I could see its dreadful snout rising upwards out of the cloud. Slowly, very slowly, the snout rose up, and the indigo circle went up with it.

"In the dead stillness of that room I got a strange sense that all eternity was tense and utterly still as if certain powers knew of this horror I had brought into the world.... And then I had an awareness of something coming... something from far, far away. It was as if some hidden unknown part of my brain knew it. Can you understand? There was, somewhere in the heights of space, a light that was coming near. I seemed to hear it coming. I could just see the body of Bains on the floor, huddled and shapeless and inert. Within the swaying veil of cloud the monster showed as a vast pale, faintly luminous mound, hugely snouted—an infernal hillock of monstrosity, pallid and deadly amid the redness that hung in the atmosphere of the room.

"Something told me that it was making a final effort against the help that was coming. I saw the indigo circle was now some inches from the floor, and every moment I expected to see it flash into streams of indigo fire running down the pale slopes of the snout. I could see the circle beginning to move upward at a perceptible speed. The monster was triumphing.

"Out in some realm of space a low continuous thunder sounded. The thing in the great heights was coming fast, but it could never come in time. The thunder grew from a low, far mutter into a deep steady rolling of sound.... It grew louder and louder, and as it grew I saw the indigo circle, now shining through the red gloom of the room, was a whole foot off the floor. I thought I saw a faint splutter of indigo light.... The final circle of the barrier was beginning to melt.

"That instant the thunder of the thing in flight which my brain heard so plainly, rose into a crashing, a world-shaking bellow of speed, making the room rock and vibrate to an immensity of sound. A strange flash of blue flame ripped open the funnel of cloud momentarily from top to base, and I saw for one brief instant the pallid monstrosity of the Hog, stark and pale and dreadful.

"Then the sides of the funnel joined again, hiding the thing from me as the funnel became submerged quickly into a dome of silent blue light—God's own colour! All at once it seemed the cloud had gone, and from floor to ceiling of the room, in awful majesty, like a living Presence, there appeared that dome of blue fire banded with three rings of green light at equal distances. There was no sound or movement, not even a flicker, nor could I see anything in the light: for looking into it was like looking into the cold blue of the skies. But I felt sure that there had come to our aid one of those inscrutable forces which govern the spinning of the outer circle, for the dome of blue light, banded with three green bands of silent fire, was the outward or visible sign of an enormous force, undoubtedly of a defensive nature.

"Through ten minutes of absolute silence I stood there in the blue circle watching the phenomenon. Minute by minute I saw the heavy, repellent red driven out of the room as the place lightened quite noticeably. And as it lightened, the body of Bains began to resolve out of a shapeless length of shadow, detail by detail, until I could see the braces with which I had lashed his wrists together.

"And as I looked at him his body moved slightly, and in a weak but perfectly sane voice he said:

" 'I've had it again! My God! I've had it again!' "

7

"I knelt down quickly by his side and loosened the braces from his wrists, helping him to turn over and sit up. He gripped my arm a little crazily with both hands.

" 'I went to sleep after all,' he said. 'And I've been down there again. My God! It nearly had me. I was down in that awful place and it seemed to be just round a great corner, and I was stopped from coming back. I seemed to have been fighting for ages and ages. I felt I was going mad. Mad! I've been nearly down into a hell. I could hear you calling down to me from some awful height. I could hear your voice echoing along yellow passages. They were yellow. I know they were. And I tried to come and I couldn't.'

" 'Did you see me?' I asked him when he stopped, gasping.

" 'No,' he answered, leaning his head against my shoulder. 'I tell you it nearly got me that time. I shall never dare go to sleep again as long as I live. Why didn't you wake me?'

" 'I did,' I told him. 'I had you in my arms most of the time. You kept looking up into my eyes as if you knew I was there.'

" 'I know,' he said. 'I remember now; but you seemed to be up at the top of a frightful hole, miles and miles up from me, and those horrors were grunting and squealing and howling, and trying to catch me and keep me down there. But I couldn't see anything— only the yellow walls of those passages. And all the time there was something round the corner.'

" 'Anyway, you're safe enough now,' I told him. 'And I'll guarantee you shall be safe in the future.'

"The room had grown dark save for the light from the blue circle. The dome had disappeared, the whirling funnel of black cloud had gone, the Hog had gone, and the light had died out of the indigo circle. And the atmosphere of the room was safe and normal again as I proved by moving the switch, which was near me, so as to lessen the defensive power of the blue circle and enable me to 'feel' the outside tension. Then I turned to Bains.

" 'Come along,' I said. 'We'll go and get something to eat, and have a rest.'

"But Bains was already sleeping like a tired child, his head pillowed on his hand. 'Poor little devil!' I said as I picked him up in my arms. 'Poor little devil!'

"I walked across to the main switchboard and threw over the current so as to throw the 'V' protective pulse out of the four walls and the door; then I carried Bains out into the sweet wholesome normality of everything. It seemed wonderful, coming out of that chamber of horrors, and it seemed wonderful still to see my bedroom door opposite, wide open, with the bed looking so soft and white as usual—so ordinary and human. Can you chaps understand?

"I carried Bains into the room and put him on the couch; and then it was I realised how much I'd been up against, for when I was getting myself a drink I dropped the bottle and had to get another.

"After I had made Bains drink a glass I laid him on the bed.

" 'Now,' I said, 'look into my eyes fixedly. Do you hear me? You are going off to sleep safely and soundly, and if anything troubles you, obey me and wake up. Now, sleep—sleep—sleep!'

"I swept my hands down over his eyes half a dozen times, and he fell over like a child. I knew that if the danger came again he would obey my will and wake up. I intend to cure him, partly by hypnotic suggestion, partly by a certain electrical treatment which I am getting Doctor Witton to give him.

"That night I slept on the couch, and when I went to look at Bains in the morning I found him still sleeping, so leaving him there I went into the test room to examine results. I found them very surprising.

"Inside the room I had a queer feeling, as you can imagine. It was extraordinary to stand there in that curious bluish light from the 'treated' windows, and see the blue circle lying, still glowing, where I had left it; and further on, the 'defense', lying circle within circle, all 'out'; and in the centre the glass-legged table standing where a few hours before it had been submerged in the horrible monstrosity of the Hog. I tell you, it all seemed like a wild and horrible dream as I stood there and looked. I have carried out some curious tests in there before now, as you know, but I've never come nearer to a catastrophe.

"I left the door open so as not to feel shut in, and then I walked over to the 'defense'. I was intensely curious to see what had happened physically under the action of such a force as the Hog. I found unmistakable signs that proved the thing had been indeed a Saaitii manifestation, for there had been no psychic or physical illusion about the melting of the violet circle. There remained nothing of it except a ring of patches of melted glass. The gutta base had been fused entirely, but the floor and everything was intact. You see, the Saaitii forms can often attack and destroy, or even make use of, the very defensive material used against them.

"Stepping over the outer circle and looking closely at the indigo circle I saw that it was melted clean through in several places. Another fraction of time and the Hog would have been free to expand as an invisible mist of horror and destruction into the atmosphere of the world. And then, in that very moment of time, salvation had come. I wonder if you can get my feelings as I stood there staring down at the destroyed barrier."

Carnacki began to knock out his pipe, which is always a sign that he has ended his tale, and is ready to answer any questions we may want to ask.

Taylor was first in. "Why didn't you use the Electric Pentacle as well as your new spectrum circles?" he asked.

"Because," replied Carnacki, "the pentacle is simply 'defensive' and I wished to have the power to make a 'focus' during the early part of the experiment, and then, at the critical moment, to change the combination of the colours so as to have a 'defense' against the results of the 'focus'. You follow me.

"You see," he went on, seeing we hadn't grasped his meaning, "there can be no 'focus' within a pentacle. It is just of a 'defensive' nature. Even if I had switched the current out of the electric pentacle I should still have had to contend with the peculiar and undoubtedly 'defensive' power that its form seems to exert, and this would have been sufficient to 'blur' the focus.

"In this new research work I'm doing, I'm bound to use a 'focus' and so the pentacle is barred. But I'm not sure it matters. I'm convinced this new spectrum 'defense' of mine will prove absolutely invulnerable when I've learnt how to use it; but it will take me some time. This last case has taught me something new. I had never thought of combining green with blue; but the three bands of green in the blue of that dome has set me thinking. If only I knew the right combinations! It's the combinations I've got to learn. You'll understand better the importance of these combinations when I remind you that green by itself is, in a very limited way, more deadly than red itself—and red is the danger colour of all."

"Tell us, Carnacki," I said, "what is the Hog? Can you? I mean what kind of monstrosity is it? Did you *really* see it, or was it all some horrible, dangerous kind of dream? How do you know it was one of the outer monsters? And what is the difference between that sort of danger and the sort of thing you saw in the Gateway of the Monster case? And what...?"

"Steady!" laughed Carnacki. "One at a time! I'll answer all your questions; but I don't think I'll take them quite in your order. For instance, speaking about actually seeing the Hog, I might say that, speaking generally, things seen of a 'ghostly' nature are not seen with the eyes; they are seen with the mental eye which has this psychic quality, not always developed to a useable state, in addition to its 'normal' duty of revealing to the brain what our physical eyes record.

"You will understand that when we see 'ghostly' things it is often the 'mental' eye performing simultaneously the duty of revealing to the brain what the physical eye sees as well as what it sees itself. The two sights blending their functions in such a fashion gives us the impression that we are actually seeing through our physical eyes the whole of the 'sight' that is being revealed to the brain.

"In this way we get an impression of seeing with our physical eyes both the material and the immaterial parts of an 'abnormal' scene; for each part being received and revealed to the brain by machinery suitable to the particular purpose appears to have equal value of reality that is, it appears to be equally material. Do you follow me?"

We nodded our assent, and Carnacki continued:

"In the same way, were anything to threaten our psychic body we should have the impression, generally speaking, that it was our physical body that had been threatened, because our psychic sensations and impressions would be super-imposed upon our physical, in the same way that our psychic and our physical sight are super-imposed.

"Our sensations would blend in such a way that it would be impossible to differentiate between what we felt physically and what we felt psychically. To explain better what I mean. A man may seem to himself, in a 'ghostly' adventure, to fall *actually*. That is, to be falling in a physical sense; but all the while it may be his psychic entity, or being—call it what you will—that is falling. But to his brain there is presented the sensation of falling all together. Do you get me?

"At the same time, please remember that the danger is none the less because it is his psychic body that falls. I am referring to the sensation I had of falling during the time of stepping across the mouth of that pit. My physical body could walk over it easily and feel the floor solid under me; but my psychic body was in very real danger of falling. Indeed, I may be said to have literally *carried* my psychic body over, held within me by the pull of my life-force. You see, to my psychic body the pit was as real and as actual as a coal pit would have been to my physical body. It was merely the pull of my life-force which prevented my psychic body from falling *out* of me, rather like a plummet, down through the everlasting depths in obedience to the giant pull of the monster.

"As you will remember, the pull of the Hog was too great for my life-force to withstand, and, psychically, I began to fall. Immediately on my brain was recorded a sensation identical with that which would have been recorded on it had my actual physical body been falling. It was a mad risk I took, but as you know, I had to take it to get to the switch and the battery. When I had that physical sense of falling and seemed to see the black misty sides of the pit all around me, it was my mental eye recording upon the brain what it was seeing. My psychic body had actually begun to fall and was really below the edge of the pit but still in contact with me. In other words my physical magnetic and psychic 'haloes' were still mingled. My physical body was still standing firmly upon the floor of the room, but if I had not each time by effort or will forced my physical body across to the side, my psychic body would have fallen completely out of 'contact' with me, and gone like some ghostly meteorite, obedient to the pull of the Hog.

"The curious sensation I had of forcing myself through an obstructing medium was not a physical sensation at all, as we understand that word, but rather the psychic sensation of forcing my entity to re-cross the 'gap' that had already formed between my falling psychic body now below the edge of the pit and my physical body standing on the floor of the room. And that 'gap' was full of a force that strove to prevent my body and soul from rejoining. It was a terrible experience. Do you remember how I could still see with my brain through the eyes of my psychic body, though it had already fallen some distance out of me? That is an extraordinary thing to remember.

"However, to get ahead, all 'ghostly' phenomena are extremely diffuse in a normal state. They become actively physically dangerous in all cases where they are concentrated. The best off-hand illustration I can think of is the all-familiar electricity—a force which, by the way, we are too prone to imagine we understand because we've named and harnessed it, to use a popular phrase. But we don't understand it at all! It is still a complete fundamental mystery. Well, electricity when diffused is an 'imagined and unpictured something', but when concentrated it is sudden death. Have you got me in that?

"Take, for instance, that explanation, as a very, very crude sort of illustration of what the Hog is. The Hog is one of those million-mile-long clouds of 'nebulosity' lying in the Outer Circle. It is because of this that I term those clouds of force the Outer Monsters.

"What they are exactly is a tremendous question to answer. I sometimes wonder whether Dodgson there realises just how impossible it is to answer some of his questions," and Carnacki laughed.

"But to make a brief attempt at it. There is around this planet, and presumably others, of course, circles of what I might call 'emanations'. This is an extremely light gas, or shall I say ether. Poor ether, it's been hard worked in its time!

"Go back one moment to your school-days, and bear in mind that at one time the earth was just a sphere of extremely hot gases. These gases condensed in the form of materials and other 'solid' matters; but there are some that are not yet solidified—air, for instance. Well, we have an earth-sphere of solid matter on which to stamp as solidly as we like; and round about that sphere there lies a ring of gases, the constituents of which enter largely into all life, as we understand life—that is, air.

"But this is not the only circle of gas which is floating round us. There are, as I have been forced to conclude, larger and more attenuated 'gas' belts lying, zone on zone, far up and around us. These compose what I have called the inner circles. They are surrounded in turn by a circle or belt of what I have called, for want of a better word, 'emanations'.

"This circle which I have named the Outer Circle cannot lie less than a hundred thousand miles off the earth, and has a thickness which I have presumed to be anything between five and ten million miles. I believe, but I cannot prove, that it does not spin with the earth but in the opposite direction, for which a plausible cause might be found in the study of the theory upon which a certain electrical machine is constructed.

"I have reason to believe that the spinning of this, the Outer Circle, is disturbed from time to time through causes which are quite unknown to me, but which I believe are based in physical phenomena. Now, the Outer Circle is the psychic circle, yet it is also physical. To illustrate what I mean I must again instance electricity, and say that just as electricity discovered itself to us as something quite different from any of our previous conceptions of matter, so is the Psychic or Outer Circle different from any of our previous conceptions of matter. Yet it is none the less physical in its origin, and in the sense that electricity is physical, the Outer or Psychic Circle is physical in its constituents. Speaking pictorially it is, physically, to the Inner Circle, what the Inner Circle is to the upper strata of the air, and what the air—as we know that intimate gas—is to the waters and the waters to the solid world. You get my line of suggestion?"

We all nodded, and Camacki resumed.

"Well, now let me apply all this to what I am leading up to. I suggest that these million-mile-long clouds of monstrosity with float in the Psychic or Outer Cirde, are bred of the elements of that circle. They are tremendous psychic forces, bred out of its elements just as an octopus or shark is bred out of the sea, or a tiger or any other physical force is bred out of the elements of its earth-and-air surroundings.

"To go further, a physical man is composed entirely from the constituents of earth and air, by which terms I include sunlight and water and 'condiments'! In other words without earth and air he could not *BE*! Or to put it another way, earth and air breed within themselves the materials of the body and the brain, and therefore, presumably, the machine of intelligence.

"Now apply this line of thought to the Psychic or Outer Circle which though so attenuated that I may crudely presume it to be approximate to our conception of aether, yet contains all the elements for the production of certain phases of force and intelligence. But these elements are in a form as little like matter as the emanations of scent are like the scent itself. Equally, the force-and-intelligence-producing capacity of the Outer Circle no more approximates to the life-and-intelligence-producing capacity of the earth and air, than the results of the Outer Circle constituents resemble the results of earth and air. I wonder whether I make it clear.

"And so it seems to me we have the conception of a huge psychic world, bred out of the physical, lying far outside of this world and completely encompassing it, except for the doorways about which I hope to tell you some other evening. This enormous psychic world of the Outer Circle 'breeds' if I may use the term, its own psychic forces and intelligences, monstrous and otherwise; just as this world produces its own physical forces and intelligences—beings, animals, insects, etc., monstrous and otherwise.

"The monstrosities of the Outer Circle are malignant towards all that we consider most desirable, just in the same way a shark or

a tiger may be considered malignant, in a physical way, to all that
we consider desirable. They are predatory—as all positive force
is predatory. They have desires regarding us which are incredibly
more dreadful to our minds when comprehended than an intelligent
sheep would consider our desires towards its own carcass. They
plunder and destroy to satisfy lusts and hungers exactly as other
forms of existence plunder and destroy to satisfy their lusts and
hungers. And the desire of these monsters is chiefly, if not always,
for the psychic entity of the human.

"But that's as much as I can tell you tonight. Some evening
I want to tell you about the tremendous mystery of the Psychic
Doorways. In the meantime, have I made things a bit clearer to
you, Dodgson?"

"Yes, and no," I answered. "You've been a brick to make the
attempt, but there are still about ten thousand other things I want
to know."

Carnacki stood up. "Out you go!" he said using the recognised
formula in friendly fashion. "Out you go! I want a sleep."

And shaking him by the hand we strolled out onto the quiet
Embankment.

Other Tales of
Mystery and Suspense

Other Tales of
Mystery and Suspense

The Goddess of Death

I T WAS IN THE latter end of November when I reached T—worth
to find the little town almost in a state of panic. In answer to my
half-jesting inquiry as to whether the French were attempting to land,
I was told a harrowing tale of some restless statue that had formed
a nightly habit of running amuck amongst the worthy townspeople.
Nearly a dozen had already fallen victims, the first having been pretty
Sally Morgan, the town belle.

These and other matters I learnt. Wherever I went it was the same
story. "Good Heavens! what ignorance, what superstition!" This
I thought, imagining that they were the dupes of some murderous
rogue. Afterwards I was to change my mind. I gathered that the
tragedies had all happened in some park nearby, where, during the
day, this Walking Marble rested innocently enough upon its pedestal.

Though I scouted the story of the walking statue, I was greatly
interested in the matter. Already it had come to me to look into
it and show these benighted people how mistaken they had been;
besides, the thing promised some excitement. As I strolled through
the town I laughed, picturing to myself the absurdity of some people
believing in a walking marble statue. Pooh! What fools there are!
Arriving at my hotel, I was pleased to learn from the landlord that
my old friend and schoolmate, William Turner, had been staying
there for some time.

That evening while I was at dinner, he burst into my room and
was delighted at seeing me.

"I suppose you've heard about the town bogey by now?" he said
presently, dropping his voice. "It's a dangerous enough bogey, and
we're all puzzled to explain how on earth it has escaped detection so
long. Of course," he went on, "this story about the walking statue is
all rubbish, though it's surprising what a number of people believe it."

"What do you say to trying our hands at catching it?" I said. "There would be a little excitement, and we should be doing the town a public benefit."

Will smiled. "I'm game if you are, Herton—we could take a stroll in the park tonight, if you like; perhaps we might see something."

"Right." I answered heartily. "What time do you propose going?"

Will pulled out his watch. "It's half-past eight now; shall we say eleven o'clock? It ought to be late enough then."

I assented and invited him to join me at my wine. He did so, and we passed the time away very pleasantly in reminiscences of old times.

"What about weapons?" I asked presently. "I suppose it will be advisable to take something in that line?"

For answer Will unbuttoned his coat, and I saw the gleam of a brace of pistols. I nodded and, going to my trunk, opened it and showed him a couple of beautiful little pistols I often carried. Having loaded them, I put them in my side pockets. Shortly afterwards eleven chimed, and getting into our cloaks, we left the house.

It was very cold, and a wintry wind moaned through the night. As we entered the park, we involuntarily kept closer together.

Somehow, my desire for adventure seemed to be ebbing away, and I wanted to get out from the place and into the lighted streets.

"We'll just have a look at the statue," said Will; "then home and to bed."

A few minutes later we reached a little clearing among the bushes.

"Here we are," Will whispered. "I wish the moon would come out a moment; it would enable us to get a glance at the thing." He peered into the gloom on our right. "I'm hanged," he muttered, "if I can see it at all!"

Glancing to our left, I noticed that the path now led along the edge of a steep slope, at the bottom of which, some considerable distance below us, I caught the gleam of water.

"The park lake," Will explained in answer to a short query on my part. "Beastly deep, too!"

He turned away, and we both gazed into the dark gap among the bushes.

A moment afterwards the clouds cleared for an instant, and a ray of light struck down full upon us, lighting up the little circle of bushes and showing the clearing plainly. It was only a momentary gleam, but quite sufficient. There stood a *pedestal great and black; but there was no statue upon it!*

Will gave a quick gasp, and for a minute we stood stupidly; then we commenced to retrace our steps hurriedly. Neither of us spoke. As we moved we glanced fearfully from side to side. Nearly half the return journey was accomplished when, happening to look behind me, I saw in the dim shadows to my left the bushes part, and a huge, white carven face, crowned with black, suddenly protrude.

I gave a sharp cry and reeled backwards. Will turned. "Oh, mercy on us!" I heard him shout, and he started to run.

The Thing came out of the shadow. It looked like a giant. I stood rooted; then it came towards me, and I turned and ran. In the hands I had seen something black that looked like a twisted cloth. Will was some dozen yards ahead. Behind, silent and vast, ran that awful being.

We neared the park entrance. I looked over my shoulder. It was gaining on us rapidly. Onward we tore. A hundred yards further lay the gates; and safety in the lighted streets. Would we do it? Only fifty yards to go, and my chest seemed bursting. The distance shortened. The gates were close to.... We were through. Down the street we ran; then turned to look. It had vanished.

"Thank Heaven!" I gasped, panting heavily.

A minute later Will said: "What a blue funk we've been in." I said nothing. We were making towards the hotel. I was bewildered and wanted to get by myself to think.

Next morning, while I was sitting dejectedly at breakfast, Will came in. We looked at one another shamefacedly. Will sat down. Presently he spoke:

"What cowards we are!"

I said nothing. It was too true; and the knowledge weighed on me like lead.

"Look here!" and Will spoke sharply and sternly. "We've got to go through with this matter to the end, if only for our own sakes."

I glanced at him eagerly. His determined tone seemed to inspire me with fresh hope and courage.

"What we've got to do first," he continued, "is to give that marble god a proper overhauling and make sure no one has been playing tricks with us—perhaps it's possible to move it in some way."

I rose from the table and went to the window. It had snowed heavily the preceding day, and the ground was covered with an even layer of white. As I looked out, a sudden idea came to me, and I turned quickly to Will.

"The snow!" I cried. "It will show the footprints, if there are any."

Will stared, puzzled.

"Round the statue," I explained, "if we go at once." He grasped my meaning and stood up. A few minutes later we were striding out briskly for the Park. A sharp walk brought us to the place. As we came in sight, I gave a cry of astonishment. The pedestal was occupied by a figure, identical with the thing that had chased us the night before. There it stood, erect and rigid, its sightless eyes glaring into space.

Will's face wore a look of expectation.

"See," he said, "it's back again. It cannot have managed that by itself, and we shall see by the footprints how many scoundrels there are in the affair."

He moved forward across the snow. I followed. Reaching the pedestal, we made a careful examination of the ground; but to our utter perplexity the snow was undisturbed. Next, we turned our attention to the figure itself, and though Will, who had seen it often before, searched carefully, he could find nothing amiss.

This, it must be remembered, was my first sight of it, for—now that my mind was rational—I would not admit, even to myself, that what we had seen in the darkness was anything more than a masquerade, intended to lead people to the belief that it was the dead marble they saw walking. Seen in the broad daylight, the thing looked what it was, a marble statue, intended to represent some deity. Which, I could not tell; and when I asked Will, he shook his head.

In height it might have been eight feet, or perhaps a trifle under. The face was large—as indeed was the whole figure—and in expression cruel to the last degree.

Above his brow was a large, strangely shaped headdress, formed out of some jet-black substance. The body was carved from a single block of milk-white marble and draped gracefully and plainly in a robe confined at the waist by a narrow black girdle. The arms drooped loosely by the sides and in the right hand hung a twisted cloth of a similar hue to the girdle. The left was empty and half gripped.

Will had always spoken of the statue as a *god*. Now, however, as my eyes ran over the various details, a doubt formed itself in my mind, and I suggested to Will that he was possibly mistaken as to the intended sex of the image.

For a moment he looked interested; then remarked gloomily that he didn't see it mattered much whether the thing was a man-god or a woman-god. The point was, had it the power to come off its pedestal or not?

I looked at him reproachfully.

"Surely you are not really going to believe that silly superstition?" I expostulated.

He shook his head moodily. "No, but can you or anyone else explain away last night's occurrences in any ordinary manner?"

To this there was no satisfactory reply, so I held my tongue.

"Pity," remarked Will presently, "that we know so little about this god. And the one man who might have enlightened us dead and gone—goodness knows where?"

"Who's that?" I queried.

"Oh, of course. I was forgetting, you don't know! Well, it's this way: for some years an old Indian colonel called Whigman lived here. He was a queer old stick and absolutely refused to have anything to do with anybody. In fact, with the exception of an old Hindoo serving-man, he saw no one. About nine months ago he and his servant were found brutally murdered—strangled, so the doctors said. And now comes the most surprising part of it all. In his will he had left the whole of his huge estate to the citizens of T—worth to be used as a park."

"Strangled, I think you said?" and I looked at Will questioningly.

He glanced at me a moment absently, then the light of comprehension flashed across his face. He looked startled. "Jove! you don't mean that?"

"I do though, old chap. The murder of these others has in every case been accomplished by strangling—their bodies, so you've told me, have shown that much. Then there are other things that point to my theory being the right one."

"What! you really think that the Colonel met his death at the same hands as—?" he did not finish.

I nodded assent.

"Well, if you are correct, what about the length of time between then and Sally Morgan's murder—seven months isn't it? —and not a soul hurt all that time, and now—" He threw up his arms with an expressive gesture.

"Heaven knows!" I replied, "I don't."

For some length of time we discussed the matter in all its bearings, but without arriving at any satisfactory conclusion.

On our way back to the town Will showed me a tiny piece of

white marble which he had surreptitiously chipped from the statue. I examined it closely. Yes, it was marble, and somehow the certainty of that seemed to give us more confidence.

"Marble is marble," Will said, "and it's ridiculous to suppose anything else." I did not attempt to deny this.

During the next few days, we paid visits to the park, but without result. The statue remained as we had left it. A week passed. Then, one morning early, before the dawn, we were roused by a frightful scream, followed by a cry of deepest agony. It ended in a murmuring gurgle, and all was silent.

Without hesitation, we seized pistols and with lighted candles rushed from our rooms to the great entrance door. This we hurriedly opened. Outside, the night was very quiet. It had been snowing and the ground was covered with a sheet of white.

For a moment we saw nothing. Then we distinguished the form of a woman lying across the steps leading up to the door. Running out, we seized her and carried her into the hall. There we recognized her as one of the waitresses of the hotel. Will turned back her collar and exposed the throat, showing a livid weal round it.

He was very serious, and his voice trembled, though not with fear, as he spoke to me. "We must dress and follow the tracks; there is no time to waste." He smiled gravely. "I don't think we shall do the running away this time."

At this moment the landlord appeared. On seeing the girl and hearing our story, he seemed thunderstruck with fear and amazement, and could do nothing save wring his hands helplessly. Leaving him with the body, we went to our rooms and dressed quickly; then down again into the hall, where we found a crowd of fussy womenfolk around the poor victim.

In the taproom I heard voices and, pushing my way in, discovered several of the serving men discussing the tragedy in excited tones. As they turned at my entrance, I called to them to know who would volunteer to accompany us. At once a strongly built young fellow stepped forward, followed after a slight hesitation by two older men. Then, as we had sufficient for our purpose, I told them to get heavy sticks and bring lanterns.

As soon as they were ready, we sallied out: Will and I first, the others following and keeping well together. The night was not particularly dark—the snow seemed to lighten it. At the bottom of the High Street one of the men gave a short gasp and pointed ahead.

There, dimly seen, and stealing across the snow with silent strides, was a giant form draped in white. Signing to the men to keep quiet, we ran quickly forward, the snow muffling our footsteps. We neared it rapidly. Suddenly Will stumbled and fell forward on his face, one of his pistols going off with the shock.

Instantly the Thing ahead looked round, and next moment was bounding from us in great leaps. Will was on his feet in a second and, with a muttered curse at his own clumsiness, joined in the chase again. Through the park gates it went, and we followed hard. As we got nearer, I could plainly see the black headdress, and in the right hand there was a dark something: but what struck me the most was the enormous size of the thing; it was certainly quite as tall as the marble goddess.

On we went. We were within a hundred feet of it when it stopped dead and turned towards us, and never shall I forget the fear that chilled me, for there, from head to foot, perfect in every detail, stood the marble goddess. At the movement, we had brought up standing; but now I raised a pistol and fired. That seemed to break the spell, and like one man we leapt forward. As we did so, the thing circled like a flash and resumed its flight at a speed that bade fair to leave us behind in short time.

Then the thought came to me to head it off. This I did by sending the three men round to the right-hand side of the park lake, while Will and I continued the pursuit. A minute later the monster disappeared round a bend in the path: but this troubled me little, as I felt convinced that it would blunder right into the arms of the men, and they would turn it back, and then—ah! then this mystery and horror would be solved.

On we ran. A minute, perhaps, passed. All at once I heard a hoarse cry ahead, followed by a loud scream, which ceased suddenly. With fear plucking at my heart, I spurted forward, Will close behind. Round the corner we burst, and I saw the two men bending over something on the ground.

"Have you got it?" I shouted excitedly. The men turned quickly and, seeing me, beckoned hurriedly. A moment later I was with them and kneeling alongside a silent form. Alas! it was the brave young fellow who had been the first to volunteer. His neck seemed to be broken. Standing up, I turned to the men for an explanation.

"It was this way, sir; Johnson, that's him," nodding to the dead man, "he was smarter on his legs than we be, and he got ahead. Just before we reached him we heered him shout. We was close behind, and I don't think it could ha' been half a minute before we was up and found him."

"Did you see anything—" I hesitated. I felt sick. Then I continued, "anything of *That*—you know what I mean?"

"Yes, sir; leastways my mate did. He saw it run across to those bushes an'—"

"Come on, Will," I cried, without waiting to hear more; and throwing the light of our lanterns ahead of us, we burst into the shrubberies. Scarcely had we gone a dozen Paces when the light struck full upon a towering figure. There was a crash, and my lantern was smashed all to pieces. I was thrown to the ground, and something slid through the bushes. Springing to the edge, we were just in time to catch sight of it running in the direction of the lake. Simultaneously we raised our pistols and fired. As the smoke cleared away, I saw the Thing bound over the railings into the water. A faint splash was borne to our ears, and then—silence.

Hurriedly we ran to the spot, but could see nothing.

"Perhaps we hit it," I ventured.

"You forget," laughed Will hysterically, "marble won't float."

"Don't talk rubbish," I answered angrily. Yet I felt that I would have given something to know what it was *really*.

For some minutes we waited; then, as nothing came to view, we moved away towards the gate—the men going on ahead, carrying their dead comrade. Our way led past the little clearing where the statue stood. It was still dark when we reached it.

"Look, Herton, look!" Will's voice rose to a shriek. I turned sharply. I had been lost momentarily in perplexing thought. Now, I saw that we were right opposite the place of the marble statue, and Will was shining the light of the lantern in its direction; but it showed me nothing save the pedestal, bare and smooth.

I glanced at Will. The lantern was shaking visibly in his grasp. Then I looked towards the pedestal again in a dazed manner. I stepped up to it and passed my hand slowly across the top. I felt very queer.

After that, I walked round it once or twice. No use! there was no mistake this time. My eyes showed me nothing save that vacant place where, but a few hours previously, had stood the massive marble.

Silently we left the spot. The men had preceded us with their sad burden. Fortunately, in the dim light, they had failed to notice the absence of the goddess.

Dawn was breaking as in mournful procession we entered the town. Already the news seemed to have spread, and quite a body of the town people escorted us to the hotel.

During the day a number of men went up to the park, armed with hammers, intending to destroy the statue, but returned later silent and awestruck, declaring that it had disappeared bodily, only the great altar remaining.

I was feeling unwell. The shock had thoroughly upset me, and a sense of helplessness assailed me.

About midnight, feeling worn out, I went to bed. It was late on the following morning when I awoke with a start. An idea had come to me, and rising, I dressed quickly and went downstairs. In the bar I found the landlord, and to him I applied for information as to where the library of the late Colonel Whigman had been removed.

He scratched his head a moment reflectively.

"I couldn't rightly say, sir; but I know Mr. Jepson, the town clerk, will be able to, and I daresay he wouldn't mind telling you anything you might want to know."

Having inquired where I was likely to meet this official, I set off, and in a short while found myself chatting to a pleasant, ruddy faced man of about forty.

"The late colonel's library!" he said genially; "certainly, come this way, Sir Herton," and he ushered me into a long room lined with books.

What I wanted was to find if the colonel had left among his library any diary or written record of his life in India. For a couple of hours I searched persistently. Then, just as I was giving up hope, I found it—a little green-backed book, filled with closely written and crabbed writing.

Opening it, I found staring me in the face, a rough pen-and-ink sketch of—the marble goddess.

The following pages I read eagerly. They told a strange story of how, while engaged in the work of exterminating Thugs, the colonel and his men had found a large idol of white marble, quite unlike any Indian Deity the colonel had ever seen.

After a full description—in which I recognized once more the statue in Bungalow Park—there was some reference to an exciting skirmish with the priests of the temple, in which the colonel had a narrow escape from death at the hands of the high priest, "who was a most enormous man and mad with fury."

Finally, having obtained possession, they found among other

things that the Deity of the temple was another—and, to Europeans, unknown—form of Kali, the Goddess of Death. The temple itself being a sort of Holy of Holies of Thugdom, where they carried on their brutal and disgusting rites.

After this, the diary went on to say that, loath to destroy the idol, the colonel brought it back with him to Calcutta, having first demolished the temple in which it had been found.

Later, he found occasion to ship it off to England. Shortly after this, his life was attempted, and his time of service being up, he came home.

Here it ended, and yet I was no nearer to the solution than I had been when first I opened the book.

Standing up, I placed it on the table; then, as I reached for my hat, I noticed on the floor a half-sheet of paper, which had evidently fallen from the diary as I read. Stooping, I picked it up. It was soiled and, in parts illegible, but what I saw there filled me with astonishment. Here, at last, in my hands, I held the key to the horrible mystery that surrounded us!

Hastily I crumpled the paper into my pocket and, opening the door, rushed from the room. Reaching the hotel, I bounded upstairs to where Will sat reading.

"I've found it out! I've found it out!" I gasped. Will sprang from his seat, his eyes blazing with excitement. I seized him by the arm and, without stopping to explain, dragged him hatless into the street. "Come on," I cried.

As we ran through the streets, people looked up wonderingly, and many joined in the race.

At last we reached the open space and the empty pedestal. Here I paused a moment to gain breath. Will looked at me curiously. The crowd formed round in a semi-circle, at some little distance.

Then, without a word, I stepped up to the altar and, stooping, reached up under it. There was a loud click and I sprang back sharply. Something rose from the centre of the pedestal with a slow, stately movement. For a second no one spoke; then a great cry of fear came from the crowd: "The image! the image!" and some began to run. There was another click and Kali, the Goddess of Death, stood fully revealed.

Again I stepped up to the altar. The crowd watched me breath-lessly, and the timid ceased to fly. For a moment I fumbled. Then one side of the pedestal swung back. I held up my hand for silence. Someone procured a lantern, which I lit and lowered through the opening. It went down some ten feet, then rested on the earth beneath. I peered down, and as my eyes became accustomed to the darkness, I made out a square-shaped pit in the ground directly below the pedestal.

Will came to my side and looked over my shoulder.

"We must get a ladder," he said. I nodded, and he sent a man for one. When it came, we pushed it through until it rested firmly; then, after a final survey, we climbed cautiously down.

I remember feeling surprised at the size of the place. It was as big as a good-sized room. At this moment as I stood glancing round, Will called to me. His voice denoted great perplexity. Crossing over, I found him staring at a litter of things which strewed the ground: tins, bottles, cans, rubbish, a bucket with some water in it and, further on, a sort of rude bed.

"Someone's been living here!" and he looked at me blankly. "It wasn't—" he began, then hesitated. "It wasn't that after all," and he indicated with his head.

"No," I replied, "it wasn't *that*." I assented. Will's face was a study. Then he seemed to grasp the full significance of the fact, and a great look of relief crossed his features.

A moment later, I made a discovery. On the left-hand side in the far corner was a low-curved entrance like a small tunnel. On the opposite side was a similar opening. Lowering the lantern, I looked into the right-hand one, but could see nothing. By stooping somewhat we could walk along it, which we did for some distance, until it ended in a heap of stones and earth. Returning to the hollow under the pedestal, we tried the other, and after a little, noticed that it trended steadily downwards.

"It seems to be going in the direction of the lake," I remarked. "We had better be careful."

A few feet further on the tunnel broadened and heightened considerably, and I saw a faint glimmer which, on reaching, proved to be water.

"Can't get any further," Will cried. "You were right. We have got down to the level of the lake."

"But what on earth was this tunnel designed for?" I asked, glancing around. "You see it reaches below the surface of the lake."

"Goodness knows," Will answered. "I expect it was one of those secret passages made centuries ago—most likely in Cromwell's time. You see, Colonel Whigman's was a very old place, built I can't say how long ago. It belonged once to an old baron. However, there is nothing here; we might as well go."

"Just a second, Will," I said, the recollection of the statue's wild leap into the lake at the moment recurring to me.

I stooped and held the lantern close over the water which blocked our further progress.

As I did so I thought I saw something of an indistinct whiteness floating a few inches beneath the surface. Involuntarily my left hand took a firmer grip of the lantern, and the fingers of my right hand opened out convulsively.

What was it I saw? I could feel myself becoming as icy cold as the water itself. I glanced at Will. He was standing disinterestedly a little behind me. Evidently he had, so far, seen nothing.

Again I looked, and a horrible sensation of fear and awe crept over me as I seemed to see, staring up at me, the face of Kali, the Goddess of Death.

"See, Will!" I said quickly. "Is it fancy?"

Following the direction of my glance, he peered down into the gloomy water, then started back with a cry.

"What is it, Herton? I seemed to see a face like—"

"Take the lantern, Will," I said as a sudden inspiration came to me. "I've an idea what it is." And, leaning forward, I plunged my arms in up to the elbows and grasped something cold and hard. I shuddered, but held on, and pulled, and slowly up from the water rose a vast white face which came away in my hands. It was a huge mask—an exact facsimile of the features of the statue above us.

Thoroughly shaken, we retreated to the pedestal with our trophy, and from thence up the ladder into the blessed daylight.

Here, to a crowd of eager listeners, we told our story; and so left it.

Little remains to be told.

Workmen were sent down and from the water they drew forth the dead body of an enormous Hindoo, draped from head to foot in white. In the body were a couple of bullet wounds. Our fire had been true that night, and he had evidently died trying to enter the pedestal through the submerged opening of the passage.

Who he was, or where he came from, no one could explain.

Afterwards, among the colonel's papers, we found a reference to the High Priest, which led us to suppose that it was he who, in vengeance for the sacrilege against his appalling deity, had, to such terrible purpose, impersonated Kali, the Goddess of Death.

Terror of the Water-Tank

CROWNING THE HEIGHTS ON the outskirts of a certain town on the east coast is a large, iron water-tank from which an isolated row of small villas obtains its supply. The top of this tank has been cemented, and round it have been placed railings, thus making of it a splendid "look-out" for any of the townspeople who may choose to promenade upon it. And very popular it was until the strange and terrible happenings of which I have set out to tell.

Late one evening, a party of three ladies and two gentlemen had climbed the path leading to the tank. They had dined, and it had been suggested that a promenade upon the tank in the cool of the evening would be pleasant. Reaching the level, cemented surface, they were proceeding across it, when one of the ladies stumbled and almost fell over some object lying near the railings on the town-side.

A match having been struck by one of the men, they discovered that it was the body of a portly old gentleman lying in a contorted attitude and apparently quite dead. Horrified, the two men drew off their fair companions to the nearest of the afore-mentioned houses. Then, in company with a passing policeman, they returned with all haste to the spot.

By the aid of the officer's lantern, they ascertained the grewsome fact that the old gentleman had been strangled. In addition, he was without watch or purse. The policeman was able to identify him as an old, retired mill-owner, living some little distance away at a place named Revenge End.

At this point the little party was joined by a stranger, who introduced himself as Dr. Tointon, adding the information that he lived in one of the villas close at hand, and had run across as soon as he had heard there was something wrong.

339

Silently, the two men and the policeman gathered round, as with deft, skillful hands the doctor made his short examination.

"He's not been dead more than about half an hour," he said at its completion.

He turned towards the two men.

"Tell me how it happened—all you know?" They told him the little they knew.

"Extraordinary," said the doctor. "And you saw no one?"

"Not a soul, doctor!"

The medical man turned to the officer.

"We must get him home," he said. "Have you sent for the ambulance?"

"Yes, sir," said the policeman. "I whistled to my mate on the lower beat, and 'e went straight off."

The doctor chatted with the two men, and reminded them that they would have to appear at the inquest.

"It's murder?" asked the younger of them in a low voice.

"Well," said the doctor. "It certainly looks like it."

And then came the ambulance.

At this point, I come into actual contact with the story; for old Mr. Marchmount, the retired mill-owner, was the father of my *fiancée*, and I was at the house when the ambulance arrived with its sad burden.

Dr. Tointon had accompanied it along with the Policeman, and under his directions the body was taken upstairs, while I broke the news to my sweetheart.

Before he left, the doctor gave me a rough outline of the story as he knew it. I asked him if he had any theory as to how and why the crime had been committed.

"Well," he said, "the watch and chain are missing, and the purse. And then he has undoubtedly been strangled; though with what, I have been unable to decide."

And that was all he could tell me.

The following day there was a long account in the *Northern Daily Telephone* about the "shocking murder". The column ended, I remember, by remarking that people would do well to beware, as there were evidently some very desperate characters about, and added that it was believed the police had a clew.

During the afternoon, I myself went up to the tank. There was a large crowd of people standing in the road that runs past at some little distance; but the tank itself was in the hands of the police officer being stationed at the top of the steps leading up to it. On learning my connection with the deceased, he allowed me up to have a look round.

I thanked him, and gave the whole of the tank a pretty thorough scrutiny, even to the extent of pushing my cane down through lock-holes in the iron man-hole lids, to ascertain whether the tank was full or not, and whether there was room for someone to hide.

On pulling out my stick, I found that the water reached to within a few inches of the lid, and that the lids were securely locked. I at once dismissed a vague theory that had formed in my mind that there might be some possibility of hiding within the tank itself and springing out upon the unwary. It was evidently a common, brutal murder, done for the sake of my prospective father-in-law's purse and gold watch.

One other thing I noticed before I quitted the tank top. It came to me as I was staring over the rail at the surrounding piece of waste land. Yet at the time, I thought little of it, and attached to it no importance whatever. It was that the encircling piece of ground was soft and muddy and quite smooth. Possibly there was a leakage from the tank that accounted for it. Anyhow, that is how it seemed to be.

"There ain't nothin' much to be seen, sir," volunteered the policeman, as I prepared to descend the steps on my way back to the road.

"No," I said. "There seems nothing of which to take hold."

And so I left him, and went on to the doctor's house. Fortunately, he was in, and I at once told him the result of my investigations. Then I asked him whether he thought that the police were really on the track of the criminal.

He shook his head.

"No," he answered. "I was up there this morning having a look round, and since then, I've been thinking. There are one or two points that completely stump me—points that I believe the police have never even stumbled upon."

Yet, though I pressed him, he would say nothing definite.

"Wait!" was all he could tell me.

Yet I had not long to wait before something further happened, something that gave an added note of mystery and terror to the affair.

On the two days following my visit to the doctor, I was kept busy arranging for the funeral of my *fiancée's* father, and then on the very morning of the funeral came the news of the death of the policeman who had been doing duty on the tank.

From my place in the funeral procession, I caught sight of large local posters announcing the fact in great letters, while the newsboys constantly cried:

"Terror of the Tank—
Policeman Strangled."

Yet, until the funeral was over, I could not buy a paper to gather any of the details. When at last I was able, I found that the doctor who had attended him was none other than Tointon, and straightway I went up to his place for such further particulars as he could give.

"You've read the newspaper account?" he asked when I met him.

"Yes," I replied.

"Well, you see," he said, "I was right in saying that the police were off the track. I've been up there this morning, and a lot of trouble I had to be allowed to make a few notes on my own account. Even then it was only through the influence of Inspector Slago with whom I have once or twice done a little investigating. They've two men and a sergeant now on duty to keep people away."

"You've done a bit of detective-work, then?"

"At odd times," he replied.

"And have you come to any conclusion?"

"Not yet."

"Tell me what you know of the actual happening," I said. "The newspaper was not very definite. I'm rather mixed up as to how long it was before they found that the policeman had been killed. Who found him?"

"Well, so far as I have been able to gather from Inspector Slago, it was like this. They had detailed one of their men for duty on the tank until two A.M., when he was to be relieved by the next man. At about a minute or so to two, the relief arrived simultaneously with the inspector, who was going his rounds. They met in the road below the tank, and were proceeding up the little side-lane towards the passage, when, from the top of the tank, they heard someone cry out suddenly. The cry ended in a sort of gurgle, and they distinctly heard something fall with a heavy thud.

"Instantly, the two of them rushed up the passage, which as you know is fenced in with tall, sharp, iron railings. Even as they ran, they could hear the beat of struggling heels on the cemented top of the tank, and just as the inspector reached the bottom of the steps there came a last groan. The following moment they were at the top. The policeman threw the light of his lantern around. It struck on a huddled heap near by the right-hand railings—something limp and inert. They ran to it, and found that it was the dead body of the officer who had been on duty. A hurried examination showed that he had been strangled.

"The inspector blew his whistle, and soon another of the force arrived on the scene. This man they at once dispatched for me, and in the meantime they conducted a rapid but thorough search, which, however, brought to light nothing. This was the more extraordinary in that the murderer must have been on the tank even as they went up the steps."

"Jove!" I muttered. "He must have been quick."

The doctor nodded.

"Wait a minute," he went on, "I've not finished yet. When I arrived I found that I could do nothing; the poor fellow's neck had been literally crushed. The power used must have been enormous.

" 'Have you found anything?' I asked the inspector.

" 'No,' he said, and proceeded to tell me as much as he knew, ending by saying that the murderer, whoever it was, had got clean away.

" 'But,' I exclaimed, 'he would have to pass you, or else jump the railings. There's no other way.'

" 'That's what he's done.' replied Slago rather testily. 'It's no height.'

" 'Then in that case, inspector.' I answered, 'he's left something by which we may be able to trace him.' "

"You mean the mud round the tank, doctor?" I interrupted.

"Yes," said Doctor Tointon. "So you noticed that, did you? Well, we took the policeman's lamp, and made a thorough search all round the tank—but the whole of the flat surface of mud-covered ground stretched away smooth and unbroken by even a single footprint!"

The doctor stopped dramatically.

"Good God!" I exclaimed, excitedly. "Then how did the fellow get away?"

Doctor Tointon shook his head.

"That is a point, my dear sir, on which I am not yet prepared to speak. And yet I believe I hold a clew."

"What?" I almost shouted.

"Yes," he replied, nodding his head thoughtfully. "To-morrow I may be able to tell you something."

He rose from his chair.

"Why not now?" I asked, madly curious.

"No," he said, "the thing isn't definite enough yet."

He pulled out his watch.

"You must excuse me now. I have a patient waiting."

I reached for my hat, and he went and opened the door.

"To-morrow," he said, and nodded reassuringly as he shook hands. "You'll not forget."

"Is it likely," I replied, and he closed the door after me.

The following morning I received a note from him asking me to defer my visit until night, as he would be away from home during the greater portion of the day. He mentioned 9:30 as a possible time at which I might call—any time between then and ten P.M. But I was not to be later than that.

Naturally, feeling as curious as I did, I was annoyed at having to wait the whole day. I had intended calling as early as decency would allow. Still, after that note, there was nothing but to wait.

During the morning, I paid a visit to the tank, but was refused permission by the sergeant in charge. There was a large crowd of people in the road below the tank, and in the little side lane that led up to the railed-in passage. These, like myself, had come up with the intention of seeing the exact spot where the tragedies had occurred; but they were not allowed to pass the men in blue.

Feeling somewhat cross at their persistent refusal to allow me upon the tank, I turned up the lane, which presently turns off to the right. Here, finding a gap in the wall, I clambered over, and disregarding a board threatening terrors to trespassers, I walked across the piece of waste land until I came to the wide belt of mud that surrounded the tank. Then, skirting the edge of the marshy ground, I made my way round until I was on the town-side of the tank. Below me was a large wall which hid me from those in the road below. Between me and the tank stretched some forty feet of smooth, mud-covered earth. This I proceeded now to examine carefully.

As the doctor had said, there was no sign of any footprint in any part of it. My previous puzzlement grew greater. I think I had been entertaining an idea somewhere at the back of my head that the doctor and the police had made a mistake—perhaps missed seeing the obvious, as is more possible than many think. I turned to go back, and at the same moment, a little stream of water began to flow from a pipe just below the edge of the tank top. It was evidently the "overflow". Undoubtedly the tank was brim full.

How, I asked myself, had the murderer got away without leaving a trace?

I made my way back to the gap, and so into the lane. And then, even as I sprang to the ground, an idea came to me—a possible solution of the mystery.

I hurried off to see Dufirst, the tank-keeper, who I knew lived in a little cottage a few hundred feet distant. I reached the cottage, and knocked. The man himself answered me, and nodded affably.

"What an ugly little beast!" I thought. Aloud, I said: "Look here, Dufirst, I want a few particulars about the tank. I know you can tell me what I want to know better than anyone else."

The affability went out of the man's face. "Wot do yer want to know?" he asked surlily.

"Well," I replied. "I want to know if there is any place about the tank where a man could hide."

The fellow looked at me darkly. "No," he said shortly.

"Sure?" I asked.

"Course I am," was his sullen reply.

"There's another thing I want to know about," I went on. "What's the tank built upon?"

"Bed er cerment," he answered.

"And the sides—how thick are they?"

"About 'arf-inch iron."

"One thing more," I said, pulling half-a-crown from my pocket (where-at I saw his face light up). "What are the inside measurements of the tank?" I passed him over the coin.

He hesitated a moment; then slipped it into his waistcoat-pocket. "Come erlong a minnit. I 'ave ther plan of ther thing upstairs, if yer'll sit 'ere an' wait."

"Right," I replied, and sat down, while he disappeared through a door, and presently I heard him rummaging about overhead.

"What a sulky beast," I thought to myself. Then, as the idea passed through my mind, I caught sight of an old bronze luster jug on the opposite side of the room. It stood on a shelf high up; but in a minute I was across the room and reaching up to it; for I have a craze for such things.

"What a beauty," I muttered, as I seized hold of the handle. "I'll offer him five dollars for it."

I had the thing in my hands now. It was heavy. "The old fool!" thought I. "He's been using it to stow odds and ends in." And with that, I took it across to the window. There, in the light, I glanced inside—and nearly dropped it; for within a few inches of my eyes, reposed the old gold watch and chain that had belonged to my murdered friend. For a moment, I felt dazed. Then I knew.

"The little fiend!" I said. "The vile little murderer!"

I put the jug down on the table, and ran to the door. I opened it and glanced out. There, not thirty paces distant was Inspector Slago in company with a constable. They had just gone past the house, and were evidently going up on to the tank.

I did not shout; to do so would have been to warn the man in the room above. I ran after the inspector and caught him by the sleeve.

"Come here, inspector," I gasped. "I've got the murderer."

He twirled round on his heel. "What?" he almost shouted.

"He's in there," I said. "It's the tank-keeper. He's still got the watch and chain. I found it in a jug."

At that the inspector began to run towards the cottage, followed by myself and the policeman. We ran in through the open door, and I pointed to the jug. The inspector picked it up, and glanced inside.

He turned to me. "Can you identify this?" he asked, speaking in a quick, excited voice.

"Certainly I can," I replied. "Mr. Marchmount was to have been my father-in-law. I can swear to the watch being his."

At that instant there came a sound of footsteps on the stairs and a few seconds later the black bearded little tank-keeper came in through an inner door. In his hand he held a roll of paper—evidently the plan of which he had spoken. Then, as his eyes fell on the inspector holding the watch of the murdered man, I saw the fellow's face suddenly pale.

He gave a sort of little gasp, and his eyes flickered round the room to where the jug had stood. Then he glanced at the three of us, took a step backwards, and jumped for the door through which he had entered. But we were too quick for him, and in a minute had him securely handcuffed.

The inspector warned him that whatever he said would be used as evidence; but there was no need, for he spoke not a word.

"How did you come to tumble across this?" asked the inspector, holding up the watch and guard. "What put you on to it?"

I explained and he nodded.

"It's wonderful," he said. "And I'd no more idea than a mouse that it was him," nodding towards the prisoner.

Then they marched him off.

That night, I kept my appointment at the doctor's. He had said that he would be able to say something; but I rather fancied that the boot was going to prove on the other leg. It was I who would be able to tell him a great deal more than "something". I had solved the whole mystery in a single morning's work. I rubbed my hands, and wondered what the doctor would have to say in answer to my news. Yet, though I waited until 10:30, he never turned up, so that I had at last to leave without seeing him.

The next morning, I went over to his house. There his housekeeper met me with a telegram that she had just received from a friend of his away down somewhere on the South coast. It was to say that the doctor had been taken seriously ill, and was at present confined to his bed, and was unconscious.

I returned the telegram and left the house. I was sorry for the doctor; but almost more so that I was not able personally to tell him the news of my success as an amateur detective.

It was many weeks before Dr. Tointon returned, and in the meantime the tank-keeper had stood his trial and been condemned for the murder of Mr. Marchmount. In court he had made an improbable statement that he had found the old gentleman dead, and that he had only removed the watch and purse from the body under a momentary impulse. This, of course, did him no good, and when I met the doctor on the day of his return, it wanted only three days to the hanging.

"By the way, doctor," I said, after a few minutes' conversation, "I suppose you know that I spotted the chap who murdered old Mr. Marchmount and the policeman?"

For answer the doctor turned and stared.

"Yes," I said, nodding, "it was the little brute of a tank-keeper. He's to be hanged in three days' time."

"What—" said the doctor, in a startled voice. "Little black Dufirst?"

"Yes," I said, yet vaguely damped by his tone.

"Hanged!" returned the doctor. "Why the man's as innocent as you are!"

I stared at him.

"What do you mean?" I asked. "The watch and chain were found in his possession. They proved him guilty in court."

"Good heavens!" said the doctor. "What awful blindness!"

He turned on me. "Why didn't you write and tell me?"

"You were ill—afterwards I thought you'd be sure to have read about it in one of the papers."

"Haven't seen one since I've been ill," he replied sharply. "By

George! You've made a pretty muddle of it. Tell me how it happened."

This I did, and he listened intently.

"And, in three days he's to be hanged?" he questioned when I had made an end.

I nodded.

He took off his hat and mopped his face and brow.

"It's going to be a job to save him," he said slowly. "Only three days. My God!"

He looked at me, and then abruptly asked a foolish question.

"Have there been any more—murders up there while I've been ill?" He jerked his hand toward the tank.

"No," I replied. "Of course not. How could there be when they've got the chap who did them!"

He shook his head.

"Besides," I went on, "no one ever goes up there now, at least, not at night, and that's when the murders were done."

"Quite so, quite so," he agreed, as if what I had said fell in with something that he had in his mind. He turned to me. "Look here," he said, "come up to my place to-night about ten o'clock, and I think I shall be able to prove to you that the thing which killed Marchmount and the policeman was not—well, it wasn't little black Dufirst."

I stared at him.

"Fact," he said.

He turned and started to leave me.

"I'll come," I called out to him.

At the time mentioned, I called at Dr. Tointon's. He opened the door himself and let me in, taking me into his study. Here, to my astonishment, I met Inspector Slago. The inspector wore rather a worried look, and once when Tointon had left the room for a minute, he bent over towards me.

"He seems to think," he said in a hoarse whisper, and nodding towards the doorway through which the doctor had gone, "that we've made a silly blunder and hooked the wrong man."

"He'll find he's mistaken," I answered.

The inspector looked doubtful, and seemed on the point of saying something further, when the doctor returned.

"Now then," Dr. Tointon remarked, "we'll get ready. Here," he tossed me a pair of rubbers, "shove those on.

"You've got rubber heels, inspector?"

"Yes, sir," replied Slago. "Always wear 'em at night."

The doctor went over to a corner and returned with a double-barreled shotgun which he proceeded to load. This accomplished, he turned to the inspector.

"Got your man outside?"

"Yes, sir," replied Slago.

"Come along, then, the two of you."

We rose and followed him into the dark hall and then out through the front doorway into the silent road. Here we found a plain-clothes policeman waiting, leaning up against a wall. At a low whistle from the inspector, he came swiftly across and saluted. Then the doctor turned and led the way towards the tank.

Though the night was distinctly warm, I shuddered. There was a sense of danger in the air that got on one's nerves. I was quite in the dark as to what was going to happen. We reached the lower end of the railed passage. Here the doctor halted us, and began to give directions.

"You have your lantern, inspector?"

"Yes, sir."

"And your man, has he?"

"Yes, sir," replied the man for himself.

"Well, I want you to give yours to my friend for the present."

The man in plain-clothes passed me his lantern, and waited further commands.

"Now," said Dr. Tointon, facing me, "I want you and the inspector to take your stand in the left-hand corner of the tank top, and have your lanterns ready, and mind, there must not be a sound, or everything will be spoiled."

He tapped the plain-clothes man on the shoulder. "Come along," he said.

Reaching the tank top, we took up positions as he had directed, while he went over with the inspector's man to the far right-hand corner. After a moment, he left the officer, and I could just make out the figure of the latter leaning negligently against the railings.

The doctor came over to us, and sat down between us.

"You've put him just about where our man was when we found him," said the inspector in a whisper.

"Yes," replied Dr. Tointon. "Now, listen, and then there mustn't be another sound. It's a matter of life and death."

His manner and voice were impressive. "When I call out 'ready', throw the light from your lanterns on the officer as smartly as you can. Understand?"

"Yes," we replied together, and after that no one spoke.

The doctor lay down between us on his stomach, the muzzle of his gun directed a little to the right of where the other man stood. Thus we waited. Half an hour passed—an hour, and a sound of distant bells chimed up to us from the valley; then the silence resumed sway. Twice more the far-off bells told of the passing hours, and I was getting dreadfully cramped with staying in one position.

Then abruptly, from somewhere across the tank there came a slight, very slight, slurring, crawling sort of noise. A cold shiver took me, and I peered vainly into the darkness till my eyes ached with the effort. Yet I could see nothing. Indistinctly, I could see the lounging figure of the constable. He seemed never to have stirred from his original position.

The strange rubbing, slurring sound continued. Then came a faint clink of iron, as if someone had kicked against the padlock that fastened down the iron trap over the manhole. Yet it could not be the policeman, for he was not near enough. I saw Dr. Tointon raise his head and peer keenly. Then he brought the butt of his gun up to his shoulder.

I got my lantern ready. I was all tingling with fear and expectation. What was going to happen? There came another slight clink, and then, suddenly, the rustling sound ceased.

I listened breathlessly. Across the tank, the hitherto silent policeman stirred almost, it seemed to me, as if someone or something had touched him. The same instant, I saw the muzzle of the doctor's gun go up some six inches. I grasped my lantern firmly, and drew in a deep breath.

"Ready!" shouted the doctor.

I flashed the light from my lantern across the tank simultaneously with the inspector. I have a confused notion of a twining brown thing about the rail a yard to the right of the constable. Then the doctor's gun spoke once—twice, and it dropped out of sight over the edge of the tank. In the same instant the constable slid down off the rail on to the tank top.

"My God!" shouted the inspector, "has it done for him?"

The doctor was already beside the fallen man, busy loosening his clothing.

"He's all right," he replied. "He's only fainted. The strain was too much. He was a plucky devil to stay. That thing was near him for over a minute."

From somewhere below us in the dark there came a thrashing,

rustling sound. I went to the side and threw the light from my lantern downwards. It showed me a writhing yellow something, like an eel or a snake, only the thing was flat like a ribbon. It was twining itself into knots. It had no head. That portion of it seemed to have been blown clean away.

"He'll do now," I heard Dr. Tointon say, and the next instant he was standing beside me. He pointed downwards at the horrid thing. "There's the murderer," he said.

It was a few evenings later, and the inspector and I were sitting in the doctor's study.

"Even now, doctor," I said. "I don't see how on earth you got at it."

The inspector nodded a silent agreement. "Well," replied Dr. Tointon, "after all it was not so very difficult. Had I not been so unfortunately taken ill while away, I should have cleared the matter up a couple of months ago. You see, I had exceptional opportunities for observing things, and in both cases I was very soon on the spot. But all the same, it was not until the second death occurred that I knew that the deed was not due to a human hand. The fact that there were no footprints in the mud proved that conclusively, and having disposed of that hypothesis, my eyes were open to take in details that had hitherto seemed of no moment. For one thing, both men were found dead almost in the same spot, and that spot is just over the over-flow pipe."

"It came out of the tank?" I questioned.

"Yes," replied Dr. Tointon. "Then on the railings near where the thing had happened, I found traces of slime; and another matter that no one but myself seems to have been aware of, the collar of the policeman's coat was wet, and so was Mr. Marchmount's. Lastly, the shape of the marks upon the necks, and the tremendous force applied, indicated to me the kind of thing for which I must look. The rest was all a matter of deduction.

"Naturally, all the same, my ideas were somewhat hazy; yet before I saw the brute, I could have told you that it was some form of snake or eel, and I could have made a very good guess at its size. In the course of reasoning the matter out, I had occasion to apply to little black Dufirst. From him, I learned that the tank was supposed to be cleaned out annually, but that in reality it had not been seen to for some years."

"What about Dufirst?" I asked.

"Well," said Dr. Tointon dryly, "I understand he is to be granted a free pardon. Of course the little beast stole those things; but I fancy he's had a fair punishment for his sins."

"And the snake, doctor?" I asked. "What was it?"

He shook his head. "I cannot say," he explained. "I have never seen anything just like it. It is one of those abnormalities that occasionally astonish the scientific world. It is a creature that has developed under abnormal conditions, and, unfortunately, it was so shattered by the heavy charges of shot, that the remains tell me but little—its head, as you saw, was entirely shot away."

I nodded. "It's queer—and frightening," I replied. "Makes a chap think a bit."

"Yes," agreed the doctor. "It certainly ought to prove a lesson in cleanliness."

Bullion

IT WAS A PITCHY night in the South Pacific. I was Second Mate of one of the fast clipper-ships running between London and Melbourne at the time of the big gold finds up at Bendigo. There was a fresh breeze blowing, and I was walking hard up and down the weather side of the poop-deck to keep myself warm, when the Captain came out of the companion-way and joined me in my traipse.

"Mr. James, do you believe in ghosts?" he asked suddenly, after several minutes of silence.

"Well, sir," I replied. "I always keep an open mind, so I can't say I'm a proper disbeliever; though I think most ghost yarns can be explained."

"Well," he said in a queer voice, "there's someone keeps whispering in my cabin at nights. It's making me feel funny to be there. I've stood it ever since we left port; but I tell you, Mr. James, I think it's healthier to be on the poop."

"How do you mean, whispering, sir?" I asked.

"Just that," he said. "Someone whispering about my cabin. Sometimes it's quite close to my head, other times it's here and there and everywhere—in the air, you know."

Then, abruptly, he stopped in his walk and faced me as if determined to say the thing that was in his mind. "What did Captain Avery die of on the passage out?" he asked, quick and blunt.

"None of us knew, sir," I told him. "He just seemed to sicken and go off."

"Well," he said, "I'm not going to sleep in his cabin any longer. I've no special fancy for just sickening and going off. If you like I'll change cabins with you, as you don't seem over troubled with superstitions."

"Certainly, sir," I answered, half pleased and half sorry; for while

353

I had a feeling that there was nothing really to bother about in the Captain's fancies, yet—though he had only taken command in Melbourne to bring the ship home—I had found already that he was not one of the soft kind by any means. And so, as you will understand, I had vague feelings of uneasiness to set against my curiosity to find out what it was that had given Captain Reynolds a fit of nerves.

"Would you like me to sleep in your place tonight, sir?" I asked.

"Well," he said with a little laugh, "when you get below you'll find me snug in your bunk, so it'll be a case of my cabin or the saloon table." And with that it was settled.

"I shall lock the door," I added. "I'm not going to have anyone fooling me. I suppose I may search?"

"Do what you like," was all he replied.

About an hour later, the Captain left me and went below. When the Mate came up to relieve me at eight bells I told him that I was promoted to the Captain's cabin and the reason why. To my surprise, he said that he wouldn't sleep there for all the gold that was in the ship; so that I finished by telling him that he was a superstitious old shell-back. But he stuck to his opinion, and I left him sticking hard.

When I got down to my new cabin, I found that the Captain had made the Steward shift my gear in already, so that I had nothing to do but turn in, which I did after a good look round and locking the door.

I left the lamp turned about half up, and meant to lie awake awhile listening; but I had gone over to sleep before I knew, and only waked to hear the 'prentice knocking on my door to tell me it was one bell.

For three nights I slept thus in comfort and jested once or twice with the Captain that I was getting the best of the bargain; but he was firm that he would not sleep there again and said that if I was so pleased with it, so much the better as I could take it permanently.

Then, just as you might expect, on the fourth night something happened. I had gone below for the middle watch and had fallen asleep as usual, almost as soon as my head was on the pillow. I was awakened suddenly by some curious sound apparently quite near to me. I lay there without moving and listened, my heart beating a little rapidly; but otherwise I was cool and alert. Then I heard the thing quite plainly with my waking senses—a vague, uncertain whispering, seeming to me as if someone or something bent over me from behind, and whispered some unintelligible thing close to my ear. I rolled over suddenly and stared behind and around the cabin, but the whole place was empty.

Then I sat still and listened again. For several minutes there was an absolute silence; and then, abruptly, I heard the vague, uncomfortable whispering again, seeming to come from the middle of the cabin. I sat there feeling distinctly nervous; then I jumped quietly from my bunk and slipped across silently to the door. I stooped and listened at the keyhole; but there was no one there. I ran across then to the ventilators and shut them; also I made sure that the ports were screwed up, so that there was now absolutely no place through which anyone could send his voice, even supposing that anyone was idiot enough to want to play such an unmeaning trick.

For a while after I had taken these precautions, I stood silent; and twice I heard the whispering, going vaguely now in this and now in that part of the air of the cabin, as if some unseen, spiritual thing wandered about trying to make itself heard.

As you may suppose, this was getting more than I cared to tackle; for I had searched the cabin every watch, and it seemed to me that there was truly something unnatural in the thing I heard. I began to get my clothes and dress; for after this I felt inclined to adopt the Captain's suggestion of the saloon table for a bunk. You see, I had got to have my sleep, but I could not fancy lying unconscious in that cabin, with that strange sound wandering about; though awake, I think I can say truthfully, I should not really have feared it; but to submit myself to the defencelessness of sleep with that uncanniness near me was more than I could bear.

And then, you know, a sudden thought came blinding through my brain. The bullion! We were bringing home thirty thousand ounces of gold in sealed bullion chests, and these were in a specially erected wooden compartment standing all by itself in the center of the lazarette, just below the Captain's cabin. What if some attempt were being made secretly on the treasure, and we all the time idiotically thinking of ghosts, when perhaps the vague sounds we had heard were conducted in some way from below! You can conceive how the thought set me tingling; so that I did not stop to realize how improbable it was, but took my lamp and went immediately to the Captain.

He woke in a moment, and when he had heard my suggestion he told me that the thing was practically impossible; yet the very idea made him sufficiently uneasy to determine him on going down with me into the lazarette, to look at the seals on the door of the temporary bullion room.

He did not stop to dress, but just pushed his feet into his soft slippers, and reaching the lamp from me, led the way. The entrance to the lazarette was through a trap-door under the saloon table, and this was kept locked. When this was opened, the Captain went down with the lamp, and I followed noiselessly in my stockinged feet.

At the bottom of the steep ladder we paused, and the Captain held the lamp high and looked around. Then he went over to where the square bulk of the bullion room stood alone in the center of the place, and together we examined the seals on the door; but of course they were untouched, and I began to realize now that my idea had been nothing more than an unreasoned suggestion. And then, you know, as we stood there silent amid the various creaks and groans of the working bulkheads, we both heard the sound—a whispering somewhere near us that came and went oddly, being lost in the noise of the creaking woodwork, and again coming plain, seeming to be in this place and now in that.

I experienced an extraordinary feeling of superstitious fear; but, curiously enough, the Captain was affected quite otherwise; for he muttered in a low voice that there was someone inside of the bullion room, and began quickly and coolly to break the sealed tapes. Then, very quietly, he unlocked the door, and telling me to hold the lamp high, threw the door wide open. But the place was empty save for the neatly chocked range of bullion boxes, bound and sealed and numbered, that occupied half of the floor.

"Nothing here!" said the Captain, and took the lamp from my hand. He held it low down over the rows of little numbered chests, and suddenly he swore.

"The thirteenth!" he said with a gasp. "Where's the thirteenth? Number Thirteen!"

He was right. The bullion-chest which should have stood between No. twelve and No. fourteen was gone. We set-to and counted every chest, verifying the numbers. There they all were, numbered up to sixty, except for the gap of the thirteenth. Somehow, in some way, a thousand ounces of gold had been removed bodily from out of the sealed room.

In a very agitated but thorough manner, the Captain and I made close examination of the room; but it was plain that any entry that had been made could only have been through the sealed doorway. Then he led the way out and, having tried the lock several times and found it showed no signs of having been tampered with, he locked and sealed up the door again; sealing the tape also right across the keyhole. Then, a sudden thought seemed to come to him, he told me to stay by the door while he went up into the saloon.

In a few minutes he returned with the Purser, both of them armed and carrying lamps. They came very quietly and paused with me outside of the door where the two of them made very close and minute scrutiny both of the old seals and of the door itself. At the Purser's request, the Captain removed the new seals and unlocked the door. As he opened it the Purser turned suddenly and looked behind him. I heard it also—a vague whispering, seeming to be in the air; then it was drowned and lost in the creaking of the timbers.

The Captain had heard the sound, too, and was standing in the doorway holding his lamp high and looking in, his pistol ready in his right hand; for to him it had seemed to come from within the bullion room. Yet the place was as empty as we had left it but a few minutes before; as, indeed, it was bound to be of any living creature. The Captain walked across to where the bullion chest was missing, and stooped to point out the gap to the Purser. A queer exclamation came from him, and he remained stooping while the Purser and I pressed forward to find what new thing had happened now. When I saw what the Captain was staring at you will understand that I felt simply dazed; for there right before his face, in its proper place, was the thirteenth bullion chest; as indeed it must have been all the time.

"You've been dreaming," said the Purser with a burst of relieved laughter. "My goodness! but you did give me a fright!"

For our parts, the Captain and I just stared at the re-materialized bullion chest, and then at one another. But explanation of this extraordinary thing we could not find. One thing only was I sure of, and that was that the chest had not been there five minutes earlier. And yet, there it was, sealed and banded, and wedged in with the others as it must have been since it was placed there under official supervision.

"That chest was not there a few minutes ago!" the Captain said at length. Then he brushed the hair off his forehead and looked again at the chest. "Are we dreaming?" he asked at last, and turned and looked at me. He touched the chest with his foot, and I did the same with my hand; but it was no illusion, and we could only suppose, in spite of the tellings of our eyes, that we must have made some extraordinary mistake.

I turned to the purser.

"But the whispering!" I said. "*You* heard the whispering!"

"Yes," said the Captain. "What was that? I tell you there's something funny knocking about, or else we're all mad!"

The Purser stared puzzled, nodding his head.

"I heard something," he said. "The chief thing is, the stuff is there all right. I suppose you'll put a watch over it?"

"By Moses, yes!" said the Captain. "The Mate and I'll sleep on that blessed gold until we hand it ashore in London Town!"

And so it was arranged. So much had the feeling impressed us that something threatened the bullion that we three officers had to take it in turns to sleep actually inside of the bullion room itself, being sealed and locked in with the treasure. In addition to this, the Captain made the petty officers keep watch and watch with him and the Purser through the whole of each twenty-four hours, traipsing round and round that wretched bullion room until not a mouse could have gone in or out without being seen. And more, he had the deck above and below thoroughly examined by the carpenter once in every twenty-four hours, so that never was a treasure so carefully and scrupulously guarded.

For our part, we officers began to grow pretty sick of the job, once the touch of excitement connected with the thought of robbery had worn off. And when, as sometimes happened, we were aware of that extraordinary whispering, it was only the Captain's determination and authority which made us submit to the constant discomfort and breaking of our sleep; for every hour the watchman on the outside of the bullion room would knock twice on the boards of the room, and the sleeping officer within would have to rouse, take a look round, and knock back twice, to signify that all was well.

Sometimes I could almost think we got into the way of doing this in our sleep; for I have been roused to my watch on deck, with no memory of having answered the watch man's knock, though a cautious inquiry showed me that I had done so.

Then, one night that I was sleeping in the bullion room, a rather queer thing happened. Something must have roused me between the times of the watchman's knocks; for I wakened suddenly and half sat up, with a feeling that something was wrong somewhere. As in a dream I looked round, and all the time fighting against sleepiness. Everything seemed normal, but when I looked at the tiers of bullion chests, I saw that there was a gap among them—some of the chests had certainly disappeared.

I stared in a stupid nerveless way, as a man full of sleep sometimes will do, without rousing himself to realize the actuality of the things he looks at. And even as I stared, I dozed over and fell back; but seemed to waken almost immediately and looked again at the chests. Yet, it was plain that I must have seen dazedly and half dreaming; for not a bullion chest was missing, and I sank back again thankfully to my slumber, as you can think.

When, at the end of my "treasure-watch", as we had grown to call our watch below, I reported my queer half-dream to the Captain. He came down himself and made a thorough examination of the bullion room, also questioning the sailmaker who had been the watchman outside. But he said there had been nothing unusual; only that once he had thought he had heard the curious whispering going about in the air of the lazarette.

And so that queer voyage went on, with over us all the time a sense of peculiar mystery, vague and indefinable; so that one thought a thousand strange weird thoughts that one lacked the courage to put into words. And other times there was only a sense of utter weariness of it all, and the one desire to get to port and be shut of it, and go back to a normal life in some other vessel. Even the passengers—many of whom were returning diggers—were infected by the strange atmosphere of uncertainty that prompted our constant guarding of the bullion; for it had become known among them that a special guard was being kept, and that certain inexplicable things had happened. But the Captain refused all their offers of help, preferring to keep his own men about the gold, as you may suppose.

At last we reached London and docked; and now came the strangest thing of all. When the bank officials came aboard to take over the gold, the Captain took them down to the bullion room where the carpenter was walking round, as outside watchman, and the First Mate was sealed inside as usual.

The Captain explained that we were taking unusual precautions and broke the seals. When, however, they unlocked and opened the door, the Mate did not answer to the Captain's call, but was seen to be lying quiet beside the gold. Examination showed that he was quite dead; but there was nowhere any mark or sign to show that his death was unnatural. As the Captain said to me afterwards:

"Another case of just sickening and going off! I wouldn't sail again in this packet for anything the owners like to offer me!"

The officials examined the gold and, finding all in order, had it taken ashore up to the bank, and very thankful I was to see the last of it. Yet, this is where I was mistaken; for about an hour later, as I was superintending the slinging out of some heavy cargo, there came a message from the bank, to the effect that every one of the bullion chests was a dummy filled with lead, and that no one be allowed to leave the ship until an inquiry and search had been made. This search was carried out rigorously, so that not a cabin or a scrap of personal luggage was left unexamined; and afterwards the ship herself was searched, but nowhere was there any sign of the gold; and when you come to remember that there must have been something like a ton of it, you will realize that it was not a thing that could have been easily hidden.

Permission was now given to all that they might go ashore, and I proceeded once more to supervise the slinging out of heavy stuff that I had been "bossing" when the order came from the bank. And all the time as I gave my orders I felt in a daze. How could nearly seventeen hundredweight of gold have been removed out of that guarded bullion room? I remembered all the curious things that had been heard and seen and half felt. Was there something queer about the ship? But my reason objected. There was surely some sane, normal explanation of the mystery.

Abruptly I came out of my thoughts; for the man on the shore-gear had just let a heavy case down rather roughly, and a swell-looking man was cursing him for his clumsiness. It was then that a possible explanation of the mystery came to me, and I determined to take the risk of testing it.

I jumped ashore and swore at the man who was handling the gear, telling him to slack away more carefully; to which he replied "Ay, ay, Sir." Under my breath I said:

"Take no notice of the hard talk, Jimmy. Let the next one come down good and solid. I'll take the responsibility if it smashes."

Then I stood back and let Jimmy have his chance. The next case went well up to the block before Jimmy took a turn and signalled to the winch to vast heaving.

"Slack away handsome!" yelled Jimmy, and let his own rope smoke round the bollard. The case came down, crashing, from a height of thirty feet and burst on the quay.

As the dust cleared, I heard the swell-looking person cursing at the top of his voice; but I did not bother about this, for what was attracting my attention was the fact that there among the heavy timbers of the big case was a number of the missing bullion chests.

I seized my whistle and blew it for one of the 'prentices. When he came I told him to run up the quay for a policeman. Then I turned to the Captain and the Third Mate, who had come running ashore, and explained. They ran to the lorry on which the other cases had been placed and, with the help of some of the men, pulled them down again on to the quay. But when they came to look for the swell stranger who had been looking after the unloading of the stolen gold, he was nowhere to be found; so that after all, the policeman had nothing to do when he arrived but mount guard over the recovered bullion, of which I am glad to say not a single case was missing.

Later, a more intelligent examination into things revealed how the robbery had been effected; for when we came to take down the temporary bullion room, we found that a very cleverly concealed sliding panel had been fitted into the end opposite to the door. This gave us the idea to examine the wooden ventilator which came up through the deck nearby from the lower hold. And now we held the key to the whole mystery.

Evidently there had been quite a gang of thieves aboard the ship. They had built the cases ashore, packed them with dummy bullion chests, and sealed and banded them exactly like the originals. These had been placed in the hold at Melbourne as freight, under the name of "specimens". In the meanwhile, some of the band must have got at our carpenter who had built the bullion room, and promised him a share of the gold if he would build the secret panel into one end. Then, when we got to sea, the thieves must have got down into the lower hold through one of the forrard hatches and, having opened one of their cases, begun to exchange the dummies for the real chests by climbing up inside the wooden ventilator-shaft, which the carpenter had managed to fit with a couple of boards that slid to one side, just opposite to the secret panel in the wooden bullion room.

It must have been very slow work, and their whispering to one another had been carried up the ventilator shaft which passed right through the Captain's cabin, under the appearance of a large, or-namented strut or upright, supporting the arm racks. It was this unexpected carrying of the sound which brought the Captain and me down, to nearly discover them; so that they had not even time to replace the thirteenth chest with the prepared dummy.

I don't think there is much more to explain. There is very little doubt in my mind that the Captain's extraordinary precautions must have made things extremely difficult for the robbers, and that they could only get to work then when the carpenter happened to be the outside watchman. It is also obvious to me that some drug which threw off narcotic fumes must have been injected into the bullion room to insure the officer not waking at inconvenient moments; so that the time I did waken and felt so stupid, I must have been in a half-stupified condition, and did *really* see that some of the chests had gone. These were replaced as soon as I fell back asleep. The First Mate must have died from an over-prolonged inhalation of the drug.

I think that is all that has to do with this incident. Perhaps, though, you may be pleased to hear that I was both handsomely thanked and rewarded for having solved the mystery. Also, for many years after that, I sailed as Master of the very ship in which this occurred. So that, altogether, I was very well.

The Mystery of the
Water-Logged Ship

THE BIG STEAM-YACHT *White Hart* was driving along easily at half-speed through a dark, starless night in the North Atlantic. The Captain was pacing the bridge with Swanscott, the owner. At the little steam steering-wheel one of the four quartermasters stood drowsily, for the yacht almost steered herself, as the saying goes, and the man had little to do but listen for eight bells.

Abruptly the Captain stopped in his tracks, staring away over the bows; then, whipping round upon the helmsman, he roared at the top of his voice:

"Starboard your hellum! Smartly, now! Smartly, now!"

As the little wheel spun swiftly under the man's hands the Captain turned back quickly and stared over the bow into the darkness.

"What is it, Captain? What is it?" Swanscott was saying, glancing on every side through the darkness.

"What have you seen?"

"Light just under the starboard bow, sir," the Master answered. "It should be broad on the beam now."

He turned to the helmsman.

"Steady!" he called.

"Steady it is, sir," answered the man, and put the wheel over.

The Captain and the owner stood together and stared into the utter darkness to starboard; but the minutes passed, and never a sign of any light was there.

"Don't see anything, Captain," said Swanscott.

"Neither me!" replied the Master, and blew his whistle.

He gave word to the man who answered it to relieve the lookout for a few minutes and send him aft to the bridge. When the man arrived he asked him whether he had seen a light just off the starboard bow.

"Yes, sir," replied the man. "I thought I did; but it was gone before I could be sure. Then you starboarded, sir, and I knew you'd seed it, too. But I ain't seed it since."

The Captain dismissed the man forrard, with a word of warning to be smarter in future. Then he readjusted his night-glasses and took another long look out into the darkness to starboard; but nowhere could he see the light.

"Most mysterious!" said the owner. "What do you think it was?"

"Well, sir, it may be one of those fool timber-boys running dhowls across home and tryin' to save oil. I've known 'em do that, and just shove a lantern over the rail, if anything comes too near. They deserve hanging!"

"We ought to see her spars with the glasses," said Swanscott, "if she were as near as you think."

"Yes, sir," answered the Captain. "An' that's what's puzzling me. It might be someone got adrift in a boat; but they'd never hide the light till we'd got 'em safe. What do you say, sir? Shall we turn on the searchlight and just have a look round? You're in no hurry."

"By all means," said Swanscott. "This is interesting."

The Captain rang the engines to dead slow, and then whistled for a couple of the hands to come up and unhood the big searchlight, which was mounted on a platform at the after end of the bridge. Five minutes later the great jet of the light flashed out into the darkness to starboard, and swept round in a huge semicircle as the Captain revolved the big projector.

"Ah!" said Swanscott, who had come up beside him. "There she is. You were right."

For directly in the rays of the searchlight, apparently about a mile distant, there showed plain, with every detail of rope and broken spar standing out clear in the brilliant light, an iron, square-rigged ship.

"Derelict!" said the Captain. "Lord, we've had a shave! See how low she is in the water, and her fore and main topmasts gone. She's in the carrying trade; look at the deck cargo of her. It's shameful! Shall we take a closer look at her, sir?"

"Certainly, Captain."

The Master rang to half-speed and motioned to the helmsman, who muttered "Aye, aye, sir," and put the wheel over a few spokes. They steamed down for the strange vessel, and in a few minutes had passed under her stern and reversed about a hundred yards to leeward. Here they rode easy on the slow swells, with the searchlight playing full upon the derelict ship. Her condition was plain now to be seen. Her fore and main topmasts had gone, as I have said, with all their yards and gear; also the spike-boom had been carried away over the bows. Her mizzen t'gallant and royal masts also were gone; but the mizzen topmast was standing, so that she rolled there in the gloom, a derelict dripping hulk, with little more than her naked lower masts and yards above the deck to show what she had been.

"That's a fine thing to have floating around in the dark!" said the Captain, examining her through his glasses. "That's the sort of thing that accounts for the missin' packets. Just fancy hittin' it under a full head of steam! I'll bet that's what's ended the *Lavinia*, if the truth could be known."

Here he referred to one of the North Atlantic boats which had been reported missing just before they left home.

"Yes," said Swanscott thoughtfully. "It might have been us, if you hadn't spotted the light. But where the deuce *is* the light?"

This neither of them could decide; for the whole length of the dripping rail was unbroken by any sign of light or life, and beyond it there rose in great mounds the timber masses of her deck cargo. After a further time of watching and keeping the searchlight going, Swanscott suggested that he would go aboard and have a look round, and whilst the boat was being lowered he hurried below to wake his friend Hay, who, he knew, would be keen to accompany him.

When they both came on deck the boat was in the water, with the First Officer in charge, and a few minutes later the two of them were standing on the water-soaked decks of the derelict, with below them the dull pounding of the imprisoned timbers as they rolled sluggishly, grinding against the deck-beams and hatch-coamings in the water-logged hold. The hatches were off, and odd whiles some heavier roll than usual would send some of the water slopping up out of the hold over the coamings of the hatches, and all the time there was the lonesome swish of water upon the dripping decks and the low groan of the great masses of timber as each roll threw new stresses upon them and the bulk of water in which they floated. So that just to look down through the open mouths of the holds was to have dank thoughts and dismalness, with the grim suggestiveness of desolation and the nearness of the ocean deeps, which came to the mind as they stared down into that gulf of gloom and water and soaked timbers.

Swanscott and Hay, with the Officer and two of the men, explored the whole of the vessel—that is, all that was still above water. Forrard they found the fo'c'sle empty and glimmering wet and dank in the light from the lamps. All the bunks had been washed out, and below them, under their feet, was the same suggestive pounding and grinding of timbers and the sullen roll of the great bulk of water imprisoned in the holds.

"Makes me feel creepy," said Hay. "Let's get out of here!" and he led the way out of the gloomy iron cavern, where the very decks seemed to have grown soft and mushy with the long and continual soaking. Then away aft, and here they looked down the poop skylight into the darkness of submerged cabins, and, for all they knew, into places where dead men rolled to and fro hideously in the black waters.

"Ugh!" said Hay, again expressing the general feeling. "Beastly! Let's leave her!"

And they went aboard the yacht. Here, however, more practical things were discussed.

"Yes, sir," said the Captain. "You ain't in no hurry, an' if we go jog-trot for a couple or three days, we needn't strain ourselves or tow the blessed stern out of us. It'd be a blessing and a duty to all shipping if we was to remove her; for sink her you can't, not without you took her to pieces or blew her to pieces. I know. I've tried. She'll float as long as them timbers has any sort of framework to hold 'em together. An' then there's the salvage."

This was talked over in all its bearings, and Swanscott told his Captain that he could "take the job on", and he'd make him and the men a present of the yacht's "share". The only thing he stipulated was that a crew should not be put aboard of her unless it was a certainty that she would not sink under their feet.

"Sink!" said the Captain. "She'll not sink this side of the Judgment, not that way."

And so it was arranged. Volunteers were called for, and out of those who stepped forward four were chosen. These were put aboard the derelict, and some food and water. One of the boats, with which she was well supplied, was sent astern at the end of its painter as a precaution, lest, as the Captain said, "the im-bloomin'-possible" happened, and the wreck did sink. The sidelights were lit, and a very long spring was shackled on to the tow-line so as to ease the "pluck" of the deadweight of the "tow" as much as possible. The Bo'sun was sent aboard with the four men to take charge, and the Captain told him to put a man on the fo'c'sle head to watch the tow-line, and that the helmsman must steer by the yacht's stern-light. Then he went ahead with the line, and took a strain, and so began to jog forward through the night, slow and easy, with that dismal "tow" about a quarter of a mile astern.

For a while after they had "got going" again Swanscott and Hay walked the bridge with the Captain, discoursing on the danger of just such lonesome derelicts as the one they had come across that night. Presently the talk came upon the light which the Captain insisted he had seen. Both Swanscott and Hay were of the opinion that it must have been one of those strange "fancy lights" which sailors sometimes see suddenly at night through overstraining the eyes. On his part, the Captain was positively sure that he had seen a light; but more than that he would not say at first, until Hay perceived that if they ceased to "rag" him he might be got to explain what was at the back of his silence. He gave Swanscott the hint to cease "baiting", and by showing a sympathetic attitude they coaxed the Captain finally into admitting seriously that what he had seen must have been what he called a "sailors' light."

"A what?" said Swanscott, half amused, half impressed by the old man's earnestness.

"A sailors' light, sir," said the Captain. "It's always give as a warnin'. My father, as was fifty-five year at sea, an' died there, seen it three times, an' if he hadn't took notice he'd have smashed up his ship every time. He always said it was the spirits of them that's drowned warnin' the sailors. I half believes it, you know, and half don't. When I'm ashore it seems just sailors' talk; but on a night like this— Well, you know the feeling yourself. You saw she was *empty*, not a soul aboard. And I *know* I saw that light. You think I'm mistook; but if I hadn't seen something, where'd we be *now*? I tell you it's as queer one way as the other."

"I think I understand your attitude," said Hay. "Anyway I must admit that the sea's a place to breed fancies, especially at night, and with old wrecks and drowned men knocking around," and he peered away into the darkness, where the lights of the derelict showed astern in the gloom. "All the same, you know, Captain, we mustn't get superstitious. It may have been that you saw nothing really, but you had a premonition."

The old man snorted.

"What's the difference, mister?" he said. "What's the difference?"

Presently, leaving the Mate in charge, the Captain went below with the two friends, and they sat awhile in Swanscott's cabin having a whisky before turning in. Then, just before they said good-night, the old Captain raised his head and looked round the cabin as if he were listening.

"That's a pretty smart squall we're into," he remarked; "hark to it!" For outside in the night the wind was going over them with a scream, as one of those heavy squalls which wander the seas alone passed them. "That'll wet 'em!" he said, meaning the four men and the bo'sun who were in the derelict. "Guess she'll just be lumpin' it aboard. Well, they'll get dry on the salvage."

He drained his glass, and set it down in the fiddles; then once more raised his head, with that suggestion of listening and half-expecting. Abruptly he jumped from the locker.

"I knew it!" he said, reaching for the door-handle. "She's parted! I thought she was ridin' different."

He opened the door and hooked it back, then ran for his oilskin coat and sou'wester. The two friends did the same, and followed him on deck. Here, at first, they were half stunned by the storm of wind and rain which met them. They struggled to the bridge after the Captain, and heard him singing out to the Officer that the "tow" had parted from them. He did not attempt to blame the man; for he knew by experience that up there in the wind and rain the altered "scend" (motion) of the yacht would be less felt than down in the calm of the cabin, where the senses were not bewildered by the blinding force of the rain and wind. Also, the rain made a curtain between the two vessels, so that it was no use expecting to locate her by her lights until the squall had passed, as Swanscott and Hay discovered for themselves, and by then she might have soused them out, or be slewed off before the wind, and so hiding them.

The searchlight was unhooded and turned astern; but so heavy was the rain that the light simply made a glittering tunnel amid the raindrops, and was lost in strange rainbows in the night, without showing any sign of the missing vessel.

"You think they're all right, Captain?" asked Swanscott anxiously, for he began to fear that the wreck might have foundered, in spite of the Captain's sureness of her powers to float beyond the Judgment.

"Certain, sir," said the Captain. "Just wait till the squall's eased a bit, an' you'll see her."

"There she is!" he said a few minutes later, as the squall cleared away to leeward. "There she is! My goodness, she's drifted more than I'd have thought! A power more than I'd have thought."

She was plain now in the great jet of the light, about three miles astern, and running off before the wind.

"That's queer, Mr. Marsh," said the Captain to the First Officer, who was standing near, looking through his night-glasses. All that top-hamper aft ought to have brought her up into the wind, dead sure."

The Mate agreed, and the Captain told him to run the yacht down to leeward of the wreck, which was done. Here, with the glare of the searchlight full upon the derelict, they ranged up to within thirty or forty yards of her, and hauled. Yet the most inexplicable thing greeted them—*nothing!* There came no answering faces to the rail, nor any answering sound across the quietness left by the departed squall; nothing, save, as it seemed to Hay, who was the most impressionable, a strange little dank echo of their hail, that seemed to beat back at them vaguely from the dripping iron side of the ship.

"Good Lord!" said Swanscott, "what's up, Captain?"

"I don't know, sir," said the old man, seriously enough. "I don't understand it one bit. We must go aboard." He turned to the Mate, "Where did that hawser carry away, Mr. Marsh?" he asked.

"Didn't carry away at all, sir," replied the officer. "Must have come free off the bollard or the bitts, or wherever that fool Bo'sun made it fast!"

"Mighty queer," said the Captain, and went down to see whether the boat was all ready; for he was in trouble to discover what had happened, and intended personally to investigate this curious happening.

Presently he and the two friends, with three of the boat's crew, stood on the soaked decks and looked round. The Captain looked forrard and aft; then he put his hands to his mouth:

"Bosun!" he sang out. "Bo'sun!"

But there came back only the little hollow echoes from the high bulkhead of the t'gallant fo'c'sle, and the low break of the half-poop. He turned to one of the men.

"Back into the boat, my lad, and go across to the yacht. Ask Mr. Marsh to pass you down two ox three lamps. Smart, now!"

When the lamps arrived they were distributed among the party, and a thorough search was made; but nothing was found. The four men and the Bo'sun had gone utterly and entirely; and the only supposition that could be made was that the wreck had shipped a heavy sea during the squall and washed some of the men overboard, and that the rest had been lost in trying to save them; for it was folly to suppose that one sea, or even a series, would remove five men from the *different* parts of the decks of the derelict; for except under the circumstances suggested by the Captain, if the wreck had been much swept by water, the crew would have taken refuge in the rigging until the squall was gone. And you must know that all the time under their reasoning everyone was vaguely uneasy. The explanation was possible, just barely possible, but certainly improbable. But then, again, so was any other explanation that anyone had to offer. Hay thought of the Captain's talk about "sailors' lights," and stopped himself; for it made him uncomfortable and miserable; so that in a less impressed mood he would have reproved himself for feeling superstitious.

"And you know," said the Captain in an undertone to Swanscott and Hay, "you know she ain't sloppin' any water aboard to speak of, an' I can't see how she done much in that squall. It was stiff, that's so; but there was no time for the sea to rise. It's a corker."

Presently they left the wreck and went aboard the yacht for a consultation. Here it was decided finally to wait for the morning, and then to see what could be done in the way of blowing the wreck to pieces, though the Captain was not sanguine, for, as he said: "You can't get at 'er to put the charges in."

It was at this point that the Second Mate arrived on the scene.

"I hope you'll forgive me, sir," he said, looking at the Captain and the owner. "I feel it's cheeky of me to push myself in like this; but the Mate tells me you're giving up the idea of our salving the derelict," and he nodded towards where she lay, with the searchlight still playing upon her.

"Yes," said Swanscott gravely. "We can't allow anyone else to risk it aboard of her, even if we could get them to go. I'm very grieved indeed about what has happened."

"Well, sir," said the Second Mate, "let *me* go. I'll go alone. I'm not afraid. I'll lash myself secure and rig a few life-lines. The salvage money means a lot to me, sir. I wish you'd let me."

At first both the owner and the Captain were firm that no one else should be allowed to risk their lives aboard the somewhat mysterious wreck; but in the end he showed himself so determined and without fear that they allowed him to have his way, and, more than this, to take three of the men with him, if he could induce them to volunteer; which, indeed, he managed by sheer force of personality, persuading them and holding up to them that their share of the salvage money would more than double their wages; for it had been agreed by the owner and the Captain that the bulk of the salvage should by rights belong to the plucky Second Mate and the three men who accompanied him.

"And a good sailorman he is, too," said the Captain, "an' plucky as they're made."

The tow-line was once more passed, and the Second Mate himself saw to the making fast of it; also to the re-lighting of the side-lights, which were found to be out. Then he rigged life-lines along the decks, and so prepared to meet whatever danger there was ahead.

Presently the yacht took up the tow, and the watches settled down somewhat; but no one went to sleep, for the loss of the four men and the bo'sun had upset everybody; the curious mystery that hung about their death had tinctured the general gloom with queer thrills and wonderings.

For a good hour the yacht went forward at a slow pace through the night, and her side-lights could be seen burning clearly about a hundred yards astern, for the Captain had given orders to shorten the tow-rope.

The Captain and the owner and his friend were all grouped together under the weathercloth on the weather side of the bridge, and the old man was spinning them a yarn about another curious happening which had come to him one night in mid-ocean some ten years before. Abruptly his tale was cut short by an astonished shout from the Mate:

"My God! She's parted again, and both lights are out!"

"What!" yelled the old Captain, and jumped into the after corner of the bridge, where he could see, unimpeded by the angle of the weathercloth. "Yes, she's gone again, mister. There's some devilment in this. Man that searchlight—smart, now! Starboard your hellum. Smartly now, my lad!"

This latter to the man at the wheel.

The yacht came round in a big curve, and half a minute later the great beam of the light drove out through the darkness to port. It swept across the empty miles, showed nothing, and abruptly drove back again in a wider circling. Then they saw the derelict, a good two miles away to port.

"Got her again!" sang out the Mate. "Lord! How's she got left all that way?"

The man's astonishment was plain; and the Captain was equally surprised.

"Full speed ahead!" he shouted. "Keep the light on her," and within six minutes they were reversing to leeward of her. The Captain leaned over the end of the bridge and hailed: "Mr. Jenkins!" he shouted (that being the Second Mate's name). "Mr. Jenkins!" But there came no answer, beyond the vague echoing of his voice from the iron side of the ship, and strange little mocking echoes which seemed to sound vaguely about her empty, lumber-stacked decks.

"Starboard lifeboat!" shouted the Captain.   Then, to the Mate:

"Bring up half a dozen rifles and cutlasses, and arm the crew. Put a lamp for every man in the boat. Call the other watch. Pass them out rifles and ammunition, and have the port lifeboat ready to lower away. Keep the searchlight going."

"Aye, aye, sir," answered the Mate, and hurried away to obey, whilst the Captain turned to the owner and Mr. Hay.

"I don't know what it is, sir," he said. "But if you're coming, you'd best have some sort of weapon, and your friend too. There's something devilish aboard that craft, you mark my word; but whether carnal weapons is any use, the Lord He knows. I don't."

Five minutes later they were away in the boat and aboard of the derelict, gazing fearfully round, not knowing what they might see. Yet from end to end they searched her; from the dank and water-sodden fo'c'sle to the deserted wheel, where, but a few short minutes before—as you might say—one of their shipmates had stood. And now everywhere the silence, and the utter mystery that shrouded the end of the nine men who had gone utterly during the night, leaving no trace of any kind to tell what extraordinary thing had happened.

When the search had been completed the Captain gathered the men together, whilst he held a short consultation with his owner and Hay, in which it was decided to stand by the wreck during the rest of the night, and to make a more drastic search by daylight. As they talked they could hear under their feet the constant dull grind of the timbers, and the low, hollow boom and swirl of the great bulk of water in the holds rolling and rumbling to and fro; and this, combined with the peculiar and frightening mystery which now hung about the vessel, made everyone very thankful when the Captain gave the word to get down once more into the boat and return to the yacht.

During the remainder of that night the yacht steamed slowly round and round the derelict, keeping her searchlight playing full upon her; and so the dawn came in presently, and they prepared to make their great attempt to solve the mystery. As soon as the day had broken properly two boat-loads of men, fully armed, were sent aboard the wreck, the Captain, Swanscott, and Hay accompanying them. Then, the search began in earnest. Every piece of timber on the decks was shifted, lest they should prove to be shelters for anyone or anything; the fo'c'sle was visited, and the forepeak examined; but only to find that even here the water had entered, showing that she was full, fore and aft. The after-cabins were inspected; for it was found that a couple or three feet of air-space existed between the poop-deck and the surface of the water; though, indeed, the rolling of the vessel sent the great bulk of fluid from side to side in a manner that nearly drowned the searchers, whilst several were hurt more or less by the blows of the various objects afloat in the saloon and cabins. Yet nowhere—though not a cabin was left unexplored—did they find anything remarkable; only everywhere the dismalness of the water, and the smell of dampness and brine; and all the while, under the feet, the great bulk of water in the holds rolling to and fro, and the dull grinding and pounding of the water-logged timbers.

The search occupied the whole of the day, and all day the yacht had towed the derelict landwards, for Swanscott had sworn now to tow her into port, even though they towed only by day and removed the men to the yacht at right and stood by for each dawn.

In the late afternoon the Captain removed most of the men to the yacht, leaving half a dozen with their rifles to guard the man at the wheel, under the command of the Third Officer.

"What on earth can it be, Captain?" said Hay that evening at dinner for about the hundredth time. "Could it be an octopus?"

"No, sir," said the Captain. "You don't get octopuses in these seas. The devilment's something in that packet herself. She's a wrong 'un."

"How do you mean—a wrong 'un?" asked Swanscott seriously.

"Well, sir," said the Captain, "I don't quite know what I do mean, except just that. If I said she was haunted, you'd laugh; but she's a wrong 'un, you mark my word, sir. I'll have those men aboard here again as soon as ever it gets dark."

"Well, Captain," said Hay, "it's getting dusk now," and he pointed at the open ports. "I know I'll feel happier when they're aboard again."

Even as he spoke there was a loud shouting on deck, and the Mate's whistle was heard blowing shrilly.

"My God!" said the old Captain, "she's parted again. My God! We're too late; we're too late!"

They rushed on deck after him, and here they found that it was as the Captain had said. The "tow" had just parted, and showed dimly away astern in the dusk. Something extraordinary was happening aboard of her, for strange cries and sounds came over the sea, but never a shot to tell of any fight.

In two minutes the boats were manned, each main armed, and the yacht was running down at full speed on the derelict, her searchlight playing upon the wreck, yet showing nothing. She dropped the two boats within fifty yards, and they raced to the side of the wreck. There was a scramble aboard, with Swanscott and the old Captain leading; lanterns were passed up, and the rest of the men followed, whilst the searchlight played from end to end of the derelict craft. There was an absolute silence as the Captain put his hands to his mouth and sang out:

"Mr. Dunk! Mr. Dunk!" which was the Third Mate's name.

There came no answer; and the search began again, every man nervous, and glancing fearfully behind and on every side. Yet not a sign of any kind could they find of the men or of their arms, nor anything to show that there had been any struggle. The wreck looked as if no living thing had stood aboard of her for months.

"Into the boats!" said the Captain, and there was the beginning of a rush, which, however, he checked. "Easy now, lads! Easy! Easy!" he shouted. "Keep your heads!" And so in a few minutes they were all back on the yacht.

On the bridge Swanscott held a long talk with his Captain, with the result that all night they stood by the derelict; steaming slowly round and round her, and keeping the searchlight full upon her. The next morning the Captain and the two friends went aboard the wreck with the carpenter and two boat-loads of men, who were set to work building a big, roughly made, but powerful shelter on the poop, using for the purpose the timbers which comprised the deck-load. This was finished by the afternoon, and a strong sliding door was fitted. There were left also a number of openings round the sides and in the roof; but these were crossed closely with iron-bars which the engineers supplied.

Returning to the yacht, Swanscott called all hands together and told them that he intended to pass the night in that shelter aboard the wreck, and that he wanted volunteers to accompany him. At first no one offered; but suddenly one of the firemen said he had no wife, and he would risk it, and after that others followed, until a dozen had come forward. These Swanscott took aboard with him, all armed, both with rifles and revolvers and cutlasses; they were all naval reserve men, and knew how to use their weapons. He gave directions to the Captain to hide every light, and keep the masthead light and sidelights unlit, also the searchlight. The yacht was to lie about a hundred yards away, and the instant he fired a shot the searchlight was to be flashed upon the wreck, to and fro, to see whether anything could be seen. No sound was to be made in the yacht, and there was to be no smoking; whilst every man left aboard was to line the nearest rail, and be ready with his rifle, but no shot to be fired until the Captain passed the word. This was the general trend of the orders for the night.

As soon as Swanscott, his friend Hay, and the dozen seamen and firemen had entered the shelter he pulled across the sliding-door and secured it. Then, having passed the word for absolute silence, and stationed a man at every barred opening, he settled down to wait. Presently the dusk was upon them, and soon the night, and after that the darkness, slowly intense, almost unnaturally so it seemed to Hay, whose more sensitive spirit was open to a thousand vague influences. Far down under them, as the ship rolled, they could hear the gloomy motion of the water in the holds, and odd whiles the dull grind of the sodden baulks would change into lumpish poundings and bodgings as there came a heavier swell under the vessel. Of wind there was none, save occasionally a little breath that would come sighing out of the night, making slight eerie sounds through the barred openings, and passing on again into the distance, leaving a double silence, because of the contrast. And so the hours passed on. Every now and again Swanscott would tiptoe quietly from man to man to make sure that all were awake and watching; but, indeed, there was little fear of anyone sleeping in that dark silence, for there was an utter weirdness and suspense in the night all about them, as it might be said, and each man was tensely awake; so that Swanscott had to be careful when he made his rounds not to touch any man suddenly, lest he cry out or turn blindly upon him in the darkness.

Then, after a great time had passed; there came a sound foreign to all the natural sounds of the ship and the slight movements of the men. It seemed to Hay, who was the first to notice it, that a vague, strange noise passed up through their midst. It was quite distinct from the dull booming of the waters in the hold, and could not be mistaken for any sound of the sea conducted upward by the framework of the vessel. It was near, very near, among them, so it seemed; and Hay heard the breathing of the men stop, as they harked, fiercely tense, to this thing, which might betoken some unknown horror right among them.

Then Swanscott realised that it was necessary to *learn*, and he struck a match. As the light flared up the men moved nervously and restlessly, but they all saw that the shelter was empty of everything except themselves.

There came a further space of silence; then, abruptly, Hay knew that something was near the shelter; it was more as if his spirit knew than any coarser sense. He reached out and touched Swanscott, and Swanscott thrilled under his touch, so that Hay perceived that he too had learned. Then Swanscott slipped from his hand, and there was not a sound in the shelter; thus Hay perceived that the men also were aware of something, and held each his breath—listening.

Suddenly, like thunder in that confined space, a shot was fired, and the flash lit up Swanscott's face momentarily. The following instant a great glare of light blazed upon the structure, pouring in at the barred openings and showing each man tense and strained, holding his weapon ready, and looking blindly towards where Swanscott stood with his smoking revolver in the middle of the shelter. He was staring upward through one of the barred openings in the roof. The blinding glare of the searchlight swept away from the house, leaving all in darkness; but now Hay was at one of the openings, and saw the huge shining jet of the light sweep forrard along the decks of the wreck. Then with a jerk it lifted and poised itself in mid-air, motionless, showing every detail of the mizzen-mast right above their heads. Hay saw something incredible, and craned his head more, so that he could see higher. There were dozens of strange men coming down out of the night—coming down from aloft—down the mizzen rigging. There was a sound of confused shouting from over the sea from those in the yacht, and still the searchlight burned relentlessly, showing those strange men constantly descending out of the night.

"Stop!" shouted Swanscott abruptly. "Stop, or we fire!"

"Onto them; lads!" shouted a voice far up in the night. "Wipe them out!"

There was the report of a weapon up in the darkness, and a bullet struck the bars of the opening just above Swanscott's head. He replied with his revolver, and three of those black descending figures toppled headlong. Then there was a sound of distant firing, and Hay knew that the riflemen in the yacht had opened on the strange men who were coming to wipe them out. He saw a dozen black figures sag and fall away—some went into the sea, but more on to the decks. Then the shelter was ringing with the noise of rifle fire, and he found his own pistol spitting viciously in his hand, and saw more than one figure at which he had aimed come downward.

In five minutes all was over, and the Captain of the yacht was alongside with a fully armed boat's crew, whilst the men in the house came forth and joined them. Swanscott gave an order, and led the way aloft, followed helter-skelter by his men. He went up over the mizzen-top, and saw a man sagging forward out of the top of the hollow steel mizzen-mast. They removed the man and entered the mast, where they found rungs fitted down the inside. This led them downward right to the keelson, in the bottom of the ship, where one side of the mast had been cut away and hinged on to form a door. Through this strange doorway they stepped, and found themselves in a huge hall, which was plainly the hold of the vessel. It was lit with electric light, and there were electric fans spinning.

Swanscott was utterly amazed. The hold of the derelict was full of water. He had seen for himself. Then, suddenly, he understood. It was only the upper part of the vessel that was full of water. Whoever had arranged that strange and mysterious craft had put an iron deck across the 'tween-deck beams about midway down the broad part of the hold, and extending from end to end of the vessel. By this simple expedient they had made the whole lower part of the vessel a huge water-tight tank of iron, about two hundred feet long and about fifteen feet deep, by about thirty-seven wide at the widest part. Ventilation had been arranged up and down the hollow steel masts; as also the methods of ingress and egress; though, as Swanscott discovered afterwards, they had other methods which they used for passing in and out of bulky objects, and this was by means of a concealed hatch under the galley, which led an iron shaft right down through the water with which they had filled the 'tween-decks, even as the hollow steel masts went down.

The missing men were all found ironed "head and tail", but safe and well, save for the rough handling which they had experienced. They each told the same story—how they were seized before they had any idea that anyone was near them, and those who struggled were stunned or drugged and so removed from sight; the idea obviously being to frighten the yacht away from attempting to tow them.

The object of all this planning and mystery was revealed when they came to examine the contents of the underwater hold. Here they found an immense amount of bullion, which had evidently been removed from the missing steamship *Lavinia*, of which previous mention has been made. Questioning one of the wounded, it was made finally plain that the derelict had been planned for an elaborate piratical cruise on a gigantic scale. There was, as Swanscott knew from the papers, an immense amount of gold being shifted that week from east to west, contrary to the usual conception of the "gold-current", and this old iron ship had been fitted up like this with the sole idea of transferring the gold from the transatlantic liners to the secret hold of the apparent derelict. That she had succeeded with the *Lavinia* the bullion bore silent witness. But where was the *Lavinia*? No questioning could elicit this; so that it was plain there could be only one answer—at the bottom of the sea, where, but for the interposition of the yacht, it is likely enough each of the succeeding gold ships would have followed her with all hands, minus only their gold. It was certainly a somewhat ghastly discovery.

The method of procedure was simple: the apparent derelict, on seeing its victim approach, would put up a distress signal; the liner would stop to pick them up; then the succoured would turn upon the saviours, and the rest can be easily imagined. Perhaps, also, there were a certain number of confederates aboard; but of this there can be no surety.

The strange sound which so disturbed the watchers in the shelter was the creeping of one of the pirates' spies up the hollow mizzen-mast, which passed through the centre of the shelter. The timber baulks were to explain why a ship apparently full of water did not sink. One final little mystery was also cleared up. The reason why the derelict appeared to drift so fast was that she was aided by an electrically-driven screw deep down under the counter, by means of which she was able to keep her position on the track of the liners, or to retire discreetly, as suited best the purposes of her masters—the gold thieves.

The Ghosts of the Glen Doon

THE *GLEN DOON* WAS reputed to be haunted—whatever that somewhat vague and much abused term may mean. But it was not until Larry Chaucer went aboard of her to stay the whole of one dark night in the company of her silt-laden, stark hold, that this reputation became something more than a suggestion of peculiarness that hung always around the hulk's name.

The *Glen Doon* was a dismasted old iron vessel, lying anchored head and stern off one of the old ramshackle wooden wharves a couple of miles above San Francisco. She had turned turtle in the bay some five years before the period now mentioned, and drowned ten of her men, who were down in the hold chipping the beams. For twenty-four hours after she upended her bottom to the sky the crowds of would-be rescuers who came around her in boats could hear the tap, tapping of the imprisoned men in the hold as they tapped with their hammers against the iron bottom of the ship for help that was never to come; at least, not in a practicable form. It is true that an attempt was made to cut through the iron skin of the ship, and so get the men out that way; but, unfortunately, as soon as a hole was drilled the inevitable occurred—the imprisoned air in the hold, which had buoyed up the capsized vessel, began to whistle out shrilly.

The blacksmith-mechanic, who was attempting to rescue the men in this impossible fashion, had no conception of what this escape of air must ultimately mean. He continued to drill holes, and as each hole was drilled a new note was lent to the shrill whistling of the pent air. Finally, someone cried out that the vessel was foundering. At that, the blacksmith took up a heavy, forty-pound sled and hit the iron inside of the circle of holes which he had made. At the second blow, the tough iron bent a little to one side, making a gap from hole to hole. Instantly, the shrill piping of the outrushing air changed to a deep mellow tone as the air gushed out through this fresh aperture.

There came a loud shouting from the boats around, that the vessel was going. The water was almost level with her bilge keels, and the blacksmith took a jump for the nearest boat. As he did so, a hand came through the hole which he had made and waved a moment, desperately, yet aimlessly. Then the *Glen Doon* went under. This is the true history of the vessel which was now attracting the attention of the public.

Seven months later she was raised, half-filled with silt, and towed to her present position, some hundred yards off one of the lone old wharves above the city. She had been put up for auction, and bought by a small syndicate of men who, however, had found no use for their purchase up to the time with which I am dealing, and had, therefore, allowed her to remain where she was for five long years, their only attentions being a little repair to insure that the stopped leak was safe.

In the course of the years there had grown up, as was natural enough, rumours that the old iron hulk of the *Glen Doon* was haunted.

Reports were plentiful enough on the water-front that the sounds of ghostly chipping hammers might be heard aboard of her in the dead of night. A grimmer tale there was also going the round, that some youth had spent a night aboard of her with the intention of discovering the ghosts. He had been missing in the morning. Yet too much credence could not be given to this vague account, for no one knew either the name of the youth or the night on which he was supposed to have made his experiment. So that, as likely as not, it was but a manufactured tale. At least, this was the opinion of those who were disinclined to be credulous. Unauthenticated, it proves nothing; yet is a definite part of the halo of peculiar mystery with which the hulk became presently surrounded.

It was at this point that Larry Chaucer—son of a rich man and somewhat of a young "sport"—put his finger into the pie, as one might say, and discovered something genuinely disagreeable something, if we may judge from after events, that must have proved very dreadful in every sense of the word.

His action arose out of a bet made in his father's billiard-room, that he would stay the night aboard the hulk, alone. He had been ridiculing the flying stories of ghostly happenings aboard the

Glen Doon, and one of his friends, who held that there might be "something in it all", had grown warm in argument—finally nailing his opinion with a bet of a thousand dollars that Larry Chaucer would not venture a night aboard of her alone, without a boat to let him ashore.

Larry, as might be supposed from a young, high-spirited man, jumped at the bet, and set two thousand against his friend's one, that he would stay that very night aboard. He stipulated, however, three things. First, that they—his friends—should accompany him aboard the old iron hulk, and there aim him to make a thorough search of her; for, as Larry said, he was not going to run his head into a nest of hoboes who were "working the haunting game" just to keep strangers away. Second, that the whole business should be kept a secret, as he did not want a crowd of practical jokers "playing the fool", as he termed it. Third, that his friends should keep a watch upon the hulk through the night, both from the wharf and from a boat. This would enable them to vouch that he kept the conditions of his bet faithfully.

Larry's stipulations were accepted by his friends, who determined as they said, "to see through with the business", and make a night of it.

As it turned out, it was the very stringency of these preliminaries and stipulations generally, that made the results so extraordinary; for they eliminated almost all chance of a normal explanation being sufficient to explain away the very peculiar and disagreeable happenings which followed.

When the night came, Larry Chaucer and his friends, armed with innumerable dark lanterns, which had exhausted 'Frisco's supply, went down in a big crowd to the old wharf, which was utterly deserted. They cast loose several of the boats that were hitched to the piles, and pulled off to the old iron hulk.

The night was very dark, for the moon was not yet up. It was also exceedingly quiet, and the crowd of young fellows preserved admirable order and silence; for it had been agreed that nothing in the way of "playing the fool" should be done. Also, as is quite possible, the darkness and the quiet and the curious reputation that the hulk had already earned, tended to subdue them.

It was when the leading boat was within some thirty or forty yards of the hulk that Larry, who was steering, whispered, "Hist!" And the men at once ceased rowing, those in the boats behind followed their example, questioning in low voices as to what was wrong. Then they heard it, all of them—a distinct, faint noise of hammers at work in the old wreck. They were listening to the dull ring and clatter of chipping-hammers at work, somewhere far down in the old iron vessel.

"Pull on, you chaps," whispered Larry, after listening for a little while. "It's some darned asses playing the goat! We'll catch them at the game, and scruff them."

Larry's idea was whispered from boat to boat, and a move ahead was made; but, for all that Larry was so sure there was nothing abnormal in the sounds, very many of the young men would have preferred to make their investigations in daylight. As they drew close to the ship, and the tall iron side of her loomed up dull and vague in the darkness, the strange sounds of the tapping and clanging hammers were extraordinarily plain, yet queerly thin and remote, and difficult to locate. At one moment it was as if the unseen hammers were tapping, tapping, and beating against the other side of the iron wall of the ship's side, which rose up before their faces—as if, merely on the other side of that half-inch skin of iron, incredible nothings wielded ghostly hammers. This is how it effected the nerves of the more imaginative and sensitive, but on Larry the sounds produced merely a growing excitement.

"For goodness' sake, be smart, you chaps!" he kept whispering. "We've got 'em properly on toast. They're all down in the hold. We'll ghost 'em!" He leaned an oar up against the ship's side as he spoke, and swarmed up it. He climbed aboard, took a quick look round, and then stooped and steadied the top of the oar whilst others followed, the men in the other boats also beginning to shin up their oars.

"For the Lord's sake, be quiet, you ijuts!" he whispered fiercely to two of his friends who had bungled their climb and fallen back, with a crash, into the boat. He leant inboard, looking over his shoulder, and listening; but still, somewhere below his feet in the darkness of the hold, beat the faint, impossible refrain of the unseen hammers. As he listened, for that one moment, he got a sudden quick, new, little realization that it was down in that same hold, just under his feet, that the men had died when the last of the air went out.

"Blessed rats in a cage!" he muttered unconsciously; and leant outboard once more to encourage speed.

As soon as all were aboard, between forty and fifty young men in number, there was a whispered consultation after which some were sent to guard at every hatchway and opening from the hold below. There was a tense, silent excitement growing among them all; for they were about to have an adventure—make a capture, perhaps. Bound to, if there happened to be human hands attached to those hammers down in the dark hold. Of course, there were others who thought otherwise, and shivered a little, rejoicing in the number of their companions; but, in the main, the youths were prepared to meet good flesh-and-blood haunters, and to deal with them accordingly.

"Mind," whispered Larry Chaucer, "no shooting. We'll be hitting each other. Use your hands and clubs, my children. There's enough of us to eat 'em."

The lanterns had been lit, and now a group of men to each open hatchway, all stood in readiness for the signal to jump below. And all the while, down in the darkness, sounded the faint tap, tapping of the hammers, seeming strangely far away and remote, so that sometimes it would be as if there were no sound at all down there; and then, the next moment, the noises would rise clear and distinct.

And then abruptly the hammers ceased, and an absolute stillness held all through the ship.

"Down, my sons, down!" shouted Larry. "They've heard us!"

And he dropped with a quick swing on to the hard puddled silt which half-filled the vessel. In a moment the others had followed, and the great iron cavern of the hold was full of light as the young men shone their lanterns everywhere. To the general amazement, there was nothing to be seen anywhere. The interior of the ship was empty, except for the silt, which had set like cement.

"Not a blessed soul!" called Larry breathlessly, and shone his light round unbelievingly. "Why, I *heard* them; so did all of you!"

No one answered, and each man found himself looking over his shoulder with a queer nervousness. The silence was brutal.

"Oh, they must be somewhere!" said Larry at last. "Scatter and search!"

This was done, and the whole of the hulk searched, in the forepeak, deck-houses, cabins, and finally in the silted-up lazarette; but nowhere in all the ship was there any sign of life. Finally, the search was concluded, and the youths gathered around Larry, asking him what he was going to do.

"Stop here, of course, and rook old jelly-bags of that thousand he owes me," replied Larry, referring to his friend's bet. There was a general outcry against this, for there was a feeling that until the mystery of the tapping was cleared up, the hulk was not exactly a healthy place in which to pass the night.

"I'll bet those beastly bodies are still down there in all that mud in the hold," declared one youngster, Thomas Barlow by name. "That's what's wrong with her!"

"Don't be an ass!" said Larry. And refused to alter his intentions, even when Jellotson (alias "Jellybags") offered to withdraw the bet. Finally, after much persuading, they had to leave him; though he had great difficulty in preventing a dozen of the more determined from stopping aboard to keep him company through the night.

"And mind you, all," he called out to them, as they pushed off in the boats, "no silly jokes. I've got my gun, an' I'll just lead anyone who shows up. In the nervous state I'm in, I'm likely to shoot first and inquire afterwards."

There was a general roar of laughter from the men in the boats at the thought of Larry Chaucer being nervous. And with that, they gave way, shouting a final goodnight, not dreaming that they had heard the last words of the man who had been their leader in many a revel.

The boats reached the old wharf, where a council was held. It was finally arranged that six men in one of the boats should lie a few hundred feet outside of the hulk, whilst those who remained would keep a watch on the shore side from the end of the wharf, thus ensuring that no one could come from, or to, the *Glen Doon* without being seen. This arrangement proved the more practicable, as the moon was just rising, full and big, filling all the upper bay with vague light, and showing the old hulk plainly where she lay, a few hundred feet away.

Volunteers were called for the boat, and when this had been sent to take up its position, the rest of the young men made a back-to-back camp on the wharf—which consists of sitting in a row, back to back, each thus obtaining both warmth and support from the man behind, and presumably he deriving the same in turn. In this way they settled down to smoke and talk the long hours of the night, leaving, however, a couple of men in each of the boats, so that these could be brought instantly into use if anything happened on the wreck.

It was some time after midnight that the youngster, Thomas Barlow, insisted that he could hear something. You will remember that he was the one who had made the somewhat uncomfortable

suggestion concerning the whereabouts of the bodies. His asser-
tion made a sudden stir through the watchers, and everyone listened
intently. Yet for more than a minute not a sound was audible to
anyone except young Barlow, who insisted that he could hear the
faint tap, tapping of the hammers.

"It's your fancy, young 'un," said one of the older men. But
even as he made the remark, several of the men cried out, "Hush!"
In the succeeding silence many of them heard it, very faint and
remote, the ghostly tap, tap, tapping, ringing strange and vague to
them across the quiet water of the bay. The six men who were
lying off in the boat, upon the far side of the hulk, also heard the
low sounds in the general stillness of the night, and the man at the
tiller suggested that they should row in upon the *Glen Doon* and
give Larry Chaucer a hail, to ask whether he was all right. The rest
of the men, however, objected that to do so would be to nullify
the conditions of the bet; pointing out also that if Larry needed
help he had only to shout, for they were not two hundred yards
distant from him. Even as they argued the matter there came the
sound of a pistol-shot from aboard the hulk, echoing sharp and
startling across the bay.

"Pull, boys!" shouted Jarrett, the man at the tiller. "Something's
wrong with Larry! Get her out of the water now! Make her walk!
We should never have left him!" There sounded a rapid succession
of shots aboard the old iron hulk—one, two, three, four, five, then
a blank silence. This was followed by a loud, horrible—peculiarly
horrible—scream, and then again the silence.

"Good heavens! Pull!" yelled the boat-steerer. "That's Larry!"

They heard a confused shouting from the wharf, where their
friends were watching, and the rattle and rolling of oars as the other
boats were driven towards the hulk, fully laden. Yet the men in the
outward boat were the first to reach the *Glen Doon*, the boat-steerer
shouting out Larry's name at the top of his voice. But there was
no answer, nor any sound of any kind at all from the deserted
blackness of the wreck.

The boat was hooked on, and the men shinned up the oars, as
Larry had shown them earlier in the night. They reached the decks
and turned on their lights, each man reaching for the "gun", which
was wont to repose snugly on such occasions in the convenient but
unsightly hippocket. Then they began the search, shouting Larry's
name continually, but he was nowhere to be seen about the decks.
The other boats were alongside by this, and the rest of the young

men joined in the search.

It was in the main hold that they found something—Larry's pistol, every chamber emptied; and his dark-lantern, crumpled into a twisted mass of japanned tin. *Nothing else of any kind.* No sign of a struggle, not even the uncomfortable stain that tells of a wound received. And there were nowhere any marks of struggling feet—*nothing*.

They were all in the naked hold of the old vessel now, standing about, looking here and there uncomfortably, some of them frankly nervous and frightened of the vague horror of the Unknown that seemed all about them. In the unpleasant silence, someone spoke abruptly. It was Jarrett, the man who had been acting boat-steerer. "Look here," he said, "there's something aboard this ship, and we're going to find it."

"We've searched everywhere," replied several voices. As they spoke, a number of the men put up their hands for silence, and everyone was quiet, listening. They all heard it then. Something seemed to go upward in their midst, through the vacant night air that filled the hold. Yet the lanterns showed an utter stillness and emptiness. *It was among them*, whatever it was, and the light showed them *nothing*.

"Heavens!" muttered someone; and there was a panic, and a mad, foolish scramble for the deck above.

When they got there, out of the surrounding horror of the hold itself, they got back something of their courage and paused, clumped in a group, listening.

"What was it? What was it?" they questioned; but the black gape of the hatchway sent up no sound.

Presently, as the full significance of the whole affair came upon them, they gathered into a council, keeping their lights all about them, and staring all ways as they talked.

"We can't leave him here, *if* he's here, or until we know something," said Jarrett, who was acting in this crisis somewhat as a leader. "A boat must go for the police, and we must send for his father."

This was done, and within a couple of hours a squad of police were alongside in their launch, accompanied by "Billion Chaucer". The chief of police himself had come with the expedition; for the son of Chaucer, the millionaire, was an important personage; or, at least, his father was, which came to the same thing.

"What does it all mean, anyway?" asked Mr. Chaucer. They

told him and the chief together. At the end of the telling, Mr. Chaucer had a conference with the chief, with the result that the launch went off full speed for more help. In the meanwhile the young men were asked to get into the boats and make a cordon round the old ship, after which the chief and his men began to search in a thorough and systematic manner; yet they found *nothing*.

By the time that the early dawn had come in, the launch had returned, towing a string of boats, with a further squad of police and a large number of semi-official "helpers"—that is to say, labourers—the intention being to empty the hold of every ounce of silt and to strip the wreck to her bare skin. As the chief said, Mr. Larry Chaucer had come aboard, and there were scores of witnesses to prove that he had never left the vessel; therefore, he must be *somewhere*, and he was going to find out. He had no belief at all in the supernatural. "Ghosts be blowed!" he said. "It's dirty work somewhere!"

In the course of the day they not only emptied the ship of every particle of the silt, but they stripped and ripped away all the old rotted bulkheads, until there was little more than the mere iron skin of the ship left. Yet, nowhere did they find any sign to tell of the fate of Larry Chaucer. He had gone utterly out of all human knowledge.

The search was abandoned at nightfall; but a squad of six police were left aboard, with instructions to keep a regular watch day and night; also—at Mr. Chaucer's expense—a patrol-boat was stationed off the hulk, and relieved every six hours. For a fortnight this went on, and at the end of that time the mystery was just as impossible as at first.

At the conclusion of a fortnight the patrol-boat was withdrawn, and the detectives sent ashore, leaving the old iron hulk to brood alone over her mysteries through the dark nights. Yet, for all that the police had apparently deserted her and thrown up the case as hopeless, there was still a continual watch kept upon her officially from several points ashore, both day and night. Moreover, a secret patrol-boat kept in her vicinity at nights. In this way three weeks passed.

Then one night, the police in the patrol-boat heard the faint tap, tapping of hammers aboard the old iron hulk. They ran silently alongside, and put half a dozen armed detectives aboard quietly, with their lanterns. These men located the sounds in the great empty hold, and taking a grip of their courage, as we say, climbed down into the blackness without a sound. Then, at a whispered word of command from the officer in charge, they flashed on their lanterns and swept the rays over the whole of the great empty cavern. But there was not a sign anywhere of anything, beyond the clean-swept iron plates of the ship. And all the time, from some vague, unknowable place in the darkness, sounded the low, constant tap, tap, tapping of the hammers.

They returned to the decks, and switched off their lanterns. Then settled down, still in absolute silence, to watch, taking various stations about the deck of the vessel. Two hours passed, during which a faint mist had cleared away, allowing the moon—which was once again near the full—to make indistinctly clear (as moonlight does) every detail on the poop and down on the maindeck, while the broken masts and parted tangle of gear showed in black silhouettes against the pale light.

It was in the third hour of their watch that the six men saw something come up above the port rail and show plain in the moonlight. It was a man's head and face, the hair as long as a woman's, and dripping with sea water, so that the cadaverous face showed white and unwholesome from out of the sopping down-hang of the hair. In a minute there followed the body of the strange man, and the sea water ran from his garments, glistening as the moonbeams caught the drops. He came inboard over the rail, making no more noise than a shadow, and paused, swaying with a queer movement full in a patch of moonlight. Then, noiseless, he seemed to glide across the deck in the direction of the dark gape of the open main hatchway.

"Hands up, my son!" shouted the officer in charge, and presented his revolver. His voice and hand were both a little unsteady, as may be imagined. Yet the figure took no heed of him, but dropped noiselessly out of sight into the utter dark of the hold, just as the officer fired. Simultaneously there came a volley of shots from the other police; but the strange man was gone. They made a rush for the hatchway and leaned over the coaming, flashing their lanterns down into the bottom of the ship, and long the 'tweendeck beams; but there was nothing. They climbed hurriedly down into the hold and searched it fore and aft. It was *empty*.

When they returned once more to the deck the patrol-boat was hailing them. The officer had heard the shooting and had run down to discover what was happening. The detective officer gave a brief account of what had occurred, and sent a note by the patrol-boat to the chief of police, stating the brief facts. An hour later the chief was with them. He instituted a fresh and even more rigorous search, but found nothing of any kind. Yet, as he said, the man had come aboard and gone down into the hold, and in the hold he must still be, seeing that he had not returned.

"It's where them sailor-men was drownded!" muttered one of the detectives, and several of his companions murmured their agreement with the suggestion of belief that lay at the back of his remark.

" 'Twas a drowned man, right enough, as come aboard," one of them said definitely. "A walkin' corpse!"

"Shut your silly mouth!" said the chief, and he walked up and down for a little, puzzling. Then he wrote a note, which he gave to the officer of the patrol-boat. "Deliver at once, Murgan," he ordered.

At dawn, in response to the chief's written order, there came alongside of the hulk a couple of boat-loads of mechanics in their blue dungaree slops. Under the direction of the chief of police, the whole of the interior of the vessel was mapped out and apportioned to the mechanics, who were ordered to drill holes at stated intervals, right through the side of the ship, fore and aft. In this way, it was speedily proved, beyond all doubt, that there was no such thing as double sides to the hulk, for the points of the drills could be seen coming through into the sunlight on the outside of the vessel.

When it had been proved that there was no such thing as a secret recess above water, the chief gave orders to drill holes right through the bottom of the ship. This was done constantly and regularly all along; and each time that a drill bit through, the sea water spurted up into the men's faces, proving beyond doubt that there was no such thing as a secret double bottom. As each hole was completed, it was "leaded", that is temporarily plugged with lead, prior to filling it later with a red-hot rivet. In this fashion, very little water was allowed to come into the hulk.

It was now proved as an indisputable fact that the *Glen Doon* floated there nothing more than an empty iron shell upon the water. There was no place aboard her big enough to have hidden a fair-sized rat and, what was more, there was no possibility of her having any secret hiding-places aboard, for this last drastic test had definitely settled the point. There remained now only the stumps of the hollow, steel lower masts, and that these were empty was soon shown by lowering a lantern into each, on the end of a long cord. The *Glen Doon* was nothing more than a thin iron shell; yet a living man, and what had passed for a second living man, had gone down into that naked hold and disappeared utterly and entirely.

"She orter be sunk. She's one of them devil-ships!" remarked one of the mechanics, wiping the sweat from his face. He had heard a full account of the curious happenings from some of the detectives. "I'm goin' ashore. I don't like *this*!"

At that moment there came a loud "Ha!" from the chief of police, who had remained in the hold, walking up and down with a puzzled frown. The others had come up into the sunlight, disliking the uncomfortable sensation that the great gloomy cavern bred in them. Yet now, at the chief's shout, there was a general scurry to get down to him, to learn what had caused him to shout to them.

They found him standing near the mainmast, staring through a small pocket microscope at something on the mast.

"You're a lot of beauties, you are!" he called to them as they drew near. "Look at this!"

They found that he was pointing to a few stray hairs that appeared to have got stuck upon the mast, but a more careful scrutiny with the microscope showed that they had really been nipped into the steel itself—in other words, that there was an almost invisible opening in the hollow steel mast.

The chief beckoned to a couple of the mechanics and set them to work with their drills, and presently, with a couple of long jemmy-bars thrust into the holes they bored, they were able to prise open a beautifully fitted curved door of painted iron that exactly matched the colour and curve of the hollow mast. A careful search at the bottom of the interior of the mast showed them a diminutive steel lever which, on being wrenched round, allowed the metal floor of the inside of the mast to drop downwards, discovering a small shaft, about six feet deep, which led straight down into some strange, secret apartment hidden under the bottom of the ship. As the police paused there, they saw the flash of a light and heard men's voices.

Descending the small shaft, revolvers in hand, the officers found themselves in a curious room, so enormously long that it gave them the impression at first of being a tunnel, just sufficiently high to enable a man to stand upright with comfort. Later, when the mechanics came to examine it, they pronounced it to be formed of a series of old boilers, joined end to end, so as to be watertight, and suspended several feet below the ship's keel by iron struts; the means of ingress and egress being through the little shaft that led down from the foot of the hollow mainmast. They found, also, that there were similar shafts leading up to the feet of both the fore and mizzen masts, though these were used chiefly for ventilation purposes, being fitted with small electric-motor fans, driven from a dynamo, which was used also in certain illegal processes of silver-plating, and was driven in turn from a small gasoline engine within the long tunnel-like room.

There were six men in this tunnel-shaped apartment. Five of them were skilled workmen, and very badly "wanted" indeed for the identical work at which they were now caught—coin-punching, as an Americanism has it; in other words, coining.

They were taken like so many rats in a trap, and made no attempt to fight, realizing the hopelessness of their position. The sixth man, the detectives recognized as the "drowned sailor". He, having swum off to the ship to warn the gang that the detectives had crept quietly aboard, and so to get the coin-punchers to stop working the machinery which had so misled everyone—the sound being very faint and far-seeming after having been conducted up from underwater to the ship through the iron stays which supported the long room of boilers in place.

In an account of this kind, I have nothing to do with the sentences that were accorded to the men, but will refer only to those points which are not yet made clear. The fate of Larry Chaucer was never definitely known. It appears that there was a considerable number of men in the gang, and these worked a week at a time in relays of five in the boiler-tunnel room. As it happened, the five men and the scout who were caught were able to prove conclusively that they were up at Crockett on the night on which Larry disappeared. His body was never found, and his end can be only guessed at.

It is evident that he must have been waiting silently down in the hold when the door in the mast was opened, and so discovered too much to be allowed to live. He was probably knocked on the head and lowered into the boiler-room, his body being disposed of later. There is no doubt that, had he not found out something definite, he would not have been molested, for it was no part of the original plan of the coiners to attract attention to the hulk by suggesting that she was haunted. This was, indeed, a very great misfortune for them in every way.

The sound which had seemed to pass up through the crowd of young men in the hold had been the slight rustling noise made by one of the gang swarming up inside of the hollow mast to take a peep from aloft, so as to find out what was happening. The mast, of course, passed up through the centre of the hold, and was therefore in their midst, but no one had dreamed that the faint, peculiar noise proceeded from it. Indeed, it is unlikely that any of them really knew that the masts were made of anything but solid, painted wood; though, of course, this is only a conjecture.

The crumpled condition of Larry's lantern was probably due to its having been trodden on by some of the gang, when they captured him.

I believe that I have now touched upon all the uncleared points. With regard to the scout, he must have noticed, from the shore, the flash of the detective's lanterns, and swum off, in preference to boating, because it was the way least likely to attract attention. He was a Mexican, and the hairs in the mast were obviously trapped from his plentiful growth, which has been commented upon earlier.

Mr. Jock Danplank

"MARY," SAID MR. JOCK Danplank, "we're going to do these people down one, or die like heroes! What say?"

The speaker, a Britisher who had weathered the States, looked down at his exceedingly pretty and diminutive American wife, and smiled grimly. And she, in return, stared meditatively at him, at the same time "snying" up her nose in a fashion peculiar to herself.

"Of course, we shall level up, J.D.," she agreed. "If only your uncle had finished what he was saying"—she paused; then, "seventy-seven feet due east—seventy-seven feet due east—" she muttered thoughtfully, and tailed off again into silence and thought.

"East of what? East of what?" she exclaimed abruptly. "He must have meant east of some important object. Oh, why— Anyway," she concluded, "it'll be funny if we can't go one better than that Britisher cousin of yours."

"You forget, Mog, that *I'm* British," said the big man, grinning mechanically.

"You?" said his wife, indignantly. "Why, you're quite half American, and nearly as good as some real ones I've known."

"Thank you, dear," said her husband, gravely; and broke into talk. "Here we have the case in a few words," he said. "My Cousin Billy was Uncle Gerald's favourite. I rubbed my uncle up the wrong way when I was a young chap, and got slammed out of his will. I go abroad to dig up the blessed earth until I find the golden acorn. Somehow I miss the acorn, but, anyway, I got you under the mistletoe, Mog, an' guess I'm not sorrowing!"

His wife grimaced, and threw her gloves at him. He caught them neatly, and continued:

"Meanwhile, Cousin Billy—who's a bit of a hog in my humble opinion—fails one day to hide some of his funny work from my

393

uncle, who is fearfully upset, and cuts him whack out of the will in turn, whilst I am taken once more into favour, as being perhaps a bit more wholesome-smelling than Billy; though, as the will said flat out, 'too thoughtless in my speech to my elders and betters.' Perhaps I was."

"I'm sure of it," said his wife, firmly.

"Anyway," continued her husband, "here you have me back into the to the tune of a hundred thousand pounds—that's five hundred thousand dollars, Mog! But the estate goes to Cousin Billy through the entail. You won't understand that, but it doesn't matter. Cousin Billy has the estate; I have the cash; at least, I mean that was uncle's intention. Uncle dies of old age, and shock at Cousin Billy's little goings on. On his death-bed he calls his solicitor across to him, and begins to tell him something, but gets no further than 'seventy-seven feet due east', when his speech fails, and he never delivers the rest of his message. After the funeral, the will is read. Consternation and well-earned agony of Cousin Billy, on learning that the estates and the mortgages are his, and the personal cash and effects mine. Consternation, also, later, on the part of the solicitor, who, on going through uncle's papers and personal matters, can find no traces of cash or 'paper' to represent the said five hundred thousand dollars mentioned in the will. He puzzles over final words of uncle's, but is no wiser.

"Meanwhile, he has cabled across to me. (Lucky he had my address!) We arrive, are told everything. We puzzle, and are no wiser, either. We take up quarters at the venerable village inn—my Cousin Billy not feeling in hospitable mood—and here we are, rightful owners of one hundred thousand pounds, and puzzling our little heads to know what uncle meant when he said, 'Seventy-seven feet due east—' What you might call something in the nature of a conundrum, with the solution in Heaven. At least, I hope so."

Jock Danplank ended his summary of the situation, and sat down on the arm of his wife's chair. He fumbled in his inside coat-pocket, and brought out a small packet of papers, methodically banded together with elastic. He removed the elastic, and selected a paper which he proceeded to unfold and glance through.

" J.D.," said his wife, suddenly. "If that's the will, let me have a look at it. I'll bet there's something you wise men have overlooked. Let me see it."

"Here, madam!" said her husband, and handed the paper to

her. "It's not the will itself, of course, but it's an official copy, or whatever it's called."

Mrs. Jock Danplank made no reply, but read steadily at the document for some minutes, with occasional little snorts of impatient disgust at the twisted phraseology and the economical punctuation.

"What's this about your uncle's writing-table being left to you?" she asked, suddenly looking up at him.

"Oh, that!" said Jock Danplank. "He to left it me as a sort of keepsake, I s'pose."

"J.D.," said his wife, earnestly, "you're an ass. Send for it at once."

"If you mean," said her husband, "that you expect to find anything in it, you're just mistook, my Mog. Old Jellett, the lawyer, and his confidential clerk have been through it in detail; why, he even had a professional cabinet-maker to overhaul it for any secret drawers or recesses——"

"Why," interrupted his wife, who had not been listening, "there's a cottage as well." She had been running her glance down the will, and had come to the item further on. "A cottage and gardens, J.D."

"Yes," assented her husband. "That's where the table is, I understand. The place used to belong to my Aunt Lydia. I remember it when I was a boy; the cottage used to be a little farmhouse then. I suppose uncle must have had the place rebuilt, and turned the fields round it into gardens and private grounds. Jellett tells me it's quite a decent little place, and that uncle was quite fond of it—used to run down there for quiet weekends from town, instead of opening some of the rooms at the Hall."

"Well," said Mary Danplank, "why aren't we there, instead of here?"

"Oh," replied her husband, "one hardly likes to go rushing in too soon. We'll take a walk over to-morrow, if you like, and have a look at it."

"We'll go right over this minute."

The big man rubbed his clean-shaven cheek a moment, meditatively, then swung a powerful knee off the arm of her chair, and stood up.

"Very well, Mog," he said. "Perhaps you're right. We'll go and look after our own interests personally, right away."

"Oh," said Mrs. Jock Danplank, laying her cheek a moment

against his sleeve, "you're almost as nice and sensible as a real American, J.D."

"Thank you, Mog," said her husband simply. And together they went downstairs into the main street of the village.

The landlord was at the door, bowing respectfully a listening ear to a dissipated young man sitting in a smart dogcart with tremendously high wheels.

"Yessir," said the landlord. "Yessir—yessir." And between each he nodded profoundly. "Dinner for six gents? Yessir. All shall be as you say, sir."

"Hullo, Billy!" shouted Jock Danplank. "Glad to see you're still alive. How's the mare going?"

His cousin turned in his seat, and glared at him.

"Hang you!" he roared, at last. "Speak when you're spoken to."

"Sore about it still, Billy, eh?" said Jock Danplank, loosing his wife's hand gently from his sleeve. "Better be civil, though, Billy. You look out of condition."

But his cousin confined his attention now markedly to the stout landlord, who had been expectantly rubbing his hands during this passage between the cousins.

"At seven sharp," were his last words; and, with that, he whipped up his horse, and bowled away at a smart trot stationwards, without so much as a further glance at Jock Danplank.

"Nice specimen, Mog, for a cousin," said Jock. And then they set out in the direction of the cottage.

The door was opened by a dear old lady, who proved to have been Uncle Gerald's housekeeper. She asked them in, carried off Mrs. Danplank to quite the most charming little bedroom she had ever seen, and won her little American heart by her homely, motherly way of speech and natural kindliness.

Later, there was tea, also scones, in one of the sunlit afternoon rooms downstairs; and then old Mrs. Hartleytres took them on a tour of inspection.

There were four small but most exquisitely shaped and furnished rooms downstairs, excluding offices and the mahogany panelled hall. The fourth room proved to be Uncle Gerald's study. It was done in the deepest rose-tinted shades, and all the outer wall of the room was one long window, out of which opened two glassed doors, French fashion, into a veritable circular sea of rose blooms, to which the window was the only visible entrance. The effect was marvellously beautiful, and Jock Danplank's diminutive wife uttered an exclamation. But, as it proved, it was not the sight of the rose-tinted room and the world of blooms beyond that had stirred her to exclaim; it was rather the fact that in the very centre of the room was a gigantic writing-table of old red Spanish mahogany, in the top of which was inlaid a curious pattern in roses, radiating outward from a common centre.

"J.D.," said his wife, "the table!" And she ran forward to study it. "Why," she remarked, after looking at it a little, "it's a fixture, I do believe. Your uncle must have had some real reason for mentio——"

She paused abruptly, and looked at old Mrs. Hartleytres.

"Yes, ma'am," said the old housekeeper. "Mr. Jellett, the lawyer, has said the same thing to me. He's been here a dozen times to look at that table; he and Mr. Baker, his chief clerk. They even had a workman in. Mr. Jellett told me he suspected a secret drawer; not the money, ma'am, but a paper to tell where it is. You see, I was present at the reading of the will. Sir Gerald Gwynn was very kind, he left me a thousand pounds."

Mr. Jock Danplank walked over to the table and pushed it, first one way and then the other, but it did not move. "Firm as a rock," he muttered, and stooped to look at it; but his wife was already down on her knees, lifting the carpet away a little from one of the pedestals.

"It's built into the floor, J.D.," she said, with a note of excitement in her voice. "What's that been done for?"

Her husband got down also on his knees, and examined it. He looked up presently at Mrs. Hartleytres. "Did the lawyer have this table lifted?" he asked.

But the old housekeeper shook her head.

"No, sir," she replied. "That table's never been moved since Sir Gwynn had it put there. He had some queer ways, if you'll forgive me for saying so; and such a to-do as there was about the fixing of that same table, you never heard."

Mr. Jock Danplank walked towards the window. "J.D.," his wife called after him, "if I don't find anything, I'm going to have this table lifted, and the floor underneath taken up."

"Very well, Mary," said her husband. "Perhaps it will be as well, if it can be done without harming things."

His wife resumed her search, and he walked out into the circular garden. It was exceedingly beautiful, the roses having been trained to make a perfect circular wall of bloom right round, excepting where the French windows opened into the place. In addition to the rose trees, there were numbers of beautifully sculptured groups and figures set around the garden, and in the centre was a very fine specimen of the "Fighting Gladiator", done in bronze. The ground was one beautiful level of marvellously cultivated grass, smooth and even and pilelike as velvet.

"Splendid!" said Jock Danplank, looking round him with the deepest appreciation. "Simply fine!"

"Yes, sir," agreed the housekeeper; "I believe this is the second finest rose-garden in England. Sir Gwynn loved this place." She sighed a little. "Poor gentleman," she said, "he was dreadfully lonely. I dare say that made him so—so peculiar at times, and so eccentric."

Mr. Jock Danplank nodded, and rejoined his wife, to continue the tour of the house.

By the time this had been done, evening had set in. And when they got down again to the study, and found that a cheerful fire was easing out the first touch of autumn chill, they appreciated old Mrs. Hartleytres' suggestion that they should send back the boy with the trap, and stay the night.

"Have your boxes sent over in the morning, ma'am, and stay here for good," she suggested. " 'Tis your own place now."

"That's hoss-sense, Mrs. Hartleytres," said Jock's wife.

And so it was arranged that they should at once enter into so much of their fortune as was discoverable.

Now, I am particular to give the following somewhat trivial details with exactness, as there happened that night a somewhat strange and disturbing thing.

During the evening, whilst Jock Danplank smoked and meditated quietly, his wife went once more through all the various drawers of the big writing-table in one final effort to discover some signs of a secret recess, but without success. Later, her husband took his cigar out into the circular rose garden; and the two of them traipsed round happily on the short-cut grass, enjoying the sense of togetherness in their "very own" grounds. But in no case did they trample on any of the flower-beds; nor, on returning, did Jock Danplank leave the catches of the French window unfastened.

Yet, see what happened. In the morning, Mrs. Danplank was awakened by voices under her window

"I'm sure you're mistaken, Mr. Biggle."

"I'm not mistook, Mrs. Hartleytres, ma'am!" said a husky, shrill voice, which was evidently that of the head-gardener, "When I come, Mrs. Hartleytres, ma'am; there was the great silly footmarks all acrost my beds—dang un! beggin' your pardin', Mrs. Hartleytres, ma'am; an' there was the French winder open, showin' as 'ee come out last night for a smoke-o an' a walk round. No, Mrs. Hartleytres, ma'am, I'll say wot I 'ave to say; Mr. Danplank ain't no gennelman to do such a thing, not so how he was twenty times Sir Gerald's own nevvy, which he couldn't be. It'd make old Sir Gerald turn in 'is grave an' 'ave the cold shudders, which 'ee 'as, if 'ee was to larn of sich a thing. It would that!"

"Hush, Mr. Biggle!" said the voice of the old housekeeper. "You've no right to speak like that of young Mr. Danplank. There's some mistake. And, anyway, the flower-beds are his own."

"Eh!" said the shrill, husky voice again. Poor old Sir Gerald's mebbe tearin' his hair this very minnit in 'ell—not but 'ee wer' as bald as a hegg—just to think wot things is comin' to, Mrs. Hartleytres, ma'am."

"Hush!" said the housekeeper's voice again. "They're sleeping up there, Mr. Biggle. You must see Mr. Danplank yourself when he comes down."

In the bedroom, little Mrs. Danplank was shaking her husband vigorously.

"J.D.! J.D.! J.D.!" she said shrilly in his ear. "Wake up! Wake up! There's been someone in the house, and they've been on Biggle's flower-beds. You're sure you fastened the window last night?"

"Absolutely!" said her husband, sitting up. He got out, and began to dress; and presently the two of them were investigating matters downstairs.

Little Mrs. Danplank went immediately to the big writing-table, and directly afterwards she called out:

"Someone's been at this table during the night, J.D.! Someone's been at the table; all the drawers have got mixed; they've not been put back according to their numbers! Look!"

Her husband ran across from where he had been examining the catch of the big French windows, and stooped to look at the table.

"You're right, Mog," he said, very seriously.

In the same instant his wife dropped on her knees, and lifted back the carpet quickly from around the pedestals.

"I knew it!" she said bitterly. "I knew it! The table's been moved! See, the screws have been taken out! Here's one of them on the carpet! Oh, J.D., *suppose* they've discovered where the money is! Oh, if only we could have caught them! Who do you think it is?"

Mr. Jock Danplank was squatting now beside his wife, examining things, with a very grim face.

"I'll bet you a thousand dollars, Mog, to a red cent it's my gentle Cousin Billy," he said, at last. "I'd like to have caught him. Stand away a moment, dear."

She obeyed him, and, with one prodigious heave, he lifted the table, tilting it backwards so that he could look underneath; but there was nothing. He propped the table securely in this position with a chair; then, going down on to his knees, he investigated minutely, with the aid of a candle, both the floor and the underneath parts of the pedestals. His wife also joined him in his examination; but at the end of twenty minutes, or more, they had to admit that there were no signs of any secret receptacle.

Yet Mr. Jock Danplank was not satisfied, for, ringing the bell, he asked whether there was such a thing as a brace-bit and a narrow-bladed saw in the house. These were finally obtained from the gardener's workshop, and Jock Danplank began immediately to bore a series of holes in the floor in a line. Then, with the saw, he connected them, until he had sawn across one plank. He repeated the operation several feet away, and finally lifted out the portion of plank he had cut away; but he found the space between the floor and the ceiling below to be perfectly normal in design, as he proved by looking between the beams by the aid of his candle, and also by piercing a small hole through the plaster of the ceiling beneath.

"Nothing there, dear," he said to his wife. "Cheer up, Mog; we mustn't be disappointed. I don't believe for a moment that whoever's been messing with the table last night found anything."

"J.D.!" said his diminutive wife soberly. "You don't know one bit whether the thief found anything or not. You're just trying to comfort me. Whoever it was must have known something about the table. If it was your Cousin Billy, I'll bet he knew something we didn't; and I'll bet you J.D., we'll never touch a cent of all that money that your uncle meant you to have."

"We'll see, Mog," said her big husband quietly. "We'll have breakky now, and then I want to be quiet and think."

They informed old Mrs. Hartleytres that someone had broken into the house during the night, and meddled with the table. The old lady, dreadfully shocked and disturbed, repeated to them what they already knew, about the gardener finding footmarks on his flower-beds.

"And a dreadful way he is in, too, ma'am, about it," she said.

How much the gardener was upset, Mr. and Mrs. Jock Danplank discovered for themselves on emerging some time later, through the French window, into the rose garden. They found old Biggle standing over his two men and a boy, and giving fierce attention to the remedying and obliteration of the defacing footmarks. On seeing them approach, he whipped off his dirty old cap, and came remorselessly towards them.

"Mr. Danplank, sir," he said, his shrill, husky voice trembling with suppressed anger. "I take it as very thoughtless of you, sir, to go traipsing over my flower-beds, like as if they was dirt—which I won't say, they ain't, but not to be walked over, sir. I was pretty near minded to give notice, I was that, sir; but I thought as I'd give you one more chance, sir. But I will say wot I thinks, sir, an' that is as it wer' a wicked an' cruel thing to do!"

Mr. Jock Danplank stood a moment, and looked down at the little old gardener. Then he laughed a little, very quietly, and held out his hand.

"Mr. Biggle," he said, "I respect your attitude in the matter, and I give you my word that I have not walked over your flower-beds, and should never dream of doing such a stupid thing. You may be interested to know that there has been some stranger in the garden during the night; for the study has been broken into, and some of the furniture disturbed. I hope you've not cleaned up all the footmarks, as I want to take a pattern of one or two, Mr. Biggle."

Mr. Biggle, now thoroughly restored to his normal temperature, hastened to stop the work of repair; but it was too late. Not a single footprint had been left untreated, much to his as well as to Mr. Jock Danplank's annoyance; for he was grimly desirous of getting even with the desecrator.

"It'd make old Sir Gerald turn in 'is grave; it would that!" he kept repeating vehemently in his shrill, husky voice. "Not as I ever thought the old gennelman would rest comfortable nohow," he concluded. "Never still a moment, as you might say, Mr. Danplank, sir, day or night. All night I've known 'im walkin' round this 'ere garding. All night, Mr. Danplank, sir."

"You don't mean to suggest, Mr. Biggle, that it is my uncle who's been tramping over your flower-beds, I hope?" said Jock Danplank.

"Wot? Old Sir Gerald hisself!" said Mr. Biggle, very seriously.

"Why, Mr. Danplank, sir, 'ee'd as soon think of walkin' on 'is own face; not as I say 'ee could do it, mind you!"

The following morning there was fresh trouble, for Mr. Biggle insisted on calling Jock Danplank at six o'clock in the morning to come out and look at something he had discovered in the garden. This was nothing less than an immense hole which had been dug bang in the centre of his largest flower-bed. The hole was fully six feet deep and about ten across, and roughly circular. All round it the earth had been trampled by more than one pair of feet; and, as for the flower-bed itself, it was completely smothered out of existence beneath the pile of earth which had been thrown up out of the great hole.

Mr. Biggle's state of mind had passed beyond any hope of easement from words. At times mechanically, at half-minute intervals, he assured Mr. Danplank that old Sir Gerald would turn in his grave; but his imagination got no further, for he seemed temporarily stunned with the excess of his stupefied rage.

Jock Danplank himself was more than a little angry, but he was also more than a little excited. Evidently someone—Cousin Billy, he named that someone to himself—had certain reasons for supposing that the treasure was buried somewhere in the garden. In that case, there might be real hopes of Jock Danplank finding it for himself; *unless* those who had dug that great hole had actually discovered and removed the money during the night. Somehow, Mr. Jock Danplank had an inward conviction that nothing had come out of that hole, except the earth that lay piled around. Yet he could not be sure, of course, and felt proportionately anxious.

After considerable cogitation, he decided to see the whole business through himself, and make no complaint to the police; and, with this intention, he arranged with Mr. Biggle that a watch should be kept in the garden at nights by Mr. Biggle and his three men, assisted by himself.

In furtherance of this idea, he went up to town next day, and invested in two bull-terriers, who were tied up each night near to the French windows opening into the rose garden. And so the watch of the garden began. Mr. Jock Danplank assigned to himself the first watch, which extended from dark to midnight, and which was invariably shared by his diminutive but plucky wife. They kept their watch from a little shelter erected temporarily among the flower-beds, and cunningly screened by a number of newly planted rose bushes.

Yet it seemed that it was going to prove truly a case of locking the stable door after the horse is stolen; for a week passed without the least sign of anything suspicious.

"Oh, J.D., I'm sure they've found it!" said Mrs. Danplank more than once, towards the close of that week. "How shall we ever be able to prove it. They've got it, and we may just as well stop watching now."

Yet the very next night something happened; for about two in the morning, Mr. Jock Danplank was awakened by his wife shaking him furiously.

"J.D.! J.D.! J.D.!" she was whispering shrilly in his ear. "Wake up! Wake up! There's something happening in the garden! The dogs have just gone mad. Hark!"

Jock Danplank did listen, and surely the dogs were filling the night with their crazy barking; then there was the sound of a man shouting; and in a moment big Jock Danplank was out of bed, and into his slippers and dressing-gown.

He dashed into the study, slipped the catch of the French windows, and raced into the garden, shouting to Mr. Biggle, whose watch it was.

" 'Ere, sir, 'ere!" he heard the old gardener shouting in the distance, and he raced towards the call, cutting across rose-beds ruthlessly. He found old Biggle sitting, moaning a little, in one of the smaller circles of olden turf which lay between the rose bushes on the farther side of the garden.

"Tripped on summat, Mr. Danplank, sir, an' wrenched my ankle somethin' horful," the old man explained, gritting out the words with pain. "Take care wot you're doin' sir, there's a rope stretched across 'ere, somewheres, that's wot caught my foot, sir. I thought I saw someone runnin' when the dogs started; an' I did a sprint after 'em, but I fouled summat with my foot. Strike a light, Mr. Danplank, sir."

He struck a light, as the old man requested, and looked around him.

"Why, Biggle," he said suddenly, "there's a surveyor's broken tape or something here. Th— Why, look, man, the turf's all lifted here!"

And so it was; and in the centre of the little grass circle there was stuck a large wooden peg, to which one end of the measuring-tape was attached; the other end he discovered eventually was fastened to the bronze "Fighting Gladiator" which stood, as has been mentioned, in the centre of the rose garden. This, however, later. In the meanwhile, Jock Danplank had unhitched one of the dogs, and, taking him by the chain, followed his tracings of the intruders' footsteps. These led across the garden, cutting ruthlessly across beds, eventually to the outer surrounding hedge, through which a gap had been burst. This led out on to a ten-acre meadow, beyond which was the high road; so that Jock, knowing the man or men had a good start, wasted no more time, but hurried back to old Biggle, whom he found now surrounded by the two under-gardeners and Mrs. Danplank.

"We'll carry him into the house, and then get spades and see what's underground here," said Mr. Jock Danplank. But old Biggle refused to be moved. He sent his two underlings for spades and pickaxes, also for a couple of hurricane lamps. When these were brought he insisted on holding one, whilst the other he gave to Mrs. Danplank to hold.

Then the digging commenced, and for two hours went forward breathlessly, in every sense of the word. Yet nothing was unearthed, though by that time the hole stretched almost across the little opening, and was fully as deep as the men's shoulders. Another two hours of digging followed; and then the delving was abandoned, for it was obvious that there was no treasure there; and that Cousin Billy—for so Jock Danplank named the intruder to himself—was once more very distinctly off the mark; for this second attempt made it plain that the first had been unsuccessful.

With this knowledge came the comforting realisation that the treasure was still unmoved; and for the next week Jock Danplank and his wife took the hint that the measuring-tape had given them, and tried every imaginable measurement about the gardens, and even had a narrow hole sunk diagonally under the statue of the "Fighting Gladiator," to make sure that warlike gentleman was not standing guard over their gold; but everything led to nothing. Finally, in a moment of inspiration, Mrs. Dunplank suggested excitedly that they should measure seventy-seven feet due east through the French windows from the gigantic writing-table.

At this suggestion, Jock Danplank grew almost as excited as his wife, for it seemed to explain the reason for the special mention of the table in his uncle's will. The measurement was made from the centre rose of the inlay of the table-top, and the bearing taken by compass. Where the end of the tape came out on the smooth-grown grass, Mr. Jock Danplank thrust in his pocket-knife. Then, with the aid of old Biggle—whose ankle was now recovered—and the two under-gardeners, a huge circle of turf, some fifteen feet across, was removed, and digging operations commenced.

This was in the early forenoon. By late evening the hole had been sunk ten feet deep, and the attempt was then abandoned; for it was plain that treasure was a stranger to that place.

It took old Biggle a week to get that turf replaced to his liking, and all levelled up; and after that it seemed just useless to search the garden any further. Yet, because of what had already happened, and because, likewise, of a certain pugnacious determination in Jock Danplank, the night watches were not discontinued, but kept up as usual.

In this fashion a month passed, without incident; two months, and finally the half of a third; so that Mr. Jock Danplank began to think that no further attempts would be made in the line of midnight excavations among his flower-beds. And then something happened.

Mr. Danplank had ceased himself to participate in the watching, leaving it to Biggle and his two under-gardeners, who arranged it between them, and took off so many hours each day to make up for the extra time put in.

Thus it happened that instead of crouching out in the gardens, Mr. Danplank and his diminutive wife passed their evenings in the cosy study; and because of this, they happened to notice something that otherwise they might not have noticed.

"The dogs are very quiet to-night, J.D.," remarked his wife, as she sat smoking cigarettes and reading.

"Yes," said her husband. And relapsed again into reading.

Said his wife some half-hour later:

"J.D., I'm sure there's something funny about the dogs to-night. I've not heard a sound from them all evening. I'm going out to have a look at them."

"Hey?" said her big husband, lowering his newspaper, and stretching himself. "What's that, dear?"

"It's the dogs," she said rising. "I don't know. I've a feeling there's something wrong. I'm going to see."

She walked across to the French windows, opened one of them, and called to the dogs, who had their kennels one on each side of the windows, only a few yards away. But instead of a frenzy of answering barks, only a perfect silence greeted her.

Jock Danplank dropped his paper, and crossed to the window.

"Funny!" he muttered, as the silence remained constant. He stepped outside, and walked to the left-hand kennel, calling the dog by name. He reached the kennel, and stooped.

"Mary," he said quietly, "bring that electric-torch off the mantelpiece."

His wife ran quickly, and was back in a moment with the torch. He took it from her, switching on the light, and shone it down at the ground before the kennel. Bella, the bull-terrier bitch, lay stiff, with a piece of half-eaten meat still between her clenched jaws.

"Um!" said Jock Danplank, speaking even more quietly than before. He walked across to the other kennel, and held the light. The dog, Jerry, lay half in and half out of his kennel, and he was just as still and rigid as his wife Bella.

"This," said the big man, straightening up, "grows interesting. I fancy, Mog, with the blessing of Fate, we may have a little fun ahead of us to-night. But I'm sorry for the dogs. Go inside, dear, and shut the window. I shall be back in a few minutes."

His wife obeyed, for she was able to diagnose those times when her husband had, as it were, taken the helm. In a short time he returned.

"Now, dear," he said, " draw the curtains over the windows while we make a few arrangements in here. I've had a word with Biggle, and he's got his two men with him in the shelter; also, you'll be interested to hear that he appreciates a suggestion I made concerning the water-hose. You'll remember that the hydrant comes up near the shelter. Now, we'll pull this couch out a bit, and shove some cushions and a rug down on the floor at the back. You run upstairs and put a light in our bedroom, as if we were going to bed. Bring my camera down with you; it's got fresh plates in. You might also bring that snap-flashlight of mine. Oh, yes, and my stick out of the hall, as you come back. I'll be ready by then."

When little Mrs. Danplank returned, she found the study in darkness and the curtains drawn back, once more exposing the windows.

"Here, Mog," said her husband's voice. And in a moment his hands took the camera, stick, and flashlight from her, and guided her down on to cushions at the back of the drawn-out couch.

"Now, my little lady," he said, "you take charge of the flashlight, and when I nudge you let there be light. I'll attend to the rest of the photography. I've what you might call a suspicion that we shall have a visitor right here in this room before long, and I guess we'll take his picture free of charge. But if I'm mistaken, and he sticks to his old bad habit of digging holes in the garden, why, then old Biggle'll slip round and give us word, and we'll go picture-makin' outside. I'll run up now and turn out the bedroom light, then Mr. Cousin Billy—for I've quite a notion that will be the name of our visitor—will think we've gone nicely to by-by, bless him, and he'll have a comfy feeling that he can go ahead. You see, I'll bet he's watching even now from some corner or other."

When Mr. Jock Danplank returned, he ensconced himself comfortably with his wife at the back of the couch; and so their watch began. For two hours they remained silent save for occasional whispers, their gaze fixed upon the windows. Another half-hour passed, and the clock in the room struck two, musically, in the darkness. A minute later little Mrs. Danplank gripped her husband's arm sharply, for suddenly a man's head had become silhouetted against the lesser darkness of the outside night.

"Cousin Billy!" said Jock Danplank, in a low voice. "He's trying to lift the drop-latch with a knife, or something."

"Ssh!" whispered his wife anxiously; and after that they were absolutely silent. A minute passed, and then another. Twice they heard the latch jingle a little as the knife half lifted it out of its snick, then suddenly the window opened, for the latch had been lifted clear; and the next instant the intruder was standing motionless in the opening, evidently listening.

For a few moments he stood thus, and they could interpret the tenseness of his attitude. Then he came right into the room, closed the window very quietly, and began to fumble with the curtains. These he managed eventually to draw, and the next instant a little beam of light darted here and there about the room; he was evidently using some kind of electric-torch or lamp.

He walked across the room, and from where they lay behind the couch they heard the key turned very quietly in the lock. He had locked the door to prevent any surprise in the rear, as might be said.

The man went swiftly then to the big writing-table, lifted off a litter of papers that were on it, and deposited them noiselessly upon the floor. Then for fully ten minutes he examined the surface of the table, as the two watchers were able to see by raising their heads above the back of the couch. The man appeared to be pressing with his thumb here and there upon the top of the table, giving little, almost noiseless grunts each time; and both Jock Danplank and his wife grew excited with the thought that perhaps they were about to learn the hiding-place of some paper that should tell them where their money had been put away.

Suddenly there was a little grunt that plainly marked pleased surprise and excitement upon the part of the intruder. He appeared to be pressing hard upon the table with the tips of the fingers of his right hand, and at the same time attempting to rotate his arm, as though trying to unscrew something. A moment later the rapid movement of his elbow denoted that he was actually unscrewing something that squeaked faintly. And suddenly he gave out a gasp, and lifted some object from the table, which he examined by the light of his electric lamp.

Jock rose boldly from behind the couch to stare, and saw that the man held one of the inlay-roses in his hand—the rose evidently screwed out of the table-top like a plug. As the man turned it over, Jock saw that there was a thin cord attached to the underside; and instantly it was plain to him that his cousin—for such he knew the intruder to be—had at last solved the whereabouts of the treasure.... "Seventy-seven feet due east...."

Jock saw it all now. Seventy-seven feet due east of the spot touched by that rose, when the rose was laid due east out on the grass outside at full stretch of that thin cord which evidently connected it with the recess in the table from which it had been unscrewed. What a cunning notion!

Evidently his Cousin Billy had knowledge how to use the rose; for he switched off his lamp, and, drawing the curtains, he opened the window. He stepped out noiselessly into the garden, and proceeded across the grass, drawing the cord after him. In a minute he returned, and examined the surface of the table; then, switching off the light again, he went out once more, and appeared to make some adjustment of the position of the rose upon the grass.

Half a dozen times, perhaps, he came back, and switched on the light to examine the table, and each time Mr. Jock Danplank and his wife dived out of sight again behind the sofa. And each time that he returned noiselessly to the garden, Jock and Mrs. Danplank rose and stared after him through the darkness. Suddenly Jock Danplank comprehended.

"Mog," he whispered, "the inlay of roses on the table is a sort of fancy compass. What fools we were never to twig! He's laying the direction by the branch of roses that points east through the window. That must be why my uncle was so particular about fixing the table exactly. See?"

"Yes," whispered his wife, who was trembling with excitement, in the darkness beside him. "What a good thing we never took a flashlight of him, J.D., when he first came in, we should never have known then. He's a bad man, but he must be clever."

Cousin Billy came in quietly once more and examined the table. He must have been satisfied that the direction was now right, for he went out again, and stayed out. They could see him dimly. He appeared to be about halfway towards the centre of the rose-garden. Then they saw him walking in a bent position due east, as though he were trailing something out across the turf.

"He's measuring seventy-seven feet to the east of the place where the rose touches the ground," said Jock Danplank. "As soon as he gets to his favourite exercise, Mog, we'll slip out and look on from close quarters. This is what I call decent of Cousin Billy; he's doing his level best to help us."

A few minutes later, after the silent man out on the grass had walked to and fro a great many times between the rose and some point to the eastward of it, he gave a low "miau" like a cat; and immediately there came two figures out of the darkness of the rose bushes to the south of the garden. These joined him, and directly the watchers saw the vague gleam of shirts and bare arms through the darkness, as coats were abandoned by all three; then came the faint noises of drying implements cautiously used.

"Now," said Jock Danplank, and helped his wife hurriedly into her coat. "Come along." And he led the way silently through the French windows, out into a little winding path that led them deeply among the rose bushes, and so to the shelter upon the far side, where old Biggle and his two under-gardeners sat, peering silently through the bushes at the three men of the night who were mauling Mr. Biggle's choice turf, there before his very eyes.

"Biggle," said Jock, stealing silently into the shelter, "my wife and I have come to join the audience. I think we may conclude, Biggle, that we have them now——eh?"

"We 'ave 'em, Mr. Danplank, sir," replied Biggle, rising and offering his seat to Mrs. Danplank, with nice courtesy. "The Lord 'elp 'em, Mr. Danplank, sir, when I gets my hands on to 'em. Leastways, I should say 'elp me not to do murder when I starts on 'em."

The old man's tone made it clear that he burned and trembled with passion at the visible and audible proofs of outrage to his garden that was going on within thirty or forty feet of them.

"Old Sir Gerald would turn in 'is grave——" began Biggle.

But Mr. Jock Danplank interrupted his assurance with a question regarding the hose. "They'll need a wash, Biggle, after that dirty work, you know," he said.

"All's ready, Mr. Danplank, sir, as you ordered," said Biggle; "an' I've told Bill an' Jarge they'm to show their lanterns so soon as you whistles, sir."

After that, for maybe a full hour and a half, Mr. Danplank allowed his cousin and assistants to indulge in their hobby of hole making to their heart's content. Then, thinking that it was about time, he drew his wife quietly out of the shelter, and ensconced her with himself among some rose bushes away to the right, from which they commanded a view of Cousin Billy's operations.

"Now, Mog," he whispered, "get that flashlight all ready. When I tell you, blaze away."

He stared hard into the darkness, and could vaguely see the heads and shoulders of the three men working furiously but silently in the big hole they had made. He aimed his camera—a twin-lens—at the hole, then whistled shrilly. As the whistle went across the dark garden the sounds of digging ceased instantly, and then, in the darkness, two jets of light shone out, flashed through the bushes, swung round to and fro, and settled on the sweating faces of Cousin Billy and two other men.

Jock Danplank focussed rapidly, and even as he did so there came the sharp his-hissing of the great hose as Biggle turned on the hydrant. Then Biggle got to work. The powerful stream of water arched through the night, glittering in the light from the two bull's-eye lanterns, and smote Cousin Billy full in the face. There was a yell and a splutter, and in the same instant of time Mr. Jock Danplank gave the word to his wife. She pressed the trigger of the flashlight, and instantaneously the whole of the visible gardens flashed out in a blaze of white and blinding light, each leaf fluttering in the night breeze showing clear-cut and vivid. It lit up the face of Cousin Billy as he essayed madly to scramble up out of the big hole that was rapidly becoming a lake. He swore incredibly, screaming out his oaths with gasps and bubblings, as the remorseless Biggle kept the hydrant full upon him. The darkness felt upon the gardens with an effect upon the senses as of thunder. But still the hose played on, directed by the aid of the lanterns. The two other men had disappeared with the first arrival of the water, and were gone away through the bushes

And now at last Cousin Billy achieved the almost impossible, and ascended out of the pit of his discomfiture. As he did so the flashlight blazed out again, showing him dripping mud from head to feet, and the hose searching him from top to bottom in every sense of the word.

"Send you a proof to-morrow, Billy!" shouted Mr. Jock Danplank as the darkness fell for the second time. "Good-night, old man!"

There was no reply, only a smashing and rending among the rose-bushes as Cousin Billy left at a high rate of speed, the hydrant following the sounds remorselessly until he was out of range.

"Now," said Mr. Jock Danplank, when things had subsided a little. "Get some buckets and bail out." He handed his camera to his wife, and threw off his coat. When the buckets were brought he was first into the hole, up to his knees in mud and water. In twenty minutes the hole was dry, more or less, and digging was resumed. Morning found them still digging, and nowhere any signs of treasure.

Mary Danplank brought them out hot coffee, and tried hard to hide her bitter disappointment. It was plain that almost their last hope of finding the treasure had gone. The men all came up out of the hole, and stood round, drinking, and almost sullen with disappointment and fatigue.

"It's no use, Mog," said Jock Danplank, at last. "I'm beginning to think the talk about money in the will must have been all rot. Uncle was a queer chap. I expect he got a bit off his balance towards the end, and just imagined he'd got more than he had. He must have spent it all doing this place up. He— *By Jove!*"

His speech ended in a shout. He hove his cup and saucer bang down on to the grass, and dashed into the house. A moment later he gave out a great bellow.

"The compass! The compass! Where's the compass!"

He discovered it even whilst he shouted, put it down on the table, let it steady, and then spied along it.

"*Found it!*" he roared. "Found it, by gum! The table's not been put back straight since we shifted it. The hole's twenty feet too much to the south. Shift the rose to the north! Shift the rose to the north!" He waved one big hand energetically, and his wife ran to obey. "Yes, yes, that's it Mary. Put it down there—just there. Right. Now the tape; measure off—measure off! More to the north. There! Got it. Stick something in. Right! Now spades!" And he came dashing out through the window.

An hour later they found the money, every sovereign of it. If you please, it was packed neatly in old distemper tins, of the washable variety. That's all, except that Biggle was very much troubled for a year to come, until his turf once more resumed its velvet look of ages. Even then his trained eye saw imperfections. Meanwhile, Cousin Billy had received his "proofs", accompanied by the following little note:

"Dear Billy,—Herewith the proofs. We think they're immense. Treasure safe to hand. Congrat. me, old man.—Your affec. cousin,

"Jock."

The Mystery of Captain Chappel

I

"I AIN'T ENOUGH KNOWLEDGE," Cobbler Juk was saying, in a narky voice, "not to be what you'd call scientific. But I got the brains I was born with, and I uses my eyes!"

"Well, uncle," replied the big policeman, who sat on the end of the bench, smoking, "I don't know as this wants any scientific idees."

"A lot you know," said the little man moodily. "Ole Cap'n Chappel was killed between the porch of the Spread Eagle and the corner of Dobell's beat, an' that's no more than a hundred yards, as you might say. An' there's none of you knows to-day, more'n Adam, who done it."

"It's right we can't get on the track of no one," replied the big policeman good naturedly; "an' that's what I'm here for, uncle. The chief spoke to me to-night, an' said as you might have a try on the quiet, just same as you found out that 'sault and rob'ry case. He'll give you a ten-pound note for your trouble if you get hold of any sort of a cloo; but you've got to keep it quiet as you're in it, or maybe he'll get into a bother over lettin' an amachoor come messin' around——"

"Amachoor!" said the cobbler hotly. "You're fine perfessionals, ain't you! Lordy!"

"*We* don't think as you're an amachoor, uncle, up at the station," said the big policeman cunningly. " I tell you, uncle, you can do it. It's just the case as suits your style of thinkin' out the most likely way it'd come about. Be reasonable an' have a try."

"I'm not struck, nevvy, on detectiven'," said the old man perversely. "I got the gift, I know; but it's a sneakin', pryin', think-evil-of-yer-feller-men sort of job, an' no work for a decent-hearted man. Half the time it's just keyhole-listening or sniffing up someone else's

413

drain—there's no blessed hero work in it, except the silly stuff you reads. You can tell the chief I'm stickin' to my own last. I prefers honest cobblin'! I tell you, detectives is nothin' but lawful sneaks pryin' out other sneaks."

Old Cobbler Juk was in a contrary mood; but his nephew knew how to humour him.

"The chief said as how he'd be willin' to pay you five bob a day expenses while you was on the case," remarked the big policeman, who was clearly very much off duty. "Jack's good enough to do all the mendin' as'll need doin' this week or two. That'll leave you free; an' you'll be earnin' a steady wage—"

"Shows what you know!" snarled his uncle, interrupting. "I'd lose every blessed customer I got if I was to let Jack try his hand to the patchin'. All the same, you can tell the chief I'm on the job. I s'pose if I'm built to be a sneak, I must be a sneak; but it ain't no work for a decent man. No, you can't tell me nothin' about the case. I know more now than you an' the chief and the whole blessed lot of you. I've been studying it over quietly this last two weeks. It amounts to this:

"On Toosday night; and that's a fortnight gone now, at twenty-five minutes to ten by the market clock, and by Captain Chappel's own watch—which was a good 'un too! —the old chap said good-night to Master Claud Atkins, the saddler. That's just a way of speakin'; for, as you know, nevvy, it wasn't exactly good-night; but the other way round, owing to the two of 'em having drunk too much, and Saddler Atkins—who don't know a piece of good leather when he's shown it!—sayin' as the old cap'n's watch was no chronometer, but a common lever. That's how everyone knows the time of the business so exact; for they got out in the porch of the Spread Eagle to test it by the market clock, and found it right to a second, you might say.

"Ole Cap'n Chappel wanted to make the leather man take back what he'd said, but Claud Atkins had drunk just enough not to know what was best for him, and he started in to call the cap'n. Cap'n Chappel never was a man to stand that sort of thing, drunk or sober—as Atkins should have known, if he'd not known a bit less of faces even than he does of leather. Consequence was that the old cap'n knocked him flat, and then staggers off happy as a lord down the street.

"Saddler Atkins gets up, as soon as he sees the cap'n gone, and steps outside, talkin' brave. But, as he didn't attempt to follow the cap'n, no one took anymore notice of it all, and never would, only that one minute later, and that's exactly twenty-four minutes to ten, P.c. Dobell starts blowing his whistle; for he'd come to the corner of his beat, not a hundred yards from the porch itself, and found the cap'n, dead as a brad, with his head broken.

"Now, you know this, and the whole town knows it; and there's not the least doubt about the time being correct, for the reasons I've given, and because, in the second case, Dobell always looks at the market clock each time he comes to the corner. Therefore, you have the case like this, nevvy: Old Cap'n Chappel was killed in the one minute that lies between twenty-five and twenty-four minutes to ten on last Toosday night, in the hundred yards of Talbot Street that lies between the corner of P.c. Dobell's beat and the porch of the Spread Eagle.

"Dobell was quite sure that there was no living soul in the street when he reached the corner, and the night was that quiet that he could scarce have missed to have heard anyone run away. Now then, nevvy, what killed Cap'n Chappel? That's what you're all asking your silly selves, an' the only answer you can find is Saddler Claude Atkins, him that's so fat he couldn't do the distance in twice the time. An' as for killin', he ain't got the good, honest pluck to kill a mouse, let alone a man!

"You leave it to me now, and just tell the chief he can stop scarin' that fool Atkins, and let him out of gaol right away, so's he can run along home and let his wife bully him. Come along of me now, nevvy, an' I'll show you good common-sense detectivin', I will that!"

II

"Now," said old Cobbler Juk; having reached the place where Captain Chappel had been found, "I've been all over this a half-dozen times and more, and I've come to my own conclusions. But I'll start in earnest; an' maybe I'll get it through the likes of such thick heads as yours and the chief's as the old buffer was killed in a mighty different way to what you got thinking. Saddler Atkins! Lord, nevvy, why didn't the chief arrest our black tom, if he was needin' a desp'rate character?

"See here, now!" he continued. "This is where they found the cap'n. It's a hundred yards from here to the porch of the Spread Eagle, and ten yards to the corner of Dobell's beat; and P.c. Dobell must have come on the cap'n within twenty or thirty seconds after he was killed, and not a person in the street. Atkins could never have done it, leavin' out that he was afraid of the cap'n, for he left the other way; and he's too fat and short in the wind to go faster'n a slow walk. Then, again, the cap'n was a mighty tall man, and he was hit smack on the top of the head. That'd need a tall man to do; an' the saddlers just five-foot nothin', except round the waist. I'm away up now to have a talk with the chief, and try to get some sense into his head."

This the cobbler did, with such good results that the saddler was shortly released.

"Look here," said the cobbler, who went to see him at his house. "I got you out of that muckery; an' I'll do you one more good turn. Don't you go foolin' around after dark, or maybe you'll get what old Cap'n Chappel got!"

The saddler went very pale.

"Eh, Mr. Juk!" he said, trying to speak easily. "What's that? What d'yer mean, Mr. Juk?"

"You knows what I means!" said Cobbler Juk quietly, looking him hard in the eyes. "You got more idea of what killed the cap'n than anyone on earth—'cept me! An' perhaps just one other as I got in my mind. No; you needn't tell me nothing. I can find out what I wants without screwin' you. If I am doin' sneak-work I'll do it as clean as maybe. Good mornin', Mister Saddler Atkins. You never did know a piece of good leather when you saw it, nor ever will. I'd not say the same, though, about skins!"

And the cobbler went away, laughing at some hidden wit in his remark. But the saddler certainly never laughed. He just sat back in his chair, very pasty-faced and very breathless.

" G'lord!" he muttered presently, "what's *he* know?"

III

"Uncle, wake up! Wake up!" said the cobbler's big nephew the following night, shaking him vigorously.

The old man woke, and turned with a snarl.

"What the divvil——" he began; then, seeing that his nephew was in uniform: "What is it, nevvy? What is it?" he asked, in a changed voice. "It's not the——"

"Saddler Atkins!" interrupted the policeman. "We just found him, not ten minutes ago, in Varley Street. Stone dead as they makes 'em. Killed same way as the cap'n, to *my* thinkin'; an' not a cloo of any kind as could tell us what did it; nor there ain't nothin' touched on the body——"

"Whist, nevvy; my boots, quick!" said the cobbler, beginning to dress rapidly. "I got to see just where he was found 'fore the silly fools touch ought. I s'pose he's at the station?"

Twenty minutes later Cobbler Juk and his nephew reached the place where Saddler Atkins had been found. The old man had been so eager to get there that he had actually run half the way, the big policeman having to jog-trot to keep up with him.

For several minutes Jut searched around, using his nephew's lantern; and once or twice he picked up things and slipped them into his waistcoat pocket.

"Now," he said at last, "we'll have a look at old Saddler Atkins. Poor little fool, I warned him fair an' square——"

"What's that, uncle?" gasped the big policeman, for he was again at his lumbering jog-trot in the wake of his energetic relative.

"Not but he fair deserved what he got!" continued the old man, taking no notice of his nephew's question.

"Did you know, uncle, as the saddler might be murdered?" the big man managed to blurt out as they drew up at the station. "You ought not to have held back infermation as might have led to the arrest!" he added.

"Go an' boil your big head! I want to see the body!" was all the "information" that the Law—as represented in the body of his nephew—received.

"That's all I need," said Cobbler Juk, after he had seen what he wanted.

He lowered his voice to a whisper.

"Look a here, nevvy," he added. "If you're anxious to get a promotion, just you keep an eye on old Councillor Tompkins. He'll maybe take the next ticket for heaven! Not but he'll deserve it, and the world be better an' heaven the worse for him goin'."

Cobbler Juk spent a couple of busy days; but on the evening of the second day, when his nephew called at his shop, he found the old man patching a split upper.

"It's restin', nevvy," Cobbler Juk explained; as the policeman sat down on the end of the bench and pulled out his pipe, "After this divvil's sneak-work I been on, it's clean an' wholesome to feel a bit of honest wax thread in me fingers. An' it helps one to think."

"Have you come on anythin' as 'elps you, uncle?" asked the constable. "The chief asked what you was doin' to-day, an' I told him I couldn't say as you'd got a proper cloo yet, but I thought maybe you'd an idee. Have you got a cloo, uncle?"

Cobbler Juk held his bristle up against the light, and stared at it meditatively.

"Don't be in a hurry, nevvy," he said, speaking slowly. "This here is sure a great mystery. Not but I got some strange notions in my head, an' maybe a cloo or two that'll prove wonders in a while; but it may take a bit yet. Meantime, nevvy, see you to take care that Councillor Tompkins comes to no harm after dark. I leave it to you how you do it. I'd not be surprised but this case brought you promotion, if you ain't as big a fool as you looks.

"When you come to go over the case," he continued, still in meditative fashion, "it just looks queerer and queerer. There was the cap'n steppin' away from the Spread Eagle, full of good liquor an' life, one minute, an' then the next minute him stone dead in the open streets, an' the policeman lookin' half a mile every way for what killed him, an' not a soul in sight, nor a house nor a turnin' for anyone to run into anywhere handy, with the road runnin' there between them high, blank walls. An' no natural motive, as you might say, 'cept the little fat saddler man wantin' to have revenge! Ech! Ech! Ech!"

And the old man broke into an amused, dry laughter as he glanced sideways at the baited constable.

"An' then the mystery gettin' stranger still; for there ain't no motive, anyway; is there, nevvy, for anyone waiting to bash the saddler. An' now we're expectin' this night-murdering-thing to come for old Councillor Tompkins—"

"Do talk sense, uncle!" said the big man. "If it's so as you knows anythin', it's your dooty to tell the authorities—"

"Meanin' the likes of you and the chief," interrupted Juk. Then, with a sudden dropping of his half-bantering, half-thoughtful manner, he said: "Tell the chief, if you like, nevvy; only bang goes your chance of promotion. Miss a bit of your sleep for once, same as I been doin', an' as I should have been doin' when it come on yon poor saddler divvil. Miss a bit of sleep this next night or two and watch the councillor. His house's on your beat. No! I'll not say another word; only mind you, nevvy, I'm dead to earnest. There's death stalkin' old Tompkins, an' he'll go sure, if you or I don't save him. Not but I mind all that much, so that I bottom the mystery proper. The three of 'em 'll no more than have come by their own devil's 'arnings. Good-night, lad! I'm to my bed."

"Night, uncle," said the policeman, and rose. "You're early. I've all night off these next three nights, an' I'll see as the old councillor don't come to no harm."

IV

"H'm!" grunted Cobbler Juk to himself, the following night. "The lad's doing very well. But, for all's sakes, why don't he hide his great silly carcass!"

Old man Juk was sitting among the bushes on the west side of Councillor Tompkins' house. It was a little after eleven p.m., and a dull loom of moonlight behind the clouds made things vaguely seen around. Before him, about thirty feet away, there showed the window of the councillor's room, with the light somewhat low within, as if Tompkins had only his reading-lamp lit. From time to time a shadow crossed the blind, showing plainly the councillor's heavily marked profile.

"Old man Tompkins has sure got the trapses on him!" muttered Juk to himself. "I guess sin's a pretty poor investment in the end."

He turned, and started towards where, about a dozen yards away, he could see the big figure of his nephew; in private clothes, standing under a group of three small trees, evidently keeping a constant watch on the window.

"Nevvy!" he called, scarcely above a sharp whisper. "Nevvy!"

The night was very quiet, save for odd, restless little winds that set the trees and bushes rustling mournfully at times; so that Uncle Juk's sharply pitched whisper reached the policeman, and he came at once.

"Sit here beside me, lad," said Juk. "I don't want you arrestin' me just when you ought to be arrestin' the divvil himself!"

"I never thought as you was here," said the constable. "Look at 'is shadder on the blind. He's got the jumps. He was like that all last night, too. Never stirred out of the house for two days, as I knows."

"Things is like to happen to-night, nevvy," said Cobbler Juk. "I been hard at it all to-day, an' all yesterday; an' part of last night I was here with you, but you never saw me, you policeman you. An' now I'm thinkin' things is sure goin' to happen. But don't you do nothin' till I tells you, not so what you sees. There's some proper devil's work forrard. Just keep your club handy, an' move quick when I gives the word. S-s-s-t! What was that?"

The two men turned their heads and looked towards the bushes to their right. Something seemed to be stirring them in a way that was plainly never the wind. Abruptly, not twenty feet away, something that looked like a huge, black image rose noiselessly out of the bushes and stood motionless. It appeared to be about seven feet high, and was completely black but it was the head that most attracted and disgusted the two hidden watchers. The head was like nothing either of them had ever seen. It was something abnormal.

The thing began to go through the bushes in an upright position with a queer noiselessness. The head of it was all the time directed towards the window, as if it saw nothing else. It came out clear of the shrubs, and went up close against the window, and here it paused. It seemed to be nosing against the glass of the window, like an animal; and suddenly Cobbler Juk and the policeman heard a curious, infernal croaking quality in it.

"Lord!" whispered the cobbler. "What is it? What the divvil is it?"

And he lifted his head up a little above the bushes to see better, but his nephew grabbed at him and pulled him back.

"Don't; uncle!" he muttered. "Don't be a fool!"

The big constable was shaking.

"Get a hold of yourself!" snarled the old man. "An' leggo my collar!"

His nephew loosed him and pulled himself together, for he was a plucky enough man, only this monstrous, unnameable thing was something so entirely beyond all that he had ever conceived of. As for old Juk, he rose slowly into a kneeling position, and stared with an incredible curiosity.

The thing at the window continued the peculiar croaking grunt, and there came a sound like a low whining, which might have been from the creature itself, or from the rubbing of something against the glass.

Abruptly the shadow of the councillor showed upon the blind, and the nest instant the blind itself was drawn up with one swift movement. The snout of the thing at the window was raised, as if the creature were looking at the councillor. The two watchers could see it, black against the half light of the room within.

At first it was plain that Councillor Tompkins saw nothing. The floor of the room stood some feet higher than the ground outside, so that the man was staring out over the head of the thing that peered up at him. Juk could see that he was looking round the garden, from side to side, with quick, jerky movements.

The creature outside had ceased its horrible croaking grunts, but now it emitted a series of them, louder than any it had made, and within them an incredible note of malevolence, so it seemed to the old cobbler. The councillor glanced down, and abruptly he must have seen the thing, for he jumped back a couple of paces, then stopped and stared.

Perhaps for some five seconds he stood motionless, whilst the creature made not a sound. It was as if the man and the monstrous being outside looked mutually at one another. Then movement came to the man. His hand went into his side coat-pocket, and he took a couple of swift steps sideways to the lamp. But even as he did so the creature gave forth a kind of dull, croaking roar, and hurled itself at the window bodily. The glass smashed into atoms, and the sashes crumpled inwards.

"Come on!" shouted Juk; and left the bushes at a run, with his nephew after him. From the window there came still the crash of smashed glass and woodwork, and a flash from the lamp inside showed for an instant that the thing was half in and half out. The lamp went out suddenly, and directly afterwards there came three red spurts of fire and the sharp thuds of sound that a firearm makes when loosed off in a confined space.

Juk was at the window now. Within the room there was a scuffling, and then a strangled gasp, which was lost immediately in a mutter of that dreadful grunting. There came an instant of absolute silence, broken by a dull, heavy thud, and then again the croaking grunts broke out, just as Juk leaped forward into the absolute darkness of the room, with everywhere the stench of smashed lamp in the air.

Cobbler Juk had his nephew's lantern in his hand, but it had jolted out as he jumped for the window. He snatched at the matches in his vest-pocket, shouting to his nephew, who was even then climbing through the window, to wait for the light. He scraped a match savagely across his thigh, but the match broke. He snatched at another, just as the thing rose out of the darkness and dashed past him out the window, hurling the big constable out on to the grass as if he had been a child rather than an exceptionally powerful man.

"Look out there!" shouted the cobbler futilely.

But his nephew lay on the turf, half stunned, whilst the creature went bounding into the bushes and disappeared.

Juk hove the lantern down; and ran back to the window. He jumped through, and, without waiting to see what had happened to his nephew, he sprang in among the bushes, following the faint sounds that seemed to come back to him from somewhere ahead out of the darkness. Yet, in a moment, he heard nothing, and soon came to the confines of the garden without having seen a thing.

"Lost it!" he snarled to himself. "A fine mess I've made of it!"

He ran down a side-path to the road, and looked up and down so far as he could see; but there was nothing visible in the immediate gloom. He went, running, a hundred yards up the road, and then back again the other way, but saw not a thing; neither, though the night was still, could he hear a sound. He stood listening awhile, then shouts and lights through the trees showed him that Councillor Tompkins' household was awake, and had come down to investigate the cause of the window-smashing and the shots. He heard his nephew shouting his name at the top of his voice.

"Here! Coming!" he called back; and began to run up the path to the house.

When he reached it, he climbed in through the smashed window.

He found that the councillor had been killed by a heavy blow on the head, in a similar fashion to the way in which both Captain Chappel and Saddler Atkins had been murdered. After this he directed his nephew to telephone to the station, whilst he took a further look round.

"I'll get someone as knows what killed the councillor and the others tomorrow night," he told his nephew grimly at the end of his look round. "Then we'll get to the bottom of this here divvilment."

V

"A dog's nose for me, miss," said the cobbler, "an' not too much gin, please. M'yes, my nevvy'll have a shandygaft, miss. I don't hold with young folk drinkin' strong likkers, special them as has to uphold law an' order."

He grinned perversely to himself.

Cobbler Juk and his nephew, who was in private clothes, were sitting in the public bar of the Slade Arms, and the time lacked a few minutes to eight on the evening following the death of Councillor Tompkins.

"Now then, nevvy," said the old man, you didn't show up so grand last night—not but what I was near as bad. We got to get this man that'll sure come in here to-night, an' when we got him we got to make him tell what he knows about yon thing we saw last night. We ain't goin' to collar him right off. We'll go out after him, an' see where he goes; and then you can put them wristbands of yours on an' cart him away to the station for a talk with the chief."

They sat down for an hour, during which a large number of customers came and left. Abruptly Juk leaned forward, and touched the constable on the arm.

"Now then, nevvy, we'll just follow him;" he said; and he jerked his thumb slightly towards a big negro who was leaving the bar at that moment.

The man looked rough and powerful, and had something of the appearance of a mariner who had made enough money to live ashore in comfort; for he was wearing quite a well-cut suit, double-breasted, with an inflamed tie, and a tie-pin that winked like a true diamond.

The two of them trailed the man as far as the outskirts, and saw him put his latchkey into the door of a respectable looking house, with "Apartments" in the window.

"Come along," whispered Cobbler Juk quickly. "We'll nab him outside. It'll only mean a lot of broken furniture if we let him go in. Come on!"

He led the way, at a run, and his nephew after him. Together they got hold of the negro, but found they were in for more even than Juk had expected.

The man was immensely powerful. He tore the old man's grip from his arm, and hurled him backwards, then, with the speed and skill of a man accustomed to using his hands, he turned on the big policeman, and upper-cut him savagely. He followed the blow by a terrific drive on the mark, which drove the constable into a heap on to the pavement. Then, with one bound, he was down the steps; but here Cobbler Juk rose and pluckily grabbed at him. Yet the negro proved himself no brute, now that he had only the one small opponent. He freed himself with a swift, easy strength, without attempting to strike, much as a grown man might free himself from the grip of a boy; then, with marvellous speed, he sped away out of the gate and into the night.

"Lost him!" groaned Cobbler Juk. "Wonder why the big divvil didn't plug me good and hard?"

Then he went slowly up to his nephew, who was huddled very still.

He rang the bell, and as soon as the man of the house came they got the constable inside and on to the floor, where, between them, they brought him round, all the while that the cobbler explained something of their errand.

"Now," said old Juk as soon as the policeman came round," you lie quiet there a bit; I'm itching to have a look into that nigger's room. I'll give up detecting for good an' all if I ain't on the track this time."

Half an hour later he was downstairs, with a number of things stuffed into a pillow-case. "If you're feelin' fit now, nevvy," he said, "we'll away to the shop, an' I guess I've one or two things as 'll s'prise you. Come along."

VI

"Wait while I get goin'," said Cobbler Juk, sitting down on the little bench in his shop and reaching for his last.

"Now, you just listen, nevvy, while I gets it all straightened out. I'll tell it all to the chief in the morning, an' I guess I'm goin' to bother 'im for that ten pounds he offered me.

"You'll mind that I had a look round on my own after old Cap'n Chappel was killed. You told me just after he was found, an' I an away up as soon as you'd gone, for I was cur'us to see what I could make of it, though I never meant to give way to detecting. Well, nevvy; that's when I got my first cloo. Quite near where old Chappel was picked up I got these."

He reached over to his table, and lifted an old tobacco-box out of the litter. From the box he took five broken matches, which he spread out gently on the palm of his hand for his nephew to examine.

"Can't see no cloo there, uncle," muttered the big man, scratching his head after a prolonged and earnest stare. "They're just used matches."

"Wait a bit, lad," replied Cobbler Juk, "while I jumps on a peg.

"I got proper interested in the case, an' I did some inquirin' round. Things was pretty easy to come on. I found as old Cap'n Chappel an' the saddler and Councillor Tompkins was wonderful pally; especially when you come to think they was different in position. I drummed up with Mister Timmins, the councillor's butler, an he was able to tell me a s'prisin' lot that I'd never have thought on maybe for a divvil of a while by me lonesome.

"I spent a matter of five and fourpence on that tub, treatin' him, before I'd got all he knew; an' that wasn't much; only sometimes he'd heard the three of 'em, after a tidy little dinner, get warm and merry, and crack some mighty funny yarns over their wine.

"You'd never have thought it, nevvy, to look at the saddler, and him like a little bladder of fat, as you might say; or the councillor himself, for that matter, with him bein' so mighty respectable an' a good enough citizen, too; but, if I was to believe some of the yarns that old Timmins told, them three men had been to sea together on some mighty rum doin's; an' a lot of it to do with poachin' seal skins, or whatever they calls it.

"Well, the next thing I did was to go to old Mulberry, the photographer, an' make him an offer for three old prints he'd got of the three of 'em. He'd had 'em in his showcase, with a hundred more, till they was all faded. I got the three for ninepence; an' I sent the three pictures off to an old chum of mine in Liverpool, with a bit of a letter, sayin' I'd like to know what he could find out for me.

"Well, I guess, nevvy, it was all right what the butler had told me. My friend knew old Cap'n Chappel by reputation, an' he said he'd been a proper bad lot; had one ship confiscated for poachin' or something, an' done time.

"He got news for me about him we've called Saddler Atkins. He wasn't a saddler at all; he was a furrier or somethin' of that sort; an' he sailed with the cap'n. (I always said he never did know a piece of good leather!) His name wasn't Atkins, but Frames. As for the councillor, he was a shipowner in a small way; an' he fitted the cap'n out for his last trip, an' went with him; an' from some accounts, it seems they was suspected of doin' a bit more than sea-poachin'; an' that there's more 'n one good ship they robbed, an' murdered all aboard, an' then sunk. At least, my friend says there's a lot of funny tales went round the docks, but nothin' that no one could prove. Only they all three came off that last voyage with a heap of cash, an' never went back to sea again. They'd a fresh crew when they come back; so that no one could trace anythin' proper against 'em.

"An' after that they come inland a bit, to our town; and just settled down away from the sea, as if they was glad to be quit of it. My friend said in his letter, maybe they wasn't anxious to be in a seaport, where folks as knew too much about 'em might come on them any time.

"Now, don't get impatient, nevvy. I'm comin' to the cloo of them matches. You see, what my friend said about them not bein' anxious, maybe, to live in a seaport, where they might be recognised, got me thinkin' they might have some mighty bitter enemies; an' maybe one of them had found them out, and meant getting even for some dirty thing they'd been concerned in away back in the years.

"Anyway, I guessed, if it was someone as they'd harmed, the saddler would be put away next; an' I warned him. He took it serious, too; an' I'm mighty surprised he went out after dark, seein' he must have known somethin' of what might be after 'em. I'd have warned Councillor Tompkins same time as the saddler, but I guessed that Atkins would pass the word on to him, an' you see, I wasn't so sure about the councillor; for my friend couldn't trace out his part at first. I only knew for certain from a second letter he sent me, that I got the evening the saddler was killed. That's what made me middlin' sure he'd be the next; an' so I sets you to keep an eye on him."

Cobbler Juk, broke off his talk, and reached his palm out to his nephew.

"Take another look, nevvy, at them matches," he said. "Do you see there ain't one of them but's broke in half with a little twist to the wood, an' without one of 'em bein' broke clean in two. Well, now, I used the bit of brains I was born with. I says to myself: Mister Juk, what's five matches, all *broke the same way* an' lyin' in the same spot, close to the body of a murdered man, mean? Well, says I to myself, it's mighty likely as the one that broke one match broke all; an' it's like that he stood there a goodish bit, waitin'; for if he'd struck all them matches in a hurry he'd never have stopped to fumble them afterwards an' twist 'em in his fingers, fiddlin' like. And, I says to myself, I got to find who waited there, an' what he was waiting there for.

The next thing I had to help me was when the saddler was done out. You'll mind how I went there straight away. Well, lad, I found seven more of them matches spread up and down the pavement, all twisted the same way; here they are."

And he pulled his snuffbox out of his vest pocket, and poured seven matches, broken and twisted in the same way as the first five.

"I knew then, in my mind, for certain, that what killed the cap'n had sure killed the saddler, or leastways, the same man had been near about the same time. And I wanted to know what that man knew. Only, this occasion he'd walked up an' down, waitin'; an' longer than he'd waited for the cap'n; for he'd lit his pipe more often. Mind you, this ain't sure; for maybe the wind had blown out some of the matches, an' he'd had to strike extra; only in that case he'd not have stopped to fidget with the matches, waitin', I'm thinkin'—see, nevvy?

"Now I got a fresh notion. The man that stood near where the cap'n had been murdered would sure have been noticed standin' while he was waitin'. And I got to wondering why he'd walked up and down, same as when he held ready for the saddler. Then I minded that he'd sure never stood in the street at all; for he'd have been seen by P.c. Dobell as he was running away. And then it was that I got good and strong on to the job. The man that had been near when the cap'n was killed was never in the street at all. He'd been leanin' over the high, blank wall, waitin', an' smokin' while he kept a watch for the cap'n coming out of the Spread Eagle.

"And the blank wall on that side is the wall of the Spread Eagle bowling-green; so that the man had been in the Spread Eagle, and slipped out on to the bowling-green; an' had stood on an old barrel—as I found after—and looked over the wall, smokin' while he waited for the cap'n to leave, which he always did, nevvy, about half-past nine, as we know.

"I put in a good many hours after that, going round to the different bars and gettin' chummy with the barmen and sweepers. I got them to keep all the sweepings for me, and I went through them each day; for it was pretty like as the man that went into the Spread Eagle would go into other pubs.

"Yesterday but one I located a number of them twisted matches in the floor sweepings of the Slade Arms; an' all that evenin' I sat there, watchin' the different men that came in an' had a drink an' a smoke; but I couldn't get onto no one. I did the same last evenin'; but he must have been in before me, and left; for there was some of them same twisted matches on the floor near the bar.

"Both evenings, after I'd left, I come along quietly to see how you was gettin' on, nevvy; for I was pretty sure they'd not let the councillor rest long. And now I got the whole business in my fist, as you might say—"

He stopped, and stooped for the pillowcase, which he began to untie.

"You saw that great, unnatcheral creature last night, nevvy," he continued— "well, here, I brought along the devvil's head."

And he teemed out of the pillow-case a huge, stuffed seal's head.

"It was yon nigger, without a doubt, lad," he continued. "He was stripped last night, an' he'd fixed this thing up on his top knot. An, I guess it meant a deal to yon wicked old Tompkins as we've no idee of. Them three rogues had sure been concerned in some dirty job as harmed the nigger. Did you notice the sound he made with his mouth, an' never a word he said to-night? Well, I'm wondering what they must have done on him way back in the years. If he's caught, maybe we'll learn, an' maybe we won't. But I hopes as you policemen, you'll never lay a hand on him. I'd be very well pleased. I believe he gave them three divvils no more than was comin' to them; an' he let me off gentle to-night. I don't forget that.

"I should think, nevvy, as he'd been concerned in their sealin' business, an' maybe worse; an' when I thinks of it, I gets wonderin' if they'd cut the poor heathen's tongue out, so as he couldn't give 'em away; yet so as they could use him. What so be it is they done to him and others, I'm mighty sure it was as bad as could be. I always said yon saddler man never did know a piece of good leather when he saw it!

"Good-night, nevvy. You go along to the station an' make the proper report. I'll come up an' see the chief in the morning, an, I'll be askin' for that ten pounds of mine. An' if you wasn't so mighty big in the body an' small in the head, it could have been yours, if you'd use your eyes and the bit of brains you was born with! Good-night, lad."

The Home-Coming of Captain Dan

FOR A STORY OF exact fact, I think that this is just about as extraordinary as a professional storyteller could desire. It concerns the treasure of Captain Dan, known in his youth as merely Dan, in the village of Geddley on the South Coast.

With the youth of Captain Dan, which occurred—if I may so phrase it—prior to 1737, I have nothing to tell, except that, being "wild like", and certainly lacking in worldly "plenishings", he was no credit to the respectability of that quiet seaport village.

In consequence of this double stigma of commission and omission, he went away to sea, taking his wildness and his poverty along with him; on which it is conceivable that the respectable matrons and maidens of Geddley sighed, though, possibly, with somewhat different feelings.

There you have the whole tale of Dan's youth in a few words; that is, so far as Geddley is concerned.

Twenty years later he returned, with an ancient and ugly scar from right eyebrow to chin, and two enormous iron-bound chests, whose weight was vouched for by the men he hired to carry them to the old Tunbelly Hostel, that same Tunbelly Inn being fronted on the old High Street Alley, which has been done away this twenty years and more.

Now, if young Dan had lacked of friends and kindliness in his wild and youthful days of poverty, the returned *Captain* Dan had no cause for complaint on such score.

For no sooner had he declared his name and ancient kinship to the village than there were a dozen to remember him and shake him by the hand in token of those older days, when—as they seemed strangely to forget—there had been no such general desire to grip hands and invite him to sundries of that which both cheers and inebriates.

Yet, at the first of it, there seemed to be every reason to suppose that Captain Dan had forgotten the slights and disrespect that had been put upon the one-time Dan; for he accepted both the hands and the liquors that were offered to him; and these, I need scarcely say, were not stinted when word of those weighty iron-bound chests had gone through the little port; for there was scarcely a man who could refrain from calling in the Tunbelly to welcome "Old Dan, coom back agen. Cap'n Dan, sir, beggin' your pardin!"

As that first evening of warm welcoming of the returned and now *respectable* citizen of Geddley wore onward, Cap'n Dan warmed to the good liquor that came so plentiful and freely, and insisted on dancing a hornpipe upon the bar-table. At the conclusion of the warm applause which followed this feat, he declared his intention of showing them that Cap'n Dan was as good as the best— " 'S good asser besht," he assured the bar-room generally a great many times; and finally shouted to some of them to bring in his two great chests, which was done without argument or delay, a thing, perhaps, easy to understand.

They were set in the middle of the floor, and all the men in the room crowded round, with their beer-mugs, to watch. But at this point, Cap'n Dan proved he was quite uncomfortably sober; for he ordered every man to stand back, enforcing his suggestion with a big, brass-mounted pistol, which he brought very suddenly out of a long pocket in the skirts of his heavy coat.

Having assured himself of a clear space all around his precious chests, Cap'n Dan pocketed the big, brass-mounted pistol, and pulled out a big snuffbox from which he took ample refreshment. He then dug in amid the snuff with one great, powder-blackened forefinger, and presently brought to view two smallish keys. He replaced the snuffbox in his vest pocket, and set the keys against the side of his big nose, exclaiming, with a kind of half-drunken knowingness, in French: *"Tenons de la verge d'une ancre!"* which most of those present understood, being sailormen and in the free-trade, to mean literally the "nuts of the anchor"; but used at that time as a marine catch-phrase, as much as to say, "the key of the situation"; though often used also in a coarser manner.

"Tout le monde a son poste!" he shouted, with a tipsy laugh; and turned to unlock the nearer chest.

There were two great locks on each chest, and a separate key was used for each and the interest was quite undoubted as the cap'n turned back the bolts and lifted the lid of the chest. Upon the top of all there were four long wooden cases containing charts. These he lifted out, and put with surprising care upon the floor. Afterwards there came a quadrant, wrapped in an old pair of knee-breeches; then a compass similarly wrapped in an old body vest. Both of these he put down upon the four chart-cases with quite paternal tenderness.

He reached again into the chest, lurching, and hove out onto the floor a pile of heavily braided uniforms, a pair of great sea boots with iron leg-guards stitched in on each side of the tops, a big Navy cutlass, and two heavy Malay knives without sheaths. And all the time, as he ladled out these somewhat "tarry" treasures, there was no sound in the big, low-ceilinged room, except the heavy breathings of the interested menfolk of Geddley.

Cap'n Dan stood up, wiped his forehead briefly with the back of his hand, and stooped again into the chest, seeming to be fumbling round for something, for the sound of his rough hands going over the wooden inside of the chest was plain to be heard.

Presently he gave a satisfied little grunt, and immediately afterwards there was a sharp click, which, as the landlord of the Tunbelly told certain of his special cronies afterwards, was a sure sign of there "Bein' a secret lock-fast" within the chest. Be this as it may: the next instant Captain Dan pulled a thick wooden cover or partition, bolted with flat iron bands, out of the chest, and hove it with a crash onto the floor. There he stooped, and began to make plain to the men of Geddley the very good and sufficient reason for the immense weight of the two great chests; for he brought out a canvas bag about the size of a man's head, which he dropped with a dull, ringing thud onto the floor. Five more of these he brought out, and threw beside the first; and all the time no sound, save the breathing of the onlookers and an occasional hoarse whisper of excited suggestion.

Cap'n Dan stood up as he threw the sixth bag upon the others, and signed dumbly for his brandy-mug, with the result that he had half a score offered to him, as we say in these days, gratis. He took the first, and drained it; then threw it across the room, where it smashed against the far wall. Yet this provoked no adverse comment even from the fat landlord of the Tunbelly; for those six bulging, heavy bags on the floor stood sponsors for many mugs, and, it is to be supposed, the contents thereof.

It will be the more easily understood that no one bothered to remark upon Cap'n Dan's method of disposing of his crockeryware when you realise that the captain had squatted down upon the floor beside his bags, and was beginning to unlash the neck of one. There was not a sound in the room as he took off the last turn of spunyarn stopper; for each man of Geddley held his breath with suspense and expectation. Then Cap'n Dan, with a quite admirable unconcern, capsized the bag upside-down upon the floor, and cascaded out a heap of coins that shone with a dull golden glitter.

There went a gasp of astonishment, echoing from man to man round the room, and then a chorus of hoarse exclamations, for no man here had ever seen quite so much gold at one time in his life. Yet Cap'n Dan took no heed, but, with a half-drunken soberness, proceeded to unlash the necks of the five other bags, and to empty them likewise upon the contents of the first.

And by the time that the gold from the sixth bag had been added to the heap the silence of the men of Geddley was a stunned and bitter and avaricious silence, broken at last by the fat landlord of the Tunbelly, who, with a nice presence of mind, came forward with the brandy-keg under his arm, and a generous-sized beer mug, which was surely a fit spirit measure for the owner of so prodigious a fortune.

Cap'n Dan was less appreciative of this tender thoughtfulness than might have been supposed, for, with a mixed vocabulary of forceful words, chosen discriminately from the French and English, he intimated that the landlord of the Tunbelly should retire, possibly with all the honours of war, but *certainly* with speed.

And, as the stout proprietor of the Tunbelly apparently failed to grasp the full and imperative necessity of speed, Cap'n Dan plucked his big brass-mounted pistol from the floor beside him, and let drive into the brandy-keg which reposed, as you know, under the well-intending arm of the fat Drinquobier, this being, as you may as well learn here, the landlord's name. The bullet drove through the little keg, and blew out the hither end, wasting a deal of good liquor, and scored the head of Long John of Kenworth, who came suddenly to a state of fluency, but was unheeded by the majority of the men of Geddley, who were gathered round the stout landlord of the Tunbelly, where he lay like a mountain of flesh upon the floor of the taproom, shouting at the top of his fat and husky voice that he was shot, and shot dead at that—which seemed to impress his customers with a conviction of truth.

But as for Cap'n Dan, he sat calmly upon the floor beside his heap of gold coinage, and began unemotionally to shovel it back into the six canvas bags, lashing each one securely, as it was filled. Presently, still unheeding of the death-cries of the very much alive landlord, he rose slowly to his feet, and began to replace the gold in the big chest, replying to Long John of Kenworth's rendering of the Commination Service merely by drawing forth a second heavy pistol, and laying it ready to his hand across a corner of the chest.

In course of time, the fat landlord having discovered that he still breathed, and Long John of Kenworth having considered discreetly the possibilities of that second pistol, there was a period of comparative quiet once more in the big taproom, during which Cap'n Dan methodically completed his re-storage of his goods in the chest, and presently locked it securely with the two keys.

When this was finally achieved, a sudden silence of renewed interest came down upon the men of Geddley as the captain proceeded to unlock the second chest, which, though, somewhat smaller than the other, was yet considerably the heavier.

Cap'n Dan lifted back the ponderous lid, and there, displayed to view, was the picture of an enormous skull, worked in white silk on a background of black bunting. It was evident that the captain had forgotten, in his half-drunken state, that this lay uppermost in the chest; for he made now a hurried and clumsy movement to turn back the folds of the flag upon itself so as to hide the emblem, which was uncomfortably familiar in that day. Yet that the men of Geddley had seen was obvious, for there came a general cry from the mariners present, some of whom had been privateersmen and worse, of "The Jolly Roger! The Jolly Roger!"

Cap'n Dan stood a moment in a seeming stupid silence, with the flag all bunched together in his hand; then suddenly he turned, and flirted it out wide across the floor, so that the skull and the crossed bones, surmounted by a big D, showed plain. Underneath the D there was worked an hour-glass in red wool. The men of Geddley crowded round, handling the flag, and criticising the designs with something of the eyes of experts; some of them, and notably Long John of Kenworth, saying that it was no proper Jolly Roger, seeing that it held no battleaxe.

And on this a general and forceful discussion ensued, which ended in a physical demonstration of their views on the part of Long John of Kenworth, and a square, heavy privateersman, during which Cap'n Dan hauled the flag out of the midst of the discussion, and began to bundle it back into the chest, which he did so clumsily that he disturbed a layer of underclothing which covered the lower contents, and, displayed to view that the chest was nearly two-thirds full of smashed and defaced gold and silver work of every description, from the gold hilts of swords and daggers, to the crumpled golden binding of some great Bible, showing burst jewel-sockets from which precious stones had been roughly prised.

At sight of all this new treasure, the value of which was plainly enormous, a great silence came upon the room, broken only by the scuffling and grunting of the two who were setting forth their arguments upon the floor of the taproom. So marked was this silence that even these two at last became aware of something fresh, and scrambled to their feet to participate. And they, also, joined in the general hush of astonished awe and avarice and, what cannot be denied, renewed and intense respect for this further proof of the desirable worth of the returned citizen of Geddley.

And the cap'n, realising in his half-drunken pride the magnitude of the sensation he bad created, and the supremeness of the homage that he had won, shut down the lid of the chest and locked it with the two keys, which he afterwards returned to the snuffbox, bedding them well down into the snuff, and shutting the box with a loud snap, after he had once more refreshed his nose sufficiently.

"Be you not goin' to turn out t'other, cap'n?" asked Long John of Kenworth, in a marvellously courteous voice—that is, considering the man.

"Non," said Captain Dan, with that brevity of courtesy so admired in the wealthy; for it is likely enough that the wealth contained in those two great chests was sufficient to have bought up the whole of the port of Geddley, and a good slice of the country round about it, lock, stock, and barrel, as the saying goes.

Now, when the captain had so wittily described his intention, he pulled out a small powder-flask from his side pocket, and proceeded, in a considerable silence, to recharge the fired pistol, which he did with a quite peculiar dexterity, speaking of immense practice, and this despite his half-drunken condition. When he had finished ramming down a couple of soft-lead bullets upon the charge of powder, he primed the lock, replaced the flask, and announced his intention of turning in—i.e., going to bed—which he achieved with remarkable speed by dragging the two chests together in the middle of the tap-room, and using them as a couch, with his rolled-up coat as a pillow; and so in a moment he composed himself with a grunt, his loaded pistols stuffed in under the coat, and his great right hand resting on the butts.

And so he seemed to be instantly asleep. Yet it is a curious thing that once when Long John stepped over towards him, after a bout of whispering with several of the men in the room, Cap'n Dan opened one bleary eye, and, without undue haste, thrust out one of his big pistols in an indifferent manner at the body of Long John, whereat that gentleman stepped back without even attempting to enter into any argument on the score of intention.

After this little episode, the cap'n once more returned to his peculiar mode of slumbering; but there was no longer any whispering on the part of Long John of Kenworth and his mates. Instead, a quite uncomfortable silence obtained an unwonted permission in the taproom broken presently by the departing feet of this man and that man, until the place was empty, save for the fat landlord, who leaned against the great beer-tub and regarded the sleeping captain in a meditative and puzzled fashion.

The landlord's pondering was interrupted disagreeably; for slowly one of the sleeping captain's eyes opened, and a curiously disturbing look was fixed upon the fat landlord for the space of perhaps a full minute. Then Captain Dan extended a great hand towards the landlord, and in the hand was one of his big, brass-bound pistols, the muzzle towards Master Drinquobier. For a little space the captain directed the pistol thus, whilst the landlord shrivelled visibly in a queer, speechless fashion.

"Tenons de la verge d'une ancre!" said Captain Dan, even as he had said it once before that evening.

He tapped the pistol with his other hand to emphasise the remark, and sat on the bigger chest, still looking at the landlord.

"So," he said at last, speaking in English, "you're thinkin' to go halves with Long John o' Kenworth, ye gowk Tunbelly. You 'm waitin' now, beer-hog, to give them the signal; to enter when I'm gone over, ye soft; an' think to fool Dan easyways; an' I knowin' what ye meant, an' they only without in enter-porch, ye fat fool! Out with you, smartly! Out, I say!"

And therewith he flung the loaded pistol at the landlord's head; but he dodged, quite cleverly, for so fat a man, and the weapon exploded against the wall with a great crash of sound; whilst the landlord ran heavily for the door, tore it open, and fell headlong out into the passageway, whilst within the empty taproom the captain sat on the chest and shook with a kind of grim laughter.

Presently he rose from the chest, after he had heard the landlord go scrambling away in clumsy fright upon his hands and knees. He stood a few minutes, listening intently; then, seeming to hear something, he ran with surprising nimbleness to the door, pushed it silently to, and set down the socket-bar across from side to side, so that the door would have to be broken down before anyone could enter. Then he bent forward to listen, and in a little while heard the faint sound of bare feet without in the passage; and soon a soft, gentle fumbling at the door.

"Depasser!" he shouted, roaring with a kind of half-laughter, half-anger. Then, in English: "You've overrun your reckoning, my lads! Get below and turn in!"

And, with the word, he turned unconcernedly from the door and went back to his rough couch, and presently was sleeping unemotionally, whilst without the door the men, who had come with some hope of surprising him, departed with muffled but considerable fluency, and an unabated avarice.

And thus, and in this manner exactly, was the home-coming of Captain Dan, pirate (presumably), and now (certainly) a most desirable citizen of the port of Geddley.

Captain Dan waked early, and rolled off his uncomfortable bed. He walked across to the shelf where the brandy kegs were stored, and helped himself to a generous tot; after which he went over to the door, unbarred it and opened it, and bellowed the landlord's name, calling him also old Tunbelly and beer-hog, and cursing him between whiles in both French and English, until he came tumbling clown the creaking stair in a very fluster of dismay.

Breakfast, was Cap'n Dan's demand. Breakfast, and speedily and plentifully, and if the maids were not up yet, then it was time they turned out, and old Tunbelly could prepare the meal himself and serve it to him in the taproom, upon one of his big chests. Meanwhile, he applied himself methodically to the brandy keg, varying his occupation with occasional bellows through the quiet of the inn for the meal he had ordered.

It came presently, and he squatted sideways upon the narrow chest and set to work. As he ate, he asked the landlord questions about this and that woman of the port, who—when he had gone off to sea all these twenty years gone—had been saucy maids, but now were mostly mothers of families, if he could believe all the fat Drinquobier told him.

"Eh," said Cap'n Dan, wiping his mouth with the back of his hand, "there was some saucy ones among the lot when I was a younker. An' how's young Nancy Drigg doin'?"

"She be Nancy Garbitt these thirteen year, Cap'n Dan, sir," said the landlord.

Whereat the, captain ceased his eating a moment to hark the better. "Eh?" he said, in a curious voice at last. "Married that top-o'-my-thumb Jimmy Garbitt? *Dieu*, but I'll cut the throat of him this same day! The sacred man-sprat! The blandered bunch o' shakin's!"

"He'm dead these yere two years, cap'n," said Drinquobier, staring hard at Captain Dan with half-frightened and wholly curious eyes. "I heerd oncst 's ye as sweet-ways on Nancy. No offence! No offence, cap'n! Seven, Jimmy left be'ind, an' all on 'em maids at that."

"What!" cried Captain Dan, with a sudden strange anger, and threw his brandy mug at the landlord's head.

But afterwards he was silent for a time, neither eating nor speaking, only frowning away to himself.

"An' Nancy Drigg herself!" he asked, at length. "How 'm she lookin' these days, ye old Tunbelly? Seven on 'em! Seven on 'em, an' to that blundering bunch o' shakin's! Why don't ye answer, you bilge-guzzlin' beer-cask! Open your face, ye— ye—"

"Fair, cap'n, sir; fair an' bonny like, Cap'n Dan," old Drinquobier interjected, with frightened haste; his frontal appendage quivering like a vast jelly, until the form shook on which he sat.

"Ah!" said the captain, and was quiet again; but a minute afterwards he made it pointedly clear to the landlord that he needed a timber-sled to be outside of the inn, speedily. "An' half a dozen of thy loafer lads, Tunbelly, do ye hear! An' smart, or I'll put more than beer betwixt thy wind and water, ye old cut-throat, that must set a respectable townsman to sleep with his pistols to hand all the long night in this inn of yours lest ye an' your louts do him a mischief! Smartly, ye beer-swiller, wi' yon sled, an' smartly does it, or I'll be knowin' the why!"

And evidently smartly did do it, as we say; for in a very few minutes Captain Dan was superintending, pistol in hand, the transferring of his two great chests to the sled, by the hands of a dozen brawny longshore men who had been fished out of various handy sleeping places by the fearful landlord.

Cap'n Dan sat himself down upon his chests, and signalled to the horse-boy to drive on. But, as he started to move, the fat landlord discovered, somewhere in his monstrous body, the remnant of a one-time courage, and came forward towards the sled, crying out that he would be paid for liquor, bed, and board.

At this Cap'n Dan raised one of his pistols; evidently with the full intention of ending, once and for all, the entire agitation of the landlord's avaricious soul. But, suddenly thinking better of it, he drew out a couple of guineas, which he hove in among the little crowd of shore-boys, shouting to them to get their fill of good beer to the hatchways, and the change might go to pay his debts to Drinquobier. He did this knowing full well that no change would the landlord ever see out of those two guineas; and so sat back, roaring with laughter, and shouting to the horse-boy to "Crack on sail an' blow the sticks out o' her!" Which resulted in the lad laying his cudgel repeatedly and forcibly across the hindquarters of the animal, which again resulted in the beast changing its walk to a kind of absurd amble, which in its turn resulted in the sled bounding and bumping along down the atrociously paved street dignified by the name of the High Street Alley, so that the last the group around the doorway of the Tunbelly saw was the broad, heavy figure of Cap'n Dan jolting and rolling on the top of his great chests, and trying to take aim at the horse-boy with one of his big brass-bound pistols, the while he bellowed to the lad to shorten sail, and likewise to be damned as before.

And so they went, rattling and hanging round the corner, out of sight; the clatter and crashing of the heavy sled punctuated twice by the reports of the captain's pistols. After which he was content to hold on, and curse the boy, horse, sled, the landlord of the Tunbelly, and the road, all with equal violence, until, in a minute, the lad once more got the horse controlled to a walk, and was cursing back pluckily at the cap'n for loosing off his pistols at him. And this way they came presently to a little house in the lower end of the alley, where the boy stopped the sled and his cursing all in the same moment, and pointed with his horse-cudgel to the door of the little house, meaning that they had come to the place.

At this Cap'n Dan got down lumberingly from the top of his big chests; and suddenly, before the boy knew his intention, he had caught him by the collar of his rough jacket, and hoist him bodily from the ground. Whereupon the lad, full as ever of his strange pluck, set-to to curse him again—so well as he might, being half strangled—and to striking at him with the horse-cudgel.

Immediately the captain plucked the cudgel from him, and then, setting the lad's feet to the road again, he hauled forth a great handful of gold pieces, which he crammed forcibly down the back of the boy's neck, shaking with queer, noiseless laughter the while.

"A good plucked 'un! *Dieu*, a good plucked 'un!" he said; and loosed the lad suddenly, applying one of his big sea-boots with indelicate dexterity, to intimate that he had no further need of his services.

Whereupon the lad, who had ceased now to curse, ran off down the alley a little way, and commenced to shake himself, until all the gold had come through; after which he gathered it up, and, calling to his horse, mounted the sled, and away so fast as the brute would go.

Meanwhile, Cap'n Dan was pounding at the door of the house, and shouting lustily the name of Nancy Drigg, outside the door of Nancy Garbitt; until presently a startled feminine face came out of a lattice above, and seeing him, she screamed out, "Dan! Dan!" and withdrew hurriedly from sight.

"What do you want?" she, asked presently, from within the room, and not showing herself.

"Open!" shouted the cap'n; "afore I has the door down. I'm coom to board wi' ye, Nance. Open, I say!"

And he commenced to kick at the door with his great sea-boots.

"Husht now, Dan! You 'm the drink in you, or you'd no think to shame a lone woman this fashion. Husht now, an' I'll coom down and let 'ee in."

Whereupon the cap'n ceased from his kicking, and turned round to survey the various heads that had been thrust from the casements of the alley about, to discover the cause of the disturbance.

"Bon quart! Bon quart!" he called, at first good-humouredly; but, changing his tone as he saw they still continued to stare at him, "Bon quart! Bon quart!" he roared angrily; and aimed with one of his discharged pistols at the head of the nearest.

The flint snapped harmlessly, and the head dodged back; but the captain hauled a fresh weapon from the skirts of his long coat, and, seeing that he was still spied upon from a window higher up, he let drive in sound earnest, and very near ended the life of the onlooker; after which the alley might have held only the dead for all the living that displayed themselves to his view. He turned again, and commenced to kick upon the door, shouting. And in the same instant it was opened by Nancy, hurriedly wrapped about with her quilt.

"Husht now! Husht now, Dan, an' coom in sober-like," she said, "or 'tis only the outside of the door I'll have to 'ee."

The captain stepped inside, and turned on her.

"Nice wumman ye, Nancy Drigg, to splice that blandered bunch o' shakin's, Jimmy Garbitt. An' seven ye've had to him; an' not a man in the lot—an' little wonder; ye that could not wait for y'r own man to come home wi' the fortune I promised ye, but must marry a top-o'-my-thumb. Shame on ye for a poor-sperreted wench; an' me this moment wi' the half o' oor silver penny to my knife chain that we broke all them years gone; an' never a throat I cut but I ses, 'There be another gold piece to my Nancy!' An' you go spliced to that—"

"Husht, Dan!" said Nancy at last, not loudly but with surprising firmness. "You be proper an' decent wi' me, Dan, an' good care I'll take of 'ee, an' put up wi' 'ee so well as I may, for owd sake's sake. Put no word at poor Jimmy, an' nowt to trouble my maids, or out ye go to the sharks o' Geddley, an' clean they'll pluck ye, as well ye know."

"An' well they fear me, an' well can I mind my own!" said the captain warmly, yet unmistakably more civil in his manner; for he felt that if Nancy Garbitt would take him in, then, at least, he need fear no traitors in the camp, as the saying goes.

"I'm troubled wi' a sick pain in th' heart, Nancy, an' can't last long," he said, after little pause. "Will I pay ye a gold piece every week-ending, or will I pay ye nothin' an' you have the will of me when I go below?"

"I'll trade on no man's death, Dan; an' least on yours," said Nancy. "Pay me the guinea-piece each week, an' well I'll' do by 'ee, as you know, Dan. An' do 'ee be easy with drinkin' an' ill-livin', an' many a year you 'm boun' to live yet."

And so it was arranged:

"An' you keep the seven brats out of my course!" said the cap'n.

"Dan!" said Nancy.

"*Pardieu*, Nance! No ill to it! No ill to it!" apologised Cap'n Dan. "You 'm pretty lookin' yet, wi' the sperret that's in ye, Nance," he concluded.

At which compliment Nancy's eyes softened a little, so that it was like enough that she still had in a corner of her heart a gentle feeling towards this uncouth sea-dog of a man who had been her lover in her youth.

And this way came, and settled, and presently died, Captain Dan; and with his death there arose the seven-year mystery of the treasure, which to this day maybe read in the "Records of the Parish of Geddley; by John Stockman, 1797."

And regarding the length of life still coming to him, Cap'n Dan was right; for he lived no more than some eighteen or nineteen months— date uncertain—after the arrangement mentioned above. And these are the concluding details of his life.

For some months he lived quietly enough with Nancy Garbitt, paying her regularly, and amenable to her tongue, even in his most fantastic fits of humour, whether bred of drink or of his state of health. Eventually, however, his little room was broken into one dark night whilst he slept. But the captain proved conclusively that he was well able to defend both life and fortune; for he used his pistols and, later, his cutlass to such effect that when the raiders drew off there lay three dead and one wounded on the floor of his room, whose groans so irritated Cap'n Dan that he went over to him, and, picking up one of the overturned lanterns from the floor, passed his cutlass twice or thrice through him to quieten him, remarking as he did so: "I knew I'd ha' to fix 'ee, Tunbelly, afore I was done wi' ye." (For he recognised the landlord's corporation, despite the masks which he and all the robbers had worn.) "An' here's luck—an' you're sure goin' easy."

And he jabbed him conscientiously for the last time.

The direct result of this raid was that Cap'n Dan resolved to build himself a house that would make him and all his treasures secure in future from an attack of this sort. To this end he had masons by coach from a great distance—as distances were counted great in those days—and, acting as his own architect, he planned out a strange great house in the form of a ship in masonry, with a double tier of iron-barred windows in place of ports, and three narrow towers like modern lighthouses, to take the place of masts, with stairs inside so that they could be used for look-out posts.

There was one great door in the stern, which was hung on pintles, from the sternpost, like a huge and somewhat abnormally shaped rudder. Somewhere below this ship-house there was built a strong-room, though this was not known till later; for as soon as the masons had done their work they were sent back to their own towns, and in this way the secrets of the house were hidden from the men of Geddley.

It may be as well to say here that this peculiar house, minus its three towers, which had long since been removed, was to be seen almost intact as late as 1871. It had become built in, "bow-and-stern", into a terrace of houses, which still form what is known as Big Fortune Terrace, and was then an inn, run by one Thomas Walker, under the name of the Stone Ship Inn. "Very much in!" used to be the local and extraordinarily witty joke, according to the "New Records" of Geddley, which we owe to Richard Stetson, a citizen, I imagine, of that same quaint seaport.

To revert to Cap'n Dan. As I have said, he concluded his house and "shipped back" his masons to their varied and distant homes, by this means hiding from the men of Geddley all possible details concerning the construction of his stronghold.

Presently he removed with his two great chests of treasure to his new house, and thereafter very little of his doings appear to have been worthy of remark; for, saving an odd walk down to Nancy Garbitt's little cot, or a still rarer visit to the Tunbelly—now under the care of a new landlord—Cap'n Dan, sir, as he was latterly always addressed, appeared but little beyond his own great rudder-door.

After his removal he still continued to pay Nancy her guinea per week, and often assured her, that when he died she should own the whole of his treasure.

And presently, as I have intimated; he died. And certain grave lawyers, if that be the right term, came all the way from Bristol to read his will, which was quaint but simple. The whole of his wealth he left to Nancy Garbitt and her seven daughters, the one condition being that they *must first find it*, one day in each year being allowed only for the search. And if they had no success within and including seven years from his death, then the whole of the treasure—when found—must be handed over entire to a certain person named in a codicil to the will, which was not to be read save in the event of the gold not being found within the said seven years.

As may be imagined, the sensation which this will provoked was profound, not only within the parish of Geddley but throughout the whole county, and beyond.

Eventually, certain of the masons who had assisted in the building of the stone ship-house heard of the will, and sent word that there was a specially built strong-room under the foundations of the house, very cunningly hidden, and under it again there was a sealed vault. For a remuneration one of their number would come by coach and assist at the locating of the place.

This, of course, increased the excitement and general interest; but it was not until the 27th day of September of that year that the search might be made, between the hours of sunrise and sunset, the stone ship-house being occupied meanwhile by the lawyers; caretakers and seals liberally spread about.

On September 26th the mason arrived, accompanied by two of his fellows; the three of them being hired by Nancy Garbitt to act as expert searchers on her behalf. For; very wisely, she had steadfastly refused the enormous amount of "free" aid that had been tendered by the men of Geddley, collectively and singly, from day to day.

The 27th dawned—the anniversary, had Nancy but remembered, of that day, so many years gone, when she and young Dan had broken their silver penny. Surely the date was significant! Nancy Garbitt and her seven daughters *and* the men of Geddley stood near the door of the stone ship-house, with the three masons. As the sun rose into sight the lawyer knocked on the door, and the caretakers opened it and stood back for Nancy, her daughters, and the three masons to enter.

But the men of Geddley had to remain outside, and there waiting, many of them remained the whole of the livelong day, if we are to believe the worthy John Stockman.

Within the house the masons went confidently to work, but at the end of a short time had to acknowledge themselves bewildered. There had been surely other masons to work since they had been sent away, or else the grim old sea-dog himself had turned mason in those last months of his life, for no signs of the hidden entrance to the strong-room could they discover.

At this, after some little discussion, it was resolved to break down through the stone-built floor direct into the strong-room, which the masons asserted to be immediately below a certain point, which they had ascertained by measurements. Yet the evening of that day found them labouring, still lacking the whereabouts of the strong-room. And presently sunset had put an end to the search for a year. And Nancy Garbitt and her seven daughters had to return treasureless to their small cot in the alley.

The second and the third and the fourth years Nancy and her daughters returned, likewise lacking of treasure; but in the fifth year it was evident to Nancy and her maidens that they had come upon signs of the long-lost strong-room. Yet the sunset of the "day of grace" cut short their delving before they could prove their belief.

Followed a year of tense excitement and conjecture; in which Nancy could have married off her daughters to the pick of the men of Geddley; for to every sanguine male it was apparent that the treasure was almost in sight.

Some suggestion there was of carrying the stone ship-house by assault, and prosecuting the search to its inevitable end without further ridiculous delay; but this Nancy would not listen to. Moreover, the strength of the building, and the constant presence of the armed legal guardians thereof, forbade any hope of success along these lines.

In the sixth year Nancy Garbitt died, just before sunset on the day of the search. Her death was possibly due, in part at least, to the long-continued strain of the excitement and the nearing of the hour when the search must be delayed for another whole year. Her death ended the search for that time, though a portion of the actual built-in door of the strong-room itself had been uncovered.

Yet already, as I have said, it had been close to the time when the search must cease.

When the 27th day of September in the seventh year arrived, the men of Geddley made a holiday, and accompanied the seven Misses

Garbitt with a band to the great door of the stone ship-house. By midday the door of the long-shut strong-room was uncovered and a key the lawyer produced was found to fit. The door was unlocked, and the seven maidens rushed in—to emptiness.

Yet, after the first moment of despair, someone remembered the sealed vault which lay under the strong-room. A search was made, and the covering stone found; but it proved an intractable stone, and sunset was nigh before finally it was removed. A candle was lowered into the vault, and a small chest discovered, otherwise the vault was as empty as the strong-room.

The box was brought out into daylight and broken open. Inside was found nothing but the half of a broken silver penny.

At that moment, watch in hand; the lawyer declared that the hour of sunset had arrived, and motioned for silence where was already the silence of despair. He drew from his pocket the package that held the codicil, broke the seal, and proceeded to read to the seven maidens its contents.

They were brief and startling and extraordinary in their revelation of the perversity of the old sea-dog's warped and odd nature. The codicil revealed that the gold for which they had so long searched was still left to Nancy, but that it lay under the stone flags of their own living-room, where the captain had buried it at nights all the long years gone when he had lived at Nancy's, storing the removed earth in the chests in place of the buried gold.

"Seven children have you had, Nancy Drigg, to that top-o'-my-thumb, Jimmy Garbitt," the codicil concluded, "and seven years shall you wait—you who could not wait."

That is all. The money went to the children of Nancy Garbitt, for, by the whimsy of Fate, the woman for whose reproval all this had been planned was never to learn, and the bitter taunt of the broken silver penny was never to reach its mark; for the woman, as you know, was dead. And so ended the seven years' search. And, likewise, this history of the strange but persistent love-affair of Captain Dan, sea-dog and pirate.

Merciful Plunder

CAPTAIN MELLOR, TRADING ALONG the Adriatic coast, had put in at one of those small seaports which found themselves involved in the wars so common in the Balkans. He had stayed the night ashore with a business acquaintance whose veranda, under its cane mat sun roof, commanded a magnificent view over the red slates of the village beyond which he could see his own ship as she lay at anchor, among a dozen others, in the bay.

From the mountains to his left there came every now and again the monstrous far-off grunt of a big gun. For days a prolonged fight had been waging. At times the far-off grunting would merge into a ponderous grumbling of sound, then, the continuous mutter dying away, there came the vast *hrrump, hrrump* of the rifles in the unseen fort that lay round on the eastern shoulders of the hills which sloped away into the sea in the curve of the coast.

Each time the fort fired Captain Mellor felt the iron-framed chair under him tingle, and the windows behind him jarred and thrummed to the huge, ugly sound. Even the silver and green leaves of the olive trees all about the châlet seemed to quiver oddly with the great throb of the vibrated air.

Suddenly he sat up in his chair, his cup of coffee halfway to his lips. Through the still air of the eastern morning came the cries of a lad in agony.

He sickened as he heard with incredible clearness the awful sound. He had refused to go down into the village to see the butchery which the war authorities had dignified with the name of execution, though his friend, a Frenchman, had joined the onlookers at the scene. But he knew by the cries that the punishment was being carried out for twenty of the band of forty youths of the enemy who had been caught

445

the day before fighting out of uniform—a youthful band of "death or glory" irregulars.

And so, hour later; sitting on the quiet balcony amid the silent olives, the drowse and rest of the hushed morning about him, Captain Mellor listened to his host's account of the punishment.

The Frenchman shook with emotion as he described it. He declaimed against it all, though the youths had been taken fighting, out of uniform, upon their own initiative, and firing from ambush against the natives of the place where he lived and did business.

"And to-morrow," he ended, "the osser twenty will be executed, they say."

"No, they won't!" cried Captain Mellor. He jumped up from his chair, mopped his forehead with his red cotton handkerchief, and sat down again.

The Frenchman shrugged his shoulders. He continued his tale of horror and emotion till at last the captain interrupted him.

"If you don't like that sort of thing you should have kept away," he told him. "I don't like it, so I didn't go. After all, I expect the boys got what was coming to them."

"But, *monsieur—Sapristi!* It is terrible so to speak."

His friend's callousness shocked him, and he burst out afresh in horror; but Captain Mellor refused to show overmuch sympathy. Yet without seeming to be interested he managed to get a certain amount of very definite information from the excited Frenchman.

He discovered, for instance, where the second batch of prisoners was locked up. Also how they were guarded. And one or two other details which joined on, as one might say.

"Well," he said at last, "let's finish our business. I am sailing some time to-night."

Later that day the two men went down into the little town and took a walk round the palm-lined public square, where stood the low scaffold in readiness of the next morning.

With the terrible insouciance of the East—for even the Near East is touched with this quality of insensitiveness to the merciful fitness of things—the scaffold was neither more nor less than one of the town's fête platforms, used at half a dozen big festivals in the year.

When Captain Mellor saw it, the front was draped with the black funeral trappings which the townspeople hang round their doors before a funeral. And crowded on the platform were scores of the natives of all ages, standing with strangely morbid pleasure upon the very spot where those boys had met their deaths a few hours previously.

"Come on," said the captain to his friend, "this sickens me."

He dragged the Frenchman down to the water front, where stood the municipal hall. Farther along the quay side was a tall building, outside of which stood a guard, leaning on his rifle.

"Up there, captain," said the Frenchman, "up there where you see the barred window. Zat is the room at the utmost top!"

"Sorry for 'em," replied the captain callously. "But I guess they'll be all right this time to-morrow!"

"Ah!" exclaimed his friend. "You are of all the most hard man I ever speak to."

Yet when Captain Mellor stepped into his boat and was pulled off to his ship that night, he had achieved a knowledge of local geography that would have amazed his friend. He had spurred the little Frenchman by his callous remarks to enlarge upon every detail concerning the twenty prisoners who were to die in the morning. The Frenchman had been incurably voluble and profuse with explanations, intent only to waken some pity in this Englishman.

And all the time Captain Mellor had shrugged his great shoulders and answered inhumanly. But always he had used his eyes, even while he used his ears to take in all the information that his friend insisted on deluging him with.

It was the Frenchman who had suggested they should go to inspect the prisoners. He knew the officer in charge, and he was sure of getting permission. The captain showed no enthusiasm, but submitted to be dragged to the prison. Here after a brief talk, his friend, accompanied by his officer acquaintance and one of the guards, invited him to come and see "the birds".

Never would the captain forget what he saw! The room was just under the roof, and the windows shut fast. There was dirty straw all over the floor, and the prisoners, most of them, were lying silently about.

Not one of them looked up or showed any sign of interest. They were all of them under eighteen, and at least half of them were boys of fourteen and fifteen. Some were wounded and roughly bandaged, and all of them showed marks of ill treatment.

"They'll be gone this time to-morrow," said the sergeant in *patois*, laughing and stubbing out the lighted end of his cigarette stump against the bare leg of one of the prostrate youths. "*Pouf*, they are pigs! Come on out," he added as he led the way downstairs again.

Thus it was that Captain Mellor, as be stepped into his boat that evening, had by the use of ears and eyes and some aid of good fortune, the following knowledge stowed in his big head:

He knew that the twenty boys were locked in the topmost room of that four-storied house which was owned by the mayor of the town. The house was built quite by itself on the edge of the road, with, at the back of it, the sheer, blasted rock face of the cliff that, further to the north, ran out into a long dwindling point of black rock. This cliff stood up within fifteen feet of the rear of the house and rose at least a hundred feet above it.

With regard to the house, the windows of the top room were all barred, and the roof was, like all other houses in the place, of red tiles wired down to the rafters underneath.

The top floor was just one big room, entered by a door at the head of the long flight of stairs. The door was covered with sheet iron on the inside, and the same kind of sheet iron had been nailed over the rafters so as to hide the backs of the naked tiles and prevent them from being removed by any prisoner.

The floor immediately below the prison room was also without partition, and was in use as a temporary guard room; three soldiers being stationed there while the fourth stood on guard at the main entrance to the house. The lower floors were used as temporary offices and headquarters by the military authorities.

The guard at the main entrance was relieved every two hours, and the prisoners were fed morning and evening, and inspected day and night every time the guard was relieved.

From this mass of information which Captain Mellor had accumulated some idea may be had of the good use he had made of his friend's eternal volubility, and of his brief visit to the prison.

When he got aboard he sent word to the chief engineer that he wanted him.

"Is it away we are, George?" asked the chief as he entered the captain's cabin. "It's not sorry I am to be goin'—the murderin' brutes! Did ye see the doin's this mornin'?"

Captain Mellor shook his head.

"Were you there, Mac?" he asked.

"Aye, I was that!" replied the chief engineer. "It was disgusting. Plain beheadin' I've seen, an' plain hangin'; but yon was just brute's work. I tell ye I had me work cut out to keep me hands in me pockets—I had that!"

"Mac," said the captain, "there's twenty more of those boys.

They're going to be treated in the same way tomorrow morning. Mac, are you game to stop it?"

"You can't stop it, George; not without you've a whole bonnie regiment like the Gordons to clean them devils out an' set the dirty place on fire!" answered the chief.

"Mac," said Captain Mellor, "I've seen the prisoners. I've been up in that dirty, stinking room with them. Yon Frenchman ashore knows the officer in charge, and they took me up. I went so that I could see how the coast lies; and all the time I told the little Frenchman and the officer that I reckoned such scum was better off the earth. They'll never suspect me if I happen to let loose the whole bunch, Mac.

"I pretended I wasn't much interested; but I saw everything there was to see. It's the end house to the north, and the cliff's no more than fifteen feet from the back of the house. But the windows are all barred. A good length of two-and-a-half manila, a block, a short spar and a file, and a couple of men to give me a hand, and I'll engage to be at sea this time to-morrow with all that bunch of youngsters. I'll land them down the coast in their own part of the world, and I'll cover the ship's name up. Are you game, Mac?"

"An' what'll happen if we're caught, George?" asked the chief. "I'm thinkin' they'll be no very merciful!"

"Shoot us on sight, I s'pose," replied his captain. "Are you game to try it?"

"A file'll no do for them bars, George," said the chief. "It's a good thing, man, you've the sense to ask an engineer to come wi' ye. I'll bring a hack saw an' some oil; an' I'm no thinkin' it's the bars as will trouble us. I'll speak to Alec. He was wi' me ashore along wi' the mate this mornin' an' he'll be eager to bear a hand."

"What did the mate say about the thing, Mac?" asked Captain Mellor.

"Not much! But ye know what Mr. Grey is. He just hooked his fist into my arm an' said he thanked God he was English; which I said nothing to, for I'd sooner be English myself than one of that lot ashore! You ask him. I'm betting he's spoiling to do something useful, George."

"And you'll get your crowd below, Mac, will you, and have steam up ready?" said Captain Mellor. "I'll tell the second to heave her short so we can break the hook out and away the moment we get back."

"Aye," said the chief engineer grimly as he turned to leave the cabin. "The moment we get back, George. Maybe they'll have to wait eternity for that same moment, I'm thinkin'!"

II

Four hours later when the night had come down deep and silent upon the Adriatic, Captain Mellor brought his boat near in to the end of the low point of rock where it sloped down and disappeared under the warm, still water.

"Shove the grapple over quiet," he said. "Sound carries a mighty long way on a night like this. Pay out now. Right. Make her fast there. She'll ride just clear of the rocks. Mac, jump ashore with Alec, and one of you hold the painter while I pass you out the gear."

Ten minutes later the four men were climbing the long slope of the point, the captain and the mate carrying a thirty-foot spar, and the two engineers a coil of two-and-a-half-inch manila, a pulley block and a few of the tools of their profession. Behind them in the darkness the double-bowed boat was moored with her stern toward the grapple, and her bows toward the end of the low point, so that in a hurried retreat they would be able to haul her close in with the painter in a moment and jump aboard.

Half an hour's walk brought them to the top of the cliff at the back of the prison.

"Quietly now," muttered the captain. "Keep away from the edge while I go and have a look round."

He lowered his end of the spar gently to the ground and went forward cautiously.

"Further along," he told them when he came back.

When they reached the edge of the cliff, creeping, they found they were directly above the prison house, and Captain Mellor and the mate got to work at once to rig the spar out over the cliff.

Mac and Alec had been gone but a few minutes in their search for some large stones to hold down the heel of the spar when a woman's scream was heard some sixty or seventy feet away.

"Hark, man! What's that?" asked the captain.

A few moments and the second engineer came up breathless.

"For all sakes come, captain," he gasped. "The chief's got a woman back there in the bushes and he can't quiet her. He doesn't understand a bit what she's talking."

Quickly the three men ran through the bushes to where the woman was hysterically shouting at the engineer.

"What is it? Who are you?" asked Captain Mellor in the *patois* common in the north of the island of Euboe.

The woman gave a cry and, whirling round on him in the darkness, sank to her knees.

"Aie," she called out. "They killed my son this morning. My youngest they kill to-morrow—"

"Whist ye! Whist ye now," muttered the chief. "Ye'll have us all hanged."

The woman caught the captain round the knees and poured out mad entreaties. He loosed her arms and, taking her by the shoulders, shook her with a quiet violence that seemed to bring her suddenly to her senses, for she became instantly silent.

Then the captain explained to her why they were there. He showed her how she was robbing her boy of his one chance of life by making any sort of outcry up there on the top of that lonely cliff on a quiet night when sound would travel far.

"I am no more than a she-dog that you may beat or strangle if I make one sound," was what she replied.

"They killed her eldest boy this morning," explained the captain to the others. "To-morrow the youngest one is to die."

"God help her!" said Mac. "Well, maybe we'll save the other for her."

"Aye," answered the captain. "We'll save the other boy for her, God willing. Now get going, all of us. Mr. Grey, back to the spar!"

He turned and spoke gently to the woman, telling her to hunt round for pieces of rock and bring them to the cliff edge. The two engineers cast about them again for bowlders while Captain Mellor followed the first mate to where the spar lay.

Fifteen minutes later it was rigged out some fourteen feet over the side of the cliff. The two-inch manila rope had been rove through the sheave in the outer end, and the inner end of the long spar had been covered with a mass of heavy pieces of rock so as to withstand the weight of a man upon the tackle at the outer end.

It was Captain Mellor who went down first, for he had to get into communication with the boys to prevent any of them making an outcry in their surprise at seeing someone at work on the bars of their prison.

He was lowered slowly down and got his feet on to the sill of the window, then, while he gripped a bar with one hand he reached between with the other, and began very gently to knock steadily on the glass.

Fear had made the boys abnormally sharp-witted. In a moment the panes vibrated slightly as if the catch were being slid up. Then slowly and cautiously the window was pulled open.

"S-sh!" whispered the captain, beginning to explain matters. Before he had finished every lad in the room had crowded round the window.

"Now, not a sound," he warned them. "When does the guard come round?"

The guard, they told him, had just been round, and telling them to go back and lie upon the floor as if asleep, he gave the signal to be hauled up again.

"All serene Mac," he told the chief. "You can lower me down now, and I'll stand on the sill and send the bowline up for you. You come along down and cut those bars out. Now, then, down with me, smart."

Five seconds later Mac was beside him with his feet thrust in between the bars on the sill, and his weight taken by the bowline in which he sat so as to be able to use both hands at his work.

"Now, George," he said, "you stand by me with the oil can an' I'll have two o' these bars out inside o' fifteen minutes. I know this dirty Spanish iron! It's like bad butter with the sunstroke. Ye could almost cut it with the back of your finger!"

Yet in spite of the chief's contempt for what he termed "Spanish" iron, the bars proved reasonably healthy metal, though the tempered hack saw ate into them with marvelous ease.

But there was one thing which could not be achieved, and that was silence. The "bite" of the small saw seemed to fill the room and to go echoing with a minute, diabolicalshrillness down the "well" formed by the back of the house and the side of the cliff.

Oil proved ineffectual to bring silence, and so did soap, a cake of which the chief had brought in the hope of making the saw work quietly. Yet the bars must be cut, and as speedily as possible, and so the risk of being heard must be taken along with all the other mad risks they were running.

A three-foot length of the first bar had been cut clean away and the chief had started on the second when the thing Captain Mellor had feared happened. There was a sudden sound of feet on the stairs leading up to the prison, and the lad nearest the window whispered shrilly:

"They come. They come."

Mac had heard the sound at the same moment. He stopped his saw and swung away silently to the same side of the window as Captain Mellor.

The steps came steadily up the stairs, and light showed all round the edges of the door.

"Quick!" cried the captain in *patois* to the youth at the window. "Take this!"

He thrust the cut-out portion of the bar at him. "Shut the window quick, and lie down. Pretend to sleep. If he sees anything you must hit him with the iron. If you fail *you* die."

He swung away from the window as the lad pushed it shut, and caught the bowline in which Mac sat. He heard the key turn in the lock as the lad closed the window. A moment of intense suspense, then a burst of light and the noise of a door as it crashed open against the right-hand wall.

The two men outside heard someone enter the room and shuffle about among the boys. There came dull thuds and cries. The captain thrust his body entirely out of line with the window, and his weight was supported partly by the bowline and partly by the toe of his right boot, which he kept on the extreme corner of the ledge.

Leaning to the right somewhat he saw, by looking into the room, the cause of the sounds. The guard, with drawn sword in one hand and a lantern in the other, was kicking the youths lustily as he walked round among them.

"What devil's work are you up to now?" he growled. "I heard your noise. Tomorrow you'll have no chance of speaking. Better talk now, you pigs!"

But as he got no reply, only groans, as he stepped brutally on the bodies lying about the floor, he appeared satisfied there was no cause for alarm, and again telling them that to-morrow would rid him of them forever, he concluded his inspection and made for the door.

At this moment a cruel thing happened. A sudden gust of wind blowing round the lofty house, pushed one of the French windows open. The lamp in the guard's hand flickered, and he whirled round.

With a suspicious cry he crossed the room to the window, held up his lamp and discovered the sawed iron bar.

"Arre!" he exclaimed, whirling round and flashing his lamp upon the floor where lay the lad who had stood at the window. Once, twice, three times he kicked him, then the lad jumped at him, the solid bar between his hands.

Before the bayonet could be raised the heavy bar came down and the guard with it, He lay there very quiet on the floor.

"Shut the door and lock it, one of you," commanded Captain Mellor through the bars. "Put out the lamp, and make no noise." Then to chief he said: "Get savage with that bar, Mac. We've got to be out of this inside ten minutes."

Without a word the chief swung back into place and fitted the blade of his hack saw into the nick he had already been sawing. Then grimly disregarding all precautions he drove the little tempered saw back and forth in one long skirr of sound which seemed to set the whole "well" singing with the shrill echo.

"Through!" he cried, and, reaching up for a second cut, the shirr of sound again filled the black depth below them, echoing to right and left among the absolute silence of the cliff face.

Suddenly there was a sharp snap. Mac swore softly under his breath and fumbled in his pocket for a spare blade.

"Swing to the side, Mac," cried Captain Mellor, sensing what had happened. "I'm going to give a heave on the bar."

"It's scarce half through, George. Ye couldna budge it, strong as ye are," replied the chief.

Nevertheless, he swung away a foot, for Captain Mellor had a reputation for strength which he could never hope to justify to a better end.

As the captain stooped, bending his great knees and gripping the lower end of the bar with his right hand, a voice from somewhere below in the building called out:

"Peldra! Peldra!! Peldra!"

"They're shouting for yon man the lad clouted!" muttered Mac. "I'm thinkin' we're done this trup, George. I canna see to fix this blade an' me hands all on the go wi' excitement! Whist, they're comin'!"

Steps were on the stairs—heavy steps running up. Inside the dark room hopeless fear took the lads as they huddled together. The captain put all on the hazard of his strength. He bent his knees again, gripped the bar with one enormous hand and the bar went upward with a curious dull bang.

Diving into the room, the bar still in his hand, Captain Mellor sprang for the door. A hand was fumbling for the knob. In that instant the captain turned the key, letting the lock come back quietly.

The handle shook, and a voice called out twice: "Peldra, Peldra!" And another voice from below called out loud and clear:

"Open the door, Marx; open the door!"

It was the voice of the sergeant who had stubbed out his cigarette on the leg of one of the youths that morning.

"It's locked, sergeant," replied the half-drunken guard outside the door. Then he called out a contradiction as the door gave way before his push.

"Peldra!" he said, drunkenly, stumbling into the room. "Where's the lamp?"

From his place behind the door the captain heard the sergeant coming up at a run. In the threshold the man butted heavily into the guard, sending him spinning. A moment later the sergeant struck a match and, holding it high above his head, stepped into the room, his saber ready in his right hand.

"Peldra!" he called sharply. "Where are you?"

Then, as if sensing danger, he whirled round just as Captain Mellor sprang from behind the door. As the man cut at him Captain Mellor caught the blow on the iron bar he held. Striking with his weapon sidewise he knocked the saber out of the sergeant's hand, and, dropping the bar, he used his fists.

The match had gone out, but he could see the man dimly outlined against the window. As he shouted an alarm, the captain's right fist caught his jaw violently and he fell with a thud to the floor.

"Mac," called the captain, "start getting these boys slung aloft smart!"

With a few brief directions to the youths he struck a light and began to feel round for the guard, who, with drunken cunning, was creeping out of the door in search of help.

Captain Mellor sprang for the man, whose howl was stopped by the captain's forceful way of snapping his jaws together. Then before he could recover breath a handful of dirty straw was forced into his mouth, and his elbows strapped behind him with his own belt. His trouser legs were skewered together with his own bayonet.

The insensible sergeant was strapped up much as was the drunken relief guard. The third man, Peldra, was beyond the need of such treatment.

Captain Mellor shut the door gently and locked it. Outside the window the chief was silently sending the lads up through the darkness, one after another.

"Thank God!" muttered the big captain. "Get aloft, now, and send the bowline down for me," he whispered to Mac.

The moment he reached the cliff top he took command.

"Unship the spar. Handy now. You lads, stand back there. Mr. Grey, and you, Alec, carry the spar. We'll leave nothing for a clew. I'll hump the rope. Mac, you take the block. Get on ahead, all of you."

Presently he had them all on the march, going silently through the dark that lay heavy upon everything. He took the rear. In front of him the Greek woman was carrying her son in her arms, easily and lightly crooning a murmur of *patois* over him as though he were a baby.

Two hours afterward, with his "merciful plunder" aboard, Captain

Mellor was leaning over the after-rail of his bridge, staring at a far-off blur of lights on the horizon—the lights of the little town where, in the public square stood that brutally incongruous scaffold which would greet no youthful victims on the morrow!

Captain Mellor still trades along the Adriatic coast. And to this day, such is the irony of life's rewards, the little Frenchman never meets him without a resentful memory of his grimly brutal harshness of heart.

Often he refers to the miraculous escape of the doomed boys. And always the captain grunts unsympathetically. Then the little Frenchman mutters as he crosses himself devoutly:

"But the good God was kinder than you."

The Haunting of the Lady Shannon

I

CAPTAIN TELLER HAD HIS men aft for a few brief words as the *Lady Shannon* wallowed down-channel in the wake of the tug. He explained very clearly that when he gave an order he expected that order to be obeyed with considerable haste or there would be "consequences".

Captain Teller's vocabulary was limited and vulgar, and his choice of words therefore unpleasing; but there was no mistaking his meaning; and the crew went forward again, shaking their heads soberly.

"Just wot I said," remarked one of them, "he's a 'oly terror!"

In this there seemed to be a moody acquiescence on the part of the others; all except one, a young fellow, who muttered an audible threat that he would stick his knife into anyone who hazed him.

"That's wot you thinks," returned the first speaker. "You just 'ave a try, an' you'll find 'arf a bloomin' ounce of lead in yer bloomin' gizzard!"

"That's so," added one of the older men with conviction. "Them sort allus carries a gun in their pocket, handy-like."

But the young man looked at the other two with a sullen, somewhat contemptuous stare.

"They wouldn't dare if you chaps stuck up to them. It's just because you let them haze you. You run if they breathe on you!"

"You just wait a bit, young feller," replied the second man. "Wait till one on 'em gets his knife into yer. I've sailed with them kind, an' you 'aven't. They've ways an' means as you've no idea of. You'll learn quick enough if you runs foul of one on 'em!"

The older man finished his warning with a solemn shake of the head, to which the young fellow replied nothing; but, turning, went into the fo'cas'le, swinging his shoulders unbelievingly.

"He'll be gettin' 'arf murdered," remarked the first man.

"Aye," returned the other. "He's young an' thinks he can 'old 'is own; but Lord help 'im if he runs foul of the after-guard!"

And they also went into the fo'cas'le.

Aft, in the "glory hole", three of the 'prentices—all youngsters—sat and regarded one another with dismayed looks.

"What an old brute he must be!" exclaimed Tommy, the youngest. "If my people had guessed he was like that there would have been ructions and no mistake."

"Well, youngster," put in Martin, an older lad who had done the previous trip with the skipper, "you're in a hot shop right enough; but you'll find it a darned sight hotter if you go talking like that with the door open. They can hear every word you say up on the poop; that is, if there's not much wind."

Tommy looked startled.

Martin continued, addressing the three of them: "See here, youngsters; what you've got to do is to fly like mad if they sing out for you to do anything, and whatever they do, never answer one of them back. Never!"

He repeated the last word with emphasis.

Tommy's eyes grew rounder.

"Why?" he said breathlessly. "What do you think they would do?"

"Do? Goodness knows! Anything, I believe. Last trip they treated one of the ordinaries so badly that the poor chap went queer—silly. Mind you, he acted like a goat and gave both the second mate and the skipper slack; but they knocked all that out of him and some of his brains as well, I believe. Anyway he went half-dotty before the end of the voyage."

"Why didn't the men interfere?" questioned the boy, warmly.

"Interfere? Not they! And if they had the old man would have shot them down like a lot of sheep."

"Didn't you tell when you got home?"

Martin shrugged his shoulders.

"Not I. The youngster cleared out—disappeared. Besides who was I to tell, and what could I have said? They'd have shut me up anyway."

"I'd never have come on the same ship again—never!"

"That depends," replied Martin. "I tried to get shoved into

another but it was no use. And wouldn't I have looked pretty now if I had gone 'round telling how Toby the ordinary seaman was used by the old man and the second? Wouldn't I be in for a nice time of it, eh?"

Tommy nodded gravely; yet his eyes were reproachful.

"Still, I think you ought to have told, even—"

"Oh, stow it!" exclaimed Martin, cutting him short. "Wait until you've had the old man down on top of you; then you can begin to gas."

Tommy wisely made no reply, but began talking with the two others in a low voice; while Martin lay back in his bunk and smoked.

II

During the next few days the *Lady Shannon* had a fine fair wind which took her well away from the land, the captain making a course sufficiently to the westward to clear the bay.

Now that they were in blue water there was no mistaking the after-guard's intentions to make things hum for the "crowd". There was no afternoon watch below, and work was kept up right through the second dog-watch, while instead of turning the men to washing down at 6 A.M. it was buckets and brooms—and holystones—as soon as the morning watch was relieved at 4 o'clock.

All this as may be imagined developed a very fair amount of grumbling among the men; but after three or four had been laid out by the first and second mates with the aid of a belaying-pin the grumbling was confined to the inside of the fo'cas'le, and the crowd bade fair to submit quietly enough to treatment far worse than would be meted out to any convict in one of our prisons.

Yet, as it happened, there was one man with sufficient pluck to make a stand for the sake of the manhood within him, and this was Jones, the young fellow who had sworn he would not be hazed.

So far he had been sufficiently fortunate to escape the attentions of the second mate, in whose watch he was.

On the twelfth day out, however, came violent friction between them. The men were holystoning at the time, and the second, on the lookout for trouble, was "bouncing" 'round the decks and keeping them at it. Suddenly he saw Jones biting off a chew.

"Darn you, you terbaccer-eating hog!" he roared. "You just

throw that plug over the side an' put some of your dirty beef on ter that stone!"

But Jones did no such thing. Instead, he slipped the plug back into his pocket. In an instant the second mate was beside him.

"I'll teach you not to do what I tell you!" he snarled, and pushed the kneeling man over on to the muddy decks with a rough thrust of his boot.

Jones fell on his right side and the plug of hard tobacco tumbled out from his pocket among the slime of water, dirt, and mud-coloured sand. Immediately the second stooped for it and the next instant it was over the side.

"Get a hold of that stone!" he bellowed. "Smart now, or I'll knock the dirty face off you!"

He gave a clumsy kick with his heavy seaboot as he spoke.

The kick took Jones in a slanting graze across his right shinbone and he gave a curse of pain. Then he scrambled onto his knees.

"Thought that'd fetch you!" said the second mate grimly. "Get ahead with that there stonin' if you don't want any more!"

Jones made no reply and no move to go on with his work; but just stared wrathfully up at the officer.

"— you!" he burst out at last.

"That's it, is it!" exclaimed the second, and ran to the starboard pin-rail from whence he took a heavy iron belaying-pin. He returned at a run.

"Now then you dirty son of a sea-horse!" he roared. "I'll show you! You open your blabby mouth to me!"

He raised the pin as he pointed to the holystone.

"Pick it up!" he shouted. "Pick it up an' get to work or I'll knock you inter next week!"

Jones picked up the great lump of holystone with an air of apparent submissiveness, but instead of beginning to work it across the gritty deck he suddenly raised it in both hands and brought it down with a squashing thud upon the second mate's right foot. The officer gave out a loud yell of agony, dropped the belaying-pin, raised his injured member, slipped and came down stern-foremost among the muck of sandy mud.

The next instant Jones had flown at him like a tiger and taking him by the throat had forced him down upon his back and commenced banging his head against the deck. The men had ceased their stoning and were looking on in mingled terror and delight.

All at once from the direction of the poop there came the sound of running footsteps; they passed along the narrow gangway which led to the little bridge, standing upon four stanchions in the middle of the after part of the main-deck.

"Ther old man!" called some one in a voice of fear; but Jones, mad with anger, was past noticing.

The following moment the skipper's face appeared over the bridge-rail, his face livid with rage. He held a revolver.

"Jeerusalem! You strike my officer! Take that! An' that! An' that!"

He was firing indiscriminately among the men upon the deck. Evidently he had been drinking, for though it was plain that he desired to perforate Jones, he only succeeded in shooting one of the other men through the calf of the leg.

Then, save for Jones and the second mate, the decks were empty of men. They had run like sheep. Up on the bridge the captain was clicking his revolver impotently. It had not been loaded in all its chambers, and he had fired off the full ones.

From further aft the first mate appeared in his shirt and trousers. He caught sight of the struggle from the break of the poop, and straight away made two jumps of the ladder on to the main-deck. Reaching the place where Jones was worrying the almost senseless officer, he took a flying kick at him, but with no effect. At that he stooped and caught him by the collar, reaching at the same time for the heavy pin which the second mate had dropped.

"Let go, you rotten fool!" he shouted, raising the pin.

"Let go, you——!" obscenely echoed the skipper from the bridge overhead.

At the same time he hurled his empty revolver at Jones. The flying weapon took the first mate on the top of the head and he went down in a heap without knowing what had struck him.

From the doorway of the 'prentices' berth there came a shrill "Hurray!" in a boy's voice. It was from Tommy, who had thus involuntarily voiced his delight at the turn which the affair had taken. The skipper caught the word and turned wrathfully. He saw Tommy and immediately threw his leg over the edge of the bridge-rail. Dropping to the main-deck, he went for the boy.

"You puppy-faced poop ornament!" he snarled. "You dare ter open your biscuit-hatch at me!"

He seized him by the back of the neck and ran him to the starboard rail. Here, grasping the end of the mizzen lower topsail brace, he shifted his grip to the youngster's arm. Then with the heavy brine-sodden rope he struck the boy furiously, beating out from him little gasping sobs. In his savage, half-drunken state he took no note of where he struck, and under one of the blows, which caught Tommy across the back of the neck, the boy went suddenly limp within his grasp.

Behind him there came a curse in the mate's voice, a dull thud and a quick choking cry from Jones, another blow, followed by a slight gurgle and then silence.

The skipper opened his hand and Tommy slid down onto the deck—quietly; then tossing down the rope-end across him he turned rapidly to see the first mate, recovered from the result of the misaimed pistol, in the act of dragging the limp body of Jones off the second mate.

Taking not the least notice of the huddled boy upon the deck, the captain walked forrard a few steps and looked down at the insensible second. Then he roared for the steward to bring some whisky. When this was brought they forced some between the second mate's lips and when he came 'round applied the bottle to their own; after which, with the help of the steward, they got the battered officer to his room.

Returning on deck the skipper sang out for two of the men to lay aft and carry Jones forrard. Tommy had been removed to his bunk by the 'prentices, immediately the captain and the mates left the deck and now Martin was busily engaged in bathing his head with some salt water.

III

It was two nights later, in the first watch. The second mate had shaken off the effects of his hammering sufficiently to return to duty. To himself he had vowed that Jones—if he lived—should suffer terribly before the ship reached port. But Jones was still in a state of semiconsciousness, due to the blows that the first mate had dealt him; so that for the present the second mate had to curb his hatred and wait.

Four bells had gone and it was full night, with a bright moon shining. For a while the captain and the second mate had paced the poop, conversing on various topics, chief of which was the grinding of all insubordination out of the men. Presently in response to an order of the captain's the second mate made his way along the narrow gangway—elevated some ten feet above the main-deck—to the little bridge on its four teak uprights.

Upon the bridge was placed the "Standard" compass. In addition to the compass there were a couple of rows of wooden ornamental poop-buckets, while up through the deck of the little bridge rose a ventilator. Nothing else was kept upon the bridge; so that what followed the captain was enabled to see plainly. He saw the second mate step up to the compass and peer in at the lighted card. Then came his voice—

"Sou—"

It broke off horribly with a hoarse scream and the captain saw him throw up his arms and fall backward on to the bridge deck. Completely astounded and puzzled the skipper ran hastily along the gangway to him.

"What's up with you, Mr. Buston?" he asked, stooping over him; but the second gave back no reply.

At last the skipper reached for the binnacle-lamp. Slipping it from its place he threw the light upon the prostrate mate. It showed him the face, curiously distorted. From that his glance passed to a thin stream which trickled from beneath the man. He knelt down and turned him half over. The blood came from the back of the right shoulder.

He stood up, releasing the body, and it fell back with an inert sagging of the shoulders. He felt dazed and frightened. The thing had happened before his eyes, within twenty feet of him; yet he had seen nothing that would account for it.

The bridge stood up above the main-deck like an island and was reached only by the gangway which led from the poop. But even if this had not been so it did not seem possible that any one could have touched the second mate without the captain being aware of it. The more he turned the matter over the more he realized how inexplicable it was. Then a sudden idea came to him and he glanced upward. Had a knife or a spike been dropped from aloft? He thought not. Had that been the case then the instrument would have been visible—and there was none. Besides, the wound was behind.

Had it been caused by anyone dropping a knife or spike, then it would have been in the head or top the shoulders. There was a similar objection supposing that a weapon had been thrown at him from the deck below. In that case the wound would have been in the front or one of the sides. It was no use; he could not solve the mystery.

He gathered his wits somewhat and bellowed one of the 'prentices to go and call the mate. Another he sent forrard to order every man, watch below well as watch on deck, to lay aft. He would at least know the whereabouts of each of the crew.

The first mate came running with his gun in his hand. It was evident that he was incurably expectant of trouble. While the men were mustering the skipper told the first mate all that he knew.

As soon as the men were aft the captain made each one pass below the bridge under the light from the binnacle-lamp. Every man was thus discovered to be there, except Jones. Then the 'prentices were mustered, and all came forward except Tommy. As soon as this was done the skipper told the men to and see if the missing man and boy were in their respective bunks. In a few minutes the first mate returned to say that they were. Then the captain dismissed the men; but without telling them of the tragedy which had occurred.

As soon as they had gone he turned to the first mate.

"See you 'ere, Mr. Jacob," he said. "Do you think as that dirty carkiss forrard is as bad as 'e seems?"

"Yes, sir," replied the mate. "It's not him, if that's what you're thinking. He looks as if it was his turn next to slip off the hooks."

"An' ther b'y?"

The mate shook his head.

"No, sir. He's not got over that warming you gave him by a long chalk."

"If I thought—" began the skipper; but broke off short.

"Yes, sir?"

The skipper threw the light down on to the dead man.

"Wot's done it?" he asked in a voice denoting that he was at the end of his imagination. "Wot's done it?"

"Well sir, it must be one of the lousy crowd forrard."

"One of ther crowd! Do you think as one of them'd be livin' if I'd thought as it was them!"

The first mate made no reply, and the captain continued.

THE HAUNTING OF THE LADY SHANNON 465

"It ain't nothin' 'uman as 'as done this 'ere."

He stirred the body with the toe of his boot as he spoke. "You think, sir—"

"I don't think nothin'! I'm a long way past thinkin'. Why! I saw 'im killed with me own eyes. He was just struck dead standin' 'ere in ther moonlight. There weren't nothin' come near 'im, an' there ain't no signs of a knife, nor nothin'. I reckon as it's someone as 'e's done for, some time or another."

The mate glanced 'round the decks, silent and ghostly under the moonlight. Though he was a fairly intelligent man, it was plain that he felt a chill of unease.

The skipper went on with his uncomfortable theorizing:

"It's a dead man's ghost!" he said. "W'en that hog forrard, as you done for, slips 'is cable, strikes me as you'll be'aving a call— sudden!"

He touched the body with his foot, suggestively.

"I didn't know that you were superstitious, sir," said the mate.

The captain turned and looked at him steadily. "You knowed right then," he said at length. "I ain't, but I ain't a blind fool neither! An' when I sees one of me officers knifed before me eyes, an' nothin' in sight, you can bet as I give in ter facts. I never was narrer, an' wot me eyes shows me I believes. You can take it from me right off as ther's something in this 'ere packet as ain't 'uman."

He waved the light over the dead second mate. "I reckon as 'e's been a bad un!" he remarked, as though to himself.

Then, as if coming suddenly to his everyday self, he gave a slight shiver which he turned off into a shrug.

" 'Ere, Mr. Jacob, let's get outer this 'ere," he said.

And he led the way, followed closely by the first mate, off the bridge. On the poop he turned to the mate.

"You take charge, mister. I'm goin' down for a snooze. I reckon you can shift 'im —" jerking his thumb toward the bridge— "as soon as it's daylight."

IV

During the following day the captain indulged in a heavy, solitary drinking-bout; and on finding out from the steward that the skipper was hopelessly drunk the first mate took upon himself to put the second over the side. He did not fancy another night with that thing aboard.

That the first mate had taken the extraordinary event of the night to heart, was common talk in the fo'cas'le; for he relaxed entirely his bullying attitude to the men and in addition on three separate occasions sent word forrard to learn how Jones was progressing. It may be that the skipper's theorizing of the preceding night had something to do with this sudden display of sympathy.

With the captain being drunk, the first mate had to take all the night-watches. This he managed by having one of the older men up on the poop a portion of the time to keep a lookout, while he himself got a little rest upon the seat of the saloon skylight. Yet it was evident to the man whom he had called to keep him company, that the mate obtained little sleep; for every now and again he would sit up and listen anxiously.

Once he went so far as to call the man to him and ask if he could not hear something stirring on the bridge. The man listened, and thought perhaps that he did; but he could not be sure. At that the mate stood up excitedly and ordered him to go forrard and find out how Jones was. Much surprised, the man did as he was bid, returning to say that he seemed queer and that the men in the fo'cas'le thought he was slipping his cable and would the first mate go forrard and have a look at him.

But this the mate would by no means do. Instead he sent the man along to the fo'cas'le every bell and between whiles he himself stood by the rail across the break of the poop. Twice he called to the man to come and listen, and the second time the man agreed that there certainly was a noise on the little bridge. After that the mate continued to stand where he was, glancing 'round about him frightenedly, a very picture of shattered nerves.

At half-past two in the morning the man came back from one of his visits forrard to say that Jones had just gone. Even as he delivered himself of the news there came a distinct grating sound from the direction of the bridge. They both turned and stared; but though the moonlight was full upon everything there was nothing visible. The man and the mate faced one another—the man startled, the mate sweating with terror.

"My—!" said the man. "Did yer 'ear that, sir?"

The mate replied nothing; his lips quivered beyond his control.

Presently the dawn came.

In the morning the skipper appeared on deck. He seemed quite sober. He found the first mate haggard and nervous, standing beside the poop rail.

"I guess you'd best get below an' 'ave er sleep, Mr. Jacob," he remarked, stepping over to him. "You look as if you was spun out."

The first mate nodded in a tired manner but beyond that made no reply. The skipper looked him up and down.

"Anythin' 'appened while I was—was below?" he asked, as though the mate's manner suggested the thought.

"Jones has gone," replied the mate harshly.

The captain nodded as though the mate's reply answered some further question.

"I s'pose you dumped 'im?" he said, nodding toward the bridge, where the second mate had lain. The mate nodded.

"Seen—or 'eard anythin'?" beckoning again toward the bridge.

The first mate straightened himself up from the rail and looked at the skipper.

"Directly after Jones went, there was something messing about yonder." He jerked his thumb toward the bridge. "Stains heard it as well."

The captain made no immediate reply. He appeared to be digesting this piece of information.

"I sh'd keep clear of ther bridge, Mr. Jacob, if I was you," he remarked at length.

A slight flush rose in the mate's face.

"I heard from one of the boys that young Tommy seems pretty shaky this morning," he replied with apparent irrelevance.

"— ther b'y !" growled the captain.

Then, glancing at the mate—

"You think—"

His gaze followed the mate's to the bridge and he did not finish.

It was noticeable after the mate had gone below that the captain for the first time made inquiries as to the state of Tommy's health. At first he sent the steward; the second time he went himself. It was a memorable fact.

V

That night the captain and the mate kept the first watch together. At the beginning, before it was quite dark, they paced the poop and kept up an irregular conversation; but now that it was night they had drifted to the forrard poop-rail and there leaned, scarcely speaking once in a couple of minutes.

To a close observer their attitudes might have suggested that they were listening intently. Once it seemed there came a faint sound through the darkness, from the direction of the bridge, whereat the first mate babbled out something in a strained, husky voice.

"You keep ther stopper on, Mr. Jacob," said the skipper, "else you'll be goin' barmy."

After that there was nothing further until the moon rose, which it did board away on the starboard bow. At first it gave little or no light, the horizon being somewhat cloudy. Presently its upper edge came into sight above the "Standard" binnacle, framing the bulging brass dome with a halo of misty light that gave it for the minute almost a curiously unreal spectral appearance. The light grew plainer, casting grotesque but indistinct shadows.

Suddenly the silence was broken by a strange husky inhuman gurgle from the bridge. The skipper started; but the mate never moved; only his face shone white in the glowing light. The captain could see that the little bridge was clear of all life. Abruptly as he stared there came from it a low, incredible, abominable laughter. The effect upon the mate was extraordinary. He stood up with a jerk, shaking from head to foot.

"He's come for me!" he said, his voice rising into an insane quavering shout.

From forrard and aft there came the sound of running feet. His wild cry had brought out the crew. From the bridge there came a further sound, vague, and, to the captain, meaningless. But it had meaning to the mate.

"Coming!" he screamed in a voice as shrill as a woman's.

He sprang away from the skipper's side, and ran stumbling along the narrow gangway to the bridge.

"Come back, you fool!" roared the captain. "Come back!"

The mate took no notice, and the skipper made a rush for him. He had reached the bridge and flung his arms about the "Standard" binnacle. He appeared to be wrestling with it. The captain seized him by the arm and tried to tear him away; but it was useless. Suddenly as the skipper struggled something bright flashed over his shoulder, past his ear, and the mate went slowly limp and slid down upon the deck.

The captain wrenched around and stared. Exactly what he saw no one knew. The grouped men beneath heard him shout hoarsely. Then he came flying over the bridge-rail down among them. They broke and ran a few yards. Something else came down over the rail. Something white and slender that ran upon the captain noiselessly. The captain dodged, rushing sidewise with his head down. He butted into the steel side of the deck-house and crumpled up.

"Catch it, mates," shouted one of the men, and ran among the shadows.

The rest, inspired by his courage, closed about in a semicircle. The decks were still very dim and indistinct.

"Where is it?" came in a man's voice.

"There—there—no—"

"It's on ther spar," cut in some one. "It's—"

"Overboard!" came in a chorus, and there was a general rush for the side.

"There weren't no splash," said one of the men presently, and no one contradicted him.

Yet whether this was so or not Martin, the oldest 'prentice, insisted that the white thing had reminded him of Toby the ordinary seaman, who had been hazed to the verge of insanity by the brutality of the captain and officers on the previous voyage.

"It's the way his knees went," he explained. "We used to call him 'Knees' before he went queer."

There is little doubt but that it was Toby who, in his half-insane condition, had stowed away and worked out a terrible vengeance upon his tormentors. Though, of course, it cannot be proved.

When after a sleepless excited night the crew of the *Lady Shannon* made a search of the bridge they found traces of flour upon the bridge-deck, while the mouth and throat of the ventilator in the center of the bridge was dusted with the same whiteness. Inspired by these signs to doubt their superstitions they unshipped the after hatch and made a way to where the lower end of the ventilator opened above the water-tanks. Here they found further traces of flour and in addition discovered that the manhole-lid of the port tank was unshipped. Searching 'round, they saw that a board was loose in the partition enclosing the tanks from the surrounding hold. This they removed and came upon more flour—the ship was loaded with this commodity—which led them finally to a sort of nest amid the cargo. Here were fragments of food, a tin hook-pot, a bag of stale bread and some ship's biscuits; all of which tended to show that some one had been stowed away there. Close at hand was an open flour barrel.

Toby had crawled at night from his hiding-place to the ventilator and, concealed there, had stabbed the officers as they came within reach.

Tommy regained his health, as did both Captain Jeller and Jacob, the mate; but as a "hardcase" skipper and a "buck-o-mate," they are no longer shining examples.

The Heathen's Revenge

C HERE ARE STILL MANY people who refuse to recognize that in spite of evolution, education, progress—call it what you like— there remains a tremendous difference between the East and the West. And that East of the "Near East" and West of the "Far West", there are minor details of life that differ somewhat from what the white man considers to be the right and proper order of things.

For instance, it is no misstatement to say that there are places where the heathen maintain the dignity of the gods against the efforts of the missionary or the stranger.

And again, it is no untruth to say that a beautiful white girl is about as safe in some parts of this globe as a bag of gold would be in a healthy riot of the unemployed.

These facts, however, are ignored by a large proportion of our stiff-necked countrymen who never venture off our tight little island. Hallett was once of the same opinion, but experience taught him different, to his cost.

He had gone a little East of the Near East and done his vigorous utmost during one long year of what he termed innocently enough: "missionary work" to create for himself and his Cause a healthy and well-deserved hatred—that is if you view his "work" from the hea- then's side of the road.

What exactly Hallett did, above all his other offences, to raise the undying hatred of Jurwash—a somewhat ragged native in the eyes of any European but the holiest priest of a tribe of priests, in the eyes of the native—I do not know. I can well imagine it was something idiotic and brutally insulting—and also very innocent! It depends, of course, how you look at it. If you had Jurwash the Holy, I have no doubt your views would have been quite as serious as his. Which was about as serious as it could be.

Before the end of that year, Hallett did one more act of idiocy to crown his twelve month's vigorous war with the religious self respect of the heathens. He wrote home to Mary Kingston to come out to him, telling her that at last he had made such headway in his work that their marriage was possible and they could, I suppose, live happy ever after.

The girl came out, and the vast machinery of revenge which Jurwash had set into motion to get even with Hallett the Insulter of his god was checked for a time while the priest considered this addition to his problem. We in the Police Secret Service know many things hidden from others. Eventually, when Jurwash had done considering, the machinery of vengeance went forth again, and Mary Kingston disappeared.

I was alone in my office when Hallett dashed in. A young man of enormous build and strength, intensely earnest to the point of fanaticism in regard to his work, simple and honest but, unfortunately, a little lacking in imagination and sensitiveness.

"She's gone!" he shouted, gripping my arm in his excitement. "She's disappeared."

I got the details after some questioning; then, knowing I should have to act quickly, I hurried him away with work to do, though I knew perfectly well he was too upset to be of use in such methods we were likely to follow.

Mary Kingston had gone. Her disappearance left no trace whatever, but we in the S.P. spread our feelers out over the four quarters of the earth, and in ten minutes I had dispatched two of my men on special work. Another I sent with a squad with instructions to follow Hallett at a distance.

In the evening two of the men returned and made their report. I knew that unless I could persuade Hallett to leave the place, he was as good as dead, or worse. Knowing him as I did, I judged that persuasion would be useless, but would have to be tried before I resorted to other methods. And with that idea in view, I set off in the direction of his house.

Halfway there I fell in with the man and his squad who was supposed to be guarding Hallett's house. To my questions about his charge he replied that all was well. Why, I asked, had he left him unguarded? I asked him so quietly that he shook, as well he might, knowing all that lay behind my question.

I gave the beggar a note to give Abdual, the keeper of the wands, and ordered him to send Number 4 with a relief squad. Abdual was no sparer of his wands, as many knew to their cost. Then, marching back the squad, I posted them about Hallett's place and went in to argue with him.

As I had suspected, he refused to budge.

"I shall move heaven and earth to find her," he said, pacing the room like a caged animal. "She's being held for ransom by some of those ignorant tribes. Surely you can do something. Offer some reward… send a troop out into the surrounding country. Anything rather than this waiting!"

I put a few careful questions to him, taking care to keep from him all that I knew. It never occurred to him that Jurwash knew the whereabouts of the girl. Had he suspected that, I have no doubt it would have taken more than my squads to hold him. He would have gone straight to the very doom the priest had prepared for him. Before leaving him, I got him to promise that he would leave everything in my hands till the following day.

When I got back to the office, I gave personal and strict directions concerning the relief squads. It is wise, in the East, to give personal attention when a friend may be involved in any trouble. As I have said before, the heathen orders the minor details of life on a plan peculiar to the ideas of the Western Mind. Only by having the house guarded by my men could I hope to find Hallett alive in the morning. Therefore I sent a squad of men commanded by Number 4 and Number 5. Officer Number 4 keenly desired promotion. Officer Number 5 was of a jealous nature, and the fear of an ambitious junior is apt to stimulate a good service. It is a very sound method to work on.

Early the next morning I went to see Hallett and found the men posted as arranged all round the house, dilligent in their watching and officially alert… too much so as I soon learned. No Hallett was to be found, yet both sergeants and the men protested that he had never gone past them. As a thorough search revealed nothing, I gave another note to the chief sergeant for my friend Abdual, the keeper of the wands. Those same wands would cover the whole of them as well as the men of all the reliefs during that night. I guess Abdual's arm ached that day.

Immediately on reaching the office, I sent a messenger out who returned with the information that Jurwash, accompanied by others of his tribe, had gone off in the night. Three men whom I sent out later brought back a certain unwashed native whom we thrashed till he confessed that word had been carried that night to Hallett indicating that Jurwash could give him news of Mary Kingston.

As might be expected, when Hallett got to the place where the guide led him, there was no Jurwash the Holy, only one of the heathens who professed to know that the priest had set off into the desert. This information, as Jurwash had directed, was given to Hallett after he had been invited to turn out the contents of his pockets. Nothing more would, or could, the man tell me, though we thrashed him right well—except that my friend had gone off on foot, running in pursuit of that fiend.

Having got all the information I could, I dismissed the man who was promptly caught and thrashed again in the courtyard by my men who thus eased their own pains from Abdual's wands, and tried to punish the unfortunate beggar for the indignities they themselves had suffered. But this wasn't for my notice.

Knowing now how Hallett had gone, I sent a fast squad, mounted, to scour the desert ten miles to the south, while I picked a troop of fifty men who, if necessary, could ride with me further into the desert. At night, with the return of the fast squad unsuccessful, we put off, thus beginning the search which I had foreseen from the first.

A few miles hard riding to the south brought us news of our quarry, with always the same tale. Jurwash the Holy, with his followers and a white man, bound, had ridden that way. Knowing something of the mind of the native and the power of that particular priest, I always believed the second story—which generally came after an application of the wands—and which is a very sound method to go on.

Two months later we were still hot upon the track of Jurwash, though we could never come upon him. At last, tired of scouring the desert and with our provisions running perilously low, I made a camp and sent off twenty of my men to bring back the things we were so badly in need of. During their absence, I sent out ten men daily to inquire and search, feeling pretty certain that we were near the place where Jurwash had camped.

One night about a month after the messenger had gone, we had word from a ragged native who crawled into our camp whining for food, that Jurwash the Holy was living in a great tower which lay about a day's journey to the southeast. But though we rode hard a day and a night we found nothing, which made me regret that I had not followed my rule and beaten the heathen, instead of showing mercy toward him—which to the native mind is a foolish thing to show. This again is another truth which I have proved through many years.

The relief party not having returned when we reached camp, we rested a day, but still convinced we were on the right track, I put off the following day with ten men, riding twenty miles due south. Towards dusk, just as we were about to turn towards camp again having met with no success, we were fired on from all sides. When I came to myself, I was surrounded by natives, two of whom were busy staunching the blood flowing from a wound in my forearm. From time to time they forced me to drink something which revived me and puzzled me at the same moment for it is not the way of those beggars to first try to murder you and then to patch you up. Something much worse evidently lay at the back of it all.

Later, when my senses began to quicken, I noticed that there seemed to be a great troop of natives gathered around. Someone came up and tied a bandage over my eyes and mounted me on a horse, and we began to move in what I fancied was an easterly direction. For three nights we travelled, lying hidden during the day, and all that time I was made to keep the bandage over my eyes. Otherwise I had nothing to complain of, but that didn't decrease my wonder as to what the end was going to be.

As far as I could guess, it was the dawn of the third day when we rode into some great echoing gateway. Here I was dismounted and led down a few steps into what I imagined was an underground chamber. When I attempted to remove the eye covering, a voice that I recognised as the Holy Priest's warned me to drop my hand.

"You shall suffer no harm if you obey," he said, and having heard a good deal about the methods of Jurwash and seen the results of his handiwork during many years in the S.P., I obeyed his command.

After eating a messy preparation they brought me, Jurwash himself took me by the elbow and led me out, up the steps and along stone passages which gave back in strange echoes the sound of our footsteps.

"Come quietly," said the priest. "You shall learn how the gods of the heathens deal with those who treat them with indignity."

The sneer in his voice when he used our own words "gods of the heathens" told me I must prepare myself for his vengeance.

At the end of the passage we entered what felt like a vast apartment, judging from the echo. Here I was brought to a standstill while someone placed an iron band round my body. This in turn was attached to a clanking chain and then someone removed my bandage. It was some moments before I got my eyes focussed to the dim light, but I soon realized that I was standing with my back to the wall, chained securely round the waist and blinking into the gloom of the subterranean cavern.

I could make out no figures of my jailors, though a faint bluish glow of light in a downward direction told me I was standing upon a height, and then out of that thick gloom arose a strange whimpering.... I have heard many sounds that were unpleasant, but nothing like that. It filled me with horror, knowing as I did to what awful lengths those beggars will go.

The bluish glow increased till I made out a perfect circle of light which grew gradually brighter and sent out a peculiar smoke.

As the brightness increased and the smoke rose higher and higher in a slow, wavering ring of fire, I heard again that whimpering coming out of the shadow down to the left of the flame. Something seemed to move from where it came and I distinctly heard a slow chink, chink, as though something fretted in its chains. And all the time that horrid whimpering.

As time went on, the flame round the circle grew greater, and then it was I saw the thing lying in its chains and whining. Once when it raised a blackened stump and waved it aimlessly to and fro with a monotonous movement I shouted in a loud voice, "Hallett!" But no notice was taken of my call, and knowing the ways of our captors, I guessed it was wiser to keep a firm hold on myself, and I watched closely.

It wasn't long before I saw a change come over the crouching figure outside that ring of fire. It appeared to be listening acutely for some sound too subtle for ears, much as I strained them for any further devilment that might be lying in wait for us. My eyes were sore with peering into the smoke and through the flame, and when I turned them onto the figure again, I saw that it was lying down on its left side with its ear to the ground, listening. Now, I've lived a long time among the heathen, heard much and believe what I've seen, and at that moment my blood ran cold.

Rising to its feet, the figure stood peering through the flame separating it from the inner circle. Then I saw that it was staring at a little door opening under the thighs of a graven image squatting in the middle of the floor, and towering up into the rolling clouds of luminous smoke above. Through this door came a priest dressed in what they called "full raiment", and dragging a trembling, almost naked girl. Immediately the whole place echoed with the howling from that poor chained being, straining his chains and tearing at his fetters in vain efforts to burst through.

A second priest followed the first through the door, dressed in "half-raiment" and carrying wands. The girl was dragged by the two of them to the knees of the god and chained fast by a silver chain. This done, somewhere away in the darkness beyond came a low tinkle of a bell, and the second priest stepped forward and beat the girl seven times. The place was filled with the terrible howlings of that mad figure tearing at its chains. A second time that bell sounded above the hideous din—and what was done was bad for anyone to look upon. Three times the girl fainted, and the figure dashed itself about on the edge of the flames in its vain attempts to get at the men. I went mad and screamed like any woman, rather than a man who had witnessed the things in the East for half a lifetime.

And suddenly, as I tore wildly at my bonds, Jurwash appeared beside me, and I sprang at him, hoping to squeeze the very life out of him.

"At dawn, each day," he said, stepping swiftly out of my reach, and turned his wicked face towards the flame.

Whether the priests were preparing to go on with their fiendish work or not I can't say, but at that moment Jurwash said something in a voice of command and leaped down swiftly towards the fire. I saw then that the figure was working quietly and as though inspired at the fastenings of the chain which bound its ankles. One of them was loose, and Jurwash had noticed this and ran at him with a knife. Before he could strike, however, the figure twisted itself up and struck out with the loosed chain, and Jurwash the Holy died the death he deserved. One mighty wrench at the second chain, and the figure was free—a madman free to wreak his vengeance on his torturers.

Within the circle the two priests stood as if petrified, not knowing what to do, so sudden had been the turn of events. And then the figure dashed through the flames and the two priests went to their deaths without seeming to fight so far as I could see, but the two of them died swiftly.

"Hallett! Hallett!" I yelled, but he was fumbling with the fastening which bound the girl, and in a moment he had her free and was running, stumbling through the doorway, with this burden in his blackened arms.

In the light of the dying flame, I worked frantically to free myself. My knife, which fortunately had not been taken, was a poor tool with which to pick out the staple from the wall; but patience and good luck brought success at last, and my chains fell clattering to the ground. Another moment and I was wrapping my coat about my face and dashing through the flames to the doorway which might lead to freedom or death. No one appeared in the silence of that place to bar my escape down those passages along which I felt sure Hallett had carried his precious burden. A small door at the end of one turn was open, and immediately I was out in the dawn among the great sand dunes. Looking back to see if I was followed, I could see nothing but a small hole at the bottom of a huge dune.

Far ahead something was stumbling about with a bundle in its arms. I shouted again and again, forgetting in my eagerness to catch him that it was a mad thing to do, but the figure still stumbled on, and looking round from time to time to see if I was pursued, I could see no living thing in sight; neither could I tell which dune it was that held that underground temple of horrors.

After a long chase, I caught up with Hallett who, when he saw me, laid the girl down at my feet and said, "Hallo, Burton. I've killed that Jurwash," and collapsed in a heap on the sand.

Fortunately my men found me later that same day and carried us back to camp. For three days we searched the dunes but never came upon the one which hid that underground temple. At each and all I cried, "Here it is," but it never was the one we looked for. And so at last, weary and beaten, we turned north again for the edge of the silent desert.

The Halletts live today among green trees and green valleys. How much of that terrible past Mary remembers, I don't know. She never refers to it. Hallett's mind, we all know, is blank, mercifully. He will take you into his gay garden and show you his roses or his potatoes which, maimed though he is, seem to thrive under his care. They are far more important in his present life than ever the heathen's soul will be. So far as he is concerned, the latter can continue in his own particular brand of sin, calling it religious self-respect, or whatever he likes. We in the S.P. call it something else.

A Note on the Texts

WHENEVER POSSIBLE, TEXTS FOR this series have been based on versions that were published in book form, preferably during Hodgson's lifetime. The major exceptions to this rule are the stories that appear in volumes edited by Sam Moskowitz. Moskowitz was known to have access to original manuscripts and other source materials. Some stories were published only in serial form, and have been taken from those primary sources.

Over the years, many of Hodgson's stories have appeared under variant titles, which are noted below. As a rule, the titles used in this series are based on the first book publication of a story, even if the story previously appeared under a different title, in serial form.

Specific textual sources are noted below. The only changes that have been made to the texts have been to correct obvious typographical errors, and to standardize punctuation and capitalization. British and archaic spellings have been retained.

The House on the Borderland is based on the 1908 Chapman & Hall edition.

"The Thing Invisible" is based on its publication in *Carnacki The Ghost-Finder* (Eveleigh Nash, 1913). It was originally published in *The New Magazine No. 34* (January 1912).

"The Gateway of the Monster" is based on its publication in *Carnacki The Ghost-Finder* (Eveleigh Nash, 1913). It was originally published in *The Idler No. 88* (January 1910).

"The House Among the Laurels" is based on its publication in *Carnacki The Ghost-Finder* (Eveleigh Nash, 1913). It was originally published in *The Idler No. 89* (February 1910).

"The Whistling Room" is based on its publication in *Carnacki The*

Ghost-Finder (Eveleigh Nash, 1913). It was originally published in *The Idler No. 90* (March 1910).

"The Searcher of the End House" is based on its publication in *Carnacki The Ghost-Finder* (Eveleigh Nash, 1913). It was originally published in *The Idler No. 92* (May 1910).

"The Horse of the Invisible" is based on its publication in *Carnacki The Ghost-Finder* (Eveleigh Nash, 1913). It was originally published in *The Idler No. 91* (April 1910).

"The Haunted *Jarvee*" is based on its publication in *Carnacki The Ghost-Finder* (Mycroft & Moran, 1947). It was originally published in *The Premier Magazine* (March 1929).

"The Find" is based on its publication in *Carnacki The Ghost-Finder* (Mycroft & Moran, 1947).

"The Hog" is based on its publication in *Carnacki The Ghost-Finder* (Mycroft & Moran, 1947). It was originally published in *Weird Tales 39, No. 9* (January 1947).

"The Goddess of Death" is based on its publication in *The Haunted Pampero* (Grant, 1991). It was originally published in *Royal Magazine 11, No. 6* (April 1904).

"Terror of the Water-Tank" is based on its publication in *Out of the Storm* (Grant, 1975). It was originally published in *Blue Book Magazine 5, No. 5* (September 1907).

"Bullion" is based on its publication in *The Haunted Pampero* (Grant, 1991). It was originally published in *Everybody's Weekly* (March, 1911).

"The Mystery of the Water-Logged Ship" is based on its publication in *Grand Magazine No. 75* (May 1911).

"The Ghosts of the *Glen Doon*" is based on its publication in *The Red Magazine No. 64* (December 1, 1911).

"Mr. Jock Danplank" is based on its publication in *The Red Magazine No. 72* (April 1, 1912).

"The Mystery of Captain Chappel" is based on its publication in *The Red Magazine No. 193* (April 15, 1917).

"The Home-Coming of Captain Dan" is based on its publication in *The Red Magazine No. 217* (May 1, 1918)

"Merciful Plunder" is based on its publication in *Argosy-Allstory Weekly 170, No. 4* (July 25, 1925).

"The Haunting of the *Lady Shannon*" is based on its publication in *Out of the Storm* (Grant, 1975).

"The Heathen's Revenge" (AKA "The Way of the Heathen") is based on its publication in *Terrors of the Sea* (Grant, 1996). It was initally published as "The Way of the Heathen" in chapbook form in 1988.

The Complete Fiction of William Hope Hodgson is published by
Night Shade Books in the following volumes:

The Boats of the "Glen Carrig" and Other Nautical Adventures
The House on the Borderland and Other Mysterious Places
The Ghost Pirates and Other Revenants of the Sea
The Night Land and Other Perilous Romances
The Dream of X and Other Fantastic Visions